Look for these other great titles!

Dar Tania – October 2016, "a 100 page story", 105 pages
Malcor's Story – November 2016, 400+ pages
Bomoki's Gate – April 2017, 550+ pages
Dar Tania II: Set's Dream – August 2017, 250+ pages
Khalla's Play: Merakor I – January 2018, the book in your hands now!

For more information about the stories set in the Forsaken Isles, its characters, author, or whatever else inspires you to contact me at:

www.forsakenisles.com   or   www.erickbarnum.com   or
www.facebook.com/forsakenisles

If you enjoy the story, please leave a review on Amazon and Good Reads; thank you!

Edited by Tony Reynolds and Ben Duffy

# Table of Contents

# Map of Taysor

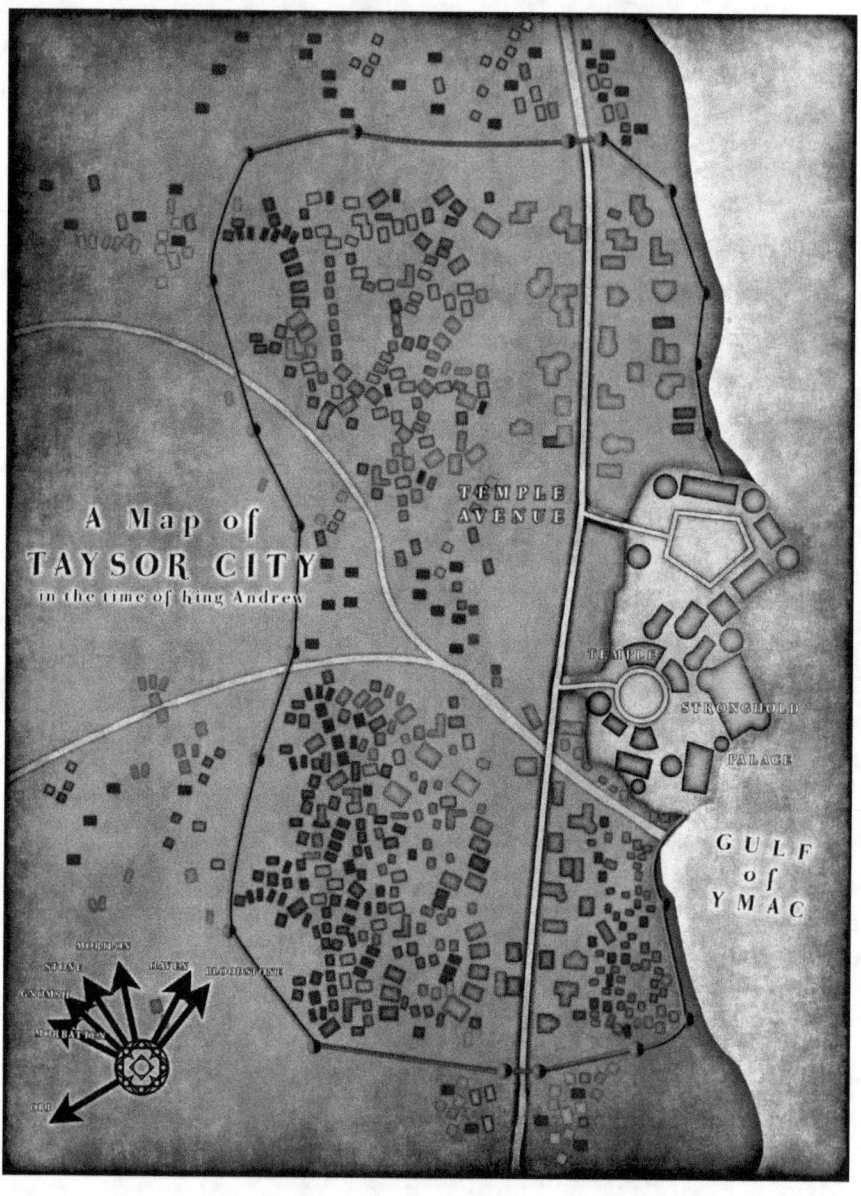

# Map of Taysor - The Temples District

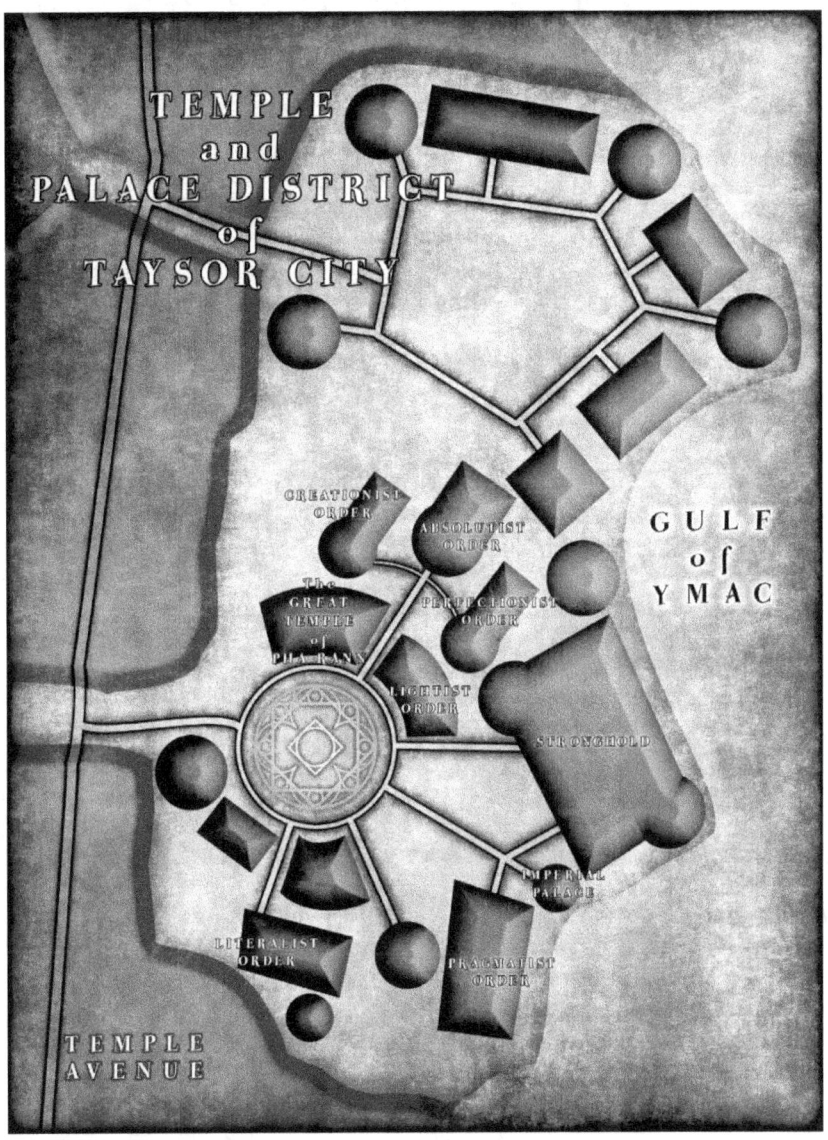

# Foreword

Khalla's Play follows the events described in the book, Bomoki's Gate. However, a reader does not need to read them in order. The important connection between the two is that the head of Morbatten's Thieves Guild, called Perdition, did an errand for the Ice Dragon Patriarch in Bomoki's Gate. This errand resulted in a reward: an ancient map showing the location of a long lost Tower of Sorcery. The implication of the reward is that this particular Tower of Sorcery was buried during a cataclysmic explosion and so survived where all thought it destroyed over 3,000 years ago. Secretly buried hundreds of paces below the Arati Grasslands, the chance that it might be intact and not looted by the dark elves pulls at their lust for adventure and treasure.

The head of Perdition is always named Marcello. Marcello's real name from Bomoki's Gate is Ash Bowker. Ash involved an old wizard named Halgrim in earning this reward. Join Ash and Halgrim as they attempt to put together a team and go to Merakor, the ancient civilization destroyed ages ago. There's a problem. Bomoki's Gate is the story of Morbatten going up against the Jade God of Necromancy. The outcome of that is the events told in Khalla's Play.

While some of the characters have continuations from the prior book, here is what you need to know. There are Thieves Guild-type groups in each of the various nations of the Forsaken Isles. Some act like crime families, others as gangs. In Morbatten, these guilds that existed prior to the year 800 DAR, were morphed into national spy, infiltrator, saboteur, and other functions and repurposed as channels for the military. Named Perdition, agents report variously to the Temple of Tiamat, the Military, or the Circle. The Circle is an elite group of heroes chosen by merit by the dragons that rule Morbatten.

Writing this book, I found myself caught up in challenging some fantasy tropes and unrolling the covers on the Forsaken Isles more and more. It was a fun story to write. The focus on writing compelling characters gave me a chance to show how Tania affects normal people, and those in other countries. Elves, which have not really had a strong role in the other books, take front and center stage through the new Marcello, the Elf Khalla. Though the elves have their own nation, their leader is lost in memory of Merakor and distant from his people. Over the years, some elves have defected to Tania and adopted Tiamat as their Goddess. Khalla comes from such a group.

Unlike the slender, waif-like elves in most fantasy, I like my elves hearty if dispassionate. They can live forever, but it's a rare mindset that can endure that long without having issues. They have pointy ears though, so don't worry! That trope is intact, though the ear-pointedness is slight. The thing that makes them elves was their creation at Pha Rann's hands to be more connected to the natural order. Pha Rann created humans to be curious about the natural order. Connection versus curiosity and a different perception of Time's flow is the primary separator between the two races. Elves age as a function of emotional involvement that pull them into Time's flow after they reach maturity. There is another elf introduced in this story, the Lady Inviress. She'll have a much larger role in the sequel.

Let's talk about thieves. A thief is a dexterous, nimble, quick-thinking, and often charismatic person who chooses to use their natural talents for non-lawful means. In Tania, where everyone is tested in their teens, such individuals become candidates for either the Military or Perdition. After all, these hallmark attributes are exactly what you would want in an officer, an archer, an engineer, a tactician. The difference lies soley with the person's interests and Tania allows great latitude in letting candidates determine their own course. If the candidate chooses, or is chosen by Perdition, they are trained and established as an agent.

Finally, let's talk about what it takes to produce a book. As the writer, these characters live in my heart and soul. They are my friends. Telling their story is fun. Making it believable and fun for you, the reader is the challenge and one where my editors and illustrator really come through. Thank you to Tony, Ben, and Darko for the 5th installment in the Forsaken Isles. If you enjoy this story, please put a review on Amazon and Good Reads. Thank you!

# Chapter 1 - Dark Whispers

She struggled against her confines. *How long have I been stuck in here*, she wondered. She felt groggy and disoriented. Oddly, she did not feel hungry. She looked down at her hands, struggling to see them because of her breasts. The narrow space, she tapped it and felt stone, made it hard to move. She hissed and purple light began to glow along her body. It showed just a finger's space around her hand and the rest of her body. The inner surface of the stone glittered with golden runes. She blinked a few times to clear her eyes. She wished that she could rub them but the stone prevented any movement. The runes became readable when she traced them with purple fire.

The ones in front of her face read: *Your name is Syand. You are a fallen human. The world sees you as a vampire. You built this to hide you from clerics and paladins that would slay you. You are the Queen of the Dark Legion. You serve Secret Kallis.*

As she read it, she recognized the runes and the writing as her own. She clenched her fists and then began to press on the stone. Though it moved an inch, she could not lift it herself. She looked around hoping she had written instructions for how to get out of the stone. *Am I in a coffin?* The weight pressing back on her when she stopped pushing stabbed her mind with a needle of claustrophobia. She resisted the urge to scream. She found her mind drawn backwards in time, to her first glimpse of sunlight. She remembered something rushing at her and then she fell, literally, to this place. Recovering, the sun burned her skin and she thrashed about before her instincts helped her regain self-control. The balm of clouds, the chirping of birds, the pitter-patter of rain washed the nightmare from her mind.

In the stone, Syand took a shuddering if calmer breath. She moved her hands around her hips and found a lever under her right thigh. She pressed it. Below her, in the stone, she heard a gear twist and then something snapped. The lid unweighted and she easily moved it to the side. Sitting up, she could see more clearly in the room's dim light.

Two oil lamps flickered to the side of the only exit from the room. A chest draped with leather armor and a gown caught her eye. A small table just to the side of her coffin - It does look like a coffin after all, she noted - caught her eye. It held a crystal decanter full of red fluid. "This isn't blood, is it?" she said picking it up and smelling it. Relieved it was not, she took a drink and felt hot fire in her throat. Slices of cheese and crackers pulled at her hunger and she took a few bites before she found them completely unfulfilling. She drank the rest of the decanter and called out, "Is anyone here?"

From the darkness, a man and a woman, both nude and scented with perfume, stepped forward. The female said, "Lady Syand, we are pleased to see you awake. Our records showed you would. I am Ydriss. This is my husband Renault."

Renault continued. "You must be hungry. We are ready to feed you."

Syand felt her eyes lingering on them and wondered aloud, "Am I vampire?"

The man said, "You are never satisfied with either answer, my lady. All we know is that when you awaken from these sleeps, you hunger for blood."

The woman touched the man's shoulder and said, "And other sustenance." She had a clawed finger cap and cut his arm. "We are ready."

Syand leaned forward and licked the blood. Unlike the wine and cheese, this blood offering filled her and she pulled the two tightly into her embrace. When sated, she leaned back on the hard stone floor and laughed. The two humans lay unconscious. Her appetite surprised them and her. Something had changed.

Drunk on their blood and from the updates they gave her as she drank, Syand knew that she was the head of Dark Legion, a thieves guild operating in Taysor in the time of High King Andrew. She knew, but did not believe, the stories that the Jade God had been slain by Morbatten. *Preposterous*, she thought. The woman, in a fit of passion, had cried out her last update about a team seeking to retrieve material from the Jade God.

Syand stood opened the chest. It contained items of a personal nature, some even sentimental. She put these to the side and donned several magic rings, an earring of blood red ruby, and then her armor. Two short swords rested against the sides of the chest, ready to be drawn.

She pulled these out and swung them. Both carried strong magic. On one she had written "Drinker" on the blade in the strange language of her masters. The other bore the name "Mirror." Drinker would capture the wounds of her enemies and allow her to recover her own pain from theirs. Mirror bounced spellcraft back at the caster. She loved her blades and kissed them. "I've missed you, my darlings," she said as she sheathed them at her waist.

She touched the earring and thought, "Dark Legion, I am awake. Meet me in the assembly hall in an hour. Bring me any proof that the Jade God is truly dead." She sensed a general acknowledgement of her command.

At the bottom of the chest, a precious book lay. Full of her own writing, it detailed the long course of her life since falling to Tehra. She pulled out a single folded sheet of paper, most precious of all her treasures. Syand carried it over to the man, Renault. She took his finger and touched his bloodied finger to the page. The blood swirled on the strange page's surface until a sentence appeared:

For what, would you know?

Syand dabbled the man's finger in blood splatter from their hours of feasting and wrote:

*Who rules in Orcus' stead?*

The runes resolved and began to shift: Nientro's name appeared and then halfway through the name 'Crea' became bright. 'Malcolm' danced over the two and then it shifted back to Nientro until all three vanished and a strange new rune appeared. It seemed to war with the first three names. "The Three Vampire Generals of Tania rule for Orcus?" Syand said aloud. "That cannot be right." Syand sat back and pondered all she knew.

Nientro was known to one of her masters. They had sought Nientro out, in Bloodstone. Though he had the hunger and ambition of a vampire, he was irrecoverably bound to the Jade God. Syand chuckled as memories came back and with them, Dar Ana – the Tanian High Priestess of Bloodstone – had managed to break Nientro's bond to the Jade God. The Three Vampire Generals had been key in Tania conquering and taking the rest of the undead fortresses in that valley. Syand burst into laughter when the delectable memory of her master's rage came to her. How he had railed against the lost opportunity of capturing one like Nientro to their true god!

She wanted to ask more. Renault would not notice or care about another question… "No, this is too tempting. Orcus is dead. Long live the Three Vampire Generals!" she cried out mockingly. "It's about time one of us became a god." She snickered. The idea was as old as time and ultimately futile. The Jade God did not allow ascension by the undead.

Syand felt certain the masters would not allow someone like her to ascend either.

Spite and jealousy threatened her but she calmed herself. The temptation to use Renault for more questions was too much. She had learned ages ago that more than two questions always resulted in the cursed artefact taking the blood-provider's soul... and once, almost Syand's. It was a dark memory and one she did not wish to flirt with again. Of course, she had only asked one question, and Renault would not mind losing his soul for Dark Legion's glory. Ydriss might object, but who cared? Her reaction could very well be the test for her becoming a vampire.

With quiet determination, Syand pulled out the special page. Renault's blood flowed sluggishly and he required more cutting. Syand wrote with Renault's finger:

*For more blood, show me the current state of Orcus.*

The blood swirled into the page and vanished and then a scene appeared slowly. The page required more blood. Syand bled Renault until his heart fluttered weekly. At last, the drawing showed Orcus sprawled out on his back. His head rested against a ruined fortress. His mighty sceptre lay broken and severed. Tanian encampments and banners of the Isles' nations flew around the sceptre as work teams dismantled it. Water, smoke, and battle raged all around the carcass. Syand licked her lips at the scene. *So tempting to learn more*, she thought.

Syand folded the page and put it back in her book. She clasped this to a chained binding at her waist. With a last look at the two humans, Syand walked out of her room and headed towards Dark Legion's assembly hall. Renault would recover, but be permanently weaker. He might not even notice it.

Syand found the assembly hall well-populated by some half of her guild. The others conveyed a general sense of not being able to make it, and well-wishes for her glorious return. Syand stepped up to the stage and looked out over the motley group of 40 humans. They came from all walks of life: male, female, old and young. The common thing that bound them all together was her blood. She had recruited each and every one of them. They were not allowed to recruit on their own. By their blood, Syand knew they were all loyal. She smiled and pushed her love to them all through the bloodstone earring. To some, she pushed the nearness of their transformation to vampire.

"Thank you for joining me. As you can see, I am not dead." Sporadic laughter twittered through the group and Syand continued. "Orcus is though! What shall we do with this? I would know. How are the other guilds, the surviving ones, I mean? Who is left to challenge us?"

The group began offering up what they knew, one at a time. Syand would point to the next person and so they went. It took a while, as she had been asleep for eight years. This sharing marked them as different from the other guilds. "Dark Legion does not keep secrets from itself," Syand said. "So, I tell you this. Orcus is truly dead. The Vampire Generals of Tania seem to have taken or are trying to take Necromancy's seat. This changes necromancy as we know it."

Syand flexed her arms and smiled at the legionnaires. "Some of my kind are going to be stronger. I can already feel it in me. Much stronger. Who knows what else will change because of it? For Dark Legion, we will rule Taysor! Here are my instructions. Recall any teams we have sent to Bloodstone. We will reposition them to infiltrate whatever process Tania would use to control the bounty of Bloodstone and the Jade God's falling." From her earring, she heard whispers of compliance. "I would also watch our friends in the game. This grand game may come crashing down without us doing anything at all. I would have the Legion understand on what the game stands and against what we might break the game. Effective immediately, let all our friends know that the Legion is entrenching. We will guard what is ours. We love them all. We will cut our take from all by half."

Their discussion lasted late into the night, or day; Syand did not know. Her resting place was secret; only Ydriss and Renault knew its location. Dark Legion's headquarters lay under a large tavern in the most dilapidated section of Taysor's eastern side. Everone called it, Offhand. When she at last slipped up to the streets, she found the city in all its might just before daybreak. It was quiet.

She could not remember any other time in her many centuries where the grand city stood this still. The human leader, Culridge, joined her, and explained it. "With all the heroes and fighters gone to Bloodstone, everyone is worried about martial law. Worse, the detonations caused by Tania – one of which took out the Northern Cross Guild – have cast a pall over everyone. High King Andrew has been gone for almost 8 months now."

"So, this quiet is a cowed population waiting for a savior? Pathetic. Culridge, we are going to take this city. We've never been as strong as we are right now. I want all intelligence on the other guilds. Bring me any Northern Cross survivors."

Culridge bowed and said, "It shall be done. We've been watching them. Only five of the lieutenants survived Kieran's folly." He was about to say more when he realized Syand was gone. Her teeth piercing his throat and a sensual reassurance that his time had come at last turned his pain sweet. "Yes…" he groaned through the tears in his neck.

As his mortality burned away, Syand enjoyed watching how the sunlight began to burn him. She touched her earring and summoned aid. "You know what to do," she said as they carried Culridge into the shadows. They had an eagerness in their steps. Syand had not made a vampire in decades. If Culridge, then perhaps they too would at last receive this reward.

Syand moved deftly to the rooftops. She did not like sunlight, but unlike weaker vampires, it was only a dislike. Thankfully, of those among the fallen humans who sought out blood to survive Time's ravages, she had ended up with enough magic to protect herself without again falling under the Necromancer's sway. She ran and jumped from roof to roof, landing with an eerie quiet that only disturbed roosting pigeons. Soon, the slanting roof tops of the warehouse district and her arch-rival, the 521 Guild, could be seen. If what her crew told her was true, she would find 521 going about their normal business operations. They favored gambling, smuggling (on the edge of the law), and prostitution. 521 shied away from being anything other than socially controversial. Cordelle was such a prude that way.

Syand skidded to a halt along the gables and peered down at the burly enforcers. They seemed alert, but not particularly on guard. With a smile, she dropped behind them and entered the warehouse that fronted for 521's real headquarters. Within a minute she found their leader, Cordelle, playing the role of a busy shipping superintendent. He relished the part and Syand spotted a city watch officer questioning some of the shipping lists. 521's guildmaster had been an actual shipping superintendent back when young. These past eight years had not been kind to him. Going from mid-thirties to forties, she expected him to look more resilient. Instead, gray hair and an even thinner frame made him look in his fifties. *Maybe it was a disguise?,* she mused.

She sauntered up to the watch officer and trailed her fingers behind his ears and neck. Leaning forward, she bit his ear softly and asked, "See anything you like?"

The officer tensed up and then relaxed as Syand mentally sent him a command to relax. "I bet we could buy anything you want in a place like this." She breathed these words into his ear and added, "With enough gold." Her sashay towards Cordelle gave 521's leader a moment to compose himself. Syand had been gone a long time. He was not happy to see her again and failed in hiding it.

When she turned back to the officer, he was fumbling his way out. Triumphantly, she twirled back to Cordelle and let her hair whip about her comely face. "Do I bill you for this intervention?" she asked.

Cordelle tapped a pen against his ledger and watched the officer leaving. Pensively, he said, "Not sure yet. We had a shipment of dolls go to the wrong place." Though Syand did not know what significance the dolls had, it meant something to Cordelle.

"Dolls?" she laughed and imitated one of the prostitutes.

"No, actual dolls. Some of them had other stuff, but that's fate. They got into the hands of some noble-born and well, you know how that is." Cordelle reached down into a sack by his foot and pulled out a doll and tossed it to Syand. The painted clay head bobbed on the cloth strips that filled its tiny form. "They're cute. Selling 'em for 3 copper. Want one? Hadn't heard you was up and around, Syand. Long time. Ten years?"

"Something like that. I came to see if 521 remained strong, and if you had any doings in Bloodstone with the Jade God's death." The doll contained a narcotic smoking powder that created a barely-noticeable euphoria. People liked its smell and used it to de-odorize their homes, if they could afford it. The Temples considered it evil. "I'm not surprised. If I remember correctly, you were testing this. Congratulations on making it work."

Cordelle jumped up onto a crate and sat down just a pace back from Syand. He winced. "It was a lot of work, but very profitable. I assume you have something you want to discuss? Let's go somewhere more private. I hope you won't mind a few guards? Since I last saw you, I have a new mage. Jace. I think you'll like him."

They walked down under the warehouse into Cordelle's office. Once away from public eyes, Cordelle's back straightened and his voice became stronger. Syand noted how he easily bypassed the various traps and safeguards in the staircase. His advanced age was a disguise, and Syand laughed. Though none of the traps were active, they helped remind her that Cordelle was probably a force to be reckoned with. Once in his office, he offered her wine and sat back on his plush chair. "Why do you care about Bloodstone?" he asked.

Syand sat down opposite him and sipped at the offered wine. "The Necromancer's fall; doesn't everyone care about it? I can feel it. Can't you? All that god body just laying there. I had a vision of the god being cut up and controlled by Tania. Tell me the body of Orcus is not interesting."

Cordelle smiled. "Yes, I can feel it. What magics we have in necromancy, they feel stronger. I'd imagine you feel it on a personal level. I bet all your... kind do. You look fantastic. Why did you really come here, Syand?"

Syand leaned forward and gave him an eyeful of her cleavage while licking the rim of her wine glass. When he stoically did not look, she laughed at him. "I've missed you, Cordelle. Also, the Jade God's body... why aren't we raiding it?"

Cordelle looked at her over-the-top attempt to flirt with him and laughed, even though it darkened her countenance. Syand did not like being laughed at and he knew it. "Tania controls Bloodstone. Tania set this plan centuries ago. I'm sure they're harvesting the Jade God since the instant he fell. Going there would be suicide for us. And, we've been busy rebalancing business with Northern Cross's sudden retirement." He pulled out a map and spread it on his desk. "While you've been gone, we worked out some arrangements. I'm happy to renegotiate with you. Culridge never quite seemed to get it. I was offering up the parts Dark Legion has always cared about. The Twins had some issues with it, but Culridge struggled to understand that I offered alliance."

"You helped me?" Syand placed her hand on her breast and feigned shock. "So generous, Cordelle! But, you see, I want more. I want Orcus."

"Orcus is suicide. I toyed with the idea, but The Twins sent a team. You just wait. Plus, I have some other brands in that fire." Cordelle toasted her. "Maybe, if things work out, we can reach an arrangement either way. 521 will have a stake in the god's black market."

Syand stood back and adjusted her top. For a moment, she held her breasts and leered at Cordelle so that he could see what he had just turned down. "Not all of us would consider it suicide. The Legion might make a run."

"The Twins are already there," Cordelle said. "They sent a team after Northern Cross vaporized. And Rogue? They might be there. I've instructed 521 to steer clear of it. Can you imagine what The Temples would do if they found any of us with the Necromancer's body parts lying around here? If The Twins don't share, I have informants near the

Temples that will drop a few clues here and there about The Temples. You see? We just need to wait it out."

Syand laughed cruelly. "And the Rogues? Will you rat them out as well? I doubt you would. Grant's your little pet, isn't he?"

Cordelle raised his glass and pointed to the door. "Please leave now, Syand. Before things get unpleasant. If I find anything that might interest you, I'll send word. I'm sure we can work out a deal but right now, there's nothing to deal in. If you do get any, I'd like to make you an offer." He rolled up the map. "Take a look at this. I would see 521 and Dark Legion as friends, or if not, a truce."

Charged by the blood in her veins and years of rest, Syand imagined ripping Cordelle's head off and bowling it up the stairs into the warehouse. Her keen hearing detected the sounds of men coming to ensure she left. The stealthy tread of enchanted boots told her Cordelle's mage stood ready as well. She whirled to leave. There was always something else about this place. It was not specific to Cordelle. It had always been this way. An uneasy feeling she could not explain. She wondered if the Dark Legion's tavern, affectionately named 'The Offhand,' felt this way to normal humans.

* * *

Khalla probed her lock pick into the tiny opening past the tensioner tool held tight by her thumb. Rocking the probe up and down, Khalla felt the telltale gaps of seven spring openings. With seven, this would be a complex key. She moved the pick in deeper and felt another; that's eight. She paused. This lock's key would be long and have at least eight raised ridges on it. On a hunch, she flipped the pick upside down. It dismayed, but also excited her, that the bottom line of the lock's channel held another three. There could be more past the eighth position, she found herself thinking. Leave it to Ash to design such an insane lock.

She braced her fingers against the lock and wiped sweat from her forehead. Though early spring, the day had begun warm and refused to cool as the afternoon dragged on. I could be anywhere, doing anything more enjoyable than this. She swore under her breath and fumbled for her other set of tools and a longer rocker.

Careful to keep tension on the lock, she inserted a longer tool used for exploration. Tactile sensation mattered when picking locks. The slightest touch, incorrect pressure… and this was Morbatten. She doubted Ash would invest in a lock like this without it also having magical safeguards or traps. "If you could talk, Door, what secrets would you whisper to me?" she asked it with some frustration. "You're practically my other lover."

Past the sixth channel, she found another three channels. Her longest pick would not reach that far. She almost began laughing. Ash had known someone would someday attempt to pick this. *Maybe even me,* Khalla wondered. Rather than set it with traps or magical glyphs, he instead offered the would-be thief a lock mechanism that could only be picked by abnormally long tools. Only one shop in all of Tania would have or custom-make such a lock or pick: Ash's shop. This design was an invitation to any would-be thief. Khalla almost laughed at the prospect of walking into Ash's shop and asking for exactly the type of tools needed to open this lock.

The door itself looked magically warded. That was what had appealed to Khalla about the lock in the first place, though she assumed Ash would have a more compelling or challenging set of traps in the lock itself. *I can't believe he hasn't just explained this to me. What's so secret in his life he keeps it here?* Upstairs, Ash would be waking up soon. Khalla blew hair out of her face and leaned her forehead against the door. All this time together and Ash kept this one room secret from her. Of all his houses, estates, and shell businesses, only this one room remained off limits to her.

She stood and stretched. Her back popped as she cracked her neck and twisted side to side. "Another time, door," she said returning to Ash's master suite. She grabbed a tray and put some Imperic tea and spring fruit on it. She mused on the several years of failed attempts and brushed aside annoyance. All this time just getting into the room without Ash knowing she knew, and then finally getting a chance to pick the lock... *I'm annoyed with myself that I can't easily pick it.* But, another thought objected that she was actually annoyed at Ash's keeping this secret still. *Ash really should have told me about this by now,* she thought. She now came and went throughout all of Ash's properties. But, the door and whatever lay behind it remained closed to her.

Khalla clenched her stomach and put the frustration aside. Dark whispers in her heart suggested that if Ash loved her, he would have shared the door's secret with her already. She pressed those voices aside, but did not want to. Her feelings had changed after Bloodstone. When Ash named her Marcello, she began feeling a growing sense of angst that she needed to be doing something. Specifically, Khalla felt it was time to put these distractions away. If Ash could not trust her, maybe she needed to put him away?

The master suite door opened on its quiet hinges and she found, to her relief, Ash still and unmoving, in the position she had left him. Maps of the ancient empire of Merakor lay pinned to the walls of the suite Ash also used as an office. *Copies of ancient maps*, she corrected herself. No one would ever stab a dagger into one of the actual maps left over from that age. They were priceless. Head sketches of candidates for the expedition group dotted sections, as did other key players. "Hey, lover boy! Wake up! The sun will be setting soon."

Ash groaned and threw a pillow at her. "Stupid elves never sleeping," he muttered. "Did I really get drunk with minotaurs last night?"

Khalla put the food and drink on the gilded side table next to Ash's head. She sat down by him, careful to sit so that when he opened his eyes, he would see all best parts of her. She smiled and pried his eyelids apart. "Yes, though the word 'with' implies you were part of the group. In reality, they laughed at you until you were unconscious. They drank. You became drunk. You may have danced for them."

Ash moved up to put his head on her lap. "It's a thing with them. They won't take you seriously until you show them you're serious. Tauran ale though, blech. If I boiled hair in water and poisoned it, it would taste better. I'm sorry I wasn't better company."

She caressed his hair back from his face and did not say anything. He knew she did not sleep. "The hour after sunset," she reminded him, "is when you are meeting the Mage's Guild to discuss the Merakor trip."

Ash nodded and kissed her stomach. "Have you been exercising, Khal? You smell active." She felt him lick her navel. "And vigorous."

Khalla caught his hand and said, "Oh, no you don't. Just because you retired from being guildmaster, does not mean I have time for all of this affection. Nice as it is." She reached out and grabbed the cup of tea. "You can make love to this."

Ash leaned up so she could leave the bed and whistled at her appreciatively. "I'm glad you're coming to Merakor with me," he said. "I'd immediately grow homesick for your lovely... smile." He toasted her with his cup of tea and took a sip. He tasted the medicinal herbs Tania used to counter the toxins in Tauran liquor. He started feeling better. His other option would be to visit a Shrine of Tiamat and ask for a prayer to remove the poison from his body. Since no one forced him into a drinking contest with the Taurans, it would cost him to seek the Goddess' help. Maybe Tiamat would, but Her priestesses did not like using their divine powers to counter poor behavior and bad life choices.

Khalla bent over, in a most fetching way, to retrieve the prior day's applicants from Ash's courier bag with the Adventurer's Guild. "That's the kind of talk that gets you in trouble with females. You're lucky I'm so giving." She flipped through the parchments. "No, I think your bigger problem is that you don't have a single elf volunteer for this suicide mission. I'm only going because I'm certain the mess you'll leave behind with Perdition will be far worse than an entire continent controlled by the Drow."

While Ash sipped at the tea, Khalla held her hands up like a scale. "This hand is the Drow and 3,000 years of evil. This other is the mess you'd leave me if I stayed here." She tilted to the right and pretended to fall over. "Maybe you should go to the Drow by yourself? Once there, you can leave a mess behind that could very well destroy all of them!"

Feeling much better thanks to the tea, Ash stood up and stretched. "But, what about fame and glory? You'll be the first elf – well, that we know of – to have gone back to Merakor. I mean, it's historic. You're so many firsts. My first love. The first Elf as Marcello. The first Elf to be loved by Marcello. The first Elf to make love to Ash in Merakor..."

Khalla began pinning new applicants up on the wall. "Glory?" she asked, ignoring his other comments. "Do I look like a paladin? I was part of the team that slew Orcus. That is sufficient for my life. I'm still concerned that 'god slayer' isn't enough for you."

"Well, that was last year, in the past. Today is the beginning of a new and glorious day. If all goes well with the Mage's Guild, I'll pick up some battle mage candidates. Then, we'll make love. Then, we'll go back to the Spiked Horn Tavern and talk with the minotaurs. If that goes well, they'll agree to send one of their named officers with us to Morilon, or someone better. To celebrate that, we'll make love again."

Khalla put her fingers on his lips. "You talk too much, and your order is all wrong. As Marcello, I don't have time for all that. You need to prioritize. Since you forced me into this role as top thief slash rogue slash spy slash agent of the empire, I barely have time for you. You have no one to blame but yourself."

"I'll take what I can get, Khal. Right now, I'm going to remember you just like this and hold your image with me through the Mages Guild meeting. You ready? Of course, you're ready. Let's go then!"

Two hours later, Ash kissed Khalla goodbye. The Mages Guild, with its large central tower ringed by other towers of different heights, gleamed with illuminated stained glass windows against the early evening sky. The air crackled here. Ash looked around taking it all in. Everything here catered to wizards. Anyone with magical talent came here at least once, most many times. The treasures in those towers…

Halgrim rocked side to side impatiently and glared at Ash. To counter Halgrim's dour mood, Ash grinned and waved goodbye to Khalla. Most of Halgrim's weight seemed to rest against a white bone staff, but Ash knew better; it was part of the mysterious artificer show Halgrim wore in public. Similar to how Ash used different personas for different tasks, Halgrim used props and his age to hide who he really was – a top-ranking artificer and a pre-archmage. No one, who did not already know, would ever guess that even the withered looking hands hid a vibrant mind and powerful spell casting ability. An errand boy held two large canvas bags full of rolled parchment, also part of the disguise. "Look at me," Ash imagined Halgrim mocking. "I'm too old to carry my own stuff."

"I see you dressed to the occasion," Halgrim observed pointing to the Ash's black leather armor, cloak, throwing knife bandolier, and general rogue-type gear. He pointed to Khalla as she rode off to the south. "You should have brought her."

"I see you dressed the part as well," Ash chuckled and pointed to Halgrim's sandals. Though the official Guild robes noted Halgrim's level as a Pre-archmage level 1, or 'Prearc 1', the sandals – not boots – showed a certain flaunting of protocol.

"At my age, I can wear what I want." Halgrim sniffed and beckoned the errand boy to follow him towards the central tower.

Once they crossed the guild's threshold, the compound became clearer. While the large central tower remained, many other towers rose up around it. Distance-distorting magic made the off-limit towers seem far away.

A guild representative stood ready and waiting for them. He called out, "Master Halgrim! So good to see you. To what do we owe a visit after so many years? I was at your retirement party. If you don't remember, I'm…"

Halgrim interrupted him. "Galvess. I remember. You look well. Is Dar Reznor ready for us? I've heard he has been absent these days."

The apprentices with Galvess and in the area all looked up at the mention of Halgrim's name. Not many Prearcs came and went by the main gate. Since the fall of Orcus in Bloodstone last winter, the higher-ups had practically vanished. Galvess smiled and said, "As far as any of us know, the guild master is ready for you. We take a lot on faith since Orcus' death."

Halgrim waved his hand and said, "I've come to make good on my dues and need to consult with the Council. Since our official request was granted, I figured I might as well get caught up and come out of retirement."

Ash stepped forward and bowed low, playing the role of fighter-attendant, possible bodyguard. He presented the scroll given him by Dread Lord Ynt'taris. Unrolling it just long enough for the representative to see Ynt'taris' draconian seal, Ash stated, "The great mage Halgrim has sent word and been granted an audience with Dar Reznor. Please take us to the Council."

Galvess blinked several times. "No one has seen Dar Reznor in months… but I'm sure he'll be here." Ynt'taris seal discomfited him. The apprentices began speaking in hushed tones. The Ice Patriarch's involvement was so rare the Mages Guild had not a single actual one in its archives.

Ash put his arm around Galvess and said, "And here you are delaying the great Reznor. I've heard that he's a member of the Circle. Wow, I'd hate to keep him waiting with how busy you keep saying he is."

Halgrim looked around and pointed to a tower in the distance. "Come, it's that one."

"Indeed, that is the Council tower, but I have no word that Master Reznor is even here." The apprentice sounded frantic and followed them in a flutter to make them stop. "If he isn't…"

Ash pushed the representative toward Halgrim's indicated tower. The tower rose up before them just fifty paces away. Ash pressed a gold coin into the young man's hand and said, while smoothing his robes, "You do good work here. Keep it up. Carry on."

The greeter quickly faded behind them with each step towards the Council tower. "You didn't take too much, I hope?" Halgrim speculated.

"Naw, just a few trinkets." Ash began handing them to Halgrim's errand boy. "Tell the poor man he must have dropped these." He handed over a deck of illusion cards, two wands, a necklace, an earring from the man's ear, and four rings off the mage's fingers. "It's a rather grim commentary on mages that I can literally take all of this and he has yet to notice they're missing."

The boy, wide-eyed, nodded and turned to head back when they reached the door. Ash shouldered the satchel of scrolls he had been carrying for Halgrim. "Well, Halgrim, this is it."

The old wizard nodded and knocked the door. The *knock* spell, for a typical mage, would pop a sealed door open. Halgrim's blew the door off its hinges. Phantasmal lights glimmered along the door frame as the doors creaked and then the left side door collapsed off its hinges. Halgrim smiled. "This is how you enter this tower. Such a simple spell, but it's a great way of announcing one's arrival with a flourish. After you, Ash."

A solitary man sat in a room that made up the entirety of the tower. Twenty thrones created a circle of empty chairs. The tower's height rose up above them and twinkled with star light. Dar Reznor waved and called out, "I'm glad to see you haven't lost your touch!"

Halgrim bowed to Reznor and walked into the circle of thrones. "I may have retired, but you know how it is, Master. I get antsy sometimes and keep in practice. Dar Reznor, might I introduce…"

Reznor finished the sentence, "Ash Bowker, formerly and perhaps still Marcello. You played a pivotal role in Orcus' fall. We've met. I'm not surprised to see you here. Dread Lord Ynt'taris ordered the Council to keep an eye out for you, Ash. I guess I expected a request for a battle mage. I never considered that a reluctant Prearc would come out of retirement. Are we to be speaking about Merakor? I do not wish to presume. Ash, no offense, but a Prearc coming out of retirement is my priority as guildmaster."

Halgrim and Ash both bowed, formally to their hands and knees. "Yes to Merakor," Halgrim said. "Yes, I am. Un-retiring that is. The prospect of adventure and Merakor is simply too much to resist."

Reznor bade them sit in the thrones near him. At his hand gesture, unseen servants unrolled and held open the various parchments and scrolls so they could all be seen together. Wine and food appeared. "I can bring in other members of the Council if needed. The white dragon Ynt'taris though, he does not like his dealings made public. Even the god emperor cautioned me to keep this close. I urge you to do the same, at least about the Dread Lord's involvement."

Ash remembered how the white patriarch of ice-breathing dragons had literally frozen time to give him the Bomoki mission that earned the Merakoran map as its reward. He picked up a platinum chalice full of elven wine and toasted Dar Reznor. "As you deem best, Dar Reznor. We live to humbly serve the empire and Dread Lord Ynt'taris."

Reznor scanned the parchments and pointed to one. "You intend to enter the Arati Grasslands. While the Mage's Council does not know it, the white patriarch has shared the purpose of your map with the Circle. I must tell you that King Malcor is most interested in your adventure too. How did he call it? Ah yes: 'A bold quest the likes of which we have not seen in ages.' Ironically, this suggests that slaying the Jade God was not a bold quest." Reznor rubbed his eyes and Ash noted the telltale signs of stress and fatigue. "Young paladins make my head hurt."

Reznor continued. "You see, sometimes the Dread Lords do not share everything they know. In this case, the god emperor knows that there is in fact a Tower of Sorcery there. Ynt'taris told you this but he did not tell you who owned the tower originally. Also, the god emperor cautions that Ynt'taris may have other interests in this than a simple reward."

Ash and Halgrim both began speaking at the same time. Halgrim said, "Who's tower?"

Ash said, "The owner of the tower does not matter."

Reznor smiled and let them sort it out. Ash spoke over Halgrim and said, "The map shows us the way to the tower. The adventure is getting in. So what if you tell me the tower belonged to some archmage or even god..."

Reznor magically silenced Ash with a mere raised finger. "Ash, you see, the tower was built by our god emperor. That's why it matters."

Ash kept talking even though silenced and then understood what Reznor had just said. Halgrim hmmm'd and leaned back in the throne to think. Reznor continued. "I'm glad you understand. Not just a god, but our god. Ash, you are in my Guild and you are not a member of the Circle. You will mind your place. No matter how much Daryx thinks of you, there is a time and place for your voice. May I continue?"

Ash realized the archmage was waiting for him and said, "Yes, apologies." The silence around him had vanished. *That's how good Reznor is with magic*, Ash realized. *Halgrim would be waving his hands around and spell casting. It'd be obvious.*

Reznor began speaking. "During Merakor, the god emperor was known as a human wizard, 'Aler Alerest' or the 'Fire Mage.' Aler Alerest was as well known as Galthrest and Velthrenest were at that time. He was assumed to have died when the Drow destroyed Arati. Clearly, that was not the case. Alerius instructs me to give you something precious." A piece of vellum, flaking and pressed between two crystal panes of glass, appeared in the space before them. It levitated slowly as it revolved before them.

Halgrim walked over and looked at it. "It's the blueprints for the tower."

"Yes, at least when operated by our god emperor. A grey Slaadi, named Polgeryx, decimated the Merakoran regiments of Arati. As they fell, cries for aid went to Aler Alerest who, at that time was a golem covering for the real purpose our Dread Lords were in Merakor. Polgeryx found and used the magics of the tower to trigger a cataclysm. An area the size of Morbatten, the valley here, not the empire, became smoldering ruin. Almost a hundred thousand died in the blast. A *contingency* spell sequestered the tower deep below the crater. Polgeryx thought it all destroyed. Commit this map to memory, or transcribe it. I must however, if you make a copy, *geas* the copy to self-destruct if viewed by any other than you two."

Halgrim and Ash studied the map and Reznor encouraged them to take their time. When they both felt they had it, Ash asked, "I'm surprised the god emperor let this affront stand, why allow it? Why not take revenge? Everything I know about the Dread Lords would seem off if Alerius did not kill this Polgeryx slaad."

Reznor shrugged. "I made the same observation. Three thousand years ago, and these are Alerius' words, 'I was not as strong in magic as I am now. However, even now in that same circumstance, I would not challenge Polgeryx without the Court.' Considering that all of Merakor was falling, it's not that surprising. Tania's own history suggests that grey slaads are beyond powerful."

Halgrim noted, "The real reason must have been compelling to give up such a challenge and treasure. The only thing I can think of is that the god emperor did not want it revealed, or even risked to this Polgeryx."

"It was, Halgrim. I'm sure of it." Reznor put his goblet down and the ancient vellum disappeared. "You know how much magic is worked into even this one, of many, towers here in Morbatten. And, you have not entered Alerius' laboratory in his mountain! There is power there. Some of it, the god emperor wishes returned. The reward, besides the other things you may keep, shall be this:

"Halgrim, you will take Dar Nientro's vacant seat in the Council, as Archmagus.

"Ash Bowker, you will take Daryx's seat on the throne of Perdition and finally rule as Master of the Thieves Guild, above Marcello."

Halgrim bowed low again and pledged without hesitation. "I accept these terms."

Ash sputtered into his chalice. "I always wondered about Perdition. I knew it! It never made sense to me that I reported to the Circle, most often via Daryx. Of course, there's also the actual throne room with an actual throne in that old fortress. Daryx all but told me this himself. Sly bastard."

Reznor commented, "For almost twelve hundred years, Daryx has served in this role. The Circle agrees that you are on the cusp of joining us. This quest to Merakor will prove whether you are worthy of it, or not."

Ash leaned back heavily and slouched in the plush chair. "Prove myself, again? I'm not sure this is a reward. I am not rejecting this offer, but it hardly seems a reward to give me impossible task after impossible task."

Reznor raised an eyebrow. "Perdition's Throne is a seat in the Circle, an impossible task for anyone except perhaps you, Ash. I might also add that, while you are rewarded by Ynt'taris, your mission's success comes at considerable expense to Tania. For example, we have noticed a lack of Elves willing to go to Merakor. We'll need to do something about this. You cannot walk into Arati as Tanian humans. The Drow will take you and you'll spend the rest of your life wondering how absolute the Allegiance of Blood is." Reznor stared at them both for long moments. "Think about this. I know you know it and that's why you've been targeting Elves. What is your plan, even with Elves? Neither of you are Elves. All in all, we estimate the cost of supporting your quest in the hundreds of thousands…"

Ash interrupted, "Gold, so what? The empire is drowning in wealth. What if I do not want your support? Perdition's Throne would have made me drool a year ago, but now, after we've killed the Jade God? I saw Bomoki encapsulated in ice. I saw the Nexus of Chaos and the Endless Worlds of Orcus. It feels like I lose myself if I agree to these terms. Having seen a god fall with first row seats. That was something. It changes perspective."

"Jewels," Reznor finished. Halgrim's eyes went wide and Ash choked on his wine. To simplify commerce amongst the Circle's members and other elite, the Merchants Guild used jewels to represent a letter of credit or some other instrument as a value equivalent to 10,000 gold coins. "The Circle's help increases the chances of your success in getting those items sought by the god emperor, which incidentally boosts your own chances. Did you think an expedition to Merakor would be a jaunty ocean voyage followed by a stroll along treasure-filled boulevards?"

With each word, Ash's expression flipped between his original enthusiastic self and a more pensive and brooding one. "Hundreds of thousands of jewels? Why not just send an army then?"

"King Malcor is considering an army, but his newness as king and lingering issues in Bloodstone hold him back. To be fair, Rojo considered it often as well though Rojo's focus was the Temple. The allure of the Lost Temple of Glass, to the paladins especially, is powerful. Even the god emperor did not, none of us did until now, calculate the cost of return being so much. The Allegiance of Blood makes it quite hard to leave and come back. There are also considerable risks, not just the Drow. But the rewards are," Reznor paused for effect. "Unimaginable," he said. "And, since you're going anyway, the Circle thought we might entice you with these other offerings. If Perdition's Throne is not desirable to you, I'm sure we can come up with some other enticement."

Ash held his chalice out and said, "While I drink more of your wine, please help Halgrim and I understand why the cost. We figured the Tauran transport and the actual team would be it." Ash looked at his friend and said, "While we did talk about the Allegiance of Blood, we always left it at that Ynt'taris would not give us this map if there were not some way around it. The Ice Patriarch would know. I guess it was bundled with the Tauran transport since, obviously, they come and go."

Halgrim turned Reznor and added, "Yes, it's as he said. We figured the Taurans must have some way of doing it. You say it's expensive. I would not have guessed that much. Our own budget…"

"Is close to a million. Yes," Reznor interrupted. "It's not enough. The Drow present challenges you have not thought about yet. Transport is one thing. Having the Taurans linger for you, ready to extract, plus any other issues you might bring back to their ship is extra. You have yet to discuss cost with them. Ynt'taris arranged transport, not everything you will need from them. Now, had you gotten Elves – and the Circle hoped you might, that would help on the final expense which is solving for the fact none of you are Drow. Elves, at least, are close. 264,000 jewels is what the Merchants Guild estimates the total cost will be."

Ash rolled his eyes. "It kind of makes me long for simpler days when the quest was clear, you went to it, you did it, and boom – loot. Look, Dar Reznor, the Throne of Perdition is enticing. I'd be lying if I said I did not want it. It's the risk cost of acquiring items of high interest to the Court of Patriarchs I am worried about. No reward is worth their enmity. I had enmity from just the Circle last year and that was quite enough for me."

Reznor snapped his fingers and illusions of the two plus Khalla sprang into being. "You are the only three so far vetted to go. If you go to Merakor like this, you'll be immediately spotted, tortured, killed, and probably soul-trapped by the dark elves. They use the surface world as a proxy battlefield since the Kinslayer War. So, as an example, we need to change you from this, to that." The illusion morphed to show the three of them becoming Drow.

Halgrim wriggled his fingers and the illusion of himself as a dark elf altered to hold the staff in his hand. He added some masculine vigor to the image as well as some muscle. "I'm an old man," he said. "Humor me."

Ash laughed and added, "We look good as Drow."

"Well, the change has to hold up to interrogation by all methods. That's what makes it hard. And, you'll need a credible priestess of Lolth." Another illusion appeared. It showed an up and coming R'Dar priestess. Ash thought he recognized her from Bloodstone last winter. "This is R'Dar Alex." Reznor looked at Ash and added, "Youngest sister of the heroine Thalian, who fell in Bloodstone."

Ash remembered Thalian. Though he did not want to admit it, in weak moments, he wondered if he could not have saved her and the dwarf. He raised his cup at Thalian's name while the illusion morphed from dragon to spider priestess. Reznor continued after the illusion was properly menacing as a Priestess of Lolth, "Making this change will be unimaginably expensive and not one we can affect with treasure. Tiamat and Lolth do not care about gold. No, to make this possible will be an adventure in and of itself. Dar Kell is already handling this one with Daryx."

Reznor held Ash's gaze for a moment before adding, "I hope you understand what I am telling you, Ash. Only a member of the Circle would know of a secret deal between Tiamat and Lolth. The fall of Orcus changes many things and the Prophecy of the Spear is still unfulfilled. If you treasure anything about your life, you will keep even the suggestion of this close to your heart, and no one else." Reznor then met Halgrim's

gaze. "I'm less worried about you, my once upon a time student."
Halgrim bowed low.

Reznor tapped his fingers on the armrest of his throne and took a deep breath. "Just talking of this makes me ill at ease. So, to another issue… of course, none of you speak Undercommon so Daryx will be teaching your entire group for however long that takes once you have that party together. Thankfully, you all know their handsign though Daryx will have to help you unlearn some things particular to Tania. And, there are so many other things required to allow you to leave and return under the Allegiance of Blood. You'd be fools to not accept our aid in this regard. Trust me, it would cheaper to raise an army and not pay you at all."

On that note, Reznor stood up. "I need to return to Dragon Mountain. Please consider these things. When you have your entire team – everyone – contracted, schedule with me again, even if you decide to foolishly go on your own. It is an option after all. Choose wisely. As you put it, the ire of the Dread Lords is yours to earn."

Halgrim and Ash remained in the Council for hours, discussing the offer, its merits, and the fact that if they did this, they would become beholden to the empire.

Ash threw a dagger to stick in one of the table edges. Another dagger thunked into it just a finger's distance to the right side. "Here's the thing. We now know that there is, might be, incredibly valuable treasure there. What if we don't take the contract and just retrieve it ourselves? We'd get paid enough that you could buy a seat on the Council. I could buy Perdition or something like it. We'd be heroes instead of contractors. Also, what if we want to keep some of it?"

"You really think we can just buy a seat on the Circle?" Halgrim snapped his fingers and laughed at Ash's exaggerated frustration. "Like that? Here's a mountain of treasure, now give me power in Tania?" Halgrim stretched and twisted side to side on the chair. "I gave up my ambitions to sit on the Council years ago. But, there's an appeal to it still. I thought myself content with being a Prearc. Also, you know what they say about dragons and treasure. Do you really want to NOT take this contract? The dragons now know that we know there are extra-special things there that they care about, that is worth hundreds of thousands of jewels. You really think we could just 'keep some of it?'"

"Why not?" Ash retorted. "If we take the contract and come back with all manner of things but just so happen to miss a few of the god emperor's desired baubles, we're just as likely to be mind-flayed. They'll think we kept them, even if we fail and don't get all of their stuff! Why not have a negotiation with them after we know what we have?"

Though the discussion continued on, back and forth for hours, they did not reach an agreement before they had to attend to other matters. Ash wanted to compromise and get the list but no promises. Halgrim wanted to take the job, the offered incentives, and focus on that. Halgrim poked his staff into Ash's chest. "Listen, if the Council will open the archmagi spells to me before we leave, that alone would be worth it. My vote is yes. And Ash, you wouldn't even be conflicted by this decision if not for my help. As a friend, as your business partner, for an old man, please let your answer be agreement under these most favorable terms, before Dar Reznor and the Circle revoke it. You know how Tania is. This golden treasure is shining right before our eyes. Take it! I bet they have another team ready to go in case we say no anyway, and then we'll have competition. Is that what you want?"

# Chapter 2 – Compelling Reasons

A man in black clothing blended into the dark alleys of Taysor's streets. Scanning a boulevard lit by gas lamps, the man noted a group of night guardsmen walking away from him. Another group of carousers stumbled his way. Good, but not ideal, he thought. He made a fist and signaled for those following him to halt. Until the carousers passed, they could not cross the street.

Ten minutes passed and it was taking too long. The longer they stayed hidden in the alley, the greater their chance of accidental discovery became. He pulled his cowl and face mask back. At least it was a cool evening. Without humidity, his gear felt comfortable. He pulled out a deck of playing cards and selected the 'joker' card. Featuring a buxom lady in a short skirt and party attire, he tore the card in half. Immediately, his form became that of the image he pictured. He minced onto the street and approached the group of five men, glad to notice they did not carry any serious weapons.

Once they caught sight of the buxom party girl, they went quiet and began elbowing each other. With a wink, she led them into an alley further up. The darkness masked the poison gas ampoule she broke in her hand as they followed her off the main street. She held her breath. One stumbled towards her, hoping for a kiss and she winced. Behind the lover boy, the other four partiers slumped down unconscious. She caught the collar of the one and touched his lips with her hand. The lingering gas was enough to knock him out. "You're just not my type, boys."

After a suitable number of minutes, she sashayed back to the main street while adjusting her clothing, and tried to imitate a satisfied air. She counted a few coins and dropped them into her purse while walking back to where the rest of her group waited. Glad to see the street still clear, she blew a gentle whistle noise while strutting up to the gas lamp and leaning back against it. She wrapped her arm up around the pole and looked around trying to act like a prostitute on the prowl for clients.

In moments, her team crossed the street and they were gone. Glad to drop the illusion, the man pulled his mask and cowl back on. "Glad to be done with that," he muttered.

"Hey, Grant, you were hot!" Muffled laughter twittered about from the darkness ahead of him.

"Shut up. We've got just three more blocks and then we'll be at warehouse 521." Grant carefully put his illusion cards away. "We're lucky so far, no real guards. Stay focused."

The warehouse district abutted the Gulf of Taysor. It sat at the intersection of Clark and Gable Street, a high traffic area mostly concerned with merchants rather than shoppers. Ocean-going trade stayed close to the coasts but allowed Taysor to dominate the gulf, except along the northern coast. The Sea of Glass, a vast desert of arid death, glimmered as a heat wave on the northern horizon of the gulf. Superstition held that ghosts visible in the waves portended ill luck, even death of a loved if seen too clearly or for too long. On a clear day, like after a storm, one could see the shimmering dunes from Taysor's tall buildings.

They moved efficiently, even bypassing hidden guards as they drew near to 521. Grant stopped when he saw the entry. His eyes noted four crossbow-wielding guards with easy shots from four different positions around the entry. "Big entrance boys," he whispered down the line. "But, this is business so not killing." 521 had a certain look and Grant's team was prepared.

On Grant's signal, they took the crossbow guards by surprise. One strangled cry out of four cut off abruptly, alerted the armored street guards and what looked like a mage just inside the entrance. The wizard came out with a wand in hand. Immediately, the four guards – now Grant's team – ignited in flickering light. They saluted back at the mage. At this distance, in the night, the mage could only see the guards waving back. "They look fine. We're all a bit jumpy with Syand up and about. Stay alert." Grant heard the wizard say.

Just as the mage turned to walk back in, Grant charged in and caught the spell caster in a head lock. Nearby guards at the entrance completely missed Grant's ambush.

Pressing a dagger enchanted to cut through anything against the sorcerer's neck, Grant said, "We were told to expect a friendly welcome. Since when is 521 on high alert for usual business partners?"

The mage tried to move but Grant's dagger shut him up. "Sure, you might get a spell off or even survive this blade, but you also might not. Answer me now. Be quick about it," Grant said with a friendly smile directed at the two hulking fighters in plate armor.

"Things are always friendly for usual business. Dark Legion is active again. We're jumpy." After a moment, the mage cursed. "Tiamat burn you, Grant. You know this is standard for us, at night. Damn it." He straightened his robes and then smacked the guard who had jumped back in frightened surprise. "You, do a better job!"

Grant did not sense anything amiss. Given the nature of their contraband, it made sense. "You know me, but I do not recognize you, mage. I'm going to let you go. I hope you don't make me regret it. Because I promise you will." Grant let the mage go, slowly, and stepped back. "Where is Cordelle?"

"I'm Jace. I joined up a year ago. Cordell is…"

A big voice boomed out from above a stack of cracks and kegs in the central area of the warehouse. "I'm right here, Grant. You idiot! Leave my guards alone, they're just doing what they're paid to do. Tell your crew to come in; too many prying eyes on the streets. Be a dear and apologize to Jace, our new battle mage."

Grant spun his dagger through his fingers and dropped it back into his wrist sheath. He detected a moment of defiance from the mage and said, "You wouldn't be the first who tried to take me. I am sorry for surprising you, Jace. But, surprising people is kind of what this business is all about. I'm Grant, leader of Rogue's Guild."

Joined by his men, Grant walked into 521 shoulder to shoulder with Cordelle. They ascended the crates and found a secret door, laying open, which led back down into the pile of stored boxes. Grant pointed to the hidden opening mechanism and several mechanical traps. "Nice hideout, Cordelle. I might mimic this later."

Cordelle snorted. "You keep picking fights with my mage and you might find yourself living here as a rat. It's my new favorite punishment. We had a merchant stiff us of 10 gold. Jace turned him into a pony and we rented him to a family for their kiddy's birthday party."

They wended down stairs that were sometimes spiral, sometimes straight, and at last entered a large circular room with no apparent exit. Grant eyed the walls and was impressed to see no hidden or secret doors, at least that he could detect without being obvious about it. Cordelle moved to sit at a huge desk in front of shelves groaning under hundreds, perhaps thousands of ornate scrolls and their containers.

"Only magic to get out of this now," Cordelle explained sitting down. "Now, to business. Grant, I have to hand it to you. You're the first one to make it back with anything from Bloodstone. On behalf of my gang, thank you for coming to 521 first. We are honored. Now, if the pleasing words are done, show me your take. I hope it's gory and disgusting in a way that befits the Jade God." He rubbed his hands together and cackled gleefully. "It must have been something to see!"

Cordelle spoke in short, gruff words, the side effect of too many broken noses and jaws without divine healing over the years. Tanian clerics rarely came through Taysor and were the only ones that would heal someone as dark as Cordelle.

"It was," Grant drew the words out, "spectacular! Orcus was taller than the valley mountains and when he fell," Grant snapped his fingers and then said, "Delton, please."

Delton opened his backpack and withdrew a flat bag. Folded many times and bound, when opened, the bag would easily hold an adult human.

"A magic bag! You're getting me all fuzzied up inside," Cordelle said, rubbing his hands and stepping forward. "You must have retrieved a lot to warrant a holding bag. Tanian manufacture?"

Grant ordered, "Delton, grab us some bone, a vial of blood, and a quill from that fine Tanian bag!"

"A quill?" Cordelle said with some confusion. The mage, Jace, leaned forward too.

"Yes," Grant explained. "Up close, the Jade God's fur is more like quills, each as long as a great lance."

Delton retrieved the vial of blood first and gave it to Grant. "It's brilliant in darkness and resists magics that would dim its light," Grant explained as he passed the crystal container over to Cordelle. The crystal glass glowed as if lit by green fire. Jace spoke a cantrip and the room became dark, except for the sickly green light. "Because we were the first ones there, we got quite a lot of this before the god emperor detonated Orcus' head. You won't believe how much we stored. Go ahead, smell it."

Cordelle uncapped it and sniffed. Green vapors of light entered his nose and momentarily lit Cordelle's eyes with green fire. He snorted and rubbed his nose. "Woah, I can see your soul auras." He looked at his own arms and began laughing. "Grant, you is as dark as I is."

"A brief sniff only lasts a couple of seconds, still an interesting side effect, no? Try this," Grant offered while passing over what looked like folded leather. "We had to de-quill it, but still."

Cordelle's look of surprise when he touched the god's skin amused Grant. "I never thought a necromancy god's skin would be so... so soft." Cordelle sniffed it. When nothing happened, he asked, "It smells like cinnamon but no special anything?"

"May I?" Grant said pointing to the hide and Cordelle's shoulders. Cordelle waved him over. "Wrapping this around you, you'll feel something we can't explain, and, we've been experimenting with this all the way back. I like to think of it as your soul wanting to be free but it's trapped and so you feel trapped."

Cordelle pulled open the strip of leather, it was three paces long and two paces wide, around him. He softly counted and at five, he took it off. "That's unpleasant. I see what you mean. Too bad it doesn't have an obvious effect."

"Oh, it does," Grant whispered. In a blink, Grant had his enchanted dagger in his hand. The knife could cut anything. That special property made it rare and precious. The vorpal dagger flashed in his hand and he drove it at Cordelle's heart.

Cordelle tried to jump back, but was too slow. His face became resigned as the deadly weapon struck true. The blade pressed into, but would not cut through the skin. Cordelle pushed the leather back to help the blade cut but it would not. Grant rubbed his hand along the edge of the knife through the skin and gave his best salesman's grin. Shock and anger became replaced by loud laughter as Cordelle stepped back and shrugged the blanket of Orcus skin off. "That felt like you poked me in the chest. It hurt, but I can't believe it. If you had told me, I would not believe it!"

Grant pointed to where his knife point barely indented the leather. "My dagger should cut right through. We saw it with our own eyes though. Thousands of fighters attacked the Jade God and while some succeeded, most blades bounced right off. And, you know how Tania is. The stories do not under-tell their weaponry. Get your mage..."

"Jace. Jace and you'll be working with him to figure this out. I want it all. All that you have!" Cordelle called out.

Grant continued, "It's incredibly resistant to elemental magic as well. More so, I would hazard, than a magic item."

"How did you cut it?"

Grant said, "We pulled it. While it resists cutting, it will eventually cut with enough effort. Well, and holy water from any god allows my vorpal knife and similarly powerful blades to cut it quite easily. We've had weeks on the road, travelling mostly at night to get here from Bloodstone." Grant began to fold the skin but Cordelle wanted to play with it some more. "If you can get past the feeling, it'd make fine armor, but we're actually thinking it might be better as a shield."

Cordelle laughed. "And the quills? The bones?"

"They have interesting properties. The quills are hard like metal but bend and twist, unless it contacts blood. At that moment, just like a leech – a really big nightmare leech, it latches on and digs in. Only anti-curse magic can remove it."

Cordelle bobbed his head up and down. He wrapped himself in the skin and ordered the mage, "Jace, hit me with your best elemental magic!"

"Boss, the freezing sphere spell would…"

"Do it!"

When the ball of ice shot out and hit Orcus' skin, it exploded and encased Cordelle in ice. Seconds later, when the spell ended in a shattering of ice crystals, Cordelle marveled, "I barely felt it. I felt the cold air when I breathed." He looked at his arms as glittering ice vanished in motes of silver light all around. "I barely felt it!"

Grant held over a small bone fragment the size of a human leg. The bone material looked like jade but of such a vibrant green it hurt the eye to behold. Like the blood, it seemed to burn as if on fire. "We did not get much of this. Accessing the bone proved difficult as, once dead, Orcus' body decayed into powerful undead we had to fight through to get what we have. This fragment though weighs about fifty pounds. We have ten fragments like this and some smaller ones. Just holding the bones, it augments the force of your will. Try it, Cordelle. While holding it, touch Jace and give him an order he would not normally do."

Jace stepped back in protest, but Cordelle caught him and commanded him, "Kneel and pretend you're a cute little bunny rabbit." The bone barely touched him as Jace tried to avoid getting tagged.

When hit, the mage groaned and immediately fell to one knee. He visibly struggled to not kneel. While this happened, Grant took out a small folded packet. "We powdered some of the bone. Either inhaled as a dust or ingested, it magnifies any and all commands no matter how ridiculous.

You feel like you're going to suffocate the longer you resist. Once you obey though, well, words can't describe it. Since I have to work with Jace, I'd rather not use him as a test subject. Its effects are quite amazing. I recommend you try it with your girlfriend, to magnify something she enjoys doing. If you know what I mean."

Cordelle walked over to Jace, the powder in his hand and almost dumped it in his mouth. "Too valuable." Instead, he put the actual bone on Jace's forehead. "Obey me. I want to see this indescribable reaction. Be a cute bunny. I'll double your pay tonight."

Jace nodded, gulping as sweat broke out on his body. He dropped down to kneeling and looked up making his best rabbit face. He hopped. That was when his expression of concentration changed to a sublime and carefree smile. He hopped again and wriggled his nose. Grant took the bone and touched Jace. "I command you to be freed of this compulsion."

Jace stood back up on shaky legs. "That felt like the most loving praise raining down on me from my parents, teachers, everyone I have ever looked up to. It just went on and on. The more I submitted, the more intense the praise became until it was all I wanted. Cordelle, had you commanded me, I would have done anything for that feeling to continue. I felt... happy. I'll be honest though, right now I feel its absence and want it back so much. I can hear it, feel it, see it. I'm struggling to not curl up and beg for more. My brain tells me to avoid it, but the rest of me is falling into despair. A weaker person would find this addictive on a level beyond anything we've seen."

"Interesting," Grant said. "One of my guys described it as being in the arms of the most beautiful woman he could imagine. We all feel it differently, I guess."

"How much?" Cordelle asked.

"For what I've shown you now, forty thousand. Seven million if you want it all. We have five holding bags, each with ten thousand pounds of material. We have the most skin and quills though. This is a discount as we would prefer a single buyer and be done with it. Sure, there were other groups and they'll be bringing bits and parts of Orcus back, but it'll be marred and the Tanian patrols will have made them suffer for it. They'll want twice our price but for lesser quality."

Cordelle sat back and on a whim, he grabbed the vial of Orcus blood and sniffed it. Blinking back the pungent odor, he looked closely at Grant. The thief's aura pulsed a steady grey. It suggested caution and awareness, but no deceit. Cordelle closed his eyes and leaned back on the table. "Twice, huh? How do you figure that?"

"Tania's patrols were almost immediately augmented by paladins and dragons. If you aren't interested, I will sell it to Tania, or charter a minotaur ship and sell it to foreign buyers. Tania was already moving to monopolize everything." Grant rolled his eyes. "Our King Andrew was helping. Weakling."

Cordelle eyed Grant and carefully said, "King Andrew is not a weakling. You weren't here when the Tanians flew over the city. They detonated three bloodstones. Remember the stone Northern Cross had? I sent a team to check on Kieran. His bloodstone's explosion left a crater twenty-men deep and nearly a hundred paces across." Cordelle touched the bone and closed his eyes. "This stuff is unimaginably powerful. Remember, Grant – we are smugglers, pirates, and…"

Grant finished the pledge, "We are the secret strength of the High King. Yes, yes. The privateer's pledge. It hardly matters now though, does it? The way I see it, you had Orcus - the Orcus - killed in Bloodstone. All the magical types there were speculating as to how it would change necromancy." Grant pointed to Jace. "Ask your mage about it. I figure we have a few months before the Abyss fills that void and strikes back. The Allegiance of Blood, if real, it won't save us. I want my payday and I want out of the Isles."

Jace nodded. "I'm not active in the Mage Guilds, but friends tell me that it'll be bad when it happens. If the Tanians were right, Orcus had two throneplanes. What are the chances that an abyssal civil war for those planes stays in the Abyss?"

Cordelle touched the blood, skin, and bone. "How'd you get so much of this, Grant? Don't lie to me. If I buy this, is Tania going to come knocking on my door with a fire-breather?"

Grant was ready for this question. His own gang had been asking him about it the entire trip since leaving Bloodstone. "Simple really. Everyone knew Bloodstone would be a free for all, whether or not Tania won. With an actual god in the cascade, we fought with Tania. At a certain point, I suspected Tania might win and so I moved the team to one of the Jade God's legs. There were these giant gaping cuts along his leg. Even if we attacked, it would not have mattered and so we took blood. As much as we could get. I'm sure you heard about the volcano and the flood, and the Tauran ship, right?"

Delton and the others started cracking jokes. No one had expected to see a world galleon appear in the sky and spear Orcus just above his belly. When banter calmed, Grant held up a quill. "This is his body fur. We held on when Orcus fell and so escaped the flooding. With all the fighting going on, we set to work while others fought. Truth to tell, I feel kind of bad about it. Demons and undead were peeling off Orcus' body and we just let them go. Thankfully, they had more interesting targets than scoundrels like us."

Cordelle walked over to the shelves and began rifling through scrolls. With his back turned, he said, "The problem isn't that I don't want it, Grant. The problem is your price. There aren't that many that would be interested in buying so much on the black market, and even fewer with that price. Even pretending I had seven mil just lying around, I wouldn't want to just give it all to you." He snapped his fingers. "Like that. It's too much. If I leveraged all of 521, I might be able to meet your price. Then, once I have your fifty thousand pounds of Orcus, I'll have to sell it piecemeal over years, maybe decades. You say we have maybe a few months? That was a poor move on your side. Plus, just like the bloodstones, I bet Tania begins selling it and that'll be my competition. Maybe they'd sell this same amount for a tenth? I call your bluff, Grant. I'll offer you a million, plus another mil as a letter of credit on the good king's seal. I can have it all arranged within five days." Cordelle offered his hand.

Grant looked at it. It was a good offer. Something about transacting at this price though made him feel greedy. "A half-mil now, a mil as a letter of credit, and you get half, not all. We'll even lay it all out and you can pick the best bones, skin, and quills. I can't let you take more than half the blood. You understand. It's not half by weight. It's half by quality and then weight. I'll take my other half across the oceans and sell in foreign markets. This leaves you with a monopoly and as the largest supplier outside of whatever Tania does with it all."

Cordelle and Grant eyed each other for several long moments. Just as Cordelle was about to negotiate, Grant added, "And I need you to buy out and end all vendettas against my crew, all of us. 521 will buy them all and then destroy them."

Cordelle started laughing. "You want me to buy out Marcello of Tania, Dark Legion, and The Twins' bounties on you, huh?" *It's an interesting move,* Cordelle thought. *The value of the vendettas is two hundred thousand each, but as a guildmaster, I can buy them out for about half. Grant knows this. But, if the other guilds find out we did not end Grant's family, it becomes political. 521 would be on the line. He's basically saying that he wants me to protect him.* "Okay, but I take two-thirds of the blood. Once we buy the vendettas, you all will die a staged death and be," he spread his hands and made a "poof" sound, "reborn. You'll leave and never come back. Deal?" He put his hand out again for Grant to shake.

This time, Grant took it. Jace was already making arrangements for the half million and an extradimensional space to spread out the parts of Orcus.

* * *

Ryvane walked with Calvin through Dockside. Everywhere, the common people bowed and waved. His popularity had exploded following his bold presence against the Green Sun of Orcus. A few charmed memories of Calvin saving children, and a well-placed bribe with witnesses ensured it. Though Dockside had never had an elected mayor before, Calvin had run as the only candidate and logically won. *Humans are so easy to manipulate*, Ryvane thought She watched a small girl run up to Calvin and give him flowers. With a curtsey, the little child ran back to her mother thrilled to have met the Mayor. *They practically beg to be led, like sheep.* Perdition's creed came to her mind: Predator, never prey. She suddenly felt very glad to be part of the Tanian Thieves Guild.

Calvin handed the flowers to Ryvane. "Pretty flowers for my pretty bride to be."

*And then, there's Calvin*, Ryvane thought as she kissed his cheek and smiled. Things he would have balked at just six months ago, now came naturally and unconsciously to him. The idea of accepting a thank you gift from a girl he had literally done nothing for would have offended him back then. Today, he reveled in the attention. Any idea, any notion, if couched in some noble aspiration worked for Calvin and boy, did he work for Ryvane now. It rather made her regret her dual allegiance to the Mages Guild and Thieves Guild. "Ah, my fiancé. You're so gallant."

While walking down what passed for Dockside's Main Street, Ryvane found herself over-thinking the word 'gallant.' *Calvin is gallant*, she insisted to herself. And he treated her well. He also did not mind at all when she used her magic on him. His absolute trust, just like now, it caught her off guard. *He would probably find it exciting to learn I'm not human. No, I'm never going to tell him. Would others tell him?* she wondered.

He slapped her butt and said, "Quit daydreaming, we've got places to be."

She slapped him back and they walked more quickly to the Mercy Court. The High Judge Jeffreys waited for them. After delays on three summons, the Halfling Reggie finally knocked at their door one day. "Go. Sai has arranged it all. But, do not delay any more or this elevates to a military court."

Though they had to wait, they found Jeffreys in a good mood. They approached his bench and bowed. It felt uncomfortable to have so many people all around listening. Jeffreys addressed them loudly. "Watch Officer Calvin and Lady Ryvane, thank you for coming. Let it be known," he said, as scribes began writing. The High Judge continued, "That your affairs in Dockside do not take priority over the Mercy Court. Should you avoid direct summons again, or dare to send me excuses, you will both be stripped of your civilian and Guild rankings. Do you understand?" He looked at Ryvane for several moments and re-emphasized, "All Guild rankings."

Ryvane swore mentally. *Of course, he knows I'm in Khalla's cell. Damn.* Khalla told her once that Jeffreys sat on the Mercy Throne for the Circle.

Calvin attempted to explain, but Ryvane squeezed his hand. "We understand, my lord. Is there another matter you wish to discuss?"

Jeffreys waited until Calvin agreed. *The scribes probably wrote down that I squeezed his hand,* Ryvane thought watching the flurry of their pens scratching away at the paper. Jeffreys continued, "Only a Dar may call for popular elections and only then in their dominion. Are either of you Dar rank?"

Calvin answered this time. "No, my lord. However, Dockside has been a mess since even before the Orcus incident. Best I can tell, it fell apart and never recovered from the Kell Conflict. You charged me to set it right."

"I charged you to investigate missing persons, not provide political leadership to Dockside. Do you deny this?" Jeffreys leaned forward and glared at Calvin.

Calvin countered, "I accept it all, Dar Jeffreys. Every single word of it. The missing persons case was solved and, while a war was being fought in Dockside's streets, I ensured that no more innocents became prey. They need help. Since my election, Dockside has never run so smoothly. Do you deny this, my lord?"

Ryvane almost clapped her hands. Every so often, this fighter-side of Calvin would pop up and remind her that he might have been a paladin.

*Maybe that's why I am falling in love with him, against my better nature,* she conceded.

"The Circle agrees with your assessment. This is why you have been summoned here. While the people may have chosen you in a sham election, this is to make it official." A scribe walked around the bench and handed Calvin a scroll, rolled and sealed in King Malcor's Seal. "The Circle has found your management of Dockside acceptable. Provided the summer trade with the Taurans runs as smoothly, you will be granted official title at first snowfall. You are dismissed."

Walking out, Ryvane nearly squealed in delight. She leapt into Calvin's arms and whispered lustily in his ear, "R'Dar Calvin. Or maybe R'Dar Cal. Some of the lords, like Daryx, shorten it to a single name. 'Darcal,' I like it. We must celebrate!"

Calvin ignored those around them, frowning to see a Watch Officer embracing a scantily clad and full-figured woman. He kissed her lips and said, "Our marriage will make you R'Dar Rvyane. That'll definitely need to be shortened. How about R'Dar Vane?"

Later that night and augmented by Ryvane's magic, their celebration lasted many long hours. When they woke up late the next day, Ryvane found Calvin at his desk reading through the scroll. He waved and smiled at her. "The letter is three things. An official charter to display in the Mayor's Office. It incorporates Dockside as a mayoral district headed by the Mercy Court. No surprise there. The actual charter is pretty straightforward. So long as the canal locks to the ocean are kept working and crime is kept at levels that do not affect the innocents or the Tauran trade, I'm mayor." He held up a medallion. "This is the third, my token of office. It's enchanted to return to me no matter what."

Ryvane sauntered over to him and put the medallion around her neck. Twirling she said, "How does it look?" Before he could answer, she laughed and said, "I'm no politician." She took it off and draped it around Calvin's shoulders. "So charming and inspiring."

While Calvin got armored up for evening patrol, Ryvane bathed and readied herself for her other job, the one Calvin did not yet know about. Around midnight, she entered an abandoned looking building on the northern neck of Dockside. Walking in, she said, "Thank you all for coming." When she turned around, she found Khalla sitting alone in the main room. The single lantern with red shutters, to indicate the room secure, flickered in the darkness.

Khalla kicked an empty chair towards Ryvane. A table sat with a bottle of wine and two golden cups. "You expected your cell to be here, I'm sure. Hello, Ryvane. I dismissed them for the night. We have matters to discuss. First, I hear you're engaged. I assume you know what you're doing so congratulations. Second, Marcello asked me to give this to you." She slid a small envelope across the table. "Go ahead, look at it. I'm supposed to stay here until you've given an answer. I also have what you might consider either bad news or good news, depending."

Ryvane opened the letter and found the perfect flowing cursive of Marcello. It read:

> Hail and greetings, Ryvane!
>
> My friend Halgrim assembles a party of adventurers to travel to Merakor and seek out a Tower of Sorcery, of Aler Alerest, in the Arati Grasslands. As a mage, as a shapeshifter, as someone we trust, as someone who speaks Undercommon, I wish for you to join Halgrim's team. The team's captain, Ash Bowker, will seek you out soon to know your answer. We desire a ten-person team. Your share will be a tenth. We expect this adventure to last for one year.
>
> Your friend,
> Marcello

Ryvane blew a stray strand of hair from her face. Her body language and voice tone said 'no.' Ryvane said, "Everything about this appeals to me except the timing. Could Calvin come?"

Khalla did not need to consult with Marcello though she needed to be diplomatic. "No. A mayor needs to stay with his people. Did you know, Ryvane, that the three people Calvin is closest too have all exceeded even their instructor's assessments? Malcor is, well, Malcor. But, R'Dar Seline serves as First in the Nineteenth Legion in the paladin Order of Fire. Legion Commander Ayden, well, she is the Nineteenth's Legion Commander. All three are of Calvin's class. Ryvane, what are you doing with him? He's hardly your type or style. Marcello told me your last lover not just burned out but you almost soul-sucked him to death, with love. The Temple had to work on him for weeks to save you from murder charges."

Ryvane crossed her arms but held the letter so she could glance at it. "Calvin has a certain appeal. He's powerful in his own right." Ryvane folded her arms and looked away from Khalla. "You wouldn't understand. You're just Marcello's little love puppet, aren't you?"

*Marcello was right*, Khalla realized. After her 'crowning' at Sai R'Dar's estate, Marcello told her, "Only two cell leaders you select will know you're the real Marcello. Everyone else will believe that you're still Khalla, working for Marcello just like they do. That was just part of the show because they all think I'm just a cell leader too." Being Marcello, this conveyance of indirect orders complicated her life daily. It gave her an appreciation to why Ash had given up the role in the prime of his career.

"Calvin isn't the issue. His lack of skill, power, and practical experience is. Marcello wants adventurers, not politicians. There won't be any critical charisma-based politicking during this trip to Merakor." Khalla added after a moment, "You know that I know, right? As a cell leader and lieutenant, Marcello told me you're a rakshasa."

Ryvane deflated a bit. "How many know?"

Khalla hopped up from the couch. "I don't think it's very many. By design however, enough know to counter you killing everyone who does. But, I don't think that's why you're in Tania. And why you're a rakshasa or why in Tania – I don't know that I care, so long as your cell performs and your thing with Calvin doesn't escalate into blowing your involvement with Perdition."

"It won't. I've actually been thinking about resigning the guild." Even Ryvane blinked to hear herself say it. She took a deep breath and then rushed through it. "It's something on my mind, Khalla. Please explain it to Marcello. I'm struggling with all of this. This thing with Perdition, it was always supposed to be temporary. A side job when I wasn't otherwise engaged in the Mages Guild. I'm not a thief. You all know it. Tania wanted me because I'm the best spy money could buy. My status here as a rakshasa is always hung over my head. I'm tired of it. At some point, I'm either a Tanian like you or I'm a prisoner."

"Marcello would, I have no doubt, prefer your resignation than your membership or cell embarrassing the Guild. Calvin, this political thing, is too close to the new king; you know this, too. I know you do." Khalla stood and began to pace. After a few turns, she added, "Though, I bet you could work something out if you did this Merakor thing. What are your thoughts on that?"

Ryvane picked at the ornate edges of her goblet. "So, prove myself as a rakshasa, now prove myself for Calvin's sake? None of this seems fair, but I guess I'm not surprised either."

Khalla looked at Ryvane and felt a tension in the room she did not like. Ryvane was always temperamental but today seemed on the edge of actually resigning. She pulled another ledger from her bag. "Ryvane, this is a record that Marcello has kept about you. Regardless of what he thinks, here is what I am concerned about." She flipped to a page. It was half empty but full of names and dates. Khalla counted them.

"Since you joined Tania one hundred and eighty years ago, you have been assigned seventeen people, men and women of various races. So, not just humans. You have fallen in love with all seventeen of them. Each time, Marcello cautioned you to not burn them out. Each time, by the time you ended it, they were burned out. The first, a nobleman, took his life in 1809 DAR. The next, a noble elven lady, fell into a profound depression and is still being tended by the Sylvan Nation. Do I need to go on? Ryvane, not just for your own and Perdition's well-being, I have to ask you – are you sure you know what you're doing with Calvin?" Khalla held up the book.

Calvin's name was written by clear handwriting that was not Khalla's. A note scribbled there read: He has become dependent on charm magic for basic performance as a watch officer.

Ryvane tried to look away but it was so easy to read. Her face fell even further. "I don't mean to. It's the curse of my race. We have these powers that are so convenient to build followers. But, it quashes ambition and progress, the things that make them worth knowing. That's why Kieran and I left. He already had a harem. He did not want me because, well, complex reasons. Mainly, he saw in me what I see: I want to be a mage and not just a lazy rakshasa one who charms everyone to get her way. Part of our nature though, we fall in love or fascination so easily."

Khalla refilled Ryvane's wine cup and asked, "Do you really love him?"

Ryvane nodded but did not speak and after a minute, Khalla said, "If you do, you need to stop charming him. We all use and rely on magic, but yours is different." Khalla pulled a copied page folded into Ryvane's book. "This is a report from our Soran cell. It notes about Kieran: the rakshasa has assembled a guild. Northern Cross suffers a generational disease. They are strong and ambitious and then lose reputation and territory. Their officers become sloppy and lazy. I don't get it. Is it a rakshasa thing? The other guilds have come to expect it. Later, our agent writes that Kieran will not give up his bloodstone for fear that he will lose control of Northern Cross."

Ryvane folded her arms and hugged herself. "That's how we were raised. These powers come so easily. Even in the Mages Guild, they wanted me to specialize in charm magics. Not in your ledger is that my first master fell in love with me too. I was new and broke it off for fear of stunting my training as a mage. My next master, I was more relaxed, more confident. We had a torrid affair. I wanted a tower; he gave me his tower. It's my tower now. He committed suicide. Were I a human, I'd feel bad but because I got his tower, I don't. I accept this but know I should not. It's a part of me that is broken or was never in the rakshasi to begin with." Ryvane lifted her head up and looked at the ledger of her past assignments. "This is mostly correct. Marcello only tracked my Perdition assignments. There are another two hundred and nineteen."

Khalla took a stiff drink and tried to imagine how the Law of Innocents would apply to a rakshasa causing so much destruction. "Of them, did any, you know, work out all right?"

"Three survived and went on to have happy lives, Khalla. Just three. That's how pathetic I am. I hated seeing this when I was with the rakshasa. I hate recalling it now and I hate myself for it. It's why my resigning might be a good idea."

"That won't save Calvin." Khalla meant it to sound encouraging but the deadpan words struck Ryvane who growled softly.

"No, Khalla. I suppose it won't. Merakor might though. We'll be in danger, in a group. Calvin can focus on other things and I won't have to play the Mayor's girlfriend. Everything will be out on the table. Calvin will either live or die, but it won't be because of me." Ryvane slammed her hand on the table. "Tell Marcello that Calvin is my condition."

Khalla folded her hands across her stomach and shrugged. "Okay. Let's see what Marcello has to say about it."

Ryvane smiled, for the first time during their talk. "What is the bad or good news?"

Khalla walked around and put her hand sympathetically on Ryvane's arm. "Kieran is dead. We got word from our Soran cell months ago but Marcello has been tied up and finally asked me to tell you. Apparently, Kieran refused to go to Bloodstone or to turn over his bloodstone gem. When the Dread Lords detonated those outside of Bloodstone, the blast destroyed him, his entire guild, and well, you get the picture. I heard that Kieran was a friend?"

Ryvane deflated even more. "Kieran is, err - was a half-brother, of sorts. We were supposed to be wed in the rakshasa way, but we ran away and came here instead. He ended up in Taysor because he thought it'd be fun to operate in the shadows of a good god's religion. I came here because I was tired of being part of a society that preached goodness but practiced atrocity. It gets exhausting. Originally, Marcello wanted me to ensure that Perdition and his guild, Northern Cross, never came to blows. It became quite profitable from a smuggling perspective, which is why I'm a cell leader I guess. So, this is mixed news. Though a rival, he was not actively against me for a long time and did not resist my desire to come here alone. I feel sad at this news. Though, what you say about Calvin hurts more. A girl can dream of a knight in shining armor, but I guess that all too often, it's just another rusty suit of armor. I wish you had said that Tania is my home and it's not a jail."

Khalla nodded. "I understand. I have a bit of my own situation going on with someone I love. Over time, I find myself seeing more and more of his flaws. It gets harder to remember love. I'm sorry, and not to belabor Calvin, but there's just one more thing. I hope I can say this as a sister?"

Before Ryvane could agree or not, Khalla raced forward. "You know, we all know... you deserve better than Calvin. In fact, if I remember correctly, you taught the seminar at the Mages Guild about how charmed labor does not increase productivity. By taking away accountability, accidents and quality issues slow down what looks like a magically-easy way to gain a compliant labor force. I speculate that the same charm magic at play in a relationship is really just some sort of charade; the real feelings degrade. You taught that, right?"

Ryvane conjured another bottle of wine. "I did not know you had similar problems, Khalla. I did not mean the love puppet thing from earlier. Maybe I speak my rakshasa mind when I say these things. Calvin used to tell me he loves me. Now, he asks for magic." Ryvane poured a glass for Khalla and then drank from the bottle. When finished, she said, "What happens when I have to use magic to ensure he loves me still? Yes, it starts out well enough but it's just an appearance. Over time, the charmed person relinquishes those parts of them capable of loving strongly. That strong love is what appeals to me and my kind. Strong emotion. Our magic can capture it, like a candle flame, for a while. But, it burns out and we cannot rekindle it once lost. Magic cannot solve for a mortal's moral choice. In fact, it tries to solve for the charm magic by kindling resentment, hatred, and loathing. I tried to leave them all before it happened, but, well, you see how it turned out. I want Calvin to be different. Merakor will get us out of this mess. My mess."

"Getting out of this mess by taking him to Merakor?" Khalla laughed. "What happens when your home feels like a jail?" Khalla countered. "We're all trapped here in the cage of our own choices. Sure, we could leave, but we'd lose so much. There are powerful intangible benefits to being Tanian, to working for Perdition." Khalla took out a notebook. Its worn and re-used pages looked identical to the notebooks all the cell leaders had. She said, "The Tanian way is for you to take someone deserving of you. When they take you back, when they fight for you, that's how you know moral agency is most at play! Would you have chosen Calvin without orders from Marcello?"

Flipping back through it, Khalla said, "I'm looking at your notes for Calvin from right before Perdition left for Tania. You missed out by the way! You wrote: Noble-hearted but eminently corruptible by fame and sex. A capable fighter but an even better leader of fighters. Possessing a quality that makes people instantly like him, Calvin is a prime candidate for recruiting to Perdition. Consider Cell or Enforcer Leadership, for when a softer touch is required. Recommend testing immediately. Later, you wrote in response to a question about testing: Calvin shows no interest in advancing himself through martial training." Khalla closed the book. "Those I have loved, yes, they have been flawed. However, Calvin will not survive Merakor. I don't know enough about how rakshasi think to even guess at why you want to be with him. Marcello, and honestly me too, thought you would leap at Merakor."

Ryvane growled. "I hate it when my own words are quoted to me. Yes, I wrote these things. It's my job as a cell leader. What I left out is that Calvin has certain noble qualities I find endearing. You have no idea what it's like to live for many years and never connect in a loving way with someone." Ryvane stared at Khalla for a while and then conceded, "Though as an elf in Perdition, and the rumors I hear about you and Marcello, maybe you do?"

Khalla put her fingers to her lips and made a sh'ing sound. "I will tell you, Ryvane. It's not just rumors. Maybe someday, who knows? I could become Perdition's wife?" She laughed. "That sounds terrible."

Ryvane watched her flatly. "I don't believe you."

Shrugging, Khalla offered her the ring from her left hand. "Read the inscription."

It read: *My immortal star I chase eternally. Love, Marcello.* Ryvane flipped it back. "Nice ring. I could enchant such a thing in a few hours. Why does Marcello and his 'immortal star' want me to go to Merakor? For me, that's the real question. For decades, I have worked between the mages and the thieves. What changed?"

With a gleam in her eye, Khalla leaned forward and took Ryvane's hands. "The High Tower of Aler Alerest, in the Arati Grasslands."

Ryvane blinked and then thought for a moment while she removed her hands from Khalla's. "That tower was lost."

"That's not what the Ice Patriarch told Marcello. Think about it, Ryvane. If you stay with Calvin, it's only a matter of time before he self-destructs. He's only made it this far because you've compensated for his lack of conviction with charm magic. You know this. I could send any of our cell leaders to him with a proposition to leave Dockside, and with the right presentation of reasons, he'd leave it all. Are you going to rule Dockside as a widow?"

"No. Not at all." Ryvane stood. "I'm done with this discussion. If you want me with Merakor, Calvin comes. Tell me, Khalla, are you going to rule Perdition?"

Khalla watched Ryvane leave. She wanted to say it out loud but could not. *Yes*, she thought. *I am going to rule Perdition.*

* * *

RiVule stretched. The orc priest looked around his small cave. Everything sat in its place exactly where he wished it to be. Yet, it all felt different, as if changed, and he could not see what or where the change was. Sketches of his last project, a hobgoblin dissection, fluttered in a weak draft of air moving through the complex. Sensing a change in RiVule, his personal attendant groveled outside, asking if RiVule needed anything. He ignored the obsequious thrall.

"Has something happened with my war host?" RiVule called out to Frentoris. Frentoris carried all the armor and weapons of a high-ranking guard, but served like the best slave money could buy, yet with dignity and strength. Not many Orcs could pull off obsequious power. Unlike the thrall, Frentoris knew how to avoid being obvious about it. Plus, he was a deadly paladin with many kills.

Frentoris looked up sideways from the ground where he pressed his face. "No, master. The host remains, as always, ready for war."

RiVule pulled Frentoris to follow as he walked out of his living area. The best thing about Frentoris was the rush the large orc derived from intimidating others in RiVule's name. To reach RiVule's destination, they would cross several of the great chambers. They reached the first, a staging area used to dump hauls from the surface and prepare for expeditions. It bustled with merchants and fighters, and fighting merchants. While most bowed to RiVule, some even sincerely, a few would undoubtedly try to challenge the eccentric priest.

Frentoris scanned the area and selected the most likely challenger. The shaman stood to the side of the straight path through the great cavern. A fighter nearby chuffed and flexed. That would be the one. RiVule sensed it to and touched Frentoris with Gruustir's blessing. Strength, amplified senses, and speed quickened Frentoris' body. He pressed forward from RiVule and charged the shaman. The fighter would intercept him; his body language practically shouted it. Though Frentoris did this every day, the shaman made it dangerous with unknown magic and favor. The shaman pointed to Frentoris and the fighter charged, moving so slowly that Frentoris laughed.

Drawing his sword, Frentoris smashed the fighter aside with the flat of his blade. Gruustir desired acknowledgement this day, not death. Stronger than an ogre, Frentoris's blow sent the fighter skipping to the side where he smashed apart barrels of liquid. The shaman, not expecting this, prayed and began a spell. Frentoris sensed it as a spell to withdraw and buy time. "It won't work!" he screamed. "Gruustir take you!"

Though the shaman dodged the first sword attack, the second rang against the shaman's leather helmet. The third, Frentoris roared with pleasure, would do RiVule proud. His sword stabbed into and out just above the backside of the shaman's hips. The painful and fatal wound would end the shaman in days unless healed.

"Dog! Carrion dog meat!" the shaman swore at Frentoris. "Gruustir curse your black heart!"

"Not today," Frentoris said. "Today, Gruustir blesses me, and curses you. Master RiVule comes."

The shaman's eyes dilated at the name and then locked on RiVule as the red-robed Orc sauntered towards them. "I did not know," the shaman pled.

"You knew," Frentoris laughed. "You knew and sought to challenge him anyway! Idiot!" Frentoris kicked the shaman's knee, which broke on the metal boot. The shaman fell to hands, in too much pain to not scream in agony.

RiVule said, "It's so nice to see proper Orc respect from one of the shamans. You look good, bowed before me in pain. Tell me, Coriga, tell me I am not the most favored of all Gruustir's sons."

Coriga spat on the ground at Frentoris' feet. "Gruustir favors you, for now."

"Above all?" RiVule asked, a cruel tone in his voice.

Coriga's green skin blanched and, seeing no assistance from the hundreds of fighters all around, he at last bowed his head. "Above all, RiVule. You stand above all."

RiVule leered and turned to face all in the cavern. Compared to the rest of the Orcs, RiVule looked almost elvish. Unusually tall, slender, and only lightly-complexioned, RiVule could have passed for an ugly elf. Here, even to the orcs, he looked garish. The fighter struggled to recover his balance amid the splintered and leaking barrels. RiVule held out his hand and telekinetically pulled the fighter's neck to his hand. The invisible force snapped the fighter's neck when the rest of the body did not move. "This is on you, for challenging me," RiVule hissed at the shaman.

Twisting the body in the air so that it faced Coriga, RiVule shouted. "Fighter! Serve me now in death!" Most shamans could not even make zombies. RiVule smirked and then had to hide his own astonishment as the fighter's corpse twisted from zombie to ghast form and leapt at the shaman. In that moment, RiVule figured it out. The sense of something changing; it was this easy power.

RiVule ordered the ghast to sit and obey. Mindlessly, the ghast's sweeping claw attack became a torpid whack along the shaman's face. Necromancy, RiVule realized. It's different. He prayed to Gruustir and touched the ghast. This time he could not mask his surprise at the ghast burning away to a resurrected fighter. RiVule hoped no one else noticed. "You serve me now," RiVule said to the fighter.

Looking dazed, the fighter shook his head and swore it. He took Frentoris' offered hand and stood. RiVule pointed to the shaman's shattered knee. "Coriga, heal it," he ordered.

The shaman hissed back thinking RiVule mocked him. "I'm nowhere near the rank to do this thing! You mock me! So much power! Teach me!"

"Yes!" RiVule screamed back. "I spit in your dead heart, now heal yourself or die by my hand!"

The shaman prayed and, expecting only gentle healing, nearly lost his concentration when the ruptured tendons pulled back and re-strengthened his knee. "It's healed! How?" Coriga twisted his knee to pull the bones into their proper place as it healed.

RiVule touched the shaman's head. "Because you obey me," he thumped his chest. "Most favored of Gruustir's sons! Now, come with me. Coriga, you serve me now, too."

The group of four now marched to the next chamber. With a shaman and another fighter in tow, no one else challenged them. They quickly reached RiVule's destination: the Temple of Gruustir.

Entering it, RiVule frowned to see not a single worker anywhere. When just RiVule had worked on this by himself, progress was tedious and slow. But, after his ascension to 'Most High Shaman,' his orders to bring workers and cycle them continually resulted in leaps and bounds in its progress. With no one to question, RiVule whirled on Coriga. Stabbing his finger into Coriga's chest, RiVule hissed, "Find out and come tell me why there are no workers. We'll be in the Holiest."

RiVule watched Coriga sprint off. At least that one hasn't become fat and slow like the other priests, he thought. I might keep him. The two fighters followed RiVule into the innermost chamber of the temple. Though the outer portions still required much work, RiVule's personal touches in the Holiest rocked the fighters to their core.

The Holiest sat at the end of a wide corridor burrowed into the stone. A carved arch nearly three Orcs tall and five Orcs wide showed the telltale signs of sculptures yet to come. Crossing this, they entered a large chamber shaped as if the inside a hollowed out pyramid. Under the center point of the ceiling, a stone table flanked by statues of their god on three sides welcomed them. Even Frentoris had yet to enter this room. He usually stood guard at the far end. The other fighter, named Incer, pointed to the statues and muttered, "Heresy."

RiVule spun on Incer and hissed at him. "Do not dare lecture me on heresy! It is well-known amongst the shamans that Gruustir created Orcs to rule over the ogre and goblin races. If not to be ruled, why not also that they were created to serve? This suggests that Gruustir created ogres and goblins as well." He thumped his heart. "I know this as truth. You have no idea of what you speak. Silence your tongue before I take it."

Approaching the three statues, RiVule pointed to the Goblin visage of Gruustir. "This is for Warp. The Orc is Creation. The ogre is Chaos. I require blood. Incer, thank you for volunteering. You are to lay on the stone table."

Frentoris shoved Incer at the table. "You won't lose your life if you obey," he growled.

With fearful anxiety fading to resignation, Incer hopped up onto the table and laid back. The instant he hit it, RiVule prayed to Gruustir and paralysis captured Incer. Unable to move, Incer felt the air stick in his lungs and realized that RiVule truly held a differing level of power from the shamans, who could freeze one's movements but not restrict breathing. One of his eyes, caught mid-blink, began to twitch and ache.

"Everything is paralyzed," RiVule said. "Even your heart. What you're experiencing now is your brain consuming what little strength it has left to note these things. You'll be dead in moments. If this works, you won't die. Have faith and I will restore you, again." While speaking, RiVule cut runes of each gate into Incer's forearms and forehead.

Incer felt his body screaming for release, and the eternity of being able to think but not move while feeling every cut. Blood oozed from the arm cuts that faded without a beating heart to move it. The single rune of Creation cut into Incer's forehead seeped blood into his eyes. As the blood slowly dribbled onto the altar, it all flowed out towards the Chaos rune. "Rotate his body, Frentoris ," RiVule ordered.

With Incer's body turning, the blood twisted to flow towards Chaos. "This confirms it," RiVule said. "Frentoris, what does Gruustir tell you about Incer; shall the fighter live?"

Frentoris twisted Incer's body, now wracked by blood loss and dying, one last time. "The great god tells me that Incer is a warrior worth saving!"

Incer felt the paralysis let him go and he tried to breathe. His body shuddered and then his heart rammed blood into the deep wounds that severed his hand tendons. RiVule's smile split his face and healing began to wash over Incer, who screamed in agony as cut arteries pulled close and his racing heart began to function normally again. Frentoris said, "Incer, you are spared but must re-dedicate yourself to Gruustir, and to me. Your ignorant following of the shamans displeases Gruustir."

Choking on the pain of air re-entering his lungs, Incer screamed out, "Yes! My life to Gruustir! My sword to RiVule!"

"Behold, the glory of Gruustir," RiVule said into Incer's ear. "Like Frentoris, be reborn a paladin of Gruustir!"

# Chapter 3 – Place Your Bets

The minotaur priest, Path, lifted his heavy boots onto the dining table. Iron strips reinforcing the table's wooden surface groaned. The old table solidly carried Path's weight. A keg-sized tankard in his hand, Path looked at Calvin and suggested that more ale would help their discussion.

When Calvin signaled for another keg, Path looked around his hob-nailed boots and said in his guttural language, "Your Tauran is improving, Captain. Keep at it and you might be the first normal Tanian to master it, well, outside the Dar ranks. Many of them speak our tongue."

Calvin raised his much smaller cup and choked down the Tauran ale. Ryvane's magical ring, a gift to help with liquor consumption, glimmered as he drank. The powerful ale overwhelmed its magic though and Calvin knew he was fast on his way to an epic drunk. He was probably slurring his Tauran speech. It all hurt his head. "I want be someone all Taurans trust," Calvin said thumping his chest and patting Path's hobnailed boots. "Hear me on this idea," Calvin said, waving his hands in a big fashion, "Dockside is the Tauran's home too. We need to make it even bigger for you, our friends." He stared at Path's huge boot and wondered if Path had a hoof like some of the Taurans, or a foot.

"I like your thinking," Path said. "But, answer me this," the cleric replied while switching to Tanian Common. He touched Calvin's hand and let Baphtomet help the poor human recover a bit. "We've been trading with Tania since the Fifth Legion, since Dar Ana's ascension as High Priestess at Bloodstone. In all this time, no one has ever approached us like this. What do you want?" Path doubted Calvin could make it happen, but the wily human had proven himself with Windwalker's rescue last year, and had retained that trust in all the months since. Most humans could not. Path was not the only one impressed. Some of the other Taurans waiting here for the next world galleon to end their shore leave, had suggested Calvin as a Tauran Friend. Path had blocked such ideas as Calvin lacked the wealth and status in Tania to justify it, yet.

Bapthoment's blessing helped Calvin who tried to sit up straight and fix his slurring Tauran. Windwalker suggested Calvin might be a Friend someday. An interesting idea from an Imperial and not one Path could dismiss easily. Taurans befriended only the most powerful. Things had changed when Malcor became king after the Jade God's epic slaughter. Remembering it, Path sighed contentedly. Suddenly, Path felt that Calvin might be an interesting key to this new king. And, not just the king. Calvin also had connections with the new Legion Commander of Bloodstone, Malcor's wife Ora, and a mighty paladin in the Order of Fire, Seline. Though not singularly mighty, Calvin had interesting associations.

The Taurans had not prospered as much as they would have liked under the first Rojo. With the king's childhood friend here and wanting to be friends with them... Path resolved to make it happen. "Yes, what do you want, Mayor Calvin?" He toasted Calvin. "We've already heard. Though our business will remain as always, it's good to know we are friends."

Calvin blinked to steady the room. The dim oil lamp lights hurt his eyes and he put the cup down. "What do I want? I want Dockside to be more than it is! Warehouses, poor people, and then your ships come in through this ancient canal and lock system from the ocean way down there. Dockside should be the center of commerce and trade. Dockside," Calvin blew a 'thbbbbt' sound with his lips. "Should be Dock Central, or the Tauran Bazaar. More exotic than the Great Bazaar. Think about it!" Calvin took another sip and almost puked.

Path eyed the inebriated human and removed his legs from the table. "Tiny human. You have a long way to go before you master our liquor. Baphtomet restores you." Path jabbed his thumb claw into Calvin's forehead. It left a bleeding gash but was more powerful than the secret aid Path had just barely used. Calvin instantly sobered.

Calvin made the holy sign of Path's god, pleased he did it correctly. "I suppose I want to get drunk. Do you know what today is?"

"Then, let us get drunk! But, I cannot have you dead from Tauran ale. Tell me of this day." Path signaled for human food and liquor.

"A year ago, I woke up ready for my Coming of Age Ceremony. You know what that is, right?" When Path agreed, Calvin continued. "I was almost 18. My father is mayor of Klenna, you know. That'd be like a Tauran Imperial Officer type 4 or 5, depending. Type 5 is smaller areas, but 4 is for one thousand families, right? Everyone expected me to pass into the knighthood with flying colors. We got word that a high priestess, Shara, would be attending. Then later, more and more messages start arriving. Suddenly, I've got the entire Tanian court present! Worse, I get there and, of course, there's Malcor – again. And, of course, Malcor overshadowed everything. He still does, I suppose."

Path took a platter of food and carefully pushed a jug of mead to Calvin. "I have yet to meet the new king. I doubt I will. That is a job for a navigator." Path referred to the red-furred minotaurs, like Windwalker, who guided the world galleons through the ocean storms. "Still, being comrades with such a person brings honor to you. Are you drinking to celebrate this or because of some other reason, this overshadowing? After all, Malcor is now king. Even if you could go back, destiny would still make Malcor king… and then you would be the human who overshadowed the king in an important ritual. That, Calvin, a far more dangerous place to be. In Minos, such things are quickly resolved by combat or execution."

"Truly?" Calvin asked. He looked at his empty cup and remembered how ill it made him feel. Then, he shrugged and refilled his cup. "Well, I guess I'm lucky to not be Tauran then. I'm too small, not fierce enough." Calvin worked this subtle flattery into all his discussions with Path. It always worked with the minotaurs, and was much safer than teasing them the way human friends might. "Path, to grow Dockside, I need money. I have a few ideas. Hear me out before you say anything, please. I'm wondering about a luxury tax on Tauran goods. It wouldn't affect you as Tanians would buy and therefore pay the levy. I've also saved some money, maybe I could invest in one of your voyages? I hear that many Tanians do this. Finally, Windwalker has been telling me stories about the treasures across the oceans of the world. Any of these would bring me the funds I need to begin renovating Dockside. But, a priority would be to clear the area around Baphtomet's Shrine, to give you more space to build bigger – if you wanted to."

Path ripped meat off the shank of lamb. In his large hands, it looked like a chicken wing to Calvin. Path said, "We don't much care for levies. Whether we pay, or the buyers here in Tania pay, it makes our goods more costly and therefore less desirable. Though not a doctrine for our god, trade is a decree by our emperor. We have a long-standing agreement with the dragons that Tauran goods are subject only to the normal taxes Tanians already pay. A new tax on Tauran goods would immediately draw attention by the Circle. I do not wish for such discussions nor to report such matters back in Minos.

"To the next option, yes. Many Tanians invest either cargo for trade or directly as a share of the ship's profit. A share of a world galleon begins at 100,000. I don't believe they are selling shares. You'd have to buy a Tanian out, which is partly how these become valuable. Last I heard, your Thieves Guild had one for sale at 210,000 gold. In fact, you may want to go visit Perdition and ask about that. Before the Orcus Event – and wow, isn't it nice to just be able to say 'Orcus?' – our shares had been consistently between 120 and 160." Path looked around the tavern and leaned forward. "Since you want to be friendly with us, I will tell you that we have received many requests for off-Isles transport. Far more than ever before."

Calvin thought about Path's words. All around, the minotaurs caroused while dexterous human serving staff dodged horns and fists to deliver food and drink. Sometimes, the Taurans helped. A serving girl, struggling to bypass a knot of minotaurs screaming at each other about their exploits, was picked up and passed around to the table she hoped to deliver food to. This happened often enough it did not even faze them. Calvin still marveled at it. Their hands would easily cover his entire chest. "Do you know why? What do think is driving this, Path?"

The Tauran priest sneered. "Orcus is dead; long live Orcus! Or, whoever or whatever takes his place. The Abyss will not long abide the absence of a primordial god. We all feel it in the priesthood. Necromancy is strong like never before. Healing, cursing – things that used to take concentration and effort, I now access Baphtomet's blessings for these as easily as I might remember, well, your name. It's effortless. With no god exerting influence over necromancy, my brothers and I feel invulnerable! We know it won't last."

Calvin thought back to his Temple teachings about dominion. "I did not know that Orcus controlled all of necromancy. Why would that make you invulnerable; may I ask?"

"Necromancy isn't just undeath. It's also healing. Because of Orcus, when I healed Windwalker for example, I did not know if my prayer and faith would fully restore him or not. It ended up taking almost ten prayers to safely restore him to the living. Now? I bet I could do it in two, no, just one prayer." Path slammed his keg down on the table. "One prayer! But what do you care of such things? You just want gold, right?"

Calvin smiled. "Don't we all? So, adventuring. I can't afford a share of your galleon, but I do think I should go talk to Perdition. They have an unusual degree of power in Dockside. I need to understand that." Calvin picked at his food and then looked up. "What about a generous donation?" Path snorted and Calvin quickly added, "Or a loan?"

"How much do you need, Tanian? Amongst ourselves, we do not lend money. But, to foreigners, yes. That could work. There are rules and obligations. How much?"

Calvin thought about the land he would need to acquire, the workers, the buildings, the renovations. "I wish Ryvane were here. She has a perfect level of detail and expense, which I can send to you. I need 50 to start. That gives the land around the Shrine, clears it, and renovates the houses connecting to the Great Bazaar."

Path listened but it made Calvin uneasy that he could not read the minotaur's body language. After a long pause, Path answered him. "For 50, I could buy the land myself and do this. The Taurans have had plenty of opportunity to do so over the decades and we have not. The prospect of a larger, more glorious shrine, it appeals but who am I to question to great priest Cloudbringer? No, Calvin, if our current shrine was good enough for the greatest cleric of Baphtomet, it is perfect for me."

With each word, Calvin struggled to retain his pleasant expression and charismatic smile. He ordered another keg for Path. "So, adventuring then, my friend."

Path slammed his nearly empty keg against Calvin's small cup and nodded. "Adventuring."

* * *

Ryvane found Calvin in their house drunk. It was not the first time she had found him this way. He lay collapsed on a divan, a steel bottle of Tauran ale to the side. She noted the ring lying spent on a table adjacent the chair. "Calvin?" she asked. He groaned in his sleep. His skin stank of Taurans and she conjured a hygiene cantrip to air out the room and its occupant. A bloody gash in his forehead showed that a Tauran cleric had healed him at one point. It was becoming a pattern since the election and official endorsement. She brushed the vomit-clumped hair back from his face and softly chided him, "Getting drunk with minotaurs will not revitalize Dockside."

She sat down opposite him and tried to breathe. This was how a rakshasa's lovers always began to self-destruct. The total relinquishing of self-control was the first step. It began well-intentioned, like with Calvin wanting to get through required guard duty made easier with charm magic. Then, it became a test of trust where, somehow, magic would always correct any problem rather than personal accountability. Looking at him, she could barely see the handsome officer who had knocked on her tower one bright day about a year ago. "What am I doing?" she asked herself quietly. She opened her hand and let the crumpled Merakor invitation from Marcello drop to the ground.

She leaned forward and let long overdue tears fall. Her own doubts and concerns, the shining moments of love when Calvin was free of her charm magic, and Khalla's words about Calvin's survival chances in Merakor. After two hours, Calvin still had not moved. Ryvane wiped her face and stood. She felt exhausted but clear in her thinking; she knew what she had to do. She pointed to Calvin and said, "You're coming to

Merakor. If you love me, if you truly love me, you'll figure it out and survive, for me!"

She uncrumpled the letter from Marcello and folded it back into her pocket. Waving her hand, a small paper and quill dipped in ink at the desk and floated to her, already writing. "Dear Calvin," it read. "I need more from you. For almost a year now, we have been together in everything. When you first knocked on my tower door, I did not think it would be like this, with us ever becoming an 'us.' You were just another job for me, and I did it. I did not think I would love you. Because of that job, I did not hesitate to give you charm and other magic to make your work easier. I'm cutting that off. I know you love me. I know you'll be able to deal with this. I'm worried my magic has become, is already a crutch for you, and I would see you as my shining hero. I will tell only my shining hero the truth, about me, about everything. Until then, trust me. Let's deal with this together. Prepare yourself for an adventure that will make even your friend, Malcor, jealous! I love you."

* * *

Grant cursed and scratched his ear. Across the way, Delton flexed his shoulders under the load of his backpack. *Signal received*, Grant thought. They were being tailed. Pausing to look at a merchant's wares, Grant used the small glass window to catch a glimpse of his stalker. He expected to see a 521 shadow. Instead, he saw a young man trying not to look like a knight.

Grant stepped into the merchant's store and began bargaining for fruit. All food merchants sold mango right now, but Grant still haggled over two of the best ones. He kept an eye on the knight and noted Delton taking up position. Delton had removed a strap from his backpack, their sign for a threat. Risking it, Grant signaled directly to Delton, WHY THREAT?

Delton signed back, CUTHBERT.

Grant swore, turning it into a commentary on the fruit. HEAD TO SAFE AREA AND CONFRONT OR ESCAPE, Grant signed.

Delton acknowledged and shot back, LETHAL?

Grant bought the two mangos, complaining loudly about their paltry cost. NO. TOO DANGEROUS WITH CUTHBERT.

Delton vanished and fifteen minutes later, Grant side-stepped into an alley marked by Delton. Set up for a perfect ambush, Grant maneuvered himself into position so it would appear to the knight that he was rifling through his backpack or eating mango.

Though the young knight tried to look inconspicuous, he knew that he had made a mistake and his quarry knew. The dreadful aura of dire woe practically radiated like a fountain from the roguishly dressed man squatted over a backpack. At first, the knight had shaken off the feeling. He had come to the market to take in the sights, mingle with the people he was sworn to protect, and to see all the goodness wrought by Pha Rann for Sora's citizenry. The shock of so much evil, like a black hole, sucked the air from his lungs. So strongly had it hit the knight that he almost forgot he stood in Sora rather than some lower level of Hell. It pulled him back to Bloodstone and evil mists crawling the valley floor.

Wiping sweat from his brow, a small voice whispered in his heart, "Devin, you should get help."

"Though I stare at very heart of my enemy, my righteous might triumphs," Devin prayed back in answer. He turned into the side alley and saw the man crouched down, his back turned. Movement further down the road caught his attention and Devin realized another enemy lay in wait. Realizing that they knew, Devin summoned his armor and his sword.

A crossbow bolt struck his breastplate as it formed around his body. "Cuthbert aid me!" Devin shouted and charged forward. His holy avenger ignited into life between his hands on the downward chopping attack he leveled at the kneeling rogue.

Grant cursed, again. The enchanted bolt used by Delton should have stunned the paladin. The merchant in Haven had assured them it would work overcome resistance to magic, and specifically that it would against paladins and their divine resistance to being magically stunned. The now-armored knight must need to be hit on skin for the magic to work. Grant wished he had asked more questions in acquiring the bolt.

A burst of heat warned Grant of the oncoming sword, even though it was not visible yet. He rolled to the side. His vorpal dagger lashed out at the Cuthberic's leg greaves. Though he connected, the knight shrugged the cut off and changed his stance to favor the wounded leg. A shield appeared on the knight's arm. Worse, from the main street, onlookers were pointing and someone called out for the guard.

Grant sprang to the side hoping to draw an attack. The young knight went for the offered opening and tried to shield bash Grant. If it the shield had hit, Grant would have been wide open to the burning sword stabbing at where his stomach would have been. Grant though had already changed direction.

Grant stabbed up with his dagger and, though he did not cut the knight, he pried the armor open and shoved a bone fragment of Orcus into the armor gap. "We're friends," Grant called out, dropping his dagger into its sheath and jumping back, hands up. Delton's crossbow twanged again behind him and hit the knight squarely in the chest. "My name is Grant. Test me for this truth!" Grant prayed to every god that it would work. Paladins were notoriously resistant to magic, and a Cuthberic would no doubt be especially resilient against the Jade God.

Devin blinked and lost focus for a moment. His sword went dim and he heard many voices all around telling him to press his attack in Cuthbert's name at the same time that Grant's voice said they were friends. Unused to confusion, Devin moved forward to continue the attack when a crossbow burrowed through his chest plate. The bolt hurt, but he knew he'd survive. However, it did draw his attention down the alley to the crossbow assailant. He was reloading.

Grant pointed down the alley, "Come on! Before he reloads! We can take him together, friend! Follow me!" With all the show of a Cuthberic, Grant charged, even calling out that Delton surrender in Cuthbert's holy name.

Delton got it and threw his crossbow at Grant and ran. The Cuthberic knight, Devin, saw this and steadied his focus. When he concentrated on his friend Grant, the confusion lessened. Stopping an assailant, one attacking cowardly from the shadows with a crossbow no less, was righteous. Devin charged after Grant and joined his cries that the assassin surrender to Cuthbert's judgement.

Carefully, Delton navigated the back alleys and drew the knight back to their crew. With Grant goading the knight on, they ran into a dead end and found Delton trying to climb a building wall. The rest of the crew was ready. Nets, rope, and long poles tripped the knight and entangled him. Though his armor burst into fire, the magically resistant netting prevented the knight from attacking.

Grant yelled out, "I've got you, fiendish rogue!" and pulled Delton off the wall.

Devin cheered, "You got him! Good on you!" As a black sackcloth went over his head, Devin prayed to Cuthbert to fell his attackers.

Grant put his hand on the bone wedged in Devin's armor and commanded, "We're friends. You're going to remember the assassin escaped. I'm just a bystander who tried to help you… when I count backwards from '3.' Now, tell me: why were you following me?"

Devin answered, "You are radiating evil as if fireworks lit up the night sky during one of the holy festivals."

Mentally, Grant cursed. The Jade God's body must have overcome the magical containers holding it. This had happened during their escape from Bloodstone, but stopped being a problem when they put the material into an extra-dimensional space. "Are you sure, friend?"

Devin nodded. "I did not want to have this happen today. Though I'm always ready to combat evil, it was disheartening to encounter it here in Taysor. Why am I friends with someone like you?"

The Cuthberic's tone of voice carried impending danger. Grant deftly touched the Jade God's bone and said, "Peace, Devin. Go to sleep." Devin struggled, not wanting to and clearly confused by his body's obedience to the command. At last, Devin closed his eyes and slept fitfully.

Grant held his fingers to lips and quietly said, "We got lucky. Devin is very young and new. Look, he only has one insignia. A more experienced knight and this would have been worse. I'm sure every Cuthberic in the world is feeling drawn to us right now. You know how they are. We need to get out of the city, now." Grant transferred his backpack to Delton along with the jade bone from Devin's breastplate. "Head to Tania. Cordelle needs to pay up still. I'll meet you in our shelter in two weeks. Avoid the guards. Above all, avoid Cuthberics."

The group nodded and ran. They'd go to the poor eastern side of the city and exit the walls. If they avoided well-travelled areas, hopefully they could avoid another encounter. We were really lucky, Grant realized. If anyone could solve the containment issue, it would the Tanians. Grant could already see the dealing that would occur to mask the Jade God's body parts. He swore. Burn me! Tania already knows how to contain this. He chuckled. Of course, they did.

Grant sat alone with the knight and changed his clothes into something a normal citizen in this area might wear. Next to him, Devin groaned and reached up to his head. Grant almost knocked him out but at the last moment, caught his hand and removed the bag over his head. "3-2-1," he said. "Here, let me help you up, good knight." The congenial tone in his voice and the offered assistance put Devin at ease.

Midway through standing up, two Cuthberics came running into the alley. Though their hands rested on their swords, they frowned at Grant and then rushed up to Devin. "We feared the worst for you, Devin! Suddenly you were gone and we got sick looking for you. We felt your peril! Where did you go?"

One of the knights sniffed at the stench in the alley and eyed Grant suspiciously. Grant focused his thinking. Totally on the up and up. I only want what is best for Pha Rann. Be honest, Grant recited in his mind. Grant brushed some filth from Devin's robes. "I was running errands and saw this young paladin being shot at by some dark assassin with a crossbow. I decided to help and to ensure that Pha Rann did not lose a knight today. Ruffians," Grant spat. Good, good. No lies yet, Grant thought. "It makes me sick that this happened here. Thankfully, Devin here proved too hard to kill." Grant, hoping to change the topic, asked Devin. "Are you hurt? Did they take anything from you?"

The two paladins inspected their comrade and found no wounds requiring immediate attention. "Do you worship Pha Rann?" one asked Grant.

Grant held up his hands. "In all of grand Taysor and the many gods of Heaven, I have the misfortune to not number myself among the faithful. I blame my mother... and a nobleman who raped her. As you might imagine, I did not grow up in Pha Rann's light. Looking at your fervor though, I must admit, I find it breath-taking." Sincere truth, with a dash of unpleasantness, Grant thought. You're doing just fine.

"I'm Ajax, brother in arms to Devin here," he said, patting Devin on the arm. "That's Trevor. For your timely aid, even if you failed to capture the assailant, the Saint God thanks you."

It worked!, Grant internally gloated. He thanked Tania for teaching him this about the Cuthberics. "I'm Garrett. My pleasure Ajax. If Devin – nice to meet you, Devin – had not recovered, I don't know what I would have done. As it was, when he fell unconscious, I knew I had to stay and make sure that things worked out." Gratefully, he recalled the lesson about using an alias as a rogue. His Tanian master had spent years beating it into his memory, Nothing is more powerful than the truth. Embrace it and you'll never have problems with divine powers and truthsaying. The trick is to pass the initial test of believability. Ironic that everyone knew him as Grant when his real name was actually Garrett. He almost laughed. Tania had taught him this: Lying about one's name is the easiest trip up when dealing with the gods and their servants. You will choose a new name...

Devin rubbed his head. "Every time you talk, I hear my mother's voice. It's weird, Garrett. Brothers, it was an assassin. The murderer got away though." Devin slumped his shoulders. "I was not powerful enough."

Ajax slapped him on the back, "That's why we fight together, Devin! Next time, get your team. Or find more willing aid, like Garrett here."

\* \* \*

"What do you keep locked in that room, Ash?" Khalla had her hands on her hips, dangerously close to her sword.

Ash had just come out of the locked room. Behind him, he triggered a pressure plate to ensure it sealed shut. "Personal things, Khalla. Nothing you need to worry about." He smiled his brightest smile at her. He stepped forward to take her hand and sighed loudly when she dodged back. "Come on, we're so close to doing this. A vacation, just you and me."

"And every other member of the party... and a world galleon full of minotaurs," she shot back. "I'm not going through with any of this only to risk another coup de grace where, surprise, you have some other secret that affects me."

"I've never done that!"

"You dumped the entire Thieves Guild on me without a heads up! You forged a high priestess' signature for Rogue's Blade going into Bloodstone. Not just any priestess either! It was Dar Shara – the Shara! Do you have any idea how hard it is to always shift and account for you? The entire guild knows you screwed us with Bloodstone. What was I supposed to do, walk up to Dar Shara and have her confirm her signature on your fake contract?" She flipped her sword into her hand. "I'm not doing this anymore. Not here in Tania, and definitely not in Merakor."

Ash looked around the room. He had prepared it for any threat, against any intrusion. Yet, he realized a gap: emotional confrontation. "Khalla, don't be like this. We've been together for years. This room has never bothered..."

"Yes, it has. The first time I came here, I tried to enter. Each time since, I wondered if today would be the day you tell me, show me, or help me understand. Right now, Ash. This is when you either come clean with me, or we're through. I'm sorry that I had to build some leverage to force this but you don't seem very forthcoming when it's tender, safe, and sexy." She looked over her shoulder at the daylight streaming into the house from the front door. "I'm counting to 10 and then I'm leaving. Ten," she said slowly. "How hard can it be, Ash?" She mimicked him, "Come on in Khalla, let me show you... 9."

Ash leaned back against the door. He felt a dizzy. The thought of losing Khalla - she'd come back, he reassured himself. At '5', he heard tears in her voice. At '1', she turned and ran out the front door. Ash felt a part of himself break and leave with her.

"I always knew this would happen," he said to no one. Sunbeams in dust from the front door shot into the hallway. He could tell Khalla was not there. He walked out and looked, hoping she would be. In spite of knowing, it still hurt. He grabbed a hidden knife under the small entry table and threw it. It struck deep into the wood.

Ash walked out and blinked in the sunlight. Khalla was truly gone. He lifted his arms to the sun and stretched, "Let the disavowals begin." Resigned, he turned back into his house and locked the front door behind him. If she was serious, she would take Perdition, quickly. He had trained her to know what to do.

Halgrim was the first. It was fast. Khalla had set things in place. Ash rubbed his face and sat down on his front porch. He had expected maybe an hour, not five minutes. Though not a disavowal, a familiar from the artificer's shop appeared and said, "All of your accounts are being revoked. What happened?"

"Khalla is formally taking control of Perdition, as she should. It's nothing to worry about."

Halgrim's voice came crackling out of the tiny devil. "A woman scorned, Ash. A woman scorned. Be careful."

"She'll get over it." Both Halgrim and the tiny devil began to chuckle and then laugh. It had a decidedly evil tone to it and Ash frowned. "She will."

His insistence made them laugh harder. At last, Halgrim questioned, "You've been with Khalla, rather, Khalla has been with you for nearly ten years and this has never happened before. What did happen?"

"She wanted to know what's in the locked room."

The devil sat down in a posture of thinking. It had to be copying Halgrim and Ash could imagine Halgrim pacing or sitting down now. Halgrim said, "That explains it. She came by a few days ago and asked me a lot of questions, indirectly, about that room. At the time, I thought she was fishing for something she did not want to just ask directly. It was the room." Ash groaned before Halgrim even asked, "What's in the room, Ash?"

"I didn't tell Khalla. She's a gorgeous, perfect woman, Hal. You think I'm going to tell a wrinkled raisin of a man something I wouldn't tell Khalla?" Ash laughed back. He tried to hide the bitter undertone in his voice.

The devil watched him curiously as if to say, "You're not fooling anyone."

"Maybe I'll storm off too," the devil said in Halgrim's voice as it hopped onto the iron fence and flew away.

Ash rested his face into his arm. He could still smell her hair on his clothes. He knew she wanted to know. "She probably thinks I have a mistress or something locked in there."

He walked to the front door and closed it, careful to engage mechanical and magical locks. When he returned to the room, he removed a drawer entirely. The drawer's slot hid a rune. The rune activated powerful anti-scrying magic. Once active, Ash unlocked the door. He did not use a key. His index finger became a key. With a last cautious glance into the hall, Ash entered the room and closed the door behind him.

☐

# Chapter 4 – Blood Echoes across the Land

Ayden wiped sweat from her eyes with the back of her leather gauntlet. The looming skeleton of the Jade God filled the northeastern portion of the sky. Her sword cut out against the demon. For a moment, the blade's radiant edge distracted her. She felt guilty and realized its source: her father's sword had not seen action since Malcor made her a new one. The titan's dagger in her other hand deftly caught, twisted around, and severed the wrist of a clawing attack.

The demon pulled back, hissing at her. If it felt fear, she could not tell. Though the wrist quickly closed off the venomous blood leaking from its stump, Ayden noted its many wounds. It would not last much longer. "I was loath to use this before. It's a bit flashy," she said. She pointed the sword at the demon, its blood groove aimed in a perfect target line. "Shadowsorcere," she said. A draconian rune on her blade lost its purple glow.

Black lightning spat from the blade and struck the demon. A normal creature would dance about with energy until it fell dead, or cold, or both. The demon froze for a moment and then laughed at Ayden. "Dark energy can't hurt me!" it roared. It leapt forward.

Ayden let it get close before she willed the black lightning dancing around the demon's body to bind it. "It can't hurt you, but it can restrain you." Ayden lined up her sword again and jabbed it between the demon's disbelieving eyes. She rotated the blade and then, holding its head on her sword, she cut at the demon with Titan's Blade. Though she loved the sword Malcor had made her, Titan's Blade had come to be her personal favorite. She had a bond with it from her adventure that retrieved it. It gave her the ability to clone herself and then the clone could take the dagger and act with a close semblance of what Ayden would actually do herself. She loved it and the surreal feeling that came with seeing herself in action.

When the demon began to disintegrate, she pulled back and looked around the valley. The outspread hand served as a backdrop for their battle. All around her, priestesses of Tiamat moved. They healed the wounded, raised the fallen, and occasionally combined their might to drive out shadows and other creatures inhabiting Tania's soldiers. These fighters, the clerics marked so that they would not return to the valley for more battles against demons. The demons would never retreat or surrender and pockets of fighting still lingered near the thumb. They could not afford possessed warriors in their midst.

Ayden walked over to a group of clerics doing just this with a fighter. The man lay twitching on the ground until a dark mist steamed out of his body. It had a foul smell to it. The mist tried to coalesce but the clerics banished it. "A fight for the very body and soul of Tania," Ayden said.

"Indeed," Sir Johaness answered. "And Taysor, and Haven, and Morilon. I'll need a map to name all the places we're saving." Johaness, a cleric of Pha Rann, stood tall and proud with his group of Literalists. Ayden had been grateful to learn that their literalness only applied to how they understood Pha Rann's doctrine.

"On behalf of the Nineteenth, I thank you and your team, Sir Johaness." Ayden saw a blink, more a dark suggestion of movement behind them, and sighed. "Another group just came in." In a loud command voice, Ayden shouted, "About face! Attack!"

The group turned as one and charged toward the area just under Orcus' wrist. Rocks and debris there created a swale. Ayden jumped in with both sword and dagger in hand. She almost cut into a roguish looking man when all of her magic went dead. She still struck at the thief, but he deflected her sword with a buckler and then stabbed at her with a rapier. The Titan's Blade, everything had gone dark and with it, the weight of her armor hindered her. The rogue smiled. To the side, six rogues lifted up loaded crossbows and fired on the clerics. Though all of the bolts clanged against their plate armor and shields, Ayden also felt their divine prayers of support fade. A tiny man behind the crossbowmen pocketed something off the ground.

The thief next to Ayden kicked her as he dodged backwards. "Not so strong now are you, Tanian?" The others chuckled and turned their attention to the line of clerics.

The tiny man cried out with a shrill voice, "Hurry! We don't have much time. I can't hold this forever."

Ayden had to recall her early days training in heavy metal armor. Magical protection had more bulk than weight, but back then in her first year, it was all metal. She rolled to her knees and stood. Remembering how to move and balance came naturally to her. She flipped her sword and knife. "You made a big mistake coming here," she said to the thieves.

Though half had reloaded or grabbed loaded backup crossbows, Ayden dodged into their midst and cut one of the thieves to ribbons. The others stepped back and shot at her. "I guess you thought you'd be fighting clerics?" Ayden taunted them. "I'm the Legion Commander. We could use more slaves..." Another thief dropped to the ground before Ayden's lethal dance. In and out, another fell. Though a quarrel finally struck her, she ignored the pain and charged right at the tiny man.

"No!" he shrieked and stumbled back from her. Just when her sword was about to cut a bloody line through his neck, an ogre tackled her. She realized she had not seen the creature because it was lying in wait, hidden in the mud and rotting gore all around. Though her armor protected her, the ogre's backhand smash – and the club in that hand – sent her flying through the air.

She landed in mud and noted three other ogres with polearms sawing the skin off Orcus' wrist. The skin came away easily, something Tania still struggled with. Once the skin cleared, they cut into the wrist looking for blood. As they found it, they drained it into buckets. She looked for the clerics and saw them advancing, right over two ogres lying in the mud. Ayden realized she had stepped on one of their backs thinking they were a bump in the landscape. She called out a warning, but it was too late.

Overhead, a griffon saw the melee and a trumpet blew. "Time to leave, boys!" the tiny man trilled. Instantly, Ayden felt magic return to her world. Simultaneously, a gate opened and the thieves began diving through it. The ogres even threw the dead thieves through.

Ayden took the Titan's Blade in her hand and whispered to it. "You know what you need to do." Her throw passed the blade clear through the portal, which vanished a moment later.

Ayden collapsed back into the mud and began pulling the crossbow bolt out of her torso. One of the priests found her and together they yanked it out. "Commander, two of our unit fell but are recoverable. Also, heralds show another group attempting to take the Jade God along the left leg. Your orders?"

Ayden gagged on her words. The bolt left a gaping hole in her lung and, though the priest's healing prayer closed it, a momentary panic pulled at her. She repressed it and checked her response to shock. She would be okay. "Is Andrew still with the Gryphon Riders? If yes, route him to intercept. If not, have the Gryphons attack and have Andrew send what he can to that position. Lady Seline is to retain her forces at the Wand."

The priest saluted her, checked that her would continue healing, and ran off to convey her orders. Still sitting back in the war-ravaged landscape, Ayden let her eyes cross the outstretched hand of the dead god. Smoke and ash still filled the valley from the volcano. Bloodstone was a mess.

"And it will be for a very long time." She rolled to her knees and used her sword, Shadowsorcere, to help stand up.

High King Andrew, an unlikely ally, would no doubt accept and race to act on this order. The young king seemed to enjoy beating Ayden's own command team in execution of her orders. Still scanning their battle scene, Ayden smiled at the thought of the young king, as if she was not also a young Legion Commander. We're the same age, I think, she wondered. Her hand moved to a small medallion Tembri had given her just before they entered the Valley of Bloodstone almost a year ago. Under her hand, while he lived, it had pulsed with his heartbeat. Since his death seven months back, Ayden's world had twisted.

Some of it was good. Some bad. The good was confusing. High King Andrew, the Second Officer from the 18th Legion Revi, the Dread Lords, even Dar Ana had rallied around Ayden for Verit's command. Her objections that she was not a paladin fell on deaf ears. If the priestesses had not been so tied up keeping the god emperor Alerius alive, Ayden rather suspected that Dar Ana herself would be pressuring her and Seline to join the Temple as priestesses. Until King Andrew pointed it out, Ayden had been oblivious to why Ana spent so much time with her.

So much had changed. The Tanian war machine had been honed over 1,000 years by Dar Ana and functioned quite well even without a Legion Commander. Ayden found that it just needed a poke and a prod here and there to work. The alliance with the Sorans had nearly strained it to breaking. Tania was used to Sorans in small numbers. That Andrew seemed interested in her did, as Dar Ana put it, "Present certain strategic opportunities. After all, not since the Sage Alaura has Morbatten enjoyed a strong royal alliance. I know you mourn Tembri, but you also know he has a glorious afterlife. He will not begrudge your happiness."

A paladin ran towards her, no doubt with news of some other crisis. Her smile broke into a wide grin and she remembered that she liked being the one who poked and prodded it. The war machine was beautiful in and of itself. Right now, her unit was just a tiny gear, one of thousands, and the Titan Blade's power would figure out what that raid was about. The god emperor had been clear: Raids will be harried but allowed until the full moon. After that, kill all of them. Morbatten will not allow the Jade God's body to fuel the next generations of necromancers."

\* \* \*

Titan's Blade spun through the portal. As it twirled, a copy of Ayden's self manifested as shadow and then became real within a single turn of the spinning knife. Ayden-blade tumbled head over heels and then caught the Titan's Blade dagger mid-air in a large room full of crates. Real Ayden wants all these people dead, Ayden-blade realized. They are stealing parts of the Jade God and it must not be allowed. Ayden-blade felt her heart begin beating and reveled in the growing power of her actual wielder back somewhere in the Valley of Bloodstone. More and more, her wielder was trusting her with autonomous missions like this. As her wielder's power grew, so too did Titan's Blade. Soon, they would be able to talk to each other. She could not wait. There was so much to tell!

The smell of salt water told her she was close to the coast, probably in Taysor, but with gate magic, she could be anywhere. Her wielder did not, had never cared much for world geography, but Ayden-blade was ancient and well-travelled. All around her, activity stopped as the raiders noticed her. Then a single voice, cried out, "Get her!" Another screamed, "How did the Legion Commander get here?!" Recognition of her wielder and her power thrilled Ayden-blade.

Ayden-blade hit the gem on the dagger's pommel. A blinding flash of light lit the area. For mortals, the radiance would hurt, even blind them permanently if they did not look away or cover their eyes. Three large buckets of Orcus blood sloshed on the floor. They had taken more than other groups. It infuriated her but she could do nothing about it right now. Her wielder wanted them all dead or captured, but most importantly to not have any parts of Orcus. Ayden-blade found the tiny man and ran past him towards the only apparent exit. Titan's Blade did not make for a great punching tool, but it felt good to smash his nose and teeth in. At least her wielder had been wearing armor and the gauntlet did a spectacular job against Tiny Man's mouth.

A moment later, Ayden-blade smashed through a wooden door resting near a ladder at the end of the passage. She jumped up the ladder and through the door. She rolled through the door into a large wooden warehouse. Boats and barges swayed in gentle water. Sunlight streamed through cracks in the wooden ceiling high overhead. Dockhands turned and looked at her with studied indifference; they knew better than to get involved. Guessing there might be as many as a hundred workers here, Ayden-blade ran to the water and dove in just as she heard voices calling for her to be killed.

The cold water, still freezing from winter, did not faze Ayden-blade at all. The magic that gave her physical form did not care about temperature, or breathing. She let her armor pull her down but finding only thick muck, she cut the armor straps so she could swim. She found that the water extended far underneath the dock area. In fact, she swam up to where she guessed the ladder and passage might be. It took a while to clear the grime, but when she found smooth stone in the general shape of the tunnel, she smiled. This was the outer wall of the chamber containing all the Orcus parts.

I really shouldn't, she thought and then laughed. Time to die again! Ayden-blade found a crack and eased the Titan's Blade into it. Pressing her hands against the dock overhead, she used her feet to press the blade into the crack. The magic blade etched its way slowly into the crack. All I need is a small hole. Just one tiny hole, Ayden-blade prayed to her wielder and remembered that she also carried other items. Her wielder must truly love her to bless her with so much equipment. Her last master had not trusted her at all. I'm going to die when I do this, Ayden-blade thought. This will prove my worth to my wielder. Ayden will find me. I will not be trapped in this dark place like I was last time.

Keeping pressure on the blade, she found a small cache of potions in a toughened satchel at her belt. Inside lay a number of potions Tembri had felt would serve Ayden well in Bloodstone. Ayden-blade touched them with reverence. Though her wielder's grief at Tembri's death was becoming more manageable, Ayden-blade loved Tembri just as much and recovered at the same pace. It hurt, physically. Sometimes, the ache was so much Ayden could barely move. The loss threatened Ayden-blade and she shook her head. I only saw flashes of Tembri. I'm not Ayden, not yet.

The real Ayden had never used any of the potions. At this point, she kept them as a remembrance. She found the one Tembri had said would increase her strength many times. Ayden would forgive her – use of their equipment lessened its potency… and be impressed with her for accomplishing this mission.

She swallowed the potion and rejoiced at its magical strength. She levered her body and kicked at the stone. Two kicks later and the Titan's Blade popped through the stone into the tunnel. Mud and water began pouring in. Though unfortunate she lost the dagger, it wouldn't matter. They were phantasmal copies anyway, of real things. Ayden-blade moved down and kicked in the next section. This time, when it collapsed, it pulled the entire tunnel section in and Ayden-blade dropped into the air bubble. The portal area had been many steps below the level of the ocean. Everyone would die. The force of water and the drowning panic all around made her laugh until her skull caved in.

# Chapter 5 – Halgrim's Deal

Halgrim, the pre-archmage, stood on the roof of the Mages Guild. The impossibly high tower stood almost three hundred paces from the ground. Nothing else came close to it. Overhead, a seething ball of energy twisted and writhed as if trying to escape. Up this high, the wind fluttered Halgrim's robes. This tower and the summoning circle crafted upon its surface "watched" the empire. Halgrim could feel the energy raging all around him. This is where the archmagi came to do great magics.

From behind, Dar Reznor's voice called out. "This is where we constructed the wish spells that ended Orcus. This is where we will have to come to make Merakor work for you." Reznor walked up to the edge to stand by Halgrim. "You should not be here."

Halgrim shrugged. "I figured, with Ash's reluctance, I wanted to see what I was giving up or getting into. I don't know what Ash will decide, but I'm in. I want it all, Dar Reznor."

"You know the price," Reznor whispered.

Halgrim nodded and walked back to the summoning circle. He knelt down and conjured a knife into his right hand. When the first drop of his blood fell onto the surface, a single page of cream parchment appeared with a razored quill of white bone. "Write your name, Preac Halgrim!" Reznor ordered.

"Yes!" Halgrim cried as he traced his name with his own blood on to the page of *Mali Lynthraceae Vede Mecum*. "Know me, Darkhold!"

Halgrim's blood sank into the page and then words appeared.

> I know you now, Halgrim vell Radcliffe.
> For what, would you know?

Halgrim looked back to Reznor who stood on the edge of the glyph. "Anything you want, Halgrim," Reznor said. If you can't think of anything, the empire has a lengthy list of questions."

Halgrim turned back to the page. Reznor's voice trailed to him, "Just one question, though."

"So many questions I've always wondered about," Halgrim said. "I always knew, my Dar. May I ask, what did you ask?"

Dar Reznor said, "For Merakor, because you are helping and because I know you as my apprentice, I will tell you. I asked the Darkhold for the formula to chain souls to certain spells so that the caster's lifeforce is not drained."

"Ah, yes. Yes! I have always wondered at this. I knew you brought this to Tania, but it was through the Darkhold?"

Reznor folded his arms into his robe to get his fingers out of the bitterly cold wind. "Yes and no. The Darkhold's answer to me required many years of research to perfect and make possible. Remember, it is an abyssal god. There is a price paid and the information often suggests a path that favors the Darkhold, not us. It always answers truthfully, but tilts it to drive us to ask more questions. No doubt, you will want to ask just one more. Do not. After many years, when I finally thought I had an answer, it turned out that the Darkhold had anticipated my epiphanies along the way. My apprentice was captured and fell into its pages. It was regrettable. Be sure, Halgrim, that you do not regret your question. Any additional use of this artefact is by the god emperor's decree alone."

"Most mages in my position, they waste this chance, don't they?" Reznor inclined his head in a cryptic nod. Halgrim pressed with another question. "Tell me, Dar Reznor, what advice would you give your newest archmage to avoid wasting this question?"

Reznor met Halgrim's eyes and held them. Reznor's several centuries as master of the Mages Guild reflected back as a strong sense of will and supreme confidence. Halgrim wondered if by look alone, Reznor meant to tell him something important. When Halgrim's exhilaration slid down a step, Reznor answered at last. "As an archmage, you serve the empire. Specifically, you serve the god emperor Alerius first." Reznor held up a finger. "Dread Lord Spark next, and then the Mages Guild and Guildmaster." He help up two additional fingers.

"All of this is to serve and strengthen the empire, and not because the empire is weak. Remember, the Court of Patriarchs watched Merakor fall. No, we strengthen the empire because it must become stronger, strong enough to kill our real enemy. In going to Merakor, you are serving the empire. The best questions are those that advance the empire. The pursuit of the answer will move the empire forward with you. However, the Darkhold is a very personal matter. For some Prearcs in your position, I require specific questions. In your case, Halgrim, Tiamat grants you free will to ask what is in your heart."

Halgrim bowed low and turned back to the page. He said, "I understand, Master Reznor. Thank you." Halgrim took the quill floating near the book and cut his left wrist with it. Dipping the quill in blood, he set it to the page and wrote his question.

Reznor watched as the winds buffeting the high tower swirled their robes. The lights of Morbatten spread out before him, Reznor watched the old man and smiled. *Our path to power is a corrupting one. With just a taste, our newest archmage becomes another weapon against our enemies.*

The Darkhold's pages remained open and hungry for blood in spite of the strong winds. They lay still. The god emperor enjoyed these tests: would Halgrim do what the empire wanted or something else? *Answers we need or an archmage we need, Tania will win today either way. The only true waste*, Reznor mused, *is when a candidate writes a question we already have the answer to.*

The red gleam from the page and the manic posture by which Halgrim's eyes fixated on the page told Reznor the question was answered. Like anyone using the Darkhold, there comes a moment when a universe of possible knowledge tempts the seeker of answers to ask for more. *For what, would you know?*, Reznor could see the question in his mind.

In all the centuries Tania possessed the Darkhold, only Dar Ana and several others could use it more than a few times. The book hungered for Ana in a way that prevented it from taking her soul. The threat was always there. Reznor remembered the second time he asked. Even with Alerius there with him, the Darkhold had nearly taken his soul. He remembered how he felt himself falling forward as the abyssal runes grew larger. Then, it all fell away and despair had stricken him for days.

None of this happened with Ana. In fact, it was reversed. If the cursed pages even sensed her, it would greet her by name and prompt, *Dearest Ana, come and let us converse. For what might I entice you to me?* The prompting question never appeared for her. Even with Ana though, after a few times, the book would offer her eternal life and power to join it. Her rejection enraged the book and made it unusable for years. Reznor wrily noted that perhaps the paladins of Tania feel the same way when Ana rejects one for another she considered more powerful.

Reznor chanted softly and the book fell asleep. It drifted back into the center of the summoning circle and left only Halgrim there kneeling on the edge. For a moment, Halgrim reached out as if to grab it back. Blood continued to streak down his wrist and fingers. This was another test of will. Reznor watched to see if Halgrim would try to claim the book. If he did, the tower itself would swallow Halgrim. Morbatten could not risk another Bomoki.

Most sorcerers thought the Tower of the Archmagi a monument and landmark. In reality, the god emperor and his subsequent apprentices built the Tower to safeguard the empire from the Darkhold's use. For the archmagi, they could feel the Tower activate whenever the Darkhold awoke. The abyssal deity slept fitfully. *Sleep* magic could calm it, but only souls could satiate the Darkhold and truly quiet it. If Halgrim passed this temptation, he would feel the tower and know what fate he dodged. For most, it was a sobering reminder of the counter-balance required by the Court of Patriarchs.

The old man, bowed on his hands and knees, looked up at Reznor. Tears fell from his eyes and then he shook as the first sob hit him and he looked away from the Dar. Halgrim shook off the compulsion and slid out of the circle.

Reznor softly said, "I'm glad you resisted it, *Archmage* Halgrim of Tania." Reznor put extra emphasis on the new title. "Dar Halgrim, you may not realize it but you have passed one of the most important tests of your life. You are no longer a Prearc." *He must have asked about a loved one or some past tragedy. That's much better than a repetitive question,* Reznor thought. "Feel the Tower of the Archmagi and know its truth. In 700 DAR, Alerius and Apprentice Cystoran built this tower to contain and feed Mali Lynthracaea Vede Mecum, what you now as the Darkhold. While the tower is a place of study, and worship, it is also a golem whose purpose is to swallow up and hold any who would abuse that book. By doing this, the Law of Innocents is respected and the empire is kept safe from the archmagi."

Halgrim's eyes widened and he put his hands on the ground. The tower, with the Darkhold, quieted slowly as Halgrim's realization and emotional state quieted. Halgrim bowed his head and made a choking sound. A tear fell to splatter in the blood by the new archmage's hand. "Of course, of course. I suspected it a test but the magic of that book. I did not trust myself and so retired at this test. I knew I would fail back then."

Unmoving, Reznor watched as Halgrim's tears renewed and then turned to wracking sobs. After many minutes, the newest archmage of Morbatten stood on shaky legs. "Thank you for this, Dar Reznor. I will not let you down." A pause later, Halgrim explained, "I lost my wife when we were very young and married. She died in childbirth. I was new in my power, still in Haven. Our daughter lived though not very long. Their deaths... I was crippled with sorrow and full of anger that I did not have the power to help either of them. I thought about using my magic to save them but was scared I would fail... I know now that my magic would not have mattered, and they are happy. I feel freer than I have felt since they died."

"Yes, of a rare family illness you did not know about. That same bloodline here in Tania would have been handled very differently. Your wife would have lived. I'm unsure if your daughter would have. I take it that you got the closure you sought?"

Halgrim walked forward and dropped to his knees before Reznor. He leaned forward in the style of the formal bow only used by paladins anymore. "Halgrim, you don't need to do this," Reznor said.

"I must. This regret has poisoned my life. It is why I left the Guild... the temptation to ask this question, the risk of the answer. But, I figure Merakor may be my coffin and I had to know." Halgrim pressed his face to the stone floor and added, "My life for Tania."

Reznor gestured and strips of cloth swirled into being and bound the still bleeding slash on Halgrim's wrist. Reznor said, "Well done, Halgrim. This sense of purpose, of being part of something bigger than you, this is what separates a Tanian archmage from other mages. Behold, your first spell." A scroll appeared under Halgrim's hand. "When you have mastered this, you shall come find me, immediately. I will know whether you succeed or not. Mastering this, we will open other spells to you. My first command to you, Archmage Halgrim, is this: I order you to master this spell in the next two hours." Reznor vanished from the tower.

Still bowed, Halgrim unrolled the scroll. The spell contained the cryptic rune markings used by Tania as a block on other mages stealing it. To master the spell, to attempt it, would create a compulsion to keep it secret, to keep it safe, and to only discuss it only within the Tower of the Archmagi. Halgrim imagined the Tower might have other purposes than just containing the Darkhold. Just like that book, the scroll's runes moved about on the page and then resolved to his understanding. "I must be long overdue for this promotion," Halgrim mused to himself while wiping snot from his whiskers. The spell was easy for him. He began to chant, and let the spell of youth unwind time's ravages in his body.

An hour later, Halgrim stood up. His changed body, appropriate for a man of 35 years, rose easily. Muscles, tendon, and unwrinkled skin felt luxurious. He stretched and enjoyed the silence of his body where normally it would snap and pop with each joint protesting. Having been bald for years, his hair had returned and lay long and wild about his shoulders. He became aware of the wind, and then the capital city. "It's beautiful," he whispered to himself. His stomach growled and food appeared for him. A small note read: Congratulations, Halgrim! We await you in the Tower of the Archmagi.

Halgrim's *teleportation* spell took him from the tower's height to the ground entrance. He walked in and found the rest of the Council sitting in their thrones. The damage from Ash's knife on the tables and chairs had been erased from their earlier meeting with Dar Reznor. A few empty chairs bore name labels that Halgrim recognized and knew still fought in Bloodstone. Halgrim remembered that when he and Ash visited, the thrones were unlabeled. He paused and scanned the names, surprised to see some and pleased he had already guessed at most. The occupants of the chairs acknowledged him with respect – a hand wave here, a slight nod there. He knew them all, either personally or by acquaintance.

Three vacant thrones of fire, ice, and lightning overwatched the room from an elevated position opposite the entry. Behind them loomed a giant statue of Tiamat every bit as beautiful as the one in the actual Temple. The starry constellations of night spun in the darkness in the tower heights above them and the triple-split moon, Gates, descended on the eastern side. Though confined to the tower, the sense of massive space filled the chamber.

Halgrim bowed to the statue of Tiamat. Doing so, he realized he had just passed another test as the assembled archmagi stood and bowed to the Goddess as well. Then, Reznor began clapping and the others joined in. Soon, congratulatory hands took Halgrim's own and hearty pats on the back pulled him in. When he at last stood before Reznor again, he found the Guildmaster smiling at him with genuine warmth. "Yes, you were overdue for this promotion." Cheers sounded in agreement. Reznor pointed to an empty throne and the name placard reading 'Nientro' changed to Halgrim's name.

The throne waited for him. Tentatively, and feeling suddenly anxious, he walked to it and then sat down. Instantly, the scene shifted from the tower's main level to an open space somewhere else. *The ethereal realm*, Halgrim realized. All around him, a river of many-hued energies like fire flowed. *Tiamat's River*, he corrected himself. *I need to come here more often.*

From the side of the River, a dragon reared up and looked down at them. The magi remained in their seats in a pose of reverence. Halgrim recognized the god emperor by his titanic size and missing wing. Blood still seeped from the shoulder wound and stained the downstream flow of energy in red flames cascading towards the future. "Welcome to the Council, Archmage Halgrim." The god emperor's voice echoed in this place of primal energy. The darkness, the pain, the power, the sheer majesty of the eldar dragon pulled at Halgrim with awesome power. It stirred him to want to do something, to take action, to help. Adrenaline spiked his body and he knew: he felt dragonterror but instead of crushing him, it bade him to act.

Alerius continued. "Too long have you avoided your destiny in this Council. You see here the assembled archmagi of Tania. This seat is where you will study the higher spells, where you shall commune with your fellow archmagi, and with the dragons! This, Archmage Halgrim, is where we, all of us together, will together plot the course that we must each walk to realize the Prophecy of the Spear and Shield. This is your destiny! Your spell book has new pages added to it. Like the *longevity* spell, which you mastered in record time like we thought, you will find that each new page contains a new spell. Your task is to develop a new spell of your own and add it to our library. Once you have mastered the Tanian standard spells, each new spell that you complete will allow you to access one owned by the Council. The Council will instruct you as to how these spells interact with the Law of Innocents. There is a reason I have required their restriction."

Alerius humanshifted and joined them at his throne of fire. Favoring his wounded left shoulder, Alerius sat down and continued. "In Merakor, there are a few items of great value. For each item you retrieve, you will be granted an extra spell either in the standard codex or from the Council's. This is your payment for taking this job. I trust you will not fail us. You have no idea how jealous many of these are that you, not them, is chosen by my brother, Ynt'taris. Alas, Bloodstone calls to me and I must leave. Dar Reznor, the Council is yours."

When Alerius vanished, a pool of blood remained in the seat and dripped down the back of the throne. It showed the extent of the year-old wound. For Halgrim, seeing the god emperor so mortal shook him to the core. Everyone knew about the unhealed wound. The god emperor did not hide that the Jade God had amputated his left wing, nor that it defied healing. If anything, it created an outpouring of love and national fervor of support. As each drop fell into the River of Fire, it ignited and burned.

Reznor stood and carefully sponged the blood off the throne. "You see that our days of having an immortal god emperor draw to a close, maybe in our lifetimes, maybe longer. We cannot know. The god emperor does not know when himself but has declared his intent to ascend with Dar Kell. You see how Tehra pulls on him. You are to ponder this. Many of the spells you have already mastered contain clues and guidance about the eldar, about mortal ascension, about our destinies. Please, lift up your faith and hopes for the god emperor's continued strength."

When finished, in the perfect silence of the ethereal, Reznor remained standing in front of the fire throne and turned to face the 37 members of the Council. Halgrim had been and continued to be both surprised and not surprised to see there were so many archmagi. They, like Halgrim with his artificer shop, kept a low profile.

Reznor said, "You all see that Halgrim joins our Council. You all hear that Halgrim is tasked with a quest to Merakor. You will each, no doubt, wish for Halgrim to acquire spells from the god emperor's store that we might add them to our codex. Until Halgrim returns from Merakor, you are each enjoined from any attempts to persuade or take actions against Halgrim. His focus must be on Merakor and the god emperor's errand. Any violation of this will risk expulsion from the Council."

The group bowed their heads and Halgrim figured he would soon learn what this all meant. Though he expected Reznor or others to speak, he saw that each archmage opened their spellbook and began studying its contents. When he wondered where his was, a book appeared on his lap. The runes on it resolved to his view, *The Alerius Codex*. In sharp contrast to the emotions he had just barely experienced at the tower and with the god emperor, he now felt excitement flood him.

The first page opened as the *spell of youth*. The next page opened to a magic named *soul chaining*. Halgrim quickly understood that the price of his restored youthfulness was life taken from someone else via soul chaining. A footnote appeared as he studied through the connection and how it worked. It read: *You are restored 40 years younger through 8 prisoners each paying 5 years of their lives rather than sitting in prison for a real 5 years. Though magic is powerful, there is an equivalency at play with stronger magic of this type. Remember it. Respect it.*

Reznor's voice came to his mind. *Each of our spellbooks is watched over by a death knight attuned to us and our lives. The more we study, the more the death knight understands how to assist, but also to intervene should we use this magic contrary to Tiamat's will.*

Halgrim considered this and sent his questions back to Dar Reznor. *Do the death knights view this as a form of atonement?*

Their eyes met across the council space. The River of Fire backlit the Dar's face. The answer froze Halgrim's soul. *It is not atonement. These are ancient paladins who chose this dark sacrament to ensure there would never be another Bomoki. They hate us. They hunger to slay us for Tiamat. Do not, do not ever, give them reason to doubt your intentions.*

Khalla sat on Perdition's Throne and wondered how something so ornate could be so uncomfortable. She felt tense at a level she had not experienced in years. Even with the Bloodstone quest, even with some of the missions she had conducted solo, none of them made her feel this way. "I must have really loved the bastard," she said out loud about Ash.

The shadows all around captured the sound of her voice and she marveled at how quiet the chamber was. She hoped Ash would answer her, and hated that she hoped. She knew Ash might show up and so came dressed in Perdition's style of a spidersilk gown over slender tools of their trade. If he did not, her meeting with the true master of Perdition encouraged a certain level of formality. A satchel containing her swords, actual armor, and heavier gear rested at the throne's base.

The throne's right arm rest cushion hinged over the actual arm. She flipped the cushion up and studied the runes there. "Ash?" she called out. "I'm going to do it. This is your last chance to stop me."

She held her breath and waited. When nothing disturbed the silence, she suppressed her frustration, and touched the runes. She had solved this riddle long ago. The true guildmaster was Daryx. The Tanian runes masked the Drow spelling of that one's name. She outlined his name and waited.

After a minute, she felt a slight movement in the air and her eyes darted to the shadows under a window. From the opposite side of the throne chamber, Daryx's voice hissed at her like a serpent. "You'd be dead already in my home, little mouse."

Khalla kept her cool and turned her body to face the voice, but instead, she felt a blade at her throat. She gasped and flinched back from it, but stumbled against Daryx's chest. Stone hands and steel arms held her firm. "Dead already and yet, you wish to sit on Perdition's Throne? The true master of this throne would have already slain me."

Khalla swallowed. "Marcello named me guildmaster. Sai R'Dar and Dar Ora witnessed this. I am Marcello and I claim Perdition."

The knife withdrew and with it, the pale-skinned Drow appeared before the throne. Daryx wore spider silk trousers, same iridescent charcoal color as Khalla's gown, but no shirt. Long white hair flowed from his head, almost like a woman's except his hair had a weighty quality to it that reminded Khalla of thick spider webs. In the moonlight streaming through the small windows to her left, Khalla noted the many scars covering Daryx's body. Though she could only see his upper half, she imagined they must cover his entire body.

Daryx bowed. "Lady Khalla, since your anointing, I have wondered when we might have this conversation. I'm sure that Marcello taught you to respect the throne?"

Daryx's inflection of the word 'respect' made Khalla worried. She shook the feeling away and stood tall. She wanted to look regal and confident for this legendary member of the Circle. "Daryx, I am Khalla sere Thalis. I have served Perdition since my recruitment as a child. I am ready…"

Daryx corrected her. "Since I purchased you from a slaver in the Barony."

Khalla lost all composure at that point. Her hopes of seeming confident fell apart and she blurted out, "What? I was not a slave."

"The unwanted child of a noble elf girl who fell in love with a half-orc. You are ugly, by Gray Elf standards. You should have been cruel, raised in a world that could not appreciate your true beauty. But, I placed you with two elven worshippers of Tiamat in my estates at Adir. There, you became beautiful. Powerful. If Lolth herself said to me that you would someday sit on Perdition, I would have laughed and mocked the very idea. But, not now. Not today, little mouse. That was what I named you when I gave you to your foster parents. Khalla is a Drow name for a little mouse adept at finding homes in others' homes."

Khalla clenched her fists and recovered her straight back and careful smile. "Slave child or not, wanted or not, I am no longer a child. Marcello named me successor. I claim Perdition."

Daryx bowed. "There are conditions."

Khalla felt the anxiety begin to leave, though every statement by Daryx opened up new questions. "Whatever they are, I accept them." Her words sounded stronger than she felt.

"Do you not want to know the conditions?"

"I want to serve Tania. I may have conditions of my own." Khalla resisted the temptation to push a strand of her hair back from her face. Resisting it, Daryx suddenly stood to her side and the air of his movement, knocked the strand away. He did not touch her, but she had to turn to face him.

He said, "Very well, my conditions can wait. Tell me, Khalla of Perdition, what would you do with the Thieves Guild?" Daryx pressed her personal boundaries and it made her feel off balance.

Though she wanted to take a deep breath and work up to her point, she felt Daryx would respond better to just getting to the point. "Marcello cloaked the guild in darkness and shadows. With Northern Cross destroyed, our rivals will most likely shift. We must shift with them. If a war breaks out, Tania must come out on top. You ask what I would do. I say to you, Daryx, I would unite all Thieves Guilds under Perdition. The raiding parties in Bloodstone are a challenge we must answer." Khalla felt her words rush out too quickly, but for fear of losing composure, she raced through them. She had rehearsed this speech twice now since storming out of Ash's home.

Daryx opened his arms wide and threw his head back. "A strong vision and certainly one in alignment with what the god emperor wishes. That High King Andrew supports Tania in Bloodstone, and their Temples now view us with confusion for victory over the Jade God, is not enough. All elements of Taysor must view Tania as a power to be reckoned with. You feel that Marcello has been lax in Perdition's reputation? You are not wrong. Which of his failures would you right?"

"That the cult of Orcus thrived in Dockside is unforgivable and shows a lack of respect for our role. That, in Perdition's assault there, we left trapped prisoners and chambers unfound beneath the cult site. Any thief should have found what the Watch Officer Calvin uncovered. It is unforgivable." Daryx's laconic body language made Khalla want to be more expressive with her own. Talking about the Cult of Orcus and the minotaur Calvin had saved there, Khalla found she had to resist throwing her arms out and imitating the dark elf. That he had vanished and now stood at the bottom of the steps before the throne distracted her and she kept her posture unmoved.

Daryx walked up and held his hand out to her. She took it and he pulled her into his arms. His strength could not be resisted though his skin felt wrong and made her profoundly uneasy. He turned her to face the empty hall. The movement reminded Khalla of a dance. "Everything except treason is forgivable, maybe-Marcello. Tania is built on excellence, on resilience. Not inflexibility. But, tell me, when Perdition's halls are full of light and the R'Dar and Dar dance here, how should we punish Marcello?"

Without hesitating, Khalla answered, "He should be stripped of his role as guildmaster. I will cast him out of Perdition." Khalla felt Daryx's hand in the small of her back as he swayed her side to side and directed her gaze. There in the center of the main hall, she saw the Master Vault. It had always been there. In Daryx's arms though, it became obvious. The dragon insignia of three twisted with wings touching was not just an ornate decoration. It was the actual door. She had thought it further in the dungeon next to the copy vault.

Khalla tensed and wondered what game the dark elf played now to show her this. Am I supposed to unlock it? Ash had told her numerous times that any attempt to enter the Master Vault without sanction by the Circle would be bad, not just fatally bad either. Daryx held her firm. She had thought he was flirting with her but realized he did this to keep her off balance; it was a test. He was showing her things. He may have been pointing things out to her since he first appeared. *Tiamat burn me*, Khalla screamed mentally. *I've been so focused on how anxious he makes me feel to see this. How do I recover?* Her eyes darted to the upper balconies and she noted a winged golem she had thought a statue. It watched over the Vault. In each of the locations Daryx had pointed her, the true nature of the throne as a death trap became clear.

Khalla followed Daryx's movements and then leaned in to him and swept him into her own arms. She expected resistance but instead he leaned into it. From a hand's distance away, he smiled into her face and let his eye teeth gleam in the faint lighting around the throne. Khalla said, "I'm feeling more flexible now that I see the true nature you've shown me about this place. I will let Ash stay and become a cell leader. I would choose him as one of my lieutenants."

Daryx bowed his head. "A wise choice. Marcello does not just happen overnight. Remember this and maybe when you make mistakes, you will judge by a less harsh standard. Are you perfect, Khalla? I am glad you see this. Ash will be a valuable ally for you."

"You know that I am not perfect. And yes, Perdition's operations must be perfect."

Daryx let go of her hand and twinkling lights filled the vast throne chamber. One by one, the lights resolved into phase spiders, hundreds of them. Khalla felt her skin crawl as a tiny one materialized on her shoulder. Daryx spoke. "I sense great turmoil in your heart for Ash. The Circle is watching the Merakor adventure with great interest. We had thought your love would carry you to Merakor with Ash. He has already turned guild activities over to you. So, tell me, do you really wish him excised or is this some other emotion speaking, perhaps you are trying to negotiate with me around non-negotiable things. The webs we think we weave can bind us just as easily as catch our prey. Which are yours: binding or catching?"

A dog-sized spider blinked into being in front of her and tapped the leather fabric of her shoe. The spider seemed calm, non-aggressive. Yet when its ghost-like leg touched her foot, she felt nothing. She knew, from her studies in the Garden, that phase spiders were one of the Abyss's most terrible creatures, able to take creatures in whole or in part from this realm into another. "What are you, my lord?"

Daryx caught her close in an embrace and, with his face a finger's width from her own, he said, "I'm the King of Perdition and you are asking for my throne."

"That's not what I mean," Khalla said. She could feel her heartbeat in her teeth. The strange elf, so prominent in Tania's legends, felt casual and yet menacing at the same time.

"This bores me," Daryx said with a touch of resignation in his voice.

Khalla thought he might kiss her, but he abruptly stepped back and walked down into the sea of phase spiders. That being around Daryx made her feel on edge, as if in the midst of combat… and she bored him. She did not miss the irony of the moment. *No doubt another lesson*, she wondered ruefully. She wondered what Ash would do, what he did when his time came. She reached out to catch the enigmatic lord but the spiders formed an impassable wall between them. From the spiders, Daryx turned towards her and said. "I hope it is not lost on you that beyond the various death traps here, my pets also protect the Master Vault. The flatspace stone should have been returned here. Farant should never have gotten his filthy hands on it. Perdition has become sloppy, maybe-Marcello. Ash's atonement is satisfactory but, to your point, I expect perfection. There are other things in the Master Vault. When I learned of the flatspace artefact, my heart fell."

Licking dry lips, Khalla said, "I understand. Lord Daryx, what must I yet do?"

"The throne may not pass to you, not yet. You must resolve this emotion for Ash. Until your intent is clear and your soul is free of regret, I will not consider you a contender. Perdition watches the Dar and acts as a check against their corrupting power in Tania's legends and our next generations. Forgiveness and flexibility, with excellence - of course, are the creed of Perdition. Do not summon me again until you understand this."

Khalla wanted to scream out loud but bit her lip instead and squeezed her fists until she thought her trembling would betray her turmoil to Daryx. "I have these things. I know you watch, Daryx. I know you know. What must I do?"

Daryx turned and bowed. The move looked exaggerated with his arms sweeping wide and to the side. "Ash shrinks from an imperial request. Within two days, if he has not answered, you may take his place and earn Perdition. Prepare to be tested. In the meantime, consider the Master Vault your first test. Keep it secret. Do not enter it." Daryx paused and a barely-there grin creased the corner of his lips. "This is not Ash's secret room, Khalla."

Seeing him begin to vanish in the shadows, Khalla called out, "At least lock him out of Perdition's accounts and turn them over to me, my lord?"

Daryx nodded, and then vanished with all the phase spiders. Khalla leaned back on the throne, aware of the sweat pouring from her skin. She had seen Daryx from a distance many times. Being so close to him, she felt a level of tension comparable to some of the action she had seen in Bloodstone. She took a deep breath and smiled. She would now hold all of Perdition's assets. *If Ash doesn't miss me, miss us, he'll miss Perdition's finances*, she thought. Then, she corrected herself. *My resources. Perdition is mine.*

It took a few more minutes of thinking and letting her emotions resolve before she realized something else: *Daryx just told me I can enter Ash's room.*

* * *

Alex sat in a classroom in the Temple while a retired paladin discussed the finer details of wounds that looked bad with lots of blood versus ones that impaired function. She watched the paladin but felt she could foresee each word, each action. It bored her and she tried to at least look interested. To illustrate his lecture, he took a knife and cut into his forearm. "You can see that this looks terrible, and trust me, it feels awful."

The class laughed just like Alex knew they would. They all knew how much a knife cut hurt. He winced – probably an exaggeration – and said, "The pain is temporary though thanks to the Goddess. You train to heal. We train to ignore this type of pain. This type of wound though," he spun the knife and stabbed it into his inner thigh. He left the knife there. Alex noted how his skin turned pale white as early shock began.

He continued. "This hurts a lot more. When I remove this, there will be a blood spray. If you do not heal me within a few seconds, I will die. I hope you've enjoyed my lesson enough to save my life from this illustration?" Humor and pain mingled in his voice and the class laughed again. When he removed the blade, blood spurted out almost five paces across the stage.

Alex had to check the distance and guessed it at five paces. To teach students distance as a unit of measure, the official "pace" of Dar Tania's stride was marked everywhere. Five of Dar's paces were 4.5 for Alex. She was much taller than the first priestess.

The supervising high priestess immediately healed the instructor. He gasped as the wound closed and explained, "Ironically, the healing can hurt almost as much as the wound. The paladins train to ignore all of this, because we trust that somewhere, a beautiful priestess has our backs and is paying attention so that we do not die. In combat, the pain we feel is not important because of what you train to do for us, for the empire, for Tiamat." He saluted the class and then turned to Dar Niss. "Thank you, Dar Niss." He bowed and swept her hand into a courtly kiss.

Dar Niss pulled him close and kissed his cheek. "And thank you, R'Dar Roberts. Please, accept our blessing and thanks." Acolytes came to help the old man off the stage and Niss faced the class. "So that it is not lost on you, while Tiamat is eternal and infinitely powerful, we are not. The knights are not. You can only heal so many times before fatigue and exhaustion overtake you. Good judgement is how you learn to allocate how much healing against which wounds. Triage is how you figure out who to bless first. This is your job as a healer. While not all of you will be healers, this is an important thing to learn. It's much harder to do while dodging arrow storms and melee attacks." Alex noted that Niss's eyes lingered on her for a moment. Alex quickly assumed an interested expression.

"Any questions?" Niss called out after taking a drink of water.

Alex immediately raised her hand. Thalian had been explicit in her letter last year, before Bloodstone. Open questions, like Niss' just now, were always tests. Always ask a question. Niss looked around and appeared annoyed there were not more hands raised. She pointed to Alex. She stood and asked, "When the R'Dar cut himself, he felt pain. I have to imagine that in his three Bloodstone campaigns, the Jaden War, and the Kell Conflict, all these battles, he was wounded far worse. But, he still felt pain. Why don't the paladins become desensitized to it?"

Niss looked around the room, daring anyone else to answer. She pointed to Valaes, the only male priest in the class and a recruit from the paladins. Still young, he had tested too highly on the Temple side to remain a paladin.

Valaes stood and turned to Alex. "Some paladins do become desensitized to it. In fact, it was discovered in the 7th Class in just 10 DAR that paladins could become addicted to pain and the "healing rush." Dar Tania and Dar Ana observed this and documented it. Of course, Ana was only 19 years old in the 10th Class. Ironically, Commander Sean voiced similar concerns nine years before this. Some argue he foresaw it." Valaes was on a roll and seemed to relish talking.

He visibly forced himself to stop talking and turned back to Niss. "Dar Niss, if I may be so bold as to say more, about the priestesses?" Niss nodded and he continued. "Some priestesses also become addicted to the paladins' pain. There's something about the power of life and death, the rush of pain, the balm of healing that we can get addicted to. Commander Sean's records frequently expressed concern about it. However, it was not until Dar Tania and Ana figured this out that the negative effects became understood. Part of the paladin tests, ever since, in the 1st Rite is to screen for pain-addictive characteristics in both knights and priestesses. If any of the proctors see it, the knight is removed to either a lesser Order or to the military. The same thing happens, I would imagine, in cleric training, though I have not had the same education here in the Temple yet as I did as a paladin."

Niss clapped her hands and said, "Well-answered, Valaes. If mortal experiences, like pain, are where we derive faith in Tiamat, and healing is the miraculous reinforcement of that faith, then desensitization or anything that detracts from that has to be culled. Sure, a priestess," she caught Valaes' eye and added. "Or a battle priest could still progress, but they become limited and – let me brutally honest here – not trustworthy. If you broke your bones, Alex, and you knew the bone setter was a sadist, how would you feel knowing a sadist was coming to heal you?"

Alex answered. "Every time I felt pain, I would wonder if they did it on purpose. I see what you mean. Without the sadist question in my mind, the pain is just that – pain. When the work is done and I'm healed, I remember both and am free of the suspicion that the setter made it hurt on purpose. Going the other way, the healer needs to be free for triage without suspecting the patient is a masochist. You cannot have absolute faith and doubt in the healer at the same time?" Alex raised her voice at the end to turn the statement into a question. Another tactic Thalian suggested.

Niss applauded again. "When Malcor faced the Khasran Lich, he knew with total certainty that Dar Tembri was there for him. Even after, though they were separated in Bloodstone, Malcor knew that somewhere out there Tembri was cheering for him. We need to be this mortal anchor for the faith of the paladins and innocents."

Another hand rose and Niss pointed to the priestess. "Imogen, yes?"

"When the pain never ends though, what happens? I mean, the god emperor's wing resists healing." Imogen's voice quieted and a tremor of fear entered her question.

Niss' gentle tone told Imogen she accepted the question. "This is the Temple. All questions are fair game. Do not be afraid to ask about the god emperor's health. It is very much in our minds since Malcor ascended. Someday, you may find yourself attending to the Court of Patriarchs. Then, not only will such questions be appropriate, but the Dread Lords will interpret your hesitation as being not ready. The Necromancer took his wing. It was every bit as vicious and brutal as the stories you've heard. The Jade God controlled the sunlight in the valley when it happened. When the dominion of a god clashes with a mortal, the mortal loses – always. Even if the mortal is the god emperor. Only when the god emperor ascends can that damage be healed. Until then, we must treat him frequently for infection and blood loss."

Another voice blurted out, "So, he will leave us soon?" The voice had a panicked edge to it and Niss frowned. Alex imagined her noting the cleric and sending her off to some punishment for lacking faith. While questions were encouraged, faithlessness was not even tolerated.

"Soon to us or to a dragon?" Niss countered. "It is no secret that Alerius declared that Dar Kell and he would ascend together. I was there. I wondered if then if that moment would be good-bye. And that was when the Queen chastised me. Alerius loves us. Do you really think he will leave just when we, his grand vision, destroyed the Necromancer? You can imagine that deep within the Abyss, Set trembles in sleep and wonders, 'Is Alerius coming for me? How much sharper will the Spear be when they come for me?'"

The class chuckled and Valaes raised his arm in the paladin salute of closed fingers – The Spear. Niss returned it and suddenly, patriotic fervor swept the classroom. "Go now, and study. Tomorrow at sunrise, we will look at the challenges of broken bones, and other more incurable conditions like birth defects and disease of thought and emotion."

Outside the classroom, Alex found a padded bench near a stone window looking south and east over Dockside Lake. Ten barges had just come up from the coast and she imagined she could see minotaurs walking about on their bundled cargo loads. She was just about to open her scriptures when someone cleared his throat to her side. She looked up and saw Valaes. He bowed and asked her, "May I join you?"

She pointed to the opposite bench and said, "Yesterday, I saw twenty barges come up from Minos. Today, it's ten. Do you know how many barges worth of cargo a world galleon can hold?"

Valaes looked out the window and shrugged. "Hundreds, I would imagine. I grew up west of the Great Bazaar. My family never went to Dockside. I wish I knew." He sat down and she saw him looking at her.

His casual regard made Alex feel self-conscious. She brushed her hair back from her shoulder and asked, "Is there something else you wanted besides speculation about Tauran barges?"

Without pause, Valaes leaned forward and took her hand. It startled her. Since joining the Temple a year ago, and except for training drills, no one had touched her since she hugged her mother good-bye. He's going to ask about Thalian, she thought.

But, he did not. "In the Order of Fire, they teach us to understand our objective, set our sights and plans on it, and ruthlessly execute that plan with faith. I've always wondered if that approach would be a good way to meet a beautiful priestess."

Alex felt her cheeks blush and pulled her hand back. Valaes held it firm. She almost argued with him. She had to admit the attention was nice. Back home, the boys had flirted with Thalian and her both in equal measure. Then, once in the Temple, nothing. "I'm not high enough rank to take a paladin," she tried to say with a haughty air.

Valaes laughed and let her fingers drag away from his hand slowly. "I'm not a paladin anymore. Why must it be about taking? What about two clerics enjoying a sunset together?"

He let the question hang there as an invitation until Alex felt compelled to say something. Though she thought of a thousand possible retorts, she did not trust herself to say any of them well. Valaes pulled his knapsack open and retrieved his scriptures and some dried fruit. He offered fruit to Alex. "If I remember correctly, the Sage Alaura wrote a dissertation on bone-setting. My mentor in Fire told me the entire test is from that dissertation." He pulled out another book. This one was clearly a copy, though new. "Which I have. Would you like to study with me?"

"How do you have this?" Alex asked as she took it and flipped it open. The archaic style of Alaura's writing had been perfectly copied, most likely by a golem in the Mages Guild. "Even a copy, these are rare and expensive."

Valaes popped a dried apple slice into his mouth and said, "When you're the son of Jan Darel, and a paladin in the Order of Fire, you'd be surprised at what you can get your hands on even after you leave said Order."

Alex had heard rumors about Valaes' father. Jan Darel was the head of the powerful Alchemists Guild, and also responsible for the flow of liquor throughout Tania. Though not really a guild, it was jointly run between the Mages and the Merchants Guilds. "So, he really is your father? I guess that makes you a R'Dar then. I should be more formal with you."

"No, please don't. If I wanted that, I'd be working in the distilleries and not sitting here with you."

*That's it. I can't take this anymore. Another compliment and I'm going to take my first paladin,* Alex thought, trying to hide her reaction to his innuendo-heavy compliments, which were effectively making it hard for her to even want to study.

Across from Alex and Valaes, in the shadowed hallway, Dar Niss leaned back and rested heavily against a stone column. The turmoil of the past months had aged her considerably. None of the priestesses talked about it, but Bloodstone had exhausted the entire Temple from those like Dar Ana down to the students. For the R'Dar and higher ranked, continually healing the wounded and rumors that Alerius would die without daily healings had taxed them. Though no one used words like "breaking" or "exhaustion," Niss looked forward to a day when she could sit in her estate's manicured gardens and let the sun wash her worries from her body.

She thought about her transcendence and the many extra years she had enjoyed as a Dar priestess of Tiamat. The image of the Jade God falling backwards from the god emperor Alerius, the smoking ruin of the ram's head wand, and the dragons she worshiped crying out in jubilation had been enough. Nothing would crown that moment for Niss. She felt it in her soul. Letting these images play out again, she felt a tinge of regret about her lover Seline, but pushed it aside. "Welcome to the time of dying," she said to herself. She did not want prolonged youth and the never-ending march of seasons it brought. "I had a hundred years and not a single face remains with me except Seline's."

Her recent year with Seline and being part of the Jade God's fall were enough. Knowing this, years of youthfulness began to unravel against her acceptance of natural death. She knew the others talked about it behind her back. She rubbed wrinkles from her hand and wondered if it would hurt when Time came for her. Her epiphany in Bloodstone was that Alerius had not removed Tiamat from Tehra to save Her from Time, but to protect her from this feeling of ennui. Dar Ana lingered. The Court of Patriarchs did too.

Niss reassured herself. *Some of the greatest of us passed this way: Dar Tania, Sage Alaura, Dar Moren, my own mother... there's a mystique to it. Let them talk.* Niss watched the young lovers-to-be and smiled. *My own first love was centuries ago.* It had taken some time to accept that her destiny was to teach, to guide, and to serve rather than partner with a Dread Lord and conquer, or rule a Temple.

Niss looked at the letter from Dar Reznor in her hand. It requested that R'Dar Alex attend a meeting with the Mages Guild that night. "This is not normal," she said again. She traced Reznor's dragon crest seal. Though not everyone knew, the Dars knew that Reznor and Alerius worked day and night to repair Bomoki's Gate. She had seen powerful clerics summoned to Bloodstone and then return drained. Those returning would sleep for days before awakening to ravenous hunger and more sleep. "And the fighting continues." Niss stretched and wondered how Valaes would react, how Alex would react.

She almost walked over to give Alex the letter, but noted the hungry gleam in both their eyes. "That's a lusty moment if ever I saw one." Niss shook her shoulders and frowned her back popped and cracked. *Will Seline still love me when I'm old?*, she wondered. *Will she stay by my side as Ana was rumored to with Dar Tania?* They had last been together five months after a concert presentation by Lars in Seline's honor. That evening had been spectacular. Seline in her battle dress and then later, when she danced as she had done for the Court of Patriarchs in Bloodstone, as Tiamat's avatar. The memory made Niss hungry for Paladin Seline all over again. *And that was just five months ago.* Niss caught a glimpse of herself against a silver mirror. *In those months, I have aged from my late twenties, to what? Sixty? As Alerius says, Time came at us like a murderer.*

*I hope Seline looks at me the way Alex is looking at Valaes right now. Just one more time so I can take that memory with me to the Silver Skies.* That night, after the festivities, Niss and Seline had walked hand in hand through the Temple's eastern gardens. After a smoldering kiss, Niss had almost told Seline about her decision to pass. The time had not been right. Seline was drunk on glory and battle. Niss was drunk on centuries of time and regret. Their embraces had been frantic, bittersweet, and intense unlike anything Niss could remember. When the mages came to take Seline back to Bloodstone, Seline's last kiss and words… they were perfect. "Sweet Niss, I carry you in my heart. I love you."

Niss walked over and confronted the two. "I have a boring, but important task for you, Alex." Imperiously, she let her gaze cross Valaes. "I suppose she might need help, young Valaes." She returned her fierce gaze to Alex. "You up for it?"

Alex jumped to her feet and bowed. "Of course, my Dar. Anything." Valaes did the same.

Niss retrieved a key from her robes and pressed it to Alex's hand. "I'm being detained here for work. My estate on the Northern Road, off Second East, it needs to be ready to host delegates from Krentismar tomorrow," she lied. "Everything should be ready, but I won't have time to double-check and take care of any last minute arrangements. Would you please go, check on it, and ensure the servants have everything just right?"

Alex bowed low. "Of course, my Dar. I'll see that everything is perfect."

"I've had several gatherings there, Alex." Niss took the younger priestess's hands in her own and squeezed them. "Be a dear and stay until the morning crew arrives? I was promised no fewer than ten maids, fifteen chefs, and an orchestra! If they aren't there by the time you are hungry for breakfast, I need to know so I can make counter arrangements."

Niss tapped Valaes and caught his hand into her own with Alex's. She ordered, "Valaes, she may need some help. Will you accompany her?"

"Yes, my Dar!"

Walking away from them, Niss used an enchanted earring to tell the enchanted servants to make a mess in the pool, to heat the pool, and to set out scandalous clothes for Alex. Maybe it was the old woman in her finally coming out with Time's pull, but she began to laugh with a level of mirth she had not really felt in at least a century.

* * *

521 knew how to throw a party. Nothing like loud music, local residents, and the watch kicking back as an excuse to transact actual business. Everyone had an alibi. No one would remember anything, or would pass it off as too much drink. Jace picked up a green bone and tapped it to the dancing girl. The Orcus bone felt oily against his skin. It conjured images of beetles and worms wriggling in a carcass. Jace said, "Go and get your prettiest friends and bring them back here at midnight. We'll have a big party for them." The girl instantly stopped dancing and ran off. Jace laughed. "This is too easy. I wonder what it'll do on undead." He turned to Cordelle. "I bet it wraps them in lover's arms and replaces hunger with desire to obey."

Cordelle shrugged. "Mind control and charm is dangerous stuff. The Temples hate it. Be careful. All we need is that girl running into a Cuthberic and all this falls apart." Cordelle was inspecting the bones one by one from Grant's haul and noting their quality, weight, and dimensions. Some fit the standard Tania pace they were so big. Others he had to rely on Tanian standard fingers. As they expected, some were better quality than others. Cordelle and Jace pulled out the best ones. They would sell half and keep the other half in 521. He was about to reply when a runner burst into the room at the top of the stairs. Runners came and went. The breathlessness and urgent air of this one caught Cordelle's attention. He poked Jace.

The runner shouted down to them, "The Twins, they've been attacked. Something hit their dock stronghold and flooded them. They're gone!"

"No. Wait, what?" Cordelle said to Jace. "First Northern Cross and now The Twins? I don't believe it." He and Jace ran up the stairs and found their lieutenant, Howie, drinking deeply from a keg. Seeing it was Howie, Cordelle punched the wall. "I had hoped you'd be an urchin not knowing what it is you say. Tell me, Howie, how bad?"

Howie poured water over his head. "Really bad. Word is they raided Bloodstone and came back with some bits of the Jade God. Something followed them back. Whatever it was, it knew about their Underdocks, and cracked it all open. The entire Twins' leadership is dead."

"Any survivors?" Jace asked. When Howie shook his head, Jace pursed his lips and said, "Boss, this is 521's chance to take power. Their infrastructure is, at least, intact."

Cordelle snapped his fingers and called out, "Brings us a map!" All around them, the party continuined uninterrupted. The musician-bards, long time members of 521, knew that things like this would happen and knew how to increase the tempo and change the songs to help distract those present from the guild's business dealings.

With the map of Taysor spread out before them, Cordelle tapped 521's territory. Northern Cross had been a buffer between them and Dark Legion. Encroachments by both into the city around the blast crater had resulted in an informal ceasefire along certain streets. Cordelle tapped such an area and said, "I'm not glad where what's ours is divided halfway through a block. Streets and canals make up our shared territory. Maybe we talk to Dark Legion rather than take." Cordelle sat back on a shipping crate. "While 521's loyalty is unquestionable, bringing in all the new ones will stretch us too thin. I want it all," he said sweeping his hand around the map. "But, Dark Legion is powerful. A war between us, would we win?"

Jace and Howie looked around. Cordelle did not often speculate about strength or weakness. He always showed confidence that things would just work out. Quietly, Jace said, "Our street crews would win. It's the rumors about Dark Legion's upper leadership where I cannot say. They block scrying, so they have to have mages. They heal quickly, so they have to have clerics. We could do with more clerics, Cordelle. And their tactics," Jace shrugged. "It's like nothing we see from the other crews. They have foreign backing, and training too." Unsaid was the obvious 'who' of Tania's Thieves Guild, Perdition.

Cordelle looked at Howie and jabbed his thumb at Jace. "You agree with the mage?"

"Yes. 521 has survived by being careful. We've had a five-month stalemate on the Northern Cross territory. If we rush to take The Twins, we might lose all of Northern Cross. That's where the empire is spending all their money, too, to repair the damage and help the citizens. It's the most lucrative turf we have right now. The Twins, what do they have? Some smuggling, some contraband, gambling and brothels… all businesses we have too. But, Legion does not have as many. I suggest we approach Legion and offer a trade, The Twins for them and for us, Northern Cross."

Cordelle pointed to the bone, "But, we have these." All eyes in the room turned to the Orcus bone. "And Grant came to us. We know where he is? Another guild on our side would make us stronger."

Jace said, "Grant was seen Uptown, with some Cuthberics. Imagine that. Word is that Delton took the rest of the crew south towards Tania to book passage with the Taurans, just like our agreement. Grant might welcome rescue from the Cuthberics." Jace began to say something else and stopped. "Uh, Cordelle... why do we care about Rogue's Guild? It's just a handful of guys."

The old man cracked a grin. "It's not a crew. It's a bona fide guild, with a high king charter. Don't get so caught up on territory and business. Rogue's Guild, Grant, like the boss before Grant, they take jobs on the outside. It gives us all eyes and ears into new heroes, foreign dealings, and endears us to the next generation of leaders. It's a role. Sure, they ain't street powerful, but they are something different. Any one of them, is worth 10 of The Twins."

"So," Jace pressed. "They're adventurers for hire."

"You got it. Real tomb crawlers, dungeon delvers. Truly, ambassadors for us all to be heroical." Cordelle slapped his knees and stood up. "I've decided. If Grant were here, it might be different. But, he isn't. Send word to Legion for parlay. Howie, you and Jace will make the arrangements with them. Let word be sent to all the leaders to prepare for a fight, just in case. I want Legion to see us gearing up, around The Twins. Have a few shakers hit up the stores for protection, and find me any of Twins' leaders if they survived. Offer amnesty. Also, have the shakers hire mercs and begin doing some shows of force in Northern Cross."

Cordelle looked around. Though Jace and Howie were the main two, all the other 521 members in the area were carefully listening while going about their work or enjoying the party. Cordelle shouted, "You're not fooling anyone! A show of force! Gear up, all of you! Also, someone find out who took The Twins down!"

* * *

Jace pulled his cloak tightly about him. He hated wearing armor. It messed up his ability to easily use magic, and was heavy, and scratchy. At least it was hardened leather, though the shield was giving his neck and back cramps. Howie walked invisibly next to him. Some of these thieves had a near supernatural ability to blend into shadows. If Jace did not know this about Howie, it would seem like magic. He envied that he had not grown up in circumstances that let him find, blend, and move through the night as easily as Howie and the others did. "Just up ahead," he whispered.

The alley twisted upon itself but had no actual side streets. This path off the intersection of Clark and Gable Street led to a tavern in the center of a wide circular courtyard ringed by dilapidated houses. The Legionnaire Tavern had a notoriety that drew thieves, rogues, and rough adventurers from all over Sora to it. Carefully disguised barricades and a few checks to chase away the unwary and unintentional visitors kept the Dark Legion's headquarters as safe as any of the paladin fortresses. At the far end, a pile of trash smoldered. Jace detected the faint herbs that made the stink here bearable. Firelight cast shadows around the trash pile and two beggarly old men poked at it with sticks. Jace could imagine the number of eyes trained on him right now. Cordelle often said, "Mages make people nervous. Carry a shield and they'll relax." It had proven true too many times to question.

One of the beggars said, "We got your note. We liked the perfume and hearts on it. You come to make love to us, or to talk?"

Jace bowed and said, "To talk. Where and when?"

"If you speak for 521, it can be now. The Leader has time. Unexpected drowning of our rival left gaping wet holes in her schedule." The beggar cackled.

Jace said, "I speak for 521, but any decisions or proposals need to run through my leader. You know that. If acceptable to yours, I would talk with her now." These old men were basically throwaway guards. Too old and weak to do anything other than harass, they proved an effective mask when the actual city watch came by with clerics, or worse, paladins.

A creaking and groaning sounded and then went silent as hidden gears lifted the entire burning mess of filth to show giant stairs leading underground. Jace tossed two copper coins at the beggars and then walked down the stairs, Howie on his flank.

They reached the bottom after several hundred steps. Jace had only visited here once, with Cordelle, to exchange prisoners. That was five years ago. Since that time, nothing had changed. Chains and shackles still sat around the wall. Magical glyphs glowed on the floor more menacing than any guard. Jace noted that one of the glyphs had been augmented. He said out loud, "A dark naga spirit. Impressive. Maybe I should toss my allegiance to the Legion. Cordelle does not like to use magic this way. He likes the personal touches of an attack, or the usefulness of illusions."

Though five tunnels branched from this central landing, and even though they heard nothing, the air suddenly chilled. Simultaneously, from each of the five tunnels, a single female with dead-white skin and jet black hair stepped. She was new. Jace studied her and noted how the atmosphere in the room changed. "We haven't yet met in person, at least not alone," he said. "I'm Jace, of 521. This is Howie. We're here to speak with the Leader."

"I am Syand. We have met alone many times, though I watched you through the eyes of my legion."

Jace saw a flick of her ruby tongue and pointed eye teeth. "A vampire? So, the rumors are true. That explains a lot." Vampires in the Forsaken Isles were a problem. They could be as potent as they had been in life. They could be as strong or as weak as their master created them to be. Being ageless, they then strengthened year by year. Rumors suggested Dark Legion was led by one, hence the ominous name. "You must be at least 200 years old. Tell me I am wrong."

Four of the images remained in the tunnels and one stepped forward. White gold jewelry twinkled in the light and Jace saw just how much she wore. It had been hard to see against her skin. "I doubt Cordelle sent you to feed me, or as a social visit. With the fall of Orcus, I can move about more freely than in the six hundred years before. You should be very concerned about this."

Jace found his eyes drawn to her and remembered that vampires had a host of powers. He averted his gaze and pulled Howie to him to whisper in his ear, not to be secretive but to block Howie's gaze as well. Syand laughed softly, and the tension in the room changed to something sensual. Jace turned to face her, but found instead that she now stood behind him and Howie. She breathed on the back of his neck and he flinched away from her, dropping his shield.

The vampire proclaimed out loud so that her voice echoed down the tunnels, "Dark Legion welcomes 521's lieutenants. How may we serve the great Cordelle?"

The word 'serve' pressed images into Jace's and Howie's mind. They saw themselves in the finest clothes surrounded by beautiful women, even Cordelle was there enjoying it. In Jace's mind, he saw Syand lean forward to kiss him deeply. He gulped. "We wish to parlay about Northern Cross and Twins' territories. Cordelle would like to offer you peace: we will take Northern Cross and you will take The Twins. Assuming any of their leadership survived, you can have them too unless they seek amnesty, as per the old rules. This thing that destroyed The Twins, we would offer an alliance to find and destroy it."

"Her," the Leader said.

Howie, who seemed to struggle more with the Leader's seduction than Jace was, coughed and then repeated her word. "Her, what?"

"The destroying force of The Twins is a she. She is not someone Dark Legion is interested in fighting. In fact, The Twins rather brought this on themselves. 521 remains my only possible enemy; why do I need this arrangement? Now that I am free to roam, I can take your lives like pulling the wings from a trapped butterfly."

The power of seduction in her voice ratcheted up with each word until Jace said, "Pardon me, Syand." He took Howie's arm and enacted a powerful spell that would dominate Howie's mind. "Howie, go back to Cordelle and report that parlay is underway. Tell him that I will bring word. Go now, quickly and without drawing attention to yourself. If questioned, you are returning to the warehouse with news of a new gem merchant looking for gold wire." As the final enactment of the spell, Jace wrapped his own mind in domination under his own control.

Howie went running off. Jace bowed to Syand and said, "Thank you for not challenging me on this. My friend is not up to the discussions we are about to have."

"I suppose not," Syand answered. "But, clearly, you think you are. That's interesting. When I saw you years ago, you were a pup, eager to win approval and new in your magic." She laughed as if mocking the younger memory of Jace. "You think your magic will save you from me?"

Jace prayed to any god listening and took Syand in his arms. "If Dark Legion takes all the guilds, The Temples will come against you. You need us as a buffer against them. Besides, you've been trapped underground, my lady. I can't imagine Dark Legion has been showing you a very good time. I know too many of your lieutenants and doubt they would offer a vampire anything interesting at all. Let me show you why you will spare me and this parlay will work to both our advantages."

With the mind domination spell active, Jace had some measure of resistance to the vampire's influence over him and he twisted it upon itself to show her locked with him in deep ecstasy. She twisted his hand, nearly breaking his arm, and then leaned in to kiss him. She bit his lip enough to make him bleed and he felt her pull at his blood. He took that feeling and pushed a sense that ecstasy could only come from passion, not feeding. "There are many mules in the city, but only I am here with you now."

Syand's breathing suggested either rising passion or hunger. "I will feed on you."

"Yes, but first, I would taste a vampire." Jace did not know why he did it, but he bit her neck.

It drew a gasp from her and then she pressed her neck against his face. A single nail tore her skin at his bite so he could taste her blood. "Yes," she moaned. Then, they vanished from the cold room and reappeared in a lavishly furnished chamber of red silk blankets and plush cushions.

Jace looked around and noted a mannequin set with ancient Tanian leather armor and a two-handed sword of what had to be Merakoran design. The giant sword rested on display by two scimitars with rune markings that dated them back to what Tania called the "Lost Legions." By itself, it did not mean anything. Then, his mind was turned to the woman before him, who would not be denied. Between her vampire powers and Jace's own desire, he thought, *I've got one chance to impress this woman. Magic alone won't do it. You better do this, Jace.*

When Syand's lips found his own and they kissed deeply, she lustily breathed into his mouth and said, "Yes, you had better," as a mirror to his own thinking. *Can she read my mind?*, he wondered.

As if in answer, Syand shredded his leather armor from his torso and smiled. "I can read desire," she breathed.

Jace turned what was left of his *domination* spell's power to mask his next action. As he dexterously undressed Syand, he withdrew a vial of Orcus' blood and put it in his mouth. He began to kiss down her chest to her navel. "I bet you haven't been with a real man in forever," he teased.

"No," she moaned. "But, I want to feel..."

When Jace kissed back up to her, she almost flipped him over to speed things along, but the blood on his lip – from her and him – was too much for her to resist and she leaned up to meet him. She saw his jaw bite and then hot liquid flooded her mouth.

She smelled the pungent odor and then threw Jace away from her. Her strength sent him tumbling across the room, but then her vision exploded. The magic items in her chamber, the twisting mage, the candlelight... all flared as if coming alive. She saw Jace hit the wall about two paces high and his leg broke along with several ribs. To her vision, fireworks exploded at those points and she saw Jace's literal pain. She also saw his *domination* spell still in effect and his intent to hide a surprise from her. She looked at her own arms and saw colored auras resolve into a healthy brown tan that hid her concrete-like skin. Though it served her well like armor, she hated its lifeless color.

"What was that?" she shouted at Jace. He sat groaning, on the verge of blacking out. "What was that?!" she screamed at him again. She teleported to his side and said, "I must know."

"It's an aphrodisiac I knew would work on you. No offense…" His words struggled as a broken rib lacerated into his lungs and he began gagging on his own blood.

Syand looked around. Everything had become daylight bright with aura colors. She knew it was not daylight, but the change, so serene and beautiful that it took her back in time, and she knew she would do anything for more.

She slashed her wrist to let blood begin to fall on his lips and stabbed her other hand in his ribs, to pull the broken bones back into place. When he did not respond to her blood, she shoved her wrist into his mouth and repeated her fix on his leg. She could hear his heartbeat, erratic and faltering and for a moment, she worried. She could not remember the last time she felt worried. The fireworks of pain exploding from him, the flickering candle of his life's color dropped by degrees. Purple motes of light danced from his skin and she saw his magic begin to leave his body. It was breathtaking in its ephemeral beauty and she screamed at him. "Do not die, mage! You will live forever! Feast on Joviel's dark gift!"

When Jace began drinking her blood, she knew he would survive and detached him before he took too much from her. She wanted him alive, not dependent. He seemed to be recovering and not just from his wounds.

Jace regained consciousness to the most wonderful feelings. For a moment, he forgot where he was and that he was with a vampire. His intelligence saved him and before he opened his eyes, he said, "Syand, I did not mean that to be threatening." He reached out and felt pain. Not all his wounds had healed.

Syand interlaced her fingers in his and kissed them. "I could compel you to tell me what that was. But, I don't want to ruin this moment. You promised us both that you make this, how did you think it? – 'impressive.' How long will this last?" she asked.

"In humans, the amount I gave you, it would kill them. A single drop triggers a visual euphoria that lasts for almost an entire day. For you, who knows? You like it?" he asked. "I've never been with a vampire before. I've read about it, of course. You wouldn't believe some of the stories about how lusty your kind is." He licked his lips and tasted her blood. "Ah, you saved me. Am I going to become a vampire?"

Syand kissed his eyes open and put his hands on her hips. "Do you want to?"

Her question was the last thing he truly remembered. At some point, Jace asked her about the parlay. She replied, "How much of the aura drug do you have?"

Knowing he could not lie, he told her how much 521 had. "And, I know where to get more."

"Bring me some more. Tell Cordelle, I want ten kegs full of it. It is my price to pull the Legion back from Northern Cross territories. When I have ten kegs and I see 521 withdrawing from The Twins, the parlay will be acceptable to me." Syand straddled Jace in a bed of fur and silk just barely draping her body. Her words and red eyes burned into Jace until he could only see her eyes. "I like you as a human, Jace. You were impressive. Impress me again, and I will give you Joviel whenever you wish."

Syand's words seemed like a dream that echoed over and over again in Jace's mind. When he stumbled up onto the street and learned three days had passed, Jace felt his legs shake. The sun on his skin felt hot, hotter than normal. The words echoed and would not stop. "I do not need a monopoly on the aura drug. Give me the ten kegs though, and you can have Northern Cross. Teach me how to have as much as I desire and I will yield The Twins to 521. Help me get all that there is and you can serve me forever, Jace. A mage like you, with vampire powers, you'd be deliciously formidable."

☐

# Chapter 6 – RiVule the Exemplar

RiVule stood on Quat's mountain summit and looked north. Gruustir whispered to him that north, he would find something the Orcs needed. Visions of glory, power, and the god's power made his soul sing. "Coriga, you will stay here with the paladins. I will call for you soon. Gruustir promises me the Mighty Horde will march soon. I want all tribes pledged upon the altar, and 100 paladins."

The mountain was wide and squat compared to the northern mountains, but it rose up alone after a vast stretch of swamp. The swamp kept the northern humans and others away from the Orcs and that suited everyone just fine. The biting insects that plagued those with weaker skin did not bother an Orc at all. RiVule inhaled the southern wind and smelled spring in the Quat. He had hoped glory would be found closer to the tribes than the northern country. Yet, it beckoned and he knew Gruustir required him to go there, to Morbatten of the dragons.

"Those who resist, great lord?" Coriga simpered.

"Slay them. Eat them. Feed the weak to the strong! Schedule the feast and invite all the tribes to it. I leave you now to follow Gruustir. He speaks to me of great glory. Tell the Host we march against demons, not humans, not dragons." RiVule was about to leave but Coriga had another question. RiVule grabbed the shaman's throat and said, "You get one more question before I throw you down the mountain and feed you to the marsh trolls."

"Master, ack..." RiVule put Coriga's feet back on the ground but retained the choking grip. "Master RiVule, the War Host will expect raids against the humans. It has always been..."

RiVule threw the shaman back. Frentoris and Incer let the shaman backpedal and fall. RiVule addressed them all but glared most at Coriga. "For centuries untold, the Orc has lingered here. The War Hosts rampage and are thrown back by the dragon humans whenever we go north. They are not Orc, but they are centuries of victory strong. I would see the Orc ally with strength. It is time that the Host march against the foes selected by the great god Gruustir! The error for all other Horde Generals was they ignored Gruustir's will. Had even a single one had wisdom to see it, the saga of the Orc would be written in the great events that unfolded last winter and the green sun."

RiVule's eyes flashed red within the black mirrors of his iris. Coriga whined and crabwalked back from the priest. "The Story of the Orc will be one written in victory, plunder, and power! The dragon humans are key to this. I go now. Coriga," RiVule said looking back over his shoulder. "100 paladins will be ready to march on my command. Any who balk, you will feed them to the Horde. Frentoris, if Coriga fails us, you will feed him to the trolls alive, while healing him."

The two paladins slammed their breastplates and bowed as RiVule stepped off the ledge and slip-slided down the steep eastern face of the Mountain. Behind him, Incer pulled Coriga up while Frentoris retrieved the shaman's staff. "Come," Coriga said. "We have work to do."

RiVule walked, led by the god, for several days before he came to a northern wagon trail. The path showed the signs of wheeled carts and animals. The thought of horses and cattle made his stomach growl, but he continued fasting and turned northward. Almost immediately, on the northern branch of the road, he detected a watcher in the darkness. He prayed to Gruustir for guidance but felt only anticipation, not danger. He slowed his walking and called out in Tanian Common, "I know you're there, whoever you are. Don't be foolish."

To his side, a quiet rustling in the undergrowth made him turn. He noted the humanoid crouching there was female. She stood and stepped forward, carefully. She bowed with great respect and her words pleased RiVule. "Great priest, RiVule. I am Taisha, spawn of orc and elf. I heard stories of your departure and raced to catch you."

"Why have you done this thing? Had I wished for sex, I would have brought females with me." RiVule could tell she did not seek him for such things, but subtly wished to remind her of both her place and that he travelled alone.

Taisha remained bowed with her head low and eyes averted. She adjusted the dagger gauntlet on her left arm and RiVule saw extensive burn scarring along her arms. No doubt, she sought to cover the damage with the gauntlets. He frowned at her vanity but a thought came to him, *She walks your path.*

He said, "Taisha is not known to me. What do you hope to achieve by accosting me in the darkness?" RiVule relaxed his stance and stepped into her personal space. Considered intimate between Orc lovers, it also presented aggression absent intimacy.

She recoiled backwards and dropped to her knees again. "I have dreams, great priest. The dreams have told me to meet you here. I do not know what they mean, just that my heart would explode if I did not follow what they show. So, now I am here." She bowed even lower, mimicking the salute used by the humans to their north. "Can you teach me? What do they mean?"

RiVule bent down and kissed the top of her head and then pulled her to her feet. "It means that Gruustir has decided that I am not to walk this path alone. For this, I am grateful. Taisha, have your dreams shown you alone amidst humans?" She nodded. "Have they shown you fighting in seas of demons and elves?" She continued to nod. "Then, it is ordained that we are to walk this path of blood together. I travel to Morbatten, for the Horde and for the great ships."

RiVule turned back to the road and resumed his walk north. A moment later, he heard Taisha's stealthy footsteps join behind him. "You are trained as an assassin," he observed.

"No, my lord..."

"RiVule. Call me RiVule. When we reach the humans, they will not care that I serve Gruustir. Just RiVule from now on. So, not an assassin?"

"No. I mean, yes. RiVule, my father was Orc but I was raised amongst the elves. I learned to be quiet and to stay unseen so as to avoid their prejudices."

"This explains your beauty. It disgusts me," RiVule said spitting on the ground. "Thankfully, Gruustir must have grand plans for you to place you on my path. Let us see what the great god holds in our combined destinies." They walked in silence before RiVule asked again, "Tell me, Taisha who dreams. Did you know your father? You speak our tongue well."

"Yes, my... RiVule. To my shame, my father was an outcast from the mountain. He," she tried to continue but RiVule interrupted her.

"Why an outcast? For loving elves?"

"No, he had dreams and the dreams taught him magic." She flinched when RiVule caught her arm.

"Your father was Gren Forestan? I know this story. Does he yet live? I would speak to others who have these dreams. The destiny of the Orc is not to raid from the Mountain." He felt her blood around his nails and eased his grip on her arm.

"Yes, that was my father. He wandered until he was shadowed by Sylvan Elves. They watched him and when they saw no ill intent, when they saw him use magic to endure the winter, they began to speak with him. My mother, she fell in love with him."

RiVule began to laugh. "Love! Such stupid notions, yet, powerful ones. Gruustir tells me that these are vestigial traits left over from Pha Rann's taint in our spirits. Yet they are power!" He whacked her on her shoulder and said, "For this love of Elf and Orc, I now walk this ordained path into a tide of elves with you, Taisha... and to glory! Praise Gruustir! Tell me more!"

Taisha spoke of how the two fell in love and her mother was eventually exiled. "Gren would not convert to Krentismar or other gods, so they would not let him into Morilon. My mother, Airess, she would not leave him so she was exiled. They settled together on the southern border of Morilon. When I was born, they each taught me how to survive in a world they said would reject me. But, I remember one lesson above all: Orcs might reject me, but with strength, they will respect me."

RiVule laughed and said, "Your father Gren was truly wise in his teaching of you. Were there any other children?"

"No, RiVule. My mother became pregnant with twins but our small home was overrun by giants attacking Morilon. I was out hunting when it happened. I found my home, my family, slain. I took my revenge as I could but the elves would not restore my family. They said the damage to my mother was too much, and they would not waste Krentismar's power on someone that rejected that god. They told me to go to Morbatten. I've been here for months, RiVule. Respect, reject, they only care about what you can do not what race or color you come from. It's like another dream."

With twilight falling, a light snow began to fall. RiVule chanted mantras to himself to help pass the time and not lose focus in spite of hunger. It did not surprise him to hear Taisha's stomach protest the journey. He learned that she began her fast the same day he did. Just past the moon's zenith, RiVule saw the dancing shadows and lights of an encampment ahead to the side of the road. RiVule repeated one last time, "I live to serve, not to fight. I am not just another Orc."

Careful to make noise so they would be heard, a human sentry finally called out, "Who goes there on the path?"

RiVule focused on his best human speech and said, "An Orc. I am travelling alone with a female."

His answer caused some concern and a different voice called out, "Orcs never travel alone. Who are you really?"

This amused RiVule. Even a small war party would have already shredded these sentries to brisket. "A priest Orc travels alone."

Soon, the entire camp was awake. What must have been all their fighters came out to meet him with lanterns and weapons at the ready. RiVule opened his arms and let them see that he carried no weapons. "Like I said, a priest Orc. Alone, except for my companion."

Taisha stood behind him. In unaccented Tanian, she called out, "He speaks the truth. It is just us."

An older man who stood behind the guards edged forward. "I am Victor. This is a caravan of cloth and hand-carved art. We're taking it from Stone to Tania. Are you friend or foe?"

RiVule did not sense anything malicious about the human and for a moment, marveled at him. "With my battle host, you would all be dead were I not alone. I suppose I am neither friend nor foe. Not knowing your intent to me, how could we be friends? Yet, we are not destined by the Great God to fight as enemies."

Taisha hastily added, "We are friends, good sir." Her fluent Tanian reassured them all.

In the back, someone said, "Chatty Orcs, ain't they?"

Victor pushed past the warriors and said, "It's a cold night, though you seem unaffected. Do you need anything: fire, food? You're welcome to join us provided you give us an assurance there is not a battle host."

The god told him to break his fast and RiVule smiled. "I hunger. A war host would not talk with you. You would all be dead. By this, you know I speak the truth." Mimicking the human custom he had seen, he put his hand forward. "My name is RiVule. The female is Taisha."

Victor shook his hand and when he saw Taisha, his jaw dropped. Even in the shadows of the lantern light, her deeply-tanned complexion and clear green eyes enraptured him. Though hidden by studded leather armor and various weapons, she stood tall and beautiful. "Taisha," Victor said, offering her his hand. "Let me escort you back to camp? I thought you were an Orc as well."

"Half, actually. I'm glad you do not find me as disgusting as RiVule." She took Victor's hand. "Thank you, Victor," she said. "We are both very hungry. I'm sure we can add to your guard in exchange for a good meal. We're heading to Morbatten too."

It took the caravan two weeks to reach Morbatten. Blended in with the caravan, no one gave the Orcs any problems though Taisha drew more than a few admiring looks from the men. Victor especially went out of his way to invite her to dine with him every night. RiVule scoffed at it when they were alone telling her, "You're goblin ugly, but these humans fawn over you like a fertility idol. Is this normal human behavior?"

She replied, "Tania is open to Orcs, you know. Orcs, just like you, are quite common in this land. The humans don't see us a frightening, but as exotic. Even you, as a lord priest, may find yourself the object of desire by their females. Be careful!" and she poked his arm, leaving before his growl turned into a retaliatory strike.

He tried to chastise her, but she called back, "If you see yourself in this place for much time, we should spend more time on your speech. Do you speak Elvish?"

RiVule began to laugh. "I understand it and read it. You will translate for me."

When they crossed the Cordabad River at Crossing and entered the proper North-South Highway, RiVule began to open his eyes and mind see the empire of Morbatten. Cresting a hill, he saw Dragon Mountain and the great Temple to the north. He jumped atop Victor's wagon and moved to stand on the crate boxes to get a better view.

"We'll be there in another four days," Victor called up to RiVule.

As they entered the continuous settlements, RiVule began to point to the priestesses of Tiamat and note the paladins in the military patrols. A few noted him and it made Victor nervous. "Please," he begged. "The military is here to keep things peaceful and moving on the highway. If they see you or us as troublemakers, it'll delay our arrival and, well, it could be bad."

"These are your people, right?" RiVule countered. "Afraid?"

Taisha touched RiVule's shoulder and said, "Victor isn't afraid. He's Tanian. He knows that the military is not here to keep him, personally, safe. It's here to keep the empire safe and that means that Victor could be hurt. In Tania, it's best to the let the military be itself. There is a saying in this land, 'Let the priestesses be.' It means…"

Victor interrupted her and finished, "Hope they do not take an interest in you. You'll see. I know you serve the god Gruustir. You should visit the Temple and declare your intentions. Tania has no issues with other gods, so long as they do not detract from Tiamat."

"The great ships," RiVule said screening his eyes from the daylight.

Victor nodded, "You'll not see them from here. They're out in the ocean to the east. You might be able to see the lake at Dockside though. There are canals and locks – mechanical gears that move water to raise and lower boats – that go from Dockside down to the ocean. That's where the great ships are. You've mentioned these before. I should tell you, not many Tanians go on the minotaur ships. They're quite expensive."

RiVule shrugged. "I have seen it in a vision. The female too. We will go on the ships."

Victor slapped the reins against the ox moving his cart and swatted some bugs away from his face. "The Taurans, no offense, but I don't think they like Orcs very much. And, the stories I have heard, even moving cargo on their ships is very expensive. I'd love to sell my wares in foreign lands; I hear it is worth it. But the minimum cargo value I'd need to move is 50,000 gold." He pointed to the five wagons in his train. "That's more than I have ever had in my entire life as a merchant. I can't even imagine what it would cost to be a passenger."

RiVule hopped down and sat back next to Victor. "I am not worried about gold. Gruustir has told me it will happen. Perhaps your cargo will be part of that destiny."

Victor laughed and said, "I can't see my humble wares being part of Gruustir or any other god's plans, but I'll tell you what. Should it happen, my friend, I will go and get enough of my fellows together to meet the Tauran quota. We'll pay you an arranger's fee too. Deal?"

RiVule had his first encounter with the Tanian military five days later. He and Taisha were almost at the Great Steps, which led to the Temple. A group of children ran about the streets and one bumped into RiVule. The Orc caught the vagrant in a ghost hand that mimicked RiVule's own hand. Held off the ground by the neck, RiVule pulled his golden emblem of Gruustir from the boy's hands. He moved his other hand to heart punch and end the pickpocket's life, but Taisha caught it and whispered to him, "No, RiVule. Look around."

He almost killed the boy anyway, but noted how everyone eyed them. In that group, two priestesses stepped towards them. Paladins moved in as well. Of the two clerics, one had fire in her hair and a look of eternal youth. Frustratingly, Taisha bowed to the priestesses.

In Orc, RiVule hissed, "They would spare their thieves?"

In the same, Taisha answered, "No, worse than death. Trust me."

The transcended priestess pointed and two paladins caught the thief. RiVule twisted his hand to retain his hold, but the magic of his left gauntlet failed. If the Tanians noticed, they did not show it. The priestess said, "I am R'Dar Veron. Welcome, priest of Gruustir. How may Tiamat welcome the Beast God Gruustir this bright day?" The second part was directed at him in fluent, if accented Orcish.

RiVule smiled at her. "I seek voyage on the great ships, the minotaurs." He pointed to Taisha, "She tells me I should come to the Temple. Hopefully, this is enough? In coming here, a thief steals my holy symbol and you interrupt my just punishment."

Continuing in Orc, Veron replied, "The criminal punishment for theft here can be severe. Tell me, would your punishment end his life?" When RiVule nodded, Veron continued. "Ending his life does not serve Tiamat or Gruustir. The boy will be punished, tested, and made to serve if he does not repent. With the witnesses here, his punishment is certain. Will you let this be? Of course, were he to do this in your lands, you could punish him as you see fit. You agree that Tiamat's law reigns in Tiamat's realm?"

RiVule did. While the paladins handed him over to the City Watch, drawn to the area by the commotion, Veron took RiVule's arm and said, "I was just about to visit the Temple myself. Would you and Taisha like to accompany me?"

Gruustir told him he should join this priestess Veron. The calling was clear: take her, seduce her, take her with you. Unlike Taisha, this priestess excited RiVule and he found himself resisting the urge to strut like a young fighter. To focus, he asked about the Temple. It was everything he imagined it would and should be. "I grew up hearing stories about this place," he said. "Dragons. They would have a temple like this. Magnificent."

Veron told him about the stone used, the gold, the runes, and the three obelisks. It passed time until they ascended the stairs and Veron took him directly to Dar Shara. No cleric of Gruustir had ever walked into Tania alone. They usually came with a war host, as mercenaries, or as enemies. This had never happened before.

The knights watched with casual readiness, but Veron was well-known. They paused in the central room and RiVule asked about the lone paladin standing near the top of the central tower between the three obelisks. "That is a guardian knight of our highest order, the same as our King Malcor. I must imagine that Gruustir's genesis story may have some similar elements to Tiamat's?"

RiVule began speaking of the Orc, Goblin, and Ogre as they proceeded deeper into the Temple.

* * *

Grant hoped his crew were safely in their hideout. The three Cuthberic paladins had been hard to shake loose. Again, he thanked his stars that they were young and gullible. The city sat quiet, stifled. With so many of the Orders gone to fight in Bloodstone, it had a feeling of not-quite-martial law. It felt like the people decided to be on their best behavior so that better behavior would not be imposed on them. It made Grant's skin itch. *At least I'm not with Devin, the new Cuthberic paladin, and his friends*. Grant groaned at the days lost seeking out the "evil" assassin. Thankfully, the Cuthberics received mustering orders and took their leave of Grant on the fifth day.

He slipped into the Satin Purse Inn, a neutral hangout for the various factions. He was surprised to see it so full. Not just full, the place was bustling with more activity than he had ever seen. Sidling up to the bar, Grant's coin gave him a tankard of ale and a soft whisper in his ear about the fall of The Twins.

"521, they say," the red-haired barmaid whispered into his ear, "wanted Northern Cross's territory. Something happened. The entire leadership of The Twins was wiped out." The maid licked his ear and kissed his cheek. "It's been too long, baby Grant. We missed you."

Grant tapped another coin against the counter. "Delia, tell me more. What are the rumors? Anything about my crew?"

Delia made the coin vanish into her skimpy top and pressed even closer to Grant. "Lots. It'll cost you more than a coin."

Grant pushed over a purse with enough coin to pay her ten years' worth of wages and tips. "Drinks on the house, and your finest room. You know, I should get three Delias for this price."

She took the purse and hefted it before it too disappeared. "Just the original, baby."

A few minutes later, when the libations began to flow from an unknown benefactor, Grant slipped aside and entered the back rooms of the tavern. The penthouse suite was locked and occupied, so Grant stood to the side and waited for Delia at the next best room.

Once they were alone, Delia told him what she knew. "Someone from Dark Legion came here and said Jace had gone over to them. Yeah, I know right?" she added when Grant's eyes bugged out. Jace was Cordelle's new battle mage. *Loyalty must not last long anymore*, he thought. She pressed hima gainst the wall and unlocked the room's door. "I've heard some stories about a Tanian doing in The Twins. I don't know if that's true or not, but some of the survivors said they saw the Legion Commander, Ayden, there. Problem is, she's in Bloodstone, right? I mean, I guess they could use magic to move her around but it'd be strange to have her away from Blodostone."

They talked like this for a while before Grant asked her again, "What about my crew?"

"What about them? You going interrogate me or are you going to enjoy what you bought?" Delia blinked her eyes and slowly pulled her clothes off. Grant tried to ask another question but she stepped in to his chest and kissed him. Her hands undid his armor straps and then, at last, he returned her kisses. When Delia at last pushed him down on the bed and straddled him, she said, "You bought the best, Grant. Enjoy."

She began to massage his forearm and biceps where he touched her. "One of our agents saw Delton and the others leave by the Second East Gate. They looked normal, for your crew. We gave them word you'd joined the Cuthberics." She looked at him and giggled. "You as a Cuthberic. Mmm," she moaned. "I can almost imagine it." She dragged herself up and down his body ensuring he could feel all of her skin on his own. "Then, we get this story about Dark Legion, and 521 uniting. So, that's what's going on here and why we're so busy today. All the unaligned were called together for a special meeting. I thought you had come to check it out. Doing some recruiting of your own?"

Though Delia's sensual massage took him back to other times he had spent money with her, the unfolding of the stories did not add up for

Grant. He recalled his training: *When something is off, that is when you act. You do not wait and see. You don't have the luxury of waiting. You act, Grant. Suddenly, without warning; that is how you survive.* Marcello had never led him wrong.

Though he really wanted to stay with Delia, he lunged upwards and rolled to the side to fetch his sword. It threw Delia off him. That was when he saw it. Her legs, for just a moment, wavered in his vision. "Dopplegangers," he said. "You're always so smug but you overplay your hand. What happened to Delia?"

The doppleganger looked at him with Delia's face. She wiped a smudge of lip paint from her mouth. Looking around, Grant noted the hidden blades and spikes throughout the room. "This is a deathtrap," he said pointing his sword at her. "What happened to her?"

Delia slumped in resignation and then flowed under the bed as if liquid. Grant stabbed forward and just missed slicing what was left of her leg. Wondering how many in the tavern where compromised by these copy creatures, Grant grabbed his gear into his arms and ran for the window. Though the second level, the street outside was narrow. Amid shattering glass, Grant reached for the roof of the veranda atop a small house across the way and caught it with enough fingers to redirect his momentum to the side. He landed, naked, in a pile of straw set out for horses. Upstairs, the not-Delia put her head out the window and screamed, "Burglar! Grant robbed me!"

Grant swore, cursing Pha Rann and Cuthbert for the needless delays and obstacles. A man walked out of the tavern with a crossbow loaded and took aim at Grant. For just a moment, the two recognized each other. They exchanged nods as Bradley intentionally missed Grant. The Twins' lieutenant signaled to meet. Grant's dagger struck the wall next to him as a "yes."

An hour later, Grant allowed himself to be followed by – he hoped – Bradley. Bradley had once been part of his crew but left when a stable home and consistent pay were offered at multiples of the best Grant could do. Grant could not offer a regular work schedule. They moved into a series of twisting alleys that crossed dark streets. As they walked, they spoke to each other.

Bradley called out first, when they were finally sure no one else followed or watched them. "Grant, thank the gods! When I saw you and Delia, I hoped you had come to help sort things out. The Twins were wiped out by Tania. Dark Legion and 521 are mopping up what's left. There's talk about merging 521 and Dark Legion. You hear about Jace?" It all came rushing out of Bradley with a tone of shock and disbelief.

Grant eyed Bradley looking for signs that he might be a doppleganger. He seemed himself. "Prove you're Bradley," he called back.

"Your mother was Adellia. Your father was Tanian. Your first heist was robbing a paladin, is what you tell people. For reals, you stole food on Treedle Street." As Bradley rattled these things off that only Bradley knew from their times together, Grant allowed himself to relax a bit, not much. "You really Grant?"

Grant called back. "My last pay to you was 1,207 gold coins for the sale of art we stole from that stuffy prince's estate."

Satisfied, they put their weapons away and clasped hands. "It be good to see you, sir," Bradley said. "You have no idea how it's been since the Jade God fell. The Twins hired some dopples to help with getting stuff out of Bloodstone. Soon, we're overrun by dopples and I don't know who is who anymore. 'Keep doing it,' they said. 'It's fine,' they said. But, it's not fine, Grant! It's wrong. The godfathers, they laid it down: no monopoly on the streets. Cardinal rule number 1." To emphasize, Bradley held up a single finger and wagged it between them.

"Join my crew, Bradley. Be my spy. Why would The Twins, 521, and Dark Legion want to do this?" Grant asked. "A merger, that might explain Jace, but no one really knows who heads Dark Legion. Do you know?" When Bradley shook his head 'no,' Grant sat back and rubbed his head. "I wonder if Delia is okay, the real one. Plus, why would Cordelle or whoever from Legion risk attention from The Temples."

Bradley sat down on a barely unbroken crate. "Delia's strong. If anyone survives this, it'll be that one. Have faith. What do we do, my friend?"

Grant laughed. "There's no point in having a cardinal rule, unless there's a way to enforce it. In Taysor, there are many ways to make it happen. I'm just not sure it's my role to play enforcer. Where is Cordelle in all this?" Behind the question, Grant wondered if Cordelle had made good on the promise to buy out his contracts. "You know what? It doesn't matter. It does not even matter at all. I didn't get paid. We're going to reclaim my wares. C'mon."

Without another word, and in the practiced silence of thieves, the two darted off towards 521. Grant thought about his partially-paid deal with Cordelle. The half mil would hold them over for a long time. Grant decided, *I'll leave them some of it, for the coin and letter of credit. That'll be fair.* Grant realized he would end up with another execution bounty on his head.

Within an hour, they arrived at the warehouse where he had transacted Orcus parts with Cordelle six days earlier. Though many watchful eyes served on guard duty, the complex was vacant. Not a single of the enforcers or actual guards were present. Grant pulled out a Tanian deck of illusion cards and kissed five cards in quick succession. A family of four with a pet dog appeared and Grant pointed to the warehouse entrance and said, "Go there in 5 minutes."

Grant and Bradley worked their way through packing debris and shadows to a side entrance used by actual guild members. At the five minute mark, the illusions walked out of the shadows towards it. Grant noted thieves move forward to deter them. He did not recognize any of them from his visit to 521.

In absolute silence, Grant crossed the loading area and slipped behind a guard into the side entrance. Bradley had to pause and move more slowly to avoid detection. That was when Grant hit the guard with the green jade stone on his ring finger. "You'll remain here on guard, but you will say nothing. You will notice nothing. You are tired and you want to close your eyes for a bit is all, but you're still awake."

The guard sighed with eager ecstasy and Grant waved Bradley forward. Together, they crept into 521 and gained the stairs to Jace's extradimensional staging area. Just like outside, Grant noted the absence of the guards and then saw the dead nagas. Outside, the illusions were slaughtered by the unnaturally silent thieves. Hopefully, that would end it though Grant did not remember 521 being so bloodthirsty. Even as an illusion, it was a cute family and their pet dog.

Grant drew his sword and twisted another ring on his finger. He went invisible. Bradley moved forward knowing Grant would cover him. Entering Jace's area, they found a short woman shoving bone and skin into a magical holding sack. She whirled at Bradley's entrance. *A vampire*, Grant thought. He touched Bradley to let the thief know to be careful. The single tap was a thing in Grant's crew. *I'm surprised she is resisting the Orcus parts.* He eyed her. If she was holding a bone and he touched her... but she had packed it all up, including the blood, and skin. *I have to get that bag.*

It did not matter. She attacked Bradley without warning. The thief fell back, trying to parry her raking hands with his sword and buckler. Grant maneuvered himself carefully behind her. When Bradley screamed in pain, Grant drove his sword forward, twisting it into her back. The vampire screeched and turned to counter attack so quickly that Grant lost his grip on the blade. "Grant," the vampire hissed. "So long have I wanted to meet you."

Syand grabbed a jade bone and, swinging it like a club, advanced on both Grant and Bradley. She did not recognize the lean middle-aged one but figured it had to be Grant of the Rogue's Guild. He wore the garb of an adventurer but had the canniness of a hunting tiger. The older and fatter one, once he recognized her as a vampire, looked terrified. Something wet hit her face and began to burn. "Holy water? Seriously?" she raged and turned on Grant. "Tell me your name that I might carry you with me for eternity."

"I'm Grant," he answered as another stream of blessed water arced out at her. "Where is Cordelle?"

Syand dodged the next splash easily and then realized she had stepped into an attack. The fatter one, she remembered his name 'Bradley,' stabbed up into her. "You're clever," she said looking down at his sword piercing her thigh. "Here I thought you terrified of a little old vampire." She vanished and reappeared right behind Grant. Her arm shot forward into his back to grab his heart. She felt it, smelled the blood, and then the phantasmal illusion or shadow magic or whatever it was – A clone?, she wondered – burst apart into webs of quickly fading energy.

She spun looking for Grant, but was surprised to find him right in her face with a symbol of Tiamat in his hand. A phylactery trailed along the symbol that Grant held against his skin. "In Tiamat's holy name, I compel you to serve!" It was not Grant's voice. She heard a female's voice superimposed over Grant's. The language, ancient draconian used in Tiamat's scriptures, caught Syand and she resisted.

"You think a stolen priestess' voice will force me to obey YOU?" she shrieked. Though her body moved stiffly, she grabbed Grant's wrist around the phylactery and began to squeeze it so that the metal box pressed into his skin, until the skin tore, bone broke, and Grant screamed.

Bradley, unable to retrieve his sword, looked around. Scanning the room for anything, he noticed Grant's handsign, "USE SPEARS ON WALL." He saw the six long needles. They were not spears, clearly. They looked like oversized porcupine quills. Bradley heard Grant's arm break and raced to grab one. At the last moment, he grabbed another.

Syand forced Grant to his knees and pulled the symbol of Tiamat from his hand. Bradley tried to aim the spear and throw, but Syand moved so fast. Holding the symbol in her hand, she punched Grant in the forehead and threw him aside.

Bradley threw the spear. It missed and Syand whirled on him. Bradley felt his bowels begin to loosen and threw the other quill. It would have hit except that Syand vanished. The chill along his back told him she now stood right behind him. He whirled, on guard, and barely avoided a talon attack that would have torn his throat out.

From the other side of the room, two Grants stood up and picked up the spears. One said, "You must be fronting Dark Legion." The two Grants held the spears defensively, and moved forward cautiously. Bradley whimpered and crawled towards Grant. He saw his friend on the floor, holding an earring he had not noticed before. *It's a bloodstone*, Bradley realized. *Grant, what have you been doing?*, Bradley wondered.

"Fronting?" Syand laughed. "Not fronting. Is. Dark Legion is all of the guildmasters going back to the beginning. I am Syand. Please, scream my name as you die." Syand grabbed one of the spears. It felt alive in her hand, like a snake. It also hurt her to touch it. She dropped it, but doing so distracted her and the two Grants charged.

One of the quills skewered through her left hip. Like the spear she grabbed, it felt like a snake twisting and writhing in her pelvic bone. She swung the jade bone to deflect the other Grant and hit solidly. The Grant she hit vanished in a magical explosion of energy and lights.

Through the explosion, the real Grant stood and while cradling his mashed arm, he held Tiamat's symbol again. Syand began laughing until sunlight burst from the symbol. Her urge to laugh became a screeching cry of pain. "We are not done, Grant!" She called on her powers to leave, but the quill anchored her in place. She tried to snap the spear, but it would not break. Fearing another attack by the clone or Bradley, Syand jumped back against the wall so that the stone would push the quill out. Doing so, she stabbed the second Grant and it vanished.

Because of the sunlight shining from the dragon goddess' symbol, she could not see and her skin burned in Tiamat's shining radiance. *I should consider myself lucky that isn't Pha Rann or some other do-gooder god*, she thought as the quill finally pushed free of her hip. The gore-encrusted spear fell to the side and she teleported out just as Bradley came charging at her with another quill spear.

Bradley braced, expecting to hit the vampire. When he hit the wall, he fell back relieved to be alive. From the lack of the unnerving aura vampires carry with them, he guessed she was truly gone. Grant winced and wrapped the symbol along his arm above his destroyed right arm. Bradly pointed and exclaimed, "By Joust, your hand, Grant."

"It's okay. I can take care of this, but I need a quick favor." Grant smiled at him weakly. "You might even enjoy this."

"Anything," Bradley said.

Grant pointed to his vorpal short sword and began pulling it out. "I need you to cut my arm off at my elbow. It won't heal with the damage to the bone, and I'm about to pass out. We can't afford that..." Grant stumbled and barely caught himself before he slumped down. With a grunt, he tightened the phylactery around his hand stump to act like a tourniquet. "You must."

Bradley looked around and realized that he could never carry Grant out of here. "If you say so," Bradley grumbled while pulling Grant's sword out. Its gleaming edge sparkled like a slow lightning strike along the blade. So that he would not think about Grant's pain too much, Bradley struck quickly. It cut through the flesh and bone cleanly. For a brief moment, Bradley could see the flat slice of flesh and bone before blood covered it and the Tiamat symbol went dark.

Bradley began rummaging through Grant's pockets and found a flask that looked like it might be a healing potion. He hurriedly unscrewed the lid and poured it down Grant's throat. Grant began coughing and choking and then rolled to his stomach and screamed while also trying to be quiet. Holding his hand and trembling, Grant said through clenched jaw and teeth, "Brad, the earring on my left ear, pull it off and put on my finger."

Bradley fumbled through Grant's sweaty hair and found a single earring there. He tore it off, making Grant shudder as his ear ripped. He stabbed it onto Grant's right hand. Instantly, it flared with soft radiance and Grant began to breathe, rather like a woman in childbirth. When the stump stopped bleeding and Grant pulled the phylactery strap off, Bradley understood. "Regeneration? I've heard about these but never thought I'd see this type of magic."

Grant shuddered and whispered, "It was a gift from an old friend. It comes in handy sometimes."

Bradley watched as the stump closed and bone began to reform. "I always wondered about that," he said.

"Yeah, with so many clerics on hand, none of the mages really prioritize regeneration magic. With the Jade God's hold on necromancy, it just felt too dangerous. But, there are always those times where you almost have no choice." Grant's voice strengthened with each word. While the wound and the pain remained, the magic seemed to be helping and after a few minutes, Grant stood and began to investigate the room. "Good, she didn't take very much."

Upstairs, a commotion broke out and they understood they did not have much time. Grant pulled open Syand's holding bag and they began inserting the spears and bone fragments. Grant said with annoyance, "Jace must have most of it locked up still. I need it."

The commotion became yelling and a voice rang out that intruders had entered below. Cordelle's laugh resounded and his voice came down into the space. "Hey, whoever you are, you have to the count of five to surrender or you're all dead."

Bradley looked at Grant and saw Grant focusing. After a moment, and weakly, Grant called out with Jace's voice. "Boss, that bitch from Dark Legion, she broke in. I chased her off but she got some of the vials."

Bradley held his breath and prayed to Joust for a fair shake. The mimicry was fantastic and Bradley recalled how Grant used it for entertainment when they were both young in their professions. They could hear Cordelle say something to the group upstairs and then his footsteps came down. "Why didn't you tell me you were back?"

Grant shoved Bradley at Cordelle, who caught the leader with a poisoned blade to his throat. "Tell your crew that you need some time and everything is good," Grant hissed at Cordelle.

Cordelle slowly put his hands up and said, "Whatever you want." Bradley made the mistake of relaxing and Cordelle twisted free and called out for help.

Grant kneed the guildmaster in the groin and, before things escalated, Bradley caught Cordelle in a vise around his neck. Within a second, Cordelle's face went red as the guildmaster struggled to call for help, and to breathe. Alarmed voices called down to them. Grant recognized Howie. "Cordelle? You okay? We're coming down."

Grant mentally swore and fumbled at his pocket until he grabbed a card from the illusion deck. He tapped it to Cordelle and threw it at the stairs. If Bradley could just keep Cordelle quiet a few moments longer, the old man would pass out. From the card, an illusion of Cordelle appeared at the bottom of the stairs. Standing to the side of the stairs, Grant turned and looked up. The illusion of Cordelle copied Grant perfectly.

Mimicking Cordelle's voice, and pretending he saw Howie or whoever was running down the stairs, Grant said, "Hey, it's okay. Jace tripped and dropped some stuff. We're good. Return to your posts and keep an eye out for Dark Legion." Cordelle must have kicked Bradley because there was a stifled grunt and then things went quiet.

"You sure, boss?" Howie asked.

Grant detected the faintest tone of suspicion and waved his hand. "Yeah, we're fine. Jace, you jackass, quit screwing around."

Grant had the illusion turn so that Howie would not see the illusion's mouth move. Casting his voice to the side of the office where Howie could not see, Grant called out in Jace's voice. "Hey, Howie, since you're so eager to help, we could use some food from Happy C's." Switching to Cordelle's voice, he had Cordelle look back up the stairs and added, "See if they have any of that honey liquor I like so much."

Howie did not seem convinced but he eventually nodded and left. Grant slowly relaxed and said, "Bradley, we don't have much time."

It took them five minutes to find the locks to Jace's hidden room and disarm the traps it contained. When Bradley was distracted, Grant switched Syand's bag with an empty one of his own. Marcello had taught him to never trust when life and death lay on the line. Dopplegangers complicated everything. He called out to Bradley. "Only a few more minutes. Look, Bradley. There're some things I haven't told you about me. But, I'll catch you up on everything. Promise you won't freak out. Play it cool. The Cordelle illusion should pace at the bottom of the stairs and give us a bit more time."

His newly-reacquainted friend nodded. They entered the room and began shoving quills, skin, and bone into the holding sack. Relieved to see that Cordelle had kept the highest quality stuff and blood in his office, he noted that 521 was labelling the lower quality parts for resale. Grant closed and rearmed the door behind them after dragging Cordelle's body in with them.

"What is this stuff?" Bradley asked pointing to folds of leather and quills. "That green stuff..."

"The Jade God," Grant said. "It's all from the Jade God. My crew and I grabbed it when he fell in Bloodstone."

Bradley continued shoving it into the sack in huge arm sweeps. "I see. You sold it to Cordelle?" With Grant indicating 'yes,' Bradley kept cramming stuff into the sack. He finished just as Howie swept through the illusion and began calling for Cordelle.

Grant walked over and helped Bradley with the last table covered in green bone. Exhausted from the tension of the night and still recovering from Syand amputating his right hand, Grant was completely surprised by Bradley's attack. The poisoned blade slipped into his ribcage and twisted. Grant's breathing immediately sucked in as his lung collapsed. Paralyzing poison made his body go limp and he collapsed to the ground.

"Sorry, Grant. This stuff is too valuable to let you have it." Bradly ripped the regeneration ring off Grant's hand and relieved him of his vorpal sword and the remaining illusion deck. He dumped a bit of the bone fragments about and posed Grant in the act of killing Cordelle.

I wish I was shocked, Grant thought. The paralysis made it hard to move but he had a shot. It happened when Bradley came over to put the knife in his hand. "Stop," Grant said. Bradley was holding a green bone in his hand. "You won't remember what I tell you but you will obey. You're going to take the sack and toss it into the canal. Take my illusion card, the Ace, and use it make my own backpack not visible on me. Good lad." Outside, Howie was growing frantic. Grant checked the backpack and could feel but not see it. "Bradley, put my ring back on my finger. Good good. Now, you're going to keep doing what you're doing, but you're not going to kill me or Cordelle."

Bradley put the knife in Grant's hand and stabbed it into Cordelle's shoulder. "Business is business and Dark Legion pays very well."

Mentally, Grant cursed Bradley.

☐

# Chapter 7 – Ash Conundrum

Ash turned and entered into the Adventurer's Guild. The pyramid shaped structure dominated the road all around it. Ash enjoyed the Adventurers Guild. It always had a lot of energy in and around it. People leaving with gold in their eyes. Parties coming back with stories, sometimes treasure. Ash had active contracts here for his adventurer persona and often met Khalla here when they needed cover for getting out of Tania. Entering the main hall, he looked – knowing she would not be there – to the dark alcove adjacent the work board. She was not there, and it made him miss her. He walked over there anyway and sat down. Under the stone bench, he felt where they had carved their names almost ten years ago. "Let's have an adventure together, Ash," he could remember her saying.

Ash felt her name carved on the seat and said out loud, "We joined a caravan to Stone. The caravan was slow, exactly what we wanted. We stood guard at night and ruled the evenings."

The shadows answered him back when Khalla appeared. "Ash, I never pictured you as sentimental."

Looking up, Ash quickly wiped the hope from his face when he saw she was all business. She looked fantastic, every bit the part of a female Marcello. "I am. I just usually hide it better. I can tell you didn't come here to throw yourself at me and beg me to take you back?"

Khalla sat down opposite him and said, "Would it matter if I did? No, it would not. Here's the deal. I spoke with Daryx. I spoke with Halgrim. None of them understand your reluctance to serve Tania in something we're essentially doing anyway. I've offered to do it and take Perdition's throne. Formally take it, not just play errand girl to you. However, because of what I think is real love, I wanted to tell you this. And, give you a chance. We can go a few ways, Ash. I love you. I thought you loved me too. You can open to me and tell me what is so damn important about that cursed room that you'd give up me, give up us, for it. I want to believe that, whatever it is, I can handle it. We'll figure it out. Do you love me?"

Ash nodded his head. "You know I love you, Khalla. That you ask, it hurts." Ash put his hands over his heart. "A lot. I can't even tell... I can't speak... I... look, a long time ago, I made a deal. If I even try, I am stopped. Thinking about it with a possibility of telling you, I... it's like the Allegiance of Blood. Do you understand?"

"No. Give me a key. Your shop has them. Long. Thirteen or more channels lock pick and raker. Three on the bottom. May I break in and see?" Ash felt Khalla softening a bit. She almost took his hand. "This deal was worth it, I hope?"

Ash shrugged. "It was at the time. Now, with you, with us, it seems stupid and regrettable. There's not a lot I can do about it. I'd be magically compelled to stop you if you actually enter."

Khalla leaned back and folded her arms. "Ash, I've been trying to get into that room for ten years."

"Hence all the traps and theatrics." He laughed and said, "You are much more patient than I am." He leaned forward suddenly and caught her hand, holding it tight so she could not pull away. "I love you, Khalla. I need you to trust me on this. The deal isn't some unlivable condition that affects you or us. Maybe," he eyed her closely. "You've met Kaia?"

Khalla stood up and pulled free of Ash. "Even if Kaia, why wouldn't you tell me this years ago? You know my entire life…"

"I was Marcello. I had to know your entire life."

"And you kept this from me," Khalla whipped back to face him. A tear started growing in her eye and without wiping it, she said, "You've known and could have at least told me it was a Kaia thing. Now that I am Marcello, do I get to know?"

"I noticed you froze me out of Perdition. That was cold. But, I actually don't know. It's not a specific thing to Perdition, but to me and Kaia. Maybe you will. Have you tried? I'm sure Daryx knows." Ash waved over a serving boy and asked for wine, crackers, and cheese. "Halgrim asked once and he came to terms with it when I didn't tell him. He does not know and I believe he tried to find out with magic, demons, and scrying."

Khalla did not want to leave but also did not know what to say. "I should leave," she said. Finally, when the wine came, Khalla said, "Daryx gave you two days to answer the god emperor or else the offered Perdition deal comes to me. I'd rather it go to you. You've earned it. I never coveted this level of power. The Circle! Can you imagine me there?" she chuckled. "But, for you, you'd be a natural. I suspect Daryx prefers you too. I'm leaving. I hope you're right about everything. Either you do this and make things right with me, or I'm doing it and taking Perdition."

"I don't like ultimatums," he called to her back.

"It's not an ultimatum; it's fact. And, like our love, it requires something more from you than secrecy. You could have told me about Kaia, at least."

* * *

Khalla walked into the back room of the Mud Bar, a brightly-lit tavern just off one of the main roads east of the Great Bazaar. She was pleased to see Ciejek, her cell's lieutenant already there though she wished more had also arrived. She did not like being alone with him. He had a small decanter of elven wine open to air in the room. It masked the smell of sweat and food. "They're all accounted for, Khalla," he said. "They'll be here."

"Perfect," she replied, and sat down. It was her favorite wine and she took a careful sip. Ciejek had a fondness for drugs and poisons. "If you did anything to this, I can't tell."

He bit at his nails and shrugged. "After all this time, you still don't trust me?" Khalla took another sip and shook her head. Ciejek continued. "So, a little birdie told me that Marcello is having some problems and you might be the answer."

Khalla eyed him. Since their assault on Sai R'Dar's estate, most of the cell leaders accepted that the whole thing was part of the act put on for The Circle. Everyone knew The Circle watched the assault. Business had never been better since as cell after cell received lucrative security contracts for all of the Dar, even those not in The Circle. "I don't trust you. At all. Besides what Marcello might do to you, you should worry about what I might do to you if you had been or ever were successful in drugging me."

Ciejek raised his crystal shot glass and toasted her. "To sexy elves!" It was the first toast he had made when they met years ago. He was new to Tania then, obviously so, and not a worshipper of Tiamat. His attempts to buy exotic materials had triggered a warning to Perdition via the Alchemy Guild. Khalla had investigated and found this strange man of many talents just arrived on a Tauran world galleon. His best talent was drugs and poisons. When he did it for Tania, he was a genius. When he did for himself, he used it for pleasure and control.

She did not toast him back though she took another sip of the wine. "Dare I ask the birdie's name?"

Ciejek leaned back and tapped on the wall to summon a waiter. "We need another bottle of wine," he complained. "No one important, though

Page 123

it might have been Ash, that clothing merchant. He's just a front for Marcello, isn't he?"

Khalla masked her frustration. *Of course, Ash would spread rumors.* It was his classic move when stressed. "I wish. Do you have any idea how much money Perdition is worth?" she speculated.

He raised his glass in another toast, "Millions. And as many sexy elves as I could possibly wish for. By the way, I had to let Unir go. She just could not endure the ecstasy." He winked at her. "The others stayed."

Khalla rolled her eyes. "I don't know where you find these women or why they'd choose to be with you. Do you still call them your harem?"

He laughed. "You know I do, and there's a spot for you anytime you want in. I've told them about you and they all want to taste what it's like to be with an adventurer elf." He raised his glass again and said, "A toast! To our fearless and sultry cell leader, Khalla!"

Khalla touched the folded Merakor note in her pocket and wished that Ciejek had equal skill at recruiting adventuring elves as he did prostitutes. "I've got an inside path into what might be the biggest score in centuries, and it requires elves. You know, the kind that know how to fight. I don't suppose you know any, Ciejek?"

The suggestion of wealth piqued his interest and he leaned forward and poured her another sip of wine. "Seriously? And, yes actually. I know a few. Not my girls, but their siblings and friends. What do you need, and…"

"What's in it for you? Right, so. Here's the deal. I'll review with the rest of the group, but the recruiter will pay for leads on strong adventurers."

Ciejek pulled out his notebook and began reviewing notes and writing while watching Khalla pensively. Money always made Ciejek take matters seriously. As the other cell members started to arrive, Ciejek finally got the additional wine and food he had ordered. When the last two cell members arrived, the small room felt crowded.

Khalla noted each cell member and let memories of their work together dance through her mind. Each excelled in their profession and had done flawless work in Bloodstone as her leaders in Rogue's Blade. Besides Ciejek, she counted Bolston, Yunstir, Thraden, Zachir, Pol Nir, and Oscar. Pol Nir served as the only other female in the cell's leadership. "I trust you all with my life," Khalla said bowing to them. "Thank you for coming."

Ciejek had finished and passed the torn paper to her. "30%," he said and winked.

She ignored him. Khalla took a small amulet from around her neck and placed it on the table. A bloodstone gleamed therein and Khalla touched it. Softly pulsing red light filled the room and their discussion continued telepathically. If anyone looked in or spied on them magically, they'd see a group of friends laughing, eating, and drinking. Perdition had learned long ago that hiding from scrying was very difficult. Showing a scryer something not-quite-real was much easier.

"I have two orders of business for you all. One is personal. The other is for pay," Khalla explained. "Before I get into this, I want to talk about the personal. There are rumors since we took on Sai's estate that I am Marcello. Though not true, I fully intend to make a run against Marcello in the next couple of days. It's time we had some leadership that doesn't stick us with Dar Shara's forged name on a contract as we're walking up to Dar Shara."

The others cheered this. Not only had that stunt upset them, but it fundamentally changed the expectations of the group as they headed into Bloodstone. Being professionals, they had rolled with it. Pol Nir asked, "Timing? What do you need?" The others expressed their readiness as well.

"I need both this personal issue and the profit issue tended to. The clothing merchant, Ash, he has a room in his personal residence that I have been trying to open for nine years now. I don't trust him. He is loyal and close to Marcello. This room has a secret and I need to know what it is. It will send a message. This isn't a smash and grab thing. I'll pay you each your usual fee. Nothing else is to be touched. I'd prefer Ash not even know we were there. After our Dar estates work, this should be easy. Who's in?"

Yunstir asked, "When do you want this to happen?"

"Tonight, right after this meeting. I don't want word getting out." All but Bolston and Ciejek could do it and Khalla thanked them.

"The other matter, for profit, is this: I need help. The guild has been tasked with a mission, well, an adventure that includes retrieving priceless magical artefacts for the god emperor. The pay is beyond imagination. Marcello is having some qualms with the mission so I volunteered to do it. I'm hoping that you'll help me. This is how I supplant

Marcello and you'll become Perdition's new lieutenants. There's a lot of details, but here's the quick.

"We'd be going to Merakor, for perhaps a while. Maybe up to a year. Marcello has been seeking out elves, but except for me, he's had no luck. I have a proposal to change this so that each of you could come along. Pay will be equal shares of what we find as well as any rewards except for one: Perdition's throne. Should that happen, you each become my lieutenants and we will take Perdition into the next era." Sending so much passion and enthusiasm through telepathy while also pretending to laugh at jokes and eat dinner was hard. Khalla knew her concern could be felt by the others.

Ciejek was the first to reassure her. "None of your performance was compromised by Pol Nir's terrible pun. That was awful, Pol. Just awful. So, Merakor. I may have some friends in Morilon that would join. But, yes. If I can go, I'm in."

Oscar asked, "What happens to our cell? I have marks I've been grooming for years. I'd hate to see them all lost."

Khalla began to answer but Pol Nir did before her. "Marks are marks. You'll pick them back up when we return. Plus, it's Merakor. We might come back with so much gold we never need to cull marks ever again! I'm in."

Khalla said, "All of our current work will be transferred to other cells. Regular drill when any of us take a sabbatical and no different than when Rogue's Blade marched on Bloodstone."

Thraden loudly called for more lamb and beer. Telepathically, he said, "I'm intrigued, but need a minimum threshold. Merakor sounds good and all, but this is about dark elves and 3,000 or more years of trap setting and monsters. Assuming we make it back, what does an equal share look like? I assume it's not just us. Who else?"

Khalla, remembering her conversation with Halgrim, answered, "Anywhere between 75 and 100. So, to get a million, we'd need to bring back 100 million in treasure. Yes, it's daunting."

Thraden said, "We might not come back with anything and be lucky to escape with our lives. The greatest archmagei barely escaped with their lives and most of them went insane just getting from there to here. No, I'd need a minimum. Give me a min and I'll forgo an equal share."

"Me too, Khalla. What's the minimum? I'm in for that," Oscar said.

Yunstir said, "I'm out. Apologies, Khalla but I've been wanting to retire for some time. You know this."

"One last score, Yunstir. The biggest ever," Khalla said. Her eyes gleamed in the red-tinted light of their feast.

"Merakor," Ciejek whispered out loud in the room.

A grin split Yunstir's face. "Fine. Equal share. Toss this minimum garbage!" He slammed his mug against Ciejek and Thraden's.

Khalla eyed Bolston, Zachir, and Pol Nir. "What say you two?"

Bolston stabbed his dagger into the last piece of bread. "Aye, I suppose I'm in. Equals."

Pol Nir reached into her pocket and pulled out a deck of divination cards. She had a habit of shuffling and playing with the cards when nervous. She let the cards dance between her hands before flipping one up against her forehead so that all could see. "The Hungry Soul," she said. "This is an un-terrible omen for the mission. The Hungry Soul portends success if fed a course of greed and pain. I'll take one more card before I answer. Call it, Bolston."

Pol Nir let the cards dance in her hands again. When Bolston nodded, she punched her forehead and pinned a single card there. "The Golden Lord of Hell," Pol Nir whispered. "This quest will yield treasures we cannot imagine. I'm in. Equal share."

Khalla knew this next part would make or break the group. "The minimums will get paid first. Since there is a risk of not getting enough to pay and since equal shares above that would not be fair to the others, I propose fixed price rather than minimums. 50,000 gold. Deal?" She looked over at Thraden and Oscar.

Ciejek snorted. "You're going to regret this," he said to them out loud.

"100,000," Thraden countered. "You heard Pol Nir."

"If you believed Pol, you'd switch to equals," Bolston muttered. Someone told him and Ciejek to shut up.

Khalla put her hands on the table and stood up. "50,000. Share the risks as equal if you believe it more than that. 50 is enough to live like R'Dar lords the rest of your lives, to a point. Of course, if you went equal share, you come back wealthy enough to become actual R'Dar."

"Fine, if Thraden does it, so will I. 50,000 gold," Oscar said. Thraden nodded. Zachir sighed and agreed to. "We're in. All of us. Equals."

"Excellent," Khalla said. "I'll have standard agreements created with standard provisions for hazard and special work. This is going to be fun, and interesting. Until you hear from me about this again, normal operations. Oh, and crew, you may want to brush up on your Elvish."

The quizzical looks she got from everyone made her laugh. "Merakor. Really? The entire place is ruled by Drow."

Ciejek snorted. "We know. Why Elvish? Don't they speak some other language?"

"They were all elves. While they may have their own words and dialects after three millennia, they all speak Elvish. Whatever we encounter will be a variant on that. Lastly, don't talk about this to anyone. If you hit the Adventurer's Guild up, you'll see several postings for elven groups for heroic missions overseas. That's Merakor. Don't apply yourselves, but if you know of any Elves kick them my way. Recruitment bonuses are very high on this one. And, remember, I'm also making a run against Marcello. Stay sharp."

Khalla stood and pulled her cowl about her face. She scooped up the amulet and put it away. The telepathic connections dropped and Ciejek groaned about having eaten too much. All was as it should be, though she noted Ciejek eyeing her a little too closely. It made her feel uncomfortable and brought back unpleasant memories of the time he had tried to drug her. *After all these years, I still don't trust actually trust him*, she realized.

* * *

Delton led Grant's crew their run along a steep mountain trail ascending south of Taysor. The Shield Mountains divided northern Taysor from southern Morbatten as effectively as any military wall or border possibly could. The foothills had shaken winter but the mountain peaks looming ahead of them showed deep winter still.

Patches of ice clung to the shadowed side of the ravine wall they had followed for almost an entire day now. Behind them to the north, the delta plain of Taysor faded away as hills and rocks obscured their view.

Best they could tell, no one followed. The lack of contact with Grant made Delton worried and they doubled their pace, running day and night.

Only short naps kept them moving. *Endurance* potions helped, but they were beginning to feel strung out by the magic. The potions, normally effective for an entire day, barely carried them for an hour now. Magic could not compensate for lack of sleep and physical limits when pressed for days like this. When they finally reached shelter, there would be a long detoxification period, and possibly withdrawal. Grant always made sure they had magical gear to help with anything, but these potions were not meant to be consumed hourly.

Watching his breath steam in the mountain air, Delton sent silent thanks to their leader for the enchanted boots and cloaks that made weather extremes matter not at all. Even these, taxed this way, felt frayed. Something about their magic made them matter more when needed. In their six-day race out of Taysor's eastern gates, they had barely paused. Delton worried their gears' magic was stretching just as surely as their bodies were.

"Let's rest for four hours," Delton called out. "Finn, check the southern trail ahead and report back. I'll take first watch." By the time he finished, Finn was running silent and fast to the south. The trail wound upwards into the Shield Mountains. This path paralleled the military roads used for countless years against Tania in the Winter Wars. Also called Smuggler's Hide, this lesser known path was a favorite escape route when evading Taysor's law. The other members of Rogue's Guild had already fallen asleep. Ten days on the run with no more than three hours of rest every once in a while, and fatigue build up caused by the stamina magic did that to a person. But, they had been together through worse.

Delton hefted the pack, with its precious cargo of Jade God body parts, and prayed it would all be worth it. On a whim, he climbed a rock tower adjacent their camp. From there, he could see Smuggler's Hide and also the path ahead where Finn moved quietly. When Finn stumbled, Delton knew that they were running out of time. They had to make the hideout before they could rest.

"What's that?" he muttered when a glint of light caught his eye to the north. The city of Taysor gleamed along the horizon. It looked more comfortable than their marathon had been so far. He squinted and looked hard, crouching down and going very still. His training kicked in and he opened his mind and vision to take in everything. This way of detecting movement worked for animals and it worked for humans.

After what felt like a minute, he saw movement again. Carefully, and slowly, he pulled out a Tanian spyglass. Wrapped in leather to prevent the brass from drawing attention, Delton focused it north and swore when he saw what looked like a ranger leading a paladin and a squire along their route. "Pha Rann curses us," he added and then watched, wondering if they sought his group specifically.

The trio moved slowly. The paladin's heavy charger struggled with the uneven terrain. At last, Delton caught sight of herald markings and breathed a sigh of relief. A Cuthberic knight would be bad. This one bore the markings of the Literalist Order, a powerful and numerous order with a reputation for being reasonable. The squire looked like a warrior and trudged along in heavy splint armor. Heavily armored, the group would never catch up to Rogue's Guild. Delton guessed they were two days ahead of this group and breathed a sigh of relief. The ranger alone moved nimbly. "Must be an elf," Delton mused. He put the spyglass away and moved back down to his team.

Finn returned shortly after and reported the trail clear ahead. "Del, at this pace, we're at least three days out. Also, I know you know this, but we're all getting close to our limits. Right now, a child could defeat us with a tantrum."

Delton nodded. "Thankfully, we don't have to worry about pursuit. A Literalist paladin and two retainers are about two days behind us. They'll slow down or prevent us from being intercepted back from Taysor and the southern trail sections. We need to get to the base faster than three days."

The two looked at each other and the sleeping team. "Three days," Finn said. "That'll be pushing it. The path ahead ascends sharply across the most exposed parts of the trail." Finn pointed to the east. "I'm worried about the weather too. Grant's gear is top notch but it won't help us from slipping and slowing down."

Delton had been worried about the weather too. The eastern side of Shield Mountains had terrible sleet storms, sometimes blizzards in spring. Hearing Finn say it, Delton knew they had been lucky so far. "We'll have to keep pushing. You're right, though. I'd rather run for three days and miss the bad weather when it inevitably comes. Each hour, we're at risk of something. At least Taysor had enough militia show up for the Winter War that we don't have to worry about monsters, raiders, and the like. I've heard it was sparse and that Tania didn't even show up. We'll run and sleep when we're safe, or collapse. Grant would order the same," Delton countered but he looked at Finn with a rising question tone in his voice. *Would Grant do this?*, Delton wondered. No doubt Grant would already have them there.

Finn sat back against the rocks and rubbed his hands through his greasy hair. Like them all, Finn had dark shadows in the lines of his face and bloodshot eyes. Chapped lips had long ago bled and then scabbed over in their long run. It would all look worse but for the beards covering all their faces. Finn rubbed his eyes and said, "I don't know if he would. He'd probably give the backpack to the two strongest and have them race to the hideout while the rest of us followed as best we could."

"Damn, I knew that. I was hoping you'd say otherwise. We could do that, but I don't want to split us up. It feels wrong. We should have heard from Grant by now." Delton went quiet and jumped to his feet. He signaled Finn to wake the crew. Springtime in the mountains brought a certain ambience with it and things had just gone too quiet. Training compensated for exhaustion and the party moved into guarded positions. Handsign flashed back and forth and then Delton pointed.

A hooded figure crested the rock tower to look down at their now empty and deserted camp. Without a fire, there was no sign they had been there at all. If Delton had not just climbed the rock tower, the hooded figure would have easily blended in and appeared as a rock formation. Another figure rose up beside that one as around the camp, a sense of being watched fell over them. Delton and the team held their breath, going perfectly still. While hiding in shadows and being stealthy came naturally to them all, hiding from someone similarly trained was much more difficult than hiding from a normal person. If any of them made a mistake...

A bird call sounded from the rock tower and they heard padded boots move away from their camp. Delton signaled for everyone to remain where they were. After he counted a hundred heartbeats, Delton felt the adrenaline fade enough to think more clearly. Sadly, it also allowed the accumulated fatigue to come crashing down on him. Luck and its god, Joust, smiled on him though and he thanked all the gods he could remember when nothing happened. His thanks were interrupted when a shadowy figure detached from the side of the rock tower and walked right into their midst. The figure moved his hand over the ground and paused where one of the team members had fallen asleep.

While they could take one tracker easily, they already knew there were more. Delton did a quick calculation. If they played hide and seek with whoever these were, it would slow them down. They were too tired to play that game. It had to be now or never. He signaled for everyone to be ready as the tracker's head turned away from him.

Delton sighed and stepped out from the shadows along the wall and stretched. He pretended to be surprised by the tracker. Grant would no doubt have thrown his voice to make it seem he approached from farther away. Grant was a master of voice mimicry and ventriloquism. The tracker whirled and drew a blade.

"Woah there, friend. No need. I'm not looking for a fight." He let his hand drop to his short sword and showed he was willing to. He stretched and yawned. It was not hard to sound exhausted. "Out here on Smuggler's Hide, I don't know that I care."

"You stink," the masked man said. "I'm looking for a human named Grant. He might be with a clean-shaven man with green eyes, goes by the named Delton."

Delton opened his hands and pointed to his dirt, sweat, and grime-encrusted face. "Do I look like whoever this Grant is?" Days of not sleeping had made his eyes so bloodshot and dull, they hardly looked green. In the poor lighting, he knew they looked shadowed and brown.

The tracker relaxed and put his sword away. Delton noticed the man looked like he felt, tired. "No, but I was told that Grant would be here with his crew. Have you seen or heard of anyone like that?"

Delton shook his head and said, "You know, except for the paladin I passed a few days ago, I haven't seen anyone up here. I'm Bollister. What's your name?"

The tracker declined to answer and said, "We saw the paladin." He pulled some papers from under the leather armor covering his chest. One he opened up. It was a sketch of Grant. The other was a sketch of Delton. Delton looked healthy, fat, and devoid of facial hair. *Grant's such a genius*, Delton reflected. He had made Delton eat and eat for days and then a mage had plumped him up even more before Delton got caught by the Soran Watch for petty theft. The mage had also made Delton's eyes really pop with green color. They were more hazel. All of the team had a similar treatment and it had saved them many times, like right now.

The tracker pointed to sketches. "Have you see or do you know anything about these two men? There's a rich bounty on their heads. I could share it with you, Bollister."

*Thank the gods*, Delton thought. *I'm so dirty he doesn't recognize me.* "You know, I'm just a trapper trying to get a jump on the spring thaw before the Winter War ends. It's been a rough year with hardly anyone showing up. You know how it is." Delton held out his hand for the papers. He tapped Grant. "This one looks familiar. Actually, now that I look at it, this other one does too. I think I saw them maybe 2 or 3 weeks ago by the eastern gates."

The tracker pressed him. "The main eastern gate? Can you tell me which one?" The tracker pulled a gold coin out of his pocket. Delton pretended to be impressed.

He scratched his head and acted like he was trying to remember. Another gold coin appeared and Delton took both. "It was the northern one. You know, the smaller one by the fountains that commoners use? Yeah, it was that one for sure."

The tracker gave him another coin and said, "Many thanks, Bollister. Good day to you."

Delton pocketed the coins and said, "My pleasure. I'm kind of sad you didn't ask me about things I could give you better information on. Remember my name. I travel this area all the time. Also, if I run into these characters, how do I find you? Are they dangerous?"

The tracker, who had almost left the clearing, turned and said over his shoulder. "You don't. I'll find you." Then, he was gone.

Delton chuckled. "That was menacing." One of the team signaled, asking if all was clear, but Delton did not feel it was right. While repacking his bag and securing the gold, he carefully handsigned that they should follow him on guard.

A minute later, Delton shrugged the backpack onto his shoulders and began to climb the southern trail. He went slowly so that his team could follow at a safe distance but stay close. Turning on the ridge, he felt dizziness wash over him as he caught his breath. The height of each step made climbing slow and soon Delton felt his legs wobble. He signed, "CONTINUE ON. NO CHOICE."

By the time the sun began to fall towards sunset, Delton could see through the trees that they had nearly reached the summit. *I'm surprised I haven't been attacked yet*, he thought. The summit is the best place for an ambush. He carefully readied five of the jade bone darts and paused to wrap a cloak of Orcus skin around him as the temperature fell. With their mounting fatigue, Delton could not chance the summit being safe.

When he reached the summit, he found the summit as it had always been, completely cleared by centuries of travelers seeking rest from the rough weather that tortured the foothills of the Shield. With a glorious sky overhead, Delton noted three men stood near a campfire, not yet lit. Each held a cocked crossbow and stood ready for combat. He dropped his backpack, the signal for the others to stop, and stretched.

Delton ignored the men. They were bait to distract from the impending ambush. As he stumbled forward, he counted at least seven others hidden along the trees below the summit clearing. Careful camouflage or elvish magic probably concealed a few more. Pretending to at last see them, he raised his hand and called out. "Oh, good evening!" He heaved for his breath. "I always forget how hard that last part is. Ah, burn it all." One of the three aimed his crossbow in his direction. Delton put his hand up and waved it away. "I'm not a threat," Delton added.

"We'll be the judge of that," the crossbowman called back.

Delton held his hands up but continued walking along the foot trail. "Okay, judge. I'm exhausted. But, I can tell you don't want a stranger's company. My name's Bollister by the way. I'll find a different camp area."

The other two brandished the loaded crossbows and said, "I'm a troll if your name is Bollister."

Delton recognized the tracker from earlier and waved. "I thought we settled this? Oh, you must want your gold back. It's fine. You can have it back?" The tracker leaned up to their leader and whispered something. It made them all relax a bit. The sketch of Grant was in the leader's hand and he was looking from it to Delton.

Because of the clearing, if he went any farther, his team would not be able to cover him or reach him in time. Delton dropped the backpack letting it seem heavier than it was. "Don't care if you're a troll named Tobey, but if you keep pointing those bolts at me, you're going to make me think you're unfriendly. I don't suppose you have any water? I'm parched."

The first crossbowman said, "You're either Grant or Delton, or one of his men. Admit it."

Delton pulled a small flask of whiskey out and popped it to take a swig. "Okay, I admit it." The three immediately aimed right at him. "I'm either Grant, Delton, or his men." He took another sip. "Seriously? Whoever these people are, you think they're going to just walk up and identify themselves? I've been a trapper here my whole life. That never works. Hey, bear! Admit it! You're a bear, now give me yer fur!" He began to laugh and took another sip, letting the flask empty, and held it up.

"There's a spring over there. I'm heading that way to get some water. Good luck to your idiot hunt."

Delton continued walking towards them and made his way to where he pointed. When he got close, he threw his five darts. Two of the three crossbows twanged. Though they both missed, one hit the Orcus skin. Dodging the bolts and taking the impact of the one that did hit threw Delton's balance off enough that his own dart toss went bad. Three struck one of the crossbowmen. The other two missed.

From behind, the ground rose up as a hidden fighter jumped up and attacked Delton's flank. The sword strike was good, hitting right between his shoulder blades. It should have skewered him. Instead, the Jade God's skin blunted the attack. The force of the stab threw Delton stumbling forward to the three crossbowmen.

All around, Delton's crew ran forward firing at the ambushers with their short bows. Delton noticed the original three get distracted by the sudden onslaught. Not wishing to lose the opportunity, he leapt forward, tumbling under a crossbow swung like a truncheon, and grabbed one of the bone darts protruding from the middle one. "I'm your friend! Defend me!"

The crossbowman, caught in the middle of reloading, nodded. Locking the bolt into place, he fired nearly point blank at his friend, the tracker. Delton threw one of the darts at the other and grinned when he saw it sink in. Though the darts did not do much damage, they were quite powerful when used the way Delton just had. Soon he would have another ally; he just needed to touch the bone and give an instruction.

Finn shot at a dark shape in the trees. The figure dropped to the ground and charged him. A silent combat ensued as Finn drew his gladius and used his bow as an improvised shield. He recognized his opponent as the tracker who had spoken with Delton earlier in the day. At first, Finn thought poorly of his chances, but when the tracker began making clumsy mistakes, Finn realized the truth: they're more exhausted than we are!

The thought boosted his morale and he redoubled his efforts, worried less about precision and more about scoring hits. He thrust forward, making an obvious feint. When the tracker fell for it, he slammed the shaft of his short bow alongside the tracker's head. The blow should have sent the tracker reeling back but there was not enough strength in their attacks. This obvious sign of failure renewed Finn's worry about how they might fare. He knew what he needed to do, but exhaustion made everything he did slow and weak. At least Joust smiled on them and their opponents were similarly affected by fatigue.

The tracker tried to kick Finn back and open a space to slice at him with a scimitar. Instead, Finn blocked the scimitar with his bow. The cut string prevented the attack from having any momentum and their weapons tangled. Locked nearly face to face now, Finn slammed his forehead into the tracker's nose. The plan looked good until the tracker did the same thing. They fell back, their foreheads stinging. Finn stumbled to one knee and waved his blade around hoping to keep the tracker at bay. When the stars in his vision cleared, he saw his enemy doing the same thing.

Not trusting his footing, Finn crawled forward trying to be as quiet as possible. Though the tracker flailed about hoping to keep Finn at bay, Finn got close enough and when the scimitar moved past, he grabbed it and pinned it to the ground. His short sword found the tracker's face and he sheathed it deep in the man's neck. He held him there, in his death throes, careful to keep the scimitar pinned. After too much time, the tracker's struggles ceased and a bloody rasp of a last breath told Finn it was over.

Twilight was a terrible time to fight. The lighting made everyone essentially blind and turned terrain flat. Distances became hard to read and yet, Finn took hope from Delton standing at the summit with two crossbowmen. Several of the ambushers had fallen to bolts while Delton's group, though wounded, appeared to be quickly winning. A battle nearby caught Finn's notice and he turned to see Kasey grappling with an ambusher. Their numerous wounds, and their swords lying discarded on the ground, told the story of how their fight had gone. Finn stood up on shaking legs and drew his sword from the tracker's mouth. He thought about throwing it – he was excellent with thrown blades – but decided against it.

When Kasey and his attacker fell back, Finn charged in and tackled Kasey's opponent. Finn felt a dagger cut into his lower back. It gave Kasey the edge he needed and the next attack struck true. As Finn had with the tracker, they carefully ensured the man's death before turning to help their friends.

They must have been the last ones fighting. Delton called out, "Well done," and clapped the two crossbowmen on their shoulders. "Now that you've defended me, please help the survivors. You have *healing* potions?"

One of the men replied. "We used them all catching up to you."

"Oh," Delton answered. His knives cut their throats and they both fell over dead, completely taken by the surprise attack.

Of them all, Kasey had the worst wounds, closely followed by Finn. Delton fussed over their wounds and said, "Well, this takes care of our immediate enemies. We have a choice now, team. Do we press on for the security of our hideout or rest here until we're all feeling better? Remember, there's a paladin just a few days behind us. Maybe they can help, but maybe not. Without Grant, I leave it to you all to decide. My vote is that we continue on after we clean up and take a nap here."

Kasey raised his hand. Multiple gashes crisscrossed his palm showing that he must have grabbed a blade at some point in his battle. "I'm not as hardy as you, lieutenant. I tried a *healing* potion. It did nothing. I'm toxic. I bet the others are too. I want to keep going and get to our base, but I'm a liability right now."

Several others nodded their heads. Delton felt it too. Though he had yet to require magical healing, he knew he was close to needing it just to keep moving. He wondered, in that moment, how Grant was doing and what Grant would do in this situation. Tentatively, he said, "If Grant were here, he'd say something like, 'Who can run to the base without stopping?'" Delton tried to mimic Grant and though they smiled, exhaustion proved too much for anyone rise to the attempted humor. Delton tried to smile anyway. "Okay, the boss isn't here. We're going to make a fire. I'm going to stand guard. You're all going to sleep – real actual sleep – and do your best to recover. I'm waking you meatbags up in ten hours."

Finn asked, "You're not going to rest?"

"Not a wink, Finn. I'm going to ensure all of you do. Any disobedience and you're out of Rogue's Guild. Maybe you can go get a nice bouncer job at The Twins, or as a boring fence at 521. Now, you might have to carry me tomorrow…"

Delton looked around and saw they had all collapsed. Most just slumped forward, face first into the short mountain grass clinging to the summit. The area around them was splotched in blood. Kasey was bad and Delton tried to tighten bandages around the wounds he could see. After Kasey, he checked on Finn. Both had critical wounds that bled through the bandages. Delton prayed to Joust that they endure the night. At least their attackers had made a fire ready.

As night fell, the firelight illuminated the circle of the nearly-dead team. Delton paced the circle stopping every few turns to check on Kasey and Finn. The others had wounds too, but not as bad. Several times, Finn labored to breath and Delton tried to wake him up. Nothing helped, but the rogue stayed alive.

At one point, Delton fell back and breathed deeply while starring at the stars, but really nothing. His eyes felt so heavy. He forced himself to roll back over and to stand up. He did not trust himself to stay awake. He checked on his team, bandaged some still bleeding wounds, and added wood to the fire along with a Tanian warmth rune. The fire helped shake off the cold and he did his best to bundle the team in their bedrolls. Even with the enchanted weather gear, getting comfortable helped improve rest. The night would be cold up here in the mountains and boots and cloaks alone would not help them endure it. Tending to their bed rolls helped him stay awake for at least a few hours.

Delton startled upright and waved his short sword around. He had dozed off again. The fire had dimmed to embers and the bright stars overhead told him he must have been out for at least two hours. The respite did not help him. His legs and hands had gone numb and so Delton pulled his cloak more tightly about him and went to check on the team.

Kasey did not respond. The man's skin felt clammy and lifeless. Forcing despair away, Delton leaned over and checked Kasey's breath, and then frantically felt for a pulse with numb fingers. After a minute, Delton collapsed on top of Kasey's corpse... and dozed off again.

When Delton next opened his eyes, he found the sun already risen in the eastern sky. Delton jumped up but found his legs and feet, his arms had gone numb. He stumbled and fell over groaning in agony. The wet dew did not help improve the misery of the morning. Next to him, Kasey's blue-gray body lay motionless as spring insects began to flit about the clearing. The rest of the crew, thankfully, had survived the chill night and Delton forced himself to walk. That was when he noticed Finn, or rather the saturated puddle of blood under his back. Finn, like Kasey, had passed in the night.

Joust strike me dead too, please, Delton mentally swore. On the third lap around the clearing, he noticed a short figure leaning against a boulder. It was a Halfling and he was watching him.

Delton grabbed his sword hilt and quietly drew it halfway. "How long have you been there? What do you want?" he hissed. He meant to sound menacing but his words slurred.

When the Halfling smiled to show vampiric eye teeth. In the sunlight, Delton knew how delirious he had become. Brandishing his sword, he moved forward. "Answer me!"

The Halfling stepped up to meet him, not threatening but not exactly friendly either. He had jet black skin as if he were painted the color of the night sky. "I'm Kaia. I've been here since you summited last night. Well, if you want to get particular, I've been following your group since you left Bloodstone." Kaia walked right up and took the sword out of Delton's still tingling fingers. "You're so weak right now a stiff breeze would kill you, Delton. I like your bluffing spirit though." Kaia reached up and tapped Delton in the chest with two fingers. The force of that tap sent Delton stumbling backwards. "Here, amongst all these dead bodies, it might work against someone not aware of who you are and what you carry."

Delton stared at his hands and body, which had yet to wake up and begin working. He could not remember any other time he had felt so helpless. Numb and unfeeling, his body let the Halfling disarm him. Then, Kaia stabbed Delton's sword into the ground. Delton saw several of the Halflings swim in his vision as he struggled to remain alert. He asked, "Why? No, I mean, what do you want?"

Kaia walked over to the fire and it burst into warmth anew. "Come. Sit, Delton. What I want is simple: a trade. What you want, I think, is more complicated. I had thought Grant would be my quarry. You humans are so amusing. Who knew Grant would be so two-dimensional and typical? You, Delton, on the other hand are a complicated mess of loyalty, ambition, and possibilities. Of course, I could just take what I want from you, but I don't work that way." Kaia patted the ground by him by the fire.

Delton felt no imminent threat though something about the Halfling seemed familiar, like he would remember it if he were not so tired. "A deal. Okay, let's deal. What do you want from me exactly?" The fire gave off more warmth than it should and feeling began returning to Delton's hands. He rubbed them in the heat and felt the world spin around him with vertigo.

"Yes, let's," Kaia said. An iron kettle appeared in the fire and Kaia withdrew it steaming. "Here, sip. Drink. Recover some strength. You're so stretched by magic use and exhaustion that you're practically drowning in the River. Sorry, that's a Tanian adage. What I mean is that this tea will help you feel better but it won't actually help you. You and your team are beyond anything I might do until you all rest up."

"Beyond help? No, we've almost made it."

Kaia pointedly said, "Kasey did not make it, nor Finn, right? What would Grant say? No, you're actually quite far from making it. You see, while your base is safe, you are not. You're all walking zombies and that paladin you saw earlier? He's looking for you. He's not actually a paladin. He's a vampire wearing armor to protect him from daylight. And, your attackers last night? They were too tired from racing you to the summit to correctly identify you. I might have helped with that. You're welcome. So, my offer is quite simple: I'll help you all get to your base."

"A vampire?" Delton almost asked. Instead, he took a sip of the drink. Medicinal herbs burned his throat and he recognized several stimulants and a healing potion. Something about Kaia's manner of talking made everything he said seem reasonable and true.

Kaia pulled some cooked rabbit from the fire and offered some to Delton. There had not been a rabbit there before. "Now, why would I tell you such a thing? Not knowing is half the fun of being you. To the deal then. You have cargo that you're trying very hard to hold on to. You know it's worth a lot. But, you don't know what is happening with your leader. You don't know where you are. You don't know who is hunting you. So, at first glance, you want to get to where your leader told you to go. But, you also want to protect the cargo. And, you also want the wealth it represents, Delton. But, tell me, what is it that you truly want?"

The conversation seemed like something from a dream, where a magical creature appears and offers wishes. "What do you want?" Kaia's question prompted images of money, power, fame, adoration by beautiful women, a legacy, not having to run and fight anymore... it all ran through Delton's mind. He knew he was not thinking clearly because food kept appearing from the fire and he was talking with an impossibility – a black-skinned Halfling with vampire fangs.

Delton snorted. "I'm so tired I can barely focus, and you ask me what I truly want. It depends. I suppose right now, I just want to get my team to the base safely. Once there and recovered, I'll be able to answer this question better. Kind of an odd early morning, brink of death kind of conversation to have, isn't it?"

"Oh, these are the best kinds to have," Kaia said, patting Delton's knee. "As to the deal, what do I get if I help you all get to your safe base?"

"Well, you already know what I carry and haven't taken it from me. So, you must want something else." Delton struggled to think and after a minute gave up. "You're talking to me. I must have something you want that maybe cannot be taken?" Kaia snorted into his own tea. It gave Delton the sense it could be taken. "What do you want? I can't really push images into your mind, but let's pretend I am. What can a thief offer you?"

Kaia grew quiet and stirred the fire with a crossbow bolt. "I want to go home and rule like I am meant to. But, curse them. Curse them all. I am denied this. For now." The ferocity in Kaia's voice shook Delton while at the same time awakening a part of him that wanted to fight for and serve this strange person. "Your leader, by the way, just had his arm cut off by a traitor Grant thought was a friend. You won't be surprised to know that Grant has some assets you don't know about. He'll be all right, probably. So, now you that. Now, you tell me, Delton. Why do you serve Grant the way you do? Could you serve me that way? You ask what I want and it's that: to take back my home and rule as king of my people."

Feeling more confident and increasingly secure with this odd person, Delton answered. "I serve Grant because, for years, he has never led me down the wrong path. I've seen others doubt his leadership and perish. He saved me from poverty. He saved me from countless bad decisions by which I would have died or been imprisoned. Through these, I have come to know that not only can I count on Grant, but I can absolutely trust him even when all seems hopeless or his orders don't make sense to me. Grant has become my hope. I don't know why I'm telling this to you as a total stranger. I must be closer to death than I thought."

Kaia chuckled. "You have no idea, Delton. None at all how thin your and your team's lifeforces are right now." He watched the flames for a bit and at last said brightly, "Excellent! It's been a while since I've had a servant. I promise, I will not lead you astray. My orders to you will not make sense but the outcomes will move us both to where we want to be. Do you accept this deal by which I will save those of you still living and get you all to your base?"

Delton blinked in confusion and looked around. His team remained asleep on the edge of death. "This is just a dream," he said to the smiling Kaia. "Sure. I will be your servant and you will be my Grant."

At those words, a black disc of magic energy opened across the fire. "Go ahead, poke your head in," Kaia said. "It's your base."

Delton felt uneasy but because Kaia could have easily killed them all, he shrugged and looked in after poking his hand through. The portal opened into the common quarters of their underground base. Kaia dragged two of the team, one in each hand, through the portal and dropped them on the floor while Delton looked around. "This dream is so weird," Delton muttered as he stepped through at last. "You shouldn't be able to do this. Grant explained it to me once, something about not being able to use gates or teleportation because of anti-scrying enchantments."

"Grant is sort of correct. This location should not be accessible unless I've already been here." A few more trips and Kaia brought the bodies of their assailants through as well. "Don't want to clue anyone in to the fact you won. I'm going to keep these two." He pointed his finger at two of the dead bodies. Both twitched with dark energy as they jerked to unlife and stood up as zombies. "You two," Kaia said. "Make a trail southwards for a hundred steps and then veer off to the east. Travel fast but with heavy footsteps that leave clear foot prints. You will die at the third dawn's rise." Kaia shoved them back through the portal, then closed it.

Delton watched all this as if it were happening to someone else. "So, thank you," he said to Kaia. The room spun and blurred.

Delton woke up to find the entire group, except Kasey and Finn, washed and lying asleep on cots. The cavern was much warmer than it had been, no doubt thanks to the glowing heatstones Delton saw on the floor. Delicious smells wafted through the air and Delton struggled to sit up.

Kaia appeared from the kitchen and brought in a platter of meats, cheeses, and bread. Delton's stomach growled and Kaia said, "You weren't wounded like the others," Kaia said. "You have good luck. They'll all be out for at least another day, maybe longer. I've known humans who can war for days, but they're all paladins. It's impressive you stayed awake and alert for as long as you did. In some places, like Tania, I bet you'd be a paladin. No one would have had to save you from poverty because the Temple of Tiamat would have swooped you up into its very military embrace. It's too bad your life only offered you thievery."

"How long was I asleep?" Delton wondered.

"Three days. You've been out for three days. Well, today is the third morning. The zombies already died. I felt it just an hour ago. Here, eat." Kaia put a tray of crisped and fried meat on the cot next to him where the breads and cheeses already rested. "We have things to discuss. And, when you were a kid, before Grant, what did you want to be when you grew up?"

Delton did not feel any different but seeing his team safe and resting, he told himself that he had done the right thing. Looking at the Halfling now, with less pressing concerns than pure survival, he recognized Kaia. "You're the Halfling we've heard stories about from Tania, right? The one who makes deals to the eternal regret of those interacting with you." He tried to say the last part like a joke.

Kaia grinned and flicked the tips of his fangs with his tongue. "I'm not really a Halfling, but I'm sure you've figured that out by now. Look, I don't want you or 'us' to get overly caught up in concepts like "eternal regret." I want you to focus on doing the same things you've always done. The only difference is that you now work for me and from time to time, I might need you to do something. I like to come and go as I please so, when I'm not around, you're free to do whatever you want. When you were a kid, what was the whatever you wanted to be?"

"A healer," Delton said. "I wanted to wear a white mantle over full plate armor. I thought the war hammers were so neat." He chuckled and imagined Kaia rolling his eye, but instead saw Kaia listening intently.

Delton could not resist the food and started eating. Feeling his own ribs and seeing how sunken and ghastly everyone looked helped reinforce his feelings that agreeing to the deal was going to work out for him, for the team. The food tasted like the best meal he had ever had, the best he could imagine. A wash of gratitude came over him and he said, "Thank you, Kaia."

Kaia had gotten up and was checking on the rest of the team. At Delton's words, the Halfling jumped and whirled as if struck by something. Delton felt a mild electric tingle along his fingernails and shook it off his hands. "What was that?" Kaia demanded, eyes looking around the room and then at Delton. "What did you to me?"

Delton looked equally surprised and Kaia relaxed a bit. Delton said, "I don't know. Nothing. Something. I just wanted to say thank you. Kasey was beyond saving. I guess Finn too. Even if we'd had a priest, we were all so right on the edge. We would all be dead were it not for you. Thank you." The effect this time, no less sincere than the first, brought back the tingling feeling and Kaia felt it too. Delton saw him get goosebumps along his arm.

"Interesting," Kaia said watching the skin on his arm. He returned to his careful inspection of the team. "I've had this described to me but never actually felt it. Well, I've felt it, just not this close. Apparently being almost dead boosts how you feel about things, huh? Alerius tried to explain it to me several times. Very interesting."

"Alerius? You mean…"

"Yes, the red dragon who rules Morbatten. He's a friend."

Delton finished chewing and took another sip of water. He cleared his throat. "So, you said you weren't a Halfling. You're clearly Tanian. How does that work where I'm a Soran? And what, might I know, are you?"

Kaia's eyes sparkled, "I'm an accidental Tanian, not by choice mind you. Don't get too hung up on it. I'm a Hell Lord in exile, Delton. Welcome to the family. Are you ready for your first assignment?" Kaia's black within black eyes sparkled.

Delton felt a sense of mischief creep through his recovering fatigue. "A hell lord?"

"Yes. One of the strongest. And, my brothers await my return. Want to have some fun?"

The twinkle of red light in Kaia's eyes filled Delton with an energized sense of foreboding. In that moment, he could see a barren rockscape. No creatures moved on it but the place seethed with hidden eyes. "I don't know how I, as a human, would help a hell lord, but sure. Why not?"

* * *

Ash punched the wall and cursed at Tiamat, Pha Rann, and Joust. So many things were going so well but so many others were falling apart. He had always counted on Khalla and yet, word already came from Halgrim that she moved against him.

The Tanian adage of "dragons and women" came to his mind. It referred to the inscrutable and dire nature of either when they did not get what they want. Not a single elf had signed on once told the destination. Having been equivocal about Reznor's offer, he wondered if the Mages Guild thwarted him out of spite. It seemed like something a Tanian archmage like Reznor might do. "I should just go talk to Ynt'taris," he grumbled. The idea sounded terrible even as he said it.

His walk took him to Halgrim's shop off the Great Bazaar. It looked like it always did: small, boring, cheap. Ash walked in and shouted for Halgrim. Even if not there, Halgrim would hear him. Moments later, a serving girl came out of the back room. "Master Halgrim is busy at the Mages Guild and sends his regrets." Her musical voice rang out clear and perfect as if played by a minstrel. "He says to come back at sunset and he can talk to you. He also says that you're overthinking things and to accept the deal. Or else accept Khalla in her new role. He is particularly concerned that you and Khalla are not getting along. He adds that both he and Khalla have accepted the deal and hope you will too."

Her voice, too perfect to be human, annoyed Ash. He touched his ear and stroked the mithril spider golem dangling there. After learning that Sai's golems had personalities, he had named the spider Twist. He glared at the serving girl and said, "Halgrim, you idiot. Accepting this deal changes Merakor from a fun anything-goes adventure to a mission. Our own adventure, we live, we run, we find stuff, and we profit. If things get bad, we can escape. A mission though, suddenly we're risking our lives for things that we may not even be able to get. It's been three thousand years. Who's to say this stuff is even there still? Worse, what if the Drow have it?"

The serving girl put her hand on her hip and with that same perfect but now ironic tone of voice said, "Then we will enter the Underdark and do our best to get it. Think about it, Ash. The wonders of the Underdark! No one has been there in millenia either."

"Damn it. Tiamat burn you all," Ash said, turning to leave.

"Wait, Ash," the girl said, catching his sleeve. "Halgrim wishes to ask you if it isn't time to give up the secrets of that room. You love Khalla. She loves you. Let this end. You two are perfect for each other. Khalla knows it. It's high time you know it too. You probably meant well by telling her about Kaia, but you have to understand, for her, she still feels like you're choosing a past deal with the Halfling over her. Figure it out!"

Ash pulled free and stepped back outside. Annoyed, he turned right and walked off not even bothering to try and blend into the crowd. It took him the entire distance to the Dragon Fountain to calm down. Nearly a mile and, through the crowd, an hour of walking. He sat down on the marble lip of the fountain and then laid back to look up at the bright blue sky dotted by iridescent white puffs of clouds. The sunlight felt warm against the chill of the stone and occasional splashes of water. Birds soared in the air and Ash wished he could...

"You've only got one Elf so far," a familiar voice interrupted Ash's wishing. "And she's beautiful and skilled. A worthy Marcello."

Ash looked up and found a hooded beggar sitting next to him. Gleaming purple fire rimmed mischievous eyes that looked at him from the shadows of the cowl. Ash sat up, careful to be respectful but also mindful of the public setting. "Daryx, you do me great honor. How may I serve?"

"Secrets and secrecy," Daryx said.

Ash struggled to find meaning in the Dar's words and shrugged when it felt awkward that he did not understand. "I do not understand."

"Right now, you are putting all this effort into hiding the fact that you are not really you." Daryx rattled a cup held in bandaged hands and Ash dropped a gold coin into it. "Just a gold coin? I come all the way here to speak with you, in disguise, and all I get is a single gold coin?"

Ash ignored the taunting. Giving a beggar more would draw attention from the other beggars in the area. On a whim, Ash looked for them. He was not surprised to see that all of the beggars nearest him were disguised soldiers, from Daryx's estate no doubt. Daryx recruited the best of the best. "To what do I owe the honor of a visit like this?"

"You have potential to rule Perdition. Yet, when offered, you turn it down. Now Khalla wants it. You recommended her for it. You actually gave it to her, yes? And, she never really took it until yesterday. What are you afraid of?"

Ash stood up and began to pace. "After Dread Lord Ynt'taris gave me the map, I thought that would be enough, at least for a while. I've dedicated my whole life…"

Daryx cut him off. "And you want, you feel that you deserve a vacation?" Daryx began to laugh. "To Merakor?" The dry laugh became genuine mirth when Daryx finally coughed and said, "You don't think the god emperor knew his brother, his best friend, his fellow patriarch and ruler here for millennia, gave you this map? The tower is Alerius', not Ynt'taris'. Have you become mad since you entered into this entitled vacation mindset? You're not that naïve, Marcello."

Listening to Daryx, Ash felt the words stab at him like daggers. A quiet, if paranoid, voice had been whispering this to him for months. *Of course, the other dragons know about it.* He stopped pacing and faced Daryx. "It sounds naïve and ignorant when you say it that way, my lord. I suppose I had hoped that after a lifetime of service, this one thing might truly be mine."

Daryx stood and put his arm around Ash. "My dear Marcello. It's all yours. No one forced you to capture a winter wolf and give it to Ora. Yet look at the rewards! Consider that you were not required to do this but did and now, at a whim, you could speak with Ora, the Ice Priestess. Many already consider her the Queen of Morbatten! You did not have to take the kinetic ice to Bomoki, but did in a most creative way – not even knowing the reward. If we go farther back in time, you have had an amazing career. What isn't yours that you still hope for something that is, as you said, 'mine?' Had Ynt'taris offered you the reward up front would you have balked at the Ice Patriach? No, Marcello would have said something about 'pleasure to serve' and 'patriotic duty.'"

Talking this way, it made Ash feel a compulsive restlessness grow. He also felt a tugging in his mind and his heart began to race. Maybe sensing it, Daryx dug his fingers into Ash's shoulder. "You made a deal with the Halfling Kaia, like so many others. Do you regret it now?"

Ash found he could not speak and so nodded his head. Someone was approaching the room and its secret, which Ash must defend at all costs. He had felt it for years with Khalla. The difference this time was intent to enter at all costs. He knew Khalla wanted in, but her stealth defeated her ever actually entering. The disquiet he was feeling could only mean that Khalla or someone else was going in, no matter what. Realizing the room would soon be breeched, Ash began to sweat; Daryx was not going to let him leave. He felt the faint tinglings of Kaia's geas on him, that he must do something.

"Daryx..." he whispered through dry lips. He fingers twitched and he quickly picked out the fastest route out of the Dar's perimeter. Just as he noted it, a woman in the garb of a mother stepped into his vision. She carried a basket of fruit, and Ash noted the jewelry and hidden wands of a sorcerer.

"No," the Drow responded. "Secrets die. This one must die so that you may live, Marcello. I chose you, not Khalla. She is worthy, but Merakor is more important than a lover's squabble. Perdition is more important than Merakor. Khalla may very rule after you, but she is too young and as of yet immature."

"I could die," Ash whispered.

"Marcello is dead. Long live Marcello!" Daryx spat back at him sarcastically. "If you move, I will slay you right here. You won't be the first Marcello I have trained up only to later slay."

\* \* \*

Far across town, Khalla led her team towards Ash's house. "Nice area," Ciejek commented. They all wore the clothing of higher paid workers and servants. The others commented on the neighborhood too. No one bothered them.

When they reached Ash's estate, Ryvane was waiting for them. Khalla deftly popped the door open with the key Ash had given to her years ago. That drew a wolf whistle and Khalla punched Ciejek, hard. "Focus," she ordered. Ciejek gave her a wounded look and stepped back. *Fun Khalla was gone*, he kept reminding himself since Bloodstone.

In no time, they stood in the room before the door Khalla had wasted years trying to pick. She noted the dagger mark on the surface and wondered if Ash was all right. "Ryvane, I've tried to pick this lock forever. At this point, I just want the cursed door open."

Ryvane nodded as the others pulled out heavy tower shields and lined them up in front of the door. Once the shields were in place, Ryvane pointed the wand at the door. Khalla had witnessed many *knock* spells cast before, but Ryvane's had a brutal quality to it. The door thudded as if struck by a battering ram. Ryvane triggered the spell again and then gave the wand to Khalla. "Keep triggering it at the lock."

Ryvane began casting her own spell and this time, the lock and hinges began to heat, pulsating in waves until they glowed red and began to melt. The edges of the wooden door around the hinges began to burn and smoke filled the room. Ryvane enacted a cantrip to clear the smoke, and then changed her spell and cast a different one. This spell crystallized the door into ice. Twisted by the *knock* spells battering it and the lock and hinges melting, the sudden temperature change caused the door and the surrounding stone frame to explode apart.

A number of needle darts fired from the door frame. The trap types were specific to thieves, hidden and aimed at blind spots in Tania's thief training. They smacked into the tower shields.

Ryvane took the wand back from Khalla and pointed it at the door. Her spell slammed against the door and it cracked apart. The smoking ruin of the entry had just barely cleared when Khalla jumped forward and dove through it. Doing so, she barely avoided being hit by *paralysis* magic that radiated into the outer room. Ryvane and the others, except Pol Nir, were partially caught and paralyzed. "They're all right," Pol called to them. "We'll be tied up, but I'm coming through once the traps are done discharging."

"Use Ciejek as bait," Khalla called back.

Pol smirked at Ciejek and said to him, "Aren't you lucky you haven't ruined my life yet?" The door behind them attempted to seal itself shut, but Pol slammed a prybar into the gap and wedged the door open. A moment later, sleeping gas began hissing into the room. "It's going to be a while, Khalla!"

* * *

Back at the fountain, Ash felt the door break and fell to his knees as magical sirens activated in his head. He saw Khalla and her cell break the door open. Khalla dove through and was in the room! Most of the traps were failsafes designed to incapacitate. Ash did not want to kill whoever found his secret... well, he wanted the option to kill whoever found it.

The sensations flooded through him and Ash realized that maybe he should not have stacked them all that way. The mental visual of Khalla in her agent gear tore at his heart and he dropped to his face on the stone ground at Daryx's feet. His body trembled as he fought to resist running to defend the secret. He screamed into the dusty stone at his face, "Yes, Daryx. I regret it every day since I met her!"

Daryx put his hand on Ash's head and chanted in the alien language of the Drow. It reminded Ash of a prayer but made his skin crawl. Resigned peace replaced the knot of dread in his gut. Any minute now Khalla would know and Ash would either live or die, would either retain her love or would not.

Daryx patted his head and said, "If she truly loves you, your secret is survivable. And, you will be free. I'm shocked Khalla waited this long. You have no idea how annoying your secret has been to me, Marcello."

Khalla uncovered leather flaps on her bracers and soft magical light glowed to illuminate the room. Simple stone, elementally bound, formed a cube to mask its presence from the outside and along hallways and other interior spaces. To her trained eyes, the room exactly matched what she thought it should be. So, at least there were no other secret rooms in this area. The stone to the outside of the manor's walls had to be at least a pace thick. Ash had built this room to be impregnable.

A coffin-like box stood upright along the wall at the end of the room opposite from the door drew her eye. The coffin, after her recent time in Bloodstone, heightened her fear and she forced herself to take a deep breath. Gingerly, she stepped towards it, eyes searching for pressure plates or other trap mechanisms. She found none.

With each step, the room grew colder until she felt the coffin's surface and realized how deadly cold it was. Using a knife, she scraped at the gray ice she had thought was stone. Chips peeled off, then larger pieces, and she saw a face inside. She quickly cleared an area but felt her hand begin to tremble when enough ice cleared that she could see. It was Ash.

Ash, frozen and speckled with ice, rested in the box. His face was crusted with frost, but she could tell by his skin color that he was not dead. "What is going on?" Khalla muttered while chewing her lip.

From outside, Pol Nir called, "Everything okay? You need help, boss?"

"I'm fine," Khalla said, trying to sound okay. Ash's eyes sat closed and lifeless in the freezing box. "No traps in here. Hey, I need some time. No one come in, okay?"

"Got it. They're all paralyzed still anyway, and sleeping gas now too. All's clear out front too. Let me know," Pol Nir shouted.

Khalla used her arm sleeve to clear the rest of ice. It *was* Ash, there was no doubt about it. But as more frost cleared, she noticed that it also was not Ash. At least, it could not be the Ash she knew. His left arm lay bound to his side and she could tell from it shape that the limb was wrong; it was too small and the fist was in the wrong place. Frustration and anxiety grew in her heart and she shoved the coffin to its side. It thudded to the ground and she called out, "Pol, I'm okay. Stay where you are," to the team outside.

She looked for a way to open the stone but it eluded her. "Pol, I need Ryvane's *knock* wand. Just throw it in here."

A moment later, the wand clattered in and Khalla aimed it at the edge of the box. Thankful that Tania included training for the use of magic items like this, Khalla recited Ryvane's activation word. The box trembled. At the second pulse of energy, the box cracked open. Khalla tucked the wand into her belt and pulled at the cracks until the stone cut and blistered her fingers into a bleeding mess. Still, she kept lifting until the lid gave way.

Khalla put her arms around Ash and pulled him out. The cold body slid out on ice forming around it. She felt for a pulse and looked for some magical rune or anything that might revive him. Not finding any, she looked for several scars Ash had. This Ash had none of those.

The withered left arm nagged her and she unwrapped it. As the linen binding came undone, she found her suspicions confirmed: it was a birth defect. The arm terminated into long curled fingernails just below a tiny upper arm and malformed elbow. Unsure if she felt horror or terrible fascination at it, Khalla realized she had never seen any children or adults in Tania with defects like this. The Temple tended to remove them at birth. What happened to them, no one knew. Elves did not really have birth defects like this and while Orcs and other races might, Khalla did not spend enough time with them to know.

Hoping for answers, Khalla unwrapped more of the bindings but did not find other defects. She feared that there might be chaos marks, but at least along the upper torso, she found none. Prying his eyes open, she noted dull cataracts along the left eye. "Oh Ash, what happened to you? Who are you?" Though not dead, the frozen body was not alive either and did not answer.

Back at the Great Bazaar, Daryx locked Ash in an embrace. Not brotherly or tender, the embrace conveyed a threat against leaving. Ash carefully held Daryx and prayed to Tiamat for help. "Did you know," Daryx said, "that all of Kaia's deals are recorded for The Circle to review? For the most part, we only ever check when someone rises to R'Dar and later to Dar. I've known this whole time and it did not change my assessment of you as Marcello. Why are you so concerned that Khalla will fall out of love with you?"

Ash whispered. "She holds my life in her hands. That was the deal. A chance at life free of the curse of my birth. A life free of that until my secret is discovered by someone who loves me. Did Kaia tell the Circle that if Khalla rejects me, I will die?"

Daryx nodded. "That's why I'm here for you, child of dragons. What your parents did, what your mother did, is unforgivable. She was punished. Not horribly, but in an appropriate way. Your father never knew you existed, which is as it has always been with high ranking priestesses. The god emperor has long observed that mortal love is irrational. I suppose divine love is as well."

Daryx tilted Ash's face to his own so that Ash would see him. "Do you think she'll choose to love you still?"

# Chapter 8 – R'Dar Alex and Valaes

Alex and Valaes held hands as they walked away from the Mages Guild. Niss' estate had been a gift. One they had enjoyed until time took them to their meeting with Dar Reznor. The magic of their time together, and now this strangest of offers, made it hard to talk. Valaes squeezed her hand reassuringly.

Strangers on the road gave the young priestess and dashing priest room as they walked by. Their attire, and the emblems of their service to Tiamat, ensured their space. Many of the older citizens pointed to their holding hands and wished them well. Finally, Alex broke the silence. "Merakor… is real."

Valaes nodded. "And we've been invited."

"Ordered," Alex corrected him.

"You're the sister of a hero. I'm the son of Jan. We were invited. But, yes. Maybe it was a firm invitation."

Alex leaned into him and gave him a hug. "Either way, Merakor."

He nodded. They walked east towards Dockside. Reznor had told them where to go. A broad intersection continued their path to the warehouse district. Instead, they turned northwards and walked along the edge of the Temple Mount. As they walked, the housing went from well-maintained and trafficked by people on the street to shoddy and ill-maintained. The farther they went, it eventually became abandoned. Though they felt watchful eyes on them, no one bothered them. As clerics, they could go anywhere in Tania and be safe. Still, neither had been in this area and they felt on edge.

Another hour and they found a ramshackle building, just as Reznor had described. Entering, they found that it fronted a tunnel entrance into the Temple Mount. Alex prayed and gentle light began radiating from her hand. The tunnel proved only several hundred paces before it opened into a box canyon with steep cliff walls rising on all sides. The west and north cliffs no doubt rose to the Temple itself another thousand paces above them.

Before them, the ancient fortress of Perdition loomed. Valaes whispered, "I thought this was a legend too."

Walking up the wide boulevard to the massive gates, Alex found herself holding Valaes' hand too tightly. She eased up, then let go. "I assume we're being watched. Let's enter this place like servants of the dragons."

Valaes nodded and they squared their shoulders and steadied their pace. When they reached the gates, they found a small human sized door built into the right side. Ajar, they could see a tiled courtyard beyond it. "Hello!" Valaes called. Only echoes and reverberations from the high cliff walls answered him. They shrugged and stepped through the door.

The walls and gate framed a giant courtyard with an old keep built in the center. High towers forming the points of a star would have allowed siege weapons to fire in any direction. Gray stone tile, just like the Temple had, raced out in all directions from the gates to the central keep. A straight boulevard of stone stretched out before them. They could only see it because traffic over centuries had slightly polished it. Valaes was about to walk forward when Alex caught his hand.

"Thieves Guild," Alex said. "There must be traps. Combine with me, please." He nodded and began praying to do so. It unnerved Alex how easily that command had come. *Maybe Tiamat wants me to lead, she wondered. Or, Valaes is just that used to following priestess orders from his time as a paladin?* Valaes' combination prayer merged his power to her like a warm sun. It brought with it his power and some of what he felt. Alex felt an excited energy and realized she was feeling his attraction for her. Even in this place, he wanted to kiss her, hold her, and be with her. The thrill of it and knowing he found her that attractive almost broke her composure.

Now combined, the two prayed and their quiet song harmonized until, between them and the central keep, stone tiles began to glow. Each glowing tile meant an unknown number of traps. They nodded and began to walk, careful to let their tremulous song ring out in the silence of this hidden place. They avoided the glowing tiles and walked a meandering but safe path. It took an hour to reach the central keep. Tall stairs led up to the keep's entryway some twenty paces above them.

A male voice interrupted their climb. "Well done, you two." They looked up and then dropped to their hands and knees before Daryx and Dar Shara. "To detect traps, in the safety of Morbatten, you are wise."

Daryx held his hand out, which Dar Shara took, and they descended the stairs. Behind Shara, the Dread Lord Armageddon appeared. He stayed at the top and looked out over the courtyard. When his gaze passed over Alex, she felt her skin prickle with heat, like campfire embers falling there. Dar Shara said, "I would expect no less from the sister of R'Dar

Thalian, hero of Bloodstone. Her courage and wisdom clearly stayed in the family. Tell me, Alex. Are you better than she?"

Alex felt compelled to answer and her words stuttered out of her. She did not want to answer impetuously but Shara's command gave her no choice. "My Dar, Thalian should have lived. I blame her lack of foresight for her death. I would be better than she was. I believe I will be."

Shara touched Alex's head and said, "Rise, daughter Alex. It is not a sin to hate the failures of those we love. Thalian, like you, served with all of her heart and soul. While it could be lack of foresight, there are not many who would endure the trial she faced at the end. When you get back to Dar Niss' estate, you will receive a messenger with an account by King Malcor. It describes the foes she faced and how her life ended as well as the purpose. If you are wise, like Thalian, you will understand what her sacrifice meant and why the Queen loves her. I command you to read this and let go of any ill feelings for you sister. You must be free for the adventure ahead."

"Thank you, my Dar," Alex said.

Daryx squatted down by Valaes. "Another battle priest. Another paladin turned cleric. The frequency of battle priests is climbing since Tembri's afterlife. This should please the empire. Tell me, Valaes. Which prayers do you orient your calling around?"

Without hesitation and with confidence Alex felt herself envying, Valaes said, "*Combine, resurrect,* and *firestorm.*"

"Combine?" Daryx asked in surprise. "Have you figured out how to weaponize this one?"

Valaes nodded. "Yes, my lord. It acts as a form of domination. Though I cannot control my opponent, I am able to access their experience and draw on their skills to make me more powerful. It's quite potent against sorcerers and creatures with innate abilities."

"Shara!" Daryx exclaimed. "This, I must see! Go on, I will not resist."

When Valaes saw that Shara approved, he began to sing the *combination* prayer again. Alex noted key differences from her experience with him earlier. For one, he did not touch anyone. Also, he seemed intently focused on Daryx and the words of this most basic prayer kept lilting and twisting. When finished, Valaes clapped his hands and purple *faerie fire* sprouted along his arms to outline his entire body. Valaes gestured and Alex began to levitate.

Daryx chuckled and showed some concentration in his eyes, but nothing happened. "You've taken my Nobleborn powers. How interesting! Did you take my resistance to enchantments, I wonder?"

"The advantage of combination," Valaes explained, "is that it's not an attack, nor is it even discernible to my target. Unless I take powers that can only be used infrequently, my target might not even know that it happened." Valaes steeled his voice and added, "In testing with the other battle priests – who thought I was insane to do this – we found it ignores creatures' magical resistance. Dread Lord Spark allowed us to test and I was able to breathe lightning, though it seared my mouth and broke my vocal chords. And, well, I died... But, it proved it is possible to capture a dragon's breath weapon. Of course, the Dread Lord cooperated and allowed it to happen."

Shara touched Alex's hand and removed the *levitation* effect. She said, "Valaes, that's quite an achievement. I am wondering why it was never reported to me. Nevermind, I will find out." Daryx and Shara both complimented the battle priest and then turned their attention back to Alex. Shara continued, "As Dar Reznor explained, the Merakor quest requires sacrifices. Specifically, I am here to ask you – and Valaes as well it seems – to play the role of Lolth clerics. Merakor is controlled by Lolth and this mission requires a freedom of movement and action that only a priestess of Lolth can bring."

Both Alex and Valaes found themselves watching Daryx as Shara said this. His impassive, if bemused, expression told them nothing. Shara continued, "This next part, I tell you in total confidence. You may only discuss it with members of The Circle. Please understand this. Tiamat has, for many ages, had an alliance of sorts with Lolth." Shara looked sideways at Daryx and, seeing the Drow impassive, she explained. "It's less an alliance and more of an understanding. I'm not even sure that's the right word for it. You'd think after centuries, we would have a better way of describing it. Daryx?"

The Drow shrugged. "Lolth is not able to make alliances. I would say my Goddess is fascinated with the dragons. It's a fascination."

Shara smiled and turned back to Alex. "There you have it. It's a fascination. A fragile one, like a single strands of webs. If you are both agreeable to this, and no one in the Temple will force you to make this choice or judge you ill for saying no, you will both be stripped of your emblems of Tiamat and they will be replaced by Lolth's. The Allegiance of Blood and other *geas* magic will bind you to Lolth. All of your clerical powers will be intact and you will not remember that you ever served

Tiamat. The magic will twist your thoughts so that you firmly believe, even under interrogation, that you serve Lolth. In fact, Tiamat will be powering you."

Shara paused and Daryx spoke. "You will do things that no cleric of Tiamat would ever do, that would require atonement if you did. That is Lolth's way there. But, you will be exonerated of these things, though perhaps your conscience will not let go so easily. I have been in Tania nigh on one thousand years and I am still haunted by regret from my time with the Drow." He laughed, "And my ways still make Tania uncomfortable. That is how deep Lolth's webs are spun."

Shara pulled Alex and Valaes to her step and embraced them both. Holding the backs of their heads, Shara said, "You will see marvelous things. You will do terrible things. But, Tiamat wishes for this to be. You are instructed to write letters to yourselves so that you remember this talk and also remember why you are doing it, and that I command you to forgive yourselves. Alex," Shara said, kissing her cheek and then her lips. "You will be a dire priestess of spiders." She then kissed Valaes the same way and said, "And you shall be her slave. Go now."

As they left, Daryx called out. "You have three days. Look for my servants then and plan to join me at my estate to study, and practice, until the world galleon leaves. Let your loved ones know you will be gone for up to three years."

* * *

RiVule and Taisha walked down the broad boulevard named East-West Minor. The humans gave them wide space and RiVule thumped his chest and mocked them to Taisha. He might have been more boisterous except for the cityscape tantalizing his eyes. Every three intersections a canal flowed with clear water to the south and it drew his eyes up to the three mountain peaks looming over the city. Without meaning to, they entered the Great Bazaar. Taisha suggested they see the Dragon Fountain and, free of the crowded merchants and shoppers all around, they arrived.

"What is this?" RiVule asked as he pointed to a beggar hugging a human of apparent wealth. "Why does the human not strike the fool down?"

Taisha put her hand on RiVule's arm. "Caution, great priest. These people, this religion does not care for society and rank the way our hordes do."

RiVule growled and then put his hand on her own. "I see. The human there is not a shopper." He pointed causally and Taisha caught sight of RiVule's interest. Dressed as a shopper, the human lounged against a lamp pole with his gaze locked on the beggar and the surrounding crowd.

Taisha noted a bandolier, just hidden by the short cloak, holding at least three wands. "Yes, a mage. That beggar, or the one being held by him, are not what they seem either," she said. "Very astute, Lord RiVule."

It became a game as RiVule quickly spotted another six bodyguards. When they identified one as a priestess, RiVule chuckled and strolled in her direction. Taisha tried to hold him back, but could not stop the foolhardy priest. RiVule walked towards the priestess and in a loud voice called out a challenge. "Cleric! Why sulk in shadows? Has Tiamat fallen so far that you do not proudly honor Her Name?" RiVule thumped the Gruustir symbol hanging as a medallion around his neck and pointed to the tattoo on his forehead.

The priestess looked concerned and quickly looked around to see if RiVule had drawn attention to her. RiVule pressed towards her, only stopping within sword distance. Taisha ran to RiVule as the other guards subtly moved to protect the priestess. "RiVule," she hissed in Orc. "This is a bad idea."

RiVule ignored her and spread his arms to the sun overhead. "I am RiVule, chosen of Gruustir. I am come to see Morbatten and grow weary of talk. My soul burns for combat against a dragon priestess. Will you not face me?"

Taisha crashed into his back and he heard her sword out of its scabbard. They stood in the center of a circle of weapons, all enchanted, all bearing dragon markings. The beggar and the human eyed them as well. Taisha noted the glowing purple eyes in the beggar cloak and felt her stomach knot with fear. Only one person in Tania had eyes like that. "RiVule…" she whispered but her voice was lost in the din as the guard mage enacted an *illusion* spell to mask their confrontation from onlookers' view.

"I am Dar Interi, priestess of Takhissis. I meet your challenge," she said tssing her cloak back. Fiery red hair burst into actual flame as a bladed mace appeared in her hand and shield materialized on her arm. "I do not know this name: RiVule. Are you truly chosen of Gruustir?"

RiVule answered her with a roar. "Too much talk!" His arm enlarged to the size of an ogre's and he punched Interi's shield. She raised it to block, clearly not interested in a real fight. "To the death!" RiVule said as his fist connected with augmented strength. The blow sent Interi stumbling back into the guards behind her, and left a dent in the shield.

RiVule saw Interi discard her shield and begin to pray. "You waste too much time singing!" RiVule said laughing. He jumped forward, mixing ogre strength with Orc dexterity. He cleared the distance and punched her again just before her prayer completed.

A column of fire erupted where RiVule had been and Taisha shrieked. "I'm not fighting!" RiVule heard her yell as she rolled out of the fire. Though burning, she quickly patted the fire out of her clothes. RiVule noted her hair had burned away completely. She was guilty of human vanity and considered her hair beautiful. RiVule howled in laughter.

The beggar said to Taisha, in perfect Orc, "But, clearly he is - fighting. Who are you?"

Interi finally brought her mace up to block another battering ram-like punch. The blades cut into RiVule's hand and he screamed out to Gruustir for the *regenerative* blessings of the trolls. His other hand twisted into a caricature of an ogre arm but ended in a more delicate set of fingers with black talons. This hand began twisting as if spell-casting and then lightning crackled from it at Interi as the other fist, already scabbed and healing, slammed down at her again.

The priestess vanished and reappeared behind RiVule to smash her mace at his leg. RiVule allowed the mace to hit and caught her neck with his black taloned hand. "Vanish again. I dare you," he hissed at her. Though his leg was shattered, he shifted his weight to the other and while squeezing with the clawed hand, slammed both hands together. Interi tried to vanish again but RiVule's taloned hand jerked and twitched but retained its hold on her.

"*Forbiddance*," RiVule said reverently in Orc. His hands closed together with a thunderclap and then he threw Interi back from him.

Spinning on his good leg, RiVule whirled through the circle of steel and said, "Are there no gods here who can stand against me?!"

Taisha was about to explain RiVule to the beggar, when the beggar vanished from her and reappeared before RiVule. "My goddess is here, *chelicera*. If you continue to disrespect…"

RiVule attacked the beggar. Though Daryx ducked, RiVule caught the beggar's cloak. RiVule's eyes gleamed when it became apparent he faced a Drow. RiVule put his head back and roared to the sky. The earlier boasting changed in pitch, becoming manic and insane with combat lust. "Yes. Yes!" RiVule leapt forward to press his attack.

Daryx dodged the attack and touched RiVule's side. With a blade, it would have been a lethal strike. RiVule's eyes went wide and he spun about to backhand Daryx, but missed again. Another tap, this time on the back of his neck, made him realize he was now twice dead. "That word, *chelicera*, what does it mean?"

"Spider...," Daryx said as he tapped RiVule's inner knee. Such an attack would cripple and if a cut deeply enough, bleed out the victim in seconds. "Fangs," Daryx finished as he drove the palm of his hand onto RiVule's heart.

Though not a hard hit, RiVule felt a sensation in each of the touched areas. RiVule thought he heard the Drow whispering in a language that must be Undercommon. Suddenly, an effect he had felt many times before bound him. The sensation spread out from each of the touch points, then seized his heart and lungs. Poison of a type common in cave-dwelling spiders took hold of RiVule and locked his movements. The priestess Interi protested. "My lord, I did not require assistance!"

RiVule began to laugh but felt his lungs unable to move. Lack of air threatened asphyxiation, but RiVule did not care nor did he want to let his victory over Interi go. He laughed and, though his words garbled for want of air, he said, "You're *sclavus*."

As he lost consciousness, he thought he heard Taisha say, "He means that by winning, Interi becomes his slave."

Interi moved to attack again but the Drow prevented her. *How interesting*, RiVule thought as he blacked out.

RiVule came to in the quiet of his mind, careful to keep his eyes closed and not move. He immediately noticed that he was not bound and did not seem drugged. He strained to hear and thought he detected Taisha's voice speaking in Tanian Common to others, possibly the priestess Interi. How he relished the glaring anger in that one's eyes when he named her sclavus!

Feeling no one near him, he prayed to Gruustir and felt the burning passion of the god in his chest. He opened his eyes and sat up. He lay on a plain but elegant bed in a stone room. The stone had the look of everything in Tania, of smooth seamless stonework as if carved from a monolithic block of granite. Light runes glowed behind tiles backcasting light onto the walls.

RiVule stretched, loving how the post-combat tension left him feeling relaxed. He had been well treated. Leaving the room, he found a corridor stretching to his right to Taisha's voice. To the left, it passed several doors and opened into a larger room full of silver radiance as if reflecting off water. RiVule turned left.

As he drew near the hallway's end, his skin began to tingle with a sense of divine power, not Gruustir's. It reminded him of spiders, the big ones in the The Quat. Entering a large domed room, he noted giant clusters of amethyst growing in pockets along the walls. Far ahead of him, a dark grey stone slab sat in a ring of liquid. That plain stone had a holy sense to it but looking at it, even thinking about it, made his skin crawl as if being swarmed by insects. It was sacred to some god. Changing his focus, RiVule sought some kind of marking but finding none, he turned back to the stone table and approached it.

The flat rock lay large enough for an ogre and appeared to float in silver liquid, the radiance of which filled the cavern. The amethyst crystals refracted it back, creating points of lavender shade everywhere. RiVule saw a narrow stone walkway over the liquid to the slab and was about to step onto it when the Drow called out from behind. "Unless you are here to offer sacrifice to Lolth, I suggest you not approach the altar."

RiVule's eyes widened and he retracted his foot. "Lolth is known to Gruustir," he said. "The writings of the prophets say they were once even lovers."

Daryx entered the chamber. "I am Dar Malyx, or Daryx. This is my altar to the Spider Queen. I am Her Servant. While you are welcome here, as a worshipper or as a sacrifice, I do not want to see Gruustir's Chosen One slain in my home. Lolth's scriptures do not speak of Gruustir, though I will admit that there are several passages where Gruustir may have been referred to as 'strong food.'"

Daryx walked up to RiVule and offered him an amethyst monocle. When RiVule held it up to his eye, he noted that the cavern was full of incorporeal spiders, millions of them. The silver liquid was not flowing water or energy like he thought; it was baby spiders, so many they appeared as liquid. "I have not heard of Gruustir having written scriptures. I would be interested in acquiring them if we can be friends, RiVule."

RiVule snorted, "What would a Drow slave care about Gruustir?"

"Careful," Daryx said quietly. "You are a guest in my home." A phase spider appeared on Daryx's shoulder and RiVule watched Daryx stroke its barely visible form with the back of his finger. "In all of my time in Tania, I have studied all of the religions that cross my path. You might say that it's a hobby of mine. I'm curious as to what role Gruustir might play in the Abyss now that the Jade God is fallen."

*This Drow does not like being called a slave*, RiVule thought. *But, aren't they all?* He turned to face Daryx and struck his own chest. "And why is it that the saga of the Orc is not written with the fall of Orcus?" RiVule struggled to keep anger from twisting his Common back into Orc.

Daryx walked towards the slab and hopped up onto it and sat down. His expression dared RiVule to follow. "It is not written because every Chosen One raises a horde and attacks the outlying provinces of Tania, or Morilon, or Stone. The timeless tale of slaughter amongst the Orc would suggest that your prophets would benefit from writing that Tania has always defeated the hordes. Your strongest die and even our weakest fighters gain valuable combat experience."

RiVule growled and then stopped. What the Drow said was why he had come. "There is no glory in fighting the weakest," RiVule proclaimed loudly. He liked how his voice seemed to agitate the ghost spiders. "The prophets wrote that whosoever would bring Tania to its knees would earn a seat at Gruustir's right hand." A giant spider walked through the altar and Daryx towards him. It took all of RiVule's self-control to not flinch as the spider passed through him. He felt nothing and continued. "For the hordes, the prize is not Tania as much as the glory of the kill."

"So, you have a war host then?" Daryx asked.

RiVule's face split into a giant toothy grin. "Many tens of thousands. And since the Jade God's fall, we are blessed in ways no other horde has ever been." RiVule eyed the spider pit and felt a prayer come to his recollection from the writings. The prayer allowed the priest to control insects into a swarm. Maybe he could bend the prayer to control the spiders and let him cross? He smiled at Daryx and began to pray. When done, he walked boldly onto the narrow bridge and hopped up to sit by Daryx. The spiders did not notice him. Or, if they did, they paid him no heed.

"I've never known a shaman to master such a complex interaction with a god," Daryx commented. "Only a priestess of Tiamat has ever dared join me here. Since you are here, let me show you something." Daryx pressed the stone by his leg and a panel opened, softly lit by glowing faerie lights. Daryx's fingers glided across several markings and, around them, the cavern vanished.

RiVule found himself drifting in space with Daryx next to him. To their left, stars appeared, each burning with faint but noticeable colors. Daryx pointed to a pale yellow one. "That is Set's dominion." He pointed to a brilliant purple one and added, "That is the Gate of Chaos; Demos-Gorgos' realm."

RiVule pointed to a tinted silver star to his right and said, "That is Gruustir's realm. I can feel it in my bones." Daryx nodded. "Why do you show me this?"

"Because the Abyss is in upheaval and no one knows how it will come back together. Tania has interesting doctrines regarding these things. For example, according to the god emperor, Alerius, Gruustir resides in what the dragons call the Second plane of the Abyss."

RiVule frowned. "Why not the First?"

"According to the dragons, the First is hotly contested by every Abyssal power and Gruustir grew weary of it and so took the Second instead. From there, he can freely take control of the First at his pleasure. The great god Gruustir is strong enough to control two dominions."

RiVule eyed the Drow and wondered, "Why do you say this to me? First plane, Second plane. Two planes or all. Gruustir is the god of Orc, Goblin, and Ogre. His name and the mighty feats of his creations must be written in Bloodstone."

Daryx bowed. "The Saga of the Orc is one we welcome. The other races lack a RiVule to lead them, guide them, and control them to a higher calling."

"I will…"

"Your Mighty Horde is all Orc, no?"

RiVule wanted to strangle the arrogant, lecturing Drow but wondered if he would drift endlessly in this strange place if he did. A small voice suggested he would be lucky to survive a direct confrontation. "It is all Orc. Yes, the other races struggle with leadership. After Bloodstone, I will unite them all!" RiVule pointed to a bright star and asked, "What is that one?"

Daryx replied, "It's actually a chain of what the Tanians call Nexi. The one you're pointing to is named Mali Lynthracae Vede Mecum, or the Darkhold. You'll notice the other stars in a line with it?" For a moment, one such star flared and Daryx noted, "That is Lolth's, or the demonweb pits. A colorful if inaccurate depiction of what phase spiders enjoy."

Daryx moved his fingers over the rune panel and the Abyssal stars fell back to a glowing cyan cross set in a circle. "This is our world, Tehra," Daryx explained. "You'll notice that the longest leg of the cross extending past the circle is gyrating. Since the fall of Orcus, it is has been this way. Before, it pointed solidly to the Chaos Gate. If you watch this long enough, as the philosophers do, you'd see that Tehra dances closer to all three gates. This is why all clerics are enjoying a surplus of power. I have to imagine that you came for a purpose. It cannot be that a Chosen One with such a powerful horde came to Tania after all these centuries as a coincidence. Why are you here, priest of Gruustir?"

RiVule waved his hand through the star-filled expanse. "Do you have a map of Tania and what you call The Quat?" Daryx touched more markings in the rune panel and the stars vanished to be replaced by an aerial view of Morbatten.

"So big," RiVule said with genuine appreciation. "My horde is strong enough to take that, those, and that one. And hold it." He spoke without bluster and pointed to the area between The Quat and the capital city. "We could perhaps take that the city, but it would over-extend my horde and leave us susceptible to counterattack by the time Tania brings its armies and dragons back from Bloodstone." Annoyance crept into RiVule's voice, "Bloodstone has no saga of the Orc!" He struck his chest. "My horde should have been there!" He spat this and jabbed his finger at the space where Bloodstone would be if Daryx's map showed it.

"How many is your horde?" Daryx asked.

Suspiciously, RiVule hesitated and then declared, "Eighty thousand warriors. We have two thousand shamans. One hundred paladins. All of goblinkind, trollkind, and Gruustir's children rally to my banner." Again, the matter-of-fact tone suggested RiVule spoke truth. "But, this first time, it is for the Orc."

"You have paladins?" Daryx asked before catching his own surprise. "I had not heard of Orc paladins outside of Imperius and Tiamat…"

"Traitors!" RiVule hissed.

"How is this possible after so long? Ahh, I have a theory." Daryx brought up the map of the Abyssal Nexi again. "The Jade God's fall creates a pull that draws Gruustir closer to Tehra. We cannot see it in this symbolic representation, but that would explain it."

"Taisha will be my next paladin," RiVule stated.

"So, you have a horde and claim you can take these areas. Yet, you are here speaking with me. Clearly, you want something. Is it a role in Bloodstone? King Malcor would welcome the Orcs to the valley as allies. The saga of the Orc could yet be written in the blood of demons and undead lying in wait there."

"That is part of what I seek for Gruustir. It is a start. What must happen for King Malcor to agree to this?" RiVule jumped down from the altar and kicked one of the phase spiders off the bridge. Though his boot harmlessly passed through the creature, it turned and hissed at him.

Daryx came down as well and the amethyst cavern reappeared around them. "I would see Taisha become Gruustir's paladin. May I? Following that, we will go together and meet Dar Malcor. Tell me, RiVule, would you meet The Circle as an enemy offering truce, or as an ally?"

Expecting "enemy" as the answer from the war-lusting Orcs, Daryx felt only wonderment when RiVule answered. "Ally."

* * *

"Why?" Howie screamed as he slammed Grant's face with a brutal back-handed punch. The steel gauntlet broke Grant's jaw in new places and several teeth came loose.

A hired priest healed Grant so he did not pass out. 521's lieutenants laughed when Grant began screaming at the pain of exposed teeth nerves and the raw pain in his broken jaw. The cleric looked nervous and said, "Had I known I would be multifixing someone, I would have tripled my price."

Howie glared at him. "Too late to re-negotiate. You saw it: Grant killed Cordelle. We're not… multi-flexing, or whatever, him, at least not yet. Just keep him alive." Howie withdrew a long needle from a leather toolkit. It looked like a digging spike sharpened into a narrow needle. He let Grant focus on it and then stabbed it right through Grant's torso just below the collarbone on the right side. Grant grunted and then screamed.

"Try harder!" someone taunted.

The cleric grabbed Grant's jaw and twisted where it had become dislocated. It popped back in and the cleric felt along the jaw to where the biggest crack lay. "Expose the skin here."

Howie took a large dagger and rubbed it in salt and then sliced open Grant's cheek at the spot. The cleric pulled the skin back to the bone and then rubbed a thick paste on the crack. The bone began to heal there. "This will only repair the crack so he can speak with less pain. It's still cracked and not set correctly." The cleric then prayed for healing before Grant went unconscious from the salted pain. Grant spit bloody phlegm at the priest. "This is disgusting, and not what I agreed to do here."

Ignoring the cleric, Howie pulled up a chair and sat right in Grant's face. "You wanted to say something?"

Grant nodded. His eyes looked glazed, pupils wide open and unfocussed. "Didn't kill Cordelle. Dark Legion." Bloody drool fell from his swollen lips.

Howie punched Grant in the nose, cutting upwards to drive the nose bone into the brain. The cleric swore as Grant began to convulse, only just catching him before he died. "Damn you, if you do something like that again, Howie, I'm out of here!"

"You're going to stay and do this until your debts to Cordelle are repaid!" Howie screamed at the priest. Two enforcers pulled the priest back into a chair and shoved him into a sitting position.

"Why not take Cordelle to a temple then? He doesn't have to stay dead!" the cleric protested.

Grant's head seemed to rotate on a swivel. "Howie, you're a necro-humping piece of dung..."

Howie plunged the salted dagger into Grant's chest and twisted. "No!" the priest cried out. "I can't recover..."

An unearthly voice, disembodied, rang out. "Contingency."

Grant's body disappeared leaving Howie twisting the gory knife in the air. Howie whirled, seeking Grant's body. "What was that?!"

"Contingency," someone said. "Isn't that a Tanian wizard spell?" The priest said he did not know.

Grant reappeared in the Shield Mountain hideout that had long served as his guild's safe haven. He fell to his knees and began vomiting blood as the contingency spell blasted his body with healing magic. His vision swam and he saw Delton running towards him. The rest of the crew leapt into action as well. He felt Delton catch him and ask, "How can we help?" before Grant collapsed.

Delton looked up at Kaia who said, "I had nothing to do with this. Though I suppose I know exactly what just happened." When Delton kept looking for an explanation, Kaia added, "If you want to know, it'll cost another deal." Looking at the rest of the team, Kaia turned back to Delton. "There is no one else here I'm willing to deal with."

Delton and Jerare lifted Grant to a cot. "His face looks awful! There are many broken bones here." They missed the bloody tear in Grant's chest because his entire shirt was a gory mess. The spike and salt flecks from the dagger showed how Grant had finally died.

Kaia said, "His jaw is broken in three places. Skull has a primary fracture that, even with healing will continue to squeeze his brain. Five ribs are broken as are all of his fingers and toes."

Delton looked up at Kaia with pleading in his eyes. "Kaia, another deal for Grant's life. Whatever it takes."

Kaia nodded and said, "This is going to be gruesome. All of you, except Delton, leave." When they were gone, Kaia took out a symbol of Tiamat. Unlike the emblems seen throughout the Isles, this one had runes and small garnets dotting its surface. Kaia pressed this to Delton's hands and said, "Congratulations, you're now a cleric of Tiamat. I suggest you spend the next few minutes ignoring what I do to Grant and realign your thinking to that of a faithful priestess named 'Olen.' You got that? When I call for it, you're going to bludgeon this emblem into Grant's head as hard as you can. You need to kill him with the blow. We need to kill him so that his body will recover all of this damage. Trust me. Hopefully Grant does not have other contingency spells in place."

For the next five minutes, Delton had to actively suppress as a gag reflex as Kaia magically healed Grant while ripping broken bones out of the man's body. The only thing Kaia said was, "He's close to his limit. The torture was ongoing for some time when the contingency triggered." The broken ribs tore free with muscle and sinew attached to them. Kaia worked quickly and brutally, not caring for anything other than keeping Grant alive. At last, he called out, "Now!"

Delton slammed the Tiamat symbol into Grant's face and felt bone break. A female's voice burst from his mouth as he sang the *resurrection* hymn. Kaia urged him, "Keep your focus on the priestess Olen's voice. Pretend it's her, not you. If you struggle, try to remember good times with Grant that created the sense of loyalty you feel for him."

The gaping wounds began to heal over newly reformed bone. "Why didn't this work with Tembri?" Delton asked. He referred to the king's battle priest, who had died in Bloodstone of multiple shattered bones. The famous story had become an opera in both Taysor and Morbatten.

"Bloodstone always had a unique connection to Orcus, even for those close to dying. Orcus wanted Tembri so this could not work. The instant he drew close to death, Orcus would take him. It became not just a battle for his body, but for his soul." Kaia caressed Grant's forehead as the emblem began to disintegrate into Grant's head. Molten metal and red gemstones fell and then dissolved into the bloody wound. "He's going to make it," Kaia said. "Stay focused. This will be over in another couple of minutes."

Olen's voice continued her prayer as more and more of Grant pulled back together. Long after the emblem had vanished, Olen's hymn rang out clear and passionate from Delton's mouth. When Grant took his first shuddering breath, Delton fell over his torso and embraced him. "You talk of loyalty but it's more than that. Grant saved my life going back to when I was just a kid in Sora's streets. Poverty wasn't just a curse; it was my life. Though fast, I was small. Grant saved me from street kids, from the city watch that would stick kids like me into chain gangs, from the knights, from myself. I once prayed to Pha Rann and asked for a guardian angel. He sent me Grant."

Kaia folded his arms and leaned back against a table. "That's a great story, Delton. Here's the truth you don't want to hear or see, even though it's in your face all this time. Grant works for Perdition. Pha Rann didn't send Grant to you; Tiamat did. Pha Rann would not have led you into this profession. Think about it."

Delton felt too exhausted to ask questions, but his lethargic mind spun into overdrive at Kaia's words. Grant always seemed to have a leg up on the other guilds. He had access to Tanian magic that Sorans struggled to get. He always passed it off as a benign but secretive patron. The Bloodstone Campaign with the Nineteenth Legion had really driven it home. When Grant had them peel off to the Sixth Fortress' northern side and they had harvested so much of the Jade God... Delton nodded. "It makes sense," he said. After breathing deeply and shaking Olen's voice from his ears, he said, "So, what's the price?"

Kaia grinned at him. If they had not spent so much time together the past few days, Delton would have found the leer alarming. "You're going on a quest. To Merakor. Don't worry. Grant is going too. He just doesn't know it yet."

\* \* \*

Khalla found Ash in his favorite restaurant and sat down opposite him. He did not even look up and his sullen demeanor weighed on her. She waived a serving girl over and asked for Elven wine. "I thought you might be here," she said quietly. "It's not like you though to be so predictable. Are you changing or are you just that resigned to losing Perdition?"

Ash caught her hand and said, "Maybe both if it means I do not lose you. Have you answered the question? Are you going to?"

Khalla frowned at the intensity of his question. The frozen and deformed body held a tattoo on the chest that read, 'Do you still love me?'

"Oh Ash, I've loved you since the day we first met. Sure, you drive me crazy with some of the things you do, but I always knew that, as Marcello, you had to act in a certain eccentric way that might not really be you. Now, of course that I know the real you doesn't have this," she said patting his arm. "I have to wonder, what are you really?"

Ash sipped the wine when it arrived. "Do you really want to know?"

Khalla gripped his hand tightly and said, "I deserve to know after all the time we've been together. Maybe start at the beginning and build up to it."

Ash nodded. "My mother was, well, still is a high-ranking priestess. She comes from a well-known family of powerful R'Dar nobles. When I was born, my condition was nothing short of scandalous. It became more so because of my father, a paladin noble. They brought mages in to *polymorph* me, but as an infant – I'm told this – it never lasted very long. Long enough for public show and display. As you might imagine, I was not loved as a child.

"So, one day when I was maybe four years old, my mother came and said that things just were not working out. She kissed me goodbye. Guards loyal to the family took me to Taysor and dropped me off in the streets. Crippled children aren't killed there. I almost died many times except an orphanage took pity on me. They called me 'Flipper.' You can imagine why.

"I hated it. I hated them. I hated everything. I was fast. With my one good arm, I could do things that most normal children struggled with. By twelve, I could one-handed juggle six balls and was put on the street as a performer. They sold me to a freakshow the next year. Eventually, I came back to Tania. Having grown up a bit and in circus garb, my mother did not recognize me when we did a performance for Gershon and the Merchants.

"That night, Kaia came to me. He offered me a deal. The price of the deal was total secrecy. I understand from Daryx that there was a bet of some kind as to how the secret would be figured out. I don't really know how they did it, but I think a mind flayer and a doppleganger were involved. After they did, whatever it was, I had my real body as it should have been."

"Wow," Khalla said, and took a deep gulp of wine. "About Kaia, I was well-prepared to say no long before he found me. At the time, it was tempting but when I come across stories like this, I realize I am a better person for having said no. I don't want that to sound condescending or judgmental, Ash."

Ash shrugged but remained unwilling to look her in the eyes. "So," he said. "Are you going to answer the question?"

Khalla pulled him forward and insisted that he look at her. "Even as 'Flipper,' I love you, Ash."

At her words, Ash went stiff as if anticipating pain. Nothing happened and after a moment, he let out his breath and smiled tentatively at her. "I love you too, Khalla."

"So, do you want to go to Merakor or not? I've been busy. I think I've got Ryvane onboard. Since we're not getting any Elves, I figure we may as well grab any of the special crew we can get." She pulled out her ledger. "She wants Calvin to come."

Ash chuckled. "I bet you had a few words to say about that. Still, if his coming means Ryvane comes, it wouldn't hurt us."

"He's a liability and you know it," Khalla countered. "But, yes. I suppose you're right. I'd rather our trip not be the one where those two realize how mismatched they are."

"Halgrim can handle Calvin if drama becomes an issue, or Ryvane refuses to charm control him. Let's sign him up. As I understand it, the

Drow will expect us to have a few slaves anyway." Ash reached out for her ledger where she had written down possible names. He saw that her entire cell's leadership was on board. He tapped Ciejek's name. "I don't like this one. The way he acts towards women, towards you is... alarming. If he wasn't such a good poisoner, I'd have booted him from the guild."

Khalla leaned forward for a kiss and their lips met. She said, "Consider him fodder. Though I sometimes wonder if Marcello should not take care of him before."

Ash tapped Ciejek's name one more time and said, "Yes, let's. You're Marcello. It's your call. I often thought about it. You know, you've changed a lot. I mean, I noticed it when you pulled Perdition together for Bloodstone. Since, it's like you're more intense."

With Perdition secured to Khalla, she sent out word to the small but growing team to meet at the East-West Major shrine at the base of Temple and Dragon Mountain the next night. The clerics secured the entire mountain so that only those already cleared for Merakor arrived to find Perdition's chapel empty. Ynt'taris sat beneath the Tiamat statue flipping through the pages of a large book. Not everyone knew it was Ynt'taris in spite of the many stories about the little girl form preferred by the ice patriarch. The Temple also had its share of prodigy girls.

Khalla went to welcome the Ice Patriarch, but a priestess waved her off. In handsign, she said, NO. HE IS HERE TO LISTEN. HE KNOWS YOU. THAT IS ENOUGH.

As the rest of the team arrived, Khalla noted them in her ledger and greeted them warmly. They each carried a letter of instruction sealed by the Mages Guild. Alex and Valaes arrived last and sat down in the front, bowing deeply to the ice patriarch. The girl looked up and measured each one of them. With Khalla's team, Ryvane and Calvin, Alex and Valaes, Halgrim and his favorite apprentice, they numbered sixteen. "This is not enough," Ynt'taris said, looking up from the book. "And, you will need more elves. One capable Elf?" Ynt'taris found Ash and gazed at him blankly for a long moment until Ash felt sweat break out over his body. "Maybe you aren't taking this seriously enough."

Ash stood and bowed. "Dread Lord, those elves loyal to Tania fight in Bloodstone with the Nineteenth Legion. We have not yet dared broach the topic of recruitment there."

Ynt'taris flipped his book shut. "Permission is granted. My daughter Ora shall see to it that you have access to the dossiers on every Elf or Half-

Elf in the Legion. Commander Ayden will be instructed to cooperate fully." Ynt'taris' eyes scanned the group. "And you will need others. There are not enough fighters. Perdition's enforcers look the part, but the skills required to scare a shopkeeper are different from murdering your enemy when they are set on murdering you in return. The Drow have no compunction against casual slaughter. Perhaps some of the veteran officers of the Nineteenth would like to join you. Ora will speak to Legion Commander Ayden about this as well."

A pressure wave popped their ears as Kaia and Delton appeared just outside the shrine door. Kaia whirled shoved Delton forward as he bowed to Ynt'taris. "Dread Lord! This is Delton, formerly of the Soran Rogue's Guild. He would like to join this adventure."

Delton looked completely disoriented but his eyes focused on Pol Nir and Bolston. He waved and then bowed low. "Delton of Sora, at your service. As Master Kaia says, I would like to join this adventure." Under his breath, he whispered, "Whatever that is."

Ynt'taris answered him. "To plunder Merakor. The team's leaders, Ash and Halgrim, will fill you in on the rest after you sign the contract."

Kaia held a scroll forward to Khalla, which materialized into his hand. "Signed. Dread Lord," Kaia said bowing. The Halfling vanished. Ash heard Kaia speak in his mind and say, "I'm impressed. You knew you had to get someone to love you against an unknown time of discovery. You've done well, Ash. Your debt is fulfilled. You are free from the curse of discovery."

Ash nodded and mentally sent his thanks to Kaia. It connected, he knew it, and he felt it like a hot spark in his mind.

Ynt'taris hopped down from the stage and said, "You have plenty of thieves. You should fit in quite well with the Drow. I would see more priests," his eyes glanced to Alex and Valaes. "Capable you might be, you will need more and more powerful ones. I have set things in motion to bring a powerful cleric. You need fighters. It is too bad King Malcor cannot join you personally. That is the caliber of warrior you need. Archmage Halgrim will speak now."

Halgrim stood and walked up to the stage. Ash had not seen him since his age reversed. He looked good and Ash had a sudden feeling that everything was going his way, again. Finally. He squeezed Khalla's thigh and she smacked his hand away. "Tonight, Khalla..." he whispered to her.

Halgrim created an illusion of the Arati grasslands and spun it in a complete circle so that everyone could see the mountains that split Merakor down its center and divided the western side from the eastern. "We are going here," Halgrim pointed to a crater. This is where a Tower of Sorcery was detonated at the end of the Kinslayer Wars. It belonged to a powerful archmage known as Aler Alerest. That name might remind you of the god emperor. You would not be wrong. Three thousand plus years ago, Alerius studied Merakoran magic and became known there as an arch mage. He was known as the Armored Mage because then, like now, his human form retains the plate armor we see him wearing. His tower was not destroyed. It was cleverly buried deep in the earth at the time of the cataclysm. We are going to salvage items of interest for the god emperor and to plunder the rest. Ash?"

Ash walked up and joined Halgrim on the stage. He pointed to the eastern coast labeled 'Overlook.' "This is where we will land. Soon, a world galleon will arrive here in Tania and begin offloading cargo. They finish in three months. Between then and now, longer if we need it, they will leave and take us with them. Taurans appreciate precision in follow through so put that in your mind as we'll be with them for several months' voyage. It would be good to be ready in exactly three months, for their sake. Once outside of the Isles, we will be able to come above deck and resume preparations. I should not need to tell you how lethally dangerous Merakor is. This is not a vacation." His eyes darted to Ryvane and Calvin. Calvin tried to look calm, like he belonged. He wilted under Ash's stare. Clearly, Calvin recognized Ash from street encounters.

"Tania is financing this operation because of the Tower's salvage. The reward for what we salvage is immense. The Circle has authorized us to offer you each R'Dar title complete with all holdings. All other treasure will be counted and divided evenly as shares. To ensure our success, the empire is paying all expenses. However, you are welcome to buy in and help for extra consideration. Buy in cost, per share, is one hundred thousand gold. It's steep, I know. Speak to Khalla if you wish to do this. Halgrim and I lead, but Khalla is going to be your go to for anything like contracts. If we find magic you are interested in, you can buy it out of your share by group vote. Understood?" Everyone nodded and Ash continued. "So, that brings us to the dark elves and the Spider Queen, Lolth. Unless any of you worship Lolth already, pay attention."

Halgrim pointed to Alex and asked her to stand. "This is Alex. She has graciously agreed to be our priestess of Lolth. You may not recognize her now because, well, she's not a Drow." Halgrim began chanting and at his words, everyone began to change. Ears became pointed, skin darkened, and eyes began to glow with purple and silver lights. "This is an illusion of what we must all become by the time we reach Merakor."

Before their eyes, Alex's clothing fell away and was replaced with black leather bands that wrapped around her thighs, over her hips and crisscrossed her breasts. Where attachments required linkages to hold the bands in place, spider emblems appeared and cinched them tight. Her long hair, already a light red, became silver. Silvered spider tattoos burst out along her exposed skin.

Valaes watched it all in fascination and said, "You look intense, Alex."

She held her arms up to look at herself. "I hate this look, but by Tiamat's grace, we will make this work!"

Halgrim waved his staff over the group. "Not all dark elves are dark-skinned. Many are just Elves who decided to join the Drow in the Kinslayer Wars, or are now the children of captives. Those that look like Alex are the pure ones, the Nobles like Daryx, who first entered the Underdark and found Lolth after the Race Wars. They are nobility and regardless of their profession, we must get used to treating them as if Daryx."

Alex stepped forward and pointed at Bolton. "You!" she screamed. "Stand and present yourself!"

Bolston looked around with a bewildered expression on his face. Alex drew her hand back and racked her nails across his face. "I said stand, you idiot male!" Her other hand began to burn with caustic darkness as she prayed to Tiamat under her breath.

Bolston's hand inched to his sword as he tried to back away but could not because of the stone benches. Seeing him not standing, Alex shot her hand forward and shrieked, "Die!"

Bolston fell unconscious as the others jumped forward to help and protect him from Alex. Seeing the group split, Valaes rose up to Alex's side. He felt his body began to change, but it felt natural when his lower abdomen split apart to reveal a tarantula spider. Armor and weapons sprouted all around his body. His four arms moved as if each had their own will and held two long swords and two maces. The long swords burst into purple fire and caustic poison leaked from the maces.

"Freeze," Halgrim said. "All of you. Bolston isn't dead, but you will all be if you encounter other Drow and fail to obey the Holy Mothers of Lolth. No matter how irrational Alex's demands, you must obey. And, it will not always be Alex playing this role. The priestesses are like Lolth in their midst. If Tiamat were here and She ordered any of us to turn on the others, would we hesitate? I would not."

Bolston was shaking his head and looked at Alex with a frightened and confused look on his face. "I thought I was dying," he said.

Alex took his hand to help him stand. He hesitated and then shrugged. She reassured him. "It's a simple *divine command* prayer. Your soul responds to the Goddess and tries to obey. You just blacked out for a moment. Don't worry. If things get rough, and they will, I can also heal… or kill." Alex smiled at him and then twisted her face in an apoplexy of rage. "Now stand up, you spineless aphid!"

This time, Bolston jumped to his feet and bowed. "Much better," Halgrim said. "Best time frame, we have three months to master this, plus the ocean voyage. While some of us know the Drow handsign used here in Tania, none of us speak Undercommon except for Alex, Valaes, myself, and Ash. And, Tanian handsign is not truly Drow handsign; we'll need to relearn a lot. Any one else speak Drow?"

Delton raised his hand and said, "Um, actually. I do. I'm sure my accent is all wrong, but my crew, we learned Undercommon." Ciejek raised his hand and said that he too had studied it enough to speak it.

"I speak it too," Ryvane called out in fluent Undercommon. "My accent is probably dated as well."

Khalla made a note after checking Ryvane's dossier and saw that this skill was absent. *I wonder what else is missing*, she thought.

"Okay," Ash said. "We've got the beginning of a team. Begin setting your personal matters in order. We could be gone for up to three years. Remember, we need to become Drow." He pointed at Alex and tried to mimic her haughty pose.

It drew a few chuckles and lightened the mood. Halgrim let the illusion drop and added, "We're looking for adventurous elves. If you find any, send them to me or Khalla. We'll pay one hundred gold for qualified referrals even if we don't add them. If we do, one thousand gold."

Ynt'taris watched this all and faded to the background. He had things to say, but no one asked. He would keep his thoughts to himself. For now. A priestess waited there with a message from Ora. Her headaches were getting worse. She asked to be taken into the mountain heights where thin air and endless cold would help her recover.

The priestess relayed this message and waited for instructions, but Ynt'taris vanished, leaving crystallized air to fall like snow where he had been standing.

□

# Chapter 9 – Vampire Games

Ciejek walked along one of the southern roads away from the Great Bazaar. While walking, he carefully checked that he was not being followed. Only when completely certain did he finally turn into a side alley and begin making his way east. After just a few minutes, he began to smell the scent of wet wood and mildew wafting from the warehouse district. Staying his course, he came up behind one of the massive wooden and stone buildings used by the Taurans to store equipment and merchandise. A Tauran guard, alert and ready as they always were, glared at him and dared him to come closer. "Just traveling," Ciejek said.

Moving to the north, the thief came to the open staging area outside a large but dilapidated human warehouse and worked his way past crates and workers of all types. The Taurans did most of the lifting and moving while merchants picked their way along the aisles with checklists. Ciejek smirked at the busy activity and thought again how easy it would be to steal any of this. He began scoping out a possible haul when caution restrained him. There were too many stories of this and they all ended with the Taurans amputating the thief's arm.

Ciejek checked again to see if he had been followed. He felt confident he was not. When he reached Dockside's lake harbor, he walked out onto a pier and stretched. A cold but humid breeze lifted off the lake's surface. A string of barges moving in both directions made their way to and from the lock system that led to the Coastal River and eventually the ocean. Taking it all in, Ciejek heard a voice from under the pier. "Nice night," the voice said trying to sound pleasant.

Ciejek let his neck crack as he twisted it side to side and said, "No bats tonight at least."

"Bats here are often hard to see."

"At least they don't breathe fire," Ciejek answered and completed the encoded message that he had not been followed. He paused and then said, "A team is being put together to go to Merakor. I'm in it. Khalla is moving against Marcello. She wants to be the next Marcello."

"Do you know who Marcello is yet?"

"No. But, if we help Khalla then she will be. And, we know who she is." Ciejek skipped a copper coin out onto the surface of the lake. "She never said who Marcello is. Obviously, she knows. I'd guess the other cell leaders know too."

Ciejek got chills down his spine when the voice said, "Dark Legion is pleased with this news. We will help Khalla become Marcello. It will be the first time we will know who Marcello is. Your orders are to stay close to her, know her, endear yourself to her. You are to be her most loyal lieutenant. Do you understand?"

"I understand and obey," he said. "There is more."

"Go on," the dark voice encouraged him.

Ciejek sat down and looked up at the rising moon. He said, "This Merakor quest... there is a Tower of Sorcery that used to belong to the god emperor. They are going to retrieve some items of power, and loot all else they can. Khalla will be going. I thought you would want to know this. It seems as if things are beginning to happen."

"So, our one chance at Marcello will be gone for many years. This is not good. We will therefore accelerate our plans. This changes nothing of my instruction regarding Khalla. Are you ready for more instructions?" When Ciejek said he was, the dark voice continued. "A war is beginning in Sora. Northern Cross and The Twins are gone. 521 is crippled and will soon bow before Dark Legion. That leaves only Rogue's Guild as a threat. While outright warfare between Tania and Sora is forbidden by the Queen's Way, our guilds may fight. Dark Legion will attack Perdition. Khalla will rise as Marcello. Dark Legion will pretend to fall to Perdition. You will be there to see it, Ciejek. When the moment arrives, you will give us Marcello."

"Is all this necessary for the master vault?" Ciejek asked. "It's special but is it this special?"

The voice hissed and seemed to retreat underwater. After some time and with only the lapping of water along the dock's supports for sound, the voice came back. "You know we desire the master vault?"

"Why else would you want Marcello? Hell, I figure you have deals like mine with half of Perdition. I'm not stupid, you know. What else could it be? If it's something in the vault, I might be able to get it and avoid the war. Call it 'Plan B'."

"Okay, Ciejek. Though we wish the entire vault were ours, there is one thing in the vault we must have. Long ago, one of our guild mistresses came from Tania. She was a priestess named Joviel. When Tania made her Marcello, she was required to bind her soul to an artefact, which Tania still possesses. It seems that this process is different for each of those in Tania's power. We desire that Joviel's soul be freed, specifically that the artefact, a sapphire round the size of a marble set in platinum to look like a pendant, be held by Dark Legion. In fact, none of our plans can come to pass without Joviel. Do you believe such a thing is recoverable without Marcello? Is there a way to access the master vault without Marcello?"

Ciejek reflected on the snippets he knew about Farant and Khalla's involvement in that. "Khalla's definitely a lieutenant. She probably knows where the vault is and how to access it. She also knows who Marcello is. If I were to give her a reason, I bet we could get Joviel's soul gem before an outright war. I know you think you would win, but as a Tanian, I'd point you to the many heroes of legend here that would suggest you lose. How many paladins has Dark Legion killed?"

The voice hissed again and with sarcasm said, "There is only one hero who might stop us, Ciejek. And, you already work for us."

"Well, not all of us get to live forever. I still want my pay. If I get this soul gem, I want to come into Dark Legion. I'll need sanctuary at the end of this anyway. There's no scenario where I get Joviel's soul and Tania doesn't kill me, or worse. They'll think I sold it, and then torture and worse happens to me. No, getting you this will end my stay here with the mortals." Ciejek looked around and wistfully said, "I'll miss lots of it."

The chill in the voice sounded worse when it chortled. "And your harem, no doubt. But, don't worry. Once with us, all of your vices can be sated, and they will be much... enhanced. Get us Joviel, Ciejek. Syand will reward you herself."

Ciejek nodded and stood. He skipped another copper coin out into the water and turned back to the land as something wet and cold rose up behind him. Ciejek tilted his head to the side and said, "Gentle now..." before he clenched his jaw in agony. The vampire's bite always hurt, but then the tingling ecstasy came and Ciejek sighed. "You're my favorite drug."

A white form, dripping wet, bit into his neck and drank deeply. Before finishing the blood meal, the creature placed a crystal vial into Ciejek's hand.

* * *

Grant blinked his eyes and looked around warily. He remembered Howie's smashing blow that should have broken his neck. With some relief he found himself in their Shield Mountain hideout. Someone said,

"Hey, Grant's awake!" but he could not place the man's voice. The dim lantern light and glow stones they used hurt his eyes and he winced trying to focus. "Delton?" he asked.

"Delton did a deal with the Tanian Halfling to save us, to save you. He's gone, Grant." Grant struggled to place the voice. His ears rang. It kind of sounded like Venter, but his eyes were not working well. "We haven't seen him for at least two days, Grant. Good news is, we made it. We have the Jade God's stuff. We have you back. The Halfling said you'd be fine."

Someone pressed warm broth to his lips and he sipped at it through sudden waves of nausea. He could tell that he must have been close to death many times to feel this awful. "How did I get here, Delton's thing?" he asked.

Another voice answered him. It was Jodi's. "The Tanian Halfling brought us all here, boss. Things were real bad. We were chased from Taysor to Smuggler's Hide. We had a battle with what looked like Dark Legion. You appeared just as we were starting to recover. That Halfling saved us. Said that you and Delton owed him."

"The black-skinned Halfling," Grant said trying not to gag on the broth. It tasted heavenly, but his stomach did not agree. "You mean Kaia. Kaia was here," he re-stated.

Venter said, "Yes, Kaia was here for almost four days. He helped us all get better. Also, Delton said to tell you that he had no real choice and that he would do it again to save us, to save you."

Jodi interrupted. "But, he also said to have you tell us the truth, about everything."

"That's right," Venter added. "Everything."

Grant tried to nod but fell back and then rolled to the side to dry heave. Everything in his mouth tasted like dried blood. When the retching calmed, he put his hands over his eyes and said, "Okay. Everything."

When he next woke up, Jodi was playing on a mandolin. The gentle strumming reverberated just enough in the stone caverns that it made the mandolin sound much better than Jodi's skill normally allowed. It was one of his favorite things about the caves. Checking, Grant guessed his stomach would allow him to sit up. Carefully, and then with Venter's help, he tried to stand. His stomach growled and Jodi stopped playing. "You should have been here, boss. The Halfling made the most delicious gourmet food. Like the best food you could ever get at The Lighthouse. You remember that place in Haven?"

"Oh yeah," Venter groaned. "It was soooo good. But, Jodi's right. The food we had while they were here was to die for."

Grant stumbled over to a table and sat down. While Jodi brought over broth and other more substantial food, Venter began to explain everything. Though tentative about eating, Grant found he could stomach crackers and even dried meat. It all tasted so good that he had to restrain himself and eat slowly.

Sipping at water, Grant said, "Okay, you guys deserve to know everything. I'm sure it was a shock to Delton, but you're all smart. I'd not be surprised if you already know or suspected. We work for Tania. Not all the time, but sometimes. The Orcus gig – that was Tania. I was approached by their guild about seven months ago. They were pretty certain Orcus would come through. They wanted us to kick a black market trade into motion. I was instructed and signed up to harvest as much of Orcus as we could. We'd be given safe haven from their military for exactly the amount of time we were there." Grant chuckled and then winced as his bowels twisted.

"You remember how hell erupted when Orcus fell, right? All the undead began peeling off, and the gates everywhere. We were in a full cascade." He dug at a knot in the table's wood. "A full cascade. Imagine that. And gods. Everywhere." He whistled softly. "Then we moved in. Remember how we'd almost get attacked by a demon or whatever and something would happen to distract it, or attack it, or pull it away from us? That was Tania."

Venter and the others listened intently. Unlike Grant, they had all recovered enough, and Delton had hinted enough, that none of this surprised them, but Delton did not have details. Jodie asked, "We still lost friends."

Grant raised his water cup in salute. "Tania would not guarantee no fatalities. That's on me. I regret it, but our work does have certain risks. They told me if Orcus came through, it would be bad. Marcello even described how bad it might become. I understand Perdition had a 30% casualty rate. We lost less than a fifth. I'm sad at the loss, but it tells me how truly good you each are at what you do."

Jodie and Venter nodded. "You couldn't know how bad it would be. If you had been able to convey it," Venter said, "I might have stayed home for this one."

The others chuckled. Jerare began laughing uncontrollably until tears fell from his eyes. "Grant, if you had said blood would rain from a green sun and the very earth would go undead and claw at me, I would have thought you were exaggerating, so you wouldn't have to pay me!"

When the laughter died down, Grant said the names of the fallen. "Finn. Kasey. These were our brothers. Their deaths are on me as your leader. I should have been here for you all." He sighed heavily and rested his head on his arms. Everything felt heavy and lethargic. "So, we were to sell it for the 'best price' we could get and report on the buyers and pricing to Perdition. Anything we harvested over that amount, we would get to keep. Tania knew this would be dangerous stuff. See, if we could sell a vial of blood for one hundred gold illegally, then Tania would price the actual stuff at one hundred and ten gold. I don't think Tania knew what the powers would be any more than we did at the beginning. Who would buy it and for how much was the second part of the mission."

While talking, Venter, Jodi, and the four others gathered around and listened. One said, "I knew it had to be something like that. Why else would the dragons leave us be?"

Grant pointed to him. "Jerare, that's exactly why they left us alone. You might remember that I climbed up and 'stood guard?' In reality, I had a token. Without that token, we'd have been glassed by the dragons. I know it. You know it. Point in fact, The Twins are gone because they tried to harvest Orcus without sanction. They're all dead now. A Tanian followed them back, it seems, and drowned them all. So, you see. The deal with 521 was for the amount Tania asked us to supply. I did not want to deal with Dark Legion because of rumors that they're actually vampires or worse."

Grant began to refill his cup with wine but his hands shook so badly he stopped. He took a pull from the bottle. "I haven't felt like this since my training days."

Venter gave him time to take a few drinks. "Boss, are you Tanian?"

Grant smiled. "No, I'm just like you. Marcello contacted me ten years ago when the Rogue's Guild was just a dream for me. They offered me the Morilon contract. Tania could not risk actual Tanian agents on that one because, you know how Morilon is about Tania. It should come as no surprise to any of you that Perdition recommended all of you to me for that job. It brought us together." Grant raised the wine bottle to each of them. "To us, the proud few, and brothers lost on the way here!"

The others toasted. Grant continued. "Northern Cross is gone. My guess is Dark Legion will front 521 through Jace or maybe Howie. You saw my condition when I arrived here. Dark Legion is more vicious than I've ever seen them and they framed me for Cordelle's death. To ensure our success, Tania put a magic spell on me they call 'contingency.' It's a type of magic that says, If Grant is about to die while engaged in this job for Tania, teleport him away to whatever he considers a safe location. I'm glad it brought me here. I didn't want to tell Tania about this place. They pay well, but you know how it is. Kaia didn't bring me here. Dark Legion was beating me to death for more Orcus blood. They have some, but they know I have most of it. I doubt they go to Bloodstone after what happened to The Twins. My guess is that they'll deem that too risky to go after and will instead want what we have as an easier source - us. Seeing how it affected their leader, I'm guessing it's potent and perhaps addictive to vampires."

Pete patted the backpack which held all of the Jade God's body parts. "So, what happens with this?"

Grant smiled. "While we did not get paid in full, but we did get one and a half million. The total price suggests that what we have left is worth maybe twenty-five million. Tania considers this our pay. Once I report on it, they'll owe us some favors but one and a half million is enough for all of us to live like kings if that's what you want. Just keep in mind, it's Tania and so there are probably other jobs they'll want. For the 521 pay, equal shares for us all, just like we originally said. I'd like to carve out some for Finn and Casey and send it back to their families. Anonymously, of course. Any objections?" There were none and Grant laughed. "Like any of you would object to this. Thirty thousand gold to the families then. That's plenty. After all, we still have death contracts on our heads."

Jodie asked, "What about Delton?"

Grant sighed. "I'm catching up on details here, but he made a deal with Kaia, right? You all know about the Halfling of Legend, right? I'm guessing you've heard stories of the genie who grants wishes for heroes?"

"Yeah, we went through that during the time Kaia was with us," Jodie said. "Personally, I was a bit upset he didn't offer me anything. He offer you, Grant?"

"He did, but Marcello had cautioned me to decline any offers. He offered me a ring that would make me move five times faster. I was very tempted. But I still said no. Maybe that's why he took Delton. So, to that point, I consider Delton alive and part of the team. He'll get his share but we'll reserve it aside here in the hideout. If he gives it back to us, then we'll split that. Fair?"

Grant reached around for his own backpack and almost fell over. Venter gave it to him. "I got most of the 521 stuff back too." He patted it and pointed to Delton's. "Obviously, we can't sell it all at once, not here, not for some time. I'm thinking that we buy passage on a Tauran ship and leave the Isles for a bit. We can set up shop in the Western Lands and sell it. It'll probably take some time but once word gets out that we have this stuff, it should go fast. My guess is that within a year we'll have traded it all," he pointed to the Orcus backpack, "for currency, gear, and other tradable goods. Twenty-five million minus expenses and hero pay for each of you allows us to fill up enough of a world galleon's berth that the Taurans will take us seriously on the way back. We'll vanish from the Isles and come back as bona fide merchants. From there, sky is the limit." He smiled weakly and struggled to stand up.

Venter refilled Grant's cup after catching him. "Not yet, boss. There's a problem though - Dark Legion."

Grant nodded. "Only a problem if they find us. From what I can see, the Jade God's bones and blood are addictive to the vampires. The quills though as exceptional weapons against them. Before he betrayed me, Bradley speared Syand with one. It went through her pelvis bone and she could not break it or removed it except by pulling all the way through. It was nasty."

"So, they really are vampires?" Jodie asked. He continued to pick at his mandolin.

Grant nodded. "They really are. Not all of them, mind you. And, they've joined up with doppelgangers. It would seem that the Pha Rannic Temple needs to update its teachings that those creatures were killed off from the Isles during the Allegiance of Blood."

At the mention of the shape-changers, one of Jodi's strings broke. Everyone turned to look at him. "What?" he said. "They freak me out. The Halfling would have known if any us were, but still." He eyeballed Venter back.

Jerare cleared his throat to ask a question. "So, the Dark Legion controls 521…"

"And what is left of The Twins," Grant interjected.

"And The Twins, and they're vampires, and they have doppels. This sounds really bad for Taysor. Why not just tell your Cuthberic friends and be done with it?" Jerare finished.

Grant sighed. "We actually don't have a way to send word, not from here. When I built this, I did not want it findable by magic. It prevents us from sending magical messages. I'd bet that without Delton's cooperation, Kaia would not have been able to find our hideout. From here back to Sora, it's too dangerous and would take too long to send word. The way I see it, we need to get to Tania. There is a Temple of Pha Rann there, or Perdition can send word for us. I doubt Tania wants the Soran Thieves Guild to become unified under vampires."

Venter nodded. "If we encounter anyone who can send a message on our way to Tania, we will have them do it as well. Deal?"

Grant raised his cup as if in a toast. "Of course, Venter. Walking to Tania is going to take some time. The mountain passes are still clogged with snow and ice. But, with some luck, we might encounter the Winter War fighters heading back to Sora, at least those that chose to go there rather than to fight the real battles in Bloodstone. On second thought, I don't trust people like that. Let's just focus on being open to the possibilities of a mage or a priest we can hire to send word, but head to Tania as fast as possible." Grant was feeling better and better. "Hey Jodie, do we still have that crate in here marked 'Winter War?'"

Jodi pointed to the corner and strummed his first chord on the repaired mandolin.

* * *

RiVule scoffed at the human paladin standing his ground against Taisha. The newly-sanctified paladin of Gruustir stood radiant in her fury. With a howl, she slammed her shield into the paladin's shield. The force and surprise of it knocked the paladin back a few steps to the edge of the training circle. RiVule saw health inflate the knight as he pushed back and then ducked under Taisha's sword.

Daryx watched with an impassive expression. "The Order of the Shield is better at group action," the dark elf noted quietly. "But, from what I'm seeing, Taisha should be able to hold and rank up to the Order of Fire."

RiVule scoffed again and spat to the side. "Then, why Daryx, are we wasting our time with this *scla*... this one?" He almost used a slur for weak fighters, *sclavus*, but had learned Daryx did not appreciate insulting language against the knights of Tiamat.

"The Order of Fire is in Bloodstone. Shield is not entirely deployed there. This one owes me a favor. If Taisha could not defeat him, I would not waste the Order of Fire's time. You should consider healing her," Daryx suggested as the paladin finally ran his sword through Taisha's side. Armor plating fell off her back hip as she screamed and twisted to break the sword free. "While admirable to so flagrantly taunt pain and death, Tania considers paladins more valuable than fighters, even more than mages in some regards. The Temple of Dragons will not appreciate so callous a disregard for her well-being."

RiVule prayed and sent healing and enhanced speed to her while asking, "Why does Tiamat care about a paladin of Gruustir?"

"It's all part of the larger plan to kill another god. We can talk about it someday."

RiVule looked back at Daryx about to say something when Taisha screamed in agony. Her opponent caught her left side open and stabbed his sword up through her rib cage. Her scream quickly fountained into bloody spittle. RiVule and Daryx watched her begin to die. "Now we see if she truly has Gruustir's blessings," RiVule commented.

Taisha's body flailed and abruptly, she caught the knight's hand at her left side and squeezed to hold him there while her other hand began smashing her pommel against his helmet. Unable to maneuver in the tight space and entangled armor, the knight tried to block her with his shield. She knocked his helmet off. A still moment displayed to RiVule and Daryx: Taisha fighting death's embrace and the knight surprised to lose his helmet. RiVule smiled when Taisha drove her thumbs into the paladin's eyes and gouged them out with her last bit of energy.

"Blessed indeed," Daryx said. "Battle lust through death, and focus. It's admirable. Tania trains its paladins for this. It takes a lot of training to let go of the fear of death and so absolutely trust."

RiVule nodded as her lifeless body slumped down beside the paladin, who clutched his face and screamed in agony. RiVule said, "Flawless victory is either to defeat your enemy or to enable that same enemy to fall to the horde." So that Daryx would see, RiVule revived her to life and, as an extra measure, restored the paladin's sight.

As Taisha blinked her eyes and felt air rush into and out of her lungs, she saw RiVule walking towards her. Then the ripped tissue around her lungs closed and she breathed sweet air. RiVule embraced her and she realized tears dribbled from his eyes. I've never seen a war priest cry, she thought. Not saying anything proved the correct response and she embraced the priest back with all her might. "So, this is what it means to be a paladin?" she asked.

RiVule nodded and switched to Orc. "Perfect victory even in death. The horde would embrace you too, brave paladin. You are the first female to be so embraced as an equal." RiVule paused as the word 'equal' felt wrong. "No, Gruustir says you are equal to Frentoris. You exceed the Horde's warriors. I am impressed."

Behind them, and with a tone of voice that showed nothing, Daryx observed, "She's a paladin. I've never seen or heard of such a thing before among the Orcs. Truly, Gruustir marches into Tehra at the beginning of a new age."

RiVule took Taisha's hand protectively. "And the saga of the Orc shall be carved into the demons of Bloodstone."

Daryx nodded. "Send word to your Mighty Horde. They are to come to Tania and pass through the Temple Gate to Bloodstone. I will make arrangements for the sentries to let them pass provided they do not menace the citizens. Being part of an empire means reserving your strength for those deserving of it." Daryx eyed RiVule and almost cautioned him again.

RiVule bowed to Daryx and waved off more explanation. "I agree. It shall be as you say, Daryx. The citizens, the Innocents as you name them, will marvel safely at the Mighty Horde."

Daryx eyed Taisha closely. "The next full moon is when Gruustir's Mighty Horde shall embark to Bloodstone. May the tunnels shatter and demons curse the day of the Horde's arrival! RiVule, Taisha is altered like Tiamat's priestesses. She is more beautiful and fierce. She is perfect."

Taisha felt herself blush but riding the euphoric wave of resurrection and RiVule still holding her hand, she repeated his words, "More beautiful. Fierce."

RiVule squeezed her hand to tell her she pleased him. Behind them, Daryx signaled for the paladin to leave. "If there are other paladins – the one hundred you mentioned, I wonder if you and your knights might be enticed away from Bloodstone to something beyond legendary."

Daryx's words stirred something in RiVule and suddenly he saw a vast expanse open before him. War and the fires of war raged all around… and Drow fell before Taisha's blades, before his divine power. Unbidden and unasked for, a single word formed in his mind: Merakor. "You wish for me to join a quest to Merakor." RiVule stated this as if daring the dark elf to tell him otherwise.

Surprised, Daryx said, "Yes, Merakor. I see that the significance of this is known to the Orcs." Daryx began to explain the general plan and mission, but RiVule cut him short.

"The vision Gruustir shows me is sufficient. There will be enemies to slay and plunder to be had. Taisha will come with me. Frentoris and Incer must lead the Horde in Bloodstone, or I'd ask them to decide for themselves, though Frentoris would come. Incer is too stained by Coriga's corrupted doctrine."

Daryx did not know the names and replied, "I'm sure you'll figure it out. And yes, there will be Drow to slay." Daryx pulled a folded paper from his pocket, similar to the one Khalla had used when she spoke with her cell. "This has the basic information. In three months' time, enough time for you to see the Mighty Horde situated in Bloodstone, you will depart for Merakor."

Taisha piped in, "You are not going, Lord Daryx?"

"I cannot. For me to leave the Isles would mean my death. Though I yearn to go home and see my enemies bleed and die, Lolth requires me to stay here and tend to the master plan." Daryx's eyes gleamed with purple lights. "No doubt my enemies are glad I have not returned."

"You will tell me their names," RiVule ordered. "We will bleed them for you."

Daryx's smile promised RiVule names. Pleasing this strange Drow would bring the Horde more alliances and more power. RiVule made a mental note and sent it as a prayer to Gruustir. "Your plan folds together, Master. The Age of the Orc dawns!"

\* \* \*

Cordelle flailed in his bonds as dark dreams rocked him awake. The light seemed dim but it hurt his eyes, and he hungered. He felt burning cords bound tight against his ankles, wrists, and throat. The blinding light came from a patch of rectangular sunlight against the wall to his side. He felt its warmth and wanted to flinch away from it. By the chill in the air, he sensed it was morning and the sunlight would eventually fall across him. "That'll be bad," he muttered to himself.

"Indeed," a cordial voice answered from across the way. "It'll burn you to death. You're not ascended, you're not eldar, you're not protected. You'll die, if that's what you want."

Cordelle twisted his head and felt his skin burn against the ropes binding him. "Who are you? Why am I here?"

"I am a humble servant of Pha Rann. My name is Michael. I am charged with learning how you came to be this way and whether or not you wish to continue in this way." Cordelle could see Michael once he looked away from the sunlight. He wore the white garb of a cleric but seemed to hide an inner strength and power that gave his words the confidence they carried. "You've become a vampire. From your screaming and other words, I'd guess you haven't lived a life much in accordance with Pha Rann's teachings. Want to talk about it?"

*Syand and Jace*, Cordelle mentally swore at their names. *Syand attacked me and then Grant arrived with Bradley. Bradley betrayed Grant?* That did not make sense. Cordelle struggled to make sense of it. The *geas* magic on Jace should have prevented his betrayal of Cordelle... *Unless it wasn't a betrayal*, Cordelle realized. "I'm a vampire?" Asking the question out loud confirmed it. Syand had been a vampire. Cordelle always suspected it of her and Dark Legion, but they often moved around and did things vampires should not have been able to do. *Maybe I should not take popular opinion as the truth about vampires.*

Michael stood up and held a mirror out for Cordelle to see he had no reflection. Angling the mirror so Cordelle could see Michael, the priest said, "You are. But, you haven't fed on or killed anyone so the good news is that when I was called to intervene, you weren't destroyed outright. It seems you were murdered and then turned by a vampire rather than created in their Dark Gift. Someone was looking out for you. Our task now, if you wish to redeem yourself, is to help me find the vampires and stop them before actual innocents are killed or made into vampires too. Taysor and vampires don't go together."

Cordelle nodded, but the rope burned his neck. "Elven rope with silver wire in it," Michael said. "That you can move against it at all tells me you're not yet lost."

"I know who it was, who did it. But, what's in it for me? You say redemption, but you also know I'm not faithful to Pha Rann. Why should I?"

Michael came around and began to untie the ropes binding Cordelle. "Revenge," Michael said. "I'm a Perfectionist. Vampires have fallen so far from Pha Rann's design that we just need to end them all. You're a vampire and you're going to help me... for revenge."

Cordelle tested the idea that he might be a vampire. "So, I'm a vampire. Just like that," he grumbled as his hand came free and he rubbed his wrist. "I don't get a choice, nothing." Freed of the enchanted rope, his skin healed quickly. But, with that healing, came a renewed sense of hunger. He felt Michael's pulsating heart right there in front of him as the priest untied his feet.

"Yes, just like that." Michael removed the last coil and stepped back. "That you did not attack me suggests you have some wisdom in you. It would not have gone well. We don't always get to choose the path of our lives, Cordelle. But, we can choose how we walk it."

Cordelle poked his finger into the sunlight. Searing pain ignited along his finger in the light and he thought he saw smoke coming off his finger. When he pulled it back after a moment, the skin blistered like the worst sun burn he had ever seen. Like the rope burns, it healed quickly... and his hunger mounted. Cordelle touched his teeth and found them sharp, so sharp in fact that they cut his finger open like a razor. "I seem to be a vampire. I should be back in my warehouse organizing my next shipments. I have hundreds of families that rely on my business..."

"Dark Legion took it all, Cordelle. It's all gone. Operations are normal, but it's not really yours anymore. I'm sorry." Michael stood with his back to Cordelle and was flipping through the pages of what looked like Pha Rannic scripture. The brightly illuminated drawings and illustrations suggested it as such.

Michael's words struck at Cordelle's core. Normally a patient and pragmatic man, Cordelle suffered a shock of agony and lancing pain from his toes to his fingertips. The priest's skin pores and hair follicles magnified to his vision and, while the steady thumping of his heart did not change.

Michael said, "You're feeling unholy wrath. For vampires, any mortal emotion goes to an extreme. I'd imagine that you're either really wanting revenge or you're so full of anger that you're thinking about attacking me again." Michael turned to face Cordelle. The serene expression and radiant light in his countenance hurt like the sun burn on his finger. "Good luck with that. If you can resist the urge to feed and help me, we might recover 521. That is what you called yourself, right?"

Cordelle nodded and fought back a desire to leap at Michael. His fingernails had grown nearly to the length of dagger blades during that moment of unholy wrath. "I'm not used to feeling this."

Michael titled his head and with an expression that said 'obviously,' turned back to his book. "I'm looking through my Order's records of illicit activities in Taysor. While we have long known about the presence of Thieves Guilds here, most have been like 521. My faith is indifferent to the guilds; you serve a purpose. However, the Dark Legion was different. It arrived out of nowhere and quietly began growing in power. It has never lost or retracted in power. Though it seems small, I have reason to believe that it is the largest guild."

Cordelle laughed and quickly quieted himself. His laugh sounded cruel and full of hate. "Dark Legion is a joke. They are dark because you can't see them. They're insignificant! Even if Syand is a vampire, they're good at battle. Nothing else! That was why I wanted a truce with them. I am not, nor is my guild, a family of fighters."

Michael let him finish. "Consider what you just said. 'Amazing battle talent.' Like vampires perhaps? Tell me, Cordelle: have you ever seen a member of the Dark Legion die?"

Though he wanted to say yes, he conceded that he had never seen any of them die. "When Northern Cross exploded, we were sorting through body parts for days. Even with The Twins, we've been fishing their leadership out of the water. Vampires cannot endure water though."

"That's a myth. You're a vampire," Michael said. "You cannot endure holiness. When an ignorant becomes a vampire, they bring all these pre-conceits with them. This drives neurotic behavior in a fallen creature already subject to extremes of emotion. While your finger burned, you can actually endure sunlight. Think about it. It's daytime and you're talking to me just fine, even though that window is open. Sure, you don't like the sunlight. But, light by itself doesn't matter. On Tehra, the sunlight is Pha Rann. That holiness is what burns you. The myths about water actually stem from *blessed water*. Commoners mistakenly assume it means any water." Michael shrugged. "I would guess that an early vampire sought to cover actual weakness and so created all these stories. Water, garlic, locking your house… these hide the true weakness of divine light, blessed water, and silver."

"Sounds like clerical mumbo jumbo to me, but okay. Where are you going with this? I'm really hungry. Please tell me that I can eat normally."

Michael smiled. "Okay, Cordelle. You can eat normally. The downside is that it won't sustain you. Vampires are necromantic. You need necromantic energy – which I can give you – or you'll become so crazed for life energy you'll take it however you can. Consider what I just said about pre-conceits. If you've heard that vampires drink blood, you might find yourself obsessing over that very thing. The truth is stranger. It's the emotion and lifeforce you need to sustain you. Brutalizing your victim enhances the emotion in their lifeforce, but it doesn't have to be like that." Michael flipped to a dog-eared page in the book and pointed. "This vampire used to be a member of our Order. He fell to vampirism back in Tania's 8th Legion. He knew it happened and retreated to holy ground where we recovered him. We could not cure him, but we learned a lot. Give me your hand."

Michael began to pray. It started out like all the hymns and prayers Cordelle heard his entire life, but it changed after the first sentence and Cordelle realized Michael reversed the syllables in each word. Through his hand, he could feel the pulsing life of Michael as hot pinpricks against his hunger. Then, like a cool breeze on a humid day, the pinpricks resolved as energy flowing into him from Michael. Though the hymn sounded dissonant and off-key, it filled Cordelle.

"You don't have to be a vampire," Michael said. "We can work together to put an end to this Syand and maybe Dark Legion. If we don't, all those people in 521 and the other guilds that you care about will fall to Dark Legion. While I'm sure there are a few you'd be okay to fall, there are many you care about. Am I right? And there's, of course, innocents who live all around the guilds."

"521 and the other guilds," Cordelle said. "We took an ancient oath to the High King. When I became guildmaster, I took the same oath my predecessor did. Though I've never met King Andrew or his father, it felt sacred at the time. I took it seriously." Cordelle fidgeted back and forth on his feet. Now that his hunger had faded, he realized how violated he felt. What Michael called 'unholy wrath' shook his body again and he fought it back. "I still do. If what you say about Dark Legion is true, all of Taysor is at risk."

Michael took Cordelle's hand and embraced him. "That is the wisest thing I have ever heard a vampire say."

The rest of the day passed quickly. Michael prayed and birds came to the window and bore away messages from Cordelle to the rest of 521. On a whim, Cordelle sent one to Grant and Delton. By nightfall, only two replied though all of the animal messengers came back perplexed. Michael prayed and after much mediation explained. "The animals found dead bodies and then living bodies. They did not know how to deliver the message to a dead person and so came back to us. That's why they are acting so strange. Pha Rann compels their errand. I'll release them. The two that completed their mission, theirs are the only members of 521 that are still alive. I'm sorry for your loss."

Cordelle pointed to Jace's bird. "Send it back and ask Jace for the secret number."

Several hours later, the bird returned with the message: 'Eight.' Cordelle began to laugh somberly. "Jace is lost too," he explained through his dark laughter. "521 adds up to eight, but the secret number is actually the name of our first guild master ever. Jace must be a vampire too."

"Your guild's mage. Jace. Thirty-seven years old. Ambitious. Loyal... until Dark Legion. Do not blame him. You would be him if I had not found and brought you here. Shall we start with him then? Unless you know where Dark Legion's actual location is, I'm expecting there is a vampire coven deep under Taysor." Michael dropped some bones while praying and looked at them. "Jace. Yes, let's start with him. He portends our best approach."

Cordelle looked over Michael's shoulder. "You drop bones and they tell you things?"

Looking up from where he squatted, Michael replied, "They told me when and where to find you. Pha Rann works in strange ways. I've come to trust this one. It works for me."

Nightfall found Cordelle shadowing Michael. The priest, like all of them in Taysor, strode boldly down the thoroughfare with no concern for the increasingly strange looks he drew as the town around him grew more and more poverty-stricken. Cordelle recognized the area as a no man's land to the northeast of the Imperial palace grounds, near the Ymac border.

The proximity of the royal family, the temples, and the paladin orders meant that most smugglers preferred to operate on the northeast side. Over time, this section of Taysor, which sat tucked behind hills and buildings, grew into a sprawl. Many guildmasters tried to tame it, but each failed because of the heavy hand of the Soran guard and watch here. Sprawling poverty rigidly bounded by law and order marked this area the thieves called Northtown. This was where people came when they wanted to be safe, but free of religious issues and their spillover into Taysor's politics.

Michael paused under a chained lantern marking a shadowy intersection of five roads. He sat down and, using his hand as a surface, shook the bones and then contemplated them. For Cordelle, the wait was testing his sanity. The bones looked carvings from a big creature, likely some monster. "Did you kill something for those bones?" Cordelle asked.

"Yes, in Bloodstone. A devil took possession of a fighter in the group. When I exorcised it, the actual devil came and attacked me. It was my first devil slaying."

Cordelle listened but his thoughts raced in unpredictable directions. Being a vampire made him think faster. He had often wondered why all the stories about vampires featured rage fits and stupid mistakes that led to their demise. "I get it," he whispered. To his vision, Michael and every other person he could see radiated life and light. "Eat me," "Take me," "Make me yours forever"... each lifeforce called to him seductively. Resisting it, the seduction changed to jealousy.

I'd kill them all, Cordelle realized. The wooden post he leaned against in the dark shadows splintered under the strength of his hand. I don't even know how strong I am, but based on the stories... Cordelle jumped and easily cleared the two-story building at his side. Though he missed landing on the roof, he easily landed on the ground on the other side of the building. As a trained thief, he could tell he made no sound. No wonder Dark Legion has been so powerful, he mused. And we just thought they were good fighters.

Michael at last received an answer and stood up. "Come on. We need to backtrack a bit." After ten minutes of fast walking, Michael turned onto one of the gaudier streets in Northtown called Abigail's. Walking west on this, he at last came to a small building. It bore no signs but muted light from the inside and music showed it to be a gathering place. Michael walked up and opened the door, much to the surprise of a Dark Legion enforcer named Bowhouser. Cordelle recognized him and also saw how Michael had lifted the door off its hinges.

Cordelle crept forward wanting to see inside. Michael pulled out a symbol of Pha Rann and in a loud voice said, "Servants of darkness! Pha Rann commands your obedience. Stand and lift your arms in the air!"

Even though Cordelle was behind him, he felt his body and soul – what was left of it anyway – twist. Against his will, he stood and lifted his arms. Over Michael's body blocking the door, he saw three others do the same. Michael said, "You three will follow me, silently. The rest of you, if you value your lives: you saw nothing. You heard nothing. We," he said pointing at the vampires, "were never here."

Something about Michael's specification of the three he could see freed Cordelle from the arms-in-the-air compulsion. Michael walked towards Cordelle and, pointing to him said to the three, "You will obey Cordelle from now on." Michael then prayed to Pha Rann in the language of ancient Merakor to enhance his faith.

Cordelle and the three vampires found themselves still in front of the tavern, but also not. Gray mist and sparkling if muted color swirled around them towards the east. Michael said, "My prayer has withdrawn us from the world to give us some time," Michael explained. The tavern disgorged all of its people. Blades drawn, they burst outside looking for Michael. Not seeing him, they divided into groups.

In the strange and quiet space, the three vampires chafed against Michael's control. One tried to snarl at him but could not make a sound except a quiet whimper. Michael said to Cordelle, "So long as we do not order them to do something contrary to their natural desires, Pha Rann allows me to control them. I did not mean to get you as well. Please forgive me."

Cordelle answered, "I recognize them all though I don't know their names. They've been with Dark Legion as long as I can remember. Vampires, whod've thought it? So, what do we do?"

"We find Jace." Michael folded his arms across his plate armor. "Jace is the starting point."

Cordelle pointed to the snarling one. "Nod your head if you know where Jace is." The vampire nodded. "Tell me what happened to him."

Clearly, the vampire did not want to but at last, like a sneeze, the words came out. "Syand made him an offer he could not refuse. He joined the Legion."

"How many vampires are in Dark Legion?" Cordelle asked.

The vampire shrugged. "How would I know? I've never counted. Many. There are at least 150 of us."

"150," Michael said, his voice trailing off as he watched the dim shapes of the Dark Legion stalking them in the real world. "How many are like Syand?"

The vampires began to struggle, quivering as they fought to resist Michael's control. He sighed. "I see," he said touching the one talking.

"You've filled your heart with darkness and your nature now prevents you from betraying your masters. I'm sorry that your life has become this. Pha Rann did not make you to serve evil." The priest touched the other two and shook his head. "I'm so sorry." Under his outstretched fingers, the three vampires instantly crumbled to dust.

Cordelle jumped back. "What was that?!" he screamed.

"A holy servant can instill fear, obedience, even permanent death in necromantic creatures," Michael explained. "Pha Rann's design ordains death for us all. I asserted that design against the necromancy and so it ends. With the fall of the Jade God, it's easier than ever before. There is no dominion separating them from me. Their day of reckoning is here. Sure, they are more powerful against the unsanctified, but as Tania proved, if their god may die, so too may they die."

"What are you?" Cordelle asked. In spite of the strange fear he felt from Michael, he had never heard of a Perfectionist doing anything like this. "Aren't you supposed to be all about doctrinal compliance?"

Though Michael agreed with him, he also explained, "It is up to each of us to find our perfect path to righteousness. My path came through Creationism and Lightism. Today, I am arbiter and judge of vampires. Tomorrow, I may be called to serve as a healer." Michael shrugged. "To each his own. So long as we remain here, and unless something truly powerful comes along, we have as much time as we need. You know these three. The bones brought us here. We must learn why."

Cordelle began sifting through the garments and pile of equipment left over from the vampires' incineration. After some time, he asked Michael, "When you found me, were there any weird things with me such as giant quill-like spears, green clubs, or small vials of dark liquid?"

Without hesitating, Michael said, "Yes. When I arrived, your crew was beating someone, Grant from Rogue's Guild, I believe. He vanished with a Tanian contingency spell. When everyone recovered from that, they turned to find me entering and attacked. I was forewarned and therefore came ready for combat. There were some almost-vampires in the group. They fled. I let the humans leave." Michael pulled his backpack off and fished around. He pulled out a small carved piece of green bone and a crystal vial. The vial must have been used because only a few drops of blood remained.

Cordelle's eyes locked on the blood and the hunger struck him. Michael noticed it and pressed his hand to Cordelle's chest. "You will tell me what these are, I hope?" he asked while sending necromantic energy into the thief. It calmed the hunger, but Cordelle felt his entire being fixated on the Orcus blood.

"It's from the Jade God, from Bloodstone," he whispered. "As a human, it was amazing. The way I am now, I feel like an addict, ready to destroy all for just a taste."

Michael almost dropped them as he realized the truth of Cordelle's words. "I felt the great evil from them, but in the midst of so much carnage, I grabbed these because it was clear they had something to do with your death and Grant's impending murder by Howie. Howie, by the way, was corrupted by Dark Legion years ago."

Cordelle felt a hot flash of anger. "You know, you could have said something…"

"Why would I do that?" Michael casually retorted. Cordelle saw a brief glimmer of fanaticism in the priest's eyes. It was scary and Cordelle reminded himself that if he overstepped his bounds, he would become a pile of ash as well.

Michael continued, "Evil always destroys itself. It's an edict as old as the Gate of Creation. Like a snake eating its own tail, evil falls to evil. Your guild thrived because you remained focused on commerce. Had you become actively evil, like Dark Legion, something like this would have happened to stop you. An evil agent in an evil guild does not require Pha Rann's intervention. There is more at stake in this endless battle than your hurt feelings. Your scope of justice is dangerously off kilter if you view 'good' through the lens of 521. Pha Rann did not design you to ply Taysor with drugs and vice. You should direct your anger at Howie, not me. Better yet, if you care for your soul, you will direct your anger at all the times you had a chance to increase Good in the world and chose instead to increase your wealth."

Cordelle felt dumb-founded listening to Michael. Each word made sense, and painfully showed him what a waste his life was. Yet, it also shook him to his core and he countered, "You make sense but, you realize that Perfectionist teaching is not accessible to common people?" Cordelle tried to adopt a humbler and less angry tone of voice. "Let me have the blood. It allows you to see auras. I can only imagine what it will do to a vampire."

Michael moved to hand it to Cordelle but paused when he saw Cordelle's shaking hands. "One moment," he said and rolled his bones on the ground. Outside their Pha Rannic shell, in the real world, several vampires moved towards them sniffing at the air but clearly unsure of what they were seeking. "Pha Rann tells me that this will be instantly and nearly fatally addictive to you, Cordelle. If you do this, and without more, you will die. Which makes me wonder how much blood was found?" Michael pushed Cordelle away from him with a warning look. "Pha Rann does not tell me what becomes of you, whether you live or die."

Cordelle licked his lips and said, "I tried this as a human. Let me try it as a vampire. It's not like I have anything to live for. You yourself said I'd be 'redeemed.' Now that I've seen your redemption, we have nothing to lose. And, if they had Grant, they were probably trying to get the rest of it."

Michael closed his eyes and began to prayerfully meditate. At last, Michael agreed. "Okay. Grant is key. Drink this. We find Jace. Then we find Grant. I'm going to need a mage, which means that you're going to have to come to the Temple of Light, Cordelle. Unless we get Jace and he helps us. Drink up."

Cordelle, in his haste to open it, broke the glass neck and swallowed the several drops. Unlike his human experience, the world exploded into light as bright as noon-day. He could see the blurring of Michael's separated from the world sanctuary and the two vampires lurking outside its protective faith. Michael burned gloriously in his vision and looked every bit as divine as Cordelle imagined an angel might. By contrast, the vampires looked emaciated and ghoulish. All of his hunger vanished and he inhaled life, feeling it coil through his body.

Michael said, "I'm going to return us to the world. If we're going up against Syand and that many vampires, you need to understand your own powers. I'll only intervene if you can't take on these two vampires sniffing at us."

Cordelle flexed his hands and nodded. Michael ended the sanctuary prayer. The vampires recoiled as Cordelle and Michael seemed to appear in a blink before them. Faster than either could react, Cordelle punched the closest in the head. It surprised Cordelle that his fist speared through the skull of his opponent and exploded gore and brain out the other side. The strength and speed of his body plus the power from the Jade God's blood uplifted him. "So this is how the gods fight!" he screamed.

The other vampire dodged out of Cordelle's reach, barely avoiding a talon rake from Cordelle's other hand. "Cordelle," he hissed, wincing when Cordelle freed his arm by pulling it through his friend's skull. The vampire shot forward and made two slashing attacks at Cordelle with scimitars.

Cordelle dodged one, but the other sliced his shoulder open to the bone. Cordelle barely felt it. There was no pain, only hunger from the wound. Cordelle stepped into the slicing attack and caught the outside edge of the vampire's arm. "I don't know your name," he said biting into the vampire's shoulder. Armor folded against his teeth and then sweet blood rich in necromantic power entered his mouth.

"My name is your death!" the vampire gasped. He brought his other hand up and the scimitar speared through Cordelle's midsection. Again, Cordelle experienced no pain but did feel his hunger increase. If analogous to the pain he might have felt as a mortal, he knew he must be nearing "death" because the unholy wrath described by Michael rose up to overtake him.

Cordelle choked it back and locked the hand and hilt in his stomach. Sliding his teeth through the shoulder armor to the vampire's neck, Cordelle could see the carotid artery in the vampire's neck and then a splash of blood flowed over and into him. Rather than drink, Cordelle chewed into the vampire's neck until he felt bone. Though the scimitar in his bowels sawed back and forth, the two remained locked until at last, Cordelle's opponent fell. Cordelle pulled the scimitar out of his guts while drinking the last blood of his foe.

"That was gruesome," Michael said. "But now we know. Tell me when the Jade God's blood wears off. Your fight drew attention, we must move now. To Jace."

\* \* \*

Calvin raised his glass to Ryvane. "I was just talking to Path the other night about adventure as a way to finance a revival here in Dockside. Merakor!"

Ryvane smiled and clinked her glass against his. Around them, other restaurant patrons smiled and pointed at the charismatic couple. Ryvane could hear them talking about Calvin. It only bothered her slightly that no one talked about her. "My vanity feels upset that no one cares about the winsome lass dining with you," she said. "Yes, Merakor. I had to pull a few strings with the guild to get you onboard, but they saw your value as a warrior and negotiator immediately."

"Should I be concerned about Dockside while we're gone? Up to three years. That's a long time." Calvin looked around the room and nodded at several of the people who raised their glasses to him. "We should be careful in our conversation."

"I am. They can't hear us courtesy of a simple spell. It'll be fine. You have helpers here and the City Watch. I've sent word to Reggie and he assures me that Dockside will be returned to you as is. Just imagine how much better things will be when you return a hero!" Ryvane was so used to charming Calvin that she had to resist it this time. She wanted to see his genuine reaction to everything. It had been too long.

He smiled at her with boyish charm and said, "If I come back. It wouldn't be an adventure if there was no risk. What if I die? What if you die, my love?"

"I'm not worried about it. In my time with the guild, Tania prepares for these things at a level you almost cannot imagine. It's all business, with risk and contingency plans aplenty. We'll both be fine." Looking into his smiling eyes, she wondered if he knew that this would be yet another lie. In all likelihood, Calvin would die. At a certain point, the clerics would not revive him. Khalla had been very clear on this point. Calvin could come at his own risk. If he proved useful and valuable to the team, the clerics would revive him as a matter of course. *If not*, Ryvane thought, *that's why I have an order in for three resurrection scrolls.*

They enjoyed pleasant and celebratory dining. Unlike so many similar nights before this, Calvin did not ask or suggest that they abscond with one of the beautiful serving girls or diners, though several presented themselves as the type Calvin would have wanted to bring home with them. It made her feel giddy and, in spite of herself, she wondered. *What happens if I tell Calvin the truth about me?*

So lost in her own thoughts, Ryvane missed most of what Calvin said. His mention of the king's name pulled her focus back to their dinner talk. She blinked her eyes at him. "I'm sorry, I zoned out. What did you say about the king?"

"Sure. You looked a bit out of it for a moment. I was just thinking that maybe it's time I visit Malcor and let him know how things are going. My father won't care about Merakor. At least, if he did, he would try to talk me out of it. But, if things go poorly, I'd like for someone to be able to tell him I died heroically. Malcor seems ideal for this, don't you think?"

*It's always Malcor with him. Hey Malcor, I'm going to Merakor. For all we know, Malcor's name will be the official seal on the god emperor's contract.* Thinking about it, she knew it would be. "That's a great idea, Calvin. My friends told me they heard Malcor was here in town. If we go through official channels, we'll never see him. However, Ora is up at the Temple these days. What if we talked to her first?"

Calvin clinked his glass against hers. "That's a perfect idea," he complimented her. "I wonder if Ora remembers me?"

"I'm sure she does. She's probably the only beautiful girl to not fall under your spell." Ryvane indicated a young woman to Calvin's side trying to catch his attention. Word had quickly gotten around Dockside that Calvin and Ryvane enjoyed extra company. For those willing, it meant they had plenty to choose from. Pointing her out, Ryvane hoped Calvin would dismiss her.

When he ignored the girl and took her hand across the table, Ryvane's heart skipped. Calvin said, "Tonight, it's just you and I. I want you all to myself. No magic."

His words, so perfectly and sincerely spoken, pulled Ryvane back to her last moments with Kieran. Calvin's similarities to Kieran were part of the reason she fell in love with Calvin so easily. "Really?" she giggled. "You don't want a real girl?"

The words slipped from her mouth and she flinched inside. Calvin raised an eyebrow at the odd comment but let it slip by. "You are my real girl, Ryvane."

"Oh my, you're on your most charming behavior tonight. Careful or you might find yourself being tested, to your limits. Imagine it." She pulled his hand to her and bit his knuckle as hard as she could. Calvin carefully did not flinch even when she tasted his blood.

"Test away, dearest."

She looked at him and whimsically said, "Ok! Here we go. Will you still love me if I'm not really me?"

"Who else would you be, Ryvane? Yes, I would still love you. Unless you're that archmage. I don't think I could handle being in love with Halgrim. It's not my thing." He chuckled. "Can you imagine?"

"Even if I'm a monster?"

"Like, what kind of monster? Malcor is supposedly a dragon and Ora clearly loves him, if what the bards are singing about is true. If a priestess can love a monster, then yes, I would still love you."

Ryvane squeezed his hand. "Not a dragon, a cat monster. Mreow!" she teased him playfully.

"Oooo, I like that," he answered.

Ryvane could not stand it anymore. She put coins on the table for their meal and they vanished from the restaurant to reappear on the top of a Mages Guild tower. The city spread out from them in all directions, but Calvin only had eyes for her.

# Chapter 10 – Dark Legion

Delia kept her eyes lowered as Syand punched her again. Delia explained, "Grant keeps escaping us. I was confronted by a Pha Rannic high priest. What's your excuse?" Syand wiped drool from her mouth and dared Delia to say anything. The vampire's eyes glowed all red with wrath, waiting for an excuse to kill.

Delia whispered, "I heard Grant defeated you. The same as he defeated me. I don't know how he knew. He's very good. I can see why you want him."

Syand backhanded her. The blow would have broken the neck of any human. "What you heard is wrong. But, you – I hired you because Grant should fall to Delia. You must have made a mistake. Do not dare make excuses! Do you have any idea how much time and money we spent to figure this out about Grant?"

Delia nodded. "I was nervous. My leg shifted. Not much but enough that Grant saw. It surprised me how quickly he went from love to war. Most humans, in my experience, cannot move so quickly. He is different. It was surprising."

Syand's hand rose again but she hesitated to strike Delia. "Different, you say. Tell me more."

Delia explained, "In passion, humans fixate on the face, breasts, and genitals. My kind, we have studied this in human males. A mistake in our copy would be invisible during sex. For Grant to notice with so many other things going on, he has had training. In talking with my team, this training is not how thieves are in most of the world's places. There are only two we know of that train this way: the Drow and Tania, because of Daryx, we think. Had I known this, we would have attacked Grant in force or I would have taken more of my team upstairs as part of Grant's seduction and capture."

Syand sat back and said, "I'm sorry I struck you. I did not know Grant was like this. Show me his face. I want to confirm it was actually him."

Delia nodded and concentrated as if flexing. Her skin tone, face, and form changed to an exact copy of Grant. Satisfied, Syand said, "Yes, that is him. So, you think he might have been trained in Tania. Is he Tanian?"

Delia shrugged. "There is no way to know. In reflection, there is circumstantial evidence. He was the first to capture Orcus' parts. He has remained independent of the other guilds all this time. He came out of nowhere. He has no real base in Taysor. He keeps his group small, which is different from all of Taysor's guilds. This is how the Drow do it by the way. Their assassins are organized into small teams, just like Grant's. I've never had experience with Tania except as hearsay and a few who barely escaped death; they execute doppelgangers on sight. So, we never go there."

Syand offered her an invitation to explain. "How would they know?"

Delia flexed her body again and assumed the form of a kerchki, kneeling but still towering over everyone in the room. "The kerchki fire giants can see through our copies." Delia returned to her female form and they continued talking. "And, if we are near any of the transcended priestesses, they feel our difference."

From the back of Dark Legion's gathering, a breathless man entered. "Syand," he called. "Our team, following Delton, they've all been killed. Jace scried it out. We've lost them."

Syand's face locked for a moment as if petrified and then her eyes went completely red again. Delia flinched back from her as did the others closest. Syand took a deep breath and said, "How much of the Jade God did we get from Cordelle?"

Everyone looked around wishing Jace were there to answer. Not a single sound broke the gathering. "So little? None?" Still no one dared make a sound. Syand raised her finger to point to the messenger and asked him, "How do you know the entire team is gone?"

The man, whose breathing had calmed enough that he could talk, realized the mood in the room was not a good one. He bowed low and said, "Jace used a crystal ball and described what he saw to me. He saw all of them killed by Delton's team."

Syand asked, "And where is Jace right now?"

He gulped. "Last I saw, he was in 521's headquarters securing items he said you would need." Even to his own ears, it sounded weak. "Jace was very business-like…"

Syand vanished and reappeared with her teeth locked in the man's throat. She ripped her head back and let his blood fountain over the room before she clamped a hand over the wound. Holding the messenger against her chest, Syand said, "Find me Jace!"

The room cleared quickly, some even activating magic to help them get out before Syand took another life. Furious, Syand pulled the dying man back to her mouth and drained him.

Delia sprinted to 521's warehouse. The rest of her doppelganger team paced her alongside the street. Every turn, every twist, she shifted her appearance so that each moment she resembled someone else she passed. Even though her team ran in the shadows and rooftops, they did the same. Living among humans, this pattern of behavior had saved them even when things felt most safe. They left the normal humans, food really, far behind.

The 521 warehouse loomed before them. No guards stood ready to intercept them. No fires burned or flickered in gas lamps. Delia noticed the utter absence of guards and then her skin began to crawl. From the hidden areas around the warehouse, ghouls rose up in beggar and warehouse worker garb. They each bore the signs of recent violent death. A strange green light glimmered in their eyes.

Delia's team came to a halt. "There should not be ghouls here," one of her friends observed. The friend preferred a human trope as his form: the barbarian. His large form and exotic appearance drew attention away from the areas he struggled to get right, like facial expressions matching mood. And, no one would ever question such an imposing figure.

Delia said, "Can we take them? I see seven." Someone else called out that they saw five more by the side entrance. "Ghouls aren't that fast. We'll ignore them for now. If they follow us, we'll burn this whole place down on the way out and let the rest of the Legion handle them. Besides, the Pha Rannic Temple should be showing up shortly with this many here."

They ran past the ghouls. They seemed faster than ghouls should have been, but it was still no trouble for the doppels to extend their legs and increase their speed. Once inside the warehouse, they moved easily down into the offices. From flickering shadows and light, someone moved about. It had to be Jace.

Delia slowed down and signaled for the barbarian to enter first. He did and was blasted with ice shards. From the angle of impact, Delia could tell Jace had been prepared and was casting from the left side. The barbarian took the brunt and though frozen, he shifted to a smaller size and stepped back. His frozen form remained against a thin layer of skin and connective tissue. He shifted his degloved front side to cover the wounds; it was a matter of doppelganger pride to never show the true damage of combat. He was still hurt; he just was not bleeding now.

Delia and her team shifted to smaller, more agile forms. She chose a pixie and darted into the room. More ice bolts shot at her, but none hit. The barbarian shattered the ice that had initially encased him and charged at Jace.

Jace held a jade green wand in one hand. Unlike Syand, whose moods you could read through her eyes, Jace's eyes danced with multi-hued rainbows. He pointed the wand at her and triggered another spell. He should not have been able to cast spells again.

Five bright points of white light streaked out at her. Though she dodged, Delia recognized the spell and knew the magic missiles would hit her. She closed the distance to Jace and went large hoping to obstruct his view of her team. The five missiles speared into her skin and burned so with such heat that she screamed in agony. Yet, her leap carried her onto the vampire and slammed him to the ground.

Jace's robes felt unnatural against her hands, greasy and scratchy at the same time. She felt her barbarian teammate land just above Jace's left side. He stomped down onto Jace's arm and morphed his leg into a writhing mess of tentacles to immobilize him. The floor splintered under the barbarian's foot.

Delia shouted, "Give up, Jace! We don't have to turn you over to Syand, though her crew will be here soon!"

Those many-colored lights in Jace's eyes glanced at her and she hoped he would agree... Instead, he head-butted her in the face and broke her nose. The force of it slammed her head back and she screamed. Though a new vampire, he was fast, she chided herself.

Jace attacked her and the barbarian with the jade wand, stabbing at them with it as if it were a dagger.. Delia jumped back and let her body liquefy to move behind Jace and meld to the wall, copying its texture. The rest of the team saw it and signaled readiness. The barbarian drew his foot back and let a battle axe form in his hands. Though the axe was part of his body, it would cut like steel. At the last instant, he focused and let the axe become silver instead. "Vampire!" he screamed.

Using the momentary interlude of creating the axe, Jace began casting another spell. Oblivious to Delia reforming from the wall behind him, he summoned two spheres of ice. Just as he was about to unleash them at his opponents, Delia lashed her arms out as two tentacles from the wall and slammed his arm back against the wall and his head. Her other tentacle grabbed his foot and rotated him around the barbarian still pinning his arm to the floor.

Ice detonations dropped the temperature in the room. It made the doppels feel sluggish and heavy. Shards of exploding ice shot out from the two spheres. In the small room, the detonations would hurt and Delia pulled Jace up sideways while moving behind the barbarian to try and block herself from the jagged ice needles firing everywhere. Moving along the wall like this, she felt a strange sensation. It felt like an earthquake, but seemed limited inside the wall. Jace felt it too and swore. "Pha Rann burn us all! Let me go!" he screamed. "We're all going to die if you don't let me go right now!"

As he thrashed his head and body back and forth, Delia noted how one of the ice sphere's explosions had stripped flesh and chipped away bone from the right side of his face. Sharp angled teeth gaped at her through lisping words as he struggled to break free. Under that strange garb, the rest of his body seemed undamaged. Delia knew that when she recovered her humanoid form, there would be pain. The wall trembled again. "Ignore him," Delia called out to the barbarian and the other doppels. "Kill him."

Jace twisted so hard one of her tentacles nearly snapped. She was not ready for the pain of a vampire bite as he chomped down on the tentacle. Flinching, she lost grip on his arm. With that arm now free, Jace punched the tentacle's base where it extended from the wall. Pain flared and Delia felt her grip on conscious thought narrow to trying to hold Jace so the others could kill him. Distantly, she saw the barbarian grab Jace's backpack and signal her, then vanish. He was not usually so circumspect. It made her suspicious and then ice shards smashed her away from Jace as he completed another spell.

The other doppels attacked the mage, hacking at his back with silver weapons. She felt their impacts, but they seemed to have no effect on Jace except to drive him back and bludgeon him. The strange skin nullified all of their attacks, she realized when a knife sliced down the cape and then cut into Jace's lower calf.

The trembling in the wall became rhythmic now. She felt the entire wall move. She felt hot pricks against her body where she touched its surface. Jace finally tore her tentacle free and Delia collapsed to the ground in her true form, sexless and gray with overly-long limbs, Delia cradled her shoulder stump and scrabbled back away from the fighting.

Jace swung her tentacle at another doppel like a club, and though it did no damage, it distracted her friend enough that Jace finally stabbed the jade green wand into the barbarian. "Protect me!" Jace shouted. His face had nearly healed from the blood sucked from her tentacles.

The barbarian nodded at Jace. With a bewildered expression, he tackled the one about to backstab Jace with a silver blade and used his body as a shield to deflect another backstab attack. "No!" they both cried out but he could not help himself. "End me!" he cried as his fist bludgeoned the assassin.

Delia had put some distance between herself and Jace, and reached into her pocket. It was not really a pocket but a part of her body used to hold things. She recovered a small ball of twisted metal bands and threw it at Jace while a *healing* potion appeared in her hand. Jace swatted the metal ball away from him, but Delia smiled and leaned back to relax when she saw it hit him. "Unless you can fly or teleport, this fight is over."

The first metal band arced out and wrapped around Jace's arm as the others fell apart from the sphere and began locking to Jace. Her friend jumped to Jace's aid trying to pry the bands off. As each locked into place, Delia smiled. The *healing* potion brought her a measure of relief. Rather than stand up, she reformed herself, minus her arm, in a standing position. "Give me the wand," she ordered.

Jace grunted as the metal bands squeezed him so tight his joints popped. "Why would I do that?" he gagged back at her. "If you try to do anything to me, your friend will stop you. We're at an impasse. Soon, the ghouls will arrive and then Dark Legion. There's plenty of time for me to figure this out."

"Is that what you think, Jace? Are you insane?" Delia looked at the mess all around and signaled for her team to neutralize the barbarian. "You think Syand is going to be kind to you? Why do you think we are here?"

A small dart hit the barbarian. The assassin walked forward and pulled the dart from their friend's back while another opened a small box. The barbarian's body oozed to the floor, melting apart like hot wax. When some of it fell into the small box, the rest of the body pulled into it and they closed it with a faint clicking sound. The room around them trembled and Delia felt they were running out of time.

Jace felt the room shift too and fear blossomed in his eyes. "Get me out of here. Let's make a deal," he said.

Delia grinned and said, "No, we'll get out of here." She patted Jace on the cheek. Though still immobilized, Jace had totally healed. "Why do you think we came here?" She found a rag on a nearby table and used it to pull the jade wand from Jace's hand.

From her hip, a small flask appeared and she withdrew it. It glowed orange. "Not just oil," she whispered to Jace. "Burning oil. I figured it out, by the way." She unscrewed the lid on the flask.

Jace licked his lips and said, "I'm not bound to Syand. We can make a deal! I'll make it worth your while!"

"Do you have more of Orcus' blood?" She saw the answer in Jace's expression. She shrugged and shook her head. "CThis entire warehouse is alive, isn't it?" Delia tossed the flask back against the corner of the room. As liquid dribbled out of it, it began to burn with a magical intensity that ignited the floor and walls around it. Acrid smoke already filled the space by the time the flask stopped rolling. The smoke smelled like burning flesh, not wood. "Clever. I always thought Cordelle the best of the guildmasters, but this Grant is so intriguing. Team, let's go."

She ran from the room as the entire warehouse heaved. Jace began laughing as he fell to his side. "You have no idea!" he screamed after them.

The stairs seemed steady but as Delia raced up them two at a time, the third step vanished and became biting teeth. Ahead of her, the rest of the team tripped and fell as the ground morphed and attacked them. "Go aerial!" the assassin cried. Though Delia managed to stretch her legs and dodge the biting step, she saw the staircase – she had another ten paces to go – grow more steeply inclined and the steps vanished as teeth sprouted from the floor and walls around her.

She shifted into a small bird, but missing her arm, she had to turn one of her legs into the other wing. She was not used to flying with an arm and a leg. She fell and tried to hop-dodge the teeth. From above, the assassin ducked a ghoul as it tried to tackle him. He reached down to her with his arm extending into a tentacle. She reached for it doing the same and the two interlocked. He whipped her up the stairs as the entire passage bit down. Jace's laughter still rose up from below. "You have no idea!" The manic tone in his voice boded poorly for Delia's team. "Ghouls! Attack them! No one escapes!"

Multiple fires burned all around Delia's team and she noticed the warehouse floor, crates, and pulleys hanging from the ceiling had begun to move. "Is this entire area the mimic too?" she wondered.

The assassin shrugged. "I don't know, but it's getting bad. I don't like this job." Looking around, he pointed to the rest of the team. They had found a stone section amidst the wooden floor planking that did not seem to shift. He offered his hand to Delia and said, "There they are. You're wounded. Hold on."

The assassin shifted to giant size and threw Delia at their friends. Though the throw was overpowered, it sent her quickly to avoid the tentacle-like chains and ropes reaching out to catch her. The assassin jumped in a seemingly random pattern and joined them as chains and ropes from overhead dropped down all around them, trying to entangle them. The ghouls did not fare well in the mess of snakes material, but the mimic left them alone. Delia's team laughed when they saw one of the ghouls fall into a mouth that opened beneath its landing. The mouth expelled the ghoul towards them however and they realized how bad it was. The last doppel in their team had to drop from giant-sized to a tiny version of itself to shed a handful of ghouls clawing into its skin. Just as it seemed their friend would begin running to them, a mass of chains that became razors fell from the ceiling. Like a snake constricting prey, the razored chains circled about their buried friend.

Delia pulled a medallion from her leg as her body made the pocket available. "I agree. This job has gone bad. You all agree?" When everyone nodded, Delia touched the medallion to her forehead and said, "Grant, if you can hear me. This is Delia. We're going to your safehouse at Ymac." A moment later, they held hands and all teleported away from the warehouse.

Dark Legion arrived to find the entire warehouse moving and burning. Tendrils the size of wagons smashed out at anything that got too close and smoke billowed out of it from all directions. They tried to enter, to see what was going on, but any who got too close had to be pulled back as they fell into biting traps in the ground itself.

Inside, Jace watched the walls come alive and bite out to him. Orcus' blood boiled in his veins still and he saw the many deaths consumed by the warehouse mimic. "Cordelle really is the best," he whispered. Teeth opened beneath him and Jace bit into the ground. The mimic's blood would not sustain him, but it was worth a try. Never before had Jace wanted to live as much as he did right now. *If I can keep the mimic from encapsulating me, it might spit me out.*

\* \* \*

Ora stood beneath the Ice Patriarch obelisk in the Temple. The chill of the stone and the white-gray veins running through it helped her feel at peace. She missed Malcor and their son, Alauren. A voice from behind her noted, "It's a strange thing that, all this time, you were right there and yet, you and I never met."

Ora turned to see Dar Shara, and dropped to a kneel. The high priestess essentially ruled Morbatten these days because everyone else continued to fight in Bloodstone. The armored plate mail of Dread Lord Armageddon clinked five paces behind her. Unlike the Court, Armageddon's barely controlled dragonterror ensured a wide circle around the high priestess. Ora bowed politely. "We actually did meet, my lady. I was very young. You oversaw my testing here."

Shara smiled and shrugged. "Dar Ora, I do not remember, but since I became aware of you, I am impressed. I had to go all the way back to Dar Tania's days and the writings of Sage Alaura to find another time when the Ice Patriarch took a Rider. That is special, and miraculous. When there is time, please consider yourself welcome to join me. I would like to know more about how these things work. The Great Sage, she was most cryptic on many points. Armageddon, though a dear friend and teacher, does not take Riders."

Ora replied, "And the same for you, great high priestess." Ora blushed and look away for a moment before firming up her resolve. "This may sound stupid and silly, but may I ask a favor?" When Shara remained pleasant, Ora pulled out her notebook and offered it to Shara. "Please, I grew up hearing stories about you. I always wanted to meet you. Before my family passed away, I had hoped to find you and I was going to say, 'Please, let me serve you, great lady.' Now, here we are talking. It feels too good to be true. May I have your autograph?" Shara took the notebook and signed her name in it while writing more. Ora looked at the Dread Lord and bowed deeply. "Dread Lord Armageddon, I know it's impossible to hope."

"I will," he said.

Ora's blush turned deep red, a stark contrast to her alabaster complexion. She gulped. Shara pulled Ora into a close embrace. "You are one of us, sister. We each serve the Goddess, but a few of us are chosen for so much more." She held Ora tightly to her. "It is clear that Ynt'taris has chosen you. The king loves you. The Court favors you. We are bound by threads of destiny and I would that neither of us walk alone." Shara kissed Ora's cheek. "Never have I felt the skin of an ice priestess."

Ora hugged her back and whispered, "Your skin burns like fire. How do you stand it?"

Behind her, Armageddon began to laugh as his body ignited in a tornado of fire. The faithful all around stepped even farther back. When those present realized it was Armageddon, everyone formally kneeled before the Son of Tiamat. The Dread Lord stepped forward and gestured for Ora's notebook and quill. Ora handed it to him and then dropped to her hands and knees. Kneeling beside Ora, Shara took her hand and whispered, "I've never seen the Dread Lord sign for anyone. Another first."

Armageddon signed his name amidst smoldering paper with his gauntlet fingertip. He chuckled throughout. If he noticed the humans kneeling around him, or how all activity in the Temple came to a halt, he did not show it. When finished, he stepped to Ora and put the notebook on the ground before her. For a moment, his eyes lingered on the crowd bowing before him and he paused before turning and walking back to his position behind Shara. As he let his mirth fade, the pressure of his terror eased. When the tornado of heat swirling around him faded at last, Shara signaled a return to normal.

At Shara's feet, Ora opened the notebook and read Shara's inscription. The high priestess' words touched her with warmth and kindness. Below Shara's words, Armageddon's signature charred the paper where he wrote, "For ice, your faith is warm."

Ora looked at Armageddon and sensed that he still smiled at her through the heavy visor masking his face. She felt his eyes on her and she mouthed, "Thank you." Armageddon chuckled again just barely managing to suppress the thermals from his body before he ignited again.

Shara looked down and read his inscription too. "The Dread Lords rarely show humor. Opposition draws it out though and we are grateful he sees you as family, Ora. I also think this might be the first time a Dar has asked for my autograph. It rather took me by surprise. Of course, when I was younger, I wanted them all too. The Kell Conflict got in the way though. I assume you have everyone? Dar Ana too?"

"No, not everyone." Ora blushed again. "And, my lady, I hardly think of myself as a Dar. You'd think Dar Kell would be easiest, but I am still missing him and Arminoth. Dar Ana is, well, after Malcor I don't know how to approach her." Ora stood up and they talked for a bit about Alauren and Malcor. "I understand," Ora questioned, "that there was a meeting and consensus to allow me to be with Malcor? Thank you for this boon."

Shara waved her hand to dismiss the notion. "As a priestess, you never know when the call might come, and you pray that he will be handsome, daring, and worthy. That you have found someone who truly is and feels love for you, is marvelous. Like Dar Tania, you never know what loves will present from where and when. That you are so young, is a good thing. Your son, Alauren, is magnificent. All priestesses are allowed love. We have Dar Tania and a much younger Dar Ana to thank for this. I did not find mine until, hmmmm." She pursed her lips and thought back. "After two hundred years of service. It gets easier to obey as the years tick away."

Ora bowed low and said, "Thank you, my Dar. I consider myself very lucky."

Shara pulled her back up into another embrace and whispered into her ear, so that no one would hear or see. "Cherish it. It will not last long. The god emperor will not long let his only shadow paladin be with only you when there could be another generation of offspring written into the Book of Genesis already. Consider this a friendly heads up and also a caution to prepare yourself and him. Rojo's resistance was not well-met by the Court, appearances and support by Tiamat aside. Also, because you're a rare ice priestess and a dragon rider, the god emperor will no doubt wish for you to have children with the paladins and others who bear any affinity to the Ice Patriarch. There are not that many, Ora. You've been cloistered in Sai's estate for some time. If you'd like, I will have the records of these heroes sent your way."

Ora nodded. "I understand what you're telling me, Shara. I don't want to know, but I guess, yes, please send me the records. Though not pleasant to hear, I know this is truth." Ora then closed her eyes and pushed herself back from Shara to reclaim some personal space. "Ynt'taris told me this would happen. Unlike the fire priestesses, this child-bearing thing will be a bit different with me. That Ynt'taris approves of Malcor helps. That the god emperor approves of Malcor also helps, a lot. When commanded by Tiamat, I am ready. Malcor will bear it with the same stoic heart he does all else." Ora bowed one last time and took her leave.

Outside the Grand Hall, she found most of the Temple engaged in normal business but she could tell they had all been straining to hear. She touched the spider golem earring on her left ear and mentally asked for help from Sai R'Dar. No sooner did she complete her thought than Reggie walked up to her. His brightly-feathered hat and plump smile bounced around as he jostled his way towards her.

Out of the corner of her eye, Ora saw a familiar face entering the Grand Hall and groaned. She did not want to be here anymore. The feelings of awe and happiness at meeting Dar Shara and Armageddon had wilted against the high priestess' different view of her love with Malcor. She had known Ana would view Malcor as a competitive trophy. She had not been prepared for Shara's empathetic if factual take on having to bear children with others linked to Ynt'taris. The titanic edifice of Tiamat's worship grew small around her. Ora felt her heart yearn for the icy mountains of the north. "Take me away from here, Reggie. Please."

A small frown creased Reggie's face as he saw her and bustled to her side. He took her hand and pulled her away as, from across the hall, Ryvane and Calvin asked to see Ora. The acolyte turned to point, but found the ice priestess had vanished.

Reggie teleported himself and Ora into a large room, luxuriously decorated and flanked on all walls by ancient tapestries and golem statues. Ora took a deep shuddering breath. "Thank you. I hoped for a miracle like you. I rather miss our days at Sai's estate when it was just Ynt'taris, you, and the other golems."

From Reggie's mouth, Sai's voice came. Though flat and emotionless, Sai's voice noted, "I felt your response to Shara's insistence that you would mother children with others. I do not understand the reaction to something you've always known would be required. Even the first priestess, Dar Tania, was not exempt from duty and that in spite of her great love and special hold on Alerius."

Ora nodded, trying to hold her composure. Since giving birth to Alauren, her body and moods had not yet recovered their former state. The fire priestesses, known for erratic and fiery mood swings, had a reputation for fits of rage following birth. Ynt'taris speculated that Ora would be different. He had been correct. She hugged herself and took a deep shuddering breath. With each breath, her temperature fell until her breath misted the humidity in the room.

Reggie put her fingers in his hand and gave her a reassuring squeeze. "Will you be okay? I've brought you to where The Circle meets. This room is secure, safe, and yours for as long as you require it."

"Thank you, Master Sai. I think I'll be okay. I find that certain threads of thought panic my mind and I begin shutting down. Rooms, even the outdoors, become small. When near the powerful fire Dar, it gets worse. I grew up hearing stories about Shara. My temple studies never brought us together. It's stupid I know but…"

"You wanted her autograph, yes. It would not be hard to arrange you to meet everyone at my estate. This interest in signatures seems at odds with your actual reactions to the real people," Sai's voice observed through Reggie's mouth. "The fire dragons, they incite emotion outside the bounds you have felt. When Shara spoke, did you wish to escape?"

Ora sat down on a plush gold-wrought chair made of some no-doubt-exotic bone. The name placard noted it belonged to Dar Cain, Lord of Taxation. "No, Sai. I found myself looking for a way to win. I wanted her to die," she admitted. A small whimper escaped her lips and she choked it back. "I have worshipped her my whole life! I wanted to be her. Why would I feel this way? I don't want her to die! She's practically holding the empire together for thirty years now!"

Reggie's form melted away and Sai rose up in his place. He put his hand on Ora's head and brushed her hair back from her glossy blue eyes. "Your temperature is overly heated. I will help. Ora, you just had your first child. Be patient with yourself. Father Alerius has noted for countless generations that rampant emotions can afflict mothers after birth for about six months sometimes longer. It all fades within two years at the longest. Becoming pregnant again will help. No ice priestess or ice rider has ever had a child. It's a new thing. With your permission, I would counsel with my father."

"Why not with Ynt'taris?" Ora asked.

"The Ice Patriarch is as possessive of you as he was the Sage Alaura. I will ask my father to include him."

Ora nodded and held Sai's cold hand. The increasing cool of the metal golem helped re-center her. "I miss Alauren." She gasped as Sai's hand became unearthly cold and she opened his fingers and put her face in it. The cold pulled the fire from her and she began to breathe more easily.

Sai touched her earing and the spider golem hanging there leapt into the master's hand. A moment later it returned to her ear. "I've added magic to your earring golem. He can become very cold now. So cold that it will hurt those around you, so be careful. That is natural and a tribute to your motherly instincts. Watch Wess and Seantir from a distance. They are taking good care of your little boy."

"Yes, but it should be me..."

"No, Ora. It should be them. Know also that Ynt'taris watches from the high places of the world." Sai titled his head as if listening and apologized. "I am summoned by Daryx and must leave. Stay here. Be safe. Whatever you need, Reggie will get it for you." Sai looked around the room and in a loud voice said, "I am Sai R'Dar, Imperial Fourth. Dar Ora has my permission to be here. You are to serve her as if me." He vanished.

* * *

Calvin swung up onto his horse and watched Ryvane do the same with hers. The Temple rose up to their left side and they had a good hour's ride back to Dockside. "I was so hopeful we'd get to meet her," Calvin said. "At least we left a message for her. I'm sure she'll reply to me."

Ryvane agreed and asked, "Rather than immediately going back to Dockside, why not grab a room at my tower? The Mages Guild is just right down there. No offense to your home, but the guild has things that I miss and I know you would like."

"Yeah?" Calvin asked with a rising tone of interest. "I like how that sounds."

They turned off the southern road towards the Great Bazaar and entered the Mages Guild. It lay quiet. Ryvane led them to her tower, which appeared and stayed ahead of her on the road even as other buildings shifted to the side, as if distorted by a lens in poorly made glass. Calvin kept his eyes on his horse's neck as he found the shifting landscape disorienting. The horse did not seem to mind.

When they reached Ryvane's tower after an hour of riding, he breathed with relief and tethered his horse. "Why haven't we come back here since that first meeting?" he asked.

"I only really work here when I have official duties to take care of. With Merakor, I've been freed of most official tasks. Otherwise I'd have apprentices here doing the work for me. With Tania, it's always binding elementals or charging magical items. It gets tedious. I found it easier to contract the work and hire apprentices to do it for me. That leaves me time for what I really love about magic." Ryvane took Calvin's hand and pulled him into the tower. "Pleasure."

Calvin smacked her butt as they stepped inside. Soft light glowed from thousands of candles. A pool of water glimmered before them. Next to it, a table of fruit and wine lay spread. Movement in the water caught Calvin's attention and he noted faint female forms moving in the water. "Friends of yours?" he asked.

Ryvane raised her arms and her attire disintegrated slowly with each sanguine step towards the pool. "Water nymphs. Yes, they are friends. Soon, you'll wonder how you've known me all this time but never experienced this. They're insatiable."

Calvin moved to unpin his cloak and felt instead feminine hands all around him unpinning this, unbuttoning that, and in seconds, he stood naked too. A hand caressed his back and he shivered, stepping forward to Ryvane.

She laid back in the water of the pool and breathed a deep heaving sigh of contentment. The radiance of the pool accentuated her breasts. She languidly splashed water at Calvin and told him to hurry up. A goblet of wine levitated to her other hand. Calvin stepped into the water and noticed how barely visible creatures in the water already kneaded and played with Ryvane's body.

Entering the water, he immediately felt it... everywhere. It startled him so that he lunged forward to join Ryvane. Instead of the usual water resistance, he felt hands and lips everywhere that helped him glide to her. Beyond arousing, it felt so invasive that Calvin found it hard to relax. Used to being with Ryvane in odd sexual situations, Calvin found himself saying something he never thought he would. "Heya, can we remove some of the distractions? I'm finding it hard to concentrate on you."

Ryvane blushed and waved her hand. Instantly, they were alone and the water cooled a bit. She raised her goblet to Calvin as one appeared for him. "To Merakor, and Dockside, and Kieran!"

Calvin returned the toast and asked, "Kieran is who? My competition?"

Ryvane pulled Calvin into her arms. "He might have been, but he died 8 months ago. He was my fiancé, of sorts. Where I come from, arranged marriages are common. Kieran and I were supposed to form a family unit. He chose Taysor. I chose Tania, but we remained friendly."

"There's a lot about you I never knew," Calvin said leaning back against the pool's edge. "For example, you have access to this and yet have stayed with me in Dockside for almost a year now. If I had all this and some scruffy watch captain came by, I would not even think about leaving this tower. This is a palace compared to our home in Dockside... if you ever considered it a home at all."

Ryvane shushed him. "That should tell you how handsomely striking you are."

Calvin kissed her. "And Merakor, wow. That's something, like Dockside politics, that I don't think I could have done without you. You're a miracle. Come here, my angel." He pulled Ryvane over onto his lap and let his fingers trail along her back.

She shivered. "I'm worried about you and Merakor," she gasped when his hands began to roam away from her back. "Stop that. This is serious. I've been to Merakor."

Calvin stopped and eyed her. "I always knew you were different, but how? No one has been to Merakor except maybe the dragons."

Ryvane pulled wet hair back from her brow and took a sip of wine, and then drank all of it at once. "Calvin, before we go, there are some things you should know about me. Secrets, in Merakor, can be deadly to me, you, us, our love."

Calvin laughed. "Nonsense. There's literally nothing that could change how I feel about you..."

As he said this, Ryvane let her human form slip away. Tiger features and wet striped fur appeared while her teeth and finger nails elongated and curved into fangs and claws. "They told me to only do this when I was completely sure; Calvin, I'm completely sure that I love you. I'm not human. I'm what is called a rakshasa. My race, we aren't even from Tehra. Those of us that came here were either summoned by wizards, or we came here because of exile." With each word, her voice became less human and more accented by the changes to her mouth's structure. Her last words sounded gruff, still feminine but more cat-like. Her body enlarged as well and then she stood so that Calvin could see her. "There's more."

When Calvin saw her two pace long tail swishing and coiling, he thanked Tiamat she had turned away and gave him a chance to regain his composure. "Ryvane, I don't remember ever hearing or reading about rakshasa before."

She nodded her head and turned to the side so he could see she was still female. "I'm every bit the female you've always known. I've earned my magic powers and place in the Mages Guild. I'm also very old by human standards, but by the same token, I'm my human form's age as a rakshasa. I may be the only one and so, not really worth talking about in the empire, right?"

She turned back to Calvin and carefully kept her face neutral as she saw Calvin trying to also keep his face neutral. She held her clawed hand out to Calvin and he gingerly took it, feeling her claws and the pads of her hand. She retracted her claws as Calvin touched each one. "The life I have led, were I where my race is, I would have died long ago. My family sent me here so that, as a female, I could learn magic and live a more meaningful life. There were considered rebels. My father arranged for my mother to escape with Kieran and I. She died a few years after we arrived here."

Calvin was trying very hard to keep his composure. "You could tear me to pieces, couldn't you?" he asked feeling her claws almost as big as his thumb. She nodded. "It's kind of sexy, but it also begs the question I asked earlier: why are you even with me?"

Ryvane took a deep breath. "I was ordered to assess you when you first came to the Dockside Watch. That's the 'Why' of how I met you. I normally don't leave my tower here; the human world is confusing to me. The 'Why I stay with you' is easy – when you intervened to save the children, when you found the minotaur Windwalker, when you began to see opportunity to improve Dockside for the people, I fell in love with you. Just because I'm not human does not mean I do not love or care about other races. In fact, I feel certain human emotions much stronger than humans do." She tried to smile seductively but could tell that a tiger face doing so looked feral and predatory. She concentrated and returned to her human form. "Is this easier for you, Calvin?"

He nodded. "You did tell me, when I first met you here in the tower, that a mage could appear however they wanted. I hope you're not testing me. Halgrim did say that we would all be going to Merakor in different forms, as Drow. Part of that training, I can imagine, will be to get into a Drow mindset." He smirked. "I imagine that a much crueler, capricious, and evil way of thinking."

"I'm being honest with you, Calvin. This secret, which I have kept from most everyone I know, could be deadly to the group or to us. As such, I need to tell everyone in the group. I wanted to tell you first. If you hate me, or find this form disgusting, I understand."

Calvin had not let go of her hand and with her fingers reasserting their human shape, he entwined her hand with his own and kissed her fingertips. "I love you too, Ryvane. We've had such a crazy time together. The miracles, my angel, that crazy Halfling, and so on. I'm okay with my angel turning out to be a shapeshifting tiger. It's kind of sexy," he admitted.

"Oh, Calvin," she purred as she slinked into his arms. "I hoped you would understand."

They embraced and when Ryvane felt Calvin's hands exploring her body, she knew things would be okay. She giggled. "The human form is a bit limiting. My kind, we feel things like this much more intensely than humans do. I'm sure you've noticed this?"

Calvin nodded. "I always wondered why you were so open to having more partners with us. While I've appreciated it, it's not something I need to be happy with you. Just tell me you don't drink blood," he asked.

Several hours later, Calvin lay asleep, cradled in a water nymph's arms. He would probably sleep for hours. While Ryvane could sleep, she did not feel a strong need to except after intense magic or when wounded in some way. She snapped her fingers and called up into the ceiling. "Bring me maps of Merakor," she said. "Also, my old Kieran notes."

Calvin woke up on a divan chair, wrapped in soft blankets. Though still nude, he was dry and clean. The smell of delicious food wafted over the pool of water. He blinked through the steam and found Ryvane in her tiger form looking over a pile of maps to the edge of the pool. Nymphs helped hold the maps open. A stack of leather bound books and scroll tubes laid strewn about the room. Though he could not read the writing, he recognized it as Merakoran.

"Good morning," he said, walking over to her and grabbing an apple off the table. "Studying Merakor?"

She nodded and pointed to the central southern part of the map. "This is Arati." Her tiger form shifted back to human and she smiled at Calvin over her shoulder. "Arati was where most of the agriculture for Merakor came from. It's interesting because it began, like Tania, as barbarian tribes. At some point, they figured out farming. Though Talkra on the eastern side also produced a lot of food, it was nothing compared to Arati." She tapped the map while Calvin eased into the hot water and joined her lounged over the edge of the pool. "You can't have a large empire without stable food. What Tania did with the Halflings here, is like Arati for Merakor. This place also had an archmage: Aler Alerest. The name might sound familiar because it's an early derivative of Alerius. He probably copied Merakor in Tania's design."

"The god emperor was a Koran archmage," Calvin restated. "I'm not surprised, I guess. Everyone knows he is a sorcerer beyond what even the legends say."

Ryvane nodded. "When Merakor fell, his Tower of Sorcery was destroyed. The cataclysm," she drew her claw in a circle around the area. Her magic left a trail of light that covered about a fifth of Arati. "It wiped out everything in this area. Because of that, the dark elves pretty much left the area alone. They had no interest in already-destroyed ruins, plus the cataclysm was obviously fueled by many magical artefacts exploding. The theory is that, from their perspective, nothing would survive such destruction. We also know the Drow General for this area, a Slaad named Polygeryx, confirmed its utter destruction. Alerius, as a dragon – and this is according to popular legend amongst the Merakoran scholars, helped Polgeryx raze what was left of the Arati military. As a dragon, he made sure the Drow would think the entire area devastated."

Calvin leaned his head against her shoulder and added, "But it was all a ruse. The god emperor as a dragon could do that with his fire breath alone, right?"

Ryvane kissed his forehead. "Well guessed, Calvin. Probably not dragonfire, but something unique to him as a dragon and a mage. The truth is that he sequestered his entire tower deep underground." She tapped the center of the circle of destruction. "At least, this is what they've told us. One thing about the dragons, and they have a long history of doing this: it's never what they say."

"It sounds straightforward. We'll go to Arati. We know where the tower was. We'll go down and find it. What's the issue?"

Ryvane turned and let her breasts slide across his chest and pulled him close against her. "We can't teleport to Arati. We can't teleport into a Tower of Sorcery. They're protected. Even with Alerius giving us the bypasses, you can't just walk into a place like this. Plus, if the Drow ever had any suspicions, they may be active in the area as well."

"Why can't we teleport to Arati?" Calvin questioned. "I thought that was the whole point of the mages."

"No one has been there in thousands of years. Dar Reznor is certain that the Drow monitor the surface for incursions like this. That's why. If they saw us teleporting in, they might be able to figure out where we came from. The Allegiance of Blood forces us to protect the Isles, even in planning. No, we have travel there overland. It'll be a long trek. Unlike here in the Isles, it'll be fraught with danger. Who knows what the Drow have done to the surface world?"

Calvin looked at her gripping his hand. "You're concerned about me but not yourself." Calvin furrowed his brow and thought. "I'm guessing this means I'm the weakest fighter in the group? Or, that someone said I was."

Ryvane stroked his hair and replied, "Inexperienced, not the weakest. You've been through training for paladins and military officers, Cal. You also found cultists of the Jade God that Perdition missed. But, have you ever had to take another's life?"

Calvin found he wanted to say 'Yes!' but, even in his Temple training, he had never been in a position for a heartstrike demonstration. Eventually, he admitted it. "In paladin training, I had people die around me but I've never personally had to take a life. I've seen it. If needed, I know I could do it. I'm guessing you have."

Ryvane said, "It's rare for a Tanian military man like you to have avoided killing. Yes, I have. Many. Not as much since I joined the guild, but on that point, there's another thing I need to tell you."

Calvin rolled his eyes. "I'm feeling a bit overloaded and outclassed here."

She nodded and took his hand. "Okay. We'll stop for now then. But, when you're next feeling up to it, my tower, I can help train you. We have a few months. Soon, we'll be studying the Drow language. Around that, I can bring monsters to my tower that you can fight against, and kill."

Calvin thought about it and at last said, "Okay, but we're going to be gone for a while. I want my squad to have training too. I also need to know what the plan is for Dockside. We can't just leave everyone! I was elected mayor. I've made inroads with the Taurans. I've made promises I need to keep."

Ryvane whispered while he spoke and Calvin recognized that she was casting a spell. A minute later, their book of plans from Calvin's mayor office appeared floating in the air. Ryvane took it from the air and flipped to the page where they had drawn out a reconstruction plan. "Look, let me be really blunt on a few things, Calvin. You've been wanting to do certain things but never cared to listen to some harsh realities. I can help, but I need you to understand and trust me on a few points."

She pointed to a warehousing area. "You want to clear this for housing. That's not going to work. Perdition uses this as a staging area for Tauran cargo that is imperial in nature. I've tried to steer you away from this area, but unless you get Perdition and the Taurans and The Circle to agree to move it somewhere else, it's not going to move." She drew her finger around it and several blocks to its three sides. "All of this is owned outright by Perdition. Your reconstruction project needs to happen in other places."

Calvin pointed to his next location. "Why didn't you just tell me this earlier? I feel like this plan has been a sore spot in our relationship. Let's go to the second spot then." Tapping an area just north and east of the preferred one, he paused and moved his finger out to a muddy island in the lake. "What about here?"

"You can't do anything with that," Ryvane said. "And, I did not have permission to outright tell you about Perdition's covert operations. I hope you can understand that."

"You're right. You're right. I've had things happen on the Watch that I can't tell you about, I suppose. So, I can't do anything with a muddy island no one cares about? Why? But, with all this interest, what if – as mayor – we committed to a construction project to build this mud bog into an actual island. We'll connect it with the bridge, but underground, we'll have a tunnel." Calvin got excited. "The tunnel will be big enough for large wagons in both directions. The Taurans can load and unload away from prying eyes and move their goods underground." He flipped through the book to some notes the two had made after swimming the dock area underwater. *Magic*, Calvin mused, *changes so many things.* "Sure there's a lot of muck down there, but it's all stone even out to the island."

Ryvane began to regret some of the things she said. Calvin was becoming passionate and, with these civil projects, that meant expense. *I should have just kept him focused on the possibilities of sex with a shapeshifting 'tiger babe.'*

She interrupted him. "I'll see what I can do. I have some contacts in the Thieves Guild. I'm sure we can hunt down Reggie as well. Dockside will be fine, even if we do nothing at all. Besides, all this verve is making me think that you held back last night." She growled at him and reached down his belly to show him she was done talking.

☐

# Chapter 11 – Rogue's Guild goes Tanian

Grant and his team moved southwards with great speed. The enchanted winter gear made it easy and being fully rested, they wanted to make up for lost time. Now that they all knew about Grant, conversation around these things went a lot easier. They spent two days traversing the Shield Mountains before they broke through onto one of the many almost-roads that fed the Winter War. Once there, they moved more quickly south. The mud and ice did not slow the group of rogues and they made fast time as if walking along a perfectly cobbled street.

On the fifth day, they saw campfire smoke and the signs of increased traffic on the road. A military encampment would no doubt be their next stop. They moved off the road and scouted it, relieved to see it was a mercenary group rather than one from the Temple. Rogue's Guild changed from their Tanian winter gear into the clothing of tired and travel-worn mercenaries. Circling the camp to come at it from the east, Grant's team drew the attention of a sentry who called for backup. When the guards were able to clearly see Grant's team of seven, they calmed down but remained on guard.

With some gentle prodding, they learned that this group had broken off from a Literalist faction army to head back to Taysor. "The pay was good, but coming here was just for show. Tania did not even show up. I guess they were serious when the said they were cancelling the Winter War. Didn't stop the Literalist General from sending a gloating letter to them though!" Their commander, a fat but muscular man named Brenton, drew more than a few chuckles from the team of what had to be close to a hundred fighters.

Grant jiggled his own coin purse and said, "We fared worse. We ended up with some Cuthberics who decided they should go hunt monsters. When we could not stand it anymore, we left. They only paid us a tenth of what was promised."

The mercenaries did not like that. "For shame," Brenton bellowed. "The damn knights always sticking it to us. We come out and slave away for this stupid war and get paid a pittance. Might I ask, what did the Cuthberics promise?"

"Ten. Each," Venter answered. "We got two."

Jodie chuckled. "Our leader needs to get his math right. We got a fifth, not a tenth."

Grant dove into the friendly banter and challenged them both. "We got the extra coin from running card games with their squires and logistics officers. That wasn't pay. My math is right!" They went at it this way for a minute until Grant whisked out some cards and began laying them out. "Maybe we can earn some more by playing with you all? How much does the Literalist Order pay these days? My last job with them wasn't the Winter War, but it paid top coin."

Brenton waved them over to his command tent and while walking, he described their contract. "It's the Literalists. We got paid a gold coin for each Tanian we helped them with, which was zero. So, I renegotiated. We ended up with twenty gold each. Not as good as an actual Winter War, but better than most of the Orders, I think."

Grant sat down at the table and began shuffling the cards. "I was small as a child and learned that, with the proper skills," he flipped the cards from hand to hand and then juggled three, then five of the individual cards to let them fall into the deck, "I could win the clothes right off the prettiest girls."

Everyone roared with laughter and Grant looked around to add, "Though I don't see any here pretty enough to woo." As the laughing turned into guffaws and rude jokes about bearded women, Grant flipped five of the cards face up onto the table. "This game is popular in my village of Southfaring in Ymac. Anyone here from Ymac?" He already knew they were not by their manner of speech. "We build a hand of five cards each. Each turn we play a card face down and make a bet as to whose card is worth more. You win if your card is higher or if you convince the other player to back down. I don't have much money, so maybe we start with a copper coin bet?"

Brenton looked around and then shrugged. "I don't know this game but for a copper, I can learn." He placed a copper penny on the table. "You're going to take all my money, aren't you?"

"Remember, we were with the Cuthberics. And, we aren't forcing any of you play or bet with coin you don't have. Don't worry," Grant reassured him. "We'll play cards up a few rounds so everyone can see how it works." He put a six-sided die on the table. "The die comes into play by adding points to your hand. But, here's the catch, you roll it and you have to add that many coins to the bet. Let's do a round."

Grant let the cards dance from hand to hand. With barely a movement of his fingers, he let the cards fall onto the table. Mesmerized by the dance of cards, Brenton chuckled as, one by one, the cards began to land face-up in front him. Grant juggled each to land in correct orientation between them both.

Brenton said, "That's quite a trick. I can see how a maiden might be enchanted by such soft handwork," he commented with an exaggerated wink at his men.

Grant grinned around the tent, enjoying the chance to put on a show and have a moment free of peril. "The Cuthberics thought this was witchcraft and banned t from the camp. Playing this, in the cold, was terrible." He pointed to each of their highest cards. "Your card is the highest possible in the deck. Knowing this, you would consider and wonder, 'Does the other guy have one too?' If we tie, we keep our coins but get nothing. So, the die roll helps with ties. Though this is a Tanian deck, the Imperial is still the Imperial even if it shows as a dragon in this deck."

Grant flourished his hand over the cards. "Meanwhile, on my side of the hand, I'm thinking that I have mediocre cards. I'd ask myself whether I think you're the kind of person to start with strength or not. You seem like you would. I'm going to play my weakest card. Hopefully, this will make you sacrifice your strongest. To mess with your mind though, I'm going to put a bet on this and roll the die." Grant rolled a two. "So, a two it is." He added two copper pennies to the table.

Brenton slid his Imperial forward against Grant's Shepherd card. "So, I win and take your 3 pennies," Brenton said thoughtfully. "What if we tied?"

Grant raised his eyebrow and said, "Then, we nullify each other and nothing happens, unless we bet. The highest bet would take all in that case. You want to try playing a round without coin?" Brenton opened his hands at the table as if to say 'make it happen.'

The acrobatic flight of cards drew applause while Grant flipped and spun them for almost a minute before letting them fall face down. Brenton watched with a smile and said, "Rather than playing games, maybe we should just have you put on a show." The two men picked up the cards and then slid one face down to the center of the table. Brenton tapped his and said, "So, I want to make a bet. I roll the die, right?" He rolled a four and placed four pennies on the card.

"I'm not going to bet," Grant said. When they flipped the cards, Brenton had played a middle power card, the Tavern. The extra bet money bumped it up to the second strongest card, the Priestess. By contrast, Grant played a weak card, the Merchant. "So, you won. Remember, we'd also have a coin here for the round. So, you take my coin and obviously your own since you won."

After the round, Brenton called for drinks and noted loudly, "Are you sure you won money at this game? You're either a terrible player or you're letting me win."

Grant's eyes sparkled and he replied, "I'm just here to relieve beautiful maidens of their clothing with card tricks. My friend over there, Roger, he's the shark. If you play him, be careful." To the back of his hand, he whispered loudly, "I'm pretty sure he cheats!"

They stayed for two hours. Grant kept the games close so that Brenton's entire group just barely came out ahead. They learned that Tania had no troops in the mountains. They learned that a Literalist army was camped directly south of their location and had several powerful priests and a mage in the group. Grant signaled that they should go and send word about Syand. At his signal, Roger threw his cards in the air and exclaimed, "Bah, Joust frowns on me again! Another busted hand." He shoved his coins across the table to the happy-looking sellsword. "I'm glad we aren't playing with gold!"

"I'm not!" his opponent retorted.

Grant tilted his head over to Brenton and said, "I think this means that the team doesn't want to risk their precious Cuthberic pay against your team's superior luck. Maybe we'll try the Literalists and their much fatter purses."

As they walked away, Grant said to Jerare, "That was fun. It's been a while since we could act like normal citizens. Well, normal for us."

High Captain Percival du Regen of the Grand Literalist Army sat back in his plush chair and wished his armor did not so effectively carry the chill mountain air directly into his bones. Resolved to not fight for Tania in Bloodstone under threat – if asked nicely his whole unit would have gone – his army represented just one of the three that joined the Winter War. He held his hand over a brazier of burning coal and waited until his steel gauntlet warmed. "Insufferable," he grumbled. "Bartholomew, if the Tanians had shown up, we could use our magic gear. Isn't there something you can do about the cold?"

Across the ravine, the Tanian encampment sat unused, but Percival du Regen stayed and placed his Order's victory banner there. Before him, the Bright Priest Bartholomew recited memorized scriptures while eyeing a map of the area intently.

"I do believe, Percival, that we may want to remove ourselves to the east." the priest said. Ten miles should position us for what is to come." The cleric's voice sounded strained. It had been a long and difficult winter. Even with the blessings of the Sun God, winter was still cold and the snow and ice made it miserable. "By your orders, we are all suffering the natural. By signed decree,… would you like to quote your commandment?"

The Tanians who came, had come with the attitude of tourists. Percival stroked his gray mustache and eyed the cleric. "No, no. I remember. Winter," he spat out the tent door into the snow. "You want to move us ten miles, now. That's what you said last month. Had we moved, we'd still be stuck in the snowfall from the blizzard the week after. No, my bright lord, I am most reluctant to rely on divination when my very bones tell me that great evil will arrive any day, any minute."

The cleric folded his fur-lined robes about him and huddled under a fur blanket. "Faith, my lord Percival. We must have faith. Had we moved, perhaps we could have become a tool for Pha Rann."

From outside the camp's bright banners, a sentry called out. "Strangers on the road!" He rang a bell and Percival winced as the sharp tone stabbed pain into his head.

"All this divine power and no one can alleviate a headache," Percival sighed. "Come Bart, let's go and see what Pha Rann blesses us with today. May it be great evil to fall beneath my sword."

"May we finally face a threat to righteousness," the priest agreed. "And, my lord, I'm happy to offer you assistance with your headache, but you commanded…"

Percival waved his suggestion aside. "I know, I know. But, I doubt the Bright God intended them to be used as a daily cureall. Some things, we must face with a stalwart spirit."

By the time they reached the small path on the northern edge of their camp, they found the sentry engaged in talk with seven road-worn men. They looked like Sorans. They sounded like Sorans. Their conversation concerned Brenton's Army, the mercs to their north. Percival sniffed at the air. Something about this group felt off, but he shrugged that feeling aside. Four calm months in the wintery mountains had him seeing evil everywhere.

The leader of the group, bowed low and with well-spoken and courtly speech greeted them. "Hail to thee, High Captain and Bright Priest. I am Grant." He went on to name the rest of his crew, careful to say their real names in case *lie detection* magic was in use. "We are travelling south to Tania, as mercenaries, to seek fame and fortune along their Barony trade routes. We had hoped, prayed really, to find the faithful that we might send a message onwards to The Temples."

Percival arched his eyebrows and looked more closely at Grant. "You hardly seem the type to seek out those of faith, if I'm reading you right. Why?"

Grant took a deep breath and said, "I'm not sure our news is suitable for everyone, but if you wish, we can explain here and then be on our way. You see, we are hoping to persuade you to send word back to Sora about deeds most foul."

Percival shifted back and forth to try and quell the numb cold in his toes. "Well, ahem, foul deeds you say? Very well. Very well. Something about your presence sets me at edge, young man." He eyed Bartholomew hoping the priest would confirm. A slight furrowing of the eyebrows was enough. "Tell us, here and then be on your way." The command was stated with an undertone of steel and Grant noted that, while the paladin was at least fifty years old, he would likely fight as if a newly-commissioned knight of eighteen.

Grant bowed, continuing his gracious and charismatic approach to the group. That new sentries and paladins arrived each moment bothered him. Like the Cuthberics, this could get out of hand quickly. At least this group did not have the same sensitivity to Orcus' body as Devin, Garrett, and Ajax.

"As we left the great city of Sora, we found ourselves in the warehouse area by Gable and Clark Street. I'm sure you know it well. We were beset by devils who tried to steal our money and take our very breath from our lungs! Two of our team died: Kasey and Finn. Pha Rann smite their murderers! We fought and we fled this way, but were chased for days. We found ourselves on a barely noticeable path leading into the mountains. Only when we had fended off the first attack and fell back into a cave to recover did we realize the truth of it."

Grant remained bowed and waited. At last, the cleric Bartholomew asked, "What was the truth you realized?"

"That we were truly attacked by fiends. Or, in this case, vampires. With the Jade God fallen, they grow bold! No doubt there is a swarm of them deep under the catacombs by Gable and Clark Street. It was our hope to ask that you send word." Grant rushed through this trying to sound sincere and breathless. He paused again as if it would be too terrible to say out loud. Only when Percival nudged him did he continue. "One of our attackers had bite scars on his neck." This was an outright lie for the group, but Grant had been attacked personally by Syand. The omission of time and sequence would not register as strongly as an outright deception. "Their leader, a female vampire named Syand, heads some organization calling themselves Dark Legion. It's very name suggests the antithesis of Pha Rann, bless His Holy Name. Dark Legion! They flaunt their evil in Northtown in clear view of The Temples!"

Though Grant's invocation of deity frustrated Percival, Bartholomew patted him on the shoulder and said, "You are lucky to be alive. But, why did you not tell the Watch? You know, back in the city?"

Venter bowed and said, "Because we were running for our lives. We ran for days and days up into the Shield Mountains. Ten or more came at us at twilight. A chance encounter saved us. Otherwise, we would be dead." Venter gulped and added, "Or worse."

Grant choked. "Or worse indeed! For there is more... it's too terrible. But, I must." He looked up at Percival and showing how he had to screw up his courage, he took hold of Percival's shoulders and said, "You must send word! This Dark Legion is aligned with doppelgangers."

Percival drew back as if smacked. "Doppels? Here? Don't be ludicrous! What proof do you have?"

"This is not an attack, but I must draw my blade." Grant said this slowly and as if terrified that he would be attacked by Percival. He pulled out the dagger that he had used in his fight against Delia, Bradley, and Syand. "The blood on this is old, but I'm sure a cleric or mage could identify at least the root of its contamination." He offered the blade on opened hands. "Take it, I pray you both and see for yourselves. Or truthsay me in this matter! My blade has remnants of doppel and vampire blood on it!" He let desperation enter his voice. "Had we stopped to tell the guards, we'd no doubt be dead by now." Another truth, if speculative... and the cleric at least seemed to be buying it.

Bartholomew picked up the dagger and sniffed it. "Not human blood, that's for sure. Doppel blood, though has a certain slimy quality, as if gelatinous. Of course, I've never seen it because there are no dopples in the Isles." He poked at it. The recent bloodletting from Syand dominated the blade though and at last, Bartholomew prayed.

Grant signaled and Jerare, who carried the backpack with the holding bags full of Orcus, withdrew into the forest and snow to relieve himself but also to put maximum distance between the backpack of Orcus parts and the priest. The blood on Grant's blade began to glow and shine with red and black streaks. "This level of darkness is consistent with a vampire, but it could be from any evil source. I suppose your story carries some truth. We should at least send word about the streets, right High Captain?"

Percival nodded. "You've done right today, Grant. Now, leave our camp. You are not welcome here. Please understand – it's not personal. But, something about your team and story is setting me on edge."

A sense of casual menace, and guards with Percival, escorted Grant's team away from the Literalists. Once they were past the outer guard perimeter, Percival called out to them, "Pray we do not meet again, Grant. We will deliver your message, but you carry evil with you. I will pray for your souls. For your own sake, I urge you to repent."

Grant signaled over his shoulder and they continued their southern march. By nightfall, which came early here in the sharp mountains, they had found a level area of the trail where they could set up camp. Things went easily. Except for raiders trying to pick off the military, centuries of war by well-equipped armies had long ago cleared and kept clear this particular region free from monsters and other threats.

Musing on this and the strange behavior by Percival, Grant watched the flames lick up the wood and send embers into the sky. The paladin must have felt the Orcus material's evil power. Against his desires, an image of Delia appeared in his thoughts. He shook his head trying to banish the thoughts of what might have happened to the real Delia at the hands of the doppels. But, her voice came to him again.

He realized it was magic. Delia had to be using one of his Tanian communication earrings to telepathically speak with him. He focused on the message and put his anger at her being in one of his safehouses out of his mind. Part of the frustration was a suspicion that Delia may have always been a doppel. She had appeared shortly after Grant's first job with Dark Legion, when he had announced Rogues' Guild and presented High King Andrews' charter.

All it would take right now for Grant to give her a piece of his mind, and then some, would be to touch his own earring. If he touched it and spoke a certain activation word, Delia's earring would explode. It probably would not kill her, he brooded. At last, he opened himself to her message. "Grant, I am breaking our contract with Dark Legion. They have become vicious and short-sighted in their attacks on the other guilds. I would ally myself with Rogue's Guild. We are at your safehouse in Ymac. Please, accept my apologies. This is real." Her voice sounded real and genuine and his mind's eye saw her looking desperate and beaten. That persistent thought came to him again: *What if Delia had always been a doppel?* He felt Delia's presence fade. She would be waiting for him to reply.

Grant poked the fire and considered the many issues around allying with her. Unless the doppels had tortured the safehouse information from the real Delia, they should not know about it. Not trusting her, he knew he could not go back to Ymac. Overland, it was weeks of travel in the wrong direction. He needed to get to Tania, board a world galleon, and get gone from the Isles. The addictive effects of Orcus' blood to the vampires made it extra important. "I wonder if they go into withdrawal agonies?" he whispered to the fire. The rest of his team slept fitfully in the cold night, but rested.

More on a whim than anything else, Grant touched his own earring. "Delia," he said. "Ymac isn't safe. I cannot trust you. There is too much history now, between us, even if you are real. But, if you are sincere in your desire to ally with me, you must find a way to reach Tania. I will be sitting at the Dragon Fountain exactly one hour after sunrise on the day of the Tanian Overflight Festival. That gives you about ten days to figure it out. In two days, I'm notifying Ymac that doppelgangers are infesting my safehouse. If you truly want an alliance, you'll bring my safehouse's armory with you as a peace offering."

An hour later, an image of Delia came to him. She looked sad and lonely. "I'm so sorry about everything, Grant. I'll be at the fountain."

Her message, clear as it was, infuriated Grant and he stood up to pace. The cryptic part was whether or not she was the real Delia, why after all this time they would break their contract, and how doppels got into Sora in the first place. Venter opened an eye and said, "You need a break, boss? What's going on?"

"Nothing," Grant replied. "Well, female problems."

Venter laughed and then stood up to stretch and shake the cold from his limbs. "It's been a while since I roughed it, Grant. Even in Bloodstone, we always had military gear. I can't recall the last time I actually slept with actual rocks in my back. So, Delia?"

Jerare shushed them and said, "I'm trying to cuddle this rock. If you keep talking about it, it'll lose its sweet mood."

Soon, the entire camp was chatting and at last, Grant asked them, "Hey, since you're all up, does this mean we should just hit the road?"

They all agreed. Venter noted that since their long chase, they had all had a hard time sleeping normally. "Very well, I think we're far enough from Percival's camp that we can teleport."

While Grant began fishing around in his backpack, Art and Roger speculated if Jerare's rock was marriage material. Jerare retorted, "Hey, at least my rock loves me. And, it's nice knowing that our leader has some backing with teeth. No offense rock, but we are not meant to be. I need someone softer. Warmer."

Pete apparently, not wanting to miss the fun added, "But, she's curved in all the right places, and the right size!"

Venter snorted. "You'll need two rocks there, Jerare. I'm looking forward to seeing some of those smoking hot dragon priestesses."

Jerare feigned shock, "I've never seen them smoking."

"No, no, no, Jer… they're not smoking that way! It's because…"

Venter slapped him on the back, "They can't get enough Soran love!" And he thrust his hips forward while laughing.

Grant withdrew a wand and a book. Be flipped intently through its pages. With a distracted tone that suggested they quiet down, he said, "If any Tanians hear you talking that way, they'll definitely smoke you."

While the laughter died down and they watched Grant, Venter asked, "Since we now know about Tania, can you tell us what you're doing?"

Grant looked up from a book of spells and nodded. "Sure, but you know, old habits die hard. Basically, each time we scored big, I bought Tanian gear and magic. This book contains scroll spells. The wand helps me cast them. We're going to teleport to Tania… unless you all want to walk the rest of the way?"

The teasing mood became appreciative and Jerare sighed, "It'll be nice to not cuddle rocks, but a real woman instead."

Though Pete cracked a joke about two curved rocks, Jerare swatted him back and insisted, "Real women. I want more than one this time. After all that running, my stamina is through the roof!"

Venter sat down next to Grant and looked at the book full of draconian script. "I always regretted that I never learned their writing," he said.

Grant seemed to have found what he wanted and put the wand in that page as a placeholder as he began looking for another page. "I'm going to use a few spells. The first will be mask our area from scrying. You guys would not believe the paranoia Tania has about scrying and being scried on. The second will be to create an illusion of us sleeping and then breaking camp and continuing to walk south. The third will summon an invisible air spirit to ensure our illusions leave footprints. From a scrier's viewpoint, we want the illusion to look real so that they don't feel the need to test it. The final spell will teleport us into Tania, into a Shrine of Tiamat that has a designated area for arriving by teleport. Any questions?"

"Yeah, how much does all this cost? I might want to buy it too with my take on our haul." Roger guessed, "Ten thousand?"

Grant laughed. "No, much more. The wand cost that much. I don't remember the book of spells. I just kind of picked up spells here and there each time I went through Tania."

"So," Venter asked, "you cast these spells and then woosh, we reappear in a Shrine?"

"That's how it should work, yes. I've actually done this several times to get out of dodgy situations. You guys remember when we were in Bloodstone at the Ford of Gran? I vanished because a vampire was about to bite me. I was gone for two days because that was how long it took for me to go from the Shrine to the Temple at Morbatten and persuade them to send me back. Once back at the Temple at Bloodstone, I then had to catch back up to you all. Teleportation is amazing magic but it can be annoying. Since I'm not a mage, I can't just do it whenever or wherever I'd like to go. On top of that, to ensure Perdition's success with what they consider dumbed-down magic, I can only teleport us to known safe locations, like certain Shrines of Tiamat." He dog-eared a page and added, "I'm almost ready."

Pete turned to Art and speculated, "All the times we got paid in Tanian currency and letters of credit, it was actually Tanian backing. Huh. I wonder if we have Tanian accounts?"

Art looked at Grant, but their leader was nose-deep into the book and fidgeting with the wand. Their camp fell quiet until Grant said he was ready. Grant enacted the scrying block. Once in place, the team quickly broke camp. Each successive spell felt anticlimactic to the group of rogues as there were no flashes of light or obvious magical effects. When Grant had them all come and put their hands on each other's shoulders and his own, it felt like a relief. The *teleportation* magic sounded stilted and awkward as Grant read it from the book. There was no woosh and Venter chuckled when he became aware the snowy mountain air was gone. The soft flickering lights of lanterns and candles, the smell of perfume, and the warm air of a dragon shrine greeted their senses.

A priestess stepped forward and bowed to Grant. In Soran Common, she said, "Welcome, Grant. It has been too long. Almost a year if I remember correctly?"

"Hi, R'Dar Maishan. My lady," he bowed. "Please meet my team." He introduced them each in turn. Though Maishan looked old enough to be a mother to any of them, they each felt and knew that she memorized their faces and names as Grant introduced them. She stood taller than them all and had a quality to her beauty that suggested she was much younger.

Grant said, "I'd like to ensure that my arrival here is kept quiet. Perhaps a donation to the Goddess would help Her smile on us?"

Maishan's barely-there smile widened and she agreed. "Very well, Grant. Or, you could convert and enjoy Tiamat's favor free of coin. But, we've had this discussion, haven't we? Your arrival will be noted, quietly, but for five hundred coins, I will not notify Perdition of your presence until I am done with work. That gives you till tomorrow at sunset before my records go out and your arrival will be known to official channels."

Grant passed the money to Maishan. She took it into her robe's pockets and asked, "Is there anything you need? You have the smell of mountain air, and unwashed men."

Jerare chuckled but went quiet when Venter elbowed him. Venter bowed and said, "We've never been in a shrine like this. Where might these unwashed men find a bath?"

Maishan walked up to Venter and smoothed his collar. "With Tiamat's blessings, you could find it here. I sense great things in you, but the rancid energy from your leader's backpack tells me you'd be better off finding cleanliness at a tavern rather than with my sisters and me." She kissed Venter on the cheek. "Maybe come back when you are more... yourself."

"My lady," Grant said bowing. "We thank you. Let's head out. R'Dar Maishan, as always, a pleasure. We'll be at the Round Cup Inn."

* * *

Radcliffe Shandervall, the Supreme High Sorcerer of the Literalist Order, pondered the message received from High Captain Percival. "Vampires at Clark and Gable?! What preposterous nonsense." He waved his hand and a map of Taysor opened in the air to his side. He traced his finger along Clark to the intersection and noted it was a warehouse district. Another wave of his hand brought over a census for the area and he strummed his fingers along the pages until it magically opened to the warehouse listing there.

"Warehouse 521, used to offload Gulf of Ymac trade from Haven, Tania, and Ori," it read. Radcliffe snapped his fingers and called out, "Scruffy, bring me a scrying sphere!"

The paladin squire standing guard outside the laboratory snapped to attention and ran off. "Idiot probably doesn't even know what a sphere is," Radcliffe grumbled. He looked for the warehouse's active inventory, ownership, and was consternated when nothing could be found on record. "That's odd," he mused.

Outside, Rising Squire Robert, or 'Scruffy' because he was trying to grow a beard, came to a halt to adjust his clothing before entering the room. "Scrying sphere," he said cheerfully as he placed a small chest on the mage's desk. "Anything else?"

"Yes, yes. Scruffy, we may need a team. Please alert the Guard Captain to prepare three, no five priests and a unit of paladins strong enough to fight vampires." Radcliffe let the word 'vampire' drawl out so he could watch Scruffy's reaction.

Robert's face lit up. "Vampires!" He quickly dropped his squeaky voice back to a more deferential tone. "Please, Mage Radcliffe, might I tell the Guard Captain that it is your desire I be assigned to said unit?"

"Can you combine with the priests?" Radcliffe countered. Scruffy's reaction said it all and Radcliffe felt sorry for the squire. He patted his arm and reassured him, "Your day will come, as it does for us all. Glory and stories enough to last a lifetime. In this case, you'll have to settle for helping an old man watch from afar. Now, shoo. Go tell the Guard Captain to make ready."

Radcliffe opened the chest and admired the sphere of flawless quartz resting in the box. Scruffy had resisted the temptation to touch it and this made Radcliffe feel the squire was already on the right path and doing better than so many others with 'mage duty.' Fingerprints and smears usually covered the sphere.

Radcliffe chanted softly and let the quartz come alive with the soft glow of magical sight. The 521 warehouse should have filled his view. Instead, a twisted morass of wood, metal, and fighting peasants met his gaze. "What? What is this?" Radcliffe adjusted his spectacles and re-centered them on his face. What should have been a warehouse instead writhed and moved. A tiny human ran forward and threw a lantern at it. Oil and fire splashed a tiny part of the warehouse, which folded over the fire to put it out. At the same time, a tendril reached out and grabbed the leg of the lantern-tosser. "What are you, warehouse?" Radcliffe asked.

Action to the north of his scrying view caught his attention and he zoomed over to see a woman with white skin wearing ancient armor. She ordered a row of archers with flaming arrows to shoot the warehouse. From behind the lady, three loping humanoids ran forward to attack her. "By Pha Ran's beard, ghouls! Clearly not peasants," Radcliffe observed as he stroked his long white beard and eyed the woman. "Let's see what you are..."

The female leader of the archers dodged the first ghoul and then short swords in each hand decapitate the next two. Archers reloaded and fired point-blank into the remaining ghouls. With the ghouls dispatched, the lady looked up at Radcliffe and his quartz sphere fractured into useless glass.

The abrupt sound of its crack surprised and scared Radcliffe. The last image showed her to have blood red eyes and vampiric-looking teeth. Thankfully, Scruffy was nowhere nearby. The mage reached out to touch the sphere, a trinket he had made in his apprenticeship many years ago. "Very well, if you want to play rough, my lady archer. Who might be a vampire..."

Radcliffe stood from his desk and called out, "Familiars! Make ready my summoning circle!" From all around, air spirits and invisible creatures rose up to the second level. Lights atop the stair rail and balcony glowed softly. Radcliffe summoned his staff to his hand to hobble up the steps.

Once there, he smiled and with great praise thanked all of the spirits that prepared the summoning circle by clearing furniture and the silk rug from the floor. His circle, the focus of all his lab-spells, waited. He stepped to the edge and tapped his staff on the circle's outermost line. Soft blue light sprang from the staff and ignited runes outward traced on the stone tile floor. Once the summoning circle was full of radiance, Radcliffe stepped inside the first ring and began to cast again. With each word of the spell, images appeared and then slid out of view. Some lingered enough to be recognizable as things on Radcliffe's mind, like Scruffy and whether he had found the Guard Captain or not. He had and they were talking.

As the Gable and Clark Street vision settled on the monstrous warehouse, Radcliffe slowed his chanting and let his view glide over the melee of peasants, fighters, and the warehouse. More and more of the warehouse burned, but he noted that the powerful female kept trying to enter the building. Each time, she had to retreat because of teeth forming in doorways or tendrils nearly snatching her.

"Could it be a mimic?" Radcliffe wondered. The entire building, as large as a city block, moved like one. How it got so big, how it existed there for so long without anyone in the Temple of Pha Rann noticing... boggled Radcliffe's mind and left him no choice but to reject the idea. Typically, mimics copied the shape of treasure chests or items of interest to inexperienced adventurers. Lucky ones escaped with a missing limb. Unlucky ones, well... no one would know their stories. "But they're always small," Radcliffe insisted.

Radcliffe attempted to follow the female. "Show me, my lady. What are you?"

Like before, Syand became aware that someone scried her. She snarled and looked up at Radcliffe and hissed at him. Her fanged eye teeth and the feral red light shrouding her eyes showed the mage what he needed to know. "Vampire, yes definitely. Percival's message was correct. I will have to let him know," he whispered.

Syand tried to end his viewing but his stronger magic outmatched her. He felt her attempt to dispel it and laughed at her imminent failure. To mock the fiend, Radcliffe instructed his familiars to keep the scrying focused on her and to record her actions.

He stepped out of the scrying spell's area and rubbed his eyes. He froze when, down below in the hallway, he heard a loud thump and muffled groan. The hackles stood on his neck and a chill swept him. Metal scraped on stone and the Radcliffe saw Scruffy's body slump down just out of the doorway. "Scruffy?" Radcliffe called out.

The feeling of menace grew in the doorway until a single figure in black leather armor stepped out. He pulled his hood back and let the mage see the blood drool from his mouth that now covered his front. The vampire tapped Scruffy's body and said, "Don't worry, old man. He'll be better than himself in a few minutes. You'll be joining us too, you know." The vampire relaxed his guard. "Oh, I see. You weren't expecting a confrontation tonight. Too bad for you. Syand sent us. She needs a strong mage." The vampire jumped forward and landed on the stairs just four paces from Radcliffe.

Radcliffe's mind raced through all the research spells he had prepared for the day. With his spell book, he might be able to repel the vampire, but in the minutes it would take to cast even a simple spell, he would be done for. He could teleport through the scrying circle, but that would put him with the female leader. Bereft of good options, he brandished his staff and said, "Bring it. Your overconfidence guarantees my victory!" Hoping he sounded as bold to the intruder as he did in his own mind, Radcliffe jabbed his staff forward.

Thinking the staff might be magical, the vampire moved aside, dodging it easily, and then caught the shaft. Radcliffe shouted a magical word. Though nothing happened, the vampire flinched against expected magic. Radcliffe stabbed his silver letter opener into the vampire's shoulder. It had been many years since the mage had last fought in combat and the tiny blade barely cut through the leathers. If Pha Rann had not reassured him he would win, Radcliffe would be praying for salvation.

The vampire hissed and caught Radcliffe's hand while a thumb nail cut a line in the mage's wrist. "Mage blood, mmmm," the rogue said licking his lips. "Can't wait till you're with us, old man."

From down below, a bright flash of sunlight and a glorious voice sang out clearly, "Burn and die, dark spawn!" The vampire ignited and, like wood, crackled as he burned ash. The oppressive feeling of undeath left Radcliffe's lab. The mage shook his hand and stepped back from the swirl of embers burning before him on the stairs.

Michael stepped in and called out, "Hello, Radcliffe? You here?"

"Oh, thank the Sun God! Michael, yes. I'm here. Praise Pha Rann for bringing you here!" Radcliffe saw a dark figure slink in behind Michael. The two seemed together but the darkness made Radcliffe point and begin to cry out in warning.

Michael held up his hand and waved the warning off. "That's Cordelle. I have been hunting a vampire coven for years and finally have a lead," Michael replied while pointing to Cordelle. "Radcliffe, please meet my partner. This is Cordelle, thieves guildmaster for the group called '521.' They operate out of…"

"A warehouse at Gable and Clark Street," Radcliffe finished. "You need to see this." Radcliffe noted the two burn marks and charred ash piles near his door. Michael must have caught two vampires just as they were entering his lab. "Four of them! So fast." He wiped his forehead of sweat and sensed the dank smell of his own fear lingering. "I would not have endured those two. Nothing in my long research career prepared me for assassins. My gratitude knows no bounds, Michael."

Something had been bothering Cordelle and watching the two men talk, it struck him. "You're The Michael, aren't you? The one everyone talks about, the Hero of the Sea of Glass?"

Michael put his arm around Cordelle and laughed brightly. "You just figure that out? Yes, I'm that one though you should not believe all you hear. Bards are especially prone to exaggeration."

Cordelle looked at Michael will borderline awe. "I've been around priests and undead. You fried those two vampires without even trying, and the others. I'm inclined to believe the stories," Cordelle whispered. "I always wondered about that. They truly cannot endure you?"

"They cannot endure the truth of the gods. While Pha Rann is my sun, other clerics have similar powers. Tiamat's priestesses take great pleasure in incinerating the undead."

They followed Radcliffe up to the scrying circle. When he saw the scene unfolding at 521, Cordelle clapped his hands and laughed. Cordelle pointed and exclaimed, "Hey, they woke up the mimic! Jace must not have been as loyal to Dark Legion as they let on."

"I thought it might be a mimic but ruled it out. It's too big," Radcliffe said stroking his chin. "How did you do this?"

Cordelle hesitated and then shrugged. "What motivates a mimic? Food and treasure. My former master captured one and learned how to keep it fed. We learned that as they get bigger, they actually eat less and sleep more. Treasure-wise, we figured out that with a real warehouse operation, so long as the net value of the treasure remained about the same and increasing, the mimic did not care. The guild's real operations insured a net increase. Also, mimics can't tell the difference between gold and silver. You would not believe how much silver bullion we have in there!" He laughed. "A *sleep* spell allowed us to remove high value items and then we would feed carrion to the mimic. It thought it was eating the thief when in reality, it was a cow or dolphin." Cordelle sighed and said, "Well, I only fed it cattle. My master sometimes fed it people. Younger mimics tend to enjoy the struggle. Wow, look at that."

The mimic continued to fight off Dark Legion as more and more vampires ran forward with oil. Connected to a canal with most of it handing over the edge of the docks, the mimic had begun to channel and pressurize water to extinguish fire and then figured out how to stream the water at its attackers and drive them back. "It's so much smarter than I would have ever guessed," Cordelle observed. "Maybe it's an age thing." Cordelle turned to Michael and said, "I have a request. I would like to spare the mimic. He has been my friend and my home since I was a young boy. While you might see a monster, I see a friend. If he survives, will you help me save him?"

Michael made eye contact with Radcliffe and said, "The Literalists here will want to see it destroyed, but we must all acknowledge that Pha Rann had a hand in creating mimics, for a purpose. Cordelle has revealed new information about intelligence, choice, and thinking far beyond any of our lore. What say you Radcliffe, shall we spare the mimic?"

Radcliffe pointed his staff at Cordelle. "How?"

"Inside, in what I would call my office, is the mimic's heart. It's the desk in my office. If we could get that, the mimic can heal. If it turns out to be murderous like it was with my master, we can kill it. Right now, it's responding to the threat of invasion and fire that was triggered when I was killed and no one placated the mimic. Jace could have were he there. I'm guessing he decided not to. Jace loved 521. This could be his revenge."

Radcliffe pointed his staff at the image of the warehouse-sized mimic as it tore into Dark Legion. "Tell me about this Jace," he ordered. "What does he look like? You know what, never mind. Come over here." Radcliffe beckoned with his hand and Cordelle stepped forward. "Think about Jace and hold his face in your mind. Then, say his full name."

At Cordelle's words, the image in the scrying vision dove into the mimic through Cordelle's office. It showed Jace being held by the wall, wrapped about in metal bands, and dropping down. The mimic had swallowed him, but Jace bit into the mimic and drew health. Michael sympathized and said, "Cordelle, I'm sorry for Jace's loss to undeath. Unlike you, he is beyond redemption. Though he feeds for survival, you can see he takes pleasure from the mimic's pain. I would guess it is more so with humans. He has killed already." Cordelle nodded and gulped. Jace looked awful.

The scrying pool swirled down to show Jace in darkness. "I have no interest in speaking with him, but you may, with Michael's permission," Radcliffe said to Cordelle.

"Jace, it's me. Cordelle." He felt awkward talking to a vision. But, when Jace's eyes flared with dim red light, it showed his fangs sucking at a mimic tendril. The mimic had pulled skin and hair off Jace's head and Cordelle could image the digestion occurring elsewhere. "Jace, I may be able to help you. Do you want help? I'm with the paladins in the Literalist Temple."

Jace's eyes frowned and he looked quizzically. Cordelle pressed on and asked, "I'm going to ask you some questions. Shake your head to answer, okay? I don't want you to die, Jace. You've been a loyal friend for too many years for it to end like this. First question, did Syand make you a vampire?" Yes. "Are there many more like Syand?" Yes. "Do you know how many?" Yes. "Did you become a vampire to save 521?" Yes. "You clearly did not placate the mimic. Was that to ensure the Jade God's body did not fall into Syand's hands?" For a moment, Jace did nothing and then shook his head, Yes and No. "You went missing for so long. I assume you met Syand. She turned you into a vampire. But, then you came back to 521 before Dark Legion's attack. Was it to get Orcus?" Yes. "Do you want to be saved?" Yes.

Cordelle stepped back from Radcliffe and the mage let go of his shoulder. "Michael, can we save him?"

The priest had folded his arms and drummed his fingers on the side of his head. "We cannot save a vampire that has committed murder. So, no. We cannot save him that way. The redemption of the grave is all I can offer. But, maybe he can conduct himself honorably, like you Cordelle, and earn an afterlife worth going to."

Cordelle turned to Radcliffe. "I understand that mages can sometimes effect magic through scrying. What options do we have here?"

Radcliffe's answer was short and to the point. "Most anything, with magic, is possible. However, helping a vampire like this, is not something I can do. It violates everything. The only offer I can give you is that I can send you to Jace. Once there, what you do..."

Michael interrupted him. "That will be sufficient, old friend. Please, send us to Jace. I cannot bear the thought of the Jade God's body falling into Dark Legion's hands. While your Order restricts you from acting on the greater good here, the life of a vampire matters not at all to the harm the Jade God might wreak on the streets of our fair city."

Radcliffe nodded and turned back to the scrying pool. "Jace is trapped in the mimic. We need to make space for you. I can't drop you there. The mimic seems to react to fire. You okay with your friend burning a bit?"

Cordelle shrugged and Michael said that vampires would all burn anyway. Radcliffe sent a fireball through the scrying image, targeted at Jace's body. As the vision filled with exploding fire and the sound of Jace screaming, Radcliffe opened a black doorway. The cloying smell of burning flesh wafted through it and Radcliffe gestured them through.

They stepped through and caught hold of Jace. Metal bands held him still and with their combined weight and the mimic's thrashing about in burning pain, they began to fall. Everything burned or was still burning.

"It's okay," Cordelle shouted. "We'll fall through into the river. This was part of a last-ditch escape plan."

Michael prayed and fire burst out from his skin and rose up in a vortex above him. The mimic screeched and they slipped more. Cordelle cried out, "I'm going to try and get my desk. You okay with Jace?"

Michael nodded and began pulling at Jace's metal bindings, hoping to accelerate their fall. Cordelle dug his claws into the mimic and whispered, "I'm sorry, old friend. I know this all hurts, but it will be over soon."

Cordelle found his office mostly untouched. The heart of a mimic did not move relative to the rest of its form. Cordelle checked and saw that all of his favorite gear and Orcus' stuff was gone. He sighed and sat down at the desk. He caressed the surface and called to the mimic. "It's time, my friend. I'm sorry you're in pain. Let's get out of here. Cordelle-Escape-521-Loving."

At his words, the desk morphed into a small ball that Cordelle could hold in both hands. He picked it up from the floor and then held his breath as the floor beneath him opened and he slid down into the water. Being night, he could not see anything, but he knew the general layout and where to swim.

He stayed in the water and arrived under the downstream warehouse docks. Holding onto the wooden supports, he saw a large splash of fire and steam explosion and knew that Michael had escaped. With the heart gone, the mimic body of the warehouse fell into a stupor... and quickly ignited. Cordelle felt tears well up in his eyes, incapable of weeping. Instead, he cradled the sphere in his arms and reassured it. "Loving, we'll find a new place, a new start. I'm so sorry for your pain." The sphere purred against his face.

Michael seemed to be struggling with Jace and for several long moments, Cordelle just wanted to leave. Looking over his shoulder, he calculated it: five days of swimming would take him to the Gulf of Ymac. He had a safehouse in the port town there. He could go anywhere. It's what old Cordelle would do. He eyed Michael and realized he was not that person anymore. He pulled up to the dock and found a boat mooring rope. "Michael, catch!" he shouted.

The priest grabbed hold and tied Jace's metal cage to it. Together, they pulled Jace to the dock side. The vampire mage was in a stupor of pain. Most of his body showed signs of digestion, partial regeneration, and then fire blisters that exposed his skeleton in places. Jace had claimed all of Cordelle's equipment as well as what looked like all of the Orcus parts he could get his hands on, which was not much. Cordelle grabbed all of this and then removed the *disintegration* wand Jace kept in a boot sheath.

Michael held on to Jace's cage and then said, "I can dispel this, whatever it is. Do you recognize it? I'm not comfortable leaving a powerful mage as a vampire. Pha Rann urges me to end him now."

Cordelle saw that Michael had already set his mind to doing it. He took Jace and kissed the mage's forehead. "Goodbye, my friend. You served me and 521 well. May you find peace in your afterlife."

Michael said, "He will suffer no pain." Jace's body ignited and crumbled to dust in the metal bands, which fell and sank into the dark canal murk.

# Chapter 12 – The Mighty Horde

Coriga punched the wall. "Why, Gruustir? Why him and not me?" He beat his chest and then slammed his forehead into the wall by the altar RiVule had built in secret. "I am stronger! Strongest!"

Coriga felt a deep sense of chastisement and looked around what the other Orcs had started calling 'the Temple.' No one was there, but the feeling of being watched remained. "Strongest!" Coriga screamed. His echo trailed down the cavern's many corridors.

Frentoris and Incer walked in. They looked concerned. Frentoris bowed in the gruff manner of their people. "Master, RiVule is strongest because it is Gruustir's will. Please stop this railing. Your voice carries to the Mighty Horde. We are ready to march!"

Coriga eyed RiVule's pet knight. "How shiny and clean your armor looks, Frentoris. So, un-orc-like. Incer, you too? RiVule has poisoned your minds. This Mighty Horde is mine!"

Frentoris remained bowing and said, "Of course it is, Great Priest Coriga. Gruustir chose RiVule, who chose you to lead this Horde."

"No! Mine!" Coriga walked to the altar and smoothed his hands on it. "No one knows where RiVule is and then we get this message to march our armies into Morbatten?!"

Frentoris and Incer watched Coriga struggle with wrath. A common trait in their people, it tended to manifest before combat and times like this with the Mighty Horde ready to march. The two paladins nodded to each other approached Coriga carefully. The priest slammed his hands on the altar and continued to rail against RiVule. At Frentoris' signal, the two paladins tackled the priest and held him tight. The shaman ordered them to let him go and began calling for help.

Though the shaman's cries were annoying, Frentoris knew that no one would help the unpopular Coriga. RiVule had selected Coriga to make an example, not because Gruustir truly supported him. Before leaving, RiVule had given them explicit instructions should this happen. Frentoris reminded them of what RiVule had ordered them to do. He said, "RiVule told us that Gruustir might touch you and show you the truth of your error, Coriga. He also foresaw that this would be lost on you, as one who clings to the old ways."

Incer, who had not been party to that divine interaction, looked between Coriga and Frentoris and asked, "What truth? And what error?"

Frentoris replied, "That we all serve Gruustir, that RiVule is high priest because he serves Gruustir with all that he is. The other shamans, like Coriga, they serve themselves first."

Several warriors came charging into the Temple. When they saw the paladins holding Coriga, they stopped and then carefully pretended to see nothing and left. They sent word back down the corridors that everything was 'just fine.'

Though he bit and writhed in their arms, Coriga quickly tired and then said, "It's over. The fit has passed. I'm okay now. Thank you."

This was part of RiVule's prophetic instruction. "You will lead us to the Mighty Horde. They await your orders to march," Frentoris said.

"Yes, yes. Let's not keep them waiting! Like a mighty machine, their feet will grind the roadways! And when they arrive, they shall fall on the demons of Bloodstone like poison rain!"

The two paladins walked behind Coriga as they moved through the many corridors to the Place of Speaking. Though the Orcs had many tunnels, large caverns served as gathering areas and homes for most of the people. A raised chamber off one of these larger caverns had acoustics such that the speaker could be heard in all of the large caverns. RiVule often meditated in the Place of Speaking. The same properties that made a speaker's voice heard everywhere brought snippets of sound from across all the Orc tribes. RiVule liked to listen for the mood of the Horde.

Coriga climbed up onto a stalagmite carved into a podium and calmed his voice to address the Mighty Horde. "Hail Gruustir!" Coriga yelled.

Against the priest's shout, the Horde roared back, "All Hail! All Hail!" The din and clamor amplified as metal shod polearms and steel nailed boots began to slam and stomp on the stone floor. Soon, the entire cavern trembled with the power of the eighty thousand warriors.

Coriga felt his skin tingle with the power, and resentment rose up in his heart. He eyed Frentoris as if to dare him otherwise and then spread his arms wide. In a higher tone of voice, a practiced one to carry over the thundering noise of the Horde, Coriga said, "For I, Coriga, we march…"

His words broke short as two long swords impaled the cleric from behind. Frentoris and Incer both twisted their swords through Coriga's right and left lungs. His death gurgle quieted the Horde within seconds. Death in the Place of Speaking had a long tradition with the Orcs. The sense of anticipation and wondering who would speak next, who would lead them, and whether it would trigger civil war, filled the mountain. Everywhere, Orcs of different tribes eyed the others and gripped their weapons.

The sound of Coriga's body falling from the podium and the metal clink of Frentoris' boot as he took the shaman's place were unmistakable. "I am Frentoris, paladin of Gruustir. I serve our high priest, RiVule! The Mighty Horde rises on Gruustir's command, and we march! To Bloodstone, and glory! Bloodstone! Bloodstone!"

The Horde breathed a collective sigh of relief. Internecine fighting had long prevented a Horde, let alone one of this many tens of thousands of fighters, from ever being assembled. Their rallying cries of 'Bloodstone!" and the prospects of what that place meant to each of them, energized their tread and they emptied the mountain in a column twenty-orcs wide. Frentoris and Incer left Coriga's body to rot and grabbed RiVule's banners.

* * *

RiVule watched the Mighty Horde and smiled at Coriga's death. It had happened exactly the way he dreamed. He pointed to the scrying pool and asked, "Impressed yet?"

Daryx and Dar Shara watched. The Dread Lord Armageddon said nothing. Shara spoke first. "So many fighters march for Gruustir. It is a powerful sight to behold."

RiVule thumped his chest and Taisha blushed with pride. "Since the Jade God's fall, our children are born stronger, healthier. Our females are stronger. Our fighters learn faster." He paced and whipped his robes about him when he turned. "It is a blessing and a sign of things, great and grand things for the Orcs!"

Daryx nodded and let the scrying magic show the Horde from the air. "We have no records of a War Host this size. The largest raided into the Baronies 235 years ago. We counted 1,509 slain. We do not know how many retreated. The god emperor has been most explicit in that he never wanted Morbatten to expand south of The Quat. That you can field an army like this is most impressive. What do you call yourselves?"

RiVule hesitated before answering. "Amongst ourselves, we call one another by our tribe names. But, when a Mighty Horde is raised, then that is what we call ourselves. This obsession with naming is not the Orc way. The Mighty Horde is what my paladins have named this group. We do not write things down as do you, Daryx. In our own legends, the Orcs once ruled these lands and numbered more than the stars at night."

"It is hard to imagine such a thing, but I see it in my mind's eye. Tania has benefited from the Orcs who, like you and Taisha, come to us with faith and Gruustir's blessings." Shara signaled the mage to let the scrying fade and leave. "The Saga of the Orc in Bloodstone will be written in the blood of many demons."

RiVule eyed them both and said, "And bloodstone gems."

"Should you find them, yes. As per the standard contract, if you find gems, we will buy them from you and Dar Ana will decide how many you might keep." Shara saw anger behind RiVule's eyes and waved her hand to dismiss it. "Do not let this continue to cloud your vision, mighty priest. In consultation with the god emperor, I have been instructed to provide to you a token of our faith in you and your god." Armageddon stepped forward and pulled a pouch from his heavy belt.

Shara opened it and withdrew two pieces of platinum and mithril jewelry: a necklace bearing an ornate medallion, and a single earring. Each held a small, flawless bloodstone as its centerpiece. Both showed signs of new craftsmanship. The medallion bore a similarity to RiVule's symbol of Gruustir, a shadowed Orc hammering a blade on an anvil. The earring was a small metal disc of curved lines with a faintly female suggestion to the design.

"This is for you, mighty priest," Shara said. She moved to place the medallion and necklace over RiVule's head, but he took it from her hand instead. She continued. "A gift from Tania and an expression of the god emperor's and Tiamat's trust in you, RiVule. When Merakor is ended and the saga of the Mighty Horde is playing out in Bloodstone, I am instructed to offer you citizenship here in Tania that you might build a Temple to Gruustir as a place for all faithful Orcs to come and worship, free of distraction. I am to reaffirm the southern boundaries between Quattrain and The Quat and recognize formally the mighty Orc empire to our south as a sovereign nation."

RiVule's eyes widened as Shara spoke. He donned the medallion and bowed to her. She touched his head and explained, "The bloodstone will amplify your connection to Gruustir. For Gruustir has not always been in the hearts of the Orc as he is with you. You will find enhanced clarity and power in your god with this stone, which we named 'Divine.'"

Not wanting to lose the moment, Shara beckoned Taisha over. "So that we never forget the miracle of a female paladin, Tiamat has approved this earring be gifted to Taisha. This was constructed by our god emperor thousands of years ago. Like most of the small and perfect bloodstones, it has a name but it is our desire that you rename it in consultation with the mighty priest." Taisha bowed and Shara carefully inserted the earring into her ear.

"What is this one's name?" Taisha asked reverently.

"Red Knight," Shara answered as she adjusted the earring and stepped back. "It is a protective gemstone that will prevent you from being controlled, charmed, enspelled without your consent, and other detrimental magical powers. The Red Knight was gifted to one of our earliest paladins 1,500 years ago. The setting was destroyed long ago so we made a new one, better suited for a female Orc. The Red Knight was enchanted to protect its bearer as part of a quest he undertook to find and capture a mind flayer. He succeeded and I bless you with his spirit to watch over you and bring you much success and glory. With your armor, it augments your defense, but you might find that even if you were naked, the stone can still protect you."

Dread Lord Armageddon spoke now. "You are Orcs. You do not understand these gifts." Dragonterror began emanating from his body. "These are unique and special. They are priceless. Each stone, by itself, is worth a kingdom's treasure. Though Tania and others might put a price on them, know that I – Armageddon – am charged to ensure that they are returned to Tania should you fall in battle or use them against Tania."

RiVule struggled against the dragonterror and tried to hide his annoyance that it did not faze Shara or Daryx at all. Taisha dropped to her knees and said, "I understand, Dread Lord."

RiVule touched the bloodstone hanging at his chest. He ignored the trembling in his hand and asked, "So valuable, what is their purpose? They are not just a gift."

The Dread Lord glowered at RiVule and suddenly the Orc priest found himself standing rising, at least if felt that way, into a flowing river of fire. Hints of dragons flying along the surface danced around him. Behind him, he saw a shadow of himself looking at the scrying pool. Behind that, he saw his encounter with Daryx. In the other direction, downstream in the flow of energy, he saw darkness. In between him and the darkness, he saw monsters and foes falling to his faith. He smiled. "So, this is the River of Fire."

"Yes," Armageddon answered. "You asked the purpose. Tania is to be a Spear against the god Set, whom even Gruustir wishes slain. The bloodstones are powerful weapons against Set and Set's Children. The bloodstones are part of the Spear. You are entrusted by Tiamat with great power, Priest of Gruustir."

RiVule's expression opened to amazement and he choked, "You wish to kill another god? Set?"

He drifted down into the flowing energy and reclaimed his sense of the world. Stunned and hardly able to speak, his mind reeled at the prospect of confronting Set. The confidence in the Dread Lord's voice came because of the vision, and the fact that the dead body of the Jade God sat in the Valley of Bloodstone to the northwest... "I want to believe," he whispered.

Shara pulled him up and embraced him. "That is how faith begins, mighty priest. Welcome, newest citizens of Morbatten."

RiVule and Taisha walked away from Daryx's estate, towards the Temple. The massive statue of Tiamat which served as the focal point of a fountain seemed to glow white ahead of them. "It's strange how these people obsess to so much detail," Taisha said pointing out that the dragon eyes all looked south and each of Tiamat's heads met the gaze of a similar statue in the Great Bazaar to the south.

RiVule took it in stride. "The wealth inherent in the construction of this place is humbling, but I would expect no less from a dragon. Should I be offended that we have yet to meet the god emperor?"

Taisha shook her head, no. "Rumors here are that the god emperor was almost killed in the battle against the Jade God. He has not been seen here in Tania since."

"What happened to him?" RiVule asked, his curiosity piqued. "We do not get much news in the mountain."

Taisha lowered her voice as a group of wealthy Tanians walked past them. A knight bowed to her and smiled, which made her blush. Before, as a common fighter, such a person would have never acknowledged her. He was very handsome. "The story is that the god emperor spearheaded the attack against Orcus himself. In his dragon form, he led the assault but was struck by Orcus and his left wing amputated. Later, Alerius ordered and personally oversaw the execution of the Jade God. If the stories are true, the last words Orcus heard were from Alerius saying, 'I wish you to die.' The wound of his lost wing has never healed, though."

RiVule paused and leaned against the white marble rail that looked down to the central canal on the East-West Major. "Gruustir wishes me to offer healing to the dragon." He sighed heavily. "This is such a strange place to be. The war host would already be cutting this white stone and taking it as plunder. Yet, just an hour ago, they freely gave us bloodstones. Never before has the Horde had a bloodstone. I can feel it burning my chest with power." Taisha touched her earring and felt the same. "You feel it too. So, here we are, Orcs drowning in wealth the Horde has never before seen... welcomed as citizens and gifted with unimaginable power. I must ponder on this. Gruustir did not suggest this as my path. War, plunder, and dominion, yes. Citizenship, friends, alliances, an epic quest to Merakor. Let's go to the Temple, no... we shall climb Dragon Mountain and offer Gruustir's aid to this Alerius."

Though the day was getting on, Taisha dared not question the priest. At the fountain, they turned north and began to ascend the Monument of Heroes to the road called Ascension. RiVule stopped before the first statue and that confused look again crossed his face. "Take this one, a statue of a Taysoran knight bedecked with symbols of their sun god. Why? Why would Tania have this here as the very first thing we see? And look! The next one is a stylized statue of one of their rangers. Yet they war endlessly with Taysor."

Taisha replied, "I wish I knew. I've never been here or seen these."

Across from the statue of the Pha Rannic paladin, a priestess statue stood with her hand outstretched so that her fingers just touched the paladin's. RiVule pointed to it as they walked beneath the monolithic forms. "This one is labeled Dar Tania. I take it she is a priestess, or was?"

"Yes, RiVule. And the nickname for their lords derives from her first name as does the name of the empire itself. As you travel Morbatten, you will see her and her lover – Commander Sean – like this everywhere. They are treated as saints for young lovers, and a model for serving their god while being open-minded about others." Taisha ran her fingers on the base of Dar's statue. "She must have been truly special."

Statues of fighters, paladins, and other heroes came into view next. Each stood nearly four paces tall and looked so incredibly lifelike that Taisha wondered if they had some form of intelligence or life in them. The weapons, except for their stony appearance and feel, looked like actual weapons. Lights glowed at their bases backed by mirrors which cast light onto the statues and illuminated their path. After several turns in the wide boulevard, they became aware that an unseen magic hastened their ascent and they already rose far above the tallest buildings in the valley. "Such power, so casually used," RiVule marveled.

They arrived at the large courtyard in front of Alerius' throne room several hours before dawn. Though Taisha felt sleepy, she also felt RiVule's desire to find the dragon and it somehow gave her strength. Without pausing to look around, RiVule walked into the massive tunnel. "Now this is a proper dragon lair," he said.

With a glance at the sparkling city below them, Taisha walked in after RiVule. "It makes me feel very small."

RiVule laughed. "You felt the Dread Lord with Dar Shara! In their eyes, we are small. No doubt, others come here and think this is to impress them, or to convey the god emperor's power. The reality," he said spinning with his arms open wide, "is to allow a dragon to fly in and out of this cavern. Can you imagine how big that dragon must be?"

A quiet voice to their side answered and said, "With both wings open, the god emperor must still furl his wings to fly through this." They turned to see a paladin standing just out of plain sight to their right side. He bowed. "You are not on the expected to arrive list. In fact, I can't remember the last time we had Orc visitors. May I know your business?"

RiVule did not stop walking but called back, "Gruustir commands that I heal the god emperor's broken wing."

The paladin caught up to them and said, "Did you know that the god emperor is not in audience today?"

"My master cares not. Gruustir wills this and so we come. For the god emperor's sake, we pray that Tiamat has similar urgency." Speaking this way to a Tanian paladin worked for RiVule and emboldened Taisha.

The paladin faded away as he stopped and they continued. Now almost three hundred paces into the tunnel, giant statues of metal appeared on either side. While most had a humanoid aspect, all held weapons and looked ready to spring into action. Unlike the statues of the heroes on the boulevard outside, they could tell these were not statues but rather golems, waiting and ready for action. "Such wealth," RiVule muttered.

Ahead of them, the outline of titanic doors loomed against glowing magical and brazier-based fire light. The doors filled the tunnel. At the bottom of the right-side door, a smaller door could be seen flanked by paladins. But, when they finally closed the distance, even that tiny door turned out to be eight paces tall. One of the knights held up his hand for them to stop. "You are ordered to wait here. The god emperor is not here, but the Temple has sent word about your arrival. We have been told to keep you here until we know whether the emperor wishes to see you or not."

From behind them, the door opened and a priestess stepped out. She appeared young yet ageless and her countenance sparkled with ember fire. The two knights bowed low to her as she passed them. "Please understand," she said. "Bloodstone is a mess still. The Mighty Horde will be welcomed by King Malcor and Dar Ana with open arms. Perhaps we could review that while we wait?"

"I have heard of Dar Ana," RiVule said. "She rules Bloodstone."

"No, she presides over the Temple at Bloodstone. I'm Dar Cassandra, or Cassie if you prefer. Though Dragon Mountain is not a Temple, it is sanctified ground to Takhissis. I am the high priestess responsible for the sacred ground that is this mountain and Alerius' throne complex. You are Gruustir's high priest, RiVule and the paladin, Taisha. I am thrilled to meet both of you."

RiVule eyed her and wondered if intimidation would get him through the door. "Behind that door lies hill-sized piles of gold, yet my mind tells me that it must have been spent building the city that is Morbatten."

Cassie laughed, her smile bright and carefree. "Surely, priest of Gruustir, you must expand your imagination. Though some walk as humans amongst us as Dread Lords, they are all most certainly dragons. It is not just the god emperor's wealth but the wealth of all the Dread Lords and then the amassed fortunes of two thousand years of heroes and quests of legend. Surely, the Mighty Horde has similar stories and stores of treasure?"

Her tone was so carefully inoffensive and happy-sounding that RiVule wanted to rage at her, but instead smiled back. "So close to the dragons, how could the Orcs amass such a trove? Besides, while gold is nice, we crave glory. I grow tired of waiting. Gruustir bid me come. If Tiamat does not likewise urge the god emperor to meet me, I will leave."

Cassie came over and took his hand. RiVule noted her marble white skin against his earthen-hued skin, calluses, and long talon-like nails. *So...*

*exotic*, he found himself thinking. The thought surprised him. Taisha had made herself more than available to him. But, Gruustir required sacrifice and RiVule had sworn his all to Gruustir. He had assumed that included the joys of the physical body. Now, sensing this human priestess' energy – *is that lust?* – he let himself open to the possibilities. Everyone knew that Tanians had no compunctions about being with Orcs. In fact, one of his great-sires had exiled himself to Tania and later his son came back to the mountain. That was RiVule's great uncle.

He looked from her hand to Taisha and he knew, however this day went, either Taisha or Cassie or both would be with him. *Probably Taisha*, he conceded. After all, no one here really knew him and by human standards, RiVule was no doubt ugly. A thought came unbidden to his mind, *Whoever you desire priest of Gruustir. Not just your great sire, RiMorel but your mother and your mother's mother descended from unions with Tiamat's priestesses. It's all part of my plan to have a Spear that will slay Set. Most mortals read the Prophecy and think of it as a literal spear. This is false. The people, their faith, their strength will be what ultimately does what the Nexal Gods could not, maybe dared not do. How Heaven will tremble when Set falls!*

RiVule shuddered when he recognized the mental voice as Cassie's. In response, she assaulted his thoughts with images of them together, later. She squeezed his hand.

In the doorway behind the paladins, an armored form appeared, taller than the paladin guards and immaculate in its confidence. Alerius' voice rumbled into the tunnel. "RiVule, Taisha, Dar Cassie, please join me in my throne room. Faithful paladins, unless my brothers return, I am not to be disturbed."

The voice carried a sinister touch of power and the weight of all the years of the world. RiVule felt tension in his body and had to consciously force himself to relax. When his body did not, he wiggled his fingers and felt sweat on his palms. The dragon king, the god emperor, the red demon of the Orcs stood before him. No other Orc had ever seen Alerius up close like this. Each War Host wanted to claim the honor of attacking the dragon. Something feral in RiVule made him want to jump forward and attack. In his heart, he knew the glory of it would be lost forever. *If a gentle voice can shake me this much, I must be careful*, he said to himself.

While the two knights bowed, Cassie took RiVule and Taisha by the hand and led them to Alerius. Armored mage indeed, RiVule thought. Alerius looked every bit the role of an unusually large human except for the all red eyes and the radiant power shining from them. Knowing nothing else, RiVule would have known this was not a human though. The serene might and strange armor that subtly shifted as the light changed suggested a depth of timeless magic beyond comprehension. Three paces before Alerius, RiVule dropped to his hands and knees in his best approximation of a Tanian formal bow. "Dread Lord Alerius, at last I meet you and bow before you as if to a god. Gruustir honors your legacy in destroying the Jade God."

In answer, Alerius turned back into his throne chamber and said, "Come."

RiVule had to choke back an exclamation when he saw the torn armor and jagged bone spiked through the plate armor where his shoulder blade should have been covered by mirrored pauldrons. The wound showed signs of having been freshly healed, but blood leaked from bone marrow and around the protrusion of bone from skin. Cassie's presence reassured RiVule and Taisha.

The throne chamber itself met RiVule's expectations for the dwelling place of a dragon god. Far larger than the largest cavern in The Quat, RiVule noted the floor tiles of polished gold ore. Entering through the smaller door, RiVule saw a throne of golden but demonic skulls to the left side of the entryway. A still pool of water lay in front of the throne. Heat waves swirled the air around the seat of Aleriu's power.

Adjacent on either side sat two other thrones each decorated in the manner of lightning and ice. Alerius walked to his throne as stone chairs rose up for each of them to sit. "You've had a long day, RiVule, and Gruustir does me honor to send you. The dragon in me is offended at this intimation that even foreign gods know of my pain. Yet, my Temple grows weary with continual healing. I am willing to submit to Gruustir's gift."

"I need to see the wound as you are, Dread Lord." RiVule winced half-expecting the dragon to be offended. Orc history was full of fatal encounters with the Tanian dragons and only one encounter with a fallen one. The fallen one had devastated the ancient war host before at last falling.

Alerius nodded and said to Cassie, "I allow this because it is a gift from Gruustir and the Mighty Horde is much needed in Bloodstone." From behind him, Alerius' body exploded into space. Long before his entire body solidified, the presence of a fiery spirit filled the cavern, which now felt too small for the humanoids standing near the thrones. Never having seen this before, RiVule and Taisha fell to their knees. Even without dragonterror, the titanic revelation of this ultimate predator struck instinctive chords in them and they remained bowed. RiVule realized that the formal Tanian bow he had been seeing was not a custom. It was the primal reaction to the dragons codified as a formal salute.

Cassie stood firm and RiVule noted that a magical pen scribed the scene on parchment back by the scrying pool as she prayed reverently. Her ruby lips pulled at his attention with the promise of later and then he forced his focus back to Alerius.

His left wing lay stripped of muscle and membrane and where bones should have spread like tree branches, snapped and shattered spikes dripped ichor. In this much larger form, RiVule saw rivulets of blood streaming from the shoulder socket. "If I may?" RiVule asked and Alerius picked him up and moved him to the wounded shoulder.

The flexion joint that should have allowed wings to pivot and move was pulverized amidst scar tissue and perhaps even diseased tendon and bone. "Great dragon, has your Temple spoken to you of infection?"

"Yes, this is known. Their healings grow more frequent and ultimately desperate. My time is running out before I must leave Tehra or die. What would Gruustir offer such immaculately cursed wounds?"

Against his will and better judgement, words came to RiVule's lips and he spoke them out loud and boldly in Orc. "*Alerius, consort of Takhissis, and voice of Tiamat in Tehra, in the timeless days of Set, you led the dragons against the Heavens. Though it was not your intent, you interrupted my confrontation with Set. Secure in my will, I knew I would win. What folly! With Time's flow came the bitterness of my certain defeat if not for you and the dragons. I seek to repay this timeless debt and be discharged from obligation of conscience.*"

RiVule lifted his hands and then leapt into the shoulder socket. A scythe of green metal appeared in his hands and began cutting away at the gangrenous tissue. Alerius grunted in pain as RiVule hastened the onset of blight and accelerated the disease. RiVule, in his own voice, called back. "I have studied the anatomy of all Tehra's creatures. You cannot heal because the Jade God infused part of himself into you and masked it from Time. As such, you decay and rot from the inside out. While the cursed nature of this wound may never permit it to heal, if we remove this remnant, we can at least prevent further infection."

Alerius groaned and called out to Cassie. "Summon the Order of Water so that they might help. I would have Dar Ana, Shara, and Kell join me now."

Within minutes, the Order of Water joined RiVule in the wound and cut deeply as they dug into the shoulder socket. Forbidden to help, but forced to bear witness by Gruustir, Taisha watched the bloody harvest and began to hum a Tanian children's song before she altered the words.

> Bones planted in bone,
> The harvest grows.
> Bleeding rife with blood,
> He knows.
>
> He feels the bone,
> He is the bone,
> That must come free,
> Must go home.
>
> Hate planted in murder,
> The harvest falls.
> Flesh stripped of meat,
> Tiamat calls.
>
> Come home great king,
> To me great king,
> You must be free,
> To come home.

Taisha's humming and mouthing of these words caught Cassie's attention and a sketch of Taisha standing in reverence, and the words of her song, appeared in Cassie's book.

The bloody harvest continued for hours, maybe days before RiVule at last cried out in triumph. Blackened dragon tissue lay in discarded heaps around the shoulder blade. Steadied by the Tanian knights, RiVule pulled a single green gemstone free. The gem twinkled with fell light and reminded Taisha of an eye. It contained something.

RiVule jumped down and ran to Alerius' head, holding the green stone aloft like a small child might with a carnival prize. "Behold!" RiVule shouted, exhaustion tinting his voice. "The Blind Dragon of Merakor's eye!" Before anyone could understand or act on it, RiVule threw it in the air as a giant war hammer appeared in his empty hands. The hammer struck the green stone at the same moment it landed on the floor.

The humans cried out in shock and surprise, "No! Don't!" they said, but RiVule ignored them and stood steady as a shockwave blasted out from the stone.

"And so, Gruustir is free to rise," RiVule said. "The ancient debt is repaid."

As the green mist and smoke cleared, a gruff and deep voice resounded in the chamber. It was Gruustir's. "Nientro, as promised for Tiamat, the last seal of Orcus to Tehra is broken."

The voice of the vampire general Nientro replied, "And the dominion of Orcus is shattered at last. Rise Gruustir, our friend. Ascend and take the 664th and share free passage in the 665th with me."

The words echoed in the chamber and when they faded, Alerius collapsed to the ground unconscious. His collapse spurred a flurry of activity the like of which RiVule struggled to comprehend. Several of the priestesses shapeshifted into dragons as gates began to open everywhere. Healing care and magic, scaled up for a titanic dragon, arrived and was applied while the strange and sexual priestess Dar Ana prayed to Tiamat and a torrent of healing energy poured from her to Alerius.

*Surely, she will die,* RiVule thought, gazing at the amount of life energy she flooded into the god emperor. *Surely... no, this is what they meant. They are exhausting themselves to preserve him.* And in that moment, RiVule captured an epiphany and held it in his mind. *They love him. They would sacrifice their own lives for him.*

He noted Dar Ana, the mythic priestess who had once visited The Quat so long ago her name had changed to 'Lady of Dragons.' RiVule noted the ageless beauty of her fire and saw a hint of the statue of Dar Tania, in Ana's focus. Her faith, her execution of that faith for the god emperor, was so perfect that it struck RiVule dumb and he stared. Taisha came near him and watched. With each beat of Dar Ana's heart, with each passing moment that knit Alerius' flesh back together, RiVule noted the wing bones were not regenerating. The Dar clerics saw this too and Ana screamed out, "Shara! Kell! Combine with me! We must save his wing!"

The three came together as one and Ana rose up, angelic in the torrent of power uplifting her. She laid her hands upon the bone and prayed. It crumbled to her touch and she cursed. "Takhissis burn me instead! My life! His wing! Your son must fly!" Whatever source of strength she had been drawing from changed, and RiVule saw the River of Fire where Ana began to pull on her own lifeforce...

Alerius reached up and caught Ana in his claws. "Daughter, no. This is not your destiny. My time for Ascension draws nigh. There is a throne for a flightless dragon anointed for me by my beloved Takhissis. I forbid what you are about to do."

RiVule heard this and saw the tearful frustration in Ana's face and realized she loved the dragon, but worshipped him as a god. The title 'god emperor' was real to her, to the mythic Ana. RiVule dropped to his knees and prayed. "Gruustir, I have been wrong in my thinking. I offered you the Mighty Horde and the glory of our conquests. I sought to kindle paladins and divine miracles for the people. I see my error, and now offer you a new pledge: my love. I recommit myself to loving you the way these Tanians love and serve the dragons."

Freed of the cursed eyestone, Alerius' shoulder bled as if freshly amputated. The necrotized bone and tissue around the wound and the Blind Dragon's Eye had prevented healing. Dar Ana slumped to her hands and knees before Alerius. She was covered in days of blood. Yet, even when barely recognizable, something about Ana drew RiVule's attention to her. Her tireless efforts to save the god emperor aside, RiVule felt Ana's love and worship for the dragon. Her voice choked with exhaustion and held-back tears, Ana said, "God emperor, you were becoming a draco-lich, like the Blind Dragon. This was too close. I offer you my life as atonement for not having figured this out. That a foreign god would intervene…"

Alerius interrupted her. "Is exactly as it should be, my precious Ana. There is no atonement needed for something even I could not see." Alerius closed his eyes and breathed deeply as his shoulder continued to bleed. "It has been ages since I suffered mortal pain like this."

"Then I will tend you until you can see again," Ana pledged.

Ana's groveling bow before the god emperor almost made RiVule laugh until he saw every single mortal bowing. He remained standing even after Taisha urged him to bow. In the silence of the moment, RiVule hit his chest and proclaimed, "Mighty Alerius, with the cursed stone removed, you will heal."

RiVule stayed with Alerius and marveled at the machine that was the Temple of Tiamat. Thousands of priestesses came in homage to add their healing prayers to the god emperor. Paladins by the score combined with the strongest of the clerics, and yet none came close to the power of Dar Ana.

On the third day, RiVule found Cassie and said, "I will have you now."

With a feral grin, Cassie said, "No, I will take you." The god emperor had recovered enough to direct Cassie and other priestesses to capture RiVule's bloodline.

A week later, when the Mighty Horde arrived bearing RiVule's banners, Alerius and RiVule stood side by side and greeted them as they passed through the massive Temple Gate into Bloodstone. Alerius' shifting to human form had reopened his shoulder wound. Though tended by clerics, it became apparent that the amputated wing would be long in healing. Watching them march through and bow to RiVule and Alerius, the image of a machine came to RiVule's mind.

With haste, he beckoned for parchment and began to draw before the inspiration fled. Alerius watched with curiosity but presided over the Mighty Horde as they passed them by. Never before had any Orc stood with The Tanian Dragon.

RiVule called over Cassie. "Your king, this Malcor, he is a forge worker, yes? Give this to him or someone like him. When made, if I am not here, this is to be riveted to the god emperor's shoulder armor. It will seal his armor over the wound and prevent the recurring damage we see when he shapeshifts."

As ferociously grinning Orcs marched past them, Alerius bowed to RiVule so that it was the last thing the last column saw. "King Malcor will situate them and the Mighty Horde of Gruustir will fall upon the fiends until they are ground to mash. So, let the Saga of the Orc begin."

RiVule bowed his head and prayed to Gruustir for their victory. He was surprised to see Alerius pointing to the still-open gate. "Would you like to see the dead god, RiVule?"

RiVule licked his lips and walked through the portal. The high mountain air of ice-locked summits assaulted his nose and lungs. Cloud haze and the burning smoke of lights along the concourses stretched out while the great Temple of Bloodstone towered to his right side. The Orcs continued their march down to the valley floor and, though the Tanians here bowed to Alerius, RiVule ran forward to see the Mighty Horde descend. He noted the burn marks and signs of repair to the Temple and its causeway.

Then, like magic, the haze lifted and he spied what he thought to be hills stretching out from north to the west. It resolved to his view and became decaying but frozen muscle. He realized it was Orcus' leg. Gryphons circled overhead and as more and more of the valley cleared to his view, he noted flocks of gryphons tracking battle on the valley floor far away.

The stink of death and unnatural things filled the air and RiVule drank it in.

"Bloodstone," he said. "Long have I dreamed to come here."

Alerius walked up beside RiVule and pointed across the valley. "The Jade God's head fell across the valley and destroyed the Sixth Fortress. Since his fall, we have fought on three fronts. The first front is what remains of the demons and devils that came here during the battle. The second is raiders attempting to take parts of Orcus for magic, fetish, and other reasons. The third is from necromancers bound to serve Orcus. We are still fighting an all-out war here, just on a smaller scale and mostly underground. Your Horde will be powerful in such combat. You wish to join them, no doubt."

"I do," RiVule breathed. "Every part of me screams to lead them and see their glory first hand."

"Dar Ana excels with this and has fought with the Orc before. You could not wish for a more effective general. Come, I wish to show you more." Alerius gestured to the Temple. "You will meet Crimson Burning and King Malcor."

Below them, in the valley, the head of the column broke into a run march, something the Orcs could do for days, and streamed out at a sprint towards the closest battle marked by the gryphons. Their shouts to Gruustir for power made RiVule's heart soar. He looked back at them one last time and then whispered, "Glory find you all. I go to a higher cause for our people."

The towers along the inner wall between him and the valley unfurled RiVule's banners. The Mighty Horde had come to Bloodstone at last. He smiled and whispered, "Gruustir, I hope you see this. It's all yours – the Saga of the Orc."

# Chapter 13 – Gaming the Game

Ayden paced back and forth in the tent and kept reaching for Titan's Blade vacant in its sheath on her forearm. It should have come back to her by now. The Ayden-copy created by the Titan's Blade should have brought it back by now. She must have died. Weeks had passed with Ayden hoping Titan's Blade would return so that she could learn who was behind the raids. However, the raids – at least those from Sora – had completely ended after her encounter with that particular group.

The mage assigned to her, R'Dar Wesley, watched her pacing and said, "Don't worry, we'll find it and get it back. It was hard to get this from Ana, but with a Corth Stone, this will be easy. I had hoped your noticing its absence would lessen over time. This restless worry reminds me of an addiction."

Ayden paused and rubbed her arm. "I feel stronger, more confident when I have it. You have no idea…" Ayden stopped. "Well, you probably do since the cursed bards sing that story everywhere. Titan's Blade is special to me. I feel like part of me is missing without it. And I'm worried that, somewhere out there, she is trapped or suffering."

"It's an enchanted knife that copies you, my lady. I doubt she – your knife – is capable of suffering. I've made some arrangements to help find it though. They should be ready soon."

"Pardon my impatience, Wesley, but, last week when every single cleric retreated to Tania, I did not think they would be gone that long. We've been forced to retreat from too many of our positions. Where are the clerics? And," she punched the table. "We've lost the Sixth Fortress, again. It gnaws at me. Now, we have eighty thousand orcs and with them, we will recapture it and more, but still. I want my dagger back."

"Patience, Legion Commander," Wesley said. "Dar Ana normally handles these but she left with all the other clerics. They just barely got back." As he tried to placate Ayden, a magical portal opened in the command tent and an apprentice mage stepped through with a large trunk. "Here we are now. See? Patience."

Ayden took the trunk from the apprentice, who clearly struggled with either its bulk, weight or both. "I'll get this." She lifted it up onto the mage's table with one hand and began fiddling with the lock.

Wesley begged, "Please don't do that, Commander Ayden. There are reasons it is locked." Wesley thanked the apprentice and moved over to the trunk. With some deftly cast magic, the lock popped and they opened the trunk to find a dark blue crystal sphere. "I've only ever seen these from a distance. My lady, if I have not stated it already, thank you for allowing me to be your mage."

The apprentice hesitated to leave and Wesley had to shoo him away. "Hurry, or the dimensional door will close on you."

"I've never seen a Corth sphere," the apprentice said as he reluctantly stepped towards the portal. "Never."

Ayden pointed to the portal and waved good-bye to the apprentice. "So, these are really special," Ayden said. "Like that special, huh? It reminds me of the larger one by Ana's Temple throne." She reached in to pick it up but stopped when she felt a buzzing in her fingertips.

Wesley caught her hand and held it back. "Only scriers can use these, Ayden. I studied it enough that I'm technically a scrier, though I've learned that I personally enjoy combat magic a lot more. Here," he said and picked up the sphere. "It's quite light." A holder for the sphere, carved in bone, rested in the box. Wesley assembled it on his desk. "These are special. They allow us to do things you should not be able to do with scrying magic. And yes, the one by Ana's throne is just like this but even more powerful. You see, Corth gave that one to Ana, personally. If you know what I mean. Ana is not a scrier and should not be able to use it either."

Ayden rolled her eyes. "Before I came here, I heard so many stories about Dar Ana. Sure, it seems credible and to her liking that some might be true. Might. But, I hardly see a god giving her a crystal ball. That's just another story."

"Believe what you will, my lady. I rather like the idea of a mage god suffering for the love of a high priestess. Maybe it's the romantic in me." Wesley sat down and began an incantation whispered to the stone. As he chanted, the blue crystal began to glow and Wesley instructed Ayden to put her hand on it and concentrate on her dagger. Images swirled and then a gleaming red light pierced the blueness of the sphere. "My dagger," Ayden said.

"Stay focused. There are lots of things that glow. Try to see the runes on the handle, the way it felt in your hand, and any unique markings. Most people fixate on something vague like, 'It was my favorite knife!' We need specificity."

Under her hand, the image shifted about and then that red haze appeared again, but it was dim. Wesley touched the sphere and suddenly Ayden's hand felt wet and slimy even though when she looked at it, it was not wet at all. She began to hear sounds but they were muffled. "Your knife is underwater, in mud." Wesley rubbed his neck and popped it as he twisted his head side to side. "Let me try something." He chanted, differently this time, and with each word, the image pulled back until they saw a warehouse near ocean docks. Piers stretched out along a boardwalk and unsavory-looking people stalked about the streets, hugging the walls for shadows. It looked uninviting.

"If my dagger is alone, then my copy was slain," Ayden sighed. "Joust, please give me a fair fight for once!"

As Wesley continued to chant, the scene shown in the orb widened until the royal palace of High King Andrew appeared. "This area is east and north of the Soran palace. I'm not the best judge of distance when scrying, but I'm guessing it would take many hours of horse riding to reach that area. Your dagger, Commander Ayden, is in Taysor, underwater, in muck."

"How do we get it back?"

"We can pull it back, carefully. It might not work because of the water. In fact, it probably won't work but we can try tomorrow. I need to prepare for it. Or I can send you there now."

Wesley sat back, expecting her to ask questions. Instead, she called out to her squire and ordered him to bring her clothes and armor of "a Soran style." Wesley had only worked with Ayden for three weeks and appreciated her drive to action. Before even meeting her, she had a reputation for decisiveness. Some of the veterans felt she was too hasty, but as the Dar rallied around her, and then the dragons, and victories piled up behind her, Tania's military culture began to change. His briefing from Ayden's prior mage had been, "You're a combat mage, good. Keep lots of combat and movement spells ready. Good luck!"

Wesley blushed when Ayden stepped behind a screen and began changing into the Soran clothes. That former mage had been more studious and had lacked combat experience. Except for Ayden's famous scars from her face to her hip, she had received healing soon enough to avoid scars elsewhere. "I really wish you would give me a heads up when you do these things," he complained. "Your paladins are going to kill me if they find me in here, fully dressed, and you changing your attire." Standing next to him, Ayden's squire nodded. At least she had remembered to step behind a privacy screen.

Ayden laughed. "We're at war and you're worried about me changing clothes? Deal with it, mage. It's not like your Guild is chaste and noble in their use of magic." Her taunt was enough of a dare that Wesley knew to take it as such rather than flirting. He had seen many a knight not respect Ayden's continuing loss of Tembri. Even the Soran High King treated Ayden with great deference.

Though Wesley wanted to argue the point, she was right. "Well, yes, but I'm not like them. For one, I'm in here in Bloodstone with you. Those mages aren't. Besides, I much prefer real women over conjured or charmed ones any day."

"Fair point, Wesley. You'll have to tell me more about your love life later. I assume you're ready to send me to Taysor?" She smoothed her leather vest and checked her sword in its frog at her waist. "I really don't like Soran fashion. I find it binding, especially in the legs and shoulders." She shrugged her shoulders and Wesley walked over.

"Here, I can help with this." He took out a small knife and cut the leather along her upper back and then down along her upper thighs. He then used a spell to lace leather straps through the extra space. "Fit better?" he asked.

"You're a lifesaver. Thanks. Okay, let's go."

Wesley moved the scrying to target an area about ten paces from where the knife lay in the mud. "Once you're through, you have your *water breathing* potion. I'll illuminate the blade to help you find it. Remember, I can see you so shake your head or wave to communicate with me."

Ayden handsigned: YOU GOT IT.

"Yes, of course. Or handsign. Just remember, my view might be off and I'm not as fast with that as you are." He handsigned back slowly: BE CAREFUL.

Wesley's *teleportation* spell materialized Ayden off the harbor street in a moment where no one was present. She quickly stepped into the sparse flow of people walking about and headed towards her knife. The nature of the neighborhood and its people felt dark and tense to her. For being a neighborhood in Taysor, it reminded her of Bloodstone. She looked up to catch Wes' attention. She signed: ALL AROUND ME, HUMANS?

Wesley focused on the sphere and then from his spellbook began to cast a spell to detect nexal shifts. When he finished, the figures in his view, even Ayden, burst into colorful light. Ayden looked golden and radiant with red cracks throughout her form. Everyone he could see in the docks was red with black cracks moving and shifting across their surface. The uniformity of their colors told Wesley they were not human.

He pulled his view of Ayden towards him until only Ayden was visible and carefully said, "Everyone around you, everyone you can see is touched by Warp and possibly undead. I only ever see sameness like that with undead or clones. Because of how they're moving, I'm guessing either vampires or revenants. Probably vampires."

"I'm going to bring one back with me. Be ready to grab us." Ayden reached the area where her dagger should be. She waited until Wesley confirmed he could not detect anyone in the area and she jumped into the ocean. The water was dark and filthy. She felt grit from it in her eyes. About three paces down, she felt mud. Without Wesley's voice telling her how to move, the current would have immediately moved her too far off course to ever find the knife. She heard Wesley in her thoughts give her instructions. *Swim back under the pier. Good, keep going. Just a bit more to your left. Good. Now, move three fingers down...*

When her hand closed on Titan's Blade, Ayden felt a tingling along her spine. Holding it, she felt whole. Stronger. Without waiting, she activated her copy and they breached the surface of the water. Ayden handsigned to her copy. SO GLAD TO HAVE YOU BACK. QUIET. Ayden-blade nodded but looked like she would burst with excitement to be reunited.

"Careful," Wesley said. "There are three vampires walking towards you."

The Aydens moved to the edge of the sea wall and held on, ignoring the cold. Ayden-blade smiled at her and mouthed 'thank you.' She then signed: I WAS GETTING BORED IN THE COLD DARKNESS. IT REMINDED ME TOO MUCH OF BLOODSTONE.

"The men are stopping near you. I can't tell if they are looking for you or what. No, they're moving on now. One keeps looking back though. Damn it, he's going back to where you were."

Ayden signed, WE WILL GRAB THAT ONE. BE READY TO TELEPORT.

The vampire sniffed the air. It smelled human. The area around The Twins barely registered any changes, yet the people in the guild had all been converted to vampires by Syand and her ilk last week. Once Delia pulled the doppels out, they had no choice for maintaining control of The Twins' territory.

"It smells like a woman," the vampire Hallistead said to himself. He looked around and enjoyed how the ocean scent was so amplified in his new body. There had not been any humans here for days, not since Dark Legion turned everyone to vampires.

He had been a porter and spent all day every day either loading wagons or loading ships. His biggest dream in life was to become an unloader because the work was easier. Without The Twins supplementing his pay to filch crates here and there, he may as well have been homeless. The Dark Gift had come suddenly amidst searing agony that had then given way to strength, sense, and power unlike any dream he had ever had in his life. His first blood was just days ago and he licked his lips at the prospect of another meal. To find a human here of all places.

He walked up to the edge of the pier and looked out at the ocean. The scent lingered but the salt water and breeze broke it up. "Take him now," Wesley said to Ayden.

Two hands grabbed his knees and pulled him forward. Hallistead was not the smartest man but even he knew vampires died in water. "No!" he screamed as he hit the surface face first. He began clawing at his face trying to protect his eyes as the salt water burned and then he was out of the water. Stone slammed into his face and two identical women pressed blades to his throat from behind. An unpleasant feeling of threat loomed behind him. He seemed to be in a tent, and not in the ocean water anymore. Still, the water on his skin and drenched clothing burned him and he shrieked trying to put out imaginary fire where the water hurt him.

Ayden said, "If you resist us at all, you will die." Ayden-copy nodded at her and they flipped Hallistead over. "If you cooperate with us... why are you doing that?"

Hallistead was shuddering and thrashing side to side. "Oh," Wesley said. "He thinks the water is killing him." Wesley intoned a cantrip and in seconds, Hallistead and both Aydens dried. Wesley said, "You know it's a myth that vampires can't cross or endure water, right? The issue is divinely-blessed water that has been sanctified to a god that hates undead."

Hallistead realized he was dry and opened his eyes. Identical women – *that smell from the ocean!* – held knives to his throat. Behind them, a scrawny mage stood with a wand lazily pointed at his mid-section. Behind them all, inside what looked like a tent, two paladins stood. The sense of threat came from them, though Hallistead realized any of them could probably kill him. He held his hands up. "I'm just a porter. Please, I don't want to die."

The identical women did not relax at all. In fact, at his words, they all seemed to grow even more tense. Ayden held up her knife and asked, "Do you recognize me? What about this knife?" He shook his head. "Okay, listen," she continued. Three weeks ago, I went to Taysor. I was following…"

Hallistead interrupted her. "Three weeks ago?"

"Yes," Ayden said with annoyance. "Is that significant?"

Hallistead nodded and then winced as his neck cut on Ayden-copy's blade. "That was when The Twins' leadership, all the higher ups, they all died. Their headquarters flooded and they drowned."

Ayden-copy began to laugh. "Oh yes! I remember now. I punched a hole in the tunnel, underwater." Titan's Blade did not retain memory well between activations.

Ayden pointed to the paladins and spoke to Hallistead. "You see the knights? If we don't kill you, they will if you give us any trouble. I'd like to at least let you enjoy a few human moments. If you can tell us what happened and what this all means, I don't know what The Twins is… maybe we can help you, or do something. I don't know. What do you want?"

Hallistead agreed and said, "I'm just a porter. My name is Hallistead. I'm not a warrior. Please."

"You're a vampire," one of the knights said. "That makes you dangerous."

"I understand. I hate vampires too." Hallistead, while standing up slowly. He felt panic in his chest and began hyperventilating. "I've only been this way a few days. I didn't want this. I didn't even know about vampires until Dark Legion came and made me this way."

Wesley pointed to a chair and invited Hallistead to sit. "I'm a wizard. Death threats aside, I'll of course kill you too. And, you're in Bloodstone by the way."

Hallistead shook his head and sat down. He finally had time to look around and noted the mannequins with different types of Tanian armor. The dragon symbols everywhere, and then the wyvern emblems on the trunk, caught his focus. While he looked around, Ayden stepped behind a screen to change out of her Soran clothing. Hallistead saw resplendent armor resting on a mannequin. It bore beautiful dragons swirling about the mirrored surface and the number "19" connected in Hallistead's head: *I'm in Bloodstone*. The wizard's words finally clicked home.

For just a moment, he wondered if he could escape. Donning her armor now, Ayden must have anticipated his thinking. "The wizard isn't lying. You really are in Bloodstone. In a forward operations camp. I give you maybe thirty seconds before you are killed if you try to escape." Ayden looked at Wesley. "Please notify the High King that one of his citizens is here and he should join us immediately."

"It's true," Wesley said. "Welcome, Hallistead."

Hallistead dropped his head into his hands and began to shudder. "I've never seen a vampire cry," one of the knights said to the other. "Must be the god's death," the other replied.

Ayden sat down opposite Hallistead and when the vampire continued to weep, she said, "I don't have time for this." She signaled the paladins. One stepped forward and clasped the vampire's shoulder.

The paladin ordered, "Hallistead, in Tiamat's holy name, I compel you to obedience. You will cease this pointless show of emotion and tell Legion Commander Ayden everything she wants to know." The dragon symbol on the knight's gauntlet burned with fire as he spoke these words.

Hallistead, though still wracked by emotion, stopped crying. With a tremulous voice, he said, "Three weeks ago, The Twins – a gang of smugglers that operates in the area you took me from – was suddenly drowned to death. There had been stories of a big haul."

"The group of Sorans that got away from us," Ayden said. "Were you part of that group?"

"No, I'm just a porter I keep telling you. The day after The Twins were killed, we were summoned by what was left of the gang. That was when Dark Legion…"

Ayden stopped him. "These terms, I don't know what they mean. The Twins is a gang, okay. Dark Legion?"

Hallistead felt sorrow and regret well up, so strong that they might break him. Then, it boiled into rage and, except for the paladin's hold restraining him, he would have ripped into the people around him. "I'm sorry," he explained. "I'm not used to being a vampire. There is a rage in me I have never felt before. The Twins was not really a gang. Think of it like a street business. They did some smuggling, and stuff that could track beneath the eyes of the Pha Rannics. Dark Legion on the other hand, while also a street business, they do hit jobs, people smuggling, slaves, whoring, and blackmail. Well, I guess all of them do protection rackets too. There are others. I don't know their names. I think 521 is one. I've heard of Cross something or another. Does that help?"

"And you worked for The Twins, which was soft stuff, right?" Wesley had a magical pen transcribing everything.

Hallistead nodded and continued. "They, Dark Legion, attacked us and then their leader, Syand, came. I watched her eat my friends and knew I was going to die when she tore into my throat. I remember her saying, 'Arise, vampire!' and that's it. Now, I'm a vampire." Self-loathing welled up when Hallistead saw them all looking at him with pity in their eyes. The paladins concentrated on controlling Hallistead as his feelings flared into hatred again. "If they weren't controlling me, I'd have attacked you all long ago." Hallistead licked his lips.

The vampire took a deep breath. "I'm okay now. So, now everyone I knew in The Twins is a vampire working for Dark Legion. They told us to keep doing our jobs and stay out of public sight. They said that anyone caught doing anything that drew the attention of the Pha Rannics would be executed, and that they would bring us food. My first food was a young man. He was already dead when I entered the room, blood everywhere. I can't stop thinking about it."

"What did Dark Legion want or expect from you?" Ayden asked.

Hallistead met her eyes and answered. "They wanted us to lay low until a signal was given. At that time, we were to attack 521 and the Rogue's Guild."

"Did they say why?" Ayden knew about Rogue's Guild. Daryx had shown her the contract with Grant and reviewed their purpose when she took command of the Nineteenth. The lord had been most explicit: *give Rogue's Guild free space to take as much of Orcus as they want, but make them earn it.*

"They said something about a new drug, the blood of some god or something, maybe the Jade God?" Hallistead sat back and cradled his shoulders as he hugged himself. "I don't know what any of it means. Dark Legion wants it all, as much as they can get. Apparently, one of those two guilds or both had lots. That was all hearsay by the way. I wasn't in any of the discussions where these things were actually said. But, being vampires – we also had doppelgangers with the Dark Legion.

I think you'd call them that, doppelgangers. We just called them 'shifties.'"

From outside, a priestess entered the tent and said, "King Anderw is here, Commander Ayden."

"Send him in," Ayden replied and stood. "Andrew, thank you for joining us. Hallistead, a porter from Ymac, has just been telling us of not so good things happening back in Taysor."

Andrew bowed to Ayden and walked over to see Hallistead. "Taysor isn't supposed to have vampires. For your cooperation, Hallistead, you have my gratitude."

Hallistead looked even more uncomfortable with the High King there. Andrew's armor, crown, and general demeanor conveyed royalty and Hallistead had grown up knowing this. "My king," he said. "I don't know what to say."

Andrew sat down next to Ayden and leaned forward. "With the Jade God, vampires were bad, but most often constrained in what they could and could not do. Without the Jade God, you have all these powers but no constraints. It's very dangerous. We cannot let this be. We must root it out. Will you help us, Hallistead? I wish I had something to offer you, but in this case, we are reliant on your aid and good will. Do you still have good will?"

The question hit Hallistead like a crate smashing into his head. "Do I have good will?" he repeated Andrew's question. "To be honest, your lordship, I don't know that I ever had good or bad will. My life was not the kind of life that asked big questions. I hate what I am. I don't understand why this happened to me. But, I hated myself before I was this. I broke the law to survive each day, did that make me bad-willed? I just don't know. But, I will do what I can to help."

The priestess who had entered with Andrew stepped forward and gave a small box to Ayden. Ayden opened it so that Andrew and the vampire could see. Inside sat three glass vials of green ichor. "This," Ayden said. "Is Orcus' blood. We are curious if you will drink this and help us understand what makes it so powerful that Dark Legion would convert an entire guild into vampires." She held up one of the vials.

Hallistead reached out to take it and then hesitated. "I'm wanting to help, but I am scared. To my eyes, this blood, it swirls and sparkles like it's alive. There is a smell about it, even sealed." His hand began to tremble.

"You can do it," Andrew said and caught Hallistead's hand. Unlike the dragon paladins, Andrew's voice and smile spoke to Hallistead and helped reassure him. "Please."

Hallistead broke the seal on the vial and shuddered, almost sexually. The scent of the god's blood overwhelmed his senses and without another moment's hesitation, the vampire drank the blood. He looked around and said, "Woah. I can see colors, everywhere. It's like being in sunlight on a warm day without clouds. I feel naked and yet safe." He looked at Ayden. "I can see colors all around you. You're golden and white and red, yet there is a darkness in your heart. My king, I can see great longing in you, but cannot say what for." Hallistead stood up and smiled at the paladins. Moving with vampiric speed, he yelled, "And I can feel that your power is not enough to constrain me!"

The paladin lost his control over Hallisted and moved to reassert it. The other paladin punched the vampire right in the face as he tried to run past them both to the exit. Hallistead almost avoided the blow with his superhuman speed.

The paladin's fist rocked Hallistead back to fall to the floor. He struggled to breathe before he remembered he did not need to breathe. He spun about and then went quiet and still as Andrew's burning sword crossed his neck. "One more move and you end," the young king stated. "Challenge me, I dare you."

Caught in the moment, Ayden eyed the young king. *He's really just my age*, she realized. She remembered meeting him the first time, before the Jade God had entered the valley. He had seemed naïve and hungry to meet and deal with the Tanians. She remembered being in council with the god emperor since and his interest in grooming the Tanian king to strengthen the alliance between the Spear and the Shield. *Like me, Bloodstone has changed him. This bravado did not exist months ago.*

Hallistead began laughing. Contrary to the dire circumstances in the tent, the vampire's mirth was jarring. He moved to wipe tears from his eyes and giggled when there were no tears. "You should have seen the look on his face..." he heaved and pointed at the paladin. "When I ran past him!"

Ayden nodded to the two paladins and signaled them to forcibly restrain the vampire. Hallistead continued to laugh even as the two knights pinned him to the ground and then shackled him in silver bands. "If we cannot trust you, you will be bound. I would not think this a matter for so much laughter."

Hallistead looked at his bonds. Though his skin burned beneath the silver, his smile remained joyous. "You have no idea, do you scar face..."

Ayden punched Hallistead so hard, one of his eye teeth broke. The second paladin commented, "If I had known full attack was okay, I'd have done more than just knock him down, Commander."

Wesley watched Ayden and reflected on how much she had changed in just the few weeks he served her. Her other battle mages all reported Ayden as being self-controlled to the point of frustration. *What is changing in her?*, he wondered. The story of her scars had become famous throughout the land and yet, Wesley could not remember a single story where Ayden lost her temper. The other mages had dismissed it as grieving for Tembri. But, there were changes in just the time Wesley had been serving her. People did not normally change so much. If anything, Ayden seemed hungry for Hallistead to attack her.

Ayden grabbed Hallistead's hair and said, "Beyond the colors and a sudden and total lack of regard for appropriate behavior, what else is going on inside your head? Our patience with you is growing short."

Wesley pulled Ayden away from the vampire and apologized to the group. "You're not going to hear this. It's nothing personal." He cast a spell that removed sound from around them. He whispered in Ayden's ear. "They cannot hear us, but hear me out, Legion Commander. Assume this is a drug. Let's not kill him. His behavior here, extended to a vampire coven, explains everything we are seeing. The drug lowers inhibitions and suddenly there is war in the streets of Taysor. What happens when the effect wears off? I have other things I want to try and we need to know how long it lasts, whether it is hours or days or permanent."

Ayden agreed and asked Wesley to end the *silence* spell. "We have agreed that, for all our sakes, we should use this opportunity to see what effect the Jade God's blood has on a vampire when it ends, if it ends. As such, I have decided that Hallistead is to stay here under Wesley and the paladins' care. Wesley, send King Anderw and I a complete report daily. When you are done, see that the vampire is given proper Bloodstone treatment." She pointed to the two knights. "You will stay and assist. Until Wesley is done, I don't want anything interrupting."

For the first time since drinking the blood, a note of fear crept into Hallistead's voice. "Ends? Treatment?" he asked while Ayden walked out of the command tent.

Ayden took Andrew's arm and made it clear he would be leaving with her. Outside, Andrew asked, "What is the plan?"

"Wesley believes there are more effects to the drug. It is likely that Hallistead will require some time to come to terms with the drug before he can adequately explain how it works. Wesley felt it might take hours, even days. If permanent, we'd like to know this too. It could explain the reports out of your city. Vampires do not normally conduct themselves in the open like this." Ayden pointed to their north where gryphons circled. "And we have more important matters to attend to, High King."

Andrew felt the warmth of Ayden's hand on his arm and smiled. "Yes, the demons to our north. I was making ready to join the battle when we received word you wished for us. Vampires in Sora! I never would have believed it."

"And doppelgangers," Ayden sighed. "It seems the Gate of Warp is broken and floods us with evil."

* * *

Ash and Khalla knew, within minutes of Grant's arrival, that Rogue's Guild had come to Tania. The shrine priestess sent word and Perdition routed it to them with a note that Grant had paid for a day's leniency. Within hours, and in disguise, Ash and Khalla entered the Round Cup Inn and smirked to see Grant and most of his team sprawled out and gorging themselves. Delton slinked along with them and named those members of the team Ash did not already know. "And, you're sure that Grant has the goods?"

"Yes, in his backpack. It's all in a holding bag. We have at least another forty thousand pounds." Delton spoke quietly, trying to imitate the Tanian way of saying one thing but talking to the real purpose in code. To a listener, it sounded like Delton had said how warm the day was for being spring still.

"Go, join Grant. Talk. We're going to steal his backpack." Ash cracked his knuckles. "I've always wondered about stealing from another guildmaster. And it's been too long since I got to do this."

Ash's playful tone caught Delton off guard. "How well do you know each other?"

"We go way back. Far enough back that this will be okay, even if I get caught. You know, I recruited and trained him," Ash said while punching

Delton in the arm softly. Ash and Khalla moved back into the shadows of the establishment and began stalking their target.

Delton went up to the bar and picked up drinks for Grant's table. Within a few moments, Venter spotted him and they all called out when they saw Delton working his way towards them. Their heavy Soran dialect drew a few looks from the Tanians in the tavern and they quickly quieted down.

"Del!" Grant said, slapping his back. "When I got home and you weren't there, I feared the worst! Even with the stories about the Halfling, I've been worried about you. But, here you are looking well-rested and healthy as a caged wolf." 'Caged wolf' was one of Grant's code terms. He was asking if Delton had been trapped or coerced.

"Here, these are for you all," Delton said pushing the drink tray to the center of the table. "Healthier than a caged wolf, you know. I'm sure the team told you; things were pretty bad. So far, I do not regret the deal I made." Delton sat down and with a wistful glance around the table, he added, "I should probably be more formal about this, but Grant, I had to leave Rogue's Guild. I didn't want to but just couldn't see a way that saved everyone. Things were bad and getting worse by the minute. I wondered if I would regret it, but so far, I just miss you all, like I'm homesick. Things here are interesting. I can see why you took so much work here."

Grant passed the mugs around and Venter raised his mug to Delton. "To Delton, the best second boss I could have ever wanted!" Amidst the team crying out "cheers!" Venter continued, "When we reached the end of the rope, when the hangman's noose waited for us, when the wolf's fangs closed on our throats, you cut a deal to save us all. You have our gratitude. We will, for the rest of our days, hold a spot at our table for you."

Delton's eyes flicked to where Venter pointed and he saw the empty chair with an empty plate set for him. A sense of loss, of what he had given up rose in his heart, and he ached. He tried to stop tears and when he failed, he wiped his eyes. "Thank you," he choked. "It's been a lot harder than I thought." He would have lost his composure entirely if he had not, at that moment, seen Grant's backpack open. Ash was good, almost supernaturally good.

Delton smiled. "To Grant!" he exclaimed. "May you always bring the most profitable and secretive contracts imaginable!"

They all began laughing and Delton sat down with them to catch up.

When Grant noticed the theft, hours later, he found a note in his backpack. It read: *Perdition claims its due. Rogue's Guild is ordered to assault Perdition. If any of your team can touch the throne, you will be granted pay for the Jade God, and a new contract.* It was signed by Marcello, and Grant swore at fate and cursed Joust's name. "We were so close to being free…" he moaned as he fell to his knees and rested his eyes. He decided to let the team sleep in real beds tonight. Tomorrow would be Delia, if she came.

Grant awoke with a start and saw sunlight streaming through the window. His lower body felt numb from sleeping on his knees at the bedside. He flopped up onto the bed and closed his eyes again. With a jerk of his head, he woke up later and panicked when he realized he had dozed off again; it was now late morning and the Overflight Festival would begin at high noon. He rushed out to find the time. Relief flooded away his anxiety when he realized it was not yet noon. He would need help to reach the Great Bazaar, but he could make it in time because he was in Tania.

He moved up to Venter's room and, as only a thief could, left a note for Venter to treat the team to a luxurious day and that he would be back by dinner, maybe with friends. The artificer shop he enjoyed when visiting Tania, which also fronted as a pawn shop for unloading magicked gear, did not let him down. Within minutes, a mage came and teleported him to the Great Bazaar. Grant walked to the fountain and pressed a card to his forehead and said, "Copy me." Instantly, an illusion of Grant appeared walking with him. "Go to the fountain and sit down," Grant whispered while holding the card to his head. "Pull your hood back and look up at the sun. Look relaxed."

The illusionary copy of Grant did as instructed. It took almost an hour, but eventually, Grant noticed a lady kept walking past the area. At first, she looked old and haggard. Later, she looked young and spry. Remembering that Delia was a doppel, Grant assumed it must be her and followed her. "Stand and walk up to the lady in the green dress," Grant whispered while holding the card to his forehead. "Call out, 'Delia!' and open your arms."

The illusion did so and the woman in green flinched, and then stepped forward hesitatingly. "Say, 'I'm here. Kill me now, like you tried to last time.' Hold your arms open and kneel."

Delia watched this play out and her shoulders slumped. She felt small and defeated. Love, human love, was supposed to be more forgiving in her mind. That Grant was already begging her to kill him would not only draw the attention of guards, but told her that he fully expected that this is why she had come all the way to Tania: to kill him, not because he believed her, not because he could not live without her. The use of illusions, something Grant did whenever he did not trust a situation or sought to manipulate it, told her that things would be near impossible with him. She almost left. She almost resigned herself to despair. But, something inside her would not let it go. Besides, in a crowd, she was safe.

Grant watched the act from the doppel's side and had the illusion draw its sword and lay it on the ground. A guard nearby took an interest in this and began moving towards them. Delia saw this too. Grant let the illusion see it. "Hurry," the illusion said. "If you're going to finish your job, now is the time. I'm unarmed. The guard can't catch a doppelganger in a crowd like this. It's a perfect betrayal. Hurry, before Dark Legion takes me and gets all the credit."

Delia shook her head and said, "No. That's not why I'm here. Grant, please…"

The real Grant pressed up from behind her and she felt a knife twist between her shoulder blades. Grant had been studying. The blade targeted her doppelganger heart, not a human one. The illusion looked at the guard and stood while resheathing his sword. "Beautiful ladies," he called out. "I'll be on my way." The guard nodded and went back to his patrol. After a minute, Grant sent the illusion to walk ahead of them.

"Why are you here, Delia? Sora does not smile on doppels. Tania has perfected extreme overreaction to your kind. It'd be so easy." Grant struggled to mask the anger in his voice. "What's your name anyway?"

"It's what I said, Grant. I am Delia." Without turning, her body morphed so she could look in his eyes. Suddenly, he pressed his dagger to her perfect breasts and her emerald eyes locked into his. "Dark Legion was a mistake. I brought your armory from Ymac also."

"You're not really Delia," Grant hissed. She was arousing him. She always had. He pressed his dagger into her skin and drew a bead of blood and pulled it into the fabric, just like real cloth. "Are these even real clothes, or just part of your skin?"

"They're part of my skin, Grant. But my satchel has the armory in one of your holding bags. I didn't know what to expect here, with you, with us. I'm really Delia. There was no real Delia. My orders were not to kill you, but to introduce you to Syand. And, those weapons in the room? They've always been there. Always! But, we usually get the penthouse suite, not a secondary room. Please, believe me. You told me about the Ymac safehouse years ago. There never was a human Delia! I made this identity up so I could help Dark Legion keep an eye on Abigail's and the other taverns. There's so much going on and now, no doubt, the Legion is going to hunt me too. I've never seen them this way." Delia grabbed the knife blade and let it cut her hand. "If you came to kill me, be done with it. I'd rather die by your hand than become a vampire. My kind, we do not do well with undeath. The unchanging nature of it clashes in bad ways with us."

"Prove it. Can you prove you're really Delia?" Grant asked. "Your kind, you kill or capture and replace. It's how you are. You make deals and betray. Prove you're the real Delia."

"Yes, yes, that is all true. But, there was no need to kill or capture, because I invented Delia. And," she squeezed his hand around the knife hilt. "I love you, Grant. The Legion found me and helped us establish ourselves a long time ago. That was before we knew they were vampires, and before they all went insane. I was Delia long before you came to the inn and we first met. Please, Grant. I love you. Please, believe me!"

"How long ago did you do this Delia thing?" Grant's words made her wince. He had completely closed his heart to her and his tone remained harsh. "How did we meet?"

She hated this, how humans reacted to her kind. Until she lived amongst them in their form though, she did not understand these bonds of loyalty and love. Even now, she did not, but she knew the patterns and behaviors that stemmed from them. The hurt in Grant's voice, the dagger at her breast, his attraction and arousal to her closeness… these would not exist without love and lust. While she could not understand love, she did understand lust, as a tool. Lust would have required her to prove herself sexually. If only Grant would give in, just a little bit.

Love and betrayal of that love, that was what held them in this moment of dagger-to-heart and yet prevented Grant from killing her. *He must know I could kill him*, she thought. *Even if he has guards, this close, he knows.* She realized that Grant wanted her to prove she was not just another doppelganger. The predatory thrill of this realization and the rush of adrenaline it brought her, made her smile and lean into the knife. A stream of blood ran down her torso now.

She swallowed and opened her eyes wide. "Grant, you already know the truth. We fell in love and have been. Yes, I lied about my nature, but look at us – you with a knife to my heart! When you first entered Abigail's eight years ago, I was there already. There's no secret I can tell you, because it was all us! You and I! You were no one and I was just another paid guard who thought she was free to fall in love. And I did, with you! What we had was special and real. I can't prove I love you but if you'll trust me – I know it's hard – I will show you every day from here on. I want us to work. We have always worked. And, I know we still can because we love each other! You have to believe me when I say that I am not just another doppel out to thrill ride someone else's life. Truly, would I have chosen a bar maid and escort girl if that's what I wanted? Had I known that Syand wanted to make you a vampire, I never would have tried to poison you. Had I known that Bradley was on Syand's payroll, I would have told you that too. Please."

She felt Grant's hands relax and then pull the dagger back. His hold on her became more like a lover's and she leaned into him and they embraced. Alone in the tiny island of their bodies, shoppers and merchants moved all about and did not disturb them. Grant stroked her hair and said, "I'm sorry I cut you."

"No, no," she whispered back to find his lips. "It's all my fault. I'll make it up to you."

When Grant's lips met hers and their kiss grew in longing and power, Grant whispered, "I'm sorry."

"For what?" she breathed lustily into his neck. Her other hand slipped between his legs. *Lust is such an effective control*, she mused. Grant felt like he might bed her right here in the plaza.

"For not loving you enough to see the truth earlier." At his words, a sweet liquid filled their mouths and Grant locked her head to his. Onlookers rushing by saw two lovers. Delia felt the liquid and tried to scream, but Grant stifled her cry with his mouth.

The poison, fatal to doppelgangers, would make him ill. R'Dar Maishan had been curious about Grant's request for something like that. "There are no doppels here, Grant," Maishan had pried. "What do you know that Tania does not? Information about doppels is valuable currency here."

Grant kissed her and stepped back as her body, locked and unable to move, began to crumble like a sand sculpture splashed by water. From behind her head, he pulled an illusion card he had pressed there during their kiss. "Activate Delia," Grant said. Instantly, an illusion of Delia superimposed over the top of the crumbling one. The illusion brushed its green dress flat and smiled at him.

Through the illusion, though hard to see clearly, Grant watched as the doppel broke apart like ceramic pottery. Spiderweb cracks preceded pieces breaking and falling apart. Grant looked around the square and then saw a shadowed alcove with a clear view of the plaza. It was a perfect spot and he bowed in its direction. He pointed to the illusion, and to be sure, he touched his earring while thinking of her. He said, "Next time, you come to me. I understand there is a war and, if you have truly left Syand, she will be looking for you."

To his side, the doppel crumbled into a pile of dust and broken rock-like debris. Grant stepped into it to embrace the Delia illusion and pick up the satchel. His feet kicked the dust pile around and he said, "I know you're there, Delia. I don't have the blood anymore. Tania has it all. Good luck with that. Let's try again. This time, you tell me what you really want. We'll be at Perdition at midnight if you want to talk."

He thought he spied movement in the shadows and a flash of light on a metal surface. "Doppels," he grumbled. "It probably wasn't Delia. Oh well, she'll know soon enough. They'd have to be insane to meet me at Perdition." He began to laugh and vanished into the crowd. The illusion of Delia continued to smooth her dress and would for at least another four hours.

In the alcove, Delia drew her sword and attacked furniture in the room. She wanted to scream, but could not. Watching Grant kill her sister, knowing Grant would have killed her too,… *and the blood is gone?!* Syand would not be happy. *Grant is supposed to love me. How can he kill me?*, she wanted to yell and kill until this rage in her abated.

## Chapter 14 – Assault on Perdition

Grant returned to the Round Cup Inn and found R'Dar Maishan sitting at a table sipping at what looked like wine from a crystal goblet. The inn's other patrons gave her a wide berth, though it looked like a young couple had just ended a discussion with her. Seeing no one else from his team, he guessed they were still asleep or had left to sightsee. Most of his team had only ever been to some of Tania's outlying villages. Though still not in the capital, they would want to see more. All in all, it surprised him that they had taken the news of their benefactor so smoothly. He sat down across from Maishan, aware that that everyone in the tavern was watching.

"Well," he began. "I just killed a doppelganger in the Great Bazaar."

Maishan nodded but could not hide the surprise in her eyes. She and Grant went way back. "Remarkable that something like that bypassed our perimeter sentries. I will be sending word to the Temple immediately."

"Let's do better than that." Grant signaled for a drink and growled in the low rhythms of draconian. Not his favorite language, he had to resort to spelling certain words he did not know how to say. "There are more of them," he said. "They think we have stuff they want, well, that another Soran g-u-i-l-d wants. But, P-e-r-d-i-t-i-o-n already took it. I told them to meet me there tonight. I'm supposed to meet Marcello there at the same time. We can take them all out."

Maishan nodded. "Your draconian is terrible," she said in fluent draconian. "I'll be reporting that to the Temple as well. You need to practice more often, Grant." She took his hand and, in a manner that reminded Grant of times past when they had been a thing, tenderly squeezed his fingers in her own. "Doppelgangers aren't at the top but they're certainly high enough in the Allegiance of Blood to warrant a Slayer, or maybe the god emperor will want to add them to the Garden. You do not want to be seen as an ally to those creatures."

"It might be worse than that," Grant replied. "What happens to a doppel that becomes a vampire?" He could not remember how to say 'vampire' and did not want to spell it. He just said it and hoped no one overheard.

"Our doctrine teaches certain things about vampires. They are a foundation on which other attributes can be added. For example, a ten-year-old boy becomes a vampire. He'd be a god among 10-year-old children, but weak by vampire standards. Early experiments by Dar Ana, after the First Cascade, suggest that this does not always become the new foundation though. With the Jade God dead, who knows? Maybe a doppel would retain their foundational nature of being able to change shape and add the vampiric foundation underneath it? It's interesting that Delia said otherwise, and seemed to know. Maybe she was part of an experiment? It seems they become vampires trapped in whatever form they were in when converted. It'd be interesting to know the answer. There is a doppelganger in the Garden, but like other Set creatures, it is under heavy guard. Not interesting enough that the Temple would humor such an experiment with Slayers on high alert throughout the Isles since the god's fall."

"I'm not asking that. I want to bring them to Perdition and we fight there. My team can take them. If we fail, Tania can finish them." He squeezed her hand and took his drink from the waitress.

"I think that can work. You will let Marcello know? You will not mind if I make arrangements... just in case." Maishan finished her drink and signaled Grant to lean forward. She surprised him by kissing his cheek. "Grant, great danger swirls about you and your team. Yet, I feel there is destiny and perhaps a touch of prophecy as well. If the occasion arises," she switched back to Tanian speech and finished. "If there is a chance, I hope you'll include me in it. Though I am aging, I do not want to die of old age. I want my life to end in spectacular fashion."

Grant smiled and kissed the back of her hand. "Maishan, my love, I will. Thank you. Back to Perdition, I have to be there before midnight. My team will assault Perdition after sunset. I don't know when the doppels might show up." He moved to lean back and then, on a whim, he asked, "I don't suppose you want to assault Perdition with us?"

Maishan had an instinctive laugh, which she quickly stopped. She thought about it. "Yes, Grant. Let's assault Perdition together. I'm in and you never have a cleric with you."

When they left and to Grant's surprise, Maishan followed him back to his room. Though Maishan had not transcended like so many of the priestesses Grant had encountered in Tania, her level of physical fitness and her passion for life equaled anything he had experienced. Seduction had been part of his training and, while he enjoyed that part of his job, being able to cut loose with someone he did not have to ply with an agenda had been part of Delia's appeal. Maishan's lovemaking occurred with ferocity and Grant pushed thoughts of Delia out of his mind. She was dead, or would soon be.

As they lay together afterwards, Maishan propped her head on her arm and looked down at him. "You know, if you join Tania entirely, they will probably extend your life."

"I'm surprised that has not come to you yet, Maishan. What happened? When we last saw each other, you had some test. Did it not work out?"

"I passed. Just because I haven't transcended yet doesn't mean I won't ever. Our history is full of older clerics who transcend and then revert to their prime twenties. My mentor suggested that the god emperor wishes for me to understand how much a blessing it is to transcend before we are allowed. Or, who knows? Maybe I passed but it's just not the Queen's will that actually rise up. I don't know right now. To be honest, I struggled with it for many months. I've made my terms with it. It's a tale as old as Tania. As I grew out of that age and some of my sisters did transcend, I really wanted it. Who wouldn't?" She smiled and twirled her fingers in his hair. "Honestly, you can't tell me that you'd rather be with a perky twenty-two-year-old than my wrinkled and drooping self?"

"You're very beautiful, Maishan. I think you over-exaggerate the relative qualities involved here. I'm not exactly in my prime of life anymore either." He pulled her on top of him and they kissed. "I see nothing wrinkley or droopey." Things would have moved on from there but a knock at his door interrupted them.

Grant sighed and called out, "Who's there?" It was Venter wanting to know what the team plan is. Grant sighed again and bit at Maishan's shoulder. "Gather everyone in the dining hall in ten minutes. Tell them to be ready for a job."

"You must think me well-satisfied with less than ten minutes of pleasure," Maishan said quietly to Grant's back.

"Hey, Venter, check that. I'll need another twenty minutes to wrap up some business here." Grant smiled up at the beautiful priestess. "We take what we can get," he exclaimed and flipped her over.

Nineteen minutes later, the two walked down the stairs. Rogue's Guild was ready though it bothered Grant that Delton was not present. "You all remember R'Dar Maishan, right?" Grant asked as he bowed and presented her to the table. "She will be joining us tonight."

"What's the mark?" Jerare asked careful to avoid noting that Grant held Maishan's hand or how close the two seemed.

"Not a mark, Jerare. It's a test. Perdition. At least one of us needs to touch the throne before midnight. If all goes well, we'll run into my old friend Delia and her doppelganger friends." Grant paused and let that sink in. "Some things you don't know yet. Besides Northern Cross, The Twins, and 521 have all been destroyed or fallen under Dark Legion's control. There's essentially only one guild in Sora now. Delia and, well, as far as I can tell, everyone tied to the neutral territories are doppelgangers working for them. While there is no way for us to know for sure, it seems some of the material we brought back from Bloodstone incites some kind of insane addiction in the vampires. Dark Legion wants it all. With any luck, they'll march on Bloodstone to take it. Compared to the Nineteenth Legion, we are a much easier target. The doppelgangers are here to get it from us, from Tania. Good news and bad news. The good news is that Tania was my other buyer for the Jade God's material, and they already took what else we have. So, we're going to get paid, again. The bad news is that, if the doppels and vamps take us, we die or become vampires and then Tania kills us."

Grant looked at each of them and waited for questions. When there were not any, Grant continued. "Perdition is unlike anything we've ever seen before, but again there is good and bad news. Tania, being how it is, mirrored all their castle designs on the Bloodstone Fortresses so that their fighters would never get lost. Perdition is no different except that it's their guild headquarters. As such, it has been created as a test for thieves like us."

Maishan interjected, "Agents. We call them agents here. Thieves steal from others for their own gain. We have those too, but our laws do not allow them to survive for long. Thieves who work for Tania are called 'agents.' I just wanted to be clear on that should any of you get caught or find yourself needing to explain what is going on. Also, most Tanians don't know about Perdition. Say you're working for me on a Temple contract. That will suffice for normal interactions. If it goes beyond that, do not try and escape. Ask for me; say nothing else. They'll send work and I'll come. They'll assume you're guilty of something."

Roger chuckled and said, "Agent of the Temple. Don't run away because it means we're guilty of capital crimes. Got it." The others laughed a bit too. "It's nice to see a pretty face behind the contract." Roger prodded at Grant. "Has Maishan always been our buyer?"

Art added, "Agent. I like how that sounds. I've never been comfortable with the term 'thief' anyway. It was never something I could tell my family about. They just knew I had work as an adventurer."

"So, Perdition..." Venter said, drawing the name out slowly. "Modeled after Bloodstone, but full of traps designed as tests for agents."

"You got it." Grant leaned forward and let his hands rest on the table so he could lean into the group. "We're going to be the first Soran guild to breach Perdition." His confidence made them all feel better. "It's going to be epic. Let's do this. Head back to your rooms, get whatever you might need, kiss your loved ones good-bye. We'll meet at Maishan's shrine, errrr, Tiamat's Shrine, in an hour."

When they had all left, Maishan whispered to him. "It's so sweet that you tried to honor the Queen."

* * *

Delia paced back and forth. Grant was supposed to have revealed more and been less guarded. Something she had once read in human literature came unbidden to her mind: *Mortal emotion is magnified in humans compared to other races. When their love is challenged and proven false, bitter revenge takes root in their souls.*

Delia shuddered as she remembered how Grant had kissed her sister and fed her poison. It was enough to make her want to release the real Delia and send her to Grant. He would kill her, or course, only to realize too late that he had killed the real Delia. She toyed with the idea. *That would be a delicious revenge for not loving me!* She still had regret and hated it when her prey escaped. Not enough regret to cause problems, but still. Her vicarious existence in Delia's life had lasted long enough that it had taken hold on her. Whether it was this love game with Grant or the countless clients who bedded her, the gauntlet of emotion and pleasure it brought the doppleganger's life was deeply addictive. Without trying, without having to build relationships, without really doing anything other than showing up in the target's skin, she had experienced sexual ecstasy, love, trust, anger, and too many other powerful feelings to bother remembering them all.

Staying separated from the target's emotional state was hard for doppels. To really pull the imitation, Delia had had to really get into the girl's head. Syand had wanted Grant captured years ago, but he came and vanished too quickly to get without actual vampires helping her. The end result was that Delia had been Delia for years. Given that a usual copy job only lasted days, Delia had begun to find it difficult to remember who she really was, how to shapechange, and how to recapture her assassin training. The allure of killing the real Delia and becoming Delia had never been stronger than when Syand almost killed her in Dark Legion's headquarters. The real Delia had been sent away to work in a dark brothel where no one had names and anything went for the right price.

To find Grant, the doppel had copied Grant after he had left. The pathetic girl was overjoyed when "her Grant" returned and told her he just could not abide another day without her. With gold, with human love everywhere, the doppel had swept her off into a house owned by Dark Legion. They had married. Her imitation of Grant had fooled the real Delia enough that she got what she needed – how to make the real Grant fall in love with her.

For a few weeks, the real Delia had lived a fairy tale romance with doppel-Grant that ended in wedded bliss. It had been a perfect score that revealed everything she needed to know about Grant to capture him. Now, the girl waited in a cage under Dark Legion's care. *It would have been a kindness to kill her*, the doppel tried to reassure itself. *But no, she lives to die now because her love, Grant, had sent her to this place after a stupid fight.* Delia burst into laughter. *I'm going to make Grant pay for not loving me.*

Flying over Tania as owls, the seven doppelgangers in her team gave the Temple a wide birth. The lighted concourse and Grand Staircase provided a perfect landmark for their real destination, Perdition. The amount of light from the great city shadowed the back side of Temple Mount past the amphitheater. A great concert there sparkled with light and magic where, no doubt, they retold some dragon story. The night's dark and flickering shadows from the city's light gave them a perfect landing place. Landing as owls, they shifted to their true forms. Long and lanky arms with slender knife-like fingers flowed out from the wings. The feathers pulled back into clay-like flesh. Their true from allowed them to quickly alter to any other shape and gave them advantages in the darkness.

Though they could not see Perdition, they knew it was down below them nestled in a box canyon that made it invisible to normal traffic on the Coastal Road. That road and Dockside glimmered with magical lights. Perdition was only ever visible from the air, or if a visitor knew the way. "Remember, our target is the Jade God's blood. Nothing else. Syand would like Grant captured… so would I. But, we get paid the same whether he lives or dies. The blood is the priority."

They all morphed into coyotes and moved quickly towards the head of the box canyon. When they reached it and looked down, they found themselves scrabbling backwards. The cliff face dropped straight down nearly a thousand paces. Perdition itself was not visible except for parts of the Coastal Road that connected to its narrow boulevard. A sense of great space and nothingness loomed before them.

Delia shifted back to her true self and pulled a small glass lens from her hip skin. When she put it to her eye, the giant fortress revealed itself in a sphere of coruscating light. "There the fortress is," Delia said. "She's set far enough back from the cliffs that no siege weapons could reach it from up here. Tania is not much concerned with aerial attack. Though, there is protective magic around the fortress." She moved side to side and studied it until she at last noticed a small iris that opened in the barrier along the Coastal Road.

Looking more intently, she saw Grant's team riding horses towards the keep. Through the magical seeing lens, she could tell they had come prepared for a fight. Seething darkness emanated from Grant's backpack. "He has the blood of Orcus in his backpack. Grant's backpack is our first target. Let's go." Delia and her team moved back into owl shape and dove off the cliff to sweep alongside the rocky ground.

Maishan listened to the wind for the awaited message. It came as if hearing a voice in her mind. "Perdition sends word that a group just scried us from the cliff tops," Maishan shouted over the pounding horse hooves on the cobblestone highway.

"That'd be Delia," Grant called back. "Be on guard. Everyone activate your illusions and go dark."

At his command, everyone in the group held up an illusion card to their forehead. In an instant, copies of themselves on their horses appeared superimposed over their real forms. One by one, they jumped off the horses and let the real horses carry the illusions forward. Grant helped catch Maishan. "Bet you did not know that horse stunts would be part of agent work, did you?"

She thanked him and then enacted a prayer that would mask Grant and their crew from scrying. Around this, she then wrapped another prayer triggered from a mage scroll. "This puts a shell of anti-magic around us. Most detection is oriented to magic, not its opposite. What now?"

"We run. Everyone, stay close to Maishan and let her set our pace! If you step outside her prayers, all of your magic will deactivate and you'll fall. We will not be able to stop and risk that you weren't seen and you'll be on your own until you catch back up to us. Should that happen, you are to move forward on your own. Someone must touch the throne before midnight. It does not have to be me. If you have a chance, by Joust, you take that chance and touch it. Win it for Rogue's Guild. Understood?" After a nod from everyone, Grant took Maishan's hand. "Now, we run!"

They began running. Though their horses outraced them, they got to see what happened when aerial assailants lashed down like raining knives onto the horses and the illusions riding them. Partially transformed doppelgangers eviscerated the horses and cut through the illusions. Of the seven, four attacked Grant's illusion and tried to take the backpack. One of the doppels adjusted a rose lens on its eye. "Delia," Grant muttered and pointed her out to the group. Though she looked right at them, they could tell the doppel could not see them.

"Maishan, can you fight?" Grant asked.

"I was born to fight, Grant!" she screamed back through her heavy breathing.

Grant was impressed. Maishan struggled to keep pace with them but kept pace she did. This was no out of shape Pha Rannic cleric. Grant took her hand to help her run and shouted, "Rogue's Guild, let's kill them. We won't get a better chance than this!"

The doppels picked through the horses, wondering where the riders had gone. "It was a plant," Delia shrieked. "He knew! They knew!" Her frustration made her body lose form and she gagged trying to assert control over her shape.

One of her team asked, "Ambush?"

Delia shook her head, no. "Distraction! They must already be…"

Suddenly, the lens in her eye went dark and her entire body felt something pulse through it. An instant later, knives and blades hit them as Grant's team attacked at full charge. Delia realized Grant had tackled her and his short sword cut deep into her belly, just barely missing her true heart. No matter, the doppelgangers were immune to non-magicked weapons.

"Now!" Grant called.

Maishan ended the anti-magic and instantly, each of the doppels found themselves stabbed and lanced through by blades that exploded with magic energy. Grant's blade ignited with fire, his favorite weapon for unknown circumstances. His initial attack had just missed Delia's real heart. Without magic, her body compensated easily and shifted her flesh away from the blade. But, when the blade's magic poured out a second later, Delia knew searing pain. Her heart quivered against the edges of the knife and she knew she was going to die as the sword's fire began immolating her from the inside out.

"Grant…" she gasped.

Grant looked down at her. The force of his charge had allowed him to tackle her off his horse's corpse and pin her to the ground. He bit something in his mouth and let venom dribble from his lips onto her face. She tried to twist her head to avoid getting it in her. "For Delia," Grant said. He twisted his sword and cut upwards into her heard. "For all of my friends. For the Allegiance of Blood!"

Delia tried to swipe at Grant hoping he would dodge and free her. Instead, Grant winced in pain as her finger razors stabbed through his armor into his shoulders and side. He refused to dodge her attack. He coughed and blood mingled with the venom, but he did not move. "Set take you, Delia…" he choked and leaned forward to kiss her. Her fingers stabbed into his lungs and blood foam fell from his mouth to hers.

"You're not a vampire yet. Where is the real Delia?" he coughed. Venom from his mouth dribbled into her own as she stuggled to murder Grant.

Around them, the rest of the crew scored another successful attack, but the other five doppels rallied into a circle and threw the attackers back. Maishan stood behind the rogues and prayed to Tiamat for Grant's team. Her prayer energized them and struck fear into the doppels. One spat back, "Your goddess will not save you from us!"

The doppels jumped forward making full use of their shapeshifting powers. The front two reached out with tentacles to entangle legs and throw them off balance while the other three attacked Maishan. "Take the priestess first!" one hissed.

Venter nimbly jumped over the sweeping tentacles and tried to attack one of the three doppels, but missed. Jerare and Roger fell to the ground as suckered limbs twisted around their legs and began to squeeze. To their horror, the squeezing tentacles detached from the doppels, but continued to squeeze their upper thighs like tourniquets.

Jodie gloated over the doppel he had backstabbed perfectly. The speed of their charge allowed him to tumble to the creature's side. Distracted by the other rogues, Jodie had stabbed up into the beast's heart. When the anti-magic ended, he carved the heart out cleanly. He saw the rest of the team failing against the five and mentally mocked them for not spending more time in combat training. Art and Pete tried to defend Maishan, but one shapeshifter made it through and tackled Maishan.

Maishan felt the air explode out of her lungs when a gray human-like mass of flesh tackled her. They rolled and when Maishan regained her senses, she looked into a perfect copy of herself. The doppelganger grinned and leapt back from her. In her voice, the doppel-copy pointed and screamed, "Look out! It copied me!" The doppel raised a dragon sceptre that appeared in its hand. "Help me!" The doppel charged forward to attack Maishan.

It felt surreal for Maishan to see herself wielding a sceptre. She had not used a weapon in combat since her days studying at the Temple, twenty years ago. "Tiamat, remove me from harm," Maishan prayed.

The doppel moved past her, suddenly unable to see or detect the priestess. Though not in the River of Fire, Maishan stood up and brushed dirt and sweat from her cleric mantle. All around her, the River raged and she wished she could access it like so many of her sisters. "It's not fair," she said. "If I were Dar Shara, I'd have already defeated these things or paralyzed them all for the Gardenkeeper." Immediately, a chastisement rose in her mind and she bowed her head. "I know, my Queen. I am not a Dar yet. But, do I not serve the same as they? Tell me, beset by doppelgangers, what would you have me do?"

An image of the combat around her filled her mind and she saw herself moving through the combat, healing the wounded, and blighting the fallen shapeshifters. "Yes, my Queen. I will ensure none survive."

The doppel copy of Maishan raged all about, "Where did the doppel go?" She swung her sceptre and moved as if to strike an invisible creature. With combat continuing all around, only Pete and Art were close enough to help. The doppel called out to them, "Help me find her. She went invisible. Hurry! Before she confuses another of us."

Pete and Art moved forward to help and, using their swords like divining rods, they stabbed about in the air and sliced side to side. When they crossed in front of the copy, the doppel attacked. The sceptre struck Pete on the side of his head with a powerful blow. The sound of bone cracking made Art jump. "No! Pete!" he yelled moving to attack doppel-Maishan.

She kicked Art and when the foot struck Art's mid-section, it morphed into a teeming mass of tendrils that held on and pushed Art to the ground with immense weight. Art saw a bloodied sceptre lift up and come smashing down at him. The force of the blow pulverized his face.

But, even as Art screamed in anticipated agony, a burning swell of healing energy flooded into him from an unseen source. He had an image of a ghostly Maishan touching his outstretched hand and the words, "Tiamat blesses and heals you. Now, defeat this enemy for Her Glory!" The sceptre hit his face again, crunching his nose and cheek bones. He felt the fatal blow, but the healing strength of Maishan's vision held him alive and then restored him to health. The pain nearly blinded him but he retaliated and attacked the doppel-Maishan.

Jerare and Roger tried to regain their footing, but with the tourniquets paralyzing his leg, Jerare fumbled and fell as the two doppels facing them counter attacked. Rending claws the size of daggers scraped across and cut through their leather armor. Jerare knocked the doppel attacking him to the side just in time to avoid his arm being caught in those teeth. *That was close*, he thought. But, he was not safe yet as a new arm full of claws erupted from the doppel's chest to attack him again. Undefended and completely surprised, Venter saw his life flash before his eyes.

Venter appeared out of nowhere and cut the doppel through from behind just as the talons began to spear at Jerare's chest. With a dagger in his other hand, Jerare severed the tentacle on Venter's leg. The rush of blood in that limb brought agony renewed but some mobility at least. Then, a warm rush as health and strength flooded into him. He looked around in wonder and saw nothing, but felt Maishan's lips on his cheek and a whispered voice say, "For Tiamat's glory, slay them!"

Grant ripped the lens off Delia's eye and held it up. Immediately, he noted the glorified aura around the doppelgangers and the magic weapons of his own team. The barrier around Perdition glowed behind him like a sunset. Maishan moved like a ghost through the combat and healed Jerare. She looked transcendent and young. Grant retained his hold on Delia's neck and surveyed the combat. Though Venter had masterfully backstabbed the creature attacking Jerare, it still moved. Throwing knives whipped out from his hands towards the doppel closest to him, the one attacking Jerare. Grant's knives pierced a new section growing out of the creature's back aimed at Venter.

Seeing them safe, Grant turned back to Delia. "Tell me," he hissed, spitting more venom into Delia's barely breathing mouth. "I have the antivenom. You don't have to die. The real Delia…"

"She's…" Delia tried to smile. The venom cracked her mouth and the burning sword in her heart foretold her death. "I love…you," and then she crumbled into sandy clods.

Grant winced as Delia's fingers disintegrated and clotted his chest wounds. He could barely breathe and fumbled for a healing potion. As always, this Delia left him with unanswered questions. What was she about to tell him? Her last act had been to close his wounds to buy him time to heal. Either Tania was wrong about doppelgangers, or Delia was a different kind.

Jerare looked up at the gray monster looming over him and felt dazed for a moment when suddenly he was looking at a mirror image of himself. The creature moved to roll him over when three throwing knives cut into the doppel's side. It shrieked and its voice quickly changed from demonic to Jerare's own voice.

"The one with knives, that's the doppel!" the real Jerare screamed. With his leg felt still numb, he tried to put some space between him and the monster. Venter lined up his sword and cut into the creature, but somehow it dodged. It gave Jerare the space he needed and he rolled away.

Jodie tackled the one with knives, even as the blades popped out. "I've got him!"

Art threw the monster, which now copied him, over his head and moved to attack. Against the shadows flickering all about from fire-rimmed weapons, it was hard to tell who was friend and foe. Those copied knew, but everyone else lost sight as the combatants clashed together and threw each other back. The doppelgangers kept changing position and copying whoever they drew close to. Grant, watching through Delia's glass, called out and threw knives at the ones he was sure were enemies.

Maishan healed the agents as they were wounded or fell, but Grant knew her frustration was growing too. Art fell and with the two so close together, Grant could not tell if it was the real Art or not. On a whim, he pulled an illusion card from his deck and pressed it to the broken clay where Delia's head had been. An illusion of Delia appeared and, as Grant did his best to imitate her doppel voice, said, "Enough! Stop this ceaseless combat! I order it. Grant, we surrender."

The monsters quivered as they stopped their movements and looked around, blinking with confusion. They had almost won. Their moment of hesitation was their undoing. Jodie and Venter backstabbed the copies. They fell looking just like Art and Roger. It hurt to see, but wide-eyed and back a few paces, another Art and Roger watched.

Grant yelled out in Delia's voice. "Stop it! Grant, we surrender! All of you, drop your weapons and go to your true forms! Now, or we all die!" Delia's illusion dropped her weapons and bowed.

Two of the three remaining doppels surrendered and followed Delia's behavior. The last one snarled though and attacked Delia. When the illusion fuzzed through the attack, it hissed, "Tricks! Kill them all!"

It was too late for the two that surrendered. Venter and Jodie cut their throats with flawless precision. The single remaining one leapt into the air and tried to escape. Maishan appeared and a column of fire rose up from the ground and burned the owl's feathers even as it tried to take flight. Grant jumped up and cut it in half.

In the burning remains and as Grant patted out the flames from his clothing, they looked at the battle scene. Two of their group had fallen and lay unmoving. Maishan moved to check on them and said, "Art, Pete, and Roger are the most wounded, though Jerare's leg is mangled. While not broken, he probably has fractures running throughout.

Thankfully, I can heal everyone. I need about an hour. Or, we leave them here and trust Perdition will take care of them?"

Grant looked at the time and heaved a deep sigh. "This was costly." He looked at Delia's remains. He added, "Though worth it. We don't have an hour to spare. Maishan, of the team, who is least injured?"

"Jodie and Venter." Jerare, Art, and Roger's faces fell. Maishan explained, "The others require careful attendance or, even with divine healing, things could get bad for them. It's a shame. I was rather looking forward to Perdition myself. I'll stay back with them. Go ahead."

Grant smiled at her and said, "Someday, Maishan. I promise, you and I will walk into Perdition together."

Maishan prayed and began dressing the laceration and stab wounds for both Art and Roger. She then moved to the others and said, "I'm going to summon aid from the Temple. Honestly, I'm surprised we haven't seen any of the Legion vampires yet. I've been curious how many vampires I can dispatch." She squared her shoulders and proudly said, "I've tested higher than vampire, you know."

Grant came over and kissed her hand. "Thank you, Maishan. Venter, Jodie, let's go!"

They sprinted, tossing caution aside, towards Perdition. Though they could not see it in the dark, the tall towers loomed in the night and they felt a chill shadow whenever they looked in that direction. Grant could see the barrier and they ran through it. All Bloodstone fortresses had detection barriers. They worked like alarms. Though Perdition's could have been so much more, it was not. Marcello knew they were coming regardless. The battle on the road would have also told anyone paying attention here that armed company was coming.

Grant skidded to a stop before the giant gates. The massive doors sat heavily in their banded iron frames. To either side, rough carvings of guardians looked down at them from statues nearly ten paces tall. In Bloodstone, these would be actual guardians enchanted against undead.

Here, at Perdition's door, Grant had no idea what they should do. "I've never actually been in Perdition. Team, assume hostile," Grant said. "Spread out. Without touching anything, see if there are traps or hidden doors. I'm curious if we can scale the wall and enter that way."

The team did so and within fifteen minutes reported back. Magical runes had been cleverly worked into the floor tiles, the obvious human door within the gate, and in the areas along the outer wall. Venter reported, "We checked the walls. There are not as many runes, for where we could see. They seem random. And, Grant. The wall runes move every thirty seconds."

Grant eyed the human door, which was his area of interest. "I did not see anything about this door. To my eyes, and with Delia's glass, it looks untrapped. I don't know if we have time to scale the wall, though that is my preferred approach."

Jodie pulled a leather-wrapped grappling hook out of his backpack and began making ready. "Let's do this. I'll scale the walls. If I make it up, you can follow. If I don't, use me as a distraction and go through the door."

They helped Jodie set a *stone-grabber* bolt into a crossbow. It would pierce into stone and then the end hook would *switch-teleport* with the grappling hook, embedding it into the stone. "Tania has such cool magic. I keep wondering why Taysor never does this."

Grant replied, "Because in Taysor, we are thieves. In Tania, we'd be agents, and heroes. It doesn't pay as well, but there are some really wonderful perks to the job." He laughed. "They get the same level of support from their entire war machine that the paladins get in Sora."

Jodie shot the bolt up to the top of the wall. Once set, the grappling hook twinkled and was replaced with the bolt's tip. "It looks like we got at least an inch of penetration into the stone. Enough to hold me. Wish me luck," Jodi said. Avoiding the rune-marked stones on the ground by the wall, Jodie began pulling himself up hand over hand.

Grant watched through Delia's lens and called out instructions whenever it looked like Jodie might bump against an active rune. When Jodie reached the top, he looked around and called back. "There's a giant courtyard, just like Bloodstone. Also, the battlements are clear of runes but there is an unnatural darkness in the causeway."

Grant wished he had sent Jodie with Delia's looking glass. He turned back to the team to ask if they wanted to try. Instead, he turned back to Jodie and said. "Stay up there and cover us. Then, join us once you see what's going on. We're going to try the door. Guys, only one of us has to touch the throne. I promise, if we die, so long as one of us touches it, Maishan will restore all of us."

Knowing that if he overthought it, he never would actually move, Grant walked boldly through the doorway. "Lady Luck smiles, or as the Tanians might say, 'Fire always wins.' It's safe enough. Come on." He waved Venter after him.

The central courtyard of these fortresses was designed as a staging area for military supplies. Perdition's sat empty and unused. The giant stone tiles that made up the area had been cracked and weathered by age. A few hardy plants had tried to break through. But, except for a few scrappy trees, the entire area looked and smelled like clean stone.

The central keep rose up from the courtyard. Ringed by towers nearly a hundred paces high, each tower in Bloodstone would have a golem siege weapon on it. Looking around, Grant observed these things and added, "If the siege engines were golem-active, there'd be more damage here." He pointed to the courtyard. "My guess is that Perdition does not need siege weapons. Like before, we sprint. Do not stop. Tag the throne, that's the goal, and let's show Perdition what Rogue's Guild is capable of!"

A road ran straight from the gate to the keep's stairs. The raised section lifted it an arm higher than the courtyard. Nearly twenty paces wide, it allowed fast movement through the gates. Everything about these keeps had been built for military movement and less for enduring siege or preventing invasion. Venter pointed to a stone at the side of the great gate. "I'd bet that one is trapped. Look at it."

Grant saw nothing unusual about the stone except that it ever so slightly looked less used than the others. "I bet you're right," he said. "You can just barely tell it has been avoided over the centuries."

Overhead, Jodie gave them an all clear and they moved out carefully but quickly, looking for the faint signs of use as their safe route. Overhead, the moon had risen against the setting of the day moon. They had maybe two hours before midnight. Running the courtyard would only take twenty minutes. Traps, and the inevitable wounds or death those traps would bring, would make that twenty minutes seem like forever. I doubt Tania will revive us if we die and never touch the damn throne. Pha Rann burn that stupid chair, Grant mentally swore.

Grant picked up his last illusion card and copied himself. "Run to the keep," he instructed the illusion. It did. For many minutes, they watched the illusion until it hit something that dispelled the magic holding it together. "Damn," Grant grumbled. "Not a trap, but some type of barrier." Delia's lens showed nothing magical.

They withdrew collapsible staves from their backpacks and began moving forward while quietly tapping. It took almost ten minutes to move three tiles on the road. "This isn't going to work. We'll never make it in time," Venter noted. "Maybe one of us should give it a go?"

"You volunteering?" Grant fired back.

Venter took a deep breath and then said, "Sure, why not? Look, let's tie together. That way if something really bad happens, you can pull me back... or find your way to me, what's left of me."

"Thank you, Venter," Grant said. He already had silk rope and was lashing it around Venter's waist. "Sometimes, we just have to suck it up and go for it, right? Maybe Perdition is exactly that. This giant scary castle and maybe there's nothing here at all. With Tania, I wouldn't be surprised."

Venter squared his body and took a coil of rope in his hand. Twenty paces of rope would give them both time to react if a trap fired. "Don't let go of me," he said trying to sound happy and unafraid. Venter shook his hands took several deep breaths before he sprinted forward. The first tile was nothing and he clearly expected there to be something. He jumped the border to the next tile and screamed when the entire thing tilted to the side.

Grant barely caught Venter and pulled him back as the entire tile rotated. They had a glimpse of darkness and stone beneath. The tiles would mash anyone to death. Venter heaved, gagging, and watched as the stone began to rock back to its original position. "Do you want me to lead this next one?" Grant offered.

"No, no. I'm good. That was close. Stay on me, Grant. I don't want to die." Venter ran forward on the center line of the stone. Though it rocked side to side, it did not rotate with the thief on its center line. It gave him confidence and he picked up speed again on the next tiles.

Venter began to sprint. It made Grant uncomfortable and he called out to slow down. But, Venter seemed to have figured it out. Some of the tiles rotated side to side and others forward and back. By jumping to the center point, Venter could see which way and then take a step before jumping again. It was marathon work to keep up speed, focus, and jump with so much strength. Venter was in the zone and they cleared half the courtyard before they encountered a new trap.

Venter landed, same as he always did. But, instead of this stone rocking side to side, Venter fell through as each half of the tile rotated independently.

Grant almost did not notice it happened so quickly, so quietly. "No!" he shouted and skidded to a stop trying to pull Venter's slack rope back.

"Don't..." he heard Venter scream and then a wet grinding noise. The rope severed as the tile halves flipped and came back up. Blood splattered and dripped all across the surface. The brutality of the trap took Grant's breath away. It was not just a trap. It was a trap designed to prevent divine resurrection.

Grant looked up at the keep. He guessed he had less than ten minutes left. He shook his arms and waved for Jodie to come. To himself, he said, "Okay, so I need to stay in the center of the stone but I won't know which axis it rotates on. That means I stay on center lines, one at a time. Or, I could fly." He was tempted. He pulled out a *flying* potion and caressed its sides. "So tempting." He decided against it. It was so obvious. If Perdition had these kinds of traps, there would definitely be mechanisms against magical flight.

Using the bloodied tile as an example, Grant found that at a certain foot pressure, the tile moved. Grant looked at the gory remains of Venter and whispered, "I've got lead this time. I'm sorry, Venter."

Grant had a few close calls where tiles adjacent to ones they could not balance on triggered gas or spring darts. These, once they saw them, could be avoided. Still, it took too long and Grant began to grow anxious about the time. "This place whittles you down, Marcello," he yelled.

With a prayer to Joust in his heart, Grant pulled out the Delia lens. His prayer was answered when the lens showed magical traps everywhere but they all seemed to trigger to magic. Grant realized, So long as I refrain from using enchanted gear, I should be okay. For fear of inviting more death traps, Grant put the lens away.

Jodie caught Grant's attention with a sharp whistle. He was signaling danger... from the keep. High atop the forward tower, a torchlight bobbed. A brighter light ignited the dark sky just barely illuminating a hint of the cliffs all around. Grant saw a fireball launch from that tower towards them. Looking back, Grant noticed bright markings on some of the tiles, only visible at a certain angle, but no doubt clearly visible to the tower's siege engines. He swore to Joust, "This is not what I meant! Run! Curse it all, run!" Of course, Perdition would have siege golems...

Grant began to run in a type of hopscotch. It made for a drunken sprint, but he cleared the area where a fireball landed and splashed fire across fifteen tiles. The magic of the fireball activated all of the tile traps and Grant made a mental note to keep clear. Ahead of him, Grant saw the other towers activate and three balls of fire moved in slowly through the air towards him. No, not slow. Just very high and very big. He had seen the siege golems operate in Bloodstone. He had never been on the other side of them. It was every bit as awful as he had imagined it would feel.

"Keep running!" Grant screamed through burning lungs.

All of the towers glowed with fire now. Grant realized he had reached ballista range when eight golden points of fire arced down towards them. The fireballs took a higher trajectory now, making them appear even slower in their celestial movement. Grant landed on a tile and felt it tilt when he realized his feet had become stuck. The tile groaned and began to rotate. "Glue!" Grant screamed. "Ditch the boots!"

Grant barely pulled his feet free and leapt for the rising face edge of his tile, which became nearly vertical. He jumped, aiming for the center of the next. He stood still, quivering as his body absorbed the shock. The tile seesawed but did not rotate. A ballista cracked down ahead of them and activated a gas trap. Thankful for the lack of wind to blow gas at him, Grant prayed the other seven would miss. So many ballistae had fired that the sky ahead of him looked like fireworks... Of death. They're all aimed at me. A catapult fireball landed fifty paces ahead of him. The trajectory was so high now that it barely rolled. It made a deep whomp with each rotation while flames clung to the shattered bolt.

The ballista bolts smashed down all around them and sent three of the tiles around him spinning. With so much fire in the sky, Grant could no longer tell where or how any might fall. Joust had answered his first prayer. He doubted his luck would hold out. "Joust, c'mon..." Grant gritted his teeth and looked for a path forward. He needed magical flight, or something as an edge. A catapult ball smashed onto the tile next to Grant. Fire blasted in all directions and Grant felt his hair singe as heat radiated his skin. "Activate magic, and pray!" he screamed.

Grant donned a cloak of Orcus skin and drank the *flying* potion. In the air around him, magical doorways opened and darts began shooting out of them in a continuous stream. Two darts hit his leg before he bundled himself into the Orcus skin and flew. He felt hundreds of darts hit, bruising his body through the skin. Some of the traps fired far stronger things, or maybe some of the siege attacks hit. Poison from the darts burned like snake venom and he thought he recognized a lethal paralytic. He had maybe two minutes of life left.

Grant slammed into the main entry hall and saw Perdition's throne far back in the three story balconied chamber. A figure lounged on the throne. He waved to Grant. "Four minutes left!"

Grant peeked out from the cloak and flew along the shadowed edges of the hall towards the throne. At first, it felt pointless but then he noticed silent blades of pure darkness tracked his movement and were just barely missing him. He increased his speed and then leapt for the throne. A sword materialized near his arm and severed it at his bicep.

The amputated arm rolled and touched the throne. Ash looked down at Grant's blood where it splattered the throne. "I suppose we'll count that. Well done, Grant."

Ash picked up Grant's severed arm and touched a rune on the throne. "Did you know, this isn't my throne anymore? I've been replaced. You might find the next guildmaster more tolerant of your sloppy Soran ways. Stopping to fight doppelgangers? Priorities, Grant. Priorities. You did well with the team. Adding R'Dar Maishan was a stroke of brilliance. I can't think of many Soran rogues that would do something like that. You innovate beyond your culture. I like that. Your team, clearly you have their loyalty. We're going to recover and restore them, except Venter. Shame about him."

Grant cradled his arm stump and tried to push the shock back. Everything felt cold and dark. Ash lifted open his eyelid and said, "Think about it: Merakor. You're going into shock and the poison is killing you. Soran training is so weak."

Grant came to with his head on Maishan's lap. She was humming. He could tell from her tone that she was happy and excited. From the echoes, they were underground. From the sounds all around, they were not alone. Grant sat up and was pleased to find that he was totally recovered. His arm looked pink and new. The skin looked and felt tender, hypersensitive to air movements. "Grant, we're deep under the Temple. They've revived your team. Whatever you did, it impressed them enough that we're going to Merakor, if we want to. Oh please, Grant! Let's do it."

Maishan looked ecstatic. Grant tried to take it all in. The chamber was massive, to say the least. He could not see the ceiling or the sides except the wall near where he and a few of the others in his team rested. "Venter did not make it," Maishan said quietly. "I'm sorry. We tried, but sometimes death is beyond us. His soul resisted coming back to his body. It happens."

"He died heroically at least," Grant said. "Who is them?"

Maishan pointed to a mage who stood next to Ash and a female elf. "The Mages Guild, the Thieves Guild, The Circle, well, everyone who matters including the Temple of Tiamat. The fact that you killed a bunch of doppelgangers played very well with the Dread Lords. You would not believe how much they hate any of Set's creations." She wiped his face off with a damp cloth and her eyes gleamed with excitement. "Merakor!'

* * *

Syand shrieked when the scrying pool showed Grant pick up Delia's seeing lens and look down at the doppel's body. Syand, in her rage, clawed the walls and left deep talon rakes in the stone. It had been four days since her last taste of Orcus' blood. She should have more by now. She needed more. As it left her body, she felt the dullness of undeath settle on her. Sure, certain emotions became more powerful, but her ability to think clearly about consequences and linearity declined. She had felt limitless, multi-threaded, and now felt as if she were suffocating.

"I need more!" She kicked the wall and then covered her ears as the shockwave and cracking stone blasted her eardrums. "Bring me Bradley!" From the catacombs beneath, she felt a chorus of approval. The other vampires had not tasted Orcus' blood but lived it vicariously through Syand. They wanted their own and a secure supply before they would come out.

Bradley was thrown into the room and groveled at Syand's feet. Syand picked the fat man up with one arm and yelled in his face. "Delia is dead! Grant lives! They're in Tania! Why Tania?"

Bradley choked trying to breathe and answer at the same time. "I don't know, I don't know! Please."

"We must go to Tania. I cannot go to Tania. You will gather the lieutenants of the guilds and take them to Tania. I will come, but in the shadows. I will watch and intervene when the time is right. Do you understand?" She yelled in his face, just inches away. He nodded. When she let go of his neck, he resumed groveling. "Spare no expense. You go to Tania tomorrow! Now, get out of here!"

Bradley moved so fast, he might have teleported. Her rage temporarily sated by the prospect of action, she yelled for Jace. When he did not appear, she yelled again and then yelled at her attendants for him. The man, her delectable male servant Renault, stammered that Jace had died in the 521 collapse. "Don't you remember, my lady?"

Syand caught him and said, "NO, but tell me again!" and bit into his neck to drain him nearly to death. Though Renault had only served Syand a few weeks, her near-to-death feedings had aged him. Already he looked like a man twenty years older than he was. The woman who served with him had done better. She seemed more able to distract Syand with other forms of feeding.

Renault's blood helped Syand think and she threw him aside like a rag doll. "Bradley will be too slow. I must go to Tania. I am going to the catacombs!"

Her departure left a stink of death but lightened the feeling of madness in the complex. The female, Ydriss, had been proud to be chosen to serve Syand. It meant she was the best of the best and had a bright future in Dark Legion. Syand's madness, though, did not match any pattern of behavior in their long history and it bothered her. "What is wrong with the mistress?" Renault asked her.

Ydriss stroked his hair, noting how Syand had just barely spared his life, again. She pressed her hand over the gaping holes in his neck. "She is not right in her head. Maybe… no, I dare not say it." There was a pattern for change. It occurred when a vampire refused to go underground and thereby threatened discovery of the catacombs. The Ancient Ones would not risk the Pha Rannic Temples finding them. "We could speak with Kallis."

Renault touched her face and said, "No, not Kallis. It must be Absalom. It is the only way if we are to survive. You should be anointed head of the Legion and yet, she murders us. Absalom," he said weakly. "Please, I'm dying, Ydriss. I can't… Kallis is too…"

Ydriss took his hand and said, "No promises. We will try Absalom first. Come." She helped him stand and together, they stumbled out of the Dark Legion complex to the street. The entire Legion had been spread far and wide to seek out Orcus' blood and Grant's team. With no other guilds to fight against, they operated with wide latitude. "There is no chance The Temples did not see the 521 complex. It may be too late for Absalom."

Renault was too weak to argue. He squeezed her hand where she steadied him on her shoulders. "I understand. We must try?"

Ydriss nodded and they slowly walked towards the bright marble palace of King Andrew. Long before they reached any of the major streets, a night watch patrol found them. Ydriss waved them over and said, "Sanctuary, with King Andrew please. We invoke Absalom for Dark Legion."

The night watchmen held their polearms in a guarded manner and looked at each other. The bloodied state of undress Ydriss and Renault were in attested to nearby dangers. They knew the term 'Dark Legion' and 'sanctuary,' but how it related to these two, they did not know. Ydriss urged them saying, "King Andrew will wish to honor this request. If you cannot understand what I ask, please consider that my husband was attacked by a vampire and is near death. Surely, you will help us?"

The captain looked at the gaping fang wounds in Renault's throat and called for a cleric. A small runner boy took off towards the Temple district and the men broke out a stretcher on their polearms to carry Renault. "Yes, yes. Of course, please come with us. The Temples will sort this out."

Ydriss declined their offer to be carried on a stretcher. The sight of the gleaming white temples made her skin crawl. "Renault, this might be the hardest thing we've ever done." He squeezed her hand.

Not understanding any of it, the guard captain tried to reassure them. "Pha Rann will set this aright. I just know it. Now, if you'll tell me, miss, do you mean the Dark Legion that kidnaps misbehaving children?"

"Something like that, Captain," Ydriss replied. "That's a cover story for a gang of thieves operating in this area. There are vampires now, and something has changed and we need…"

Ydriss saw movement on the rooftops and tried to call out a warning. It was too late. Vampires fell on the night watch and tore them to shreds in an instant. Ydriss fell to her knees to catch the stretcher and Renault's head as those carrying him rolled to the side minus their heads. A vampire rose up before her and hissed, "Absalom will not save you, daughter of the Legion. Syand will see to an eternal punishment for you!"

Fangs bit into her jugular and Ydriss felt her life begin to slip away as another vampire claimed Renault. Whispering from her attacker flooded her mind, trying to fill her with hate for Renault. "You will be bound from the afterlife until you slay Renault."

Next to her, the vampire taking Renault said the same about Ydriss. "Two revenants bound to murder each other," Ydriss' vampire cackled. "Such a sweet punishment for betraying us."

From behind, a bright light flared as if it were noonday sun. It banished darkness and shadows. Ydriss, struggling to resist her attacker, felt the vampire's body crumble to dust in her fingers. A bright angel of light stepped forward with radiant wings outspread behind him. The angel cried out, "Radcliffe, send your Order here. We have multiple vampire attacks on the night watch. We can save them, but time is short."

The angel bent over Ydriss and said, "I'm Michael. You're not dead yet. Resist the vampire." He touched her forehead and said, "Pha Rann calls you to rejoin the Light!" His other hand on Renault's head pulsed with sunlight. For the first time since Syand's awakening, Ydriss felt something she had struggled to remember: hope.

"Sanctuary for Dark Legion. Absalom," she whispered and then collapsed into unconsciousness.

Her last glimpse was of a vampiric Cordelle looking down at her from over Michael's shoulder. "That's Ydriss," the vampire said who looked like Cordelle said. "She was the human leader of Dark Legion for nearly fifteen years, until two months ago when Syand came out. She was very business like. Creepy, but kept to the King's Charter."

# Chapter 15 – Sacrifice of Rulership

Ora rubbed her head and wished she could see Alauren again. By now, the boy would be smiling and responding to Seantir and Wess, his foster parents. *But, he'll think they're his parents*, Ora sighed mentally. For all her years being prepared for this, when it actually happened, she realized how ill-prepared she was for motherhood. It killed her to think about it and she pushed it out of her head, while praying she could do the same with her heart. Now, with each day since giving him up a week ago, the pain in her heart seemed to press into her thoughts, her muscles, and her emotions swayed like a butterfly's path.

Malcor's last letter conveyed similar feelings but he did not really know what it felt like to go from being pregnant to not being pregnant. The physical changes alone took their toll and made the emotional ones worse. As King, Malcor fell into duty and watchful attention when with Ora, in those few times they found themselves together. He spoke of working at the forge and his latest side project to forge swords for Ayden, Seline, and those he felt had graced his path to paladinhood. Ayden's sword, *Shadowsorcere*, was already regarded as a masterpiece. Seline's blade, still in progress, was widely speculated to touch in the elemental realms of Fire. Malcor could not figure out what to name it. Even the kerchki wanted to see it. The sleeplessness showed around his eyes and Ora worried about him.

*If only I had a forge to distract me*, she thought wistfully. The slam of a hammer on an anvil... just the thought made her head flare with pain.

The only bright side to anything these days was the surprise alliance with the Orcs and Alerius finally getting some relief. The priestesses had never before exhausted so much of themselves every day and night. When Shara sent an edict out to not comment or offer help to Ana, Ora knew that things must be desperate indeed. Ana by herself should have been able to siphon energies from the fighting in Bloodstone to heal the god emperor. That it was not enough, and even with so many clerics healing the fire patriarch... it defied any experience in recorded history.

Before the Temple's throne, a representative from the Merchant Guild spoke about the supply chain that produced Tanian steel weapons. Ora knew about this series of connected industries from Sai's operations, but it still surprised her that the empire consumed so much ore to produce so many tools of war. The counts by weapon type were staggering. Bloodstone ate it all up and hungered ever for more. The guild representative, a middle-aged man named Caltren, cleared his throat.

"Mistress, if this is a bad time, I can leave my report for your review later."

Ora looked at him and forced a smile. "That will not be necessary. We are all pressed about by different forces these days. While I rejoice for the emperor's health, the matters you bring to me suggest dire events in Bloodstone. The Circle told me that never before had the entire war machine been so tested, and taxed. That your guild conducts itself so masterfully, I commend you, Caltren."

Caltren bowed graciously, and with a smile said, "Yet, there is something else behind this compliment. It will not offend me to give you time to recover yourself, or deal with other matters that, to the Queen, are more pressing than our mining operations." Caltren's tone said that he required something but was being tactful.

Ora looked around the Temple's throne room and yearned for the days of her seclusion at Sai's estate. *Was it being with Malcor that changed me?*, she wondered. Dar Shara and Ana had both pounced on her demanding to know the extent of Ynt'taris' training. Before she could respond, they had ordered her to review all of the Sage Alaura's writings and to verify certain gaps and questions. It seemed that the Temple had an endless list of questions long unanswered by the Patriarch of Ice.

"Without the iron mines operating at peak, it is clear from your report that either our new troops will be underserved, or that gear maintenance and upkeep will fall behind. Neither is acceptable." She rifled through a ledger at her hand and prayed for guidance. Tiamat's inspiration brought her to a note from weeks ago. It described the impact of not having clerics to assist with mining operations. She tapped it. "I am going to order at least one priestess sent to each of the mines." Caltren bowed; this was what the guild wanted. "In addition, we will send a cleric to each of the supply trains. Though, I foresee that some will be mercenaries. I assume this acceptable? Hopefully, this restores the morale and fortitude to your operations."

"We have suffered many injuries. As you know," Caltren explained. "Our veterans were sent to fight in Bloodstone and younger ones called to back here to augment the empire. We had to reactivate many we thought retired, at additional expense. This will allow us to catch back up to normal operations. Our thanks, great Queen."

Sensing a motive behind Caltren's reference to expense, Ora snapped, "For which you were compensated in renegotiated contracts. Do not press me on this, Caltren." A spear of pain shot from behind her eyes into her head flared and she waved him off.

"Of course. On behalf of Master Gershon and the miners in sore need of their Goddess, I thank you and the Great Temple of Tiamat. We all serve." Caltren bowed and left.

Ora's attendants rushed up to her. Since giving birth to Alauren, the ice priestess suffered from worsening headaches that would not go away. They resisted divine healing and defied medical understanding. It was rumored that the Sage Alaura had similar effects towards the end of her life. A heretical book, written by the Sage's husband but long suppressed, suggested Alaura had decided to not extend her life because the thought of enduring the headaches even a day longer could make her collapse. Ora knew the truth of it: realms of ice clashed with warmer ones.

A young acolyte, named Hannah, took Ora's shoulders from behind. With the skill of a bonesetter, she torqued Ora's neck and back. The loud pops and gentle easing of the strain in her muscles helped. "Thank you, Hannah. I'd never make it through these things without you."

The paladin tending the great doors opposite the Temple throne entered thsked, "Do you wish me to hold the next supplicant for a while?"

Ora shook her head and beckoned them in. When Calvin entered the room, her back spasmed and Hannah whispered, "This will never do. Sit back, my lady. I'll do what I can. The Imperics in Ori have a technique involving needles. I'll send for them and we'll try that."

"No, now," Ora insisted. "Please anything to help me do this. I'd like to make it through at least one session." Hannah pointed to a runner and the young girl raced off for the special needles.

Ora composed herself as, far down the chamber, Calvin presented his credentials to a magistrate and the paladins escorted him to the throne. Usually, there would be a line of supplicants ready to go, but with Ora, the paladins slowed it down to allow for her a break between requests. It also kept the hall quieter. By the time Calvin arrived, Hannah received a packet of the Imperic needles.

Calvin bowed with a sweeping flourish. He came dressed in courtier clothes but with the emblems of the Dockside Watch clearly showing along with the medal of his mayoral office. He looked good, if a bit out of shape. Ora tried to smile and said, "R'Dar Calvin, it has been too long since we last climbed the Temple steps together. How fares Dockside's favorite hero?"

Calvin blushed and cleared his throat. He clearly had memorized what he said next. "Lady Ora, thank you for your warm welcome and time. Since my election as Dockside's mayor, I have sought an audience with you and King Malcor. It is my hope to continue warm and friendly relations with the Imperial Throne. Also, though I am registering with the Mercy Court plans to revitalize Dockside, I am here to ask for your benevolence during my long absence from Dockside…"

Ora cut him off. "Calvin, these are all very eloquent words, but in the same spirit of friendship, I must ask you: I am tired and not feeling well. Will you get to the point, for me? Also, what absence are you talking about?"

Calvin stood straight and tall. "I'm joining a grand adventure in the hopes of raising sufficient funds to revitalize Dockside. I'll be gone a year, maybe as long as three years." Calvin added after a pause, "I may not survive."

Ora's shoulder twitched as Hannah inserted a thin needle into her muscle so that Calvin could see it. Calvin winced. The pain in her eyes dropped a notch. "If you may not survive, then perhaps the Mayor of Dockside should find alternative ways to serve his people. No member of the Dar would risk the well-being of their people. What are your contingencies?"

Calvin tried to keep his face smooth and friendly though her words deflated him more than he wished they did. "My contingencies are being registered with the Mercy Court, Dar Ora. One of them is that my mayorship will transfer to my good friend, Malcor. That is why I am here. I had hoped to speak with him in person, but his work in Bloodstone – as our great King - has not allowed this. So, I am asking of you, on his behalf."

Ora closed her eyes and felt a pinch as Hannah pressed a needle into the center point of her upper ear. The needle felt cool and, when Ora imagined a rush of heat leaving her from that needle, she felt better. "Do you remember when we first met, Calvin?"

"Of course! How could I forget?" Even with her eyes closed, Ora knew that Calvin was looking around to see who else was present and taking note that Calvin knew her. "I was on my way to the Temple as a paladin. Malcor and I were attacked…"

*And, there's the first lie. You were not attacked, Ora thought. He's going to describe our meeting as something more than it was, probably to flatter me.*

"Malcor was wounded and then you, this divine priestess, came and offered us aid. Without you, dear Ora, we would have died on the East-West Major!" Calvin's tone of recollection and friendly compliments played well to the others in the throne room.

*There's the flattery. To those that don't know the truth, Calvin and I must be very good friends. He has become political.* Ora signed behind her back for Hannah to put Calvin in his place. Hannah tapped Ora's shoulder and stepped forward.

"Mind your tone and familiarity with the Dar! This is not a parlor room or café! You stand in the Great Temple before the chosen of Dread Lord Ynt'taris. No one dies on the East-West Major. The story of your and the king's encounter with House Tor is well-known. A simple, 'Yes, priestess!' will suffice for future questions from Lady Ora. Do you understand?"

Calvin flinched back from Hannah but also noted that she was a first rank acolyte, just barely out of her training. He regained his composure when, from behind, a paladin struck the back of his knees. "Bow and show respect, sir." The blow was not so hard that it forced him to kneel, but Calvin was smart enough to kneel anyway.

"My apologies, Lady Ora, I do not know what I did to offend..."

Hannah jumped down and grabbed his oiled hair and pulled his head up. "It is not what you do, but the intent of your heart. You see us as stand-ins for King Malcor. King Malcor does not rule in the Temple of Tiamat! No doubt, you look at me and see someone beneath you. Yet, Watch Officer Calvin," Hannah emphasized Calvin's official title. "You stand on holy ground and sully us with your unholy intent."

Choking back anger, Calvin realized the mistake he had made. Hannah was right. Malcor as king, ruled the Military. The Temple ruled Morbatten. He dropped to his face and formally bowed. Hannah's toes stepped back from him and she turned to Ora. "My lady, do you wish this cur removed from the Temple?"

More than several heartbeats passed and Calvin felt beads of sweat on his face and in his armpits. His second mistake was overly-speaking to his own role regarding Dockside when just as surely, Malcor and Ora's roles had changed too. *Damn it*, he thought. Even on the way here, there was a puppet stage re-enacting the story of Malcor and Ora's "great love" and their ascension to King and Queen. Ryvane would no doubt laugh at him.

"Let him finish his request. If I am to understand, you wish – in the event of your death – that Malcor become the Mayor of Dockside?" Ora restated his request with a tinge of pain in her voice. He looked up and saw exhaustion in her eyes.

He nodded. "Yes, that is my request. I can think of no better contingency. Malcor and you have done wonders for the Klennan Armory. The Princess Clarissa is also Klennan. I can think of no better caretakers for my... err, the people of Dockside. Please, give my regards to Malcor. Tell him, please, that I think fondly of our time together and wish him all the best."

Ora nodded and dismissed Calvin. Hannah caught hold of the paladin and whispered, "She needs a rest. Please hold the supplicants for an hour."

Calvin heard this as he walked out and wondered what was going on. The Temple, so impervious to anything, suddenly felt frail to him. Adding this to the stories of clerics missing for days and returning to their posts drained, and it made the Temple seem barely functioning.

When the doors closed and Ora realized she had a break, she stretched. "Hannah, please tell me that Dar Shara or Dar Kell will be here soon to see to the rest of this? How many are there for today still?" When the knight told her, she grew even paler. "I cannot last through that many." Ora rubbed her eyes again and said, "I'm going to take a break. If I'm not back or if another Dar arrives, please have them consult the Orrery of Lord Spark, page fifty-three. That will explain my absence. I realize this obligates you all, and I... I'm sorry."

The paladin dropped to a formal salute and said, "Great Dar, your pain is our pain. I will own this."

An hour later, Ora had not returned and Hannah sought out the first Dar she could find, an instructor named Niss. When they found page fifty-three in the book, Hannah giggled and Niss burst into laughter. A single verse copied exactly from the Sage Alaura's hand read:

> Each day, Morbatten feels more like Taysor, and my heart
> yearns for the clean mountain ice at the top of the world. Master
> Ynt'taris, take me to the top of the world and show me all that I
> might see clearly, how insignificant the machinations of mortals
> truly are.

"I take it that Dar Ora is still not yet recovered?" Niss asked. "Very well." Niss snapped her fingers and her own entourage came into the room. "Ladies, we will be serving Tania for the time being. Embassy and Society," she addressed her attendants responsible for social functions. "Please clear my calendar and pull any meetings into the Temple's agenda. My guests can meet me here."

Niss found the paladin responsible for managing the crowd and told him "Please re-order supplicants based on who can present their issue in the least amount of time. Anyone that can reduce their report or business to less than two minutes, I will see them and satisfy them today. The others, you are to bump to tomorrow. However, I want you to find someone you know to be long-winded and obtuse. I will see that one second. Please inform all that they will be cut off at two minutes and I will be rendering judgement based on what I know at that time. No exceptions! I will see my first supplicant in five minutes. Use force to eject any who dissemble or otherwise waste our time. Also, open the great doors and let them all in, on my mark, in five minutes."

Niss eyed Hannah and added, "I remember you, Hannah, right? A talented bonesetter. Please tell me you know where Ora is. Will you let her know that I, Dar Niss, will be covering for her until she is ready or the Temple's Command takes over? When done, you are to send word to the Divine Arson class that they will need a new teacher. I recommend R'Dar Alex and Valaes."

The first supplicant came in and bowed. She wished to know if a priestess would be able to preside over her marriage. "Yes," Niss said. "Give your information to my assistant Galrei. Tiamat blesses your union and will attend," she pointed to an acolyte. "Tiamat bless you. Next!"

The next was a merchant, the paladin signalled him as the long-winded one, with a complaint about how a competing Dar to his own lord did something that reduced his profit. Niss interrupted him. "This is a matter for the Mercy Court, not the Temple. Guards, remove him now. Next!"

The merchant began to argue. Niss prayed and the merchant's voice amplified so that everyone could hear him in the chamber. Hundreds of people fell silent as they mentally counted with Niss to two minutes.

At two minutes, Niss stood up from the throne and in a loud voice called out for silence. Divine silence fell on the merchant who continued speaking for several moments before realizing he could not hear his own voice. In a divinely amplified voice, Niss declared, "You are all tired and frustrated. I get that. We have business to attend to and I would do so, quickly. However, the Temple's judgement is absolute! Tiamat reigns here. If your issue is not worthy of the Great Mother's time, take it elsewhere!"

At her words, the merchant fell under the draconian *charm* spell Niss directed at him underneath her speech. Like a zombie, the merchant turned and walked out, thanking everyone for hearing him. Niss allowed the entire Temple to hear his words. "Yes, I'll take this to the Mercy Court," he said. "And will be donating a tenth of this year's profits to the Temple. It's my patriotic duty to do so."

"A tenth!" Dar Niss said loudly. "So generous for someone who thinks they can circumvent the Mercy Court." Her words and this reminder of Tiamat's power quelled the supplicants into a well-ordered group of people, many who know wondered if they wanted to plead their case today. To Niss' satisfaction, a number turned and left. She folded her arms and smiled. "And so we see the power of Tiamat in our daily lives."

Dar Niss watched the merchant pass through the crowd, and then called out, "Who here is seeking a priestess for a ceremonial function?" Hands shot up as young couples raised their hands, along with those seeking the blessing of a child. "Your requests are all granted!" Niss pointed to the acolyte scheduling the young couple's wedding. "My sister here, Galrei, will be taking your names and dates. The Temple guarantees a priestess will be there to serve you in your celebrations. Please follow Galrei to the Hall of Prayers. Paladins! You are to imprison any who seek non-ceremonial requests from Galrei. Now, back to other requests - Next!" Things went much faster after the crowd saw that the priestess would use her powers to speed things along. The paladin smiled. Niss had a reputation for military efficiency.

\* \* \*

High atop Alerius' mountain, Ora breathed in the cold air and looked down into the Valley of Ancients. The longing in her heart for Alauren felt as if it would drive her mad. Behind her, the snow swirled and Ynt'taris appeared. He took her hand and she felt his preferred human form. The small girl spoke with a voice of snow drifts blowing in the wind. "Do not let this poison you. Alauren is safe. I am watching over him. Seantir and Wess are known to me, personally. In the River, I showed him you and Malcor. I feel your heart is heavy, daughter."

"Master Ynt'taris, I… yes, I am heavy. I've never been a mother before. I thought I was ready to give Alauren to the Ancients but something in me, it pulls me to want to be with him. I feel fire and heat in my neck and forehead. It burns."

Ynt'taris squeezed her hand. "Soon, like your ancestor Alaura, you will need to stay in cold places. Sai is changing his estate to accommodate you. You cannot serve winter eternal and remain peaceably amidst the other seasons. We knew this day would come. Your mother instincts are strong, Ora. I will see what I can do to bring you closer to Alauren."

"Thank you." Ora dropped to her knees in the ice and embraced the Dread Lord. Looking up into the grey sky, she blinked through ice crystals blowing in the wind. She had an image of fanged teeth coming for Alauren, and closed it out of her mind as pain rose up in her head again.

"Shhh, my rider. It's going to be okay. You see glimmers of things that might be. The River of Fire shows possible futures. The River of Ice shows prophecy written as if it had already occurred. When you are stronger, I will show you. For now, know that Alauren is touched by destiny. You and Malcor knew this. The Temple knows it. He is safe. He will be trained in the ways of old and supported by the new ways when his times of peril come. You saw this work for Malcor's benefit. Have faith in the Court."

Ora rested her head on Ynt'taris' shoulder. "Did the Sage, did she have these same pains?"

"Yes," Ynt'taris answered her softly. "Though she did not birth a child. The god emperor suspects you suffer an additional trial in what the healers have named…"

"Post birthing sorrow. Yes, I'm familiar with it."

"It is similar to what humans feel when they lose an arm. Interestingly, my brother describes a similar feeling as if his wing is still there even though it is not. The physical form gives up the spiritual one less readily." Ynt'taris dragonshifted and held his claw out to her. "Come, let's go see Alauren, even if from a distance."

"Will you tell me about the River of Ice? Dar Ana in particular has asked me about this many times." Ora climbed the dragon's forearm to his back. "I fear she will never let me be until I answer her."

Ynt'taris chuckled. "It is not her place to know, nor your place to tell her. The River of Ice is unique to us. When my consort fell, a new thing emerged. I like to think of it as the flow of her tears and blood, which I might someday follow to join her in the Silver Skies."

"It sounds beautiful," Ora said. "Take me there?"

"Yes, my rider."

* * *

King Andrew ducked behind his shield as arrow-sized spines shot from the demon. The needles ploughed into his guard and the Orcs they fought alongside. He could hear them ricochet off armor and strike stone. The grunts and choked back profanity of those around Andrew told him that many of those barbs found flesh.

A young soldier behind the king began screaming, "My eyes! My eyes!" Muffled sounds and cries for a healer reminded Andrew that, even though Orcus had fallen, Bloodstone remained one of the deadliest places in the Isles, maybe even in the world.

The demon whipped its tail from side to side to scatter the paladins closest to it. "Clerics!" Andrew yelled. "Heal the front line! We need to restrain it. Set hooks!"

While eight paladins encircled and tried to keep the demon away from the battalion, the Orcs and humans switched to hooks and barbed nets. "Throw on my mark! Front line, prepare to fall back!"

Andrew's voice boomed in the stony cavern. Magical amplification turned it into a dull roar and he prayed to Pha Rann that the paladins understood. "Now!" he yelled.

The paladins dove backwards. Thinking them in retreat, the demon lunged forward right into the nets. While the demon shredded the first net, the second and next nets quickly blanketed it. Without needing any encouragement, the Orcs drove forward to stab into the nets with hooked pole arms and spears. The demon thrashed about, still dangerous as the barbed nets swung about and entangled some of the Orcs standing too close. Limited though to attacking this way, Andrew knew they would win. He sheathed his sword and stepped back to see how bad the damage was to his command.

The clerics were all tied up in removing needles from flesh. Until removed, the victims could not be healed. Of their starting one hundred humans and Orcs, thirty-seven had fallen or been hit by the needles. Andrew noticed how the Orcs struggled to sit still and most had started pulling the quills out themselves. Tissue from their skin and muscles clung to the demon quills but the Orcs showed no pain, only fascination with the gore. One even licked it and said, "Tastes like me." The Orcs all around laughed, completely oblivious to the terrible sounds of the trapped demon being killed less than ten paces away.

Andrew took a drink from an offered waterskin and asked, "How long till we can march on?"

The head cleric looked around and guessed, "Twenty minutes, my lord. But, if another event like this happens, we will need to camp. We came prepared for healing, but this demon and these types of wounds draw too much. We were ready for fatalities, not poison and wounds that prevent combat."

Andrew nodded. "With each demon so different, we can only do our best and pray Pha Rann sees us through."

An Orc looked up and added, "Gruustir will break the demon heads!" Though wounded, the Orcs all laughed as, behind them, the demon at last fell silent from its bird-like shrieking.

Andrew pulled his command together along with Frentoris and Incer, the Orc paladins. Those two had a fanatical gleam in their eyes and a palpable hunger for more fighting. Where the humans huffed and puffed to catch their breath, the Orcs licked their lips in anticipation of more to come. "King, Gruustir says to go through that tunnel," Frentoris said pointing to the eastern tunnel. They had been following a winding but generally northern tunnel for some time.

Andrew nodded. He did not want to test the Orcs, but was also curious to see how in touch with their strange god they actually were. "Have the mages seal the northern tunnel. I don't want anything flanking us. Sir Frentoris, we need a few minutes to recover the wounded and then we continue on. Does the God Gruustir provide any other guidance? Should we send scouts ahead?"

Frentoris shook his emphatically as if to say 'no' but then said, "It does not matter to Gruustir. Scouts, no scouts, we fight!"

The tunnel past the demon widened in parts and the two paladin Orcs walked at the head. Their better darkvision allowed them to see things the humans could not. The bright lanterns and divine lights of the clerics backlit the passage. Frentoris pointed to claw marks on the wall and a blood spur to Incer. "Send back word to Andrew. We have new prey."

Andrew knew something was amiss when all of the battalion's Orcs began to charge forward. Against the pounding of their metal boots,

Andrew thought he heard something roar defiantly. Not wanting to risk the Orcs feeling abandoned, the king waved his own men forward.

They double-time marched for almost four hundred paces before the tunnel opened into a large chamber. Exquisite carvings on the walls and tunnels showed ancient Tanian craftsmanship. "We must have connected to a lost Tanian mine. Priests! Stay back and see if you can get a map bearing – and do not allow the vanguard to break our surface world connection!"

The room was a giant bowl and it took Andrew a moment to adjust his eyes to the flickering light of combat. More correctly, the room, he saw, had been an amphitheater, most likely for a Shrine of Tiamat. Water had filled most of the lower section though broken stone filled parts in. Andrew saw a hellhound – no one had seen any hellhounds since Orcus' fall eight months ago – twist its body. The beast's tail transformed into a thick bone-spiked club that smashed the Orcs off their stone towers and into the water.

"It's not water," Andrew yelled when he saw the Orcs begin thrashing about and then fall still and dead. *Is the water poison?*, he wondered.

Andrew's healer cried out to the group, "Acid! The markings on the wall correlate to an early attempt by Dar Ana to establish a permanent underground mining operation for the dwarves. It endured almost sixty years. Long enough that she consecrated this Shrine. They were driven back by one of the few recorded underground cascades in the Sixth Legion. That cascade happened here!"

Andrew whistled. "The Sixth. This is ancient." His officers sent word to the Orcs and throughout the battalion about the acid. The hellhound had no issues with it, neither did RiVule's paladins. While the Orcs had lined the shoreline and began peppering the hellhounds with arrows, the two paladins stood their ground on the shore about thirty paces from the hound. Frentoris held his sword aloft and was praying. "Can paladins affect a hellhound?" Andrew asked.

"No, King Andrew. Not even clerics can. The records here," the cleric said while flipping through the copied Tania book. "I wish we had these when we first came here a year ago. I ask that you press King Malcor for access."

"I will do so, Davidson. Come, there is fighting to be had." Andrew grabbed a young fighter rushing past him. "Send word to the officers. We will not defeat a hellhound this way. We need a different strategy. I want a plan before we attack." Andrew turned back to Davidson. "If this was part of an underground mining operation, does that mean there are bloodstones here?"

Davidson shrugged, but answered. "It's very likely. The records say this area was lost when the Cascade happened. There have been no other records of an underground Cascade. I'd guess this area is full of bloodstones. Why else would Ana consecrate a shrine here? My lord, we could…"

Andrew interrupted him. "We will send word to both Legion Commander Ayden, and to Dar Ana. Now!" He pointed to one of the mages, "Go and make it happen, and be accurate!"

Officers began moving away from the hellhound back to King Andrew. They brought Frentoris with them. The Orc looked annoyed.

"Tanian tactics…" Andrew began to say but was interrupted by Frentoris.

"We have a great foe and you wish to talk?" the Orc looked disgusted.

"You face a hellhound. This is the first hellhound we have found in eight months. Do you know what this means?" Andrew retorted.

Frentoris grinned and licked his fangs. "It means the Orcs will kill a hellhound." He whirled and ran back to the combat. He signaled all of the Orcs to redouble their attacks.

Andrew pursed his lips and turned back to his officers. "Tanian tactics are to charge headlong against a hellhound immediately to prevent it from gating in other hellhounds. That there are no gates suggests that either it cannot or that it already did. The paladins charge and once they grapple the hound, the clerics flamestrike them. We have paladin Orcs and fire magic. We will replicate this tactic but be on guard for gates! Also, we cannot target the Orc paladins. I doubt they will appreciate it." He chuckled as did his command team.

Behind them, the Orcs launched another volley at the hellhound. Their arrows splashed into the acid, but for some reason the hellhound did not press its own attack. Instead it howled at them. The sound sent chills of fear down the spines of all hearing it. Andrew shook off the feeling of imminent death and smiled, "And that explains why Tania only allows veterans to fight here."

Andrew sheathed his sword and took a deep breath. "Davidson, how long is my list of must-discuss opportunities with the Tanians right now?

You want additional records from their early legions. Would you also like a date with Dar Ana?"

These types of comments began shortly after Vel Pajor took the elves and left Bloodstone. With the Cuthberics gone from Bloodstone, the armies remaining had grown increasingly bold in asking the new king to get access to archives. That King Malcor immediately granted such requests if backed by any kind of justification, had embolded King Andrew, the Dwarves of Stone, and the Gnome armies.

When Davidson pulled a sheaf of papers from the back of his scriptures and said 'Four hundred or so, and yes, I'd love a date with Dar Ana,' Andrew commented, "And the Winter War. Maybe Malcor is right and Set would have been slain ages ago if our two nations had been able to end this conflict. Why do we still fight each other?"

Davidson healed an Orc warrior being pulled back from the hellhound battle. "Almost two thousand years ago, a Soran prince offended the Morbattanians and they declared war on us."

"This is King Roland's story, right?" Andrew saw two of his officers coming his way and signaled for them to grab one of the battle mages. "Back then, the Tanians would have been offended by everything. Roland is a hero of the Cuthberics. What was so bad that we crippled our alliance with them for millenia?"

Davidson pulled Andrew closer and spoke into his ear. "The ancient Literalists rewrote Roland's story and the Cuthberics adopted it. Roland slaughtered several of Dar Tania's chieftains with a Literalist paladin's sword. Roland then accused them of demon worship and declared war on them all. My Temple supposedly has a signed order by Roland ordering extermination of 'those vile barbarian demon worshippers.' The white dragon declared war on Roland's house, not Sora. The Cuthberics would not let an evil dragon go to war against any part of Sora and declared war back. So… that's what happened."

Andrew gagged. "You've got to be kidding me."

"I wish I were – joking I mean. I thought you knew. I mean, I just assumed that when you became king, certain truths would be shared as part of the crowning ceremony." Davidson shrugged and tucked his papers back into his scriptures and chained the book back at his belt. "And yes, I'd love a date with Dar Ana. She's everything I ever dreamed of in an evil priestess. Think she'll convert to Pha Rann and repent of her nefarious ways?"

Eyeing the list, Andrew said, "End Winter War, convert Dar Ana for Davidson's fantasy – you should add those to the list." He turned as two officers came up with one of the mages. The officers looked a bit beaten from the last combat with the needle demon. One had dents in his armor and small puncture holes in his breastplate showed how close he had come to being killed by the quills. The mage looked spent. Though a large man, he trembled and hugged himself as if freezing. "I wish to discuss hellhound strategy," Andrew said in his best voice.

The officers both snapped to attention, but the mage nearly fell over when he tried to bow. Andrew caught him and gestured to Davidson to help. "My good wizard…"

"Tristan," Davidson said. "This is the battle mage Tristan."

"Tristan," Andrew continued. "We need your help. Not spellcasting mind you, but we need to figure out how to defeat a hellhound standing in a pool of acid." They looked over at the melee between the Orc paladins and the hound. Both Frentoris and Incer seemed to have reached a stalemate against the beast. Though arrows pin cushioned the hellhound it seemed unaffected by them.

One of the officers smartly clapped his heels together and said, "We've looked and there are no routes out of this room."

Andrew frowned. "Why would a hellhound trap itself here then?"

The mage eyed everyone and tried to speak. His voice sounded raw and hoarse. "No one can see it? I was trying to explain it to my squad leader when you grabbed me. My liege, Andrew. It's not a hellhound. I mean, not like how we're thinking about it. This is my second term in Bloodstone. Have any of you heard of a hellhound getting cornered and fighting like this?"

"No, I haven't." Both officers said nearly at the same time.

Andrew smiled. "So, maybe not really a hellhound. A shapeshifter?"

The mage nodded, "One immune to acid. It's a devil or a demon or something naturally immune to acid. The question isn't why would it trap itself here but what was it doing that it failed to notice an army coming at it? It must be trapped here."

Their eyes turned to the acid. Davidson whispered, "An ancient shrine consecrated by Dar Ana."

"The Sixth Legion," Andrew added, his eyes wide. "There's something here a shapeshifter wants. Any ideas?"

Even the mage could not come up with something a demon would want in a pool of acid. "Okay, so the Orcs then have the right idea. Tristan, can you dispel the shape and show us what we're really dealing with?"

Tristan nodded, but also said, "I'm spent, my king. After this, I need a break, some ale, and lots of sleep. I can barely function as is."

"I understand. Officer Caleb will escort you back to the surface after this. When you're ready." Andrew signaled for his banner to be raised. "On my mark, all of you, magic arrows. Take aim now!"

While Tristan cast, all the fighters replaced their swords with light crossbows or short bows. A minute later, the hellhound quaked and then burst apart as the giant dog form shrank. "Fire!" By the time the first arrow thudded into the rock near where the hellhound had been, a tiny devil rocked back and forth. Seeing the arrows, it held up its hands and yelped.

To Andrew's surprise, Frentoris leapt across the way and pulled the devil behind his sword, which became a shield. When the arrows stopped, Frentoris held the devil up. It wriggled and twisted in his hand, with a decidedly resigned look on its quite human face. "Let me go!" it yelled while clawing at Frentoris.

The Orc paladin laughed and held it up. "To think such a puny thing caused us any problems at all!" The Orcs roared with laughter while Frentoris shook the tiny devil. "To make sure you do not," Frentoris said to the devil while looking at Andrew, "give us any trouble, and while you answer some questions." Frentoris tore the tiny devil's wing off and then jumped back to the shoreline with it.

Incer joined Frentoris and caught the creature's leg. Togethery, they carried the creature to King Andrew. The devil stood about a pace tall, the size of a four-year-old human. It wailed and gagged in pain as it was jerked through the crowd. Frentoris tossed it at Andrew's feet. "Human king, though its magic deceived us, we have captured what I believe is an imp." Frentoris growled at it. "Tell us, what master do you serve in the acid?"

It groveled before Andrew and hissed at the Orc paladins while cradling its wing stump. "I was supposed to become a dragon!" Its manner of speech had a very dated but very Tanian quality to it.

"How long have you been here?" Andrew asked.

"I don't know. The cavern's always the same. Centuries I bet. If you help me..."

Frentoris stepped on its other wing. To the loud crackling of wing bone, the Orc said, "You're lucky to be alive. Without the humans, my host would have already torn you to pieces and eaten you." The Orcs growled at the devil to show their filed teeth. Behind the paladins, the Orcs cheered and thumped their weapons on their armor. Frentoris twisted his heel on the wing. "What is in the acid pool?"

"Okay! Okay," the imp begged. "I can serve," the devil's eyes scanned the crowd before he pointed to the mage Tristan. "I can serve him!"

Tristan waved his hand and stepped back. "I have no wish or need for a devil familiar."

"But, the power! If you take me, our powers merge and you become more powerful... so much power..."

The imp's words trailed off as Frentoris stabbed it through its head down the imp's spine. Frentoris growled at the humans. "You wait too long. 'What can it tell us?'" he mimicked a human. "You wonder. That's where the lying and deceiving starts. You want information: these serve spell casters or are bound through a contract. No doubt, its contract is below the acid. If we want to know the truth, we must go into the acid." Frentoris brandished his sword at the acid pool.

Tristan fumbled at his spellbook. The other three mages in the group looked equally exhausted. One had been fatally wounded and just barely revived from the fight with the quill demon. Andrew agreed with Frentoris and said, "Yes, we must go into the acid. First, we need to rest and tend to the wounded. Noble Frentoris and Incer, I would ensure that our route to the surface is secure and we will rest here."

Frentoris growled low in his throat but then sniffed. "The War Host is not tired. We will walk sentry on the route to the surface." He thumped his chest and Incer made a series of arm movements to the leaders back by the acid pool. They immediately began to march out. Frentoris turned back to Andrew. "Why does this surface route concern you so much, human king? Orcs are mighty underground."

Andrew smiled while his squires began loosening his plate armor from the back. "This is Bloodstone, Frentoris. So many centuries of gods fighting here has made it so that tunnels like this, they move. If you lose the surface connection, we lose everything. Entire armies have been lost. Consider this room, from the Sixth Legion – maybe fourteen hundred years ago?" Andrew moved his fingers through some math and then said, "No one has seen this Shrine for at least a thousand years. You have not met Dar Ana, but she is a dragon priestess – maybe the most powerful of them all. Do you think someone like her, like your leader RiVule, would construct a place of worship and then abandon it for centuries?"

Frentoris' brow creased with concentration. "So, we must always keep surface open. This involves warriors."

Andrew nodded, "And something physical. Morbatten long ago figured out that something as simple as rope between the surface and us would keep the tunnels from shifting. That demon, the one we just fought, could have come here, but it also could have been trapped her forever, like the imp."

"Endless torture… waiting to die, I cannot imagine it." Frentoris watched the last of the Orcs leave. "RiVule said to me, 'Remember, humans are not Orc. Treat our allies as friends and you will see they are mighty too.' My troops are – how you say – excited from victory with demon. None of us have fought such a thing. They must fight or work, and it will make it hard for you to rest. Gruustir will watch over the surface route. Also, human king, I do not trust the acid."

"Thank you, Paladin Frentoris." Andrew bowed. "Your Orcs are strong. We are honored to have you with us." Andrew watched Frentoris leave and turned to the clerics in consultation with Davidson. "Please investigate the pool. I'd see our camp sanctified and, if you can, divine the nature of the pool. I agree with Frentoris. There is something wrong about it."

Davidson said, "As you command, my liege."

With guard rotations set, Andrew's group laid down and tried to rest. The echoes of the caverns made it hard though eventually exhaustion won out. Constant battle did that and the cold dark sapped at their strength. Andrew dozed off at some point while watching the priests at the pool's edge. He awoke with a start and grumbled. He had been dreaming about Ayden, again.

Something about her struck a chord in him. Taysor did not have many women of such dynamic capability and leadership. Davidson had commented that it was the scars on her face. "It gives her an edge and says that she can take care of herself. She's no courtier or noblewoman."

Wise words, but Andrew realized it was more than that: Ayden carried herself with quiet faith, and had won the heart of Tembri, a celebrated hero even in Taysor. Andrew felt himself competing with the ghost of Tembri and wondered, *how long to let her mourn before I say something?*

Caught in his reverie, Andrew reflected on how Bloodstone had changed both of them. *I've become harder, inured to the hell of this place. Tania has one up on us because they train knowing they will come fight in hell. Ayden knew. I need to adapt to my role here better.* It frustrated Andrew that Malcor had come out of nowhere to become king when he was just barely getting to know Rojo.

The new king though, unlike Andrew, had an entire empire ready to support him. *And here I am trying to lead my army, my people, make a new alliance, and I'm daydreaming about Ayden next to an acid pool. Pha Rann burn me,* Andrew thought with chagrin. *No wonder Ayden doesn't seem to see me this way. I need to be more heroic.* Ayden's sword was unlike anything he had ever seen.

Andrew saw a cleric stumble back from the pool. It looked like he slipped. The other clerics were lost in study or asleep. Andrew saw the priest whip around and cry out, clearly terrified but he made no sound. *Am I dreaming?* The priest, a young man… Andrew struggled to remember his name. *Yeger?* Yeger reached out and then something mist-like dragged him into the acid. It felt like a dream.

Yeger reached out to them, clearly screaming for help, but not burning in the acid. Then, he was gone… just like a dream. His body falling, the splashing in the water, his clear screaming for help, and yet Andrew had heard nothing.

Andrew tried to sit up but felt gravity holding him down on his cot. *I'm king. I get a cot.* His thinking was sluggish and simple. Those around him laid on leather cloaks and bedrolls tucked under their heads; *they are not kings.* Some of the men used their helmets as a pillow. Rune tiles, courtesy of Tania, glowed throughout and provided a modicum of warmth to those in their faint light.

Andrew had one and when he looked at it, he imagined dragons in the rune shape. They swirled and he blinked to rub his eyes. His skin felt rubbery and he noticed the mist form by the pool had appeared again. He tried to sit up again and felt the room spin.

"Guards!" he tried to yell. His voice sounded weak. "Help…" he tried to shout. He fell forward onto the paladin next to him. The man barely stirred. Though not an overtly religious man, Andrew had spent many hours studying in the various Pha Rannic temples. Something was not right here and he suddenly wished he had pursued a career as a paladin. In his mind, the knight before him became Ayden and he unconsciously reached out to pull her hair back behind her ear. The cold metal of the knight's helm jarred him back into reality. It seemed that half their clerics were gone and that mist remained as a looming presence by the pool.

Andrew had never prayed so hard as he did in that moment. "Pha Rann... hear me..."

Something moved past his face and he struggled to see it or understand it. The form resolved into a man's face and he saw a Tanian agent. The man – actually an elf - held a potion before Andrew's face and signaled for him to drink it. His hands flashed in Tanian handsign but Andrew's sluggish mind could not follow it. The man put a potion in Andrew's hand.

The agent had to help him drink the vial. The potion's effects immediately helped clear the fugue blocking Andrew's thought processes. The agent screamed into his face, "You're all sick. We got word of your find at the Temple and Dar Ana sent me. By the way, congrats on finding Ana's shrine. She says she wants to personally thank you." The agent winked at Andrew. "You know how she is."

Within seconds, Andrew could smell an acrid odor in the air. The agent opened a leather roll full of narrow tubes. "King Andrew, my name is Anders. Each of these potions will revive one person. I did not come with enough and so gave ten to the Orcs already, at Ana's instruction. She said they're better suited to this place. They'll be here in a moment and will keep our line to the surface secure. I trust you'll revive who you feel is best suited to fighting. I'm going to save the clerics."

"Thank you, Anders." Andrew cradled the head of the paladin next to him and chuckled at the thought of treating him like Ayden. *I'm still not right in my head*, he realized.

Anders moved to the pool, aware of the mist creature there and moving carefully. He touched the bloodstone earring clipped high to his ear and sent his thoughts to Ana. "My Dar, I've reached the shrine. They've suffered casualties. Confirm priority: bloodstone or Andrew's clerics? Also, do you know what this creature is?"

Ana's thought came to him immediately. "It's an aboleth. Corth K'Ven just confirmed it. For priorities, both. But if you have to choose, save Andrew's team and then slip away when you can and get the stone later. I hate being political. The king is safe?"

"Yes," Anders sent and then moved in to attack. His scimitar sliced through a mist tendril carefully coiling around Davidson's leg and pulling the unconscious priest to the pool. A globule of clear slime coated Davidson's face.

Though the tendril appeared like mist, it recoiled as if in pain from Anders' enchanted blade. Anders yelled out to the Orcs just entering the cavern and those reviving with Andrew's help. "It's an aboleth! Unless you have magic that protects your mind, do not engage. You are to fall back and attack with ranged weapons!"

Another pseudopod shot out from the pool and Anders ducked underneath it. "Well done, Anders," Ana purred in his thoughts. "Keep this up and I might recommend you to one of Daryx's special teams. You know they're recruiting for a special mission right now."

"Do tell," Anders grunted as he slid on his knees and vaulted upright to sever the hold on a cleric along the shoreline. Comatose, the cleric's armor and skin had burned away in the acid. Anders pulled the priest back then felt a tentacle wrap around his midsection and begin to lift him off the ground. He cursed Joust, knowing full well that Ana was watching and would comment on it.

She did. "Maybe you should call out to Tiamat instead? You know, if you're not up to this, I can always come myself. I mean, why shouldn't the high priestess do everything herself?"

"You know that I'm up for anything, my Dar," Anders shouted out loud while driving his scimitar down along his armor to cut the tentacle off him.

As he fell, another pseudopod smacked his face. Ana advised him. "It's trying to charm you, let it – rather, pretend to let it. Hopefully it'll pull you underwater."

Anders nodded and let his body relax even as mucus-like goo secreted from the pod coated his face. He wanted to gag and vomit, but instead he smiled and breathed the goo into his nose and mouth. Ana observed, "You're very good at this. It almost makes me reconsider you as a lover. I mean, you were highly sought after for the knighthood after all. King Andrew has rallied his guard and the Orcs are there now. I've told the Orc paladins – aren't they something? – to let you be captured."

Frentoris and Incer drove forward and recovered the cleric Anders had just saved. They grabbed two more and just as Anders was about to enter the acid, Frentoris cut the arm and grabbed him. Anders felt Ana's anger at being disobeyed… and he almost laughed when he heard her voice boom out in the cavern. "Orc! You are to let him be taken! Disobey me again and I will personally ensure you find Demos-Gorgos' monkey ass in the afterlife rather than Gruustir's!"

Frentoris let Anders go and mouthed, "Sorry." As Anders felt himself dragged back towards the pool, Frentoris kicked him in the lower back so that he fell face first into the acid.

Confused by Ana's voice reverberating throughout the complex, King Andrew ran forward to grab Anders and the last thing the agent heard was Ana's voice ordering him to stop. In his mind, as the acid covered his eyes, Ana said, "This would never happen with our own knights. Idiots!" As Anders sank into the acid, Ana's voice came back reassuringly. "I'm here with you, Anders. The aboleth will hopefully pull you down to its lair. I can't tell it's using the bloodstone, so be careful."

Anders looked around at the debris strewn about the amphitheater. "So, this was your shrine?" he thought to Ana.

"Yes, it seems like yesterday that I first danced down there on the stage, to consecrate it. You would have liked it. I wore…" and Ana projected an image of her wearing barely translucent silks.

"It's hard to concentrate with monster snot in my lungs. Please, don't make this harder," Anders sent.

Ana's bright laughter came through and Anders thanked Tiamat that, whatever it was that pulled all the priestesses away a few days ago, had ended. Dar Ana's mood often set the foundation for troop morale in Bloodstone. That her energy and humor had returned boded well for the armies. "It's good to hear you laugh, my lady."

"You have no idea how good things can be," and suddenly it sounded like Ana was right in his ear, whispering to him. She giggled.

Against this, an alien voice of cinder and ash assaulted Ander's mind. "You are mine. You serve me now. What is your name?" He heard the voice as if someone were speaking to him loudly in a quiet place. It made him feel small.

Anders pushed Ana out and responded, "I am Anders. Where am I?" he said, trying to sound nervous.

"My home, now your home. You will join others. There below you." They had descended enough that Anders had to use infravision to see. The acid was clearer than water, but made everything wavy. He noted several humanoid forms on the stage where Ana would have worshipped Tiamat to an amphitheater full of fighters. He felt his feet touch the stage and noted a pile of gear and another of treasure. A compulsion to remove all of his gear and armor hit him. He could sense that he was to remove magical gear to the treasure pile.

Ana whispered, "Do it. I won't tease you. Also, you are a hundred paces deep."

Anders began to take his gear off, acting the charm out and even faking resistance a bit. The ashen voice came to him again. "You resist now, but know that your service will be joyous, even pleasurable. It has been too long since I had new servants. An elf will greatly extend their useful life. You will be a king here," the voice projected to him. With the voice came a vision of Anders ruling a vast empire of slaves made up of beautiful female elves and humans.

"Serve me, Anders," Ana moaned. "I'll ensure you enjoy every second of it!" She laughed cruelly. "It's been so long since I encountered an aboleth. This one must think you are susceptible to sexual temptation; are you, Anders? The god emperor has noted that even young aboleths can sense a mortal's desires. They'll most often offer that first. They're quite lazy as far as monsters go. You'd think something Set designed to be intelligent would be more like a Slaad or a hag. Can you see its main body yet, or the bloodstone?"

While discarding his equipment, Anders thought, "If I remove the earring…"

Ana immediately intruded into his thoughts. "You will not remove the earring. The same way it masks your thoughts from the creature, it masks itself from all things unless they know to look for it. You're safe. Try not to think about it. We don't know how much the aboleth knows about bloodstones. I certainly don't remember ever detecting one in this or any other cascade." Ana's reassurance helped him relax. With the last of his clothing dropped into the appropriate pile, other slaves came forward.

He recognized two clerics taken from Andrew's party, not by name or personal relationship, but by their strange haircuts. A beautiful female, nude and perfect came forward to Anders next. She bore the tattoo symbols of Tiamat and the dragons dating back to the Sixth Legion. The aboleth's voice assaulted Anders again. "She will be your wife and you will breed endless children for us." The priestess smiled seductively at

Anders and opened her arms for him to see her while beckoning him to her.

Ana's voice held sadness when Anders noticed her. "One of my students, Maress. She was special to me. I had thought her dead all this time. Anders, new priority after the bloodstone. We're going to kill the aboleth. I need you to buy me some time so I can see how we might do that. Underwater, in toxic acid, all these slaves will die instantly if the aboleth dies. I had forgotten how vile and self-serving these creatures are. We have one in the Garden, you know. Syliri captured it by petrifying the entire lake it was in."

Anders tried to respond, but Maress had wrapped her legs around him and pulled his head to her breasts. It was very distracting and Ana's teasing already had him aroused. He heard Ana sigh. "Anders, seriously – at a time like this?"

"It's a thing the aboleth wants," he shot back. "If I resist, it'll be bad." Maress moaned as she held herself to him. In spite of knowing he should not, Anders found he wanted to respond and wondered if it was Maress' beauty or some aspect of the aboleth's control leaking through. He could tell the aboleth wanted Maress to have a half-elven child. If he resisted, he did not know what the aboleth would do.

He said, "I recognize you. Maress, right? Tiamat burn me, but I want to do this! I cannot! She is a priestess of my god."

The aboleth began to laugh. Its guffaws blasted through the water and gave Anders a sense it was to his right in a shadowed recess used as a side entrance connecting the amphitheater and the actual shrine. Anders felt something brush his leg and saw a white tentacle touch his leg. At its touch, sexual desire for Maress exploded in every part of his body. "Slave Anders, do this thing you already want. Take her, mate her, and give in to the unimaginable ecstasy that is yours now!"

Anders moaned and gripped Maress to him tightly but refused to enter her. "No…" he shouted.

"I'm impressed," Ana deadpanned. "With an aboleth, you are much more resistant than I would have thought."

"That's not fair," Anders shot back. "I don't see you down here pretending to enjoy being bred. And, Maress is gorgeous!. She does not look a thousand years old. Hey, wait, I think I see the main body. Does it look like a spidery blob of maybe twenty red eyes in two rows? It must be a hundred paces from me."

"Yes," Ana breathed. "Do you see the bloodstone yet?"

Anders looked around, trying to not look like he was looking around by wrapping his arms and lips over the priestess' body, who shuddered. Desperately, she tried to force Anders into her but he held her too tightly against him. Maress whispered to him, "I could love you forever, Elf. Take me, please. I'm dying for you!"

Anders shook his head and felt the bloodstone earring cuff on his ear. It made sense to take it off. The white tentacle on his leg pulsed and Anders knew he had to take it off. He reached up to take it off, when he heard a female voice order him, "Anders, the aboleth knows. This is Ana. You are in danger. Do not remove the earring!"

Anders recognized the voice but with a beautiful Maress before him, so in love with him, it was too much to want to resist. As he pulled the earring off, he heard this Ana's voice say, "Very well. Give it to your lovely Maress, as a gift."

That was a great idea and Anders smiled stupidly at Maress. "We will have many beautiful children," he groaned while thrusting into her. The earring clasped onto her ear. "This is our wedding gift."

Suddenly, the priestess' dragon tattoos ignited along her skin. They were beautiful, but also a bit scary. Maress pulled Anders to her and embraced him. "Anders, Tiamat bless you." At her words, the fugue dominating his thoughts left and Anders remembered taking the earring off. He felt Maress and knew... and knowing, he did not want to but pulled back. Ana would never let him live this down and it probably ensured he would not get a recommendation to Daryx.

With a sweet smile, Maress pressed herself against him one last time and said, "Ana is with me and has shown me why you're here. Thank you, Anders. Just because my mistress Ana prefers knights, does not mean that I do not appreciate the comfort of a man's touch."

From the recessed shadows, the aboleth shot forward to grab them both. Anders felt his body paralyze when he saw how big it was. It moved the water currents and crawled forward on feelers all around the upper half of its body. While Maress prayed, Anders tried to defend her from the monster, but noticed that time appeared to have frozen. The edges of his vision had a strange fiery cast to them, like embers rising into the night sky from a campfire. "We're out of the River's flow, for a while," Maress explained. "This gives us some time, but not a lot of time. Please tell me you have *water breath* and *acid-resistance* potions?"

Anders nodded and, holding hands, they walked to the treasure pile. He felt the tendril coiled to his leg, but it did nothing to him in this divine space. "Maress, I'm sorry about earlier, but..."

She laughed. "You're not the first I've been forced to be with here, Anders. Though you were the first to resist. I love you for that." Her eyes glassed over a bit and she shook her head. All around, the river quaked as Maress almost re-succumed to centuries of conditioned thinking. "It's still with me and my desire for you is raging still. Ana is laughing at you." Maress giggled. "It helps me. I'm sorry, Anders. We have to hurry. You have no idea how much I want to comply still."

Anders quickly put his equipment and gear back on and then gave Maress her potions. Maress found a dress and a shield in the pile and picked up a mace from one of the Soran priests. The aboleth appeared to move in slow motion but the other slaves were completely frozen. "Let's do it," she said and they began scraping the aboleth slime off of their faces.

"This is the River?" Anders asked. When Maress nodded, he said, "I imagined it would have more fire."

"We're underwater. Besides, this is not the River the Dar priestesses talk about. This prayer brings us close to it, enough that outside time seems to stop." She pointed to the aboleth which continued clawing its way to them but very slowly. "Except for very powerful." Maress cocked her head and said, "Ana is speaking to me from the River. She says she is waiting to embrace me and can't wait to see me again." For a moment, emotion overwhelmed Maress and Anders found himself cradling her in her arms. "How long has it been?" she asked.

"Nearly a thousand years," Anders said.

Maress began to hyperventilate and Anders touched the earring. "Ana, I've studied aboleths. I've never heard of one this big. I'd guess it's at least three hundred paces long, maybe longer. There are only three slaves that I can see, but I'm guessing there are many more. What's the plan?"

At his touch, Ana's thoughts came to him and he heard her singing to Maress in draconian. "Shhhh, it's okay. The river's flow is endless and what is a thousand years to our Goddess? Dearest Maress, I have walked Tehra since the beginning of Tania. I was there with Dar when she dedicated the Temple, just the same as you were here with me when we dedicated this Shrine. I will see you through this. You are not alone."

Ana's focus turned to Anders. "How do you feel about possession?" Ana asked him.

"By who, you?" Anders asked with more concern and anxiety than he wished he had in the moment.

"Well, after watching how you man-handled Maress and played the aboleth like a bard, I'd like to know what makes a man like you tick," Ana teased back at him. "I'm not giving you a choice, Anders. Maress is in shock. She won't be effective against this and you are not equipped correctly for it. Without re-equipping King Andrew, we cannot attack the creature easily. Prepare yourself. I want you to relax. This will feel weird, invasive, and yes – I'm going to know everything about you. But, it's a little fair since you might learn some things about me. Just let it happen. I need you to pretend that you're watching a play featuring you. If you think too much, feel too much, or want to do something too much, it will weaken my possession. And, Anders. I need everything. Ready?"

Anders was about to say he was ready when his head erupted in fiery agony. Needles of pain cascaded through his eyes and skin down his body. He screamed and fell over backwards. Through it all, he heard Ana telling him to accept it. "Let me in. The more you can relax, the less damaging it will be. The pain is because you're an elf and I'm not. Let it happen."

The pain spiraled up and up with no end in sight, and then it was gone. Anders felt himself still as himself, but Ana was there too. He felt a metaphor presented to him of a child sitting in the corner, quietly with his hands folded. The corner in that symbol felt like a great place to be and Anders accepted it. He could see everything through his eyes, but his body moved by itself. Ana grabbed Maress and kissed her deeply. Anders felt everything, even felt how incredibly sexual and inevitable Ana and Maress had once been and would be again. The silent child watching metaphor reasserted itself and he accepted it as needle pinpricks began firing all along his body.

Ana said, "Maress, I'm here in Anders' body. We're going to kill the aboleth, free the slaves, and recover this Shrine. I know you're not feeling well so we're going to do a few things. The first is that I'm going to charm you. Then, you're going to combine with me because you love me. Then, we're going to destroy your tormentor."

Maress nodded, still clearly in shock, while Ana kissed her lips again. Just like that, the charm went into effect. "I'm not asking you to do anything you don't want to do. Kiss me back and combine with me," Ana ordered.

Maress put her hand on Ana's shoulder and Ana prayed for the bloodstone gem. It glowed in the pile of treasure. Gleefully, Ana danced to it and picked it up. The small fingernail sized sphere welcomed her with bright red light. The golden chain that used to hold it had broken. Ana coiled it through her hands and said, "Welcome back, little one."

Ana whispered in draconian, "*Nightmare of Chaos*, hear my call and come to my aid now!" Underneath her outstretched hand, a two-handed sword of black steel with an eye-like gem set in its pommel appeared. Anders recognized the deceased Legion Commander Verit's blade. Under her other hand, another sword appeared as Ana called out. "*Twilight Fell Shining on Her Bright Eyes*!" Crossing the two swords across her chest, Ana spoke to them as if lovers. "There is an aboleth out there. It must die. For Takhissis' glory and might, I command you to strike and give me its lifeforce. I want it to feel pain and be scared before it dies!"

She then prayed to Tiamat and blessed Anders and Maress with protection from acid, adding protection against evil and chaos. Without looking, Nightmare severed the tentacle on Anders' leg. "It's time," she whispered. Anders felt them submerge under the River of Fire and come back to the underwater hell of the aboleth charging them.

Everything blurred as *Nightmare of Chaos*, and the former King Rojo's sword, *Twilight Fell Shining on Her Bright Eyes*, moved forward against the aboleth as if weilded by fighters. Tentacles moved to grab Anders and Maress, but the aboleth did not know it now faced Dar Ana.

Ana screamed at it, "Takhissis burn you, Set spawn! It is time for you to end!" Anders felt Ana's wrath as the high priestess let so much more pain than he would have thought she had flood out of her. The bloodstone hanging from her hand burst into light and Ana prayed for fire and swam forward. *I wonder what the bloodstone's power is*, Anders thought. The silent child reasserted itself and Ana's power dimmed. He felt her rage and quelled his curiousity.

The two swords cut and severed emough tentacles that the aboleth fell back. Ana moved forward with Maress' hand on her shoulder. From all around, slaves came swimming out of shadowed archways built into the lower levels surrounding the stage.

The main bulk of the aboleth, which resembled a titanic catfish, lunged forward. Long whiskers ending in feather-like fans writhed around the two rows of ill-red eyes. Anders chuckled, *I miscounted.* There are at least a hundred eyes all the way down its back.

The monster's interest clearly and fatally lay with the swords, not with the Ana-possessed Anders. A blast of heat washed over his skin as Ana summoned a dragon-shaped firestorm into the liquid acid. Anders could not see it, but knew it was there. Ana sent it surging forward at the monster.

The aboleth did not realize it was there until one of its feathered whiskers blackened and wilted. The pain made the giant fish try to dodge to the side as more of its tentacles boiled on that side of its body. Anders watched in fascination as the invisible firestorm just barely missed the mouth at the center of its face.

For the first time, all of the eyes locked on to Anders – not Ana. Anders felt the assault of its power. "Quiet, shhhh. Surrender. No need to fight…"

Ana ripped herself out Time's flow and dropped to her hands and knees. "Anders, you must resist this." Anders heard her words, but felt his hands in oil. All around him wavery and burning flow of energy coursed forwards to a giant fish wreathed in flame. The aboleth loomed giant in his future, representing the slaves, moved towards them. The swords looked glorious to the point it hurt Anders' eyes to behold them. Ana, master of this realm, laughed and cried out to Takhissis.

Touching Anders from the River, Ana said, "You feel Set's power. You must resist it, Anders! Under all of your training is a fortification of will, by the dragons' decree. Use it. Fight it." Her words strengthened him and he refocused on Ana.

The ashen voice spoke to him for the flames and commanded him. "You must end yourself that I live, Anders. Yours will be a beautiful death that will echo through my immortal life." The eyes blink in unison and Anders felt the powerful swords under Ana's control. "Either of these blades can end you and save us. Do it now!" Anders shook and felt his left hand reaching for a venomed blade at his waist.

Ana pushed the aboleth's voice out. "Anders, remember who you are. Outcast of Morilon, servant of Perdition, citizen of Tania! You are beloved by your peers, feared by your enemies, and loved by Tiamat. For this creature, you must hone your will into a spear and stab back."

He concentrated on a spear, double-edged, with a golden needle-like point. It felt right and then he wrapped it about in dragons and launched it at the aboleth. The ashen voice fell from his mind. Anders knew they were going to win. The prospect of victory excited him.

Ana's voice changed as she took back control of Anders and screamed in draconian. All around her in the River of Fire, a titanic visage of a dragon reared up from both sides of the River. Like a phantom, it swarmed around and mimicked Ana's movements until they matched exactly. Ana lifted up her voice and shouted, "Mother, hear my cry! Lend me power to burn Set's creation, to burn it all! Fire! Flames! Infinite heat!"

Ana's fury caught Anders by surprise again and he wondered how someone like her could harbor so much hurt, because he could feel it was some past pain that focused the energy. While Anders was repulsed by the aboleth, he did not actively hate it. Ana hated it in a way that forced Anders to redefine his own understanding of what the word hate meant: to actively lust for another's destruction. Considering this, the silent child metaphor nearly reasserted itself, bu the felt Ana consciously shunt it aside and let him see her soul. "Let's try this," Ana whispered to him.

An image came to him of Dar Tania. Her face was part of everything in Tania and he recognized her immediately. Dar Tania had aged and was slipping away into death. Ana held her hand in both of her own. She was bowed over the first priestess and kissed her fingers frantically. Anders had never heard the story of Dar Tania's death. His curiosity seemed to pull the story forward.

"Dar, please don't go. Without you, what will I do?" Ana was crying. "You don't have to die. Ascend! We will become gods together - Dar and Ana, the twin gods of flamestrike and firestorm!" The desperate hope in Ana's voice hurt Anders to hear. Elves did not feel emotions like this.

Dar's wrinkled hand caressed Ana's face. "Precious Ana, my knight Sean waits for me. Tiamat will do with me what She will. I do not wish to be a god. As a god, what could I ever hope to create that would even compare to you? You are my shining star, my warm fire, my daughter... I will be waiting for you..."

Tears flooded Ana's eyes and then the metaphor punched Anders in the face. He had a sense that Ana was angry at him and he stopped paying attention to the past scene. Regaining his own awareness, Ana had summoned another sword – her own sword, Morbattania – and raked it along the left side row of eyes. Of the five eyes, she blinded three. The ichor swirling out into the acid looked like tiny hands grasping into space. Finally, they were close enough to the beast to see its true size. Each eye's diameter equaled his height. The body must be five hundred paces from head to tail. The feeler stalks and whiskers would double that.

The aboleth bit upwards. The attack created a suction that pulled Ana into its maw. Rather than struggle against the draw, Ana curled into a ball and let the aboleth bite down onto her. Anders expected the venomous fangs rimming the maw to skewer him. Instead, brilliant flashes of light tingled his skin as, all around him, wherever the fangs pressed into him, spectral plate armor fragments appeared. "Anders, quit gaping. This is goddess armor. It's why I don't wear armor, none of the priestesses do. You probably thought it was some seduction control mechanism. Have faith in Tiamat, if not in me. I'm not going to ruin your body."

He saw Ana brace her feet on rows of smaller fangs and begin to press upwards using the great sword of Dar Tania as a lever. Ghostly metal boots appeared around his feet. He heard himself praying in draconian and then, all around him, fire triggered and an explosion of steam boiled the acid around them.

Ana laughed. Unlike their earlier back and forth, Ana's laughter was cruel and mocking. Anders, like everyone serving in Bloodstone, had heard story upon story of those times Dar Ana entered combat. Like a goddess conducting a celestial choir, Ana had presided over the fall of the Jade God. Only the Dread Lord Crimson Burning had been close to experience it all with her though. With Ana possessing his body, Anders felt what could only be pure pleasure at the pain inflicted on the aboleth, and hatred for it. Another flash bubble of steam erupted around her and the aboleth spit them out. With a flash, it tried to escape.

"No, you don't," Ana said. "*Morbattania*, heed my cry!" Ana sang. Her sword spun from her hands and speared out after the aboleth. "*Morbattania*, herald of all dragons, capture my foe." With unbelievable speed and precision, it struck the fleshy part of the tail. Anders did not realize it at first, but the sword had enlarged. Looking at it relative to the aboleth, he realized the sword would be large enough for a titan.

"Your sword's name is *Morbattania*?" Anders mused.

The metaphor began to assert itself and then Ana let Anders see more. Dar Tania lay in her bed. Her hair and eyes burned in ways that no other high priestess ever did. She gestured to the wall by her bed and Ana picked up a sword and gave it to her. "Yes, my love," Ana whispered. "Your sword…"

"Its name," Dar Tania rasped, struggling to breathe. "Is *Morbattania*. My daughter, Seline, she saw it in one of her visions. She was your age, Ana. She forged it, and said, 'Daddy helped me the whole time.' I believe Sean and Seline made this for me as a gift, a reminder. I want you to have it."

"A reminder of what?" Ana whispered, taking the sword and drawing it just a few fingers from the sheath. Draconian runes in Seline's strange interpretation of the dragon's writing style danced along the blood groove. It looked brutal in the Tanian way, yet something about it sang to the beauty of the Pha Rannic sun. The runes burned through Ana's wet eyes and read: **Dar Tania, with a sword, is forever a dragon**. The runes flashed brilliant gold and in flowing Pha Rannic script read the same but in Commander Sean's flowing cursive.

Dar coughed and tried to clear her breathing through asthmatic wheezing. "To remind us, Ana, that our spirits are as big as dragons. My Sean is so handsome. I wonder if I'll see him... Seline?..."

Ana bowed her head and began rocking back and forth. "No, Dar. Don't. We can still ascend..." Dar deflated and passed from Tehra. Ana held the sword to her breast and laid her head on Dar's head. Deep wracking sobs shook her body and then Anders saw the hand of a Dread Lord touch Dar Tania's head. It was Alerius. The vision ended.

Before his eyes, the aboleth writhed, trying to free itself from the sword. Each attempt resulted in green blood spurts around the blade. Ana looked behind and saw Maress still focused on retaining the combination. Behind her, several hundred humanoids appeared swimming towards them. Anders saw humans, dwarves, and a few elves. Most notably, many looked young and he realized they were children. Maress's children, the thought struck him... and then Ana reasserted the metaphor of him not disturbing her.

"Maress, break combination; I've got this now. Once the aboleth is dead, they will all drown or be killed by acid. We need to lure them all up into the cavern and out of the acid. Maress, you can do this." Ana tried to sound reassuring, but to Anders it sounded like military command. Maress nodded and broke off contact. Ana then changed her focus and the image of King Andrew filled her thoughts. "Andrew, we are sending enslaved survivors out of the acid. Be prepared to restrain and save as many as you can. We are bringing the aboleth up but cannot kill it until we have all the slaves out of the acid."

The aboleth felt Ana's distraction and lunged forward. It looked like it might tear in half where the sword pinned its body. Anders lifted his hand

and the bloodstone there glimmered in the darkness. He saw a globule of spit rolling at them. Though it seemed to move slowly, the liquid made it hard to get out of the way. He wanted to get away and was surprised when his body began to move. Ana reasserted the metaphor, practically screaming at him to not move. Pain lanced through him and he collapsed back into his corner. He understood that if he did it again, it would be bad.

Ana pointed her hands forward and called out to *Chaos* and *Twilight Fell*. The two swords danced forward at the aboleth and they sliced apart one of the severed tendrils near the monster's shoulder that had begun regenerating. Ana stepped out of the flow of Time and dropped back into the River of Fire. It put her right next to the aboleth's face and dodged the aboleth's attack. *Chaos* appeared in her hand and she stabbed it into the fish beast. *Twilight Fell* screeched past the aboleth and took up position by a tunnel leading into the shrine. The aboleth's escape was now cut off.

Ana looked back at Maress and saw her fall under the other slaves where they pinned her down. Around them, the ashen voice ordered submission. With despair, Anders saw Maress' face go slack. She caressed the face of a fighter, whose body then vaporized in a steam explosion all around them. Maress had lured them in close so she could flamestrike herself. Ana felt pleased by this and continued hacking at the beast with Chaos.

Anders felt Ana chant in draconian and saw a red line of energy lash out from Ana's heart and connect to Maress, healing her. With each cut into the monster, the line pulsed and he knew that Ana drew health from the aboleth's wounds. Strange draconian words spilled from his mouth and Anders felt turmoil in his soul. Yet Ana kept chanting. The dissonant sounds made his skin crawl and he felt his eyes begin to hurt to the point he might claw them out. A vision of the cleric's resurrection ritual, which Anders had seen just once, came to his mind and he understood that Ana was reversing this to obliterate their enemy.

The aboleth moved to bite him again, and like before, Ana let it happen. The spectral armor – *goddess armor*, the corrective thought came to him – protected him. Ana reached up and grabbed one of the fanged teeth with the last syllable of her prayer.

The effect on the aboleth was immediate. Its body began to disintegrate in a growing radius from Ana's touch on its tooth. However, as it did so, the line of energy flared bright red and Ana redirected the energy of its death back to the monster, healing it even as she took its life by the Goddess' power. Caught in this well-tended murder, the aboleth was paralyzed. Anders watched fascinated. *So this is how a Dar priestess wages war? You truly are frightening*, he complimented Ana.

Ana ignored him and summoned *Morbattania* to her hand. At the sword's touch, Anders felt his body enlarge until she could lift the titanic creature. Its slimy skin stuck to him and blistered his face and arms. His body grew towards the surface. Below them, the slaves raced upwards to save their master. Anders finally understood: Ana had paralyzed the monster on the brink of death and was using it as a lure to get the slaves out of the acid.

King Andrew and his most powerful spell casters waited outside the amphitheater. Frentoris and Incer fidgeted with their sword pommels and complained. "Waiting is not Orc."

"It won't be long now," Andrew suggested. On cue, the acid pool began to overflow as something pushed the lake to spilling. Cracks in the rock and hidden holes began to drain the acid but it made Andrew's battalion nervous.

A giant-sized Anders broke the surface with a monstrous catfish in his hand. The creature bled from the stumps of multiple amputated limbs. Eyes across its face blinked while others oozed ichor. Anders threw it to the side of the pool and then dropped to his knees. His body shrank from its giant size back to human. Acid rushed back into the pool.

A red line of energy radiated from the center of his body to the creature. Andrew had heard about aboleths and had even seen a Tanian sketch of one. It was larger than he could fathom. Andrew noticed it was disintegrating even as it healed. "Anders!" he called out, but the agent shook his head no, and gestured for him to keep back. A bloodstone twinkled from his right hand. Behind them, King Rojo's sword, *Twilight Fell*, exploded from the surface and attacked the aboleth. He saw *Nightmare of Chaos* raking eyes along the beast's spine.

Andrew pointed and yelled. "Look! Verit and Rojo's swords continue to attack on their own!"

Frentoris moved to charge forward, but Anders shouted again. "No! Stay back. It cannot die for a few more minutes."

A minute later, the acid pool broke and a woman emerged from behind Anders... *No*, Andrew corrected himself, a transcended priestess stepped out of the acid. Dragon tattoos covered her otherwise nude form. A moment later, scores of humans and creatures of other races erupted from the pool and moved to attack her. Some ran to the aboleth to try and help it. Each had a thick mucus-like capsule around their head.

Anders pointed to them and called out to the king. "Save them! Save them all! Charm, enthrall, possession, subdue them! But, we must clear their heads before I end the aboleth! That goo has to come off or they will suffocate."

Frentoris and Incer nodded and sheathed their swords. "Bash with shield," Frentoris said. He looked at the other Orcs. "If the weak ones die, the human clerics can revive them."

"Yes, smash them down," Incer agreed.

Andrew ordered his guard in and melee ensued. While a few of the slaves had weapons, none had armor. The king noted twenty acting as if they were going to attack Anders. It would be a fast battle for Andrew's team except that more and more slaves kept clambering out. Plus, dripping with acid, the fighters had to be careful when their armor and shields began to sizzle.

Andrew's captain yelled back, "Only magic gear can endure the acid! Be on guard."

Tristan and Davidson did their part. As they moved through the assailants, their spells and prayers removed the monster's hold to the point that those saved would drop to their knees and begin clawing at the gel around their heads. The transcendent priestess walked to those, unaffected by combat and ignored by the attackers. At her touch, the curse of enslavement was removed. Andrew could tell because they began screaming in agony where the acid burned into their skin. He sent his clerics in and they began the arduous process of saving as many as they could.

Anders remained focused on the aboleth, balancing its death with the healing it received. Though a few of the slaves got close enough to attack, Andrew noticed goddess armor protecting Anders and it clicked. "Ana," he said touching his bloodstone earring. "You are controlling Anders?" When no reply came, he ordered his guard to move in and protect Anders. "Treat him as if he is the high priestess Ana."

They did their best but new slaves kept coming out of the pool, younger and younger ones too. Andrew's fighters paused, though the Orcs had no problem smashing them unconscious or killing the nude humans with their shields. One of Andrew's captains caught Frentoris and demanded, "The king said to not kill, subdue!"

Frentoris shrugged the captain back and snarled at him. "I do not serve the human king." He smashed another human with a backhand and grinned at the captain. "You can sort this out later."

Near the pool's edge, Andrew moved up to stand by Anders and said, "What do you need?"

"We need them all out of the acid. Once they are all out, we will end this. And yes, I've taken possession of Anders. It's a standard part of agent contracts here, King Andrew." Anders heard Ana laugh in his mind, not at him, at the king.

Andrew eyed Anders and said, "I was not aware of this." He thought, *But, I can see Tania doing it.* He made a note to discuss it with his counsellors later. He had never understood the High King Charter for the various crime families operating out of Ymac. Now that he saw Tania using agents this way, he wondered why Taysor did not similarly use them as part of the military. Maybe they did.

Beside them, the pool continued to give up slaves while those in the hall began retrieving and removing unconscious but freed bodies from the cavern. Andrew guessed that they must have bought enough time for all of the slaves to exit the acid, summoned as they were by the aboleth's cry for aid. Anders said, "The time is now. I want all available fighters to concentrate missile fire and magic on the aboleth. On my mark."

Anders turned to the cavern and sang out in draconian, calling for all faithful to combine with him. Unconsciously, Andrew put his hand on Anders' shoulder and felt Ana's pulling at his spirit. Paladins, mages, and clerics joined with Ana... "In Tiamat's name, I release this curse." A pulse of multicolored energy pulsed out from her and struck all of the slaves. Shrieking cries of pain rang out as they clawed at the aboleth slime around their heads and their bodies blistered from the acid.

"Attack now!" Andrew ordered.

The battalion attacked. At the same time, Ana redirected the healing that had been keeping the monster alive to those now-freed slaves. A star pattern of red lines shot out and through everyone in the area as Ana drew life from the monster to heal its slaves. The arrows and magical attacks began to hit the aboleth. Perhaps by fear, or Ana's will, the paralysis ended and the creature flopped towards the pool. "No, not this time," Anders said. "There is no escape, only oblivion and Set." *Morbattania* appeared in his hand and he threw it like a spear. Mid-flight, it enlarged to the size of a battering ram. It skewered the monster through its face and pinned it to the wall. Stone dust rained down from the impact.

With its death, the slaves not already unconscious fell asleep. Anders turned to Andrew and said, "Witness, oh king, the desolation of the Sixth Legion's Shrine, and the revenge of Takhissis upon Set."

Anders moved to the acid pool and put his hands in it. He began to sing a gentle song in draconian. It brought an image of pure waters into Andrew's imagination. The acid began to heal and purify back into water.

King Andrew walked back to check on the survivors. Davidson reported that they had saved almost one hundred and fifty from the pool. "They're all in a bad way because of the acid, but they'll live with proper care and time. And, it appears that about half of them are Soran. Though…"

"What?"

"They're the children of the Tanian priestess. I'm sure of it. Many of the younger ones show signs of interbreeding diseases." Davidson sounded unsure of how to report this. "What do you…"

Andrew patted his shoulder. "Let the children of Tania be handled by Tania. We are here to help, not render judgement. We will offer our nation to them and take them as refugees if that's what we must do. I will let Dar Ana know. We must treat them gently. I cannot imagine being enslaved to that fish nightmare for even a day let alone hundreds of years."

They both looked at the obliterated aboleth. Orcs stood nearby daring each other to eat it and see if it actually tasted like catfish. King Andrew shuddered and went to check on whether their surface lines remained clear. True to Frentoris' promise, the Orcs had continued to run the line even when combat resumed. Andrew had not expected this level of discipline.

# Chapter 16 – Khalla's Play

Khalla tapped her crystal wine glass against her forehead. An ancient book, supposedly written by the god emperor himself, described the circumstances of Polgeryx's attack on Arati. "He certainly has a flair for the dramatic," she said.

From the darkness outside the room, a voice replied. It was Daryx. "Yes, the god emperor considers himself a collector of human experiences and passions. Writing, music, he has dabbled in it all. When you have infinite time and your only risk is emotional entanglements, I do believe the Court and other eldar here have taken to writing as a way of remaining dispassionate but still able to process these things in a way that does not age them."

Daryx entered the room and Khalla noted he wore loose-fitting and combat-ready clothing, but it still had a formal look to it. He sat down across from her. "Your team is almost ready. There are a few others I think you should consider." He removed a scroll tube and opened it. From within, he pulled a handful of pages. "The first is Revi. He was slotted to be Second in command of the Eighteenth Legion and stayed on to fight with Commander Verit and now Ayden. He is very capable and one I have had my eyes on for special teams."

Khalla took the page and scanned it. "Revi, three campaigns in Bloodstone. Offered a knight position but refused. Left the military and became an adventurer. Interesting. So, he's only in it for pay, glory, what?"

"Revi has contracts on three bloodstones, but has never taken or sold them, though you can be sure he has received multiple offers against them. He has a knack for what humans call 'luck.' He is also a skilled myrmidon, much like Commander Ayden. Ideally, we would be sending Ayden with you. Sadly, fortunately, however you see it, she is excelling at command. Revi is the next best bet for a fighter who can actually fight and stay true to the mission objectives."

"Very well. I will go and meet him. Who else?"

Daryx handed the next one over. "This is for a doppelganger named Delia. Everyone thinks she is dead. We resurrected her. I have secured her soul in a gem and it is safe. She will cooperate. She already speaks Drow. I'm not entirely sure how she ended up on the Isles, and she cannot stay. She should be your best friend. If not, kill her."

Khalla nodded. "Meat shield, got it."

"This next one is a special request from Morilon. The Lady Inviress Havkor. It seems that she has an interest in Merakor." Daryx passed over a paper and let Khalla look at it.

"She is very old. I know her name. She's famous in Morilon for defying everything Vel Pajor does." Her eyes went wide while scanning the parchment. "She is a dark elf?"

"Yes and no. She joined the Drow at the end but was caught up as a spy when the refugees came to the Isles. Rather than be executed, she pledged to Krentismar like the others. She is since reformed, but cannot stand the rule of Pajor's family. She's like you that way, Khalla. She was also there in Havkor when the Imperial City fell. It will be invaluable to you to have an actual dark elf in the party." Daryx smiled and added, "Since I cannot go."

"She is well-qualified no doubt. It'd be good to have a priestess of Krentismar… and practitioner of necromancy? Did I read that right? I thought Morilon did not practice necromancy."

Daryx began to laugh. "Her term for it was 'life studies.' You are correct; they do not practice necromancy." Daryx leaned forward. "But, Vel Pajor is essentially a necromantic sorcerer. Were he still in Merakor, by now, he'd be a lich. Think about that for a while and you'll see it explains a lot of the tension in Morilon." Daryx paused for a moment to see if Khalla had any comments. Then he explained. "Havkor is a royal elven name. Her grandfather was the King of the Sylvan Nation, whose capitol was Havkor. Just like Shorin for the Grays and Kinpeace for the High."

Khalla pulled at the page and chewed her lip. The thought of having a royal elven anyone made her uncomfortable. "I trust that you, that Tania, trusts her?"

Daryx laughed. "It doesn't matter. When you all leave, the Allegiance of Blood requires that we alter your memories so that the Isles can never be intentionally found. Inviress' life memories and experience cannot alter whether or not she is loyal to us, but it would be quite telling if she immediately tried to rejoin the Drow. In fact, it might help you to have an ally, which is how we will cast this. But, shhhh, this is between me and the next Marcello." He raised his eyebrow, "Or, has your newfound knowledge about Ash changed your ambition?"

"No, not all. Perdition is rightfully mine. Ash's day is done." Khalla put Inviress' page to the side. "So, why aren't you coming with us, my lord?"

Daryx sat back and looked around the room. "Since you seem so set on being Marcello, I should let you choose and redecorate a room here." He stretched his arms and when a phase spider appeared near him, he stroked it. "I cannot join you because the Allegiance of Blood protects me from being found by those who no doubt still look for me. I'm essentially trapped here on the Isles. Not that I mind. When I have left the Tehran realms on errand, I've noticed that it takes the Drow between four to ten hours to find me. I'd be good for bait. No, I'll go back when the god emperor deems it time to make us known."

Khalla continued leafing through the parchments. "May I know about the Temple of Glass?"

"What do you think it is?" Daryx countered.

"Well," Khalla said pausing in her perusal of candidates. "It's obviously a Temple to Tiamat. It's important. But, Glass? It throws me off. Tiamat did not have worshippers in Merakor, right?"

"No, She did not. No one except for the dragons, the kerchki, and Syliri. The Temple of Glass was built by the dragons just when Time began to flow. The River of Fire had not yet moved, and the consorts dedicated it as a sacred place to Tiamat. Before then, dragon breath was not fixed as it is now. The dragons had preferences, but there was no red, green, or gold. There were just dragons. Glass, as a name, was coined by the God of Scrying, Corth K'Ven, to represent the fact that it is all dragons' temple. It has unique meaning to those that know of it, or have been there. I suppose it's worth noting that Ynt'taris' consort was killed there as well. So, it has powerful significance to the Ice Patriarch."

Khalla listened intently and committed this advice and these learnings to her memory. She asked, "Is this mission part of reclaiming it?"

Daryx laughed. "I suppose, but technically no. If anything, this mission is about the Prophecy of the Shield and Spear. What do you think of the other recommendations?"

Sensing Daryx would not say more, Khalla pulled out five of the pages and passed them back to him. "These other five look good. I don't understand this one though. This is a request from our Tauran allies. Because his Blade of Stars was, as they say, 'epically speared into a god's belly,' the current emperor Cyclone has no Blade of Stars. He wishes to join the quest to Merakor and find 'a glorious afterlife piled round about by epic foes.'"

Daryx's grin became cat-like. He said, "Politically, we cannot say no to the Taurans. They are transporting you there and back. We owe them a great debt for their aid in Bloodstone. Taurans are an interesting element. Don't worry. The emperor knows he will not be an emperor in this quest. In his words, he asked that you treat him like any other fighter, just with a bit more respect. Also, he's a very powerful fighter. Not many Tanians have fought alongside the Taurans. They are formidable."

Khalla nodded and said, "I can see that. So, the team is looking really good up until you asked me to take a Sylvan Queen and the Tauran Emperor. Suddenly, I'm less concerned with logistics and more concerned with team morale and cohesion."

Daryx shrugged. "Perdition's Throne is often political. Ruling is political. So far, you've had a cell. While you've done very well with it, even you know that Ciejek is not exactly trustworthy, for example. And, you've been political with that one. How much do you really know about him?"

"Well," Khalla sat back from the desk and popped her back. "After what happened, I've made it my business to know everything about him. Had Vendetta allowed it, I'd have killed him."

Daryx stood up and turned his back to her. "Why do you need Vendetta to kill, little girl? Ciejek either deserves to live, or you kill him. As Perdition's head, will you wait on The Circle to make decisions for you? Issues like this remind me that you are still very young."

Khalla jumped up to prevent Daryx from leaving. "No, of course not! But, in that matter, Ciejek was not himself. The Law of Innocents..."

"Does not matter when compelling evidence supports self-defense. Had you killed him, we could have skipped some of this." Daryx pulled a small folded paper from his sleeve. "This is compelling evidence. Do what must be done, Khalla."

Daryx left by fading from her view until he was just gone. She blinked her eyes and took the folded paper. Something about interacting with Daryx made her uneasy. She felt tense. The words on the paper did not help: *Prop K up. No matter what, we must have her.* Ciejek's writing underneath was clear as day: *K suspects nothing. All is as planned. Soon, you will have all the blood you want.*

Khalla ran out into the hallway hoping to catch Daryx. Instead, she slammed into Valaes. The strong cleric jumped back and then caught her as she rocked back from his chest. "Sorry! Sorry, it's my fault," he said. "Khalla, oh it's you. I was just coming to see you."

"Have you seen Daryx?" Khalla asked looking around him. Her study and room at Daryx's estate was at the end of a passage. A secret door in her room wrapped back past the other rooms and allowed her to see throughout the complex, if she needed to.

Valaes stepped back and then replied, "No. Just you. Everyone is training. There's a class on Drow handsign going on right now with some ranger. The guy is amazing fast. It's funny…"

Khalla moved to walk past him, "Sorry, but I really need to find Daryx."

"Oh, okay. Well, um, I got a note from Daryx that I should report to you. Right now. Is it related maybe?"

Khalla eyed the tall cleric and paused. Ash had always told her this: when action sings in your heart, pause for a beat or two and then decide. *What do I really know about you, Valaes?* she wondered. *Wealthy son of the one of the most secretive and powerful guilds. Gifted battle priest with a bright future. In love with Alexandra. Set for greatness. He's perfect. I can't trust anyone in the guild right now. Ash, yeah, I could him, but he'd gloat about it for years.*

"Valaes, maybe. I need to do something, quickly. You up for some action?" She pulled him out of the hallway and into her room. Magic cloaked each room from outside observation, though clearly those enchantments did not apply to Daryx as the estate's owner.

Valaes laughed and said, "Hey now, I'm with someone and I know you're with Ash so…"

"It's not that. There is someone in Perdition that needs to be ended." Khalla poked Valaes in the chest. "You up for some wet work? Don't worry, cleric, my target deserves it."

Valaes grew contemplative and then shrugged. "I don't feel the Goddess guiding me either way. Sure, within the bounds of my faith, I'd love to help. Though, I might have a request."

"Go get geared up. Keep it quiet. I'll meet you at the estate exit on East-West in an hour. Valaes, do not tell Alex or anyone."

An hour later, Valaes found Khalla. She wore enchanted leather armor that looked almost like mummy wraps under civilian clothes. By comparison, Valaes came girded in plate armor. Spikes rose up from his gorget. The neckguard on his weak side counterbalanced a war hammer decorated and gleaming with many dragons coiling on each other. The artwork on the hammerhead caught Khalla's attention and she leaned forward to see better. On closer view, the dragons moved as they coiled all about each other. "Beautiful hammer," she said.

"Who're we going to be smashing with it?" Valaes asked.

"My lieutenant: Ciejek. The Circle has given me something I long craved and his time has come." Khalla pulled the hood of her cloak up over her face and they stepped off Daryx's manicured estate to the street. "What's your request?"

"When we go to Merakor, I'd like to stay close to Alex. I'm worried about her and this whole Lolth business. I realize I'll probably have to be her slave, but yes – I'd like to stay by her side." Valaes' tone of voice conveyed his concern for Alex.

Khalla nodded. "We were planning on keeping you two together anyway, but yes. I will see to it."

The East-West Major had sparse traffic. Ahead of them to the west, a wagon moved carefully. Behind them to the east, the road lay quiet and still. Valaes stepped back a pace and laughed. "I've always wondered about these Dar estates. From the streets, my father often told me not to judge them by what you can see. Who would have thought this one would be what it is?" He carefully avoided details that would point to Daryx as the owner.

Khalla nodded. "Let's look like a noble couple walking the streets together." Valaes offered her his arm and cracked a joke by saying, "So, you're an elf and I'm a human. In your long life, you've probably already dated a hundred guys just like me."

Playing the part, Khalla said, "Oh, that's not true. You're my first human. And, I'm not that old. I mean, I'm old enough but still."

"So, my love, how many have you been with? I assume elves if I'm the first human."

"Not that many, dear Valaes…"

"Wait, I'm twenty-three and I've dated five girls since I was sixteen years old. So, five in seven years, and you're one hundred. Woah, you've been with at least ninety boyfriends? Gah."

Khalla giggled. "Your math is funny and you presume elves would date like humans. We prefer to take our time. Ninety. I'm not a slut. Enough about me, tell me about Alex. A battle priest and another seems to be all the rage right now for stories. You trying to emulate Tembri?"

The priest put his head back and laughed. "To win the heart of Commander Ayden is a worthy precedent to aspire to. Did you know that Tembri was the second Augmentor? All this time, so much doctrine, and then along comes Tembri. Now, in my battle priest Augmentor classes, there are ten of us. Even we wonder why there are suddenly so many candidates, and not a single female candidate."

"Battle priest, you say, what does it mean? I know, like everyone, that Dar Ana is a Necromantic battle priestess so it's strange you're all men now. How are Augmentors different?" The day looked like it might rain and Khalla brushed her brown hair from her face. Even the hood did not keep her unruly hair from getting in her face.

Valaes said, "How far until we reach the target, and how much do you really want to know?"

She patted his bicep and was struck by the diameter of his armor. He truly was the classic strong cleric, just like Tembri. "About two hours, at this pace. And yes, I'd like to know. We're going to be in Merakor for some time together."

"Okay, but if you get bored, please say so. I can probably talk about this for days. So, since you know about Ana, you understand that she can harvest life energy from wounds she inflicts by prayer, right? Being an Augmentor is kind of like that in that it's a variation on the normal cleric or healer most people think of when it comes to the Temple. Where she can harvest and redirect life energy, an Augmentor can change the expression of that energy. For example, I had not decided what or where I would specialize until we were brought into this quest. My first Augmentor spell is a simple one that allows a priest to bridge bodies of water. Originally developed as a military spell, the Temple long ago figured out that it could be used as a weapon against water elemental-based creatures. Against them, it works very well."

Valaes eyed Khalla to see if she was bored yet. She smiled at him and said, "Still here. Still good."

His face split into a big grin. "I've always assumed that elves and magic, well... this is cool. Okay, so the first Augmentor lived a long time ago. He was burned to death as a heretic in Quattrain. Why? Because he was a man hearing Tiamat's voice. I'm glad we're past that; praise Kell! So, where was I? Yes, he wrote that with focus this spell could be used against living creatures. Khalla, he actually figured out how much water is in a human body. It's a lot. By weight, it's almost two-thirds. Elves are a bit less. Don't ask me how he figured this out. I don't know, but I assume it involved either volunteers or fresh corpses.

"So, Tembri experimented with it and figured out that the spell works in an expanding arc." Valaes used his hands to show her. "When water is divided, it's a function of faith. By focusing, I can shape this arc and make it specific enough to target something as small as a creature. But, being an Augmentor, why stop there? Water is just one element after all. So, Tembri figured out that this spell can also affect fire, air, and earth. So, when you ask what an Augmentor is I would hope that you would think of a 'more creative' priest. The truth is that if I specialize in it, really, only my study and imagination would put a boundary on it."

"And this Bridge Water prayer, this is one you've decided to specialize in?" She pointed to the canal. "Elementals drive this canal. What happens if you use it here?"

"Well, if I were a normal Tanian priest, it'd really hurt and upset the water elementals, because it's not a focused spell. I could dam up the canal though and then release it all at once without hurting the elementals. Or, I could create a pocket of air around a fish and asphyxiate it. You know, a monster fish. The more interesting application," he said stopping and catching Khalla to make an arc across her chest. "The application of removing all water from your heart or other vital organs, makes this spell an interesting and unexpected weapon. Everyone fighting Tania expects fire and dragons."

Khalla remembered seeing Tembri in Bloodstone and, before that, at various court functions. She had never realized he was an Augmentor. She knew he was special as a battle priest; everyone did. "How many spells can you do this with?"

"My testing suggests between four to six, same as Tembri if I get six. I will also be taking a healing spell, which I can use necromantically. It's strong enough to heal near death wounds. Tembri had that one too. His Augmentor ability was that he could throw it and then divide up the healing power of Tiamat. Most clerics waste their healing by either not healing enough or healing too much. There is no beyond-maximum-health threshold… though my instructor has been talking to Dar Ana about this. She has a theory she calls 'Extra Life.'" Valaes stopped because he realized Khalla was staring off into space. "Apologies, I lost you."

Khalla shook her head. "No, Valaes. It's Ciejek. He was my friend once. Some humans get corrupted. His was lust and wealth. All his pay goes to buying contracts on elven and human women to be enchanted. It's all contracted to end at a certain time." She pulled her hood back and turned her face into the wind. "He's had this coming for a long time."

Valaes remained silent. "I thought elves were immune to charm."

"In Morilon, among elves, there are ways to make it work." Khalla resumed walking. "Apparently, he wanted to do it to me, as a prank, or not. Who really knows? I was new here in Tania and did not know. He spent years apologizing."

Valaes swung his hammer over his shoulder and offered his arm to Khalla. "But, his apology is made hollow by the example he rubs in your face. A man like this must be truly insecure." His bright laugh made Khalla feel better. "The Book of Fire says that Takhissis set a fire in the heart of all men. But, we are not dragons. The challenge is to feed the fire without being consumed by it. We are not treasures to the dragons when burned all at once. My interpretation of the scripture. Well, to be honest, my recollection of my teacher's interpretation of that verse."

Valeas' good nature and mood helped Khalla feel better. The dread in her stomach and the wondering what the note meant, besides the obvious, gnawed at her. Since the incident, Ciejek had always been the first to meetings, the first to meet objectives, and the first to apologize. They had evolved an uneasy working relationship and she had even come to rely on him for certain jobs. She tried to calm her breathing and realized that the thought of confronting him was making her sweat.

Valaes suddenly stopped and caught her into a bear hug. "Though I don't really know you, you need to understand that Tiamat has great plans for your life. Be blessed, Khalla. Know that She knows you. We, the Goddess and I, we have you back."

His words broke apart Khalla's anxiety and flooded her chill hands and feet with warmth. Her thoughts resolved to crystal clarity. Same as before, she knew it was time for Ciejek's tenure in Perdition to come to an end. She had to be the 'K' referenced in the note. Daryx did not just come by that note nor would he invent such a thing as a test, not for such an enforcer like Ciejek.

Without saying anything, Daryx had told her that Ciejek was guilty of treason at the worst, betrayal at the best. She could hear his voice in her heart as surely as if he spoke to her, "Khalla, Perdition cannot be ruled by one terrified of her subordinates. Remove him."

"Thank you, Valaes. My gratitude to the Goddess is eternal. Maybe I should be more faithful?" She pushed back from his hug. "I needed that."

"You are consecrated to Her. Whether you are faithful or not, you are part of what makes Tania such a great treasure to the dragons. Take courage! Now, let us confront this Ciejek and see what we shall see."

Ciejek would have lived on the East-West Major if he had more money. Still, he lived in an upper class neighborhood close enough to the Dar estates to claim bragging rights. It was much nicer than Ash's manor, and certainly outclassed Khalla's home. He should not be able to afford it based on Perdition's pay.

A cast iron gate of black spear points ringed the manor. Manicured gardens and the tinkling sound of fountains could be seen and heard. The appearance from the street conjured such images in Khalla's mind. She could already see naked women taking their leisure. She blinked and realized there were none. Ciejek's stories and the reality would probably exist inside where the R'Dar neighbors would not take offense or grow suspicious.

They found the main gate and noted the two guardhouses to either side, one on the street and another just behind the gate. Guards stood at attention. They followed the couple but most likely were admiring Valaes' high end armor. To check, Valaes turned and waved. One of the guards came out and they began talking about armor. "The Temple gets all the best stuff," the guard complained but in a joking manner.

"Well, I won't argue the benefits of it. Of course, I don't get to sit in a nice house on a nice street and check out gorgeous women all day." He pulled Khalla to his side. "That's why I like to go walking with my own gorgeous lady!"

The two laughed and soon the other guards came out to pass the time with the gregarious priest. "So, anyone important live here?" Valaes asked. "Four guards, and you all look experienced. She must be powerful. New R'Dar?"

The guards chuckled. "Oh, I wish," one said. "The master of this home pays well and that's why we're here. He calls himself a collector of beauty. We're here to ensure his privacy. That's it."

Valaes went, "Hmmm, I see. So the gorgeous ladies are actually in there, huh? Maybe they need medical attention?"

Khalla punched Valaes and said, "You're going to need medical attention if you keep this up." The guards all burst into laughter. Khalla said, "You all seem to be enjoying yourselves. I see some ale back in the house. You want me to bring some out here?"

Before the guards could possibly say otherwise, Valaes exclaimed, "That's a great idea! Go grab us some. I'll reimburse you for it. We've been walking from the Temple and I'm parched!"

Khalla walked over and grabbed six cups. Powder fell unseen into four of the six and then she returned. A favorite of Perdition, the drug's name was Hazel. Hazel triggered a thoughtless fugue in its victims. Still conscious, they could take care of themselves. Later, they would not remember anything. If tired, the victim would fall asleep. From a passerby's perspective though, they would still be there guarding. It took effect quickly and Khalla said, "Well, you should get back to your posts. Here, we'll help you and then be on our way to the Fort."

They helped the four guards back to their respective posts and then entered the estate. Valaes closed the gate behind him and locked it. The guards said their thank-yous and then went back to street watching.

Khalla moved ahead of Valaes to the front door. She signaled in handsign to tell Valaes to enter the house and see if he could distract Ciejek. WILL POKE AROUND A BIT.

He nodded and opened the front door. Because of space limitations, Ciejek did not waste space on a foyer. The front door opened into a lavish parlor set about with plush silk cushions and seating areas. To either side of the door, nude female statues held out their hands and a hanger with a coat draped one. Elaborate paintings on all wall surfaces showed various sex acts prominently featuring females and a golden winged serpent. Valaes heard giggling behind a door to his right side and waved Khalla in. He barely saw her enter and move through the room to climb the stairs.

Valaes listened at the door and was pretty sure the giggling was from people making love. He walked around the room and found three more doors. One was a double door and unlocked. He opened it and stepped into what was the actual dining room. It had been converted to a dance area with a patio that looked out on the southern slopes of Dragon Mountain. Though still early in the evening, Valaes could see the monument lights climbing Ascension to Alerius' throne. It made him feel very much at peace to see it. Not sure why, he found himself fingering the symbol of Tiamat about his neck.

Khalla wanted time so he activated the Tiamat symbol on his hammer. Its golden light pushed back the encroaching darkness and he felt better. "Hello!" he called out. "Ciejek, it's me – Valaes. I got your invite." He walked back to the entry hall and heard the giggling had stopped. "Hello?" he called outl "Ciejek, it's me – Valaes."

Ciejek cracked the door open from the side room. He stood to the side of the door so that his nude body would be hidden. "Valaes? What are you doing here? I didn't send any invites."

Valaes let his eyes widen. "Oh, Ciejek. I'm so sorry. I thought you did! At the dinner the other day, you were talking about your place and said we could drop by. I found myself exhausted by training today and just wanted to get out. I found myself in this area so thought I'd stop by and take you up on the invitation." Valaes smiled. "Oh, no. You didn't mean it for real. I'm so stupid." He let his face fall.

Ciejek turned back to quiet the girls with him. Looking back, he said, "No no no. I was serious. I just didn't expect you to randomly show up. I mean, you didn't say anything. Look," Ciejek pushed a manicured hand off his neck. "I'm a bit busy but if you want to sit down, there's food set out and we'll join you for dinner in maybe an hour?" Someone said something sharp and Ciejek laughed. "Okay, in about two hours. Feel free to relax. Two hours, okay? Unless, naw – you're with Alex, right."

Valaes noted how dilated Ciejek's eyes were. "You okay, Ciejek? Are you using drugs?"

Laughter and giggles burst from the room behind the rogue and he winced. "That obvious, huh? Yeah, I've got a few in here. Why'd my guards let you in?" Ciejek's eyes focused a bit and became suspicious.

Valaes put his hand on Ciejek's and enacted a *charm* prayer. "You invited me remember? I'm going to sit here and eat some of this food. Because you invited me here. Go back to the girls. I'll still be here in two hours."

Ciejek grinned and said, "Thanks, Valaes. Your understanding means everything to me."

Upstairs, Khalla picked a door lock and entered what she hoped was Ciejek's room. It was not. It clearly belonged to one of the girls. Makeup, perfume, and a never-ending closet of sheer fabrics met her eyes. On a whim, she picked up an outfit and put it in a belt pouch. "Just in case," she whispered. Ash had always said to do what it took to blend in. The bed was decorated by a coiled serpent that rose up over the bed posts and looked down. The serpent motif seemed dominant. Khalla scratched her head. In his work life, Ciejek never mentioned serpents nor carried anything bearing such images. It had a religious undertone to it. It bothered Khalla that she did not recognize it. Maybe Valaes would?

The next room gave her some trouble but eventually the door lock popped and she swung the door open. It had to be Ciejek's room, or lair. Compared to the brothel décor of the rest of the home, Ciejek's room was normal. Mannequins held several suits of armor and gear from Perdition along with his preferred knives. A rack of vials and powders, meticulously labeled, hung above his desk. Khalla went to the desk and sat down, looking for traps, anything.

She heard Valaes call out and thanks to her elf hearing, she knew she had all the time she needed – two hours if she heard things right. Something bothered her though, and she found herself looking around the room with both normal vision and infravision. Nothing. A minute later, she found a small depression in the wood to the side of her right knee. When she pressed it, a locked drawer popped open. She held her breath, another cautionary teaching from Ash.

Her infravision showed a gas hiss forth from the drawer and then dissipate. She continued to hold her breath and looked into the drawer. It held Ciejek's favorite knives as well as his drug-blade. That knife could hold poison and release it by pulling a trigger on the hilt guard. It was empty, but again, just in case, Khalla filled it with fugue-inducing Hazel and placed it on her belt.

The darkness by the window continued to pull at her attention and she forced herself to ignore it and scan the room. The desk yielded another trap on a different drawer that turned out to contain nothing important except the contracts on the girls. Four elves, all young, all being paid to go under enchantment magic that would make them fawn on Ciejek and remember this as a long and happy vacation. It disgusted Khalla that there were people willing to throw their moral agency away like this. Clauses in each contract granted Ciejek ownership of any children though incentives were offered to the girls to prevent pregnancies.

* * *

Outside the window, the Dark Legion vampire cursed the fates. The idiot Ciejek had already overplayed his hand. Now, a powerful cleric and their best candidate for Marcello, whom they could not hurt, was about to find everything. *I must act fast*, the vampire thought. *Ciejek needs to die in a way that sends a message.*

The creature crawled, spider-like to Ciejek's window and looked in. The fool was distracted and engaged with three of the girls. At least the priest was not in the room. The sash to the window slid open as the vampire willed it to move.

The vampire almost killed Ciejek outright. *No, they'll interrogate him even if I kill him if it's too obvious. Still, it's worth a try.* Looking around, he saw only the girls and none of them would kill Ciejek.

A snake coiled in a cage caught the vampire's attention. The snake was one of Ciejek's favorite pets. The vampire unlatched the cage and prodded it to Ceijek. The girls, used to the snake, ignored it though one shuddered at the coldness of the vampire's unseen passing. Urging it on, the snake began to twist around Ciejek. He laughed and the girls moved about to let it. One complained though saying, "Not this game again."

Ciejek was so focused on his own pleasure that he was caught by surprise when the snake coiled around his neck and squeezed tightly enough that he could not talk. The safe word to release the trained snake was known to the girls. They yelled it, but the snake ignored them. It only sensed the vampire's desire that it squeeze and then relax. Keep him alive but unspeaking until that door opens. Then squeeze as hard as you can.

The girls, seeing just another of Ciejek's weird games, went back to what Ciejek always wanted out of these sessions. They could not do anything about the snake and Ciejek had taught them to not interrupt these planned events.

The vampire rooted around and found Ciejek's pants on the other side of the room. He slipped a vial of Orcus blood and a note into his pocket. The note read: *Varlessa, K's price is 1,000 gold for another vial. Let me know, C.*

With any luck, Dark Legion's involvement with Ciejek would never be known. The vampire returned to the girls. He could not plan on it though. Tania had a reputation for extracting information, even from the dead. The best outcome would be luck if they did not interrogate Ciejek. *Worst case*, the vampire realized, *I need to let Syand know Ciejek is compromised. It'll accelerate all of our plans. Idiot Geryon worshippers, even at their best they're still brain dead zombies.* For a moment, he looked in the thief's eyes and compelled the girls to ignore his words. "You're going to die, Ciejek. No eternal night for you, idiot. Khalla and Valaes are here. They'll learn about you you soon enough. Thank you for your service to Syand. She sends her regards but reminds you: you cannot serve Geryon and Kallis."

The vampire commanded the girls, "You're not going to remember anything until a priest of Tiamat enters the room. When either the priest or an elf named Khalla call to Ciejek, you're going to realize Ciejek is dead. He has a heart condition, remember?" Catching the attention of all three girls, the vampire expanded on his instructions, "You're all going to keep making love and you're going to remember it was like always. Nothing happened out of the ordinary except that Ciejek grew tired faster than normal and complained about numbness in his left arm." The vampire stroked the snake's head. "And the snake did what Ciejek trained it to do, squeeze Ciejek as tightly as it can."

Looking back at Ciejek, he continued, "You're going to die of a heart attack." He slowly opened a vial of liquid and poured drop after drop into Ciejek's mouth, deliberately letting it splash into his eyes, nose, and around his mouth. He laughed. "You've had this coming for a long time. Welcome to Dark Legion."

The vampire looked around, tempted to burn the entire house down. The priest looked potent, perhaps enough to destroy a vampire. Regretfully, he waved goodbye to Ciejek. The man's eyes were locked on him, probably begging. He was trying to breathe and failing. The girls continued as they were ordered and did not notice or care that Ciejek's skin tone was changing to an unhealthy pallor.

* * *

Khalla breathed more easily and could not say why. The oppressive darkness in the room had let go. She riffled through the desk and found all kinds of documents, most of which were side contracts Ciejek should have reported to her. She took them all. An envelope caught her attention and she flipped through its contents. They paper inside was copies but even so, was clearly old. The envelope was labeled 'Joviel.' She tucked it into her pouch. Next, she went to check the closets and bed. Her careful search at last yielded a secret closet near the bed. A small safe, set in concrete and magically locked, rested inside.

She rotated her shoulders and twisted her neck side to side before she began studying and investigating the runes. After five minutes, she popped her knuckles and removed a special tool that looked like a pen. Tania used enchanted runes as part of its daily life, and security applications flourished. But, with the proper tools, you could break the runes. To prevent this, most of the runes would trip a mechanical safety. Knowing Ciejek's fascination with drugs and poison, Khalla already knew it would be something like that.

The silvery pen had retractable sections. Khalla extended each section until it was as long as she was tall. Standing back, she carefully slid the tip towards the rune. A faint shock in the rod told her the mechanical trap had fired. Like at the desk, her infravision spotted a faint mist that quickly faded away. She held her breath and continued. When the razor tip encountered the rune, she pressed down and jabbed it forward. She did this a few times. When she retracted the tool, its tip had melted but the rune sat inactive.

Khalla slipped a light metal gauntlet onto her hand and reached in for the safe. It was heavy and she had to tug hard to retrieve it from the nook. The actual lock on the safe took her only a few seconds to defeat. Inside, she found three vials of red liquid. One vial was half empty. A small book held gibberish and she figured it must be a code of some kind. The writing, though, matched the cursive on the note given her by Daryx. The name Joviel appeared again. She pocketed these items and went to check on Valaes.

Valaes sat as far from the side door as possible. He held his ears in his hands and looked like he was trying to meditate. The lusty groans of the women were much louder in the hallway and Khalla realized Ciejek had enchanted his upstairs bedroom to be silent. She tossed a wadded up tangle of clothing at Valaes and he looked up. He had stuffed bread into his ears to help block the sounds. He looked relieved to see her. He pointed to the side door and rolled his eyes. Though he had comprehended handsign well, he was not fast and he emphasized: FORTY MINUTES.

Khalla nodded and signed back. PRACTICE HANDSIGN IF BORED. AM CHECKING OTHER ROOMS. WE WILL HANDLE HIM SOON.

Valaes struggled with the Drow sign language. GLAD NOT PALADIN ANYMORE, BUT STILL.

Khalla chuckled and turned to the other rooms. Room by room, she searched and quickly realized that Ciejek was living way above the means of a cell lieutenant. The women's rooms were full of expensive clothing and jewelry. *Maybe he inherited it*, she wondered. She started to feel bad for the women and then Ciejek. *What kind of a man would surround himself and fill his life this way?*

One of the side doors off the main floor and a ready-to-leave Valaes led down. "Just a bit more," she said softly. The sounds of love-making sounded almost painful behind the door. "That poor woman," she smirked.

Downstairs, she found a locked door. Khalla picked it and entered. The room felt evil to her and had a smell of body odor and sweat. Her infravision showed a human heat shape lying down along the opposite wall but nothing else. Unwrapping a light rune along her forearm, she saw a household shrine to a devil. Devil worship was rare in Tania as almost everyone worshipped Tiamat or Krentismar. This shrine was notably different from anything she had ever seen. Khalla looked around hoping there was not divine magic at play here. Khalla heard a groan from the human and turned to see.

Though smaller than the entry room, the back of the room contained a large table with wrist and ankle chains. One of Ciejek's women, at least she hoped it was one of his, lay bound and naked on the table. Candles had long since burned out. The woman's eyes were bound by silk. Perhaps sensing Khalla or having heard the door open, she whispered, "Master, is that you? Please, let me go. I have given all my pleasure to the god. I have nothing left."

Khalla looked at the table more closely and saw nothing. Except for a figurine of a winged half-man, half-snake wrought in gold, she saw nothing. She said, "The Master sent me, I'm new. This looks, um, interesting. Your pleasure has lasted how long, and how much longer must you serve the god?"

The girl whimpered and tried to rotate her hips, but the chains prevented it. Khalla saw she could easily free the girl by removing a simple cotter pin from each shackle. The girl licked her lips and tried to kiss up to to Khalla's voice. "Nine hours. I have twenty more to go." She sounded eager and yet depressed.

"Tell me the name of the god you serve," Khalla demanded.

"Geryon, the Bright Ecstasy. Oh please, I don't want to lay here in the dark anymore!" She thrashed her wrists and ankles in frustration. "Unbind me, please! I'll do anything. One day, it'll be you and I'll come free you early. I promise."

Khalla stood back and looked at the figurine. The snake idol looked beautiful and the artwork was highly refined. It was the same model as the serpent decorations throughout the house. In Perdition, she had only briefly studied Geryon. He ruled what was known as the Sixth Plane of Hell. His worshippers fixated on venom, drugs, and poison. It made sense that someone like Ciejek would worship a god like Geryon. Though Tania had no instructions for Geryon worshippers, like they did to kill Set worshippers on sight, she remembered that Perdition had presented Geryon's worshippers as dangerous. Khalla recalled something about addiction … still able to hear the girls' lovemaking upstairs, Khalla smirked. *This is exactly the kidn of god Ciejek would worship*, she realized.

Khalla said, "No. But, I'll be back to check on you. Which drug should I give you to help? I don't want to risk upsetting the master on my first day."

The girl pouted. "You can give me the white powder called 'The Glove.' It makes this worse but Ciejek will love you for it. If you're going to give me anything helpful, give me either Hazel or Open Lotus."

Khalla knew Hazel. It would help the girl lose track of time and perhaps sleep. "Open Lotus is a little strong for you and your remaining time. Tell me why you want it and I might let you have some."

The girl sighed. "Open Lotus will help me give more pleasure to the idol. It compels pleasure."

She looked around the room and found another cabinet full of powders and liquids. Ciejek had labeled everything clearly and she quickly found Open Lotus. It was a powder. "I could give you Open Lotus. How would you like to take it?" Khalla hoped the girl would describe how to take it.

The girl smiled and laughed. "Yes, give it to me. Now," she moaned. "You could join me with it. Since you're new, let me tell you, it's like nothing you've ever felt."

"No, joining you will also risk the master's displeasure." Khalla replied. "Open your mouth." Khalla sprinkled some into the girl's mouth.

The effects were almost instant. Khalla jumped back as the girl began breathing heavily and moaning. The sounds of her lust might give the girl upstairs a run for her money. "More!" the girl cried. "Give me more!" The tone of her voice became demanding and Perdition's caution regarding addiction struck Khalla again.

Checking the shelf, she found several containers of Open Lotus behind the initial powder. Hefting one, she guessed Ciejek had almost three pounds of it. Based on how little she sprinkled on the girl, Ciejek had a massive amount of it. *Where does this come from? I've never heard of anything like this, ever.* She decided to take it all. *I cannot risk unknown drugs on my streets. As Marcello, I'm going to improve Perdition's training.* Seeing the girl still lost in lust still, Khalla pondered on the fact that such a drug would debilitate her. *Maybe this is what Ciejek had tried to give me so many years ago.* She was drooling and thrashing in the restraints.

When she returned to the upstairs, she found it silent and Valaes looked relieved. SLEEPING, he Drowsigned and then gave up when he kept making mistakes. He whispered it instead. He pointed to the stairs, "More girls down there?" he rolled his eyes.

Khalla moved silently to the door and listened. She nodded and signed: THREE TO FOUR SLEEPERS. SHRINE TO G-E-R-Y-O-N DOWNSTAIRS."

Valaes eyed the stairway and looked unhappy about the news. NOW?, he signed back by pointing to the door and releasing a tight fist. His Drowsign was much faster with short ideas.

Khalla nodded and moved back. MAYBE THEY KNOW WE ARE HERE. KNOCK AND ENTER.

Valaes looked uncomfortable and said, "Do I have to?" He knocked on the door and called out. "Hey, it's Valaes. I just want to check that I can eat some food while waiting for you, Ciejek."

When no answer came, he opened the door and looked in. The room smelled like sex. Ciejek lay amidst a tangled sprawl of women, and a large snake. The smell of alcohol lingered in the air. Valaes almost left but Ciejek's skin color caught his attention. "Hello? You awake? Ciejek?" he called out and entered the room.

At Ciejek's name, the girl sleeping in the crook of her shoulder woke up and blinked at Valaes and then tried to wake her master. He did not move. The girl screamed. The other girls woke up and began to scream too. Ciejek was dead.

Valaes ran over and tapped Ciejek on the arm. Nothing. A second later, Valaes realized that Ciejek was truly dead.

"Khalla, you should come in here. Ciejek is dead." Valaes checked the girls. They all seemed okay, if so drunk they would not respond to him cogently. "I can revive them but I'm not sure Tiamat would want me helping a bunch of Geryon worshippers."

Khalla checked Ciejek, not because she doubted the cleric, but because she could not believe it. *I'm supposed to kill him.* She realized she felt robbed. "Can you send a message to Ryvane? Tell her to come to Ciejek's with a cleaner crew."

Cleanup took all night. The girls sobered up but could not remember any of the evening's events. One of the girls said, "It was a usual evening with him. He wanted lots of drugs and the snake, I guess. The only thing that was different was when the priest came. That guy," she said pointing to Valaes. "Ciejek never had company on nights like this."

Ryvane deciphered the notes quickly. It was a meeting schedule with an unknown contact at the Dockside warehouse area. No one in Khalla's cell could recall Ciejek having business there. "He probably went in disguise," Khalla decided and let it go.

Ryvane pointed to some of the cipher and said, "A lot of this about Perdition's master vault and someone named Joviel. Joviel is a Merakoran name for a Lyrion empress. She was mythology when Terest Nostram founded what became Merakor. I wonder why Ciejek would care about Joviel."

Khalla took the translated notes and said, "I'll ask Marcello to look into it."

They struggled to identify the three vials of liquid until Delton joined the investigation. He looked at it and said, "It's Orcus blood. No one here in Tania should have it. I thought we were the only ones that had any. Well, for a time 521 and Dark Legion had some. Still, to get it here this quickly seems planned."

Khalla's report to Daryx went to the Circle and within a day, a veteran fighter from Bloodstone was identified. In the fighting, he had found spilled blood from Orcus and filled a wineskin with it. He hoped it would crystalize into bloodstones. When it did not, he took it to Ciejek to fence. Consulting with Grant and the Soran Rogues' Guild, they decided that if Dark Legion had known Ciejek had Orcus blood, he would have been targeted by them long ago. Yet, when the clerics prayed to Tiamat and augured the forces behind it all, the answers came back: *Vampires, not Geryon. Beware Geryon, but he is not your immediate enemy. Asmodei watches.*

On the third day, Khalla formally asked the Temple to resurrect Ciejek 'for interrogation.' R'Dar Alex, Valaes, and the others did not think it would be approved. It was not, even with offered payment.

When RiVule became aware of the investigation, he offered to do it. "My people, we have ways to get people to talk. If I do this, it'd be best that I am left alone. Gruustir's ways are not your ways."

"Will I be able to speak with him?" Khalla asked.

RiVule replied in Orcish. "I don't care whether you do or do not. However, interrogation is more effective if I'm left alone. My methods are exquisitely painful. That should be enough to assuage your sense of vengeance?"

RiVule and Taisha left with the body. An hour later, they heard Ciejek begin to scream. Four hours later, RiVule and Taisha came out. They looked clean and fresh. Khalla entered the room and found blood splattered about the walls. It looked like Ciejek had been butchered but kept just barely alive. The sight nearly made Khalla gag. The smell in the room… RiVule said, over his shoulder, "Enough of him is left for you, in case you do not trust my methods."

Khalla walked over to where Ciejek's rib cage lay splayed open and his heard beat under a mechanism that dripped oil onto the heart. Ciejek's eyes looked mad. She could not stand it and pierced Ciejek's heart with her sword. "This is more mercy than you deserve."

RiVule pulled Khalla out of the room to where Ash and Daryx had been summoned and waited. He addressed them all. "Ciejek was a Dark Legion spy. He came to spy for them. They wanted him to find out who Perdition's leader, this Marcello you all refer to, is." RiVule smacked the door behind him where the dead body lay. "He failed but thought he could cultivate Khalla as the next Marcello. He felt she was safe to name because, as an elf, she would logically outlive the humans and eventually become Marcello." RiVule bowed to her. "You were targeted. Ciejek met weekly with a handler, a vampire. They were going to make him into a vampire too. They wanted Marcello because of someone named Joviel."

Ash asked, "Not that I am doubting your methods, but are you confident Dark Legion does not know who Marcello is?"

RiVule eyed him for a long moment and then Taisha interjected. "I saw the interrogation. There is no chance Ciejek is lying about any of this. He begged to tell RiVule everything."

RiVule waited for a moment. "Recently, since about seven weeks ago, they became interested in the Jade God's blood. Ciejek said they were mad for it and offered him wealth beyond his imagination if he could get them more. I think it's time you tell us the truth about Orcus." RiVule turned to face Daryx squarely. "Now."

Daryx laughed and hopped down to see the group. "The truth is that any god's body would be valuable. It has the powers that Grant has already shared with us. The addiction for vampires was new and, yes, we have tested and confirmed it. It is, sadly, not a lethal withdrawal, otherwise Syand would solve herself. Withdrawal enrages vampires and then they fade into a stupor which enrages them more. We're not sure how long as our subject has yet to recover. Maybe they never do. That would be fortunate for Sora."

"And Joviel?" Khalla asked.

Daryx smiled. "A matter for Marcello and The Circle to discuss. Not for here. What Ryvane told you is true. Joviel was a Lyrion empress predating Merakor. Maybe it was a hobby?"

Khalla kept her face still and let Daryx change the topic. She noted that Ash too abided by this.

Daryx said, "This is all well timed. It is likely that Dark Legion will come to Tania. As such, I have leaked word to Sora that Tania is stockpiling the Jade God's blood and other parts in Perdition. It will stay there until such time as we move it to the god emperor's mountain. Some is to be sent overseas with the Taurans, on the next world galleon as tribute to their participation in slaying the Jade God. Legion is probably already here in Tania. That they have been meeting with Ciejek is alarming to the empire. More will come. As a test of this group's ability to work and fight together, you are to prepare Perdition for attack. Draw the vampires there so that Innocents are not molested. If you succeed, we will accelerate departure to Merakor. If you fail, the Temple will ensure no vampires in the empire escape."

RiVule waited until Daryx was done. "There's another thing," he said. "Syand is not the leader. Some vampire named Kallis is. But, Ciejek thought there was another behind that one. Ciejek thought she or he might be a hell lord. He never learned."

Daryx said, "We will investigate both names. You have done very well, Lord Inquisitor."

"Lord Inquisitor. I like that," RiVule bowed.

\* \* \*

RiVule checked a list of material and paced back and forth in the large room. Perdition suited him. The dark stone, the antique veneer that suggested dust and age on the tapestry-draped walls reminded him of home. Taisha held a similar list. Between them, a pile of green bones had been laid out with clear labels. RiVule felt both irritated and impressed by the meticulous nature of everything here. "Look at this," he said. He bent over and picked up a bone fragment the size of his hand. The verdant green hue sparkled in the torch light, but to his Orc eyes, it glowed with power.

Taisha walked over and said, "It looks like another bone." She gestured to the giant pile in the center of the room.

RiVule chortled. "These Tanians, everything in its place. Like that pile of bones, this one is labeled. Look at this." He presented a small piece of parchment tied to the bone. It read: 2#, PERFECT if refined to cabochon no larger than 2 fingers. Dust everything else.

Taisha put her hands on her hips. "So, they label everything."

RiVule touched her with the bone. "You cannot speak unless I say 'Gruustir.'"

Taisha eyed him and began to say something. Though her mouth moved, she could not make a sound. "Apparently, you have not been paying attention to the notes. The bone, when touched with a command, actualizes the command. Go ahead, try and say something."

She tried but could not. With some effort, she handsigned: I DO NOT READ WELL.

RiVule nodded. "The Horde does not educate well. We will change this. The Jade God's body is powerful. I knew it would be. Tania knew it would be. Until we had this, they just did not know. It's quite literal, based on their studies. Try singing," he ordered while tapping her with the bone again.

Taisha did so and easily, her voice sang out, feminine but gruff. She began to laugh and fell silent again. WEIRD.

"Your Drow signing is getting better. Well done. I'd like you to do better than Valaes. That one is annoying. So smug." RiVule touched her again and said, "You are released from all compulsions."

"Thank you," she said, bowing. "Maybe I should pay more attention. The guarding of this, anticipating attack..."

"We're going to let them take some," RiVule spoke quietly, in Orc. "Their first foray must convince them to come full force."

Taisha nodded. "How long?" she wondered.

"A few more hours. The dark elf says they'll be here just before sunrise."

The rest of the night passed with restless pacing. When RiVule got word that Perdition had been breached, Taisha giggled. "It's about time," she said, drawing her sword. Playing the role of a vigilant paladin, she walked the perimeter, being careful to leave gaps.

RiVule stayed by the bones. Each bone had a small carving in it that had been recorded. It would allow them to scry the bone no matter where taken. An hour later, with the eastern sky lightening, Taisha stretched and said, "This long night has been dull. I'm hungry."

RiVule barked back, "I hunger too. How much?"

"Three shanks of meat should be enough after a dull shift like this," she answered.

They both saw a shadow move behind Taisha. Playing her part, she drew her sword and probed the shadows. "Did you see something?" RiVule asked.

"No, just shadows. But still." She ignited her sword with Gruustir's burning fury and pressed forward. RiVule came over to check with her.

Behind them, a vampire rose up from the bone pile. Stupid Orcs, he thought. The bones vibrated beneath his hands. Syand had said they would though they barely had any of the fragments after Grant's raid on 521. He sniffed and began looking around. A larger bone plate, too heavy to lift without drawing attention, rested on a small crate. Eyeing it, the vampire sniffed again and detected blood.

Not just any blood, it realized, and carefully ripped the side of the crate open. The two Orcs seemed oblivious to him. The vampire eyed them and felt confident his two friends could deal with them if needed.

A small vial of dark green, nearly black blood met his gaze. He had not had any but knew its effect and knew Syand wanted it more than anything in the world. He pulled the panel out and pocketed several of the vials. The panel fit into a sliding rack and had at least fifty of the small containers and it looked like the crate might hold another three sliding panels. Syand would reward him above all the others in the coven.

He heard steel ring out as the female fighter far away from him yelled, "I see you, thief! Stand and fight!"

A whooshing of flame and heat wash even this far away suggested it was time to leave. As he stood up and looked for good hiding places, he noted several more crates. He had not seen them because of the lighting, but now that he knew what to look for... he paused in awe. The upper galley around this area was full of crates. Tania had harvested tens of thousands of vials of the Jade God's blood. The vampire had to still his heart. *Syand will make me a king!*

He watched the combat and dashed to the side. A moment later, the other two hissed at Taisha and RiVule, "We're not done with you yet!" The cliché threat delivered, they retreated after their brother.

Taisha roared and went running after them, pretending to be more tired than she actually felt. Once they were gone, she whirled back on RiVule and roared, "That whetted my appetite! I will not play pretend again!"

RiVule grinned and summoned his mace. They eyed each other and then clashed in proper combat as the sun finally peaked above the eastern Shield Mountains.

# Chapter 17 – The Chase

"It wouldn't be natural if we didn't chase them," Ash said. He ran, jumping from roof top to roof top.

Khalla kept pace on the other side of the street. The shadows in the alleys below allowed the vampires to move preternaturally fast. It had surprised them both that they ran to the docks. Khalla leapt over a two-lane road and rolled to her feet on the other side. Ash thudded on his landing and cursed the lighter, stronger elves. "You need to practice your skills more," Khalla chided him. "Or, maybe you're too old?"

Ash laughed and increased his effort. He had never beaten Khalla in a race. As they neared the warehouse area, it became clear that the vampires were moving towards a dock held by a Soran merchant concern. Knowing the destination, they slowed down and let the vampires pull ahead. The two undead made a quick dash across the street where a cloud shadowed the street. Their brief exposure to the sun left a burning trail of smoke and embers and then they were inside the warehouse.

Ash and Khalla crouched down and eyed the area. This early in the morning, no one was about in this run down area. Ash said, "That warehouse is owned by a group calling themselves Cormack Dragonson. They bring things into Tania overland and then place them with the Taurans. It's been a good business for them. I wonder if they know about Dark Legion?"

"How do you know the name of the business?" Khalla asked. "That seems such a trivial thing to know."

"Well, I didn't seek out to remember it. It just sticks with me. A few years ago, you might remember, a Pha Rannic Order came through wanting voyage across the seas. I was asked to shadow them by The Circle." Ash sat down and began recovering his breath. "It was the most boring week of my life. They'd wake up, pray, march around, pray, window shop, pray... who is like that? And, it wasn't just to make sure everyone in Tania saw them. That's what I thought at first, but then it became clear that that's just how they were." Ash shook his head. "Remembering it, I'm getting bored again. Thankfully, something more important came up and I assigned Ryvane's cell to watch them."

"Does Tania watch all foreigners?" Khalla wondered. "I guess we do."

"We do. The road sentries use a hand sign for any possible targets. The Temple does a quick screen. If more is warranted, they contact Perdition. It's the primary role of Ryvane's cell. Dockside is so much her thing and, because of the Taurans, they get a lot of interesting groups coming through." He hopped up and scooted over by Khalla. The sun had now risen high enough that they no longer felt the morning chill. "Before Halgrim retired, he had a contract to watch the Mage's Guild and Bazaar. Operating a cell there is too hard. We contract it out to almost-candidates who did not pass Perdition's requirements or, like Halgrim, are friendly to us."

With the sun rising higher and higher in the sky, Ash took Khalla's hand and kissed her fingers. "It's been a rough time. We're both doing things that don't really come naturally to us, but I miss you. You're going to be great as the next Marcello."

"Speaking of which," Khalla said. "Did Daryx ever explain about Joviel?"

"He didn't have to. He knows that I know and will tell you. Joviel was an eldar human. She because the first vampire, maybe the very first. As an eldar and as a vampire, the god emperor thinks she may have been allied with the Blind Dragons."

"Oh," Khalla said and waited for Ash to continue. When he did not, she poked him. "There's more, right? There has to be."

"I suppose. It's not pleasant though. She was dismembered by ancient heroes. They could not kill her. They tried, for centuries. Apparently when you're a good hero and dedicate your life to killing someone that won't' die, eventually murder kills whatever was good in you. The so-called heroes all became vampires and death knights serving Joviel forever. Supposedly, all vampires stem from Joviel. The Three Vampire Generals wanted to find her too. They called her 'The Root.' If you look at Bomoki's writings, he wanted to find her too. Every case of vampires resisting the Jade God is linked to Joviel and a cult of Asmodei."

"So, maybe Dark Legion wants her to become stronger as vampires?" Khalla speculated.

"No, they want her eye. It's in Perdition's master vault. A vampire, with her eye, would become Joviel again." Ash sighed. "I bet you thought being Marcello would be easy. There's more."

"Tell me," Khalla whispered. She felt cold all of a sudden.

"Once you see the eye, you know she can see you. She talks to me sometimes. Offers me rewards to set her free. The whole Bomoki thing with Farant... they were probably looking for Joviel. Imagine someone like the god emperor, Dar Ana, or Syliri, but as a vampire that wants to kill everyone and rule Tehra. That's Joviel. We can't kill her. We can just contain her. That's why there are so many fake master vaults and Perdition is set up the way it is."

Khalla whipped her hair to the side and grinned at him. "This is too dark to discuss with vampires across the street. Let's talk about something else."

Ash smiled brightly. "That's a great idea. And I have just the topic: I want your answer about my past. You know me. I don't like these things hanging between us." Ash kissed her hand again and flashed his charmingmost smile at her.

"You don't know my answer, really? My actions since should tell you the answer." Khalla withdrew her hand and turned around to lean back against the roof edge. The warehouse would not be going anywhere and the vampires inside would either reveal themselves or not. Regardless, as the sun rose higher, the vampires would grow more and more sluggish.

Ash groaned. "We haven't been together since all that happened. Your actions tell me that you are putting distance between us." He rolled over and grabbed her waist tightly. "When everything about us wants no distance."

Khalla patted his head and made sure he felt it as an act of condescension. "Ash, you lied to me for all of our relationship. You knew I wanted to know and, even if I believed some compulsion prevented you, I thought we were closer than that. You should have trusted me. That you did not?" she suggested an answer to her own question. "It tells me that we are not as close as you want to pretend when everything is fine in Ash's life. There's a lot going on right now. I understand the whole Kaia thing, I really do. But, there's part of me that says if you really loved me, you would have found ways to give me hints, to tell me, to show me you cared but could not. While I'm impressed that Daryx had to threaten your death to not intervene, it shows the compulsion is not as powerful as you seem to have thought it was."

Ash bowed his head and with defeat in his voice said, "It almost killed me, Khalla. By the geas, by Daryx, you're right – I should have found a way to test it in a non-suicidal way. But, consider this from my perspective. You're Marcello. You're young and the world is moving your way. Then, one day, a beautiful young lady elf shows up, who will outlive you. She outclasses you in every way: speed, dexterity, passion, intelligence. She's the total package and you fall in love with her. Let's pretend there was no geas and I had just said, 'Oh, I was born with a birth defect. I'm blind in my left eye and my left arm is a stump.' How would that have gone?"

"That's not fair, Ash." Khalla curled her finger though her hair.

"When I see you do these human things, I sometimes forget you're an Elf, Khalla. Even Daryx has pointed out how un-Elf like you are sometimes."

"I am young, but you and others keep reminding me of this. Sure. I'm young, but I was in love with you too, you know. I told you everything. Worse, you knew I wanted into that room. You're clever. I'm sure you could have dropped hints about Kaia, geas compulsions, and secret rooms. I'd have figured it out." Khalla kissed Ash's head and squeezed his hands back. "To be honest, I'd think that you would be more interested in Grant and Delton's team. A turf war in Sora could impact us. This is too heavy for me right now, Ash."

He nodded and took a deep breath. "It is impacting us," Ash explained. "My last report to The Circle showed that our trade, even through Haven, was getting choked up. Tanian goods to them move just fine. It's the flow of goods from Sora to us. The Circle is concerned, not enough that they wanted us to do anything but enough that they want it monitored and reported on."

Khalla shoved him off her. Though he was stronger, she wriggled free and rolled back from him. "See? This is what I mean. You hand over Perdition to me and then you keep all this stuff to yourself. It's not fair to me, Ash. You've done this the entire time I've known you. I have yet to get an apology for the Dar Shara forgery. That could have been really bad. You dump Perdition on me without even asking if I want it, and then continue as Marcello for all these months. I can't do this anymore."

Ash watched her closely, hoping to see a break in her demeanor but when he saw only seriousness and frustration, he sighed and sat back. "Khalla, as a cell leader, you are in line for Marcello's spot. Being a cell leader is a test for this. You know this. So, it wasn't dumped on you, but even if it was, as your mentor, your friend, and hopefully your husband, I would expect you to be able to pick it up and continue Perdition's work."

"What did you say?" Khalla shot back at him with unnerving intensity.

"Continue Perdition's work?" Ash replied carefully.

"No, before that," Khalla pressed.

"Cell leaders are in line for Marcello's role?" Khalla tackled him and put her knife to his throat. Though intense, Ash could tell she knew he was playing with her. "The part about being your mentor?"

She jerked her knife against his throat. "One more chance. Don't screw this up, Ash."

Ash whirled his fingers and something gleamed in his hand. Khalla pounced on it and tore it free. A small platinum disc showing the dragon goddess Tiamat, gleamed on a filigree chain. It was a marriage token. "Khalla, you have been by my side for eight years. My life was smoothed by your presence," he said in Elvish. "I love you. I want you forever. Will you marry me?"

Khalla held the disc and looked at it from both sides. "I want to," she whispered.

"Then put it on. Say 'yes.' Marcello cannot be conflicted. By marrying me, you can be Marcello and I'll still be here for you. There are other advantages besides my energetic love, and our shared interests in Perdition." Ash backed off a bit. "I want you in my life. I always have. I'm sorry I struggle with some of these things."

Khalla stroked the circle of the medallion's edges. A rune on the back would ignite at her touch and just like that, they would be married. "Ash, Perdition is mine. You retired, right? For real?"

"Of course. My announcement at Sai R'Dar's estate was real. Except for the tail end of Bloodstone, Daryx would have made it official months ago." Ash put his hand around Khalla's where she held the medallion. "Khalla, will you join me? As your husband, I would do everything in my power to make up for these wrongs, and to give you new ones to be angry at me for."

"You promise?" she asked. When Ash nodded, she touched the rune. It felt warm to her touch and she felt Ash's heartbeat through it. "We are joined."

Ash embraced her and they held each other for a long moment. Khalla cleared her throat. "As exciting as this is, I never thought you would do this overlooking a vampire warehouse."

"Only the best for you, baby. What's next, Marcello?"

Khalla nodded. "I'm going to appoint you to a new cell. With Ciejek gone, we'll reorganize them in Marcello's name. You will head the Mercy Court Cell. You will continue as Marcello's lieutenant since everyone thinks you're either Marcello or his lieutenant anyway." They kissed and Khalla put her hand on Ash's chest and felt his heart beating against the rune on her finger and his chest. "I'm not going to cry," she stated. "First, I'm not going to cry because you are obviously doing this because you're worried about my answer. And I'm very mad." She took a deep breath. "Second, because there's a warehouse full of vampires down below us. You owe me a proper proposal." She poked his chest hard enough he winced. "In Morilon. My parents need to see that you are going to honor my elven heritage. Just because I'm converted to Tiamat does not mean I'm converted to human."

Ash kissed her and promised he would. "It will be a proper Elven request for betrothal," he said in flawless Elvish. "Your parents will love me." He twisted his Elvish into a nearly perfect dialectal form of High Elven.

Khalla grinned. "Then, let's go see what has become of the vampires. I've missed you but I can't let my first act as Marcello be to let Daryx's elaborate trap fall apart."

A minute later, two shadows slinked into the warehouse. It was empty. The vast space showed no recent activity. The wet smell of wood and sloshing of water underneath its superstructure made it seem bigger than it was. The high ceiling flew over their heads and reminded Ash of his underground adventure with Malcor in Bloodstone. "Not nearly as dark as Bloodstone," he signed to Khalla. She nodded.

They moved apart and began looking for any signs of where the vampires might have gone. "Underground or underwater?" Khalla signed after ten minutes of searching revealed nothing at all of interest.

"Underwater," Ash signed. "Older vampires. More experienced. New ones would never go underwater."

The warehouse had either flooded or was built into the water to smooth loading and unloading operations. The state of the roof suggested it should be in full operation. Ash did not like it. Though it pleased him to see Khalla taking it all with appropriate seriousness, he remembered other times when situations like this caught him off guard. It should be trapped if only Dark Legion vampires lived here.

By the edge of the water, Khalla waved him over. One of the vampires had mashed some algae clinging to life where cracks in the roof allowed just enough light to stream through. She pointed to scald marks in the algae where the sunlight could have burned its hand. The pain of sunburn or something else had made the vampire claw the wood. Khalla signed, WE NEED TO GO IN WATER. I CAN HOLD BREATH FOR TWO MINUTES. YOU?

Ash nodded and then after a moment, he removed his entire belt and offered it to her. He signed back. DIFFERENT IDEA. He pointed to the first pouch: DARTS AND THROWING KNIVES. NEXT IS POISON AND VENOMS. THE OTHER SIDE POUCH HAS ANTIPOISONS AND HEALING. THIS IS MARCELLO'S GEAR. DARYX ORDERED ME TO GIVE IT TO YOU BUT I LOVE HAVING IT SO MUCH. IT'S YOURS NOW. WOW, I'M FEELING SENTIMENTAL. HURRY PUT IT ON BEFORE I START CRYING.

He helped her fasten it on. REACH INTO ANY POUCH AND THINK ABOUT WHAT YOU WANT. AS MARCELLO, YOU HAVE ACCESS TO THE CIRCLE'S ARMORIES. IN OTHER WORDS, YOU HAVE INFINITE RESOURCES THROUGH THESE POUCHES. FOR NOW, JUST THINK ABOUT WATER BREATHING.

Khalla put her hand into the potion pouch and did so. Within three heartbeats, she felt a glass container tap against her fingertips. She retrieved another one. "I'm going to like this Marcello belt," she signed back.

They both tossed the small amount of slimy liquid down their throats and then slipped quietly into the water. Ooze coated the surface and they were grateful to duck under its sloshing flow. Enough light streamed in that they could see generally through the haze. The water reached down ten paces but just two paces down, a corridor opened up back under the main warehouse floor. Khalla pointed and they carefully entered. With no traps yet, they felt increasingly on edge.

Swimming in a few paces, Ash noticed a crisscrossed mesh of nearly invisible wires ahead of them. He almost signaled to Khalla but decided to see what the new Marcello could do. She rewarded his trust when she stopped just before the wires and signed back to him. I SEE HEAT SHAPES AHEAD, FROM GEAR NOT BODIES. THERE ARE SEVEN CLUSTERS OF HEAT. MAYBE SEVEN VAMPIRES?

Ash nodded and signed. FIGHTING VAMPIRES UNDERWATER IS BAD.

Khalla studied the wires and pointed to one. AM GOING TO TRAP THE TUNNEL.

Ash smiled broadly. Khalla retrieved five small fire gems from her own gear. Each thief carried a few. As a lieutenant and because of Ash, Khalla had much more powerful ones than the others. She carefully set these into the muck around the trap wires so that the reset one would vibrate along the detonation rune on each gem. At her touch, the runes glowed softly and then went dark again. Just one would be enough to collapse the warehouse and detonate the others. All five, if they detonated at the same time, would immolate the warehouse and probably flash boil the water the vampires in this enclosed space.

Khalla set the five and then placed another fire gem in the mud where a vampire might stand to reach for the reset wire. As they retreated, she placed the others so that vampires fleeing the underwater hole would set them off. They quietly resurfaced and were just about to dry off when they heard voices outside on the street. They retreated to the shadows, careful to stay on the algae to hide their dripping wet clothes.

Paelo and Viri entered the warehouse talking loudly about the great spring weather. They had clearly been here before and they carefully cased the interior as a precautionary measure. One of them spotted the wet edge of the algae and whistled the other over. They talked in quiet tones but from reading their lips, Khalla could tell they were speculating about whether one of the vampires had come out recently. Neither knew. They resumed their check. Even when Paelo was just a pace away from Khalla, they found nothing.

Viri whistled loudly. From outside, two other men came in. They carried a long crate, which they put down just as soon as Paelo closed the outside door. "Whew, this one is heavy."

The other nodded. "Extra pay. This should have been on a wagon."

"Yes," the first demanded. "Extra pay."

Viri passed them a small pouch, which both crowded around to look into. "More. Extra pay. Heavy load. Extra." From inside the crate, a faint pounding thudded and a child's voice cried out for help. The porter smacked it hard. "Shut up!" Khalla's fingers dug into Ash's hand at the sound.

Viri and Paelo growled at them. "You're lucky to get anything. You want more easy jobs, you'll take what is there and leave. Now, go."

The two porters grumbled and left. Viri followed them and signaled when they were gone. Paelo ripped the lid off the crate. Khalla gagged when she saw what was inside. Ash even seemed to deflate and his hands began dancing in handsign. "You're Marcello now, Khalla. You were never an Innocent, but you certainly cannot stand by and let those two children be fed to vampires."

Khalla nodded grimly. Ash continued. "You have a lot of latitude. You could contact Daryx and ask for help. You could summon the other cells. However, regardless of what you do, you must balance the safety of the children against Daryx's trap. A Marcello should be smart enough to balance the need for the trap to work and save the lives of the Innocents. I went wrong on this early in my own tenure. It took until the Jade God's fall to earn the Circle's trust back. I'll tell you about it later, but for now – you cannot let Innocents die. Tania will not stand for a member of the Circle who would not sacrifice themselves to save Innocents. Sure, they trusted me as a thief, but they never let me join the Circle as a formal member. You need to be better than I was."

Khalla watched the vampires lift the children out of the crate. Both looked terrified and had the raisin-look of children who had cried all their tears, were hungry, thirsty, and scared. No doubt they would cry more if they could. It broke her heart to see them looking side to side for help, for anything. Viri knelt down before one and said, "I'm sure you're frightened, but look around. There's nothing here to be that scared of, but if you aren't quiet, we'll give you reason to scream. So, shut up!"

The little girl pointed to Viri and said, "You are scary." She looked six and Khalla instantly appreciated her Tanian spunk.

*Don't worry, little one*, Khalla thought. *I am your angel.*

Viri smirked and condescendingly said, "You don't need to fear me. The monsters in the water are what you should be thinking about. They have pointy teeth and white skin. Rahhh!" he screamed in her face. The little girl fell back, still defiant but now eyeing the water with concern.

Khalla sensed Ash's skin flare hot with sweat as he resisted charging out. The other girl leaned into the spunky one and buried her face. That one stood only to the other's shoulder and could not have been older than four. At Viri's words, she wet herself. The older child stroked her hair and tried to comfort her... and Khalla felt something awaken in her mind. Like the sun bursting out from behind dark clouds, she realized that this small girl was special and had to be saved. Feeling it, her bones ignited with warmth and she imagined her body burning. Ash kissed her hand and whispered, "Hail, Marcello. I stand ready to fight for Perdition. How may I serve Takhissis' retribution?"

Khalla's mind danced, faster than ever before. She had felt chills during Tiamat worship services, and when blessed by a priestess. The feeling burning her bones now was like those times but much amplified. "We need to free the kids, kill those two, and leave no sign that the vampires are compromised. For now, we're going to attack and kill those two. On my mark." Ash nodded. She felt him crouch down and go still while tensing his muscles at the same time. An ancient relaxation technique going back to the early empire, it seemed counter-intuitive, but worked well when pouncing from a crouched position.

They watched the two vampire brutes for a few minutes while they made the girls wash and put fresh clothes on. They enticed them with food. It broke Khalla's heart to see the older one refuse to cooperate, even when they beat her. Only when they threatened the younger one – *are they sisters?*, Khalla wondered – did the older cooperate.

After some more scrubbing and cleaning, Viri seemed satisfied and pinched their cheeks. "Now you look cute and ready for a feast. You're the important guests of honor, you know."

The older girl remained defiant. "My mommy is going to find you."

Paelo laughed. "Sure she will, kid. You're tough. I'll give you that, but your mommy isn't coming because she's dead."

"No, she's not! My mommy is a priestess! You're going to burn!"

Paelo backhanded her. "She's dead because we killed her. Now, shut up and eat!"

Khalla saw the child's will break and when the girl burst into tears, Khalla signaled to Ash. Khalla and Ash swept out from the shadows like angels of death. Silent blades moved through the air. Paelo felt his heart pin and quiver on an enchanted blade. It hurt and he spun to see a rogue tumble backwards from the attack. The blade remained in his heart. Viri heard Paelo grunt and noted blood from his friend's tunic. Then stabbing pain and the grinding of bone made Viri stumble back as his spine seemed to come afire.

Khalla's sword stabbed in and then cut down Viri's spine as she set her whole weight into the strike and held on. Ash would toy with his enemy but Khalla just wanted the vampires dead as quickly and quietly as possible. Khalla latched onto her targets' backs and refused to let go.

The blade in her other hand rose and fell in a staccato burst of stabbing attacks into Viri's kidney. To Khalla, it seemed she rode the dying human, like a wild horse, for minutes. In reality, her leap carried her onto his back and then dropped him to the ground. Her knives pierced him six times before he hit the ground, already dead. Pulling free, she decapitated the undead and kicked the head to the side.

Ash leapt back and sheathed his short sword with a flair, as he bowed to the two girls. "Congratulations, lovely ladies. Marcello has come to save you." He pointed to Khalla, who looked up into the older girl's eyes. The sunken and terrified eyes glimmered with hope.

"Hi, I'm Marcello. Your mommy sent us to save you. How about we leave this place and go find her?" Inwardly, Khalla groaned. Her plan would only work if she stayed behind. "What's your name?"

"I'm Elsa. That's Winnie. Isn't Marcello a boy's name?" Elsa asked. "Are you really angels?"

Khalla put her fingers to her lips and said, "Shhh. It's my secret. You're very brave, Elsa. The Dragon Goddess is so proud of you. Today, I am honored to be your angel. The dragons know and love you both." She touched Elsa and Winnie's noses and smiled. "These bad men will never hurt you again. Where do you live?"

Elsa thought for a moment and then said, "Near the docks. The street is, umm, the number '5,' maybe. If I see it, I can tell for sure."

Khalla held her arms open and moved forward off Viri's dead body. "You both look like you need a hug. My husband is going to take good care of you. Ash, this is Elsa and Winnie. Will you take them home?"

Ash's fingers danced. "Are you sure? I'll be gone for hours." Ash beamed at the two girls. "It would be my honor, as a knight and your personal angel today, to escort two such brave girls home. Goodbye, my love." He blew Khalla an exaggerated kiss, being careful to keep the children's attention away from the dead bodies.

Khalla worried that Winnie would not let her go. The hug started tentatively and then became fiercely strong. "It's going to be okay," Khalla said. You wouldn't want to let my shining knight wait, do you? Your mommy is waiting for you."

Khalla picked them both up and gave them a reassuring hug. Ash came over to take the smaller one. "Ash, with all due haste, return to me, my love. Send word for Pol Nir to meet me here. Now, run!"

Ash had the six-year-old hold onto his back and cradled the younger one. He bowed to Khalla, and began to run. Perdition favored the fleet of foot and Ash sprinted for Dockside. The sunshine and wind in their faces lifted the spirits of the children who both yelled for him to run faster. More on a whim, Ash activated the magic in his boots and really began to stride. On the way, he found a beggar and conveyed word for Pol Nir to join Khalla at the warehouse. He prayed that he would be fast enough and Khalla would survive. Seven vampires to one Khalla, not odds he liked. He felt her heartbeat from the medallion against the one he wore around his own neck. It beat a steady counter rhythm to his own racing pulse.

Khalla looked at the bodies and the blood. Without a cleaning crew, she could not hide the fact that they were dead. Looking at the sun through the roof's broken slats, she figured she had at least another two hours before shadows from the western buildings would cast this location in afternoon dark. The girls were clearly intended as food.

She made a mental note to berate Ryvane if children had gone missing from Dockside before these two and Calvin mishandled it. She had always known the Law of the Innocents was a serious matter. But, she had never felt it as white hot fury in her core like this. "I get why Takhissis is the goddess presiding over The Circle. This must be what the dragons feel when hoarding treasure." An image of Elsa and Winnie lying dead before vampires struck her mind and she almost teared up at how heart-wrenching it was… and behind the pain of that image, she felt divine wrath. "Dread Lords, indeed," she mused.

She put her hand into one of the pouches and thought, *Something to mask the smell of blood.* A vial appeared before her fingers. It was oil pressed from the coveted Fireflowers. It was also Khalla's favorite perfume. She laughed. "Leave it to Ash to have perfume in here."

Khalla rolled the two bodies over and began cutting them, to make it look like there had been a grand fight. To make it more real, she used blood to make it look like she had been wounded. When Pol Nir entered an hour later, she found Khalla looking a mess.

"Khalla! What happened? Are you okay?" she screamed, running forward with a potion in her hand.

Khalla signaled, GOOD. KEEP THAT UP. MAKE YOURSELF LOOK WOUNDED. WE NEED TO MAKE IT LOOK LIKE WE BARELY SURVIVED THIS FIGHT. She pointed to the sloshing water. THERE ARE SEVEN VAMPIRES UNDERWATER.

Pol Nir nodded. The Imperic had an economy of movement Khalla liked. Pol Nir studied to perfect the craft of silent movement and stealthy battle technique. Perdition had welcomed her and she thrived in her craft. Her chosen specialty was sabotage and traps. They communicated with handsign and then, for practice, switched to Drowsign.

When Khalla told her about Ash finally proposing to her, Pol Nir came over and hugged her. Pol Nir began studying the scene of the battle and indicated areas for traps. TOO BAD WE CANNOT USE SUNLIGHT AS A TRAP.

Khalla nodded and signed: WE NEED TO LET AT LEAST ONE ESCAPE.

Pol Nir created a series of fire gem traps that would set a wall between them and the water. Hoping to divide the vampires and create a screen for any attempting to escape, they signed back and forth about the plan. Without warning, the floor trembled and then warmed. "Oh," Khalla signed. "I forgot to tell you that I trapped their exit too." She smiled and then they both lay down as if unconscious.

Steam humidified the air as a second detonation pushed bubbles to the surface. Minutes later, they saw three forms pull themselves from the water. "Perdition followed us and took our servants," one said in Soran dialect.

Another voice rasped back, "And trapped our resting area. Curse them all! But they left food at least to strengthen us for the long swim. Go check."

Though Khalla could not hear the vampire's footsteps, she heard water dripping to the floor as the creature approached. In the near-absence of any other sound, the slow drip of water from the approaching vampire made Khalla's skin crawl. She actively repressed it and focused on remaining still. *They swim here from Sora*, she marveled.

Pol Nir's trap exploded when a vampire stepped near Khalla's head. The heat of the flames felt good and Khalla wished she could open her eyes. The sound of at least one vampire thrashing about and shrieking also warmed her heart. She could not fathom the two small girls being here right now. It helped her steel her will.

The vampire by her head screamed out, "Shut him up! We don't want to draw attention to ourselves. Your flesh will heal when you eat. Now shut up and come forward."

A wet vampire crouched down by her head and sniffed. What she hoped was water dripped on her face and Khalla realized the other vampire stood over them both. "Elf," the one touching her head now said. "And human over there. They're both pretty. Shame to eat and run. They killed our servants."

The vampire at her head turned her face. "They're out. Our slaves drugged them before running off. Look at all this blood. It must have been a fight. This elf is cut up good. Hey, wait a moment. Isn't this Khalla, Ciejek's boss?"

The other vampire spat at him with considerable pain in its voice. "Who cares? Quit playing with your food. I'm taking the human. Elves give me the creeps."

The one at her head laughed and began fingering her medallion. He slipped it off her head. By now, Khalla realized that only two vampires were present. While there could be more underwater, this one and the other wounded one were all they had. She had planned for more to survive the underwater tunnel.

The vampire lifted her arm to its mouth and licked her skin. "Elf blood is good. I like this. I can taste human blood here too."

When the vampire opened its mouth to bite down on her arm, Khalla shouted, "Attack!"

She punched the bridge of the vampire's nose knowing it would not kill, but would hurt the vampire. It fell back holding its face and howling in pain. Khalla's other hand, not checked by the vampire, held her scimitar and she struck out at the creature's torso.

Pol Nir rolled to the side at Khalla's command. Finally able to see her target, Pol Nir asked it, "Oh, did you get burned?"

One had to live. The crate of Orcus blood was enchanted to resist rough handling. It had probably survived the flash boiling in the tunnel, though Khalla suspected they might have put it somewhere else. Khalla's vampire looked healthier and seemed more of a hedonist. Pol Nir brandished her rapier and assumed a duelist stance. "Come at me, bloodsucker."

The vampire looked at these two women, obviously spoiling for a fight. She looked confident, calm, and frightening. He had never seen an Imperic before. She was beautiful, even when so grim. The fire gems still burned and he wondered if they had set other traps. Shaking its head, he turned and ran to the water. His jump through the fire re-ignited what was left of his clothing. Pol Nir spun and moved to Khalla's aid.

Khalla engaged her vampire in a careful dance of attacks and parries. Seeing that Pol Nir's had fled, the two ladies nodded and pressed their attack. The vampire caught Khalla's sword and twisted it out of her hand and tossed it aside. "You have no idea, do you, the power of a vampire?" he said to them.

"Teach me," Khalla countered. She kicked the vampire, who easily caught her foot. Using his catch as leverage, she clipped him in the chin with her other boot and completed her backflip. The kick shoved him back to Pol Nir.

Pol Nir aimed her rapier at the vampire's heart through his back. Khalla's kick and the creature's attempt to regain his balance gave Pol Nir the perfect opening. She lunged forward and drove her rapier through his heart. He tried to twist and see her, just in time to see his friend jump through the wall of fire. "Ignite," Pol Nir said. The narrow foil burst into flames and she let go of the hilt. Another rapier appeared in her hand and she danced backwards in case the vampire should try and attack.

From its other side, Khalla said, "That's a flawless strike, Pol." Khalla's short sword skewed into the vampire's chest from a different angle.

"Thank you, my lady," Pol said with a bow, keeping her rapier aimed at the vampire.

Trapped between the two fighters, and impaled on a blade burning with enchanted fire and another one that might also erupt, the vampire realized he was going to die if he did not flee. He pounced at them both to keep them away and swept at them with his claws. The elf seemed disinterested in his actions and said, "You're going to die. The only real question here is whether you want a chance to live a bit longer? Well, do you? Surrender, if yes."

The vampire eyed them both and the wall of fire. His chest hurt. The fiery blade was not going to kill him; he was stronger than dying right now. But, his odds of escaping looked bad. He dropped to knees and gagged out, "Remove this blade."

From behind, Khalla pulled it out. "Good vampire." The two of them switched positions so that Pol Nir could cut him down if he tried anything. "I have a lot of questions to ask of you, but before we get there..." she raised her sword and cut it down into the vampire's neck to sever its head. She wanted to time it so the vile creature would know its death.

Instead, a blinding flash of sunlight filled the warehouse and Khalla's sword struck something metal. It took a moment for her eyes to adjust. When they cleared, she found a cleric of Pha Rann standing between her and the vampire. Her sword had struck his battle hammer. His entire body seemed to darken and Khalla realized she was seeing a teleportation portal. A dark form that looked like another vampire and an old mage stepped through nest. In frustration, she jumped back from the cleric wondering what was going on.

The cleric turned his hammer, each face resplendent with a holy symbol of the Daystar, and commanded the vampire, "You shall remain still." The vampire's body burned from the sunlight all around the priest. The vampire became paralyzed. Turning to Khalla and Pol Nir, the cleric bowed and said, "I did not mean to interrupt your execution, but I actually do have questions before we end this one. I am Executor Michael of the Perfectionist Order of Pha Rann, at your service."

"That one is a vampire," Pol Nir said, pointing to Cordelle. She held rapiers in both hands now. Pol's eyes went wide. "Tiamat burn me! You're The Michael! The one who defended the soldiers in Bloodstone at Haver's Point? The Battle of Helmet or something. Khalla, it's Michael!"

"Yes," the cleric said. "I am Michael, but don't let the stories spun by bards make you credit me with something I am not. I am just a servant of Pha Rann. Nothing more. And, that is Cordelle. He is helping us in hopes of earning his redemption. Though technically a vampire, he has not yet crossed to the Gate of Chaos or Warp. I humbly implore you to accept his presence. The mage is Radcliffe. His magic found you and brought us here. Agents of Tania, on behalf of the Queen's Way, I formally request that you release this vampire to me for interrogation."

Khalla looked at the paralyzed vampire quivering and slowly burning from Michael's nearness. She sheathed her sword and said, "I'm Khalla, an agent of Tania. My friend and I were about to put an end to this one for numerous crimes against Morbatten. On condition that he is executed following your questions, yes. I release him to you in Marcello's name."

Radcliffe coughed and said, "Many know Michael from the 17th Legion – Battle of Northhelm?"

Pol Nir practically jumped up and down. "Yes, that's it! I've seen the opera of that battle. The actor is, of course, handsome but nothing compared to the real Michael." Pol Nir blushed and went quiet.

Michael bowed again and said, "The opera is ludicrous but is effective at showing how Pha Rann has a design for us all, even Tanians. If you do not mind?" The cleric turned to the vampire and said, "You get two deceits. Your third lie, you die."

Pol Nir came over to Khalla and said, "It's refreshing to see a Pha Rannic be so blunt and yet pragmatic at the same time."

"Are you in love with Michael?" Khalla asked. "Don't make it so obvious."

"Right now, I'm so thankful I never converted to Tiamat. Do you think he likes Imperics?" Pol tried to smooth her hair and pulled a napkin out of her pouch and tried to clean the blood from her face. "Do you have any *hygiene* magic?" Khalla chuckled.

Michael explained the catacomb layout underneath Sora to the vampire. "I want you to tell me this – what is the safest backdoor way into your coven, the one with the fewest guards?"

The vampire tried to spit, but Michael caught his cheeks and punched him with the other hand. The vampire's face was imprinted with the Symbol of the Sun on Michael's knuckle guard. Free of Michael's divine hold, the vampire moved back to run when the cleric said, "Freeze." At Michael's command, the vampire's body locked and he fell. Cordelle had to turn him to face Michael again.

"That was your first lie – thinking you could avoid answering. The holy light of Pha Rann and the design in your soul want to answer me. Tell me." The various symbols across Michael's body began to glow towards bright noon day sun and the vampire screamed for it to stop as his skin resumed burning.

"We use a tavern, by the Ymac docks. You already know it. The basement, there's another basement you can only access from the wine cellar. There are no guards because the entire tavern is Dark Legion." The vampire seemed defeated.

"Good. See? That wasn't so bad," Michael reassured the creature. "You're an old one. Wise. I like that. You must have had to be very sneaky to last so long in Taysor."

Wild energy filled the vampire's eyes and Khalla realized it was pride. "For four hundred years, I have survived. I'd be immortal if not for Syand sending me here."

Khalla asked, "Do you swim here from Taysor?" The vampire nodded. "That's a long swim," Khalla said.

"You have no idea," the vampire replied. He looked up at Michael. "You have Cordelle with you. What if I serve you like him?"

Michael pursed his lips and said, "I'll think about it. Now, next question. How many vampires like Syand are there?"

It started as a giggle and then became harsh laughter with a cruel edge of malice to it. "There's none like Syand! None! She's insane! But, of others? She killed them all."

"How many did she kill?" Michael's left fist began to glow.

"One hundred and two," the vampire replied.

"I see," Michael said. "I've thought about it. You're not going to live forever. You're going to Hell, back to the corrupted design only Pha Rann can heal when the Gates are reunited." Michael placed his hand over the paralyzed vampire as it began to glow with increasingly bright daylight. The vampire began to cinder.

"You will lie to me again, and so my words are true. You wasted one on denying Syand; someone created her." Michael's hand pulsed and the vampire's body collapsed into a pile of dust. "And may Pha Rann judge the evil of your life against that corruption, rather than the perfection you should have been."

Pol Nir elbowed Khalla. "Much better than the Cuthberics. I like the Perfectionist order."

Radcliffe laughed. "You might not should such judgement be turned on you, young lady. Literalist Mage Radcliffe at your service."

"It's true," Michael said. "Pha Rann set forth a clear path for us all to ascend to Heaven. All life serves the Sun God anyway. For now, I am satisfied. Radcliffe, send word to the High King and notify all orders to assemble and march on the catacombs." He looked over to Khalla. "I trust this execution satisfies Perdition's requirement?"

"Yes, it does, Lord Michael. Are you going back to Sora?" Khalla nudged Pol forward. "I bet they could benefit from a real agent, Tanian style. Ask him, Pol." Khalla pointed to her. "She came to us as an Imperic interested in mastering stealth combat and perfection in movement. She has been a loyal member of my team. I would recommend her to you should you wish for a thief that is more than just a pickpocket."

Pol Nir walked forward bashfully while Radcliffe flipped through an obvious spell book. "Um, Lord Michael…"

"Just Michael, please."

"All of Sora's thieves, well the survivors, seem to be Dark Legion. Would you, err, may I join your army? I am skilled…"

"She has Marcello's commendation and approval for this mission," Khalla stated. "Queen's Way, order 5, allows Marcello to interject a Perdition agent into Soran business when Tanian interests are also at stake."

Michael nodded. He turned to Pol Nir. "I am Michael of Augrosa. Will you serve my interests in rooting out and destroying a coven of vampires from beneath the fair city of Taysor?"

Pol Nir blushed. "So heroic," she whispered to herself. "Yes, Michael of Augrosa, I will. I am Pol Nir, agent of Perdition. My contract is… until you release me." She quickly added, "And your autograph on my opera poster!" She was really blushing now and Khalla laughed.

Michael nodded. "Maybe we can do better than that. I like your attitude. Come! Let us return to the fair city."

Listening to them, Khalla felt a burst of inspiration. Daryx wanted to lure Dark Legion here. If Michael killed them all… "One moment, Michael. It occurs to me that we have more than just an interest in this. I actually have an entire team with an interest in this. Would the Temple of Perfection accept an alliance against this evil?"

The priest signaled to Radcliffe, who paused in his spell casting. Michael said, "I sense great things moving, Khalla. Tell me more."

"First, let me introduce you to everyone." She eyed Michael and shrugged. "I'm sure Lord Daryx will be pleased to meet the famous Michael as well."

Michael burst into laughter that continued well down the street away from the warehouse.

# Chapter 18 – Leadership Tested

Syand felt her fingertips buzzing with energy. News that they had found crates upon crates of the god's blood had helped her feel better. Compared to the bright lights and enhanced awareness that came from Orcus' blood, her world had faded to dark greys with a red tint. The absence of her favorite snacks, Ydriss and Renault, had annoyed her but she found she lacked appetite.

"It's probably withdrawal," she grumbled to herself. In a few days' time, she would know. Vampires did not feel the effects of drugs and poison unless they consumed it through a mortal's blood. Even then, the effects were dilute. She should not be having withdrawals. She drummed her fingers on the chair's armrest. Plush satin fluffed with exotic bird feathers created a texture that she enjoyed. At least she could enjoy something again. The past two days had been rough.

Everyone in the room pretended they were not paying attention to her. The Dark Legion had easily consolidated all of Taysor's guilds under its thumb. "I expected more of a fight," Syand said.

An enforcer nearby turned and she made eye contact with him. He quickly looked away, but Syand repeated her words more loudly. "All this time, all these plans, and Dark Legion takes it all in just a few days. Were the other guilds truly so weak?"

The enforcer looked around and shrugged. "Two of them fell before we even attacked. 521 and Rogue's was the only two what fought. And Rogue's, they just run off. That you gave us permission to share the Dark Gift meant everyone joined us. Yes, just a few days and Dark Legion is supreme, my queen!"

The fight against 521 was still talked about. The entire warehouse coming to life and attacking. They still could not figure out what had happened. It had killed over half of Dark Legion's human members and ten of the vampires. More mortals would have died had Syand not converted them to vampires. Then, as they thought they had wiped out the leadership, the individuals and teams within 521 had started striking back. Sure, it did not hurt the Dark Legion directly, but when the Legion tells a merchant, "We're your new caretakers," and that same merchant's store burns down that evening, it makes the Legion look bad. The reputational damage was incalculable.

Ydriss needed to be here to explain the time discrepancies and help convey how the lay of the land had changed since she was last active eight years ago. It bothered Syand that Ydriss could not be found. To counter all these unknowns, she had come to rely on the coven for aid. Lower level minions were sent to watch the streets at night and report back. A team had been sent to kill Ydriss and Renault or bring them home. That they were never seen again... Syand shook her head to clear it. Then, there was the matter of Delia's team. They should have reported a week ago, but there was no word. Delia had even said not to underestimate Grant. "He's not like the other bosses. He's canny." Delia's words had proven true and Syand would no longer send slaves to do a master's work.

The wall to her side bore chalk markings of all the streets and showed 'x' marks where their turf was being hit by 521. Abigail's penthouse suite was large enough that Syand had taken it over as her command post. The walls now bore sketches of Northtown. 521 had proven most resilient. This tactic of watching the Legion and then targeting the people... was a risky play. "We should send word to the Temples that 521 is burning the citizens out of their shops."

The enforcer agreed and a chorus of "Yes!", "Let's do it!", "Let the Temples hunt them down," arose from the flock of sheep grazing at her feet. Syand looked at the pitiful array of 'thieves' before her. Dark Legion had fallen, maybe too far. She resolved to kill them all when this business finally sorted itself out and start from scratch. The thought made her feel much better and she smiled.

Syand pointed to the chalk map. "Go there to the Baker Olerstead's shop. Tell him that, as a thank you for his allegiance, we are reducing his protection cost by half. Make sure 521 sees you." She pointed to the enforcer. "This is your job. Now, go." She pointed to another. "Go with him. Make sure you take something from the baker. You are to hide and watch. When 521 attacks his shop, you must capture evidence that it is 521. Once you have it, race to the Temples. Give it to the Cuthberics." She laughed. "Let the knights war with 521's ragtag street fighters."

After they left, Syand donned her own leather armor and slipped out of the tavern. "I need the night air," she said to herself. The rooftops welcomed her and she moved quickly towards 521. The entire warehouse had collapsed into the canal leaving burned out buildings all around it. Syand perched on a house and stared down at the scene. Without the fire and heaving monstrosity attacking them, it all looked like any other fire-ravaged aftermath. "What a waste."

She spotted a glint of light along a northern street and moved down to a lower roof to see. A squad of Cuthberic knights marched into the 521 area. Their polished armor and lanterns smelled new. Their young faces gleamed with fanatical devotion and Syand leered down at them, mimicking their stupid conversation in her mind. *If they only knew I was here*, she laughed mentally.

A metal ball covered in spikes smashed into the roof edge near her and she rolled to the side and back. From below, a man's voice called out. "We know you're there, evil spawn. Come out and fight us!"

Syand thought about leaving them be, but a quick mental calculation told her she would not have Orcus' blood for another three days. She jumped off the roof and landed twenty paces away from them. "Ho there, dinner. You want a fight? Sure, why not? I'm bored and Cuthbert's slaves taste good. Mmm," she licked her lips.

Cuthberics were so devout and serious in their faith that any taunting tended to knock them over the edge. All of them, without blinking, drew weapons and charged. Syand watched them. *They're real paladins*, she saw. *They'd look slower if not. That one back there, the one not charging...* she looked more closely and saw the man casting a spell. She frowned. *So, they've borrowed a page from Tania and disguised the mages to look like other squad members.*

She changed her form to gas and blew to the side. Suspecting the knights might still be able to attack her, she shifted and her incorporeal form flowed through their legs. She rose up in the face of the mage. She enjoyed watching his demeanor change as her ghost-like form became corporeal. To his credit, he noticed her but did not break his concentration. Even when she rammed her fingers into his chest, the mage finished his spell though bloodied lips. He spat at her as she threw him back in a lifeless heap.

The knights behind her had reversed their charge and she noticed how they all radiated golden light. It hurt her eyes. The first knight's sword burst into fire and he swept it at her. The prayer to his pathetic god went unanswered and she dodged it easily enough. Syand did not anticipate that the knight would try to move her on purpose. Her dodge put her in clear attack range of four more knights. Realizing her overconfident mistake, Syand tried to dodge and regain her incorporeal form, but her power stuttered and she could not access. *What did the mage do to me?,* she thought with mild but growing panic.

One sword, and then a second, struck at her. The first blow missed, just barely, but the second pierced through her thigh and made her howl in agony. The other two knights aimed at, and tried to stab her through, her chest.

Syand rolled her body, tearing the sword in her thigh from the knight's hand. It hurt enough that she screamed but as she came back up and raked her claws up into the unarmed knight's groin, the feeling of his armor tearing and the blood on her fingers made her feel better. The paladin's scream was sweet music and she sang out, "Aaaah! Yes, scream with me – for pain, for death. You're all going to die here!"

Grimly, the knights rallied between her and the mage. One of the knights retreated to tend to the mage, leaving five before her. They all took a breath. The knights, as one, stepped back and began to pray. The knight in the center of the circle presented the Cuthberic symbol on his cross guard and stepped forward. "By the divine might of Cuthbert and by the powers of Heaven, I command you to die."

The words, stated faithfully, washed over Syand like a warm breeze. Had she been younger, she might have felt scared. She smiled and stepped forward to the knight, who renewed his command. "There is no god here but Death," Syand said. She stabbed her index finger into the symbol and it cracked.

The five knights stepped back, still looking confident in their weak faith. Syand spat blood towards them and cackled. "You're so pathetic. Everyone laughs at Cuthbert, even the Sun God."

Their demeanors held Syand in zero regard and then a sword struck her in the back. Syand whirled to see the mage recovered and casting again. The knight who tended to him had just slashed her armor. "Attacking from behind, and a woman no less, Tsk tsk." Syand kicked the knight and sent him skipping down the street to slam into the mage.

The mage intrigued Syand. He kept casting, even when steel armor smashed into him. Syand moved to the mage's side and commanded him, "Look into my eyes. Let this weary fight end. I am not your enemy. Those who would take you from my loving embrace are. Turn your spells on them," she moaned seductively in his ear while pointing to the other knights. "I am your woman."

The mage refused to look at her and finished his spell. Fire erupted along Syand's side, between her and the mage. He burned too, but though he screamed, Syand screamed too as magical energy burned her armor and blistered her flesh. Then, the other knights were on her again. Goading the mage into action on her behalf was her last option. "That was your last chance, mage!" Syand spitefully yelled. "Your last chance to be with a woman. I curse you, forever!"

She had to turn her attention to the knights. In the back of her mind, she felt like she was forgetting something. After a minute of battle, she remembered when she saw torch and lantern light along all of the streets intersecting their battle. *Cuthberics never fight alone, and they have an uncanny ability to band together,* she remembered. *Even strangers will rally to their cause, and later not remember why or what drove them to do so. The Heroic Spirit, they called it.* She had been fighting too long and was now surrounded. Fortunately, the warehouse and the canal flowing adjacent gave her an easy way out.

Standing in the burned-out ruins of the 521 warehouse, Syand turned her head from left to right and counted fifty knights standing in full plate armor against her. That they had rallied so many so quickly, was their real power. *If I could trust Dark Legion to rally for me this quickly, we'd rule the world.*

The holy symbols of Cuthbert gleamed with golden light. More than a few symbols of the other Heavenly gods stood arrayed before her too. She let blood drip from her claws and licked her talon slowly. "You going to bring the sun light? You going to cheat? You're all cowards! You fight with divine magic because you're all weak!" Her voice broke the silence blanketing the neighborhood. With so many gathered, people in the nearby houses braved to open their windows. Syand saw a small child held to her mother's chest and imagined the mother telling her the Temples had caught a very bad lady.

One of the knights stood forward and lifted the emblem of Pha Rann on his shield. The knight called out. "Yes," he answered. "You have it exactly right, except that you will die and the weak shall inherit the glories of Heaven."

Syand lunged forward as if to attack him and replied, "The only god here is Warp and Ruin. If not today, you will die. Your god did not breed you for Heaven, but as food for Warp!"

Syand whirled and dove into the water as the first ray of daylight split the darkness.

* * *

RiVule turned the corner and bumped into a priest he had never seen before. The human was big, almost Orc big. "You must be the Orc priest!" the human exclaimed in perfect Orc. "RiVule. Did I pronounce that correctly?"

RiVule stepped back realizing the priest was not just big, but also a solid wall of muscle and armor. He eyed the man and noted the only compelling designs on his armor – the sun. "Your Orc is very good," RiVule answered in perfect Tanian. "But, the speaking of my name puts harder inflection on the "aye" part. You're a priest of Pha Rann." RiVule smelled corpse behind the priest and saw Cordelle. He growled and immediately moved to put the vampire under control.

Michael, with a pleasant expression, said, "That is Cordelle. He's with me. Please do not do him harm."

RiVule lowered his symbol and tried not to look confused. "Is this a human joke? I see a Pha Rannic and yet you have a vampire? What is going on? I do not like what you humans call practical jokes."

Michael reassured him. "This is not a joke. Cordelle is not quite yet a vampire and is working with me as part of redemption. He's with us. He's been working with me for several weeks now. I'm a Perfectionist, by the way. My Order and faith fight against the corruption of Pha Rann's design. We're working to restore him to a correct afterlife in Heaven."

RiVule growled low in his throat. "Your splitting of this sun god hurts my brain. But, very well. Are you summoned to the meeting with the Lord Daryx?"

Michael waved at Khalla, who joined them. She said, "Yes, Lord Priest RiVule. Michael is considering joining our group. If not, we will be going to Taysor to help Michael's temple destroy hundreds of vampires."

Michael smiled and said, "One hundred and two vampires or so. It's not hundreds, but they're all very powerful."

RiVule licked his thin lips and nodded. "I've never fought vampires like this. We have stories, and I have prayed for it. This must be Gruustir's rewarding me for my faith and tolerance. I imagined the vampires had fallen in Bloodstone. My prayers are answered!"

Michael walked beside RiVule and they talked in Orc until they reached an assembly hall. Daryx stood quietly on a stage as everyone sat down. Daryx waved at Khalla and in Drow sign, asked her to bring Michael forward. Michael replied, in perfect Drow sign, "Thank you for your hospitality, great lord. We served together in Bloodstone on a mission to purge the 8th level of the 6th Fortress."

Daryx let his face show how impressed he was. Almost too fast for Khalla to follow, Daryx signed back, "Michael, you were using a different name then. Now that I look more closely, there was only ever one Pha Rannic cleric that learned Drow handsign so well. You went by Garrett?"

Michael burst out laughing and nodded, while his fingers continued their dance. "Sometimes, the perfect mission requires a bit of subterfuge. The Garrett alias protected my Order from being formally involved in something forbidden at that time by the high king."

Michael and Khalla reached the stage. With genuine warmth, Daryx clasped forearms with Michael. "Khalla, if we can persuade Michael to join this quest, it will be a powerful thing."

Khalla bowed and said, "We shall then do our best, my Dar."

Michael asked Daryx, "Will you be part of this alliance to root out the vampires in Sora?"

"I am so tempted to once again see a Pha Rannic cleric so unleashed." Daryx pointed to Cordelle. "And full of surprises as always. Though the Queen's Way has served Tania well with the Pragmatist Order, I am often reminded by your Temple, that there are other powerful factions in Sora. May I have permission to solicit your Judge Marshall for your participation in Merakor? Khalla, you have discussed it with him?"

She shook her head, no. "Daryx, I was not sure of this. With your blessing, I will."

Michael shrugged. "I've heard enough talk that I figured it out. There are also rumors in the Temples about this quest though the purpose, the reason, the pay, and the like are, I trust, not accurate." Michael closed his eyes a moment and then nodded his head. "Though my Order has problems with your methods, Daryx, we have never doubted the outcomes of your work. Provided this team is as effective as your Marcello suggests, I cannot fathom why the Judge Marshall would not wish for a return to Merakor."

Daryx replied in Drow, "The treasures of Merakor, and lost wisdom... it will be an epic quest worthy of you, Executor Michael."

Khalla struggled to slowly piece the Drow manner of speech together. It reminded her of archaic gray Elvish with a smattering of jagged accents counter to how she spoke and understood the Elvish language.

In the theater to their side, the various teams streamed in. Many pointed to Michael with considerable interest. After a minute, Khalla felt a hand in her own and turned to see Ash. He pulled her aside and said, "You don't have to look so smitten with the priest." He was half-joking.

Khalla took in the scene of the larger-than-life priest speaking with the enigmatic Daryx. The theater was silent as everyone strained to understand the Drow language flowing back and forth between Daryx and the Pha Rannic priest. Khalla knew that Ryvane followed every word, but then she noticed the gleam in the cell leader's eyes. Ryvane looked completely smitten, and next to her, Calvin knew it. R'Dar Alex was trying to not stare and Valaes took it with good nature. He put her hand on his bicep and flexed. Khalla could imagine him saying something like, "Anyone can look big with the right tailor and armorsmith."

Khalla squeezed Ash's hand. "Sometimes, I think I'm getting the hang of it and then a new layer of Tanian society opens up to me. Right now, I am realizing that those two operate at a level I cannot imagine." She referred to Daryx and Michael. "Don't worry about me. Pol Nir has already called dibs."

Ash strained to translate the Drow and said, "An 8th level? Did I hear that right? I thought the Bloodstone Fortresses only had three sub-levels."

"That we know about," Khalla said. "Rogue's Blade heard rumors that some of the fortresses, not all, had been turned into labyrinths that just kept going when we were there. When your tunnelers are undead, maybe they just keep tunneling forever in the absence of a controlling master."

Halgrim's appearance on the stage ended their conversation as the two lords stepped back from the magic gate opening there. It was the first time many in the group had seen him since the archmagus ceremony that had made him younger. He beamed at them all. With a spring in his step, he moved forward and bowed to Daryx. "Permission to begin our discussions? If you require more time…"

Daryx said, "Lord Michael, I trust you and I shall talk again after. I will have a servant bring you to my shrine."

Halgrim said, "You are all assembled after weeks of preparation because we have arrived at a testing point. This is not the mission we trained for, but it is close to some of the scenarios we will find ourselves in against the Drow. Lady Khalla, at your command, I have plumbed the depths of magic and confirmed the tavern Dark Legion uses as their headquarters. Cordelle's information is correct. I cannot go farther as I do not know what I am looking for, and powerful magic guards the area. I yield the floor to you."

Khalla stepped forward and held a scroll up. "This is from Marcello, ruler of Perdition. It is a contract to join forces with the Pha Rannic priest Michael, and destroy a vampire coven calling itself the Dark Legion. Whether you are bound to Perdition or not, this mission is under Perdition's rules. We shall approach this as if in Merakor. That is, the teams we have organized, their leadership, and our approach shall be as follows:

"Ryvane, you shall lead the Black Guard, responsible for the Drow priestess' safety. R'Dar Alex, you are the high priestess, which the Drow name 'Holy Mothers.'

"R'Dar Alex, your team – the Priestess Team – will consist of Valaes and Michael as your bodyguards and heralds. Lord Michael, we did not know you'd be participating in this so apologies..."

Michael shook his head. "This works for me, so long as I am not ordered to contradict my faith."

Alex blushed and looked away from Michael. "No, my lord Michael. It is I who should serve."

He burst out laughing. "Yet, in Merakor, you will reign as Lolth's priestess! It cannot be me and I am content to observe and intervene as Pha Rann's design shows me."

"Halgrim and Ash, you will both serve on the Priestess team. Grant, your team will be the Scouts. You will move ahead of the Priestess. While you will serve as all of our advance, remember, the purpose is for the Priestess team.

"My team," and she spat out the Drow word for Perdition. "*Disakcion*, shall serve as house slaves bound to the Priestess. Remember, as practice, we will hold to these teams because, in Merakor, that's how the Drow engage in combat. Lord Michael, in case you did not recognize him, is a hero of Tsora and a celebrity in Tania. You may know of his exploits from the opera *Audel Pyrel*? No, well, know this: the Lord is a mighty cleric of Pha Rann and a prominent leader in the Perfectionist Order. Tania does not see many Perfectionists so it is on us to impress him, to show him beauty in our design and execution of our faith, patriotism, and commitment to defeating our enemies. Lord Michael, please, share with us what you know. Also, because the Temples are not well known in Tania, except for the Pragmatists and Cuthberics, would you please overview your doctrine?"

Rather than stepping forward, Khalla and the others faded from the area around him. The priest's charisma and infectious smile drew everyone's attention to him. "It would be my pleasure, Lady Khalla. The opera exaggerates my role in the Battle of Northhelm. Plus, in Tania, I am told your antipathy for the Cuthberics makes me look extra appealing. Since you know and love them – I'm looking at you, agents of Perdition!" His smile conveyed the joke and everyone laughed. "Let's start with that. Cuthberics believe in the absolute Good of Pha Rann. Anything not in Heaven is susceptible to evil and they dedicate themselves to destroying it. They see that each erg of evil destroyed increases the relative goodness in the world."

Michael paced on the stage and whispered something to Halgrim. In a moment, the symbol of the Creation Gate appeared. It floated behind Michael. "This is the Gate symbol of Creation. It is also the true symbol of Pha Rann. You'll notice how it looks like the sun itself. The Daystar of Tehra is Pha Rann. His light touches everything. It is perfect. The Perfectionist Temple believes that Pha Rann anticipated and ordered the flow of Time same as everything else created under this gate. Because of the other two gates, this perfect creation is sometimes lost and it is our job to find it, individually. All of our doctrines are self-directed. We believe in finding our calling and applying Pha Rann's doctrines towards elevating our own perfection as a gift of faith, a sacrifice to Pha Rann. Someday, Pha Rann will reassert the perfect design in all of us, in all of creation. I work, as a servant, to bring that day closer. So, that's me."

Pol Nir elbowed Grant and said, "He's already perfect."

Grant chuckled. Maybe Michael heard them because he smiled at Pol Nir and then radiant wings burst forth from his shoulders. "Pha Rann did not intend humans to be bound to Tehra the way we are. He gives us wings. His light dispels evil. My purpose, my perfect mission, is to defy Warp. Next time you watch *Audel Pyrel*, you might notice that, while yes, we defeated a hell lord, my purpose was to destroy the hell lord very much like how Tania engineered the death of Orcus. That was a perfect application of a Pha Rannic doctrine that ordains a god may only be killed in Tehra. Well done, Tania."

Behind him, the Gate symbol of Warp appeared. Michael touched it and let his wings fade. "This is Warp. Warp is like poison to Creation and Chaos. I can smell Warp and Ruin. It makes Chaos more destructive. It corrupts all that is good and perfect in humanity. It is the voice of jealousy and the scream of rage in your soul. The servants of Asmodei are my enemies. For five years, I have been investigating centuries of missing persons cases in the eastern sections of Taysor, around Ymac specifically."

An illusionary map of Ymac and the Temples appeared. Michael pointed to the warehouse area and then to the Legionnaires Tavern. "When I began, I knew I might uncover the seedy underbelly of Taysor's crime families. I was committed to turning over evidence to the Temples rather than turning them myself." Michael's eyes touched on Grant. "I learned of Grant's team and their predilection to copy what I viewed as Tanian tactics, which I saw firsthand through several tours in Bloodstone. I never imagined that I would find a coven of vampires behind one of these crime families. You see, Dark Legion has a long history that goes back to the founding of Merakor. Best I can tell, one of Tania's early agents fell to a vampire in Bloodstone – probably to Nientro – and was allowed to leave. Knowing he would be destroyed, he found his way to Taysor and kept a very low profile.

"This first agent would have been around the time of the 8th Legion, so about a thousand years ago? During the time since, he has raised up the head of Dark Legion as a vampire. The head serves and then quietly retreats underground into what we call the catacombs. Allow me, new friends, to set the record straight on the catacombs. Taysor did not know they were there. They are burial crypts of Krentismar's thri-keen."

Halgrim opened his hands and an illusion of thri-keen appeared. Michael nodded in thanks. "The giant insect behind me is not exaggerated in size, nor are its similarities to the praying mantis insect. A warrior, like this one, would stand two men tall. They are fast, able to fly, and jump incredible distances. They are brutal once they engage in combat with an enemy. Provided they do not consider you an enemy, they are quite docile if possessed of an alien way of being. The reason I share this is twofold. First, the catacombs are sacred to the thri-keen. That they have not ousted the vampires tells me that the vampires are careful to not defile the crypts. Second, if the vampires are enjoying the same unfettered access to necromancy since Orcus' fall that the rest of us are, they may be able to defile these crypts and raise an army of undead thri-keen against Taysor. This is exactly the type of an end game that put me in the Battle of Northhelm in the first place."

Halgrim's illusion shifted to show the same warrior but with a zombie aspect. Michael chuckled. "We'd be lucky if the thri-keen turned as zombies. In the few interactions Taysor has recorded about them, they would arise as wraiths or stronger." Michael looked out over the audience. "You are probably wondering why a Perfectionist and worshipper of Pha Rann would not be racing off to The Temples to solve this as a Soran matter. Radcliffe? I'd like to ask you to explain what your Order's protocol is for something like this."

The old mage stepped forward and coughed to clear his throat. Next to Michael and Halgrim, the mage looked ancient and frail. "Well, I'm a Literalist. You're all familiar with us. We like to join your Bloodstone adventures and other engagements, and like you, we steer clear of the Cuthberics." He paused while the Tanians laughed. "Though we get along with them better than the Pragmatists do. Michael had to persuade me to not escalate the vampire crisis. You see, Dark Legion found me and would have killed me had Michael not intervened. So, I owe him, literally." More laughter interrupted him and he waited for it to ebb. "Within an hour of receiving word, the Temple would send word to the other Temples that we march on the vampires."

Michael touched his shoulder. "And, we cannot do this because the vampires will raise the thri-keen. While the thri-keen would no doubt come to fight, the lack of contact between our races makes it so that we are likely to be viewed as the raisers of the undead. Regardless, it would take time for an effective thri-keen response and so, best case, a legion of undead thri-keen and vampires counterattack and bring the war to the streets of Sora. Unlike the attack on Orcus, there is no plan, no dragons, no countermeasure to save the people of Sora from such an enemy. The green sun was bad, but this would be far worse. As such, Khalla has negotiated with Marcello and I am pleased to have you all join Sora's crusade against the undead. You might say that my Temple is your customer in this work."

Khalla stepped forward, though she seemed dim compared to Michael's presence. "So that we are clear, our mission is to avoid thri-keen engagement and prevent this battle from coming to the streets of Sora. Though they are not Tania's innocents, Tiamat smiles on this endeavor as a further way of strengthening our nations."

Out in the audience, Calvin leaned over to Ryvane and whispered, "Who cares about the thri-keen? Why not just kill them too?"

At Calvin's question, Ryvane's frustration peaked and she shoved him. "Pay attention. This is important, to you, me, us. If you study the thri-keen, you'll know how ignorant your question is." Calvin flinched, clearly hurt by her words. Ryvane patted and held his hand so he could not let go. "It's that important, Calvin. Please, adjust your attitude." She kissed his hand and then let go. He let it linger on her arm for a moment before he let go and harrumphed away from her in his seat. Ryvane felt her stomach sink and remembered Khalla's words about Calvin.

Khalla had begun a discussion about the teams and vampires. "While Perdition and Rogue's Guild provide ample thieving skills for stealth and assassination, we are lacking in brute force. Sadly, none of the teams here specialize in enforcement and, if I'm honest, we need heavy battle warriors, not street muscle. As such, Marcello contracted the high command in Bloodstone and we are pleased to announce and introduce that Commander Revi, Second in the Eighteenth Legion and up to yesterday part of Ayden's command as her First. He will be joining us with two others: Niltan and Furis. The three of them come with the highest recommendation."

Revi, Niltan, and Furis stepped forward. Each wore plate armor polished to a mirror shine. Unlike Lord Michael's luminous armor, theirs reflected light dimly. Bas-relief engravings of dragons covered their armor. They held up their left arms and tower shields appeared, followed a moment later by long swords enchanted and glowing with dire power appearing in their right hands. Revi lowered his shield and called out to the group. "We are honored to be here! I had hoped that this vacation would not involve the undead, but so be it! May the spawn of Orcus rot and die next to his corpse! I am Revi. I specialize in sword and lance, more sword since I completed my fourth tour with the Nineteenth Legion. This," he said slamming his hand against the pauldron of the fighter to his left. "Is Niltan. He's just like me, but not as attractive to the ladies. Over here is Furis, a specialist in the long bow and deadly enough with sword."

His manner of speech and carriage were so different from Michael's that it carried the audience, more used to Tanian flair, and many began clapping their hands. The frontline fighter situation was one they had all wondered about. Revi bowed and took Khalla's hand. "I remember you as the leader of Rogue's Blade. Well met." He cleared his throat and then in Drow said, "Your eyes shine like a thousand-pointed star in which I eternally drown."

Khalla returned his bow with a curtsey and answered him back in Drow. "Beware. Such a sweet tongue must prove itself or birth spiders."

Revi struggled with her more fluent and correctly accented Drow and then shrugged. "It sounds threatening, but also challenging. And kind of sexy. Whatever you just said, I accept."

Khalla laughed and re-addressed the group. "We will have others joining us, but this is the core party. The others are probably known to you all. The first, Lady Inviress Havkor will not be joining us until we set sail. The next is known to the Scout team as Delia. Grant, she is not dead. She is being repurposed to join the mission. She will not be joining us against the vampires until The Circle is satisfied with her conditioning." Lord

Michael's face grew distasteful and he walked off the stage when Khalla used the word. *Conditioning*, in Tania, meant soul-captured and compelled.

Grant stood and said in Drow, "Delia cannot be trusted. If Tania requires her presence, I will accept it but wish my objection noted."

Khalla inclined her head to him and said, "We will note your objection. The cleric R'Dar Maishan will join us. Alex and Valaes, so that you can continue your studies, we have requested Dar Niss though she will not be coming with us to Taysor. In counsel, we feel you will be better served by having access to actual Tiamat priestesses during your Lolth transformation."

Khalla continued, "The final will add to our warrior prowess and will take some getting used to. It's a condition of our trip to Merakor and the fight against Orcus. The Tauran Emperor, named 'Cyclone', will be arriving in several weeks on the world galleon we will take to Merakor. Don't worry, Marcello assures me that he does not expect to be anything other than another fighter in our group. If you've fought with the Taurans, you know the advantages and disadvantages of having one with us. Also, of note, going back to the Lady Inviress – she is a Drow. Well, sort of. She will be our guide, hopefully the entire time we are there. When you meet her, you'll see what I mean."

Daryx then provided a banquet following a review of the more tactical plans. They would gate to Sora's Ymac area tomorrow with the goal of taking the tavern and entering the catacombs. The rules were strict: only Drow handsign and Drow language for communication with strict team cohesion. Alex would command any variables in the encounter, which they all knew were sure to occur. Daryx ended by chastising them all for not practicing Drow enough. "I know it's hard for you all, but so is dying. You need to use the Drow language and handsign as if your lives depend on it."

As the banquet began, Grant meandered over to Cordelle. "So, I guess it ended up not mattering at all that our deal fell through. I'm sorry about what happened to you." He pointed to Cordelle from head to toe. "Vampire. Tough. I'm pretty sure they were going to do this to me."

Cordelle watched Grant. "You know, we were not ever friends, but I respected you. In fact, I once considered you a possible successor for me."

Grant, seeing that Cordelle was still Cordelle, leaned back against the bar and looked out over the crowd. "It must be different. I cannot even imagine."

"Sure you can. The heightened senses, of everything. Now that I'm this way, I can honestly say – it's amazing they don't rule the world. Of course, I never knew what it was like before Orcus. Maybe it was different."

"How'd you?" he pointed to Michael.

"Oh that? That just happened. I guess I was lucky, or Pha Rann was looking after me. Michael found me and basically said he was going to kill me if I didn't fight for redemption. Ever since, I've been traveling with one of the most celebrated clerics in Taysor. Amazing huh?"

"Any regrets?"

"Of course," Cordelle admitted. "Many. I should have killed Syand years ago. I always suspected, but she was so careful. I cannot even fathom how careful a vampire must be to hide that nature. I feel like you're all staring at me, it's so obvious. Written in my soul, burned into my face."

Grant patted his arm. "I wish I knew how to help you. You know I never would have taken 521. It's not my style, but thank you for saying that." They then fell into an uncomfortable silence before Delton waved Grant over. "I'll talk to you later, Cordelle."

Away from the others, R'Dar Alex sipped at watered wine and watched. They all seemed so cheerful. All the planning and preparations had made the quest seem so far away. Now, with a mission upon her, she felt like it raced towards her too quickly. She tossed the rest of the wine back and left to find Valaes, who sat by himself. She sat down by him. "Tomorrow," she said.

He nodded. "It all felt so far away. I don't suppose we'll have much time, what with you being the priestess."

Alex leaned her head on his shoulder. "We'll make time. Apparently, I get to be a tyrant. So, you'll give me time or I'll have you flayed by necrotic tentacles." She pinched his arm.

Chuckling, he said, "Leave it to the Drow to come up with such an impractical and disgusting weapon. I'm sure tentacles make sense underwater, but for elves?" He paused and the asked, "You doing okay?"

She nodded. "It just seems so fast. I'm glad we're doing a practice, but I keep thinking of Thalian. Everyone tells me how heroic she was, but she's still dead. I miss her. I'd rather have her here than dead in Bloodstone. And, I wonder... will I stand up to the undead as heroically as she did?"

"You'll do just fine, and do her honor."

A voice intruded on them from the shadows behind their seats. "Thalian would be proud of you, Alex." They turned and saw Daryx, barely visible in the shadows even though the room had plenty of light.

"You knew her?" Alex asked.

Daryx shook his head. "No, my dear. But, King Malcor was with her when she died. I've heard the story and read the official records submitted by Helena. Thalian truly was a hero. You've learned quickly. You have what it takes. The only thing missing is you fighting with Tiamat's faith in actual combat. You have a long line of priestesses before you who, just like you, felt nervous before their first battle. Malcor speaks reverently of your sister as did the dwarves who served with her."

Daryx held out his hand and an incorporeal form appeared there. It seemed to pulse but the blur of the object made her head hurt to look at it. Valaes struggled with it too. "What is it?" he asked, and Alex felt relieved to not have to ask.

"It's a phase spider," Daryx said. "I am their caretaker here in the Isles. Many mistakenly think that Lolth is the Queen of Spiders. She is more correctly the Queen of Phase Spiders. They're smart. They're powerful in ways that will surprise you. As a priestess of Lolth, you will need an ally like this in Merakor. The Drow consider them sacred. Part of your becoming a tyrannical High Mother, Alex, is learning how to use – not care for – your allies. Hold your hand out."

When Alex did so, the phase spider vanished from Daryx's hand and appeared on her own. Needle-sharp legs dug into her hand but did not break her skin. On her hand, she could see it. It looked like a tarantula but was weighed as much as a small puppy. Daryx pulled a canvas wrapped item from his pocket and unfolded it. Glittering amethyst gemstones the size of Alex's pinky nail dazzled in the room's light. Daryx held up a choker necklace, two earrings, a ring, and a bracelet. "Amethyst soothes the spiders. You need to wear these. The spider is trained to return to them, and to not hurt wearers of amethyst. This should give you enough time to learn how to communicate with the spider. If he accepts you, it will be during combat and stress. If he accepts you, he will be a powerful ally in Merakor."

Alex noted how it did not move, but was continually materializing and vanishing its legs on her hand. It had the appearance of movement but each leg seemed to teleport by itself, just a bit. She wanted to touch it but Daryx warned her not too. "Not until it accepts you. They are quite deadly." Daryx smiled. "You must give it a name worthy of an avatar of Lolth. If it likes the name you choose, then maybe, just maybe it will accept you."

Daryx moved to leave but Alex said, "No! Wait. My lord, I don't know what to do."

"You're a priestess of Tiamat, soon to be Lolth. You had best figure it out before you lead your team against a hundred vampires tomorrow." He reached over to scratch the spider on its head and walked away.

Alex looked at Valaes with wide-eyes. "Is it just me or is Daryx one of the strangest people you've ever met?" Valaes asked. "My father has spoken about him, especially once he learned about this whole Merakor thing. Very strange."

With each step, the spider grew agitated and Alex winced when the first bead of blood appeared along her hand. "Valaes, it's hurting me. I don't know what to do."

Without saying another word, Valaes bowed his head and put his hand on her shoulder. She felt his faith and power flow into her as he combined his might to her own. Alex bowed her head and began to pray. A sharp stabbing pain in her wrist and the slick wet feeling of blood sliding down her arm told her she was running out of time. *Tiamat, hear my prayers. Please, show your servant how to tame this creature…* Her prayer already felt wrong and she struggled to recapture her mindset as all eight of the spider's legs dug into her skin. She struggled to catch her scream of pain as, all around her, the rest of the mission teams went about the banquet and got to know Revi and his two fighters.

*Tiamat…,* she began. "No," she whispered only loud enough for Valaes to hear. "This is not a creature of Tiamat. Lolth…" Valaes squeezed her shoulder but she could not tell if it was in warning or support. She wished she knew. Temple rules forbade praying to other gods. It was not a commandment so much as a rule. *Apostasy begins with calling out to strange gods.* It was carved in several places along the Temple. One of the inscriptions was said to be done by Dar Ana herself.

*Lolth, hear my plea. Your priest has gifted to me a phase spider and said that I must figure it out. I do not know what this means. Hear me and answer.* She felt a burning sensation along her arm and opened her eyes to see the spider biting into her radial artery. Lancing fire shot along the bite into her fingers and then more slowly up her arm. The spider's eyes came into focus for just a moment and Alex understood. "Lolth is an abyssal god," she explained quietly to Valaes. "She does not answer prayers. She acknowledges power. I love you, Valaes," she whispered.

He felt her tense and then she grabbed the spider and tore it off her wrist. Praying to Tiamat that the poison would be neutralized, Alex felt slicing lacerations all along her hands as the spider tried to claw its way out of her hand. She brought it up to her face and, against Valaes' shout to not do it, she bit the spider. At least, she would have if it had not vanished.

She bit into the meaty part of her thumb and tasted blood. Opening her eyes, she saw her ruined hands, and the spider bobbing across the theater. The rest of the group noticed now and Lord Michael jumped forward to help her. She saw Daryx materialize from the shadows behind the Pha Rannic and stop Michael. The poison in her blood faded but she felt something different in her. She hoped it was not Tiamat's displeasure.

Alex prayed again and stepped out of the flow of Time. Though not as potent as being able to completely remove herself, it cast the theater and those watching her into a world of blue and gray. She could see the River's flow but could not rise up and out of it, not yet. No one moved however, and she walked towards the spider. "Listen, spider. Lolth wants this too. Your priest, Daryx, wants this. You will serve me... Or I will destroy you!" The last part came rushing out of her in Drow and she pounced on the spider.

Time rushed back in on her as her teeth bit into the arachnid. It felt like biting glass and she hoped her teeth would not break. The spider whirled in her grasp again and she felt clawed legs striking at her torn hands and face. She held on and renewed her call to Lolth, not for help, but for the spider's subjugation. It felt like forever and then Valaes' healing powers warmed her. His prayer neutralized more poison and knit her wounds even as the spider inflicted new ones on her. At some point, she felt her eyes rip out of her face and yet she kept her teeth clamped on the spider and demanded its total subservience. The cold glass feel of its flesh suddenly muted and became dusty, what she imagined webs might taste like.

She turned instinctively to look around while holding her arms as shields in case the spider attacked her face again. When weight appeared on her shoulder, she felt the pinpricks of the spider's weight. It seemed to bob up and down there. It seemed tranquil. Everyone else had frozen in time. A woman's voice, distant and echoing as if from a great cavern said, "Very well, Tiamat. I accept terms. Pray your servants do not fail them."

Alex's senses reasserted themselves as the din in the room and people rushing to her aid became so loud she fell to the floor covering her ears. Overwhelmed by complete darkness and pain, she felt her body convulse into shock. She screamed and when her wrist stump and fingers touched the gaping holes in her face where the spider had torn her eyes out, she began trembling and hyperventilating. She felt Valaes' hands on her.

"Shhh," Valaes said. "We've got you. It'll be okay." He began praying for her sight to be restored while someone poured a *healing* potion into her mouth. The healing lessened the shock but increased the pain and she felt her body begin to tremble in violent surges.

Alex felt the spider bobbing on her shoulder. It seemed happy. *I'm going to name you now. Slicer.* She said its name in Drow, but her face had gone numb from the spider's venom. The spider's happiness increased. It liked its name.

"She's going into shock. Lord Michael, Lord Daryx, you will please assist me," Valaes ordered.

Valaes' tone was perfect, just what the Temple had taught – authoritative and commanding. In Tania, the Temple held dominion. And, Alex wondered why she was noticing this. She felt disembodied in a bath of agony. She reached up her ruined hand to touch Valaes' face and, to her dismay he pulled her hand down and someone restrained her. A detached part of her noted that she could see her hand's bones through the bleeding mess and ruin of her arm stump. She began to hyperventilate again... and in delirium, she prayed to Lolth. *You bitch! Your damn spider is supposed to serve me and instead it ruined me! Is this how you honor "terms?" I demand restoration...*

Another Tanian edict, not a rule but a convention with centuries behind it, was that clerics did not heal themselves unless inspired by Tiamat to do so, or in prayerful consultation with another priestess or paladin. Alex felt her body ignite as if with poison and then fingers burst forth from her wrist stumps. She felt orbs form in her eye sockets and she opened them. Valaes and Michael recoiled from her as the phase spider *blinked* and appeared on her chest. It hissed at them.

All of the wounds, all of the pain vanished, and Alex felt a darkness in her soul that she could not explain. Profanity flowed from her mouth in fluent Drow. From behind the group, Daryx began to laugh. "I see Lolth has touched you, High Mother." His Drow answer to her profanity smacked her.

His words infuriated Alex and she flipped to her feet feeling energy flowing from her as rage fueled her strength. She saw Valaes and Michael, and all the others. She reached for her mace and found it was not there. It was in her room. The spider seemed eager though, where it perched on her breasts and she realized, "I can command it now."

"Spider, silence the dark elf!" she said pointing at Daryx.

The spider vanished leaving small rips in her bodice where its legs had punctured the fabric of her dress. It reappeared on Daryx's shoulder and seemed to purr.

Daryx laughed. "You've done it, Alex. Your sensibilities and training with Tiamat will not help you tame the Abyss. Lolth and the phase spiders thrive on action, violence, and ruin. The curse of the High Mothers is that Lolth gets into every aspect of their personality and guess what? Each of those then thrives on violence and ruin. Now that you've tasted it, I bless you with retreat."

Daryx's words washed calm over Alex's anger and she took a deep trembling breath. "What was that?" she asked.

"It's a prayer I developed, to escape the Underdark. I never thought I'd have to use it in Tania, well, not with a priestess anyway." He smiled and walked forward. "The *soothe* prayer works well with Taurans and even berserkers, like our new king." The phase spider bobbed up and down on his forearm as he reached Alex and held it out for her to take. "You've felt and seen what these can do. Remember, they're not of this world. This one," he scratched its head. "Is ready to see the outer worlds. Here, she prefers a smaller size because our amethysts are small. In combat, she is huge." He pointed to where Revi, Nilthan, and Furis spoke with Delton and others from Grant's Scout team. "She is about the size of that group. Take good care of her. Remember, action and violence. The speed of your healing... my Goddess does not believe in the gentle approach your Temple teaches or that the Pha Rannics practice. Everything is explosive."

Alex, aware now of how Lolth felt in her soul, bowed low to Daryx. "High Priest, I understand so many things I studied and did not comprehend about Lolth and the Drow now." She looked down at her blood-stained and shredded clothing. "I hope future lessons are not so painful?"

Daryx lifted his shoulders up to his ears in a giant shrug. "I've never been a High Mother. You'll have to tell me. From what I've seen, and in my own training, they are all painful. The Abyss cherishes mortal agony. Maybe our agony is the only sacrifice we can offer Chaos?"

Alex nodded. "Valaes, I require bathing and tending to. You will follow me." Spoken in Drow, her command tone silenced the entire room and made Valaes blush. He sprang to his feet and followed her out of the room.

Daryx picked up a flute of wine and raised it to R'Dar Alex. "All hail your High Mother, Alskexa!"

The rest of the team saluted. "Hail!"

"Alex is not a very Drow name. Please, get used to calling her by the title 'High Mother.' The closest equivalent to her name is 'Alskexa.' Only the most powerful of you may call her that." Daryx looked around the room and pointed to them. "That means: Ash, Khalla, Halgrim, Michael, RiVule, Grant, Revi, Furis, Ryvane, the Lady Inviress, and Cyclone. The rest of you will call her by her title at all times."

\* \* \*

Delia blinked her eyes and saw the same cursed gem hovering in the air over her heart. A mage sat to her left, just out of her vision. Tilting her head to look at him, her skin stretched against the barbed hooks set to hold her immobile. She remembered there were other mages too. The light pulsing from the gem cast the mages in stark two-dimensional forms. Her skin hurt. It had been like this since the attack on Perdition. She felt movement over her and looked up, and wished she had not.

A purple-skinned creature with bulbous eyes and tentacles where its mouth should be stood over her. At the moment, it was flipping through the pages of a book. Delia felt a tentacle shift under her head and remembered. The flayer did not need to be focusing on her to affect her. At her thought, the creature looked down and leered at her. Well, if it had a humanoid face, she imagined it leered. A series of clicks and chirps sounded from it and she heard it as: *We are almost done. There is but one thing that stands between you and freedom… such as it might be.*

The words formed in her mind and coincided with the clicking sounds from its head.

Delia thought about resisting. When she did, the mind flayer sent her images of what had already happened to her. It said, *They do not derive pleasure from your resistance, but I do. It has been a very long time since I sampled doppelganger thoughts. Please, resist.* The main image that played over and over again in her mind was of the barbs in her skin. Each barb was attached to a crank wheel. Each attempted form shift, they had cranked the reels. She had no elasticity left and could not have shapeshifted if she wanted to. Where her skin unraveled and circled the wheels, she could feel the metal chain links. Tania knew how to imprison her kind. While it surprised her, it also had not, when she thought about what she knew about this country. *Yes, that is how they are.* The flayer cackled in her thinking with glee. *And, they offer you conditional freedom. Do you want to know, or should we enjoy more resistance?*

Delia licked her lips. Her tongue and skin felt like dried toad skin. "Water," she gasped. The flayer seemed amused by this and sent her images of water – vast lakes of it. Delia swam in the waters with Grant. He loved her and they drank it till they became drunk and then made love in its cool depths. "Bastard," she tried to say but coughed. The cough pulled the barbs and she tried to hold her body immobile. "What choice do I have?"

*None*, the flayer said. *Except the obvious one.*

*I choose death*, Delia thought sarcastically. *Hard choice.*

*Not an option here*, the flayer interrupted her. *Don't you know where you are?* The flayer's mental laughter hurt her head and amplified the pain in her skin. It made everything worse. *Tania will not let you die. And it is not often I am given so much latitude to ensure you make the obvious choice.*

Delia licked her lips and whimpered. "We both serve Set. Why would you help them?"

The flayer's laughter burst forth in her mind like a flower and her body convulsed against the many hooks. *You presume that all of Set's creatures serve Set. I am not surprised that someone who would attack Perdition the way you did would also be this naïve. While Set is my creator, I most certainly do not serve Set.*

"Who then," she groaned, "do you serve?"

*Myself. I am my own god. You have the obvious choice – the only one you can make. Perhaps I should let you marinate in pain for another week?* At the flayer's words, she did not just recall but relived the deaths of the rest of the doppels in her team. The flayer had vivisected them before her eyes. The flayer had locked the memories away from their physical deaths so that they drooled and gibbered with smiles on their faces as the Tanian mages harvested their bodies.

The implication of "another week" hit Delia hard. *How many weeks has it been like this?*

*Only three,* the flayer answered. *But you remember many more because of my power. We are almost at 1,000 weeks of remembrances and, while I do not wish to brag, I have not even tried to break you yet. Consider this just an appetizer to guide you to the obvious choice.*

She felt the mages moving and two came to either side of her. They held wands in each hand and had the look of those lost deep in concentration.

"What choice do I have but the obvious?" Delia rasped.

"Only that one," the flayer said. His physical voice reminded her of a bird mimicking speech. Hearing it speak Tanian made it worse. The alien flayer should have sounded sinister. Its chirping voice speaking a human language sounded comical. The dichotomy flooded Delia with a sense of the nightmarish.

Delia closed her eyes and tried to remember the last time she had felt happy. It was hard and when the flayer mocked her thoughts she realized that all of her happiest moments were borrowed from people she had replaced. "Make this choice and maybe you find your own happiness," the flayer said in Grant's voice. She realized it was not actual words but a daydream and Grant was holding her hand in the sun. It was one of her happy memories playing out as if real right now.

She nodded. "Okay, I agree." The flayer stepped back and must have signaled the two mages who, again, pulled arcs of white and silver light from the gem above Delia. Continuing in her thoughts, the flayer gave her instructions. *This is the 37th time we have tried this. To make this choice, you will hold the wands and focus on the white lightning to the gem. If, like the other 37 times, you try to escape or end yourself, we will skip the cooperation part. My patience is directed by those stronger than me, but they understand that I have limits. I caution you to not test me again.* Images of her past tries and how each attempt at resistance had failed bombarded her memory. She saw herself try to stab the gem, escape, turn the wands on the mages, turn the wands on the flayer, and she saw how futile it all was.

"What happens next?" she asked out loud.

*Your soul enters the gem and your contract with Tania is complete. Based on your keeping to the terms of your agreement, you can earn your soul back… if you even want it. Outside the bounds of your terms, you have complete control over your life. And other benefits you will learn, such as you will not ever really truly die.*

Delia took the wand in each hand and focused on the lightning connecting their tips to the gem. She felt nausea and heard the mages tell her to keep concentrating. "It will pass," the one to her right said.

The other asked the flayer. "Is she cooperating for real this time?"

Delia felt the tentacle connected to the back of her head retract. Hard spikes pulled free and she realized the dull ache there hurt because of the flayer penetrating into her brain. She could see in her mind the ridge of spikes denting into her own skull…

"Focus!" the mage ordered her.

She did and felt a sudden pressure in her lungs, as if she had too much air. "Breathe out," the mage said. "This is your soul. Just breathe it out like you'd blow out a candle. You are not going to die. It won't even hurt."

Delia did not want to. She knew she would die. She knew it was a trap. She could not hold her breath and when she exhaled, the gem flared and – it was all over.

She slumped back on the table. She felt the pain of the hooks but it seemed distant, like a recent wound not yet healed. The mages turned the wheels binding her skin and bit by bit, her body pulled itself back together. The flayer watched for a few seconds and then said in its parrot-clicking voice, "There are two parts to your choice. The first is your soul. It is collateral to ensure your obedience to Tania. Obey Tania and serve Tania as if you were a Tanian, patriotically. The second is a judgement where you get your memories back. You have access to them but I've removed the emotion that made them valuable to you. Who knows? In serving Tiamat, perhaps you'll be able to reclaim your soul from Set."

The flayer reached out his arm which ended in writing mass of small finger tentacles. A holy symbol of Tiamat burned softly in his flesh, bleeding and re-cauterizing moment by moment. "Set does not appreciate my choice." The flayer laughed, "But, I'd make it again every time."

Panic struck Delia and she reached for the memories of Grant, before he knew she was a doppelganger. Just as the flayer had explained, they were there but had the same tone as if lived by someone else. She could remember the sound of his voice and the way he genuinely made her laugh. She remembered these as happy times, but each now had a disconnection in them. "Why?" she asked.

"An incentive for the kind of behavior that makes you trustworthy," the flayer said. "At the Temple's instruction, I have made provision that the head of Perdition, Marcello, can restore some of the feelings as an incentive for good behavior." The flayer looked about to leave, but it turned back to her and looked into her face with its alien eyes. A tentacle caressed her face and the memory of Grant's touch exploded in her thoughts. Not distant, not someone else, it was his hand on her face and they kissed. It took her breath away as if a new love, a new experience. "Like this. It's an incentive. I trust you with this one memory." The flayer withdrew and exchanged words with the mages and then left.

The reels at last released her flesh and Delia felt her elasticity come back. For a moment, she thought about killing the mages and taking one of them as her new identity. The thought seemed real and possible. The part of her that wanted to do it, did not care enough to try. She tried to lift her hand and morph it to the match the mage's skin tone. It sluggishly responded.

The mage caught her hand and said, "It's normal to want to test the bounds of this new situation. Would you like a demonstration?"

Delia nodded. The other mage pulled the glowing gem out of the air. Holding it, he said, "This is your soul gem. Whoever holds it, can control you. To ensure this does not happen, we will be giving it to the Gardenkeeper. She will be here in a little while." The mage held the stone to his lips and said, "Delia, stand at attention."

Her body immediately moved off the stone slab and stood at attention. The mage did a few other commands to illustrate, even going so far as to say, "Delia, attack the mage before you."

She really wanted to. Her hands twisted to grab his arms but her mouth said, "For what reason? He has done nothing deserving of attack."

The two mages stepped back and one conjured clothing for her. "Your soul – not you – is under a *geas* not to harm Tanians unless refraining to do so would compromise your mission. This means that your free will and moral agency come to full power when confronted with a situation that targets Tanians. That same order against a non-Tanian, well – you would have already killed the person. Do you understand this?"

Delia nodded and shapeshifted clothes onto her body. Her powers worked as well as always. As she buttoned the top of her shirt, she saw a humanoid figure come to stand in the shadows of the stone entrance to the room. A glint of gold on the arm showed the figure was most likely a woman. The mage asked again, "Delia, do you understand your new situation?"

"Yes, I can't hurt Tanians. I got it. Seems kind of unfair since you'd all be able to kill me and I could do nothing..."

The female entered the room. "You are lucky you are not standing in my Garden along with Set's other minions." The figure looked up and Delia found herself gazing into eyes of sulphurous yellow. A snake slithered out from under the woman's veil and snapped at Delia. "The point of this *geas* is to ensure your allegiance to Tania and its people, which is the only condition under which you are allowed to live. We could have killed you and still can, right now. If we decide to kill you in a month, it does not matter because your death at our hands is already certain."

Delia stretched her arms and with a careful tone said, "You're the medusa I've heard stories about. I never thought I would meet you. Sometimes, I have dreams about you."

The medusa smiled faintly. "Set touches us all in different ways. The doppelgangers are allowed full control of the Dream within your body. You are given extra intelligence to use this Dream for sabotage and mayhem. The medusae, we were given to the maedar and changed. We do not share the same Dream, but yes, I'm not surprised you have seen me. Many of Set's servants have."

A mage gave the glowing soul gem to the medusa. "She joined willingly," he said.

The woman's expression softened a bit and she said, "I am Syliri. Though most know me as the Gardenkeeper. Your soul will be safe with me until you earn it back. You made the correct choice even if the outcome was already known."

"Had I not chosen this?" Delia demanded.

Syliri smiled. "Your soul would have still been taken and would be used to power our spellcraft. We have to keep your body alive when we do this. It dies in bits and pieces as your lifeforce is consumed. While this happened, you would become another statue in my Garden. I believe The Circle wishes for you to be further studied before joining the Merakor quest. Follow me."

Delia walked out of the laboratory into a maze of hallways. High arches overhead and light spells illuminated a vast underground complex. Doors ran off to the side every so often as they crossed intersection after intersection. "Only a minotaur could navigate this maze," Syliri said. "We're going to walk this until you cannot remember where you were or where you are."

It felt like hours before they stepped into a hallway that dead-ended at a large double door. Entering it, Delia felt a sense of her own smallness. In every direction, statues stood along lanes. Each statue stood on a plinth with a label. The one closest to her read: *Bodak, undead spirit of vengeance. Gaze can kill. Only enchanted weapons and spells can slay.*

Syliri led her through more twists and turns, pausing every once in a while until Delia noted the statue belonged to a shapeshifter. At last, they came to a plinth. It loomed empty and the label on it made Delia's flesh crawl: *Delia, doppelganger slave of Set. Shapeshifter.*

"This is to be your plinth should you renege on your choice. Even should you break the *geas* spell that binds you, we have your soul gem. I realize you might now or will soon feel you had no choice." Syliri placed the gem on the plinth and an illusion of Delia flashed upwards to stand there, larger than life. It rotated slowly and every so often, her form would shift from her preferred human to her true doppel state. She hated her true form. The formless body bereft of features except the eyes and mouth made her look like a featureless vampire.

"Your soul gem will rest here until the Circle decides you have earned a release." Syliri turned to leave.

"How, I mean, how do I – what do I have to do to earn a release?" Delia tried to touch the stone but an energy wall crackled and she pulled her hand back.

"Impress the Circle, or sincerely join Tania's ranks as a citizen. Merakor will, no doubt, give you plenty of chances to impress, or to betray. The question is wrong though, Delia. You probably feel betrayed by these events already; that is Set's influence in you. But, remember this." Syliri rose up over her, suddenly becoming titanic. The eyes of the snakes looking at her flashed and shifted color to the sick yellow of the medusa's eyes. The gaze and attention of a predator like this medusa made Delia want to flee and hide. She quivered when she realized this entire chamber was full of Syliri's prey, and she was just another.

The Garden and its Keeper would never let her escape. Syliri said, "I did not choose my curse. But, Tania did choose to revive you and give you this chance. Just like the god emperor Alerius gave me a choice, you have one before you. It's the only choice that matters: remain a slave of Set, or join the fight against Set. It's truly that simple. The flayer says you love this Grant person. That is more than most of Set's spawn feel. It is more of a choice than I was ever given. Do not expect empathy or mercy. Do expect brutal judgement. It is the Tanian way. You get one chance."

Delia felt a wave of anger and then sadness well up in her heart. She dropped to her knees and wished she could cry. "It's too much," she said. "Just end it now."

"Brutal judgement. I do not need a pathetic doppelganger in my Garden." Syliri picked Delia up and slithered out of the Garden. "You will be trained, judged, and trained again. The test may never end. This is where you earn your soul. Maybe, just maybe, you can take it back from the spawn Set made you into."

* * *

The gate opened on Travers Street, just two lanes off Gable. They were less than a mile walk from the tavern, and entrance to Dark Legion and the catacombs. High Mother Alskexa made a series of curt handsigns and the groups dispersed. Their Soran clothing would mask them. Alskexa took hold of Michael's arm and they strode boldly into the night. Valaes and the others walked behind them in small groups, each taking different roads to avoid the appearance of a large coordinated group.

Legionnaires Tavern was heavy with light and carousing laughter. They would never know what hit them.

# Chapter 19 – The Tavern Brawl

Syand cracked open the water-soaked chest and withdrew a vial. Enough time had passed that she was over the withdrawal and knew its symptoms for what they were. Still, the allure was too much and she downed it in one gulp. The vampire before her stank of the sea and she thanked him. "Get yourself cleaned and fed and return for your reward."

"There is so much more," the vampire said. "When we stole it from Perdition, there must have been enough blood to fill every room floor to ceiling in here. At your command, I will go back and get it."

Already the hot swirls of daylight ignited her vision and quickened her thinking. Her mind twisted and she knew – *this is all part of a trap*. Tania would come for her. She eyed the crate, the shelves, and the vials themselves. Nothing stood out as trap-worthy. "Were you followed?" He shook his head, no.

Syand hummed and sat back on her throne. The god's blood brought her a measure of peaceful thought and she plotted her strategy. "Tania knows about us," she said to her leaders. "They will come for us, for the blood. We must set a plan worthy of the nation that killed Orcus." She hissed and then began to laugh. One by one, the others joined her. "I'm going to consult with those below. Be on guard. Expand our perimeter, and move the blood somewhere safe." Syand jumped up from the throne and picked up the small crate to take with her.

An hour later, Syand turned the last blind corner and entered a large chamber. Lichen grew along stone discs and illuminated the cavern perfectly to her supernatural vision. The discs, some carved with intricate detail and others with crude markings and jagged lines ringed the large chamber. Here, so far underground, her coven did not need coffins or anything so macabre.

All of her forebears to the first, rested in this chamber. Some stood in a pose of action, like statues at the ready. Others sat, as if in meditation. A few laid down. All looked dead and unkempt in their long rest. Syand went to one of the discs and triggered a secret door to open. A small tunnel extended away from the chamber. Syand placed the crate of blood into it, then transferred fifty vials to an ornate chest. Having secured her own cache, she walked back down to the chamber floor.

Syand walked to the end of the oblong mortuary towards a half-elf. The man looked serene in his rest and wore ancient armor, elegant still in its enchantments. He had fair skin and just a suggestion in his face of elven ancestry. She knelt before his seated form and whispered, "Master Kallis, I have a gift for you." She placed the ornate chest on the ground before him as an offering.

She unscrewed the cap on a vial of the god's blood and held it before his face. The dead do not move and the undead are statuesque in their slumber, yet remain aware. Syand stayed this way for several long minutes before she noted the first visible sign of breathing. Slowly, Kallis returned to awareness.

A sheen from Kallis' eyes looked out into the darkness. Syand knelt before him and she held something before his face as an offering. "The world feels... different," he observed questioningly.

Syand felt dust and webs from his words brush her hand. "It has been many centuries, Kallis. The world has changed. Orcus is slain."

As if teleported there, Kallis' hand materialized around her throat while the other caught her wrist. She felt an overpressure of will. Kallis asked her, "How? How can a god be slain?"

Syand struggled to retain her kneeling posture before him. "Master..., Morbatten. They set a plan... the dragons..." Kallis eased his grip around her throat and she coughed before continuing. "The dragons destroyed the Wand of Orcus, and then they slew the god."

"What year is it?"

"1805 DAR, as the Tanians measure it."

"You last woke me..."

She completed it for him, "In 715 DAR, yes. Master, please. I have a gift. The dark god's blood. It will tell you all."

Kallis took the vial from her hand. "This is Orcus' blood? How strange to say that one's name. What wonders does it hold?"

"The world burns with daylight and we see in the dark as if high noon. Thoughts come unshackled and multiply. Violent action is boosted. I am burning with its power now if you would rather taste it through my flesh." Syand offered her wrist to Kallis' lips.

He pushed her hand back. "Too much, Syand. It's too much and I've been asleep too long. I must orient myself to the long passage of time. The Temple at Bloodstone was lost and then rebuilt. A war between Sora and Tania. New dragons on the Isles. In all this time, how has the Legion changed? That you awaken me… you have Joviel?"

Syand remained kneeling but sat back. "Tania's population grows by the year. Their advancements in magic confound Sora. Their military might grows ever the same. The Taurans contract exclusively through Tania for great ships that travel the oceans. A guild has grown in Tania, as you long ago predicted. They name themselves 'Perdition.' They corrupt the ancient arts for their nation's rather than personal profit. You would be ashamed to see it, Master Kallis. The Legion has kept pace. We number five times more than when you last slept. I have added more to the coven's ranks. We do not yet have Joviel, though clues abound from books copied from the Tanian dragons and studied throughout the Isles. We know who the next Marcello will be. We know where the master vault is but need Marcello to enter it."

"The world tree in Morilon is…"

"As you directed, we watch it for signs of change. During the battle of the Jade God, many leaves fell. They have since regrown. The watched-for marks have yet to appear. All is well." Syand rushed to ask, "After all this time, will you not tell me what it means? If connected to Joviel, maybe I could…"

Kallis shook his head, no. "It is an omen, nothing more. The world tree is one we must be prepared for. As I said long ago, it means the time has come for us to leave the Isles. That is all I will say on this matter. How did Orcus die? I say that one's name and feel nothing." Kallis laughed. "The Jade God was always too much to say."

Syand wished for light to draw out some of the events. "The dragons severed the three-faced wand. Then, I am told, the god stood alone in the center of the valley. Tania's new king closed the gate to the Abyss. Once that was done, they all attacked. It was a great alliance unlike anything ever before seen on the Isles. At the very last, a new god appeared – the 'Slayer of Gods,' they named it. A giant wolf of bones. With that new god at his side, Alerius enacted a spell that, with all the other attacks, dropped Orcus dead. The valley is now full of demons and devils. To our gain, necromancy is now boundless without the Jade God's will to restrict and fetter our ability to make decisions. We are stronger; but clerics are stronger too. I expect necromantic mages are as well. This is the change in the world you feel. What else would you know?"

Kallis sat quietly for some time before he answered. "I feel different. Maybe the world is the same and it is I, we, who are different. I feel, for lack of a better term, hope. Give me your arm."

She offered her arm up again and when she felt Kallis hesitate, she pressed her wrist to his teeth and punctured her artery. At the first taste of her blood, Kallis latched on and sucked deeply. As the old ones always did, he stopped just when Syand felt she would have to either die or force him off. "Your blood is sweeter than ever and, yes. The world burns. I see my friends all around, dead and unmoving. I see the thrikeen ancients. I see you standing in a field of sunflowers, wind blowing through your hair. Is this addictive?"

Syand rushed to answer yes, but realized Kallis might consider its after-effects addictive. "Master Kallis, a vial like this – and we have nearly one hundred – lasts for about fifty hours. When the effect ends, you will feel hungry and angry. The anger will storm around you for several days and then pass. The more blood is consumed, the more powerful its effects, and the anger after. It is not addictive in the sense that you do not need more and more. It's more like a potion with rage-inducing after effects when the magic ends. The god lies dead in the Valley of Bloodstone. Tania has harvested much of the god and has as much as one thousand barrels of this blood."

Kallis interrupted her. "You think that, with enough blood, we might ascend as gods ourselves?"

Syand bowed her head and nodded. "Yes, that is what I believe. I see myself, you, and others soaking our bodies in the blood and ascending to something new."

"You see Joviel! This transcendence is Joviel. That is why I have long sought her." Kallis brushed her hair from her face. "How lovely your hair blows in the solar wind..." His hand took her chin and he kissed her.

* * *

Bradley leaned back in his chair by the bright fire. Legionnaires was quiet for how it had been before the Dark Legion clamped down on everything. Usually, the various guilds would be here either to spy on each other or to barter stolen goods with each other. Bradley had done that a few times himself. He sipped the last of his ale and ordered another. The serving girl curtsied and ran off to get him one. In this den of bloodsuckers, being one of the few humans meant the other humans took extra good care of him.

The outside door opened and, to Bradley's surprise, a large cleric entered. The tall and muscular priest wore plate armor emblazoned with sun emblems. Based on the reaction of the vampires around the door, the priest worshipped the Sun God. While not uncommon in Sora, such a priest was out of place in Legionnaires. He escorted a much smaller woman. She also wore armor and carried the gear of an adventurer. The giant man deferred, clearly to the younger.

The lady pulled her hood back and Bradley recognized her Tanian heritage. She was young. The darker skin, the angular ears and nose and teeth with slightly squinted eyes, and the dark brown nearly black hair made her easy to place. The vampires in the room backed away from the cleric. Bradley and the other humans were here for this kind of thing. The girl swept her cloak to the side and, like the priest, she wore dragon-emblazoned armor marked by the divine symbols of Tiamat. *She must be a cleric as well*, Bradley decided.

The girl looked around and then moved up to the bar while the giant held open the door. Three men entered and Bradley's heart sank. "Adventurers, indeed," he grumbled. One of the three looked in his mid-forties or so with sharp intelligent eyes. An arcane staff in his hand and a bandolier of wands across his chest showed him to be a Tanian mage. Bradley looked more closely but could not tell if he was battle-trained or not. Sora had so few Tanians to study and mages almost never traveled in public, or came to places like this.

A vampire slid up next to him. "You see that? Smells sweet, but trouble I reckon they is."

Bradley shook his head. "Yes, but probably harmless. They look road weary. Maybe we were the first inn they came across."

The other two men looked like brawlers, though of different types. The smaller one wore black leather armor and carried multiple knives and short blades. The other wore heavy plate armor ridged by leather straps so that it made a dull clunking sound when he moved instead of the loud metal-on-metal clanking enemies would hear from miles away. The three men moved to the bar and sat down to order drinks. They had gold and the mage ordered Telluri Firewater, a top shelf Tanian wine. The armored fighter began asking what manner of food they could order. The mage seemed overjoyed that Legionnaires had Fire Flower brandy.

Two vampires pretended to be passed out drunk at a table near the bar and the giant cleric walked over to it and thumped the table with his hand. "You awake? Can we have this table? I'm expecting a few more, and the lady is tired."

At a signal from Bradley, the two got up and, still feigning drunkenness, pretended to stumble to a table occupied by others of Dark Legion. "Thank you, sirs," Michael said. In a strange language Bradley had never before heard, Michael said something to the young lady and she smiled and sat down. *Is that draconian?* He had never seen a Pha Rannic and Tiamat priestess together. It was such an unlikely pairing.

He walked up to their table and introduced himself. "I'm thinking Tanian adventurer party, but that language. It's not quite Elvish. Well, I may as well go and find out," he said to himself, loud enough for the vampires to hear. Bradley stood up and hefted his belt at his waist. He hit the bar first for a refill and then stopped at the table. "Ho there, you're all a strange sight for bored eyes. I'm seeing Tanians, but adventurers too?" He eyed the girl, "And maybe a foreigner? She looks Tanian. What brings you to our fair city?"

Michael translated Bradley's words into Drow and Alskexa replied. Looking up at Bradley, Michael said, "We just crossed the Sea of Ymac, and are heading home after a fruitless waste of time in the Sea of Glass."

"Ah, I've heard songs and stories about that place. Nasty and all, was it?" Bradley sat down next to Alskexa and noted how Michael watched with great concern. He would have to be careful. Priests did not exactly wander around with power markings that proclaimed their might, but from the quality of gear and likely enchantments, he seemed and definitely felt dangerous. The girl, not so much. The others, also not so much. "Was the Sea of Glass as bad as we're told?"

Michael remained standing and suggested, "It would be better if you put some distance between yourself and the high priestess."

Bradley jumped out of his seat and backed away. "Apologies! I did not know. A high priestess," he said loudly. His behavior made the giant priest frown and he lowered his voice. At least the vampires would know there were two clerics in the tavern.

Outside, Grant signaled and the Scout team moved to get visibility on all exit points from the tavern. Confirming it, Grant used a hand crossbow to signal Disakcion and Black Guard to be ready by shooting a bolt near them. In just a few more minutes...

Their plan changed when vampires began filtering out of the tavern in ones and twos. "The best plans never actually work," he complained under his breath. He picked up a crossbow at his side and aimed it at one of the vampires skulking down the street to a side alley. The bolt struck the vampire, igniting it in fire. The immolation occurred so quickly that it lit up the night and prevented that one from alerting anyone not watching. Automatically, Grant picked up a second loaded crossbow set with the dragonfire enchanted bolts and looked for another target.

The other vampires escaping saw it though, and drew blades as they ran to help their friend and attack his attacker. Black Guard moved to shutter the tavern. Disakcion closed on the street vampires. Grant had a perfect view of Ash. His mentor moved with silence and precision. Ash's attack on the vampire's heart and throat left a quivering body behind it. Ash continued his forward motion and then launched a spinning back slash. The severed head bounced and rolled aside. Ash's momentum whipped him around and he caught the the body gently to the street.

Khalla moved with equal skill if more grace that reminded Grant of a panther, or some other predatory creature. He admired her before realizing he was targeting her with the crossbow.

The first thud of a vampire thrown against an escape door in the tavern suggested their sneaky time was up. Grant aimed his bolt at one of the windows and fired. It struck a vampire jumping out of the window. Black Guard closed the window and covered their heads as the vampire ignited in mid-air. Combat erupted in the tavern. "I'm glad I'm up here with you," Cordelle said. He had reloaded the first crossbow and passed it back to Grant.

Grant burst into laughter. "You have no idea, old friend. Tanian clerics train against undead all day, every day. This is what they eat, sleep, and breathe. Ask Alskexa after. She'll tell you this is the highlight of her career to date."

Inside Legionnaires, Alskexa found she did not like this Bradley person. Grant's briefing had been spot on. "Friendly enough, but a backstabbing liar." The tension with Michael had risen enough that the vampires all around them began to filter out of the tavern when a thud from the street outside the tavern made everyone jump to their feet and draw weapons.

She turned to Bradley and, mimicking a Drow accent in Soran Common, said, "I tested very high against vampires."

The phase spider appeared on her shoulder as Tiamat's power burst forth from the tattooed symbols on her forearms, chest, and the actual symbol in her left hand. The symbol of the Dragon Queen, its head resting in the crook of her thumb and index finger, allowed wings to spread out and form a type of razor edged buckler shield. She slashed this at Bradley while vampires all around them in the common room hissed and fell back. "In Tiamat's name, I command your destruction!" she shouted.

Beside her, Michael's faith ignited his many holy symbols and pyres rose up all around the room. So furiously did some of them burn that tables and chairs caught on fire. Halgrim sent spells to douse the fires. They needed the tavern intact, for now.

Valaes entered the room and added the burning energy of his faith to the destruction. The undead cindering all around made it easy to see the humans. Bradley took it all in, dumbfounded. The vampires had promised him immortality and wealth, but also unending agony if anything like this happened. And, he had just failed to warn the coven just three hours after Syand had ordered increased security at Abigail's and Legionnaires.

Bradley backed away from them all, trying to use the brightness of the fires to create – not shadows – but relatively darker areas and blind spots to hide in. The two clerics he could not tell. The mage and the fighters with him looked scary as more of these adventurers burst in through the front door and joined in attacking the vampires. When a vampire stumbled in front of him and began to cinder to ash, Bradley threw a gemstone into the vampire's burning hands and spoke the detonation word.

The tiny gem flashed and then exploded. The blast threw Bradley back into the kitchen's staging room. Though reeling from the blast, he tucked his legs and rolled up against the stairs. He twisted and let himself fall down, backwards, into the wine cellar. The door there would allow him to alert the coven. It was just in his reach.

* * *

Calvin watched the vampires burning and darted into stab at one of them. An instant after his sword connected on the undead's supernaturally hard skin, another fighter rose up by him and decapitated him. Calvin looked at his sword and saw it notched. "I need a magic sword," he said wistfully. He summoned his shield. He had not used it much since Kaia had gifted it to him. It brought back hard memories, but in this case, it might work as a basher.

The shield appeared on his arm and Calvin moved deeper into the inn. A vampire came stumbling out to just barely avoid a fire bolt from the Scout's sniping at the Dark Legion through the windows. Calvin drove forward with his sword, acting as if he would stab the vampire in the heart. At the last instant, Calvin pivoted and swung his shield edge like a blade. It caught the vampire near its collarbone and Calvin grinned to hear the bone break.

The vampire stumbled back and eyed probable escapes. "You're going to get killed. Might as well fight me and die like a man," Calvin boasted. "Come on!"

The vampire hissed and feinted to attack and then ran. Calvin blew his hair out of his eyes and marched to the front door of the inn. He felt a blast of warmth to his side when a fire bolt caught the escapee. "Give me something," he said in terrible Drow.

He kicked the door open expecting to see carnage. Instead, he found piles of burning ash around the clerics. As the door swung closed behind him, Calvin saw a meaty older man throw something into the fire. The resulting detonation threw everyone, even Michael, away from the blast. Calvin and Revi ducked below their shields. As the fireball faded, leaving the tavern burning, Calvin noticed movement behind the room towards the kitchen. The large man landed nimbly on his feet and twisted to tumble downstairs. *That must be where the wine cellar is*, Calvin thought. He wondered why no one else was concerned about this. *This is where I prove to Ryvane and the others that I can do this.*

Looking around, Revi fended off a burning vampire trying to gouge his eyes out. Michael was helping Alskexa to stand. Nilthan parried three human attackers. Everyone looked singed and burnt. "I feel just fine," Calvin said as he swung his sword and then, raising his shield, he charged after Bradley.

Just six steps in a wide hall went down from the kitchen's preparation area to the wine cellar. Bradley was standing up, eyes wild, and fixated on a pull chain. When he saw Calvin, he grinned and reached out to pull the chain.

Calvin knew it would be bad if the man pulled the chain. Without thinking, he jumped the six stairs with his sword aimed at Bradley's center. Not knowing if this foe would also be immune to normal items, Calvin landed with his shield edge on Bradley, switching from shield to sword at the last moment before impact. Unlike the vampires, this one felt soft and appropriately grunted at the force of the shield hitting him. "Ah, a human foe," Calvin said. "Well met."

The thief, in twisting to dodge the sword, missed the pull chain and took the brunt of Calvin's armor on his ribs. Bradley felt the wind rush out of him and he skidded on the stone floor to the side of the chain. The fighter above him had a glassy look in his eyes and actually smiled at him.

Bradley felt Calvin's hands move to rebalance himself, remembering too late that the sword was in his hand. It drew across Bradley's leather gorget and sliced it apart. The blade crossed his throat. In panic, Bradley heaved Calvin off of him and over his head. His torso, bruised by the shield and still suffocating for breath, crackled in protest.

Rather than be tossed, Calvin stepped forward and shoved Bradley farther back from the chain. The pull chain secure behind him, Calvin taunted the fat thief. "Did you want this? Oh, too bad." Calvin held his shield up and aimed his sword at his opponent. "You look winded. Too many vampires feeding on you?"

"You have no idea," Bradley spat back. He moved quickly for such a large man and threw three blades at Calvin. Two hit the shield but one slipped through Calvin's defenses and dug into his shoulder armor. "Take that!"

Calvin looked at the knife in his shoulder and shrugged. "Is that all you can do?" He feinted forward to drive Bradley to dodge to his support side. When he did, Calvin kicked forward with all his might. The kick connected and slammed Bradley back against a rack of small ale kegs. "Oh no, not the beer!" Calvin mocked Bradley.

Getting farther from where he needed to reach the pull chain, Bradley resolved to fight dirty. His opponent had a disconnected not-quite-there attitude that frustrated him. It felt like he was not taking the fight seriously even though blood had begun to dribble from the dagger wound at his shoulder. Bradley held up his hands after palming more knives. He also palmed a packet of blinding powder. "See? My hands are up. You're right. What do I owe the bloodsuckers? I surren..." He threw the powder in Calvin's face.

To the Tanian's credit, he let the powder strike him and remained focused on the battle. He had already started to lunge forward. The sword tip, like a spear, aimed at Bradley's abdomen and then lifted up. The effort of throwing the powder pulled Bradley into the tip. Cold metal slipped through his armor, his skin, and then broke his shoulder blade as it exited his back. Bradley looked up and muttered, "You bastard."

Calvin's facial expression remained uncannily serene. "I can accept that, Bradley. Grant sends his regards." With powder all over his face and his eyes closed, Calvin continued, "I may not be a paladin, but I know how to fight. You, sir, have the honor of being my first kill."

Calvin grunted with effort and, while holding Bradley impaled on his sword, used his shield to decapitate the man. Tears streamed from his eyes and nose where the powder burned. It had taken all his resolve to remain focused on the task of winning. His chest heaved with the strain of combat and coughing. He felt a strange sense of satisfaction and calm. *I did it*, he thought. *All of Ry's concerns and I stayed the course and won my first kill.* Almost unbidden, a thought came to his mind. Seeing no reason to not indulge it, he whispered, "All glory to Tiamat." It felt right. It gave him chills along his body. An epiphany struck him then and he recalled all the lectures in the Temple about dedicating his actions to Tiamat's glory. He got it now. "Apologies, my goddess. I understand now." He ripped the dagger out of his shoulder and dropped it to the ground.

Calvin had long wondered what it would be like to kill, knowing the person would not be resurrected immediately. In the Temple, he had killed on command. But, knowing priestesses would recover the fallen had turned it from this thrill-inducing adrenalin rush to rote exercise. He had been killed more times than he could remember, or cared to. Standing here, he reached out with his foot and found Bradley's body. He kicked it to ensure he was still dead and felt his boot slip in blood.

One of the few things Calvin had truly studied with interest in the Officers Corp was blind-fighting, or night fighting. It seemed a useful skill and Calvin had excelled at it. He opened his eyes and through tears, could barely see. He took up a guard position by the pull chain. He hoped the powder would not permanently blind him. Even if so, the priestess or Lord Michael or Valaes would restore his sight. A laugh bubbled up from deep in his belly and he remembered the wound in his shoulder. *This must be what it feels like for Malcor when he defeats an enemy*, he thought. *I feel giddy. Invulnerable.*

Footsteps on the stairs behind him caught his attention and he whirled on guard. "Calvin?" a female voice asked. He recognized it as Pol Nir and relaxed.

Calvin pointed to the chain. "The pull chain warns the coven. I'm sure of it. I can't see. Poison in eyes, but I'm good. Do you require aid?" he asked.

"No, I'm good. I'm going to check the powder." She walked up to him and checked his eyes. "This is a Soran blinding powder but it's actually just very fine sand mixed with spices. Here, we'll wash your eyes out." She twisted the spigot on a keg and she guided Calvin under the ale. Within seconds, he felt better and could see again.

"I've never thought to drink ale with my eyes," he joked. "I'm sure they look drunk now."

Pol Nir noted the glassy look in his face and patted his cheek. She pointed to a rag and said, "Here, let's get you dried off."

With the upper tavern secured, Scout and Black Guard moved into the tavern and took control of it, setting it back to normal operations. At least, from the outside it would look like everything was normal. Their job would be to secure retreat and prevent reinforcements from heading down into the catacombs.

Disakcion and Scout studied the pull chain and, with Cordelle's help, quickly found the trigger to open the secret door. Cool air rose up from the open portal. Alskexa pointed to the yawning entrance and in Drow ordered Scout to enter. "Disakcion will follow. Standard entry and marching order. Everyone at the ready. Grant, you have point."

Grant entered with Delton and noticed, immediately the workmanship and quality of the descending stairs. Marble tiles and wall carvings rose up to faintly glowing rune tiles. The rune tiles resembled Tanian light runes but appeared to glow by virtue of non-magical power. Scout descended without issue, bypassing several traps as they found them, until they reached a large bottom platform. By Drow handsign, they passed word back that they had reached the bottom.

The stairs opened into a large spherical room. Thri-keen stone discs, each the size of a human, were carved into every wall surface where space allowed a complete disc. Three intersecting cuts into the stone formed a triangle in the center of each disc. The flat floor had pools of water on about half of the tiles. Grant imagined that if they dug through the floor, they might find an upside down copy of the giant dome underneath them.

Disakcion and the Priestess team arrived to find the Scouts huddled low to the ground and eyeing the surface. Delton and Jerare quietly moved back and, in the dim light, their fingers told that some of the water puddles masked drop tubes that fell. "We have no idea how deep. No one was hurt."

Alskexa commanded Michael to fill the area with starlight. He bowed to her and suddenly the entire room filled with cool blue gray light, like during a full moon. Points of light swirled overhead and mimicked stars. It allowed them all to see clearly. Grant motioned and pointed to the floor. Frequent use over many years had slightly weathered some of the stone. "If we stay on the edges of the discs, we'll be okay. Water or not, it doesn't matter," he signed. "Scouts will go first. We'll signal the rest of you to follow once we reach the other side. Mark the safe edges with chalk, Scout."

Alskexa ordered Valaes and Halgrim to probe for magical traps. Their attempt to do so caused the thri-keen stonework to flare with soft green light. Yet, upon inspection, no traps were found. Halgrim signed back to Alskexa: ONLY IF DISTURBED. If any magic traps existed, the traps would be masked by the ancient stonework.

After ten minutes, the Scout team signaled all clear and Disakcion crossed first. Khalla and Ash arrived to find Grant standing on a raised platform nearly two paces tall. They vaulted up and saw three passageways branching off before them. Grant signaled: CENTER IS TRAP. WE TAKE SIDE TUNNELS.

Ash and Khalla moved forward to investigate and agreed. When all four teams had arrived, Grant bowed to Alskexa and handsigned: RECOMMEND SCOUT TAKES RIGHT TUNNEL AND DISAKCION LEFT. CENTER IS TRAPPED. PERMISSION TO GO?

Alskexa smiled regally and bowed her head, yes. In Drowsign, she complimented Grant. YOUR SIGNING IS GETTING BETTER. PROCEED. IF YOU ENCOUNTER RESISTANCE, LURE THEM BACK TO US. DO NOT ENGAGE DIRECTLY AT THIS TIME. Grant noticed that when Alskexa signed 'you' that she used a derogatory Drow term for 'male.' She was really getting into this High Mother role.

Grant would have laughed except that the seriousness of the Drow and their use of these tactics made him see that, were this real and he actually did laugh, he would be executed. THIS MALE COMPLIES, he signed with a flourish and went back to lead the assault on the right side. Locking gazes with Khalla, both teams entered their respective tunnels at the same time.

Khalla led Disakcion into the left tunnel. About ten paces in, it stank like undead. She had been away from Bloodstone enough that she had all but forgotten the musty dry smell of that place. It filled the air here. Ahead, the tunnel either forked or bent and they saw light and movement. The entire team moved without sound and approached.

Khalla saw it first. The tunnel widened and had several branches shooting off to its sides. The light came from green eyes glowing four paces above her in the air. Her infravision showed her the heat shape of a giant insect. It was a thri-keen. Though Tanians considered praying mantises lucky and would take great care to not hurt them, she could not easily say the thri-keen was a giant mantis. It had the general shape, and she imagined that from a distance, she could see the similarity with the insect. *Or, she wondered, maybe it's just this one.*

The thri-keen had a feeling of age to it and it moved slowly. Not detecting any threats, and suspecting they could not cross the chamber undetected, Khalla stepped out and bowed to the insect. It ignored her. In Elven, she said, "Hail, warrior of the thri-keen. We mean you no harm."

The thri-keen continued to ignore her. *Maybe it ignores the vampires too?*, she pondered. So that she would not overthink it, she walked across the chamber, careful to give the keen plenty of space. It dragged a circular stone behind it. Khalla paused and realized it was a tombstone. The thri-keen dragged it step by step. Though gird about with ceramic-looking weapons, the giant praying mantis looked resigned. She did not know how she knew that, but she imagined the warrior must be very old to dragging its own tombstone to its own grave. The thickness of the stone meant it would weigh more than ten men could carry. She signaled the others to follow her.

They worked their way down for almost another hour before she heard a buzzing and then Alskexa's voice came to her in Drow. "You have been gone a long time. You will send someone back to inform us of conditions and we will advance, unless you say otherwise. Figure out what our advance point should be and send the scout now."

Khalla selected Oscar and sent him back with instructions to advance 100 paces past the thri-keen chamber. With any luck, if they did lure the vampires, they could retreat to the thri-keen and get it engaged in fighting the undead as well. She imagined Grant getting a similar message.

* * *

Kallis sat up from his post-feeding and coital stupor. Syand lay unmoving next to him, barely moving, hardly alive. The stone mausoleum all around him felt empty and dark. He listened to the preternatural silence that he and Syand had shattered just hours, *or was it days?*, ago. He could not remember in this dark, timeless void. It all felt wrong though.

Without being able to say why, Kallis looked at Syand's ruined body. Were she not a vampire, their coupling would have killed her. Kallis popped his neck and spine, enjoying how her blood had diffused the god's into him. He reached over and picked up the small chest containing the fifty vials. Nearly as many vampires sat in statuesque oblivion around him. He felt total apathy and imagined leaving them all.

Kallis felt that uncomfortable tug in his mind, the one that said, "Pay attention to me or else." He sighed and walked away from Syand.

Once far enough away that she would not be able to detect him, he bowed low to the ground and prayed. "My lord Asmodei, are you telling me to leave?" he whispered into the blackness.

From the blackness, a red blur loomed in his mind. As its spherical shape grew clearer, Kallis saw it cut through by dark red lines. The formless void answered him and the sound of it filled his bones with dread. Its words carried authority and stated fact that made Kallis' mind immediately latch onto it as truth. It said, "If you stay, you will die, slave. I have not preserved you this long to die now. Travel south, to Tania, and board the Tauran ship there. You will follow the one they call Halgrim. That one once contracted with me and payment is overdue."

Kallis worshipped. "Yes, Dread Asmodei." Not knowing why, he began to grovel, thankful the other vampires remained torpid and unaware. The red cut sphere groaned in his mind's vision and separated until a single red eye of veins and a black pool of eternal night at its center stared at him.

A voice growled and Kallis could not discern if the voice was real or in his mind. It made his bones grind and ache to hear it. "It is good to know one's place. A servant will come and take the blood from you. Though you diluted it, it is not good to mix your natures this way. I created you to serve Warp, not Chaos. I forbid you from imbibing Orcus' blood. It pulls at you. Do not think that Orcus was undead. He lived, like all the eldar. His blood will kill you and I require your life still."

Hearing this, Kallis' soul overflowed with joy. "That you need me another day, fills me with desire to serve. I will find this Halgrim. I will join the ship." He almost asked for help, but knew Asmodei would provide for him. He covered his head in his lanky arms as if he might be attacked. When no attack came, he looked into the terrible red eye and found it contemplating him.

Asmodei growled. "The Dragon Queen does something new under the Gates. An alliance between Warp and Chaos. Kallis, though you are not my greatest creation, you will be the first to undergo this experiment. Serve me well and I might consider your pact fulfilled."

"You speak of Joviel? Again?!" As Kallis said this, Asmodei's displeasure wracked Kallis and he screeched. Quickly changing his tone and words, Kallis yelled out, "Yes! Anything. My life for you!" Kallis groveled long after the dark presence left. When he regained a full measure of his right mind, he took the vials of Orcus blood, his favorite gear, and left. He did not look at Syand or any of the other women and men he had once loved. They were just tools.

If anything, looking at them one last time, Kallis opened himself to the truth of these many centuries. "I hate you all. You're going to die that I might live. You have no idea the evil Asmodei has prepared for you." Kallis contemplated murdering them all, especially Syand, his first created vampire. He hated that Syand had leeched centuries of glory from his Dark Gift and never once thanked him for it.

\* \* \*

Syand became aware that something was wrong when the air around her changed. Normally it lacked movement. No breeze, no motion at all was the normal state of the catacombs. Its staleness was as eternal as the darkness. Its movement heralded entry. It only happened when the tavern door moved. She blinked her eyes and moved her legs, seeking out Kallis. He had not been gentle. The blood of Orcus had given her stamina and though she had fought back with all her might, he had brutalized her, again. The last time, she had been unconscious for three weeks. She could tell by the damp sweat and smell of their blood that it had only been hours. His absence did not bother her as much as the absence of the blood vials. She thanked the gods that she had secreted some away for herself.

She struggled to clear her thinking. She felt uneasy and wondered if the tavern entrance had been breached. A legionnaire would have already arrived and would be awaiting her instructions if that had happened without an alarm. They would have signaled as well. The signal had not sounded. That meant intruders had entered, or that Syand was going crazy.

Her eyes darted to where the servant should be. The lack of a servant there, bowing, ready for her to wake up and ask questions, or demand blood, did not surprise her. Tania was coming for them. Only one other ancient was as old as Syand. She groaned inwardly. She and Brenna had both fallen in love with Kallis at the same time. Neither had known of the other, nor did they know Kallis was a vampire. His dark gift had stripped their inhibitions about each other, and also exposed the innate rivalry they each felt for him in their love match. That's what it should have been. Vampirism had elevated it into a feud and they seldom prowled at the same time as a form of truce.

Syand smiled and sauntered over to Brenna. "If we have intruders, you will be the first." She dragged Brenna unceremoniously to the room's entrance. "You can greet the Cuthberics, the Dragon Paladins, or whatever it is." She found Brenna's sword and armor and dragged them out and put them in front of her. Enchantments on the cave would activate all of them if any with hostile intent entered the outermost cavern in this crypt. Though there were multiple exits like her secret one behind the thri-keen crypts, and Kallis had clearly left by one of his own that Syand did not know about, Syand did not relish spending eternity with him. She also did not relish the idea of fighting intruders in this crypt.

On a whim, she removed her clothing and gear and dressed Brenna in it. Brenna had similar equipment though some of the other ancients had better weapons or pieces of armor and jewelry. Syand took the best of what she wanted from each. *Yes*, she thought. *There is something off.* We have intruders. She giggled. Working quickly, she positioned the unmoving vampires she hated by Brenna. Those who had served her, that she owed, or that she imagined she loved, she moved farther back. One, a young man named Everette, had been her first love after the dark gift. She paused and remembered stalking him for months on the surface world before at last revealing herself to him.

Her supernatural abilities had allowed her to cloud his recognition of her as a vampire. Thinking he truly loved her, she had at last offered him the gift. He rebelled and tried to kill her. She had taken him anyway. He was still her favorite. She opened one of the blood vials and poured Orcus' blood into his stone mouth. She then kissed it, licking the blood spilling around his lips, and let herself bleed onto his dusty teeth. He would know of her gift. He would awaken first.

She considered waiting to see who the intruders were. Thanks to Orcus, she could see the logical fallacy in that. Whoever it was had defeated the tavern guards without a single warning. They had bypassed the thri-keen. They were coming here. They were not friends and were powerful. In Sora, the Temples never skimped on fighting evil. It would be either a band of heroes or an army of heroes. *Probably.* Ydriss and Renault's defection, Jace's absence, these collectively spelled that the Dark Legion would likely fragment and then later, come back together as it always did. The last time was nearly 400 years ago. Syand had preserved Kallis and they alone had survived. Kallis had kept Brenna. It galled her to even remember.

Syand climbed the sloped side of the chamber and found the fake thri-keen stone. It had taken years to dig her own escape tunnel. She slipped behind the stone and waited with her eye at a peep hole to watch.

\* \* \*

Khalla poked her head around an opening and saw Grant's tunnel. Grant looked out and waved back at her. He pointed to the floor where tile smoothed the rough passage floor they had been walking. It was an ideal location for a magical boundary or trap. The tiles would hide the design and working of any traps magical or mechanical.

The two master thieves bowed down to the ground and studied the tiles. Khalla felt a sense of competition and realized that with Ash looking over her shoulder and her cell leader Ryvane too, she really wanted to do better than the Soran guildmaster. Knowing that Ash had recruited and trained this one in total secrecy made it even more important. She saw a small dent and carefully probed it. Grant noticed and found a similar one. She looked along the line. She found thirty dents like this along the exit from their tunnel to the chamber before them.

Wriggling her probe with barely a breath of pressure, she found a small notch and was able to pull the dent up. She did this quickly with the other twenty-nine and almost chuckled when she noticed Grant had not realized there were more. When she inserted the thirtieth probe and popped the dent, the ground trembled just a bit and dust rained down from the ceiling. This trap had not been activated in a very long time. She stood up and brushed her hands. Careful to pose with a bored look on her face, she put her hand on her hip and let a throwing spike twirl through her fingers. Grant finished and smiled up at her. "Got it," he said quietly. "You're really fast at this."

They entered the chamber though Ash pulled Khalla back and suggested that someone else enter first. He caught her hand and in Perdition tapping said: YOU DO NOT RISK MARCELLO WHEN THERE ARE OTHERS. She nodded.

Bolston entered with Grant, but both quickly ducked back and signaled they saw forms down below them in the opposite chamber. Grant crept forward and came back to report. He signed: UNDEAD, MAYBE FORTY? I SEE TWELVE. LIKE STATUES, BUT WITH ARMOR AND WEAPONS.

Khalla chewed her lip and considered. Lord Michael could probably incinerate all of them just with his faith. Alskexa and Valaes, RiVule, Halgrim, the underground chamber was a perfect setting for any kind of area effect magic. She signed back. WE HOLD HERE ALSKEXA MUST DECIDE APPROACH. YUNSTIR, THRADEN, TAKE HER WORD QUICKLY.

In the total darkness, they settled down and hoped the vampires would wait for the rest of the team. Ash tapped her arm and signed to her. THIS IS LIKE BLOODSTONE. VAMPIRES ARE NEVER GOOD.

She nodded and kissed his hand. WHY DO YOU THINK THEY'RE FROZEN?

Without hesitation, Ash replied, IT'S A CLEAR TRAP. A DISTRACTION.

SO, WE WAIT.

An hour later, Khalla heard Alskexa's voice as if the priestess were whispering in her ear. "We are coming to you. We are magically silenced so you won't hear us. Let your perimeter know."

With the teams reunited after another hour, Alskexa ordered a classic Tanian formation. "The fighters: Taisha, Revi, Calvin, and Nilthan, you will advance with RiVule and Valaes behind them. Furis, you will trail them with your bow. The clerics will keep you all healed. Lord Michael and Alskexa will linger towards the back and only take action if required. Halgrim, ready yourself to cut this group in half. I would rather we not fight them all at once. Scouts and Disakcion will move to the side of the vampires and be ready to flank into the room when opportunity presents itself." Alskexa turned to Cordelle. "The vampires might accept you. You will walk forward and see."

Cordelle nodded though he looked nervous. "I'm not much of a frontline fighter. I'm much better at being a merchant. I'll do my best."

Alskexa hissed at him. "You will do what you are told, slave. Now, go."

Cordelle recoiled but Michael's warm hand on his back helped him feel better. *She's really getting into this high mother acting. I hope she doesn't take it too far*, he thought.

Walking across the chamber felt like a 1,000-mile journey. Each step, he expected a trap. Each click of his shoes on stone, he thought the vampires would spring to life and attack him. When he could finally look down at them from the top of the stairs, he thought he recognized one, the one in front. He paused and rubbed his nose between his eyes trying to remember. He called out to her. "Brenda? No, damn it. I can't remember if that's your name. Brendolyn? No, that's too long." He bowed. "Forgive an old man his failing memory for a beauty I haven't seen since I was a much younger man."

She did not move and after a few moments, Cordelle walked onto the steps. None of them moved, but he could tell they were still alive. Their heartbeats moved slowly like the grinding of the earth and with his undead senses, he could sense their ever-present hunger. He walked up to the female and touched her face. Nothing. He looked behind them and saw many more in poses of readiness, but they all seemed to be asleep or frozen.

He stepped back and looked around. "Damn," he said out loud. "I came all this way to trade information about Grant's whereabouts, and in hope of finding Jace. Syand?" He shouted. His voice echoed in a thousand directions and continued to echo back to him for nearly a full minute. "Syand, I don't like this game. Bradley said I could come down here for this. I know you're here. I want Jace back, and to learn why I'm a vampire. Why?"

Syand could not see Cordelle but his story did explain why there had not been an alarm, or a signal. Vampires came and went all the time without scrutiny. Cordelle could have only found this with Bradley's guidance. *The fat slob probably just gave him directions rather than escort him in.* If Cordelle knew where Grant was, then that meant there would be more blood. Her skin felt itchy with the prospect of quickly downing an entire keg of it, or bathing in it. She shuddered at the pleasure of the thought. She could tell that transcendence would be sweet. After all, Joviel had done it and Kallis obsessed about her.

Cordelle called out, "Bradley did not tell me what to do to speak with the others here. Should I wait? Hello? Grant's not going to be in Sora very long. He came with a strange group of adventurers contracted out of Tania's Adventurers Guild. My sources say he'll be moving on after just a day or two. We had some IOUs to handle and he mentioned he had more of the stuff if I was still buying. Buying might be easier than burning 521's warehouse down you know? I'm sure we can work something out."

The first words began to echo back and he stopped. Syand felt frustration and craving gnawing at her mind. She knew this was a trap. She knew it, but Cordelle's words made so much sense. *And more blood!* She would do anything for more.

Cordelle had gone silent and Syand moved out of her spot to Everette. She caressed his face and whispered to him. "Everette, my love. I need you. Awake, but do not move. Take it all in. I gave you a gift. It will make you strong. Awaken the others, all of them. Speak to Cordelle and find out where the god's blood is, where Grant is. Then, you will all march forth and get it for me. Bring it all back here. Kill everyone who tries to stop you." She quickly moved back to her hidden observation point.

Khalla and the others saw movement in the room. It was a lone figure that went to one of the statues and then quickly retreated. *So, something in there is awake and listening.* She signaled to all. "Be ready. It's going to happen any second now." To Ryvane, she added, "The figure retreated to the left side. When this all goes down, I want you to use your magic. Root that one out. Ensure we do not leave ourselves open to a counterattack."

Ryvane nodded; she had seen the figure as well. Alskexa gestured for them to quiet.

After some moments, when Cordelle seemed about to return, a lone figure moved and took a deep inhalation of air. The wheezing sound faded after a second breath. The gasping and choking, and then steadier respiration reminded Khalla of someone too long underwater. The figure spoke to Cordelle.

"The god's blood, Cordelle. We seek only its blood. You say you have it. Where?" The voice had a sinister bent to it. "If you do not have more, where is the traitor Grant? We would have words with him."

Cordelle sensed the fighters shift around, tensing. He bowed to the vampires below the stairs and replied, "Oh good. I thought you might all be sleeping. I'm very new to this whole vampire thing. Is that how you sleep, armed and in armor? It seems like a terrible way…"

"You blather on and on… know your place, slave! You come with news and would speak to the ancient ones about how they cross the many years? Where is the blood, or the traitor?" Everette drew his sword. It cast a red shine on the scene and illuminated the vampires in front of him into flat silhouettes.

Cordelle put his hand on his own short sword and took a defensive step back. "Syand said to come to her with this news…"

"Now, I know you lie. Syand did no such thing! You see, she was here over a week ago and explicitly said that if she ever found you, we were to slay you on sight," he lied. It seemed a good way to hide the fact Syand had just awoken him. He knew she would approve, and her approval might have other benefits. He licked his lips at the thought. This strange blood in his mouth, the god's blood, illuminated the darkness. He could see Cordelle's fear. Everette pointed his sword at Cordelle. He now stood five paces away at the bottom of the steps. Brenna, Everette noticed, had been placed in front of the vampires with her armor and weapons ready. He wondered why and glanced back at Cordelle, who did not seem threatening. Brenna hated being in the front of anything, especially combat.

Cordelle held out his hands in a placating gesture. "You got me. It wasn't Syand. It was Bradley. I thought name dropping would help. Look, do you want the blood or Grant? Your hostility is making me think I'm talking to the wrong vampire. Who are you?"

"My name is Everette, slave. In the future, you will mind your tongue until you are worthy to know names. The blood?"

Cordelle reached into his pocket. He noticed that the other vampires, all of them, had begun to breathe and move. Eyes slowly opened just enough to see and were watching them talk. He dry swallowed and felt fear. Unlike Lord Michael's power against the undead, this fear chilled his bones. He pulled a small vial out of his pocket. "This is a token of my good faith. I can throw it to you?"

Everette held his hand out and deftly snatched the thrown vial out of the air. He popped the seal and smelled it. "Yes, this is the god's blood. But, let's be sure." He went to Brenna and emptied it into her mouth.

Already awake, the blood swelled her with power and bright colors burst forth to her vision. She put her head back and screamed as it burned like fire in her veins. "Glorious!" she shouted. She turned to the vampire to her left and kissed him deeply, sharing some of the blood with him. The effect hit him as well.

Cordelle watched it all, wide-eyed and suddenly grateful that they had never tested the blood on him. *Or tempted me*, he added ruefully. He remembered Grant showing him the material the first time.

Looking out over the vampires stretching and shuddering to life in the chamber before him, Cordelle realized something about who he was, who had wanted to be. He squared his shoulders. "Everette, you say I am not worthy to know your name, and yet, as the guildmaster of 521, I cannot remember a single tale of Everette." Seeing the vampire's eyes flash with anger, Cordelle drew his swords. "I come here to help and you insult me. If this is what the Dark Legion is, then I reject it. I reject you and your mystical fascination with undeath and your now dead god. You don't even know what it means to live. Look at yourselves! Locked in the catacombs! You're pathetic." Cordelle mimicked drinking the blood, and then dove forward to attack.

It had been years since Cordelle felt a rush like this. The vampire's senses allowed him to see, hear, and even smell what his enemies were about to do. He preferred to fight from the shadows and at a distance. In this case, he had plenty of darkness. He threw one of his swords like a javelin. Blessed by Lord Michael, the blade would hurt, hopefully kill. It struck Everette but deflected off the vampire's armor and Everette laughed. When Cordelle swung his blade in a chopping motion, the vampire vanished into smoke and reformed behind Cordelle.

Brenna smiled cruelly at Cordelle. "So young to be a suicidal vampire," she mocked him. Her long sword stabbed through Cordelle's leg armor and cracked his pelvis bone.

The guildmaster tried to dodge back, away from the attack. But, his surprise at Everette's disappearance, and the pain from Brenna's attack sent him stumbling back into Everette's arms. "Suicidal and pathetic," Everette whispered in his ear, and then threw him at the steps. "Tell us of Grant: where is he? Yield up more of this blood, or die."

Cordelle held his hip and winced. *Draw them out into the ambush*, he tried to focus. *You can do this.* "If you kill me, you'll never know." He threw his short sword and hoped it would buy him a few moments. He crawled up the stairs and heard his sword deflected by another blade. It clattered to the ground and he reached the top step.

He looked over his shoulder to see if he had any time, but found Everette right in his face, at the top step. The vampire began to say something, but Cordelle bit his nose. He had not yet fed. He did not know what it even felt like to feed. Cordelle's jaw seemed to yawn and stretch and then Everette's blood filled his mouth and the vampire reared up holding his face. Not to lose his advantage, even though the diffused blood of Orcus was burning his vision and strengthening his frame, Cordelle kicked up into Everette's groin. Maybe it was the Orcus blood, or his first meal, but his kick lifted the fighter off the ground and sent him tumbling down the steps. The fire in his belly began to knit the wound from Brenna's blade. Though still in pain, Cordelle's confidence soared. "Thank you for the appetizer," he shouted. And then, Cordelle ran back towards the two passages.

Everette blinked and groaned as Cordelle dented his codpiece and sent him falling down the stairs. Brenna caught him. "I remember you now, you Syand whore," she spat at him. "Attack Cordelle," she ordered the other vampires. She dragged her longsword on the wall along the stairs as she climbed to approach Cordelle. It drew a line of sparks that illuminated her fangs and the well-defined musculature of an ancient one. Compared to Everette, Brenna was a god and she wanted Cordelle – and Everette – to see it.

Some of the vampires could teleport in line of sight. Others could turn to smoke or shadow and move from place to place as if flowing mist. In a heartbeat, Cordelle found himself cut off from retreat by eight vampires. They all seemed to materialize before him and then one spotted the fighters hiding by the stair entryway. *That one*, Cordelle thought, and attacked.

Brenna reached the top of the stairs as her cohorts streamed past her. Without any warning, she noticed one of Cordelle's foes point and then a metal shield slammed into her. The sheer strength threw her back. Rather than risk another ambush, Brenna jumped down the stairs to the coven's crypt. Her attacker charged down after her just missing her knees with a wild slicing attack. Brenna noted the deep magic in the blade. Its magic practically screamed for vampires to die.

"Hello," a cheerful voice said. "I'm going to be your enemy tonight. Name's Revi." The attack threw her back down the stairs and completely caught her off guard. Only the onslaught of the other vampires steadied her fall. Arrows began arcing into the coven surrounding Cordelle from where Revi attacked her. She caught her balance and felt her shoulder armor come undone.

A great whooshing sound filled the chamber behind her as a wall of fire divided the room in half and blocked the stairs from the back half of the main mausoleum. Brenna swore at Revi. "Asmodei take you, human."

Revi smashed his sword pommel against his breastplate and taunted Brenna. "Is that the best you got? You've been down here a long time! Orcus is dead. Swear by his name." A vampire near Revi tried to flank attack, but a warrior armored like Revi intercepted the flanking attack against a Pha Rannic emblazoned shield.

Revi aimed his sword at Brenna and seemed to teleport into attack. She barely parried and jumped back almost into the wall of flames.

Revi frowned and sliced his sword along a vampire rushing past him. From the Cordelle chamber, Brenna heard a voice command out. "By Pha Rann's flawless light, let no undead survive this night!" The burning screams of divine immolation told Brenna that this was all indeed, a trap. She cursed at Everette. No doubt a pawn in yet another of Syand's schemes to claim Kallis for herself.

"I'm Brenna. Nice to meet you, Revi you said, right? What brings a nice boy like you to my home at such a late hour?" Fully recovered, Brenna stabbed forward and then used her supernatural speed to flank and strike at Revi's side. Like his surprise attack on her, she surgically cut the binding on his shoulder armor. "You'll not catch me like that again."

"In front of all my friends?" Revi exclaimed. "Have some decency!" He moved forward and used his shield to deflect her sword's defense and then struck squarely at her greaves. Expecting him to strike her torso, she felt his blade shear her leg armor and tumbled back.

"I see you fight as well as you lie. It's been a while since I've played with my food," she shrugged her leg armor off. "My words hold true though."

Revi shrugged and charged forward. His sword struck into where her neck would have been if she had not vanished into humid mist. He felt the mist move along his body and reform, before goosebumps could cover his skin, behind him. He twisted to defend and felt his armor falling off his body. Years in Bloodstone and combat with Ayden and others like her had taught him to stay focused. Stay the course. Don't get distracted. As Brenna turned to gloat and watch his armor fall away, Revi focused on her heart. He had carefully built a rhythm and expected pattern of gloating and flirting. He prayed for Joust to level the field, make it fair, and then struck.

Revi's blade, enchanted against undeath, flew forward. Brenna reformed her body, already smirking to see the handsome man's armor and clothing fall away. Instead, she found his sword in her heart. She tried to move, to recapture her gaseous form, but it happened too quickly. Her mind was caught expecting – even anticipating – their next tete-a-tete.

Revi's sword punctured her ribcage and skewered her heart. He drove forward until his hilt guard pressed into her breasts. This put their faces inches from each other. Revi twisted his sword side to side. "Another beautiful lady I'll never get to know." With Brenna's last breath escaping her mouth as a sigh, Revi sighed as well. A knife materialized in his other hand and he stabbed it into her torso. Only when he was satisfied she would not regenerate, did Revi step back. As her body began to slip off his sword, he withdrew and sliced across her neck. His sword cleaved her jawline down to her shoulder and her head rolled free.

Above him, Ryvane entered and stared at Revi for just a moment. Revi's battle was too much to process. He pointed to himself as if to say, 'like what you see?' "Thanks," he called out and bowed. "That look was just enough to be awkward." Brenna's head finally came to a rest near the bottom step.

Ryvane pointed to him and quickly cast a spell. A vampire attacking from behind raked his exposed shoulder and Revi whirled to defend himself.

By the next attack, ghostly armor clung to his body and the next attack hit the spectral shape of his breastplate as if steel.

Turning her attention away from Revi's combat, Ryvane walked towards the wall of fire bisecting the room. Vampires on the other side waiting patiently to cross. One even offered to pay her to vanquish the flames. Maybe it mistook her for a spell-casting member of their own group? That raised Ryvane's hackles.

To the left, her eyes traced the many thri-keen circle stones. The lone figure had come from the left side. With the fire illuminating everything, she could see well. A simple spell magnified her vision and she scanned the stones looking for anything that might suggest a great hiding place or secret exit.

After a minute, Revi pushed her out of the way as he and Nilthan threw three vampires back from attacking her. The battle in the upper chamber seemed locked. It surprised Ryvane. She would have guessed that Lord Michael by himself could have vanquished the vampires purely through the power of his faith. *Maybe Orcus' death made the vampires more resistant to that power?* She wondered at it while scanning.

She cast another spell and an eyeball the size of a human head appeared in front of her. She concentrated and another appeared. "Inspect each disk beginning over there," she pointed to the left side. "If there is space behind them, enter and show me what you see. If there is no space, proceed to the next."

While focusing on this scrying variant spell, someone pulled her aside as a lightning strike just narrowly missed her. She held her focus enough to finish the spell even as she was thrown to the ground and landed painfully. Calvin took the brunt of the lightning attack against his special shield. The electricity coursed along the shield and his arm, down his body, to dissipate in the ground.

Ryvane pushed the pain away and wondered if Calvin could withstand the electrical attack. He did, though he dropped to his knees and smiled at her weakly, before falling over unconscious. "Cleric!" she yelled out. "Calvin needs healing."

She had a job to do and Calvin would be all right. They had clerics. *Who knows? Dying might be good for him.* Her callous attitude bothered her a bit. She resolved to make it up to Calvin later, when they were alone. The first eye reached the chamber edge and found nothing. The second eye tried the same as the first and found nothing. This would take a while. Ryvane tried to remember where Everette had been standing and tried to retrace what she had seen.

Ryvane noticed that Valaes had come forward and was tending to Calvin. That removed a distraction from her thoughts and she summoned her spell book to her hand and began looking for a spell that might help. "I need something that will show me." She flipped to a spell and eyed it. It allowed the caster to detect evil. Being of a race that registered as evil, and fighting in vampire-infested catacombs, she doubted it would work. "What if I change this a bit?" A pen appeared in her hand and she scribbled some notes while the battle raged around her. She had a brief glimpse of Calvin standing up and rejoining combat with Revi and Nilthan.

Halgrim also entered the room and the attack moved to the vampires on the other side of the wall of fire. The ones farther back, like Everette, seemed better equipped and prepared. They had been watching through the flames for minutes after all. Halgrim dropped the wall of fire and, all around Ryvane, Disakcion, Scout, and Priestess clashed with the vampires. In a moment of curiosity, Ryvane watched Michael command the destruction of a vampire before him. The vampire twisted and writhed, steam boiling out of its skin, and then it fell back. One look at Michael and the other clerics was all it took for the vampire to seek out an enemy far away from them. This concentrated the vampires around Disakcion and Scout. Just as Ryvane considered it, Halgrim sent a fireball shooting at the cluster. She noticed that Halgrim had to cast from his spellbook. That explained why larger magic effects were lacking; Halgrim was not an actual battle mage.

Ryvane hated casting from her spellbook. The formality it required along with the exacting rituals she had learned and trained long ago to circumvent drove her crazy with impatience. She began to cast, grateful that Disakcion and her own cell stood to take up guard around her. The sudden release of combat magic did not let go its hold on her mind and she almost made mistakes by rushing through parts of the ritual she knew the shortcuts to. She blanketed her awareness away from the fury of battle around her. The last syllable twisted from her lips and she dropped to her knees exhausted.

When she looked up, four of the many thri-keen discs glowed. It had worked. The general evil of the vampires clashed with the divine-nature of Krentismic magic in this otherwise sanctified place. She sent her wizard eyes zipping up to those four. In the first, the eye saw a female vampire. The vampire blinked in surprise and then struck at it. Ryvane was certain this vampire must be Syand from the descriptions provided by Grant's team and Cordelle.

The seeing eye vanished. The lash back from the spell's ending made Ryvane fall over in a fit of wracking pain. The other eye entered the same area and saw the female vampire in full retreat. Ryvane barely could see through her mind's eye. The brief glimpse suggested that might be Syand. Grant and the others had provided detailed descriptions after all.

The next of the four showed a sepulcher replete with armor and weapons. The last was empty. One of the others was similarly full of equipment. The last tunnel, like the one with the fleeing vampire, retreated from the chamber much farther than her spell could trace. She pulled back and held the magic eyes where they could watch all of the four discs.

She leaned up from the floor and saw the expected victory. The teams were fighting as they should. The vampires were losing as they should. The only problem was that they were still fighting. Even against eldar vampires, someone like Lord Michael should have been more potent. It bothered her. She felt a flash of inspiration and wondered what could be powerful enough to do this. The answer: a bloodstone. Sora had, over many centuries, acquired more than enough black market bloodstones that some could have ended up in a place like this.

Khalla yanked her sword back from where she cut up into the vampire's underarm. As unpleasant as the foul blood spray was, her satisfaction at the creature's death made it tolerable. She whipped herself to the side and dodged a piercing sword strike from its fellow. The blade still sliced into her armor but thankfully did not cut her. Khalla jerked herself back to put space between the creature and herself. This combat was not going as it was supposed to. Lord Michael and the clerics were supposed to be able to turn the vampires. This was more of a breaching test, not full scale combat. Yet it had become a fight to the death.

She eyed Alskexa and saw the priestess standing her ground against two of the legionnaires. She looked imperious but bloodied and battered. *Good*, Khalla thought. The Tanian priestesses had a reputation for not taking things seriously. Grant's friend, the priestess Maishan, did much better. Though Maishan had not yet transcended like Alskexa had, she waded through battle untouched by the vampires. At her touch, wounds healed and morale rallied. *That's what a priestess should be doing*, Khalla thought. *Why can't they turn the vampires?*

Lord Michael had barely been able to turn a single one and they had all prepared for multiple infernos just from his power alone. The tavern vampires had gone up like fireworks. Krentismic holy ground could not account for why Pha Rann's power would dim here. In Drow, Alskexa had proclaimed, "A dire power stymies our power. Nonetheless, our enemies are clearly arrayed before us. Press the attack!"

Khalla saw the wall of fire extinguish and so ran towards the lower chamber. She was almost there when the thri-keen stones beneath her erupted and a thri-keen emerged. It held jagged scimitars in each of its hands and wore armor. Though the armor reflected light and looked like steel, it had a ceramic appearance to it. The creature chittered at her and with a sweep of its leg, slammed her away. Three more followed that one into the chamber. Their insect eyes looked around unblinking and they waded into the combat. At first, Khalla thought they had arrived to help. When one came at her and threw a triangular weapon at her, she realized they had come to fight trespassers. Their presence increased the peril of the mission.

"I'm not your enemy," she said in Elven, hoping the creature would understand her. She pointed to the vampires battling all around them. "These are ancient vampires. They have defiled..."

The thri-keen attacked by jumping at her while swinging four swords in its four arms. Khalla barely dodged. It dragged a great furrow through the stone where the blade missed her. She was about to attack when Venter and Jerare dove into the gap between her and the keen. "Grant said to free you up. Go do what you need to do!" She nodded and saw that Yunstir from her own cell was running over to join the fray.

The keen, perhaps sensing she would get away, threw another disc at her. She tried to dodge, but it did not move through the air in a straight like a knife or throwing star. It wobbled. As it passed her, she felt a biting sting along her forearm. Khalla withdrew from the combat and noted the weapon had cut a thin, nearly invisible line through her armor into her bone. She could barely move her arm.

In Drow, she called out. "High Mother, we must free up Ryvane. I have a theory!"

Alskexa blocked a sword with her dragon mace and nodded. When her next attack came, the priestess went all but transparent. Her attacker blinked in confusion and looked around for another foe. Only by concentrating could Khalla see her. She was familiar with this divine power. It allowed them to step out of certain situations, like combat, and move freely about the field of battle. It was a powerful advantage and one Khalla wished she had.

No more than ten paces from Ryvane, Halgrim stood in the center of the fighters casting spells to give advantage or maim and kill the vampires. The frustration on his face told Khalla volumes about what his commentary might be when they wrapped up this business. But, she felt something else, a supreme confidence she had never experienced before. It felt almost delusional. *Is this being Marcello?* She wondered if Ash felt this way every day and made a note to ask him, later. For now, at least, they stood in the center of a raging storm, and saw that the vampires were regenerating.

Through harried breaths, Khalla almost said her piece in Common. Instead, with annoyance blushing her cheeks, she spoke in Drow. "Michael said something that got me thinking. The vampires should have fallen. They should not be regenerating. That they are, there is only one magic in these lands that can do this: a bloodstone. I'm certain there is one here, probably a tower stone. It is strengthening our foes beyond what their abilities should be. We have to find it and stop it."

Ryvane purred. "That makes so much sense. I was wondering at that, but barely had time." She pointed to the four discs. "Secret chambers. Two are tunnels. One had a vampire in it, probably Syand. The other might be an exit."

Khalla turned to Alskexa and asked, "High Mother, what we seek is probably not in those four locations. A tower stone would be protected and away from a place of likely combat. I would ask a boon of the Goddess." She bowed in the Drow manner.

Alskexa nodded and said, "The Goddess awaits your request. Proceed with caution, though. Lolth is not one to be trifled with petty rivalries and greed. For Her Glory, nothing else."

Khalla knelt before Alskexa and continued, "High Mother, hear my plea. We must know the location of the bloodstone, else this battle will…" Khalla hesitated. Lolth could not care less about this battle. She reaffirmed her wording and finished. "The bloodstone will allow us to make the vampires' blood rain down upon these caverns and wash away the stink of thy foes."

Alskexa grinned and her eyes glassed over. With an otherworldly voice and an alien lilt in her voice, the priestess responded. "What you seek is under the center disc. Beware the three-fingered spider-eaters!"

Her voice choked out the last part in a dialect hardly recognizable as Drow. Alskexa dropped to her knees and began vomiting a gray water-like liquid. Ryvane and Khalla shuddered as the feeling emanating from the High Mother passed. "To think," Ryvane said with feigned cheerfulness. "We're going to be fighting against people who do this without thought or ill-effect. Makes you wonder what Lolth is truly like."

Khalla nodded and patted Alskexa on the back. The young girl sighed at her touch and then her muscles tensed. She rose up and caught Khalla's hand. "Do not dare to touch me, slave! Touch me again and spiders will nest in your eyes!" That otherworldly pressure returned and then Alskexa fell to the floor unconscious. Khalla's wrist ached where she was grabbed.

"Come on," Khalla said, wriggling her fingers to restore feeling. "We need to find the tower stone." Khalla looked around. Things had not gone right and while the thri-keen had at least also engaged the vampires, many of her own team had fallen.

She took mental stock. Calvin had fallen with three long swords through his abdomen. Revi and his two fighters guarded Halgrim and were also keeping the vampires from feeding on Calvin. Grant fought on, but leaked blood from several dire wounds; he should not be able to continue fighting like that. Delton fought nearby and was doing better at first glance, but when he whirled around to parry an attack from striking Grant, Khalla saw several crossbow bolts embedded so deeply near his heart that he was basically a dead man walking. Pol Nir fought back to back with Michael. The priest looked like he posed for a painting, but once she saw past the glamour, even he bore terrible wounds.

Khalla scanned for Ash. He fought near Valaes with RiVule and Taisha. They stood shoulder to shoulder against a pack of vampires and a thri-keen. "An unlikely alliance," Khalla complained. She touched the earring on Alskexa's ear and said, "Merakor! We must clear and hold the center stone. It's a thri-keen disc but in the center of this room. We will crack it open and I ask that Ash and Grant descend. We are looking for a tower stone. It must be deactivated. Until it is, we will not gain the advantage."

Her words struck the minds of those in the group and as one, everyone began maneuvering towards the center of the chamber. Halgrim stopped mid-spell, to the groaning complaints of Revi's team, and flipped to a different page in his spellbook. With smug satisfaction he began a different spell.

They reached the center stone and had to count crosswise several times to confirm it. It looked exactly identical to all of the other stones. "Lord Michael?" Khalla asked.

He raised his war hammer, which grew bright with radiance, and smashed it down. Around them, the vampires and thri-keen slammed into the party, tossing the perimeter into disarray. Gathered like this, they did not have much hope of lasting very long. "Revi," Halgrim cried. "Throw them all back now!"

The fighters rallied as Michael's divine hammer splintered the stone. Though identical to the others, it fractured in a way that showed hollow space rather than earth beneath it. Revi grunted and they threw their foes back. The next instant, everything became echoes. The vampires and thri-keen charged forward and slammed into an invisible wall. This repeated all around them. In frustration, the vampires tried to teleport into the circle but failed. One of the thri-keen jumped, trying to scrabble over the top of the invisible wall.

Everyone held their breath until the keen slipped and fell backwards. Frustrated, the vampires turned on the insects and vice versa. "I thought that might help," Halgrim said. The pleased look on his face made Ash burst into exhausted laughter and the others joined in.

"Thank you, sir," Khalla said. Michael's hammer blasted a man-sized hole in the disc. From below, darkness showed. "Maybe you can help our thieves not fall to their deaths, Lord Halgrim?" Sarcasm did not translate well to Drow. It came across as 'give them a lethal push, gently.'

Halgrim enacted a *levitation* spell and the two thieves crawled into the hole head first.

# Chapter 20 – Vampire Stone

"You've done well," Ash said to Grant. Ash pulled Grant to him and checked the holes in the rogue's armor where Grant had suffered almost-fatal wounds. "You feeling okay?" Using levitation, they moved slowly down the tunnel looking for traps as they went. It seemed unlikely that such a precious artefact would be unguarded.

Grant smirked. "Thanks. Maishan patched me up. I've followed your instructions exactly, but it has been hard. I'm not trained to fight through my own impending death. And, it's not often I'm having to deal with healing fatigue. You Tanians are crazy. This is twice now in three weeks I've almost died." Grant slid his hand along the stone below him and felt a non-rock texture. He paused and Ash froze at his sudden tension. "I think I found a trigger plate."

Grant slid his hands, barely touching the suspicious area, and felt the telltale signs of machine work. "I can't tell what the mechanism is."

"Can you stabilize it? I'd hate to have this be a tunnel-collapsing trap given, well, we're in a vertical tunnel. Thoughts?" Ash was already retrieving items from his belt. Being upside made it rough so he rotated himself around and helped Grant do the same.

Grant studied the mechanism and said, "Besides avoiding it, without knowing the mechanism, I…"

"Glue it," Ash said. He offered up a small pot. "It's like sovereign glue. Glob it on the trigger plate and area around it, gently. Within a few seconds, it'll dry harder than cement. Assuming it's a trigger plate, we could then whack it and it won't move."

Grant took the glue. "I've heard of this stuff before. It's rare in Sora."

Ash shrugged. "Not sovereign though. That was, to quote the Temple, "a travesty of alchemical mistakes." Just because it had a happy result, didn't mean it was perfect. For one, it comes undone too easily. And a permanent glue, while useful, isn't as useful to an agent of Perdition as a temporary but strong one. This glue will go rock solid and in about an hour, it disintegrates. It's actually liquid spider webs."

"I want some," Grant whispered. "So, I just put this on?" When Ash nodded, Grant took out some paper and scooped the glue out onto it so his hands would not become sticky. He then slowly and carefully pressed it to the trigger plate. Within a few moments, the paper firmed up and became firm. He then did this again and spread the glue all around the trigger plate. "So, that's it?"

"I like how you applied that. I wondered if you would ask. That's what I would have suggested. As noted, you've done well. By now, we could punch that trigger and the glue will hold it firm."

They put the glue away and continued down the tunnel. They found two more traps. One was a magical rune triggered by light. Being in darkness, they bypassed it and continued down. A faint red glow grew in their vision below them.

They reached the apex of a large natural cavern. Directly below, a horse-sized tower stone rested in a pool of liquid that hid the bottom fifth. They moved to the side, pointing to the statues standing in five points around the tower stone. "Khalla was right," Ash said. "It's too big for us to neutralize."

"How do you neutralize a bloodstone? I've heard of the massive explosions caused when they break, but they're also famously hard to break." Grant was crouched back against the ceiling. The floor looked likely to be riddled with traps and the statues were definitely golems. He'd bet money on it.

Ash grinned. "Marcello and Perdition have ways. If this were a small stone, we might have a problem. But, there's no way a tower stone this large began black market. It'd have been gifted or sold by Tania. As such, it will be marked." The light in Ash's eyes gave Grant some reassurance. "We need to get Khalla. Normally, I'd do this myself, but for now, it'll be Khalla. I'll stay here. Be careful, please. We have plans for you. Head back up and get her?"

Grant nodded and, in a flash, scampered back up the tunnel. Ash floated down into the center of the room and noted the dissymmetry of the chamber. Tunnels entered at strange angles and, like the one they entered through, might only be accessed by flight or magic. The entire place felt wrong, and that was compared to the vampires up above.

Khalla joined him ten minutes later. She handsigned to him: WE HAVE THREE HOURS OF LEVITATION. BROUGHT FLIGTH POTIONS TOO. Ash shared his observations with her about the chamber and she asked, WHAT DO YOU THINK THOSE TUNNELS ARE?

B-E-H-O-L-D-E-R TUNNELS. Ash took Khalla's hand and continued to sign: SECRET. DARYX ASKED ME TO SHARE WHEN TIME IS RIGHT, LIKE NOW. BLOODSTONES ARE MARKED SO EMPIRE CAN FIND THEM AND KNOW WHO HAS THEM AND WHAT THEY'RE DOING WITH THEM. THIS IS HOW DRAGONS BLEW STONES UP LAST YEAR. UNMARKED STONES ARE RARE – BLACK MARKET ONLY.

Khalla nodded her head and noted, THE MARKINGS ALLOW DETONATION BUT ALSO DEACTIVATION, RIGHT?

ONLY MARCELLO AND THE CIRCLE AND THE DRAGONS CAN. AS MARCELLO, YOU CAN DEACTIVATE IT. AS MARCELLO, ONLY YOU CAN SEE THE MARKING. ALL YOU HAVE TO DO IS TOUCH THE MARKING AND THE STONE STOPS WHEN YOU SAY YOUR FULL NAME, WHICH IS MARCELLO DO'KHALLA DO'PERDITION.

WHAT IF NO MARKING?, Khalla asked.

THEN WE GET CREATIVE AND DO OUR BEST TO DESTROY IT OURSELVES. STONE THAT BIG WILL PROBABLY COLLAPSE ALL

TUNNELS AND TRIGGER AN EARTHQUAKE. THIS CLOSE TO OCEAN MAYBE EVEN A TIDAL WAVE. LET'S PLAN ON THERE BEING A MARKING.

Khalla drank the *flight* potion while Ash tethered a rope to her belt and clipped it to his own. She moved down to the stone, wondering if she would be able to see the marking. Once she was close enough to see her ember reflection along the tower stone's polished oval surface, she saw it. The platform supporting the stone, including the golems, stood around it. The marking was underneath the platform. She signed up, MARKING IS ON BOTTOM. CANNOT TOUCH IT. MUST LIFT STONE.

The platform had a clear ring to it. He could not see the marking but knew where it was based on Khalla's looking at it. He sighed. "This is how people who know about the markings make our jobs interesting. Well, we wouldn't get paid so much if this was easy. You should see how the dread lords protect these things."

Khalla nodded while studying the platform. "We need a mage. Isn't there a magic that nullifies magic? I heard Ryvane talking about it with Grant. Maishan did something like that, anti-magic? The threat here is the golems, right? How much does Marcello get paid?"

"A lot. More than you can imagine. While it hurt that you cut me off from Perdition's treasury, Ash's treasury is doing just fine, thank you. You'll see. Halgrim is holding the force wall. I'm not sure that Ryvane is able to cast spells like that, but I can head up and ask."

Khalla waved him away as she began checking for mechanical traps. "Be careful," she signed to him.

In the hour it took to bring Ryvane back, Khalla found and disarmed five traps. The tunnels were not for beholders. They were for giant ballista bolts, each aimed at the trap and mechanisms around the stone. Some would shoot the thief. Others would trigger an avalanche. Most seemed likely to hit the stone and Khalla imagined the giant explosion that would trigger when the tower stone broke. The golems clearly had a different activation.

When Ryvane arrived, she held a scroll but it turned out to be a page torn from Halgrim's spell book. "Can we speak?" she signed. Khalla shook her head, no. Ryvane signed back, "I have an anti-magic spell. It puts a sphere around me that nullifies magic. It won't stop the golems from attacking us with missiles, but if they come into the sphere, they'll freeze. Other magics won't work, though an area effect one will. All of our own magic will end." She looked at the bloodstone. "That will not be affected. Are you sure you want me to cast this?"

Khalla asked Ash, "Without magic, how will we lift the stone?"

He signed back, "A large lever?"

Khalla felt worry gnaw at her and she turned to Ryvane. "Find one for us; it can't be magic." She turned to Ryvane and asked, "This is Halgrim's spell. So, you can't cast this. Have you ever?"

Ryvane looked away, as if ashamed, and answered, "No. If I mess up, I could go insane. Or the spell could blow up in my face. This is at least three ranks above my current ability."

Khalla pointed. "When you cast it, I want you as close to that golem right there as you can get. I'd love to immobilize an entire one. Can we affect more?"

Ryvane took in the setting again. "If you triggered them all to activate and we got them in a ring around me, yes. They're large, but Halgrim's spell should affect them if they're close to me. Or, you and Ash can gather them and I'll cast the spell on top and fall into their middle. Either way, they all need to be in a group."

Ash came up and said, "I have 5 different pole arms ready. They should work as levers. The lack of magic makes this interesting." His smile said he did not have any concerns about the impending situation.

Ryvane began to cast the spell, quietly at first. When no traps or sentinels appeared to stop her, she went faster. Khalla had never seen a mage cast from a spell book before. It looked painful. Ryvane's voice grew hoarse at one point and sweat dripped down her face and hands. Khalla could see the torn page trembling in her hands. It took much longer than Khalla was used to. Ash signed to her, "It's always this slow. Combat mages have shortcuts to go faster."

After ten minutes, Ryvane cut a word in half. The sound had a lingering potency to it and she signaled to Khalla that she was ready. Khalla and Ash alighted on the platform with weapons drawn and ready for combat. The golems, as one, turned their heads to the intruders and moved to attack. The sound of blade on blade and larger golem weapons smashing into the floor filled the room while the two agents jockeyed to corral the animated statues together. After several back-and-forths, Khalla spotted a golem on the side of the tower stone eyeing Ryvane. It held a spear. Just as the golem moved to throw it at the mage, Khalla flipped onto its arm and cut deep into where tendons would normally lie around the elbow.

The golem dropped its arm and spun. The sudden circular motion threw Khalla and she smashed against the tower stone. She flinched thinking it would explode or shock her, but except for its strange warmth, nothing happened. The markings sat right there, out of reach through the stone itself. Ash tumbled into the fray and bought Khalla time to recover though another golem swung its sword and caught his mid-section edgewise. Acting like a club against his armor, Ash's breath exploded from his lungs. He kept focus and slipped under the blade before it threw him.

Coming to his feet, he saw Khalla readying herself for another attack. Suddenly, three of the four golems went still and Ryvane dropped down between them. Her human form gone, the rakshasa stood before the one active golem and said, "I have to focus to maintain this effect. Sorry I could not get all four." Her voice had a lisping quality to it and her tail swished side to side.

Dropping the Drow language, Ash said, "It's been a while since I've seen the real you, Ryvane. You're looking good. I'll distract the active golem and see if I can't move the fight away from here. Keep an eye on those tunnels. I don't trust them."

Ryvane purred for a moment at his compliment. "If we lever slowly, I think I can help you. But, I have to maintain focus on the anti-magic, or it ends."

Ash moved out of the area quelling magic and felt the instant rush of energy that came when his magical gear lost weight and other enchantments helping movement became active. He raced to the golem and began a series of feint and parry attacks meant to prolong combat.

Khalla looked for the polearms and saw the tower stone propped up on a ring of them. Ash had positioned the miniaturized ones around the edges. Ryvane's magic, though it only affected half of them, had been enough that when enlarged, it had popped the large rock up. She shot a mental thank you to Ash and moved forward to pull on one. With all her weight, she could not lever the stone. The polearm sat nearly perpendicular to the ground. She tried another and another. "Ryvane! I need help."

The rakshasa nodded and walked over with great care. The tiger hand grabbed the long weapon next to Khalla and pulled. The greater weight, bulk, and strength of the rakshasa propped the stone up a few inches. Khalla raced to drive all of the polearms deeper in. They began to repeat this. On the third one, one of the deactivated three began to move and Ryvane had to step back. "Okay, we get three," Khalla said straining to pry her pike in deeper.

Out of the corner of her eye, Khalla saw Ash dodge a flailing sword strike and then get kicked. The kick sent Ash soaring into the air. His slack and tumbling body told Khalla he had lost consciousness. The golem charged towards where he landed with a wet thud and was sliding down the curved walls of rough stone.

"Ry, end the anti-magic. We have the stone propped up. If we keep doing this, we're going to lose. Who knows how things are up top? End it. With magic, we can lift this. Do it now!"

Ryvane ended the spell. With strength surging through both, they pulled on the pole arms, now magically enchanted so they would not bend. The tower stone flipped out of its setting and rolled free to the side. Ryvane spun about to take on the three golems while Khalla ran for the marking.

Ryvane blocked two sword strikes and felt her forearms break. Mewing in pain, she fell back unable to use her hands. "Khalla! Hurry!"

Ash's golem picked him up and threw him back across the chamber to splatter against the opposite wall. Khalla blocked all of this out of her mind because she felt the absence of Ash's heartbeat in her medallion. *He'll be okay. He'll be okay. We just need to get the clerics down here…*

Khalla found the marking and touched it. Rune images filled her mind and she intuitively deactivated it. Though the stone remained the same, and though the golems continued their attack, she felt a difference. It felt like the stone was waiting for her. She mentally reviewed the runes and realized the stone had been enchanted as anti-divine powers of any sphere. Though too general to be truly powerful, it meant that the clerics in this entire complex would be hindered in their powers. At the thought of the complex, Khalla realized how truly large the vampire coven's area was. Over and over, a single name entered her mind, *Kallis*.

A golem backhanded her away from the stone. She felt her armor absorb a lot of the damage that would have otherwise broken her body. She tumbled and recovered her footing. Ash and Ryvane lay bent and unmoving. The golem attacking Ash must have been ordered to obliterate foes because it was charging back across the large cavern to attack his corpse again. "Oh, my husband," she whispered. "No, please. No." *I'm Marcello. This isn't supposed to happen.* Another golem lifted a sabre over its head and readied to bring it down on the rakshasa.

Though not friends, Khalla appreciated Ryvane's work. "She operates with honor, even if a thief. It's not fair."

* * *

Kallis felt the tower stone go inactive. As a priest of Asmodei, the stone's power helped him resist delusions common among those who served the Lord of Warp. Asmodei had guided him to the tower stone, had taught him the ways of the Dark Gift, and enabled him to build Dark Legion. Still, after all this time, the Lord of Warp terrified him. Kallis sat back and considered what to do next. His orders to shadow the group were clear. He had to get to Tania and board the world galleon. To do anything else would invoke Asmodei's wrath.

Kallis held his hands out before him. Syand had fed him well, sating both physical and emotional hunger. Yet, contemplating existence without the tower stone or in defiance of Asmodei's wrath... he swallowed. His hands had a slight tremble. He no longer felt fear the way a mortal might, but it did still manifest subtly through trembling in his hands, or increased breathing. "As if I need to breathe," he said.

The attackers had deactivated the tower stone. That meant they were Tanians. When the call had gone out to join the fight against Orcus, Kallis had instructed Ydriss and Renault to send word of compliance to Perdition and were granted an exemption for the large stone. It did not surprise him to learn that Kieran had tried to keep his. Maybe all the tower stones were exempt as they were heavy and difficult to transport. "Dark Legion is ended," Kallis said. He closed his eyes and reached to the back of his neck. A piercing there, under his hair, held a small bloodstone. He touched it.

This stone, he had nicknamed it 'Blood Link,' connected him to any whose blood he touched to the small gemstone. Through feedings, he had connected to all Dark Legion vampires. He could not control them, but he could focus on them and generally know where they were and what they were doing. With enough focus, he could see glimpses through their eyes and send compulsions their way. He checked and found many of the ancient ones either dead or dying. Only twenty remained and he had been right: they fought against Tanians. He noted the thri-keen and smiled. "Let's see if you can handle this, Tanians," he whispered.

His sight shifted to a vampiric thri-keen lying in a crypt. The thri-keen were particular about their burial rituals and their placing of the stones. One stone for each passed warrior. Kallis figured they must all be warriors. They were less particular about what happened to the old ones who came to place stones, that were still living. Over the many long years, Kallis had secretly captured and then granted the Dark Gift to many of the keen. They were his ace, his secret, his last gift to Sorans for their hospitality. It had, and if he was honest with himself, it still bothered him that he could not communicate with the vampiric ones. They accepted strong guidance and nothing else.

He slithered into the first one's consciousness. It was an old one, maybe one of the first gifted with vampirism. "You're going to wake up. There are intruders desecrating your people's resting places. Attack them all. Kill them all. Save your fallen from violation!" This is the command he gave to most. Their crypts were solid stone and Kallis knew it would take a few minutes for them to assimilate the command and break out. To a few others, the strongest warriors, Kallis said, "The large red stone. To save your people, you must find it and break it. It's the only way to serve your god and your people with honor."

Kallis left in a hurry. The tower stone, when it exploded, would immolate most of Northtown.

* * *

Khalla grabbed Ash and Ryvane and hoped her *flying* potion would last long enough to escape. The weight of the two strained her arms and then a golem struck her from behind. She felt her back armor cleave and then pain exploded there. She tried to keep her mind on rescue and escape but both of the bodies in her arms slipped and fell. The golem charged forward to attack again and she shrank at how much of her blood stained the saber. *I wish I hadn't noticed that.* The cold along her back and growing numbness in her limbs told her she was dying. The golem jumped up to strike her again.

Khalla felt the ground tremble. A thri-keen entered the chamber. It looked wrong though, not at all like the ones they had encountered up top. This one must have jumped from one of the tunnels because stone and debris bounced up at its landing. It moved to the tower stone. *Guardians?,* Khalla wondered. The golem, so close to slaying her, turned to defend the stone. So did the others. *So, not a guardian.* The pallor of the thri-keen was wrong and then Khalla noted the feeling of chill dread. It was vampiric.

Determined to not waste her brief respite and good luck, Khalla swooped back down to recover Ash and Ryvane's bodies but slipped while trying to grab Ash, who was so pulped there was nowhere secure to hold him between his and her own bleeding. She felt shock kicking in. With haste, she pried a *healing* potion from her pouch and drank it. Whatever wounds she had taken, she realized, she must be on death's door. The shock subsided just a bit and then pain raged into her back as the wound healed enough to really hurt. She bit her tongue to keep from screaming and drank another potion. It would have to do. Five more of the undead thri-keen entered from the upper tunnels to engage the golems.

Though they had damaged the golems, the golems remained in excellent fighting condition. Khalla could tell they were outmatched by the thri-keen. She watched the combat for a moment and realized the keen were targeting the tower stone. As one engaged a golem, another would move forward and attempt to strike the tower stone. It occurred to her that, if they succeeded, all their worst fears would come true. She touched her earring and projected her thoughts to Alskexa and the rest of the team. "We have a problem. Vampiric thri-keen are trying to destroy the bloodstone. Ash and Ryvane are dead. I'm almost dead. I'm trying to escape. We need to get out of here fast."

She crawled to Ash and stuffed him headfirst into the *holding* backpack. Its extra-dimensional space would do nothing good for his body, but he was dead. She just needed to hold him until a priestess could restore him to life. She did the same with Ryvane. She heard a loud musical tone shrill in the chamber and looked back at the tower stone. The keen continued to engage the golems and one had finally fallen. That allowed one thri-keen to slam the tower stone with an axe. The stone showed no visible signs of damage, and then the axe blade shattered. The keen grabbed one of Ash's polearms and raised it to continue striking the tower stone. She got goosebumps. *Should I try and stop them?*, she wondered. *No*, she decided. *The tower stone's destruction will kill anything down here including surviving vampires. Marcello would approve of that. It is not ideal, but accomplishes and ensures our mission, except that Syand escapes - maybe.* She flew up the tunnel as another musical note rang out with a clear and then sharp trilling pitch to it. They did not have much time.

Khalla burst out of the tunnel to find the teams huddled inside the force wall. Halgrim was sweating. The room around them in every direction seethed with thri-keen who struck at the wall. Not all the human vampires were dead either. "What?" Khalla screamed. "Curse you, Joust! More of these damn bugs!"

Michael nodded and then everyone except the vampires dropped their head to their hands as, below them, another strike rang out against the tower stone. Khalla caught their attention. "Are we ready to leave?"

Halgrim flinched as a mighty axe struck the force wall just a finger away from his eyes. Sweat drenched his body and made his mage robes cling to him. "They're destroying the stone?" he muttered. "I can't maintain the force wall and also teleport us out of here. Ryvane?"

"Is dead," Khalla said. She noted Calvin's body in a pile in the center as well as the stale humid air around them. Michael pointed up and Khalla saw the vampiric thri-keen had scaled the forcewall to get over the top.

Michael pointed to the ground all around them. It was shattered and broken. "Halgrim is a mighty spell caster. He bent the spell to wrap us in a bubble until you could get back. But, it's taxing him."

"Will it protect us from the tower stone?" Khalla screamed out. Any pretense at speaking Drow had faded out long ago.

Halgrim's sarcastic response almost made her laugh. "Of course it will," he dead panned. It took his focus from the forcewall and a three-fingered claw pierced through. Halgrim had to retract the bubble and seal the opening.

Of the original group, Revi, Grant, Delton, and RiVule remained standing with them. "I don't suppose that Gruustir allows his priests to teleport?" Another musical chime sounded but it was dissonant and flat. They heard a crackling sound like paper being crumpled.

RiVule bowed and said, "I can go back to the Quat and take perhaps 10 with me. I cannot guarantee their safety in the Mountain."

"What about you, Lord Michael?" Alskexa had dropped to her knees and was trying to prevent Valaes and Maishan from dying. They lay unconscious with multiple lacerations and broken bones.

Michael looked out of the bubble at the bodies. "We lost many outside the force wall. There's nothing we can do for them. I can take some but not all. Like RiVule, I can return to my home in the Perfectionist Temple and bring some of you with me. It is a violation and one I will have to do penance for, but am willing after the heroics I witnessed today."

Khalla dropped to her knees and opened the dimensional backpack. "Be ready to make it happen the instant..."

The ground trembled and another note rang out, and then broke into cataclysm. They felt the ground beneath them inhale. Khalla felt Michael grab onto her as the others dove to either him or RiVule.

* * *

Radcliffe leaned back in his leather chair and rubbed his eyes. The constant paladin guard outside his door and inside the lab was annoying and reassuring at the same time. He missed Scruffy. He caressed the crystal ball and said, "Show me Lord Michael."

The ball filled with silhouettes of giant praying mantises and... fire. Then, a crisped and burning Michael became clear in the ball. Radcliffe recognized the Perfectionist Temple. "Guards!" he shouted. "We're going to the Perfectionists! Order all healers to the Perfectionist Temple! Now, now, now!" He paused for a moment and then attempted to scry the chamber Michael had been in. Nothing. He pulled his view back to the street level by the tavern. The Temples had set up a perimeter all around it.

Radcliffe did not recognize what he was seeing. The tavern raged with fire and then fell as cracks tore out from underneath its foundation. The cracks raced away as the entire plaza lifted up as if the very earth inhaled. And then, dropped. Houses and building in all directions for hundreds of paces collapsed into rubble. From sewer grates, spouts of fire shot into the sky or burst out sideways. In some places, the fire was so intense that it twisted in on itself like a tornado. Radcliffe looked out his lab's window and saw the eastern sky come alive with red flames. Alarm bells began to ring throughout the city. "At least we evacuated the immediate area," he shouted to the paladins. "Hurry! We're leaving now!"

He scanned the map and tried to remember how far The Temples was from this scene. While trying to calculate it, the ground trembled. From across the western side of Taysor, alarm bells began to ring as the earthquake rocked the entire city. The scene in Radcliffe's crystal ball become increasingly terrible as magical energy continued to shatter the area. Cracks in stone became trenches for fire and then molten rock began to flow downwards to the Gulf of Ymac. One of the guards came up to him and said, "Sir, you wished to leave?" Without answering, Radcliffe put the paladin's hand on the sphere... and felt his hand grow cold.

"Yes, let's go. They have someone who can explain this." Radcliffe pulled the knight towards his laboratory. "Your name is Jathan, right?"

The paladin nodded but the question served as a distraction because they stepped through a black gateway and appeared in the main hall of the Perfectionist Temple. Idealized statues of Pha Rann and the pantheon of Creation looked down on the perfect white marble floor. Lord Michael sat on his hands and knees, heaving for air still. The smell of burning and blood lingered around the Executor and the group he had brought back. The paladins all around had their weapons drawn. Amid the stack of corpses, a Tanian priestess knelt with regal disdain. Blood seemed to sweat out of her and her left side wounds had cauterized. Against the beating of her heart, the scabs had torn and began to bleed again. A phase spider bobbing on her shoulder hissed at the paladins.

Lord Michael held his hand up. His right gauntlet had been near severed from his hand and he trembled to ward the paladins back. A Tanian mage and a female elf stood with them, equally bad. The female elf tried to smile and then collapsed. The hair behind her head had burned away and steam rose from her body. Radcliffe realized he was not looking at armor on her back, but a giant bloodied scab baked there. A Tanian officer bearing the marks of the 19th Legion stood at attention. It took a moment for Radcliffe to realize the fighter was nude wearing spectral armor. All around them, corpses littered the floor.

The Tanian priestess with the phase spider called out, "We did not come here by choice! And, we will be leaving."

Michael tried to stand but stumbled. Blood sloshed out of his boots and he trailed bloody pools where he staggered forward to ward off any hostilities. "High Mother, please. You knew this when we came. Too many have died already. Do not let the perfection of your anger ruin this moment."

Radcliffe shook his head and realized he was translating the language… from Drow. *Why is Michael talking in Drow? Oh yes, the test.* The mage stepped forward and in a loud voice proclaimed, "The Literalist Order will own this calamity, and offers asylum to Lord Michael's friends. Please, I pray, let Perfection shine down and see this as a visit, not an assault."

The paladins relaxed and then a cleric ran forward and caught Michael. "Executor, you are wounded most dire."

The *healing* prayer was already washing over Michael, but he caught the cleric and said, "Battle triage. Of the unmoving, some can be saved still. Tend to them first. My wounds can wait. We will not squander Pha Rann's blessings like this when I am surrounded by fallen comrades."

The cleric bowed and let his faith wash over Khalla. To Khalla, the healing felt like standing outside in the summer on a day where the wind blew the bugs and heat away. When the prayer ended, she imagined she smelled flowers and grass. She closed her eyes and was out.

Michael dropped to the floor and laid back to look at the stained glass ceiling dome overhead. "I'm feeling kind of sleepy. Brothers, we found a coven of vampires in the catacombs, and thri-keen, and vampiric thri-keen. A tower stone blew up." He closed his eyes.

By now, others arrived even as The Temples rallied to save citizens caught in the cataclysm around the Dark Legion headquarters. Two of the paladins placed their hands on Michael's forehead and prayed for him. At their words, his complexion improved and his breathing steadied. "His heartbeat is very weak," one said. "Squire! Attend to the cleric!"

Alskexa watched Michael strip of his armor. His wounds were more severe than he had let on. Thri-keen weapons had pulverized his body and yet left his armor mostly undamaged. "Weapons that ignore armor," she mused.

Halgrim collapsed next to her and stared at the carnage wrought in the cleric's body. "He used his body as a shield, for us." Halgrim felt a deep sorrow that such a celebrated cleric would do something like this, for her, for them. "It makes me rethink our role in everything."

Halgrim patted her shoulder and she leaned her head against his arm. "Did Ash make it out with the Orc?" he asked. When Alskexa kicked Khalla's backpack, Halgrim sighed deeply. "Ash hates dying."

"We all hate dying. Tell me about it," she whispered. Her own eyes were feeling heavy.

"We were much younger. He was already working for Perdition though I didn't know, yet. I hired him to retrieve material I needed for a magical weapon. Turned out that he needed a mage, so I went with him. We couldn't find the required monster, but caught wind of a minotaur that had what we needed as part of its armor. Ash tried to steal it. Well, you can guess what happened." Halgrim looked down at her and found her asleep. He carefully let her lie down and then grabbed the backpack. "I've never seen him so emotional, except when he thought might lose Khalla."

It took some effort as the backpack was not his, but eventually he wrestled Ash and Ryvane out. The Perfectionists did not like having a dead rakshasa on their chapel floor. "So, revive her first and she'll leave. Or, I'll take her away my damn self. Go ahead, dishonor Michael's wishes in bringing us all here. As you well know, we did not come here by our magic or choice. Your Temple is protected, right? So, honor your Executor and stop acting like we're going to attack you. This is most ridiculous."

Chagrined and angered, they backed away. By pre-dawn, the fires east of The Temples had come under control but still burned. The tower stone, Halgrim speculated, was much stronger than the one Northern Cross had tried to keep. Halgrim had not really been wounded in the fighting. Exhausted from spell casting, sure, but not from action or wounds. He used his magic to remain alert. When an acolyte approached him with an offer of healing, he shooed the young man away. "Designs within designs," Halgrim said pointing to the stained glass above them. "It's your Order's particular way, right? That's a maze designed to inspire meditation."

The priest looked up and smiled. "Each path represents a different style of meditation. The Imperics use koans. We prefer to use visual and tactile aids in our prayers."

Halgrim let his eyes dance along one thread and suddenly the entire labyrinthine design came clear as a burning sun with arcs of fire lifting from its surface. He blinked and the vision was gone. "I like it." His vision felt foggy and he realized he was going blind. "Um, young cleric... maybe I could use some help. My eyes seem to be failing."

\* \* \*

Khalla tried to open her eyes but found multiple layers of thick bandages around them. She felt soft cushions around her. Somewhere, a low chorus sang a bright and airy hymn. She remembered Michael grabbing her. Images of corpses ringed by undead thri-keen came unbidden to her mental eye and she pushed them back. Fire everywhere. Choking smoke that smelled like cooked meat... Ash's dead body falling into the void of her backpack, that mental image made her shake with revulsion. She attempted to open her eyes again but a man's hands caught her and pulled her hands back. She hoped it was Ash, even though she could tell by the uncalloused texture it was not.

The man said, "Easy now. You arrived looking well enough, which was miraculous; praised be Pha Rann. After you collapsed and we could tend to you, you had multiple wounds. You might not believe it but a blade cut up alongside your spine for about the length of your forearm. Just a bit to the center and it would have killed you. Meanwhile, the tower stone's explosion burned your eyes. Your entire group is suffering from varying degrees of blindness. We need you to rest your eyes another day."

"Ash... the others?" Khalla asked. Her mouth felt dry and her lips broke apart as if sandpaper tearing. The man pressed a sponge to her lips and she drank scant drops of water. She wanted more, but he waited. Nausea hit her.

"You Tanians are a strong bunch. I'll give you that. Shock alone would have killed most anyone else, but I guess that's why you train against that, even up to death." The man paused and then pressed the sponge to her lips again. "I'm Christof. Third Acolyte of the Perfectionist Order. I understand you're one of the heroes we've been hearing so much about here since the Jade God fell. Amazing, that adventure was. I sometimes wish I had been there, and then remember that I am a healer." He laughed. "And one who appreciates having everything needed for a flawless recovery. I did see a moving performance. It was all these drums and dancers. I was expecting the story of the Jade God's fall, not dancers. You have to understand, it feels uncomfortable for an old man like me to watch beautiful young ladies dancing. Then, halfway through the performance, I realized I could understand the story through the percussion and the dancing. It was phenomenal!"

This time, the water triggered less violent nausea. She smiled weakly, and wondered if Christof was going to use her convalescence to talk her ears off. Each time he pressed the sponge to her lips, she drank more and realized the healer was counting the drops and the time between drinks. "Christof, I could drink a bucket of water. We're at only 13 drops! Please, end this agony and let me have a proper drink!"

"Healing, our way, is going to patch you up better than Tania ever would. You don't make a new bottle and immediately fill it with wine. No, no, no. You fire it. You test it. You let the glaze and crystallization set in. Only when it's perfect, do you actually use it. Your other doctor recommended this approach and I agreed. You were close to death and mistakes in healing, similar to bone setting, can be dire. Sure, resurrection can aid that but to have to do so because an error on our part would be unforgivable. What do you know about this Ash?" He tapped the medallion around her neck. "He's special to you no doubt." He pressed it down enough that she could feel the regular beating of his heart. "Do you know…"

"About his arm. Yes. So, you know too. Interesting." Khalla reached up to squeeze the sponge at her lips but found she was softly, gently restrained. "Why am I bound?"

"The wound on your back fractured ribs and scraped several of your vertebrae. We need to keep your back perfectly straight until you are healed. Your left shoulder too. Your forearms have hairline fractures throughout them. All of you is burned, not just your eyes. You found quite the rat's nest, didn't you?"

Christof gave her more water. "Lord Michael commanded that we resurrect everyone we could. A few did not make it. Most did though I understand many were left behind and are beyond us." Khalla noted the sadness in his voice. "Sometimes, the design does not allow everyone to return. They meet Pha Rann's judgement and pass on. In the case of Ash, well. That's a story for another time. He escaped. We're not quite sure where he is right now."

Khalla remembered Halgrim's words and imagined Ash resurrecting with his natural arm. Coming to with more people knowing about it, she knew he had returned to Tania. "I'm sure he went back to Perdition. Marcello will help him with his arm." She tried to focus on something other than her restraints. "Ash must have made an impression on you. I can tell you've altered my restraints to try and prevent me from doing the same. It won't work."

"I'm sure it won't. But, I will tell you this, Lady Khalla." The healer switched to Elvish and said, "You are in a state of accelerated healing. It isn't the instantaneous healing you're used to from Morbatten. If you leave, you will injure your back and may permanently damage your vision. Trust us. Don't be Ash. I give you my word and oath that we will take good care of you."

From the right side of her bed, she heard a bright voice say, "You can believe Lord Christof when he offers you his oath, Lady Khalla. When I heard you had regained yourself, I came at once." Michael's voice was most welcome though the sound of crutches and then what sounded like a stampede of healers followed him in. Their pleas for him to sit down, go slow, be careful,… hurt her ears and he shushed them all.

"Christof, if you don't mind, Khalla and I have matters to discuss. You and the rest are dismissed. I will call for you if needed." Though couched in gentle tone, the command to leave was clear. "I will call. I promise."

Christof replied, "Of course, Lord Michael. I'll be tending to the others down the hall. She is at 20 drops."

When the room quieted, Khalla heard Michael sit back and breathe deeply. "It's not often combat casualties come here. The acolytes are beside themselves with wonder at wounds they've only studied up to this point. I wished to give you a report. Are you strong enough to hear it?"

Khalla replied, "Christof told me about Ash at least. He'll be fine. In preparing for this, it seems we all knew it could be bad, but how bad, I'm dreading your next words."

Michael touched her hand softly and said, "Yes. We lost the entire Black Guard when the tower stone detonated. Some of them, it seems, had started into the catacombs. Maybe 1 or 2 survived, but until the fires are out, and we can separate innocent bystanders from the Black Guard, I am assuming they are all lost.

"From the Priestess team, we lost Valaes. He was outside Halgrim's magic when the chamber detonated. Alex does not yet know, though as the son of a powerful Dar, I expect Tania may already know. Otherwise, I have asked that the Temple send word via diplomatic channels to Jan Darel. We also lost Nilthan, for similar reasons though he fell to a horde of vampires and had begun to turn when we put the force wall up.

"From Disakcion, we lost Bolston, Corfell, and Pol Nir. I liked Pol Nir. She had a brightness to her. Dare I say it? I believe she may have converted with proper guidance."

Khalla heard sorrow in Michael's voice and squeezed his hand back. "She was a huge fan of yours, in fact of all the Soran heroes. She idealized the Ranger Bruce too. I have no doubt she would have converted. Maybe not for the right reasons but who am I to judge, Lord Michael? In your order, would you accept a convert who was in love with you rather than Pha Rann?"

She felt Michael shrug. "I would not. This Order would not, but there are others that would. I rather liked her too. In the brief time we had, I wondered when she would get past the stories. Tanian bards take certain liberties with the truth that make me uneasy.

"Though we are not sure, I'm confident that we lost the Orc paladin, Taisha. I saw her armor in a gory tangle of slain undead and thri-keen limbs. She fought without reserve or consideration for her own safety, like a berserker." He chuckled. "A berserker paladin. I'm sure she would get along well with your new king."

Khalla whispered, "Careful, Lord Michael. King Malcor is one that even we do not jest about."

"Apologies. Continuing on then. Cordelle died. Though we recovered his body, we cannot resurrect him. He fulfilled every measure of his redemption. I have sent a commendation to High King Andrew on his behalf. He did have one thing that he wished for me to give to Marcello. His mimic. He loved it. He said Marcello would know what to do with it. I have it in safekeeping in my quarters, but the Temple will not long abide my indiscretion in this matter. I would have preferred to give it to Ash to take back to Tania, had we known he would be leaving so soon.

"Lastly, Grant's team suffered extensive loses almost equal to Disakcion. Only Delton was recoverable unless RiVule is able to and did resurrect some of those he took. I have communicated with him and he indicated the Delton survived and demands to know of Taisha's fate. So, that is the tally though technically everyone died except for me, Halgrim, Revi, and you. A few more minutes without care and I dare say we would have all died." Michael let go of her hand and dipped the sponge in water. "Here. Christof is a bit of a literalist. If you tell me you want more water, I'll get you a proper cup."

"Yes, please. I promise to sip it though I am bound." Khalla held up her hand.

"Ah, yes. Ash's escape caused quite the commotion here." Michael gently untied her wrists. "Be careful. You were down there for some time. Your skin is sorely burnt." He undid the other one and then also a midsection one Khalla had not known was there. When he undid her ankles, he apologized. "We don't get many unwilling guests. We still do not know why he fled."

"He has issues with his natural form. The birth defect haunts him. He's avoided it his whole life and, I'd guess, he recently started figuring it out. I just barely learned of it a while ago. So, that's how secretive he was about it."

"I see. Tanians have an odd view of birth issues like this. Our healers, you must understand, thought something had gone wrong with his resurrection. They thought Chaos had infected him in the course of the battle. They'll be relieved to know that is not the case. Pardon me." Michael turned his head and leaned back to the hallway. "Christof!" he called out. "Tell the healers the arm was a birth defect, not Chaos. You can stop the re-sanctification ritual."

The enormity of their losses began to build in Khalla's mind while she sipped tiny drinks from the cup. It felt good to get more than teasing drops. The nausea threatened her each one but she fought it back. *Twenty dead, forever*, she thought. *Ironically, Calvin survives…* Grudgingly, she admitted, *He conducted himself better than I thought he would.*

"Twenty lives," Khalla sighed. "Marcello is going to kill me." She found it odd speaking about herself this way but, after seeing Ash do it for years, it came surprisingly easy.

Michael leaned back and agreed. "It's a sore loss to be sure. They were each valiant in their own ways. Yet, to die atop a funeral pyre surrounded by vampires is a dream in and of itself. They will be remembered."

"No, they won't. That's not how Tania works, Michael. They were chosen for Merakor!" She felt her bile begin to rise and had to force her breathing and anxiety to calm down. "They're going to blame me, or worse Alexa. She didn't put us into this mission. Gah, this drives me insane. I'm glad Sora is free of the coven. I really am, but now Merakor is jeopardized." She touched her eyes and felt her skin flexing at her elbows. It was tender. Her eyes were tender and sensitive to even the slightest pressure. Suddenly, she realized she was bald.

"They cannot blame you. Had we, had they known about the tower stone and the vampire thri-keen, this whole thing would have been different…"

Khalla interrupted him. "With all due respect, it is my guild's job to know these things ahead of time. With Merakor, like this one, we have a general idea of what to expect. But, it's been thousands of years. Who knows what unknowns we are going to face? Here, we had more control and ability to prepare. We don't even know if Syand was killed." She rubbed her head and felt scabs sloughing off. "Tania will want to know why we failed. Had this happened in Tania in say, Dockside, and that many homes were destroyed…" She grabbed Michael's hand. "How many citizens are dead?"

Michael was quiet a moment. "You seek to make the Law of Innocents equivalent in your assignation of blame? We estimate two thousand dead but won't ever really get an exact count. Had we not pre-evacuated the area around Legionnaires, it would have been worse. Had the vampiric thri-keen or the actual thri-keen attacked us, it would have been many times worse. I only rarely see this side of Tania. You are truly worried about being blamed?"

"Don't you see? The Law of Innocents holds Marcello responsible to preserve the life of the normal person as a forfeit on his own life. As his agent, Ash and I both…"

A commotion outside interrupted them and Khalla groaned when she heard Daryx's voice. *Tiamat burn me*, she groaned inside. It sounded like someone challenged him and said, "Fight me, Drow!"

Michael tensed at the challenge and stood. "Hey! You do not insult an honored guest in the Temple! When you can claim to have bested even half the number of evil creatures Lord Daryx has, then maybe, I'll let you speak this way!"

With a pleasant tone of voice, Daryx replied. "When you feel like dying, you know where to find me, paladin." The taunting voice tone changed as he entered their room. "Lord Michael! It's so good to see at least one of the group up and moving."

Khalla heard a blade being drawn. Michael began to shout and then everything went silent. Daryx said, speaking with formal Soran Court language, "You would challenge me here in your holy place? What manner of fool are you? Is this an altar of human sacrifice where your god requires your death at my hands?"

A man grunted and Khalla heard a body drop to the floor. The room remained tense even after Michael called out, "Christof, remove that one to the hospital classroom. The rest of you, you are dismissed. Go!"

Daryx took Khalla's hand. She had never touched him like this before. His skin felt sticky and something about his fingers reminded her of what spider legs might feel like. "Marcello sends his regards but desires a full report. I came to see if there is anything you are lacking? RiVule sent word days ago. He arrived in the Quat with Jerare and Valaes. Looks like Valaes will survive. So, at least there was that. I had the Mages Guild retrieve them. Ash is just fine and is resting at Sai R'Dar's estate. You're going to love his new arm! Who could have anticipated that a seemingly easy foe and situation would escalate out of control so quickly?"

Daryx's fingers tapped on her hand and she knew. Daryx had known. Of course, he had known. The tower stone was marked. He continued. "The real question is whether you let this teach you, or break you. As one of the group's leaders, do you let them be broken or insist on their learning from it?" Out loud, Daryx said, "I overheard your discussion. The Law of Innocents does not apply to Sorans. You're overthinking this Khalla. Yes, had it been in Tania, there would be repercussions. But this is why we wanted a test before Merakor. Sora is rid of a pestilence and now tastes a fraction of the bitter sacrifice Tania paid to end Orcus. Things are well and balanced in the world of the Isles."

Khalla withdrew her hand from his. She did not like how it felt. "As a leader, I think we have a problem with the Merakor team given we were just decimated."

"Good," he said. "Looking ahead is a good thing. The real thing is, would you feel this way if more of those you cared about had died, like Ash? Ryvane maybe?"

Without hesitation, Khalla retorted. "I'd feel the same but with a deeper sense of loss. As it is, I feel like I failed them all!" Raising her voice made her gag and she fell back trying not to vomit. She failed and Michael turned her head to the side as the puked up water into a bucket by her bed.

Daryx did not seem to care. "It's good you feel this way. This is a normal reaction to real peril and losing those in your command. It's easy to think of adventure as a visit to the bank where you get all this treasure. The truth, the reality is far different. There is danger and death involved. In Tania, all of you take healing for granted. Though not glad at your losses, I'm confident that this lesson has been driven home among those of you strong enough to survive. Hopefully, it makes you all stronger. Merakor will be different. This one featured the surprise element of vampiric thri-keen. Not even the Circle could have foreseen that so close to The Temples!"

Michael had a cautionary tone in his voice when he said, "This is true. We will all be joining together to put in place better guards around the catacombs. We figured the absence of activity there meant nothing was going on. I personally know I assumed the thri-keen would take care of it and, as long as we left them alone, no problems could develop. Vampires there though. It's not possible it could have happened, yet it clearly did. In some ways, it was a perfect ruse."

While Michael spoke, Daryx tapped on her leg and told her that Valaes' family had removed him from the quest, by edict. Jan Darel held enough power in Tania that either the dragons or the king removed him from the quest. Khalla nodded her head and replied, "I wish I could take the eye bandages off."

Daryx responded to Michael and said, "It happens to the best of us. One of the fighters with you, Calvin, found a group of necromancers in the burned out ruins of an Orcus Shrine, in Morbatten. Marcello's team destroyed it, but I remember several discussions with the Circle about how such a thing could happen and gone unnoticed as long as it did. After all you can do, the rest is left to faith and diligence."

"Indeed, my lord Daryx. True words, that would do anyone in my order proud to remember." Michael cleared his throat and with a more formal tone said, "I'm going to excuse myself and ensure the guards are left with strict orders to assist you. You are welcome anywhere except in the Holy Chapel. The rest of your team is in this hallway. Rest well, Khalla."

When Michael was gone, Daryx unwrapped the bandages on Khalla's hands. "The earliest stones were a bit unstable. The Black Patriarch

Screem and Dar Ana had not yet figured out how to tame the power of the nexal gates. If you were to go, as you are now, to the Eldar times or somehow were to bask in the light of the three gates at the same time, you would burn just like you did. There are no Dar priestesses here, but I need Marcello functioning. You will take a deep breath, hold it, and not scream as I call on Lolth to heal you."

Khalla nodded and held her breath. From Daryx's hand on her leg, a feeling of crawling insects spread out to cover her leg and then creep up her torso and down her feet. She felt small pricks of heat and imagined spiders eating away at her. "You're doing well. The more critical wounds will be worse. Stay quiet."

When the feeling reached her back and her eyes, Khalla felt her insides twist and strain as the feeling of health pushed scabs, pus, and old tissue out. She felt her eyes strain with pressure and then relax. With them closed, starbursts of color erupted and then silent tears began streaming down her face. Daryx touched one and said, "It's done. Go ahead and unwrap your eyes."

The first thing Khalla saw was blood on the bandage where each of her eyes had been. It was wet and recent, probably from the last time Christof changed the dressing. She took a trembling breath when she saw the skin on her hands. Blisters had broken and then bled. She looked burned. "Khalla, everyone looks like this. They're all bald too." He kissed her hand and stood to leave. "I'll be back shortly."

# Chapter 21 – Ride the Storm

Vel Pajor fumed at the door that just slammed in his face. "How dare you! Open the door now."

From behind the stone door, Vel heard glass break at his head's level. A shrill voice blasted him through the oak wood. "You dare suggest I need your approval to join the Tanians?! How dare you? Were the gods here, I would call on Pha Rann and the very Heavens to burn you in my spite!"

Vel leaned his head on the door and called out, "Lady Inviress, then surely, it is a good thing that none of them would answer your calls!" The guards behind him snickered. The mage's eyes, bright with mirth, suddenly shifted and he pulled Vel to the side of the door as the wood shuddered and then a mouth opened in the wooden surface to bite at where Vel had just been standing.

Magic flared in Vel's hand and he touched the door, which went inert and then blew inward. He walked into the room with mage armor crackling around him. "My lady Inviress, just because the dragon scum poke at you and whisper the name 'Merakor' does not mean you will be reunited with him. Or, that Krentismar would allow him entry here even should you find him. We both know you will stay and probably rejoin the Drow. I cannot allow this. I command you to drop this hostile stance."

Inviress stood by her desk. Her staff, a famous and powerful artefact, lay across its top. A wand in her hand pointed at Vel and two rings glimmered on her other hand. Her eyes narrowed at Vel's words. "You do not know what the gods will or would not. If you did, we would not be having this discussion."

"Is this a discussion?" Vel said quietly while gesturing at the damage throughout the room. A sphere of power emanated out around Inviress. When its edge reached Vel, his mage armor, his magics, and then the mage behind him, all of it blinked out. "Anti-magic?" he sighed. "Must we do this?"

"It was you and your short-sighted father who sent Invri away! For that, I hate you. Forever! I do not belong here!" He barely side-stepped her staff which struck at his face. The follow up still caught his legs and swept them out from under him.

Inviress screeched in triumph and ended the anti-magic to bring the staff down on him. "Murderer!" she yelled. "You and your father killed Invri!"

Her staff was about to connect when a guard tackled her sideways and threw her off the king. Expecting a fight, the guard slammed her face into the marble stone and then punched the back of her head to ensure she could not cast spells. Instead, she collapsed in a ragged mess of sobbing tears. "Invri," she gasped while blood poured from her broken nose.

The mage helped Vel regain his footing. "My lord?" he asked.

Vel saw the fight had left Inviress. He signaled the mage to stand ready and stay back. "Lady Inviress, I came here to explain my forbiddance. But, I see you have yet to let go of what once was. Please remember this. I was just a boy, barely a prince when my father asked – not ordered – Invri to investigate the Underdark portals opening across our lands. When the Triopolis fell, we all lost those we cared about. You were not the only one to lose someone you loved. I lost my entire family! Do not, I pray you, make us bind you, again."

The lady's sobs became harsher as she struggled to breathe. "You would take the only hope I have known in three thousand years from me? Your family murders my love and now you threaten to bind me again? I see your heart, Vel. I wonder, does Mallaforax know you delve and search for the Darkhold? I wonder," she began laughing. "The lich in your soul taints you gray. Gray Elf King, ha!"

Vel conjured a small ball of twisted metal into his hand. "You make me sad, Lady. You should be one of our Queens."

"Sylvans do not need rulers!" Inviress retorted. Her eyes went wide at the sight of the ball. It moved inexorably towards her. The bands wrapping about themselves came loose and the first grappled onto her arm. "You are too slow!" Her other hand touched the staff and she vanished.

Vel dropped to his knees to pick up the ball. "And so we lose another of the great and powerful ones," Vel said softly. He pressed his hand to the stone where her tears and blood mingled. "To love anyone this way, let alone a traitorous Drow…"

The guard, thinking the King felt troubled by the violence and bloodshed stepped forward and bowed low. "My King, I thought to prevent further magic. I did not anticipate she would surrender."

"You did well. The truth is, had she wished it, we would have had a battle. She became a Drow long before we left Merakor. Lolth named her nobility, you know. Why she came here and took the Allegiance, is not known to me. But, she longs to go back to her Invri." Vel turned to the mage. "Let word be sent. All of Lady Inviress' estate is to be impounded.

She is hereby and forever exiled. Let our embassy in Tania know she is to be remanded to Morilon and set a bounty of a bloodstone gem on her return."

* * *

Inviress appeared on gold-streaked and polished tiles. Still on her hands and knees, she felt the overpressure of the dragons, though could tell none of the dread lords were currently present. A priestess ran forward to her. By the time the priestess arrived to help her stand, Tiamat's healing power restored her.

"Thank you," Inviress said. "If you do not mind, I would like to invoke an old favor once granted me by the god emperor Alerius." She took a small token out of her pocket. It was a disc of platinum bearing a single rune. Like all of Alerius' magic, it glowed with ember energy that marked it unique.

The priestess took the disk and bowed low. "This notes you as Lady Inviress, Sylvan Elf and friend of Tania. The god emperor is not here. He is in Bloodstone. We could send word, or you could tell me your request and, in his name, I will act on it. How may I best serve you?"

"Either, whichever. Vel is no doubt going to sever me from Morilon. I would request that all of my assets be declared independent and the offered rank of Dar be granted immediately." Inviress bowed to the priestess. "Before the official embassy request arrives, it would behoove Tania to let them know I have defected."

The priestess took the token and looked at it more closely. "You are Lady Emshel Inviress. This token was given you in 612 DAR in exchange for great..." she paused for a few moments and then continued. "Great service to Morbatten. I am sending word to the god emperor." Less than a minute later, the priestess gave the token back to Inviress. "The god emperor welcomes you with open arms. We will allow some of your assets to be frozen. I am R'Dar Vir, or Virette, whichever you prefer, my Lady Inviress. The god emperor wishes to know if you view yourself returning to Tania after the Merakor quest."

Inviress' eyes flashed and she said, "It is my intent to return to Invri. Where he is, that is where I shall go. Should Invri wish to come back here, we shall. That is my intent."

"And if he is deceased?"

Page 468

The Sylvan smiled death. "Then I shall find out the cause of his death and enact a vengeance upon those who robbed him from me, wherever and to whomever that may take me."

Vir nodded. "Very well. We will place you in a protected dwelling which shall be reserved for you when you return. In the meantime, I will escort you to your new home. As a mage of power, you will enjoy all that the Mages Guild has to offer. I understand you studied with us."

Inviress began walking out of the chamber and then paused when she noticed Vir waiting and gesturing towards the inner depths of the throne chamber. "Oh, I see. Very well, lead on."

They entered the mountain and through several turns, Inviress felt the confounding magics set in this place to make it seem like a great labyrinth. She counted her steps, just like she did when she first apprenticed to Dread Lord Alerius more than a thousand years ago. In eight hundred paces, they entered a large circular room. "The Court's workshop looks the same as always," she laughd. Without being prompted, she walked over to a plain section of the wall and pressed her hand to it. An alcove opened beyond.

Vir said, "I have heard of this but have never had reason to bring a guest here. Thank you for showing it to me."

"This is where Bomoki first apprenticed and made that damn gate. This is where every archmage candidate has worked to earn the title, until the proper guild was constructed in the city. In many ways, this is more my home than Vel's rotting jail. Tiamat *burn* him."

R'Dar Vir said, "I have sent word to the Mages Guild. A portal will open shortly." As she spoke, a black doorway sliced open into the air at the end of the workshop. "As you requested, I will make arrangements with the Circle for your Dar title, holdings, and other matters. By nightfall, either I or another will visit you with more information. Safe travels, my Lady Inviress. And, welcome to Morbatten."

Inviress used her magic to clean her clothes of blood and make herself more presentable and then walked through. She expected, and was pleased to find, Dar Reznor on the other side. She bowed to him while noting the haunting figure of Daryx behind him. "I see you lurking back there, Lord Daryx," she said with a curtsey.

"As you might imagine," Daryx answered, "I rather enjoy taking you away from Vel Pajor. Ever since I learned of you centuries ago, I hoped you would join us."

"You still look just like my husband did." Inviress said to Daryx while she took Reznor's hand and stepped down from the platform marking the magical portal. She pointed Daryx to Reznor and said, "Invri and Daryx could have been brothers. That they were not warms my heart as I do not know which I might have chosen." She laughed and smelled the air as the wind blew across the high tower. The city of Morbatten sprawled out around them in all directions.

Reznor pointed west and opened his hand. A scrying view opened in the palm of his hand. Though small, it showed her estate. They caught the sign of Vel's guards milling around the outside. A fire raged in the southern portion of her marbled home and she sighed deeply to see it. "He never was one to let go of anything, not lightly anyway."

Daryx said, "We received an embassy request just minutes after R'Dar Vir contacted me. They did not say for what and I scheduled them to three days from now. With the god emperor in Bloodstone, delays come more naturally to our empire these days."

"You still call him 'god emperor?'" Inviress embraced Reznor and then stepped forward to greet Daryx. She kissed his cheek and hugged him tight. "When I hold you, I can feel that he still lives. Do you think he has survived all these ages? I must say, Daryx, when I got your note, I nearly fainted. Merakor, truly?"

"Yes, the Dread Lord Ynt'taris moved our time tables up a bit but it's all as the gods would have it be. And, about Invri, I survived. I'm sure the Lord Marshall of Kinpeace did as well. When I last saw him, he still wore the ring you gave him. Though, and I've already told you this, he turned it into an earring. He had become very much the swordsman, and most adept with a long bow."

Daryx eyed Reznor and stepped back. "Our friend here, Reznor, probably does not know that we were all once acquainted. I was not so much as that I became a comrade of Invri towards the end of my stay in Merakor. He hunted me, you know. A male priest of Lolth, can you imagine? They sent the great Invri to end me. I was surprised to find a kindred spirit, if not a very understanding one."

Reznor smiled. "I have heard stories of course, but our work so rarely allows us to discuss our histories. While I'm sure mine is an open book to you, Lord Daryx, both of you remain enigmatic to me, as does Dar Ana and those who predated my arrival."

They turned and walked out of the wind down a winding staircase. The next level below waited for them with crackling warmth from a fire and Inviress' favorite drinks. Daryx explained, "While we ready your quarters, you will stay here in the Archmagus Tower. Part of this is to make it hard for Vel to find you. The other part is that I cannot think of any other place I would trust with you."

"You're too kind. I knew Vel would not let me leave. I've basically been kept to my estate with only rare travel for Morilon's court since I came to the Isles. It's been so long, I hardly remember the passage of the years. Meanwhile, scrying and visitors showed me what transpired. Thankfully, my daughter and her daughter have progressed well in the ancient ways."

"They are well?" Reznor asked. "I've read about the situation. It's a remarkable one. Your husband was a Drow noble long before the Kinslayer Wars occurred. I've often wished to ask. May I?"

Daryx had poured them wine into crystal flutes and handed them out. Inviress looked to Daryx who finally began to speak. "Lolth was worshipped by a faction of the elves long before they ever went underground. When the Race Wars drove us under, that was a feint. We already knew where to go. Invri, in Tania, would no doubt be a paladin of Lolth. At that time, in that place, he and my parents were consecrated to Lolth. The power of that consecration helped pull the Underdark away from the surface. The consecrated were marked as what you call 'nobles.' We call them by a Drow term meaning 'Lolth bitten.'"

Inviress patted Reznor's arm. "Lolth had never had worshippers before. Her initial foray into Tehran worship, so different from Tiamat's, was a gentle touch and then, like a spider infestation, it grew and grew until it was madness. Just because I was sympathetic, I was labeled Drow and locked under Vel's guardianship. It did not stop me from loving one of them though." She leaned back into the warm cushions and said, "He was so handsome. If he is still alive, I could let my life's work be complete."

Reznor looked at Daryx and handsigned, "She seeks suicide or love? I cannot tell."

Daryx moved to the fire and prodded the embers burning there. When Inviress could not see him, and while she talked about the old days, he signed back. "At a certain age, or level of ancientness, elves either grow dynamic and move forward, or begin to fade. She is fading. Perhaps Invri's love, if he still lives and still loves her, will invigorate her. If not, she seeks a type of suicide. She wants to know and tell herself that she tried."

"My heart aches for your loss, my lady," Daryx said, turning back to her. "I regret not having been able to speak about you with him. I'm sure he would have given me a message for you had we known that all of this..." and he waved his hand around to suggest the entirety of Morbatten and the Isles, "would happen." Though they had had this conversation many times, Daryx knew she loved to repeat it.

"You're such a dear." She sipped at the wine and put it down, barely touched. "Now, tell me. When do we leave?"

Reznor answered, "The world galleon should be arriving any day now. Once it is offloaded and filled with new cargo, you and the other passengers will board it and proceed to Merakor. All is ready. I would guess 10 to 15 days before departure."

"And then from here to Invri?"

"Twelve weeks if the weather and seas cooperate."

\* \* \*

The great ship used to be a Blade of Stars. Two hundred years ago, the Emperor Unseffi took the Blade of Stars on a circumnavigation of Tehra. No Tauran had done this since the First Era and that had been as part of seeking out wild minotaurs for conversion. The Captain, named Captain, patted the railing by his side and inhaled the salt air. Taurans had practical names descriptive of what they did, only emperors had true names. "This is a good ship," Captain said. Pilot agreed and flexed his biceps against the giant wheel he used to steer the ship. It bothered Captain that they had mysteriously lost their last pilot. "Windwalker could not do a better job than you, Pilot."

The helmsman laughed. "As if I could ever equal one that close to the Emperor!"

They both laughed. Such sayings were common in Tauran where the Emperor and his direct line were always held forth as if a mystical force of perfection. Windwalker was much closer to the Emperor even than Captain.

Hundreds of paces ahead, a rogue wave swept up and over the prow. The water swept a few of the rookies not paying attention against the railings. The ship shuddered with the force of the wave and then the deck soared towards the sky as it rose up the next wave. With great laughter, mocking, and ridicule, the rest of the crew threw things at the rookies and made bets as to if any would be swept off deck.

Captain laughed as the prow lifted over the wave and the abyssal drop loomed in front of them. Soon, Pilot and the others in hearing range joined in. The ship smashed down into the ocean and another tidal wave sized mountain of water swept over them. Captain pointed to the washed up Taurans who had to be rescued before falling overboard and said, "Tie them to the mast and let them think about how water and ships interact. Face them into the waves and tell them to be mindful of their breathing!" Raucous laughter erupted at the command.

Overhead, the great sails snapped and sang in the strong winds chasing them from a hurricane to their south and east. They had ridden the edge of this storm for two weeks now in their western course. The clerics' instructions had been clear. "Stay northerly and head west," they said. *I wish I knew our port*, Captain thought with suspicion. These quests always arrived at the worst possible time, with vague instructions and the promise of great profit. Their hull sat pregnant with luxury cargo from across the world. He thought about his own cargo and the coin he might make. The profit on this trade alone would be massive, especially at the prices Captain had reviewed with Merchant prior to taking on the cargo. *I can finally acquire a harem*, he thought. Thinking of such things improved his mood and he roared into the next wave.

Mastsmith, a strong and battle-scarred Tauran, hanged back from the center mast and let the wind blow through his fur. The sea gulls and other ocean birds trailing the giant ship danced in the clouds and crisscrossed the sails in the strong breeze. Without warning, their pattern changed and Mastsmith blew a silver whistle at his neck. Everyone on the ship heard it as a high-toned shriek, uninterrupted by storm or other sounds audible to most races.

Mastsmith looked back to Captain and blew three high pips. *Land-sighting*, Captain mused. Based on the Tauran maps, there should not be land here, not even islands. "Baphtomet take them all," Captain said as he and Pilot made the holy hand sign of their god. Then it hit him, *These are the Dead Isles*. Another thought burst open like fireworks in his thinking: *A hidden land lays before me, one masked by magic and gods*. Slowly a name dawned, *Morbatten and the Forsaken Isles*. In his mind's eye, he saw dragons drifting high in the sky over a valley ringed by tall mountains. "I know these nations," he whispered as step by step more and more memories came flooding into him. The last one of all concerned a hidden chest buried in his strong room and a dire sense of urgency he recognized as a magical compulsion. "I'll be in quarters," Captain said.

Below decks, Captain retrieved the chest. He had seen it there the entire voyage. For months he had moved it around and never once questioned it or why it was there. It never bothered him and, at this point while staring at it, it bothered him that he just accepted its presence. Putting it on his desk, he now knew that this chest contained what he needed to do in order to enter the Forsaken Isles. If he did not do these things and soon, the world galleon would be destroyed by – *Reefs!* The Dead Isles' name came from his predecessor who smashed his galleon to pieces on it.

Captain almost popped the latches with his strength before a memory of how to correctly open it burst in his mind. If he opened the chest any other way, it would contain nothing or trifles. Popping it open and whispering a word that twisted his mouth in strange non-Tauran ways, the chest opened and yielded up a folded map and small ledger. Captain took the ledger and noted the truth of his galleon and the Isles. "By Baphtomet, I've made this trip 30 times!" Awestruck, he forgot to make the holy hand sign. The map showed them on the eastern edge of the Dead Isles. An ancient cataclysm involving an underground volcano had shattered the eastern edges of the Forsaken Isles, which used to be a continent. It created a barrier reef unnavigable by any but a master Navigator.

Captain took some comfort in the last 30 trips and the absence of even a single memory of his ship being damaged in reefs. Captain began his career as a navigator. Their own navigator, one of the fleet's best, had been with him since the beginning. Windwalker was the Navigator who backed up the actual Navigator. The sudden onslaught of forgotten knowledge made him dizzy and he cursed at the magic as being cow dung. Both navigators held high positions at Court. Both were considered best of the best. It all made sense now. It had bothered Captain that his world galleon had so many navigators onboard when they departed Taura. Both the First and Second and the ship's grand cleric and magi came from either navigation or piloting backgrounds.

He flipped the ledger closed and walked back up. He sent word to assemble the officers by the wheel. High up above, Mastsmith blew out the danger of approaching reefs. If they stayed this course, they would not be able to turn or stop in time to avoid them. But, Captain knew it would be all right. "Stay the course!" he growled. "But, keep marking distance to the reefs."

At the helm, Captain opened the ledger and said, "We are bound by the Allegiance of Blood." At his words, the entire command team shook their heads. Fur stood on end as compulsive magic washed over them and memories flooded back. "We are heading to Morbatten, to see the god emperor, Alerius, dragon consort of Takhissis."

At these words, the cleric and mage nodded and said, "We must repeat these words." Repeating it, they gained more memories. The ship mage, Stormsinger, said, "We will need more speed, and water elementals. Captain, I must go and make preparations. I had my entire crew load up on weather control and elementalism today. At the time, it felt strange but I'm glad now we did it."

The cleric, Cloudcaller, bowed low and said, "I too have regained many memories. We will assist with the elementals and weather, but must alter the ship's hull. With enough speed, and a shallower draw, the ship will cross over the reefs ahead. This is what we must do."

First said, "We have less than an hour to make these changes. We've done it before. Do we only ever have such short notice?"

Second laughed. "No, remember five years ago? We hit this during a hurricane, at night. But, we still did it." Second turned and began barking orders to raise all sails and trim them for speed. Incrementally, the giant ship began to tilt and surge forward. They had been skirting the surge of the storm behind to gain advantage from the wave motion. Now, the ship leapt forward and rose up only to crash down into the wave trenches before them. With each new sail's opening, the hammering of the ship into the wave fronts became more and more brutal. But, the superstructure held strong and firm. Below decks, the stone masons, a type of Tauran sorcerer, kept the ship together and enabled the stone to float, and widen. They needed to decrease its draw.

Ahead of the great ship, at the crest of the surging water, they saw a turquoise line of the barrier reef sparkling like jewels where the sun burst through the clouds and would soon set. Captain climbed up the central mast to Mastsmith and saw that they would hit the reef in less than ten minutes. Mastsmith greeted the Captain with some concern. "Captain, I trust you with my life, but against this suicide…"

"Here," Captain said, pressing his ledger into Mastsmith's hands and pointing to a tune. "Play this on your pipes."

Mastsmith shrugged. "Orders are orders, Captain." The tune was simple if discordant. The Mastsmith went through it quickly, but at the last note, all his and the crew's memories returned. The Captain felt the crew's anxiety about the reef vanish. Except for a few newcomers, the entire crew had done this trip before, some many times.

"I'll stay up here, Masty. Head below and play that tune for the masons." Captain remembered, *Windwalker was found. We got word and rejoiced, but then forgot. Our cleric, Path, stayed behind to recover Windwalker, and was successful. Soon, I'll have my Second Priest and Navigator back!* Captain put his head back and roared into the sky. Below, the rest of the crew, thinking the Captain relished in the race over the waves, did the same, and pulled the sails tighter. The Blade of Stars began to tilt with the speed and sliced through some of the large swells in front of them. Below him, the entire deck vanished. Captain could feel the water racing through his fur as if he were submerged. Remembering the new ones tied to the mast, he began to laugh. They would probably drown. But, upon being restored, they would never make stupid mistakes like that again.

Ahead of them the reef loomed larger and larger but the ship's hull already began to widen and stretch under the combined might of the magi and clerics. All around, a swell of water inflated beneath the ship as elementals gathered to help lift the ship and ensure its speed and depth could cross the reef. "Come on, crew," Captain prayed. They needed to get the speed up nearly twice as fast as any other ship in the fleet. Only this particular Blade of Stars had been designed for unrivalled speed. Once there, they had to hold it for almost a day to cross the Dead Isles. With the new hull shape and speed, they skimmed and barely noticed the wave action anymore.

Captain slid down the mast and checked those tied there. He was pleased to see they lived, and he freed their bindings. "Go help. We're past the storm." He called out, "I'll be below decks. Prepare our deck for Cyclone!"

Cyclone sat in the Captain's quarters. He felt the ship's vibration and trembling and knew they were getting close. Like Captain, memories came back to him and he stroked the red fur along his arms. The meditative pose allowed him to consider that no Tauran emperor had ever made this trip. "I regret not fighting the god," he said. His bass-ridden voice filled the room with a silky timbre. "I regret… nothing!" He flipped a dagger from behind his back and set it to dance between his fingers. Most Taurans lacked manual dexterity. A knock at his door caught his focus and he growled out, "Enter."

Captain entered and dropped to his knees. "Great Emperor, we have reached the Dead Isles. Morbatten lies a day away. We should be there just after high sun tomorrow."

"Any losses?"

"None, my liege. Baphtomet favored us with a cyclone and, as you prophesied, we rode it the entire way here." As they both made the hand sign, Captain noted the red light burning in Cyclone's eyes. "I feel your hunger for great adventure. I would join you!"

Cyclone stopped the knife and replied, "You honor me with your desire, but the next emperor requires your service, and the alliance's profits brought by Morbatten. Our nation grows strong with magic and enchantments and soon, our army will rival our navy. This is the task the great god appoints you and the next emperor. My task is to find peace surrounded by Baphtomet's enemies." He bowed his head and made the sign. It electrified the room and Captain shuddered to see the Emperor honor their god.

"Very well, Cyclone. I will send word when we arrive." Captain bowed and turned to leave, but stopped when the emperor called out.

"This is a Blade of Stars. Though not intended for me, I would see it arrive in majesty. It is a long voyage yet to Merakor, Captain. Who knows what fate brings? You may yet fight by my side."

Captain dropped to his knees again and felt a tear leak from his eye. "You do me... great honor!"

Cyclone stood and touched the tear. Licking it off his finger, he said, "Your tears taste of glory and power ahead of us! Come, Captain! Let us take this ship and put it through its true paces!" Cyclone jumped up to the deck with Captain. So close to their god, Cyclone carried a presence of awe that made the Taurans turn and then drop to their knees. "Faster!" he roared. "Get off your knees! Speed, more speed!"

As one the crew joined and their many voices rose up into the sky as if a dragon breathed air into their vast sails. The great ship tilted on its side as wind and sea magic drove it forward. Titled to its side, the massive ship cut the waves like a blade. Cyclone roared his approval and Baphtomet answered by filling their sails.

* * *

Dar Veron sat in meditation. The River of Fire swirled about her and she could not banish the Orc priest RiVule from her thoughts. Driven to distraction, she sighed and swatted an image of RiVule from the burning torrent before her. "I never saw myself as being a humanist," she said with some exasperation in her voice.

An image of her in the future took shape before fading away. It showed her and RiVule locked together in passion. The thought of it made Veron smirk. The image, under her focus, solidified and she saw a world galleon smashing through flames. She and RiVule stood on the deck as Taurans moved about ropes between the giant masts. A voice whispered in her heart, "This will happen. You are going to Merakor. Seek out Dar Shara."

*Merakor?* Veron pondered it. There had been rumors of late about a group being assembled for it. The great lord Daryx had been uncharacteristically sighted about town, and the sister of the hero Thalian – *Alex?* – had been pulled out of class for a special assignment relating to Merakor, well, to the Drow language... which meant Daryx... which meant... "I'm going to Merakor with an Orc."

Meditating in the River of Fire, Veron enjoyed a clarity of thought that defied Tehran linearity. She remembered RiVule in the image and turned her thoughts to coupling with that one. She had borne the empire many children, but always with paladins. This time, because it was not a paladin, was shockingly different. "I cannot go to Merakor and bear a child," she whispered. As soon as she formulated the thought, the answer came and an image of her child after Merakor became clear. Tiamat's fire burned in her heart and Veron bowed her head. "This is tactical. I see. You sense my curiosity and wish to bind RiVule more closely to Tania. I hear and obey." Veron bowed her head and closed her eyes again.

The River of Time flowed around her and it was some time before she felt a change. Looking upriver, she saw Dar Shara appear. A moment later, Dar Ana appeared. Then, Dar Kell lifted out of the energy seeming to explode onto the scene. The form of a shadow dragon hovered around Kell like a dark cloak. The three most powerful clerics of Tiamat turned to Veron and signaled for her to join them. "I obey," she replied.

They stepped out of the flow of Time. Rocks, a stone table, and then candle light appeared. The candles reflected in the dark pools of energy, not yet burning. It felt surreal. Across the stone, flickering ember runes reminiscent of the god emperor's scales glimmered in the heavy light. Veron stood in silence and waited for the trinity of clerics to address her. She felt a cool sensation on her left and looked sideways at it. A gate opened and Daryx entered the setting, accompanied by Dar Ora. The unlikely pair caught Veron's attention and she remembered all of the discussion around Ora. A Dar priestess, hidden away all this time by

Ynt'taris, betrothed to the new king. Ora was as mysterious as she was gossiped about. Another priestess came through, a new R'Dar long overdue for transcendence – Maishan, Veron remembered.

Daryx, Ora, and Maishan bowed to the three clerics and then Dar Kell spoke. "Dar Veron, you are chosen by Tiamat for a peculiar mission – the return to Merakor. We have prayed, waiting for Tiamat to select a priestess to serve a complex role, since the other fell."

Dar Veron had heard rumors and speculated, "You mean the secrecy around R'Dar Alex?"

Ignoring her, Dar Ora spoke now. "King Malcor is most interested in this mission and sends me to ensure you receive the blessings and support of the military."

Dar Shara added, "Takhissis chooses you for your fiery spirit of competition, and the passion to serve."

Dar Ana stepped close enough to touch Veron and took her hands. "I choose you because of our past love, and for your uncompromising integrity. Lovely Verona, you have a special ability to partition unpleasant things away. This quest is perfect for you."

Daryx walked to the stone table and unrolled a leather-bound set of tools. Veron's eyes took them in and she had to suppress alarm. The Drow's packet contained several torture implements used to peel skin and dissect flesh. She noted several ink vials and needles for tattoos as well.

Daryx must have noticed and said, "Lolth finds you acceptable. I'm not going to lie. If you continue on this path, the next part is going to hurt. A lot."

Ana squeezed Veron's hand and pulled her into a hug. "It is worth it, Verona."

Veron raised her hand and said, "May I ask a question?" When Ana squeezed her shoulder gently, Veron asked, "What does Lolth have to do with any of this?"

Daryx almost began to answer and then pointed for Dar Kell to answer. The enigmatic high priest of the Temple at Morbatten replied with clipped words. "Merakor is controlled by the Drow. There are no Lolth priestesses friendly to us. You must therefore become a Lolth priestess and serve us a Holy Mother. This is sanctioned by Tiamat and certified by us all."

His words chilled Veron and she let Ana pull her in closer. "I have served Tiamat with all of me, for nigh on two hundred years. How did the other fall?"

Daryx began setting his tools on the stone table. "R'Dar Alex, sister of Thalian, was selected. However, in trial of combat against vampires, she lost control of the team and there were unacceptably many casualties. Though atonement was offered, R'Dar Alex has declined this great honor."

Veron looked at the tools and found she had so many other questions. Instead, she calmed her racing thoughts and prayed. A cool zephyr washed through the River and tingled her skin. For just a moment, she saw herself in the form of a Drow. She called up flamestrikes in Lolth's name. It felt powerful. It felt uncomfortable too. "There is no clear answer, but I feel strength. Very well, I defer to the Temple. I will be your priestess of Lolth."

Daryx's eyes flashed purple fire and he smiled viciously at her. "Deference is not a trait any Holy Mother has. Please, strip nude and lay on the table." Daryx turned to the assembled clerics and then to Ora. "Queen Ora, Dar Malcor's intent is satisfied here. Please know, and convey to Malcor, that things move as planned. The Circle will keep him abreast of status. Ora, you are dismissed."

Ora's face flushed pink at the dismissal and then she seemed to breathe a sigh of relief. "I will." She turned to Veron for a moment. "Please know that Ynt'taris was part of your selection, Veron. He remembers you from your First Rite." Ora fell back into the flow of Time and vanished.

That Ynt'taris chose her, and remembered her, and sent Ora to say this, took Veron back to her First Rite. Like all others in her class, the never-melting glaciers atop Dragon Mountain froze them in the wind. It was snowing. Veron had stood tall and resolute even when hypothermia had set in. She had met Ynt'taris' gaze without flinching. So cold her body trembled, she had held her hand out and asked, "Dread Lord Ynt'taris, may I see the world through your eyes?"

She stripped her robes and mantle off and laid down. Daryx touched her wrists and ankles and phase spiders appeared to hold her immobile. "Veron, I wish we could make this easier. Lolth's worship requires pain. You will not be believable without that sacrifice haunting you. When this is over, we can remove it all. For now, I apologize for what I must do."

Daryx held up a peeler and prayed to Lolth, consecrating the tool to Lolth and setting its purpose as the defilement of Tiamat's symbols etched into Veron's flesh. Ana came to Veron's head and caressed her face. She placed a rolled tube of leather wrapped around a wooden dowel into Veron's mouth after kissing her lips. "We're all going to be here for you, Verona."

Shara and Kell each took a gentle but firm hold of an ankle. Daryx whispered, in Drow, "Lolth, we will begin with the mark of each consort upon your Holy Mother's soul..."

The screaming began before Daryx's metal peeler ever touched her skin.

* * *

The high summer mountains glowed with green except for the peak snows that never melted. Everything felt alive. Khalla untied the leather straps that held her hair back and let the wind blow through it. It had grown back nicely but was still much shorter than she liked it. The bargeman called out that they would be reaching the first lock in about 20 minutes. Perdition had charted this for the team. The newest members of the team, including Lady Inviress, sat under shade awnings and studied maps of Merakor. The new priestess, Dar Veron, exclusively stayed in the shade. The spider tattoos across her body and haunting pain in her eyes had made it hard for anyone to befriend her. However, Khalla had found her sharp-minded and focused on the mission ahead.

Ash leaned back and chatted with Halgrim and Grant. They all looked so handsome and Khalla marveled at her good luck. Perdition was hers. Merakor was technically under Dar Veron's leadership, and then Ash and Halgrim. But, the Perdition charter made her a leader in it as well. She mused on the friends lost and let her eyes drift to Executor Michael. Like her, he seemed lost in thought and content to watch the clouds slowly changing shape high above them.

R'Dar Alex needed time to process everything that had happened. Though she had bonded with the phase spider, Valaes' withdrawal from the mission and the weight of so many casualties had filled her with self-doubt. Khalla could hear Daryx lecturing her, "A Holy Mother does not doubt, she questions! You must overcome this." The Circle had, ultimately, kept her in but tapped Dar Veron to play the role. When Alex healed, she would be brought to them, somehow.

RiVule watched everything intently, same as he always did. His facial expression did not show if he was bored or excited or anything. If anything, he appeared lost in thought. Taisha had not been recoverable and it surprised everyone that RiVule had not called any of the Orcs to join him. He wanted to see Merakor and insisted it was Gruustir's will he do it alone.

When they reached the first lock, Khalla asked the bargeman, "There are fifteen locks, right? How long will it take to descend?"

The old man shrugged. "With an easterly breeze helping, and favorable traffic, it should take three days." He laughed. "The distance is only about 20 miles though. You'd not be the first group I'd have seen run it. Five more days run to the coast, though you can charter ships much faster than these barges on the river."

The twinkle in the old man's eyes made Khalla giggle. She felt like a teenager in this perfect moment. When the barge touched down, she grabbed her gear and said, "I'm running it. You're all welcome to stay on the barge, but it's too nice to not run. Who's in?"

Halgrim waved her off. "I'm younger but I still hate running. You go on ahead."

Ash and Grant joined her. Delia jumped up when Grant did, but his expression told her not to come. Khalla felt bad for the girl and had to remind herself Delia was a doppelganger. There were no secrets in the group. At the last moment, Revi and Furis agreed to come along.

The five jumped off when the barge bumped against the water gate. They raced along the high steel edge and then hit the trails used by ox to drag cargo. They began to run faster and faster. As an elf, Khalla quickly outdistanced everyone. Hours later, she reached the eigth lock. A statue of the Sage Alaura held a lantern while stone wings swept up from her back and vanished into the cliffside rock.

Khalla jumped onto the pedestal and scaled up to the lantern ring. The sun would soon set in the western sky and she wanted to see how far behind her the others were. Her marriage token showed Ash's heartbeat racing and she imagined him and Grant trying to outdo the other. She laughed and jumped up to catch the bottom of the lantern ring. Dangling from there, she rotated to see the eastern ocean. She could almost see the Tauran island they called Kronos. When she rotated back, she thought she heard Revi's voice. She put her hand to her mouth and called out, "Hurry! This is beautiful!" A gust of wind blew suddenly and the map tube on her shoulder slipped off. She caught the strap and called out again, "You're missing a beautiful sunset!"

Facing into the western sky, Khalla saw the tips of their heads. She felt invulnerable and alive. A giant smile creased her face when she imagined the sun setting on Merakor itself.

# Court of Patriarchs

Alerius picked up a cracked tile in his hands and glared at it. Next to him, Spark did the same but with a different tile. Ynt'taris sat back against the wall with three tiles, nearly repaired, on the ground in front of him. Though in their human forms, their dragonterror seethed and crackled where it interacted with the others. "In hindsight," Alerius growled. "I was always glad we redesigned the gate to break when used to bring others to Tehra. Tiamat's wisdom in counseling this has been proven many times over. Yet now, with the Orcus threat gone, it is regrettable."

Ynt'taris completed repairs on one tile and set it aside. "Never again shall we trust humans with this. Never!"

"Were Alaura here, you would entrust it to her." Alerius' matter-of-fact words echoed in the chamber and were met with silence. "This would go faster if we entrusted this to human hands again. Not the entire gate. Just specific tiles."

Spark let electricity crackle over the tile in his hand. "That would speed things greatly. Our magic threatens to overwhelm these tiles. If we are not careful, all gates will open to our Queen."

"So, we are agreed. Ynt'taris?" Alerius looked up as the fractured tile in his hand began to mend.

Ynt'taris stood up and stretched. "Since you bring up my Alaura, I would remind you that she warned us of Bomoki's predilection to self-destruct. The issue, she said, was that he was a 'power-obsessed mage.' If we do this, it must be under the control of those in the Temple we trust above all else. I would accept Dar Ana. I would accept Dar Shara. However, they are both too instrumental in what happens next. Dar Ora shall lead this effort. I would see this task appointed to her, and her alone."

Spark nodded. "I will accept Dar Ora. The weight of destiny on her is less now that she is granted love with her Malcor."

Alerius listened and then after a minute said, "The jewel that is Dar Ana is lessened through the Jade God's defeat. I worry for her. So much fire! Yet, she cools. A pairing of fire and ice might rekindle her spirits. Brothers, we are in agreement on the Temple's role. Where Ana goes, Crimson does as well. That is, unless you wish to join your Rider, Ynt'taris?"

Ynt'taris picked up the tile. It dwarfed the small girl form of his body, but he easily placed it on the stone bench. "I am thinking about it. Ora is yet young and inexperienced in the ways of battle and magic. Too long have I traveled alone. Maybe it is time that my rider sees the vast world and endless heavens? Counter: I will take Ora and we will begin repair on the tiles together. For those tiles we cannot, we will bring in different specialists, always different. Only Ora will see a hint of the grand design in Bomoki's Gate. We will scatter the pearls of knowledge in its re-making across all of the world."

"This is acceptable to me," Spark said. "The gnomes grow impatient that their great machines still wait on me."

"Gnomes are always impatient," Alerius countered. "It is a blink of eight months that Bloodstone took you away from them. Yet, they begrudge you eight hours." He leered. "I wonder if the Lord of Lightning is becoming overly fond of his gnomes?"

"They have heard about Merakor," Spark admitted. "How they did this, because I am not there, I cannot say. Yet, they know. They are most anxious to hear about the fate of those at Xastro. They are most anxious to retrieve the machines at Xastro. They ask, daily, if the Merakor group might investigate, scout, and send back word."

Ynt'taris picked up the next tile. "Xastro, like the other unconquered cities, is under tight guard. The Sea Patriarch yet lives, so the gnomes are safe. We saw this in our last consecration of the Temple of Glass."

Spark stiffened. "You forget the Drow magics throughout that and other regions. We do not know what they do. The gnomes of Xastro are in that area of Drow control. I tried to see, but my attempts at speaking with the Sea Patriarch were interrupted. He did not respond anyway. Does he ever?"

Both Spark and Ynt'taris eyed Alerius. The fire patriarch answered them. "Rarely. He says he is waiting for the next inversion, that we are not yet there. As always, he remains true to the Prophecy of the Shield and Spear."

"That is enough then," Spark said, turning his attention back to the fractured tile rune.

They worked in silence for many long moments before Alerius interrupted the silence. "We must prepare a diversion to the Temple of Glass in case the Merakor team needs help. I cannot fly. It must be you two."

Ynt'taris retorted, "Take the golem wing, then. Or ascend with Dar Kell."

"You set them on this course, brother," Alerius said darkly.

Spark looked at the two and said, "I will go. The gnomes wish to see and I can think of no good reason to deny them if I am going anyway."

Ynt'taris slammed the tile down, not hard enough to break it. The loud clacking sound echoed in the room. "Then, I would take my rider as well."

Alerius bowed. "If the riders are ready, take them. I have heard that Ora struggles. Is she safe, my brother?"

Ynt'taris relaxed a bit and his expression fell. "She is safe, for now. Like Alaura, the thermal energy of this world taxes her. While I can endure it, humans were not designed to exist at extremes of temperature. The world here is too hot for her. I will take her away before things become too extreme. The Temple of Ice is a possibility."

Alerius whispered, "We could divert Merakor to check on it…"

"Do not tempt me!" Ynt'taris roared. "Do not dare tempt me. To see her bones, to be in that place again." Ynt'taris shuddered and then calmed only after long moments passed. "I am not visited in my time of need. Depending on how my rider fares, perhaps we will detour and check on it. Brother Spark, should it come to that?"

"Yes, I will go."

\* \* \* \* \* \* \* \* \* \* \* \* \* \* \* \*

You've reached the end of Khalla's Play: Merakor I. The next book will follow Perdition to Merakor as they seek out the Tower of Aler Alerest. This book will be available before December 2018. In the meantime, please pick up the other books. While none need to be read in order, there are some advantages to reading them in this order:

Dar Tania – October 2016, "a 100 page story", 105 pages
Dar Tania II: Set's Dream – August 2017, 250+ pages

Malcor's Story – November 2016, 400+ pages
Bomoki's Gate – April 2017, 550+ pages

Reviews matter. If you enjoyed this, please consider leaving a 5-star review on Amazon and Goodreads. Thank you so much!

If you have specific questions, you can visit www.forsakenisles.com or my Facebook author page at www.facebook.com/forsakenisles and I would love to hear from you.